THE MASTER PLAN

"Listen, Mattie, this is what we'll do. We'll just go. We'll leave all of this . . ." She waved through the bedroom window, and the gesture took in the bland gardens, the grid of streets with their semi-detached houses that made up the nice part of town, and the sprawling, featurelessly brutal estate beyond.

Julia's grand gesture took in the whole of the dull, virtuous suburb, and rejected it. "We'll go to London. We'll find ourselves jobs, and we'll find a flat. Then we can live, can't we? We always said we would, didn't we?" It was a glittering, covetable world, distant, but now, suddenly, within reach.

Mattie smiled suddenly. "When shall we go?"

"Today," Julia said. "Today . . ."

ROSIE THOMAS

Bad Girls, Good Women

BANTAM BOOKS
NEW YORK · TORONTO · LONDON · SYDNEY · AUCKLAND

BAD GIRLS, GOOD WOMEN

A Bantam Book
Bantam hardcover edition / May 1989
Bantam paperback edition / April 1990

Library of Congress Cataloging-in-Publication Data
Thomas, Rosie.
  Bad girls, good women.
  I. Title.
PR6070.H655B3 1989   823'.914   88-7922
ISBN 0-553-28394-4

Published simultaneously in the United States and Canada

Bantam Books are published by Bantam Books, a division of Bantam
Doubleday Dell Publishing Group, Inc. Its trademark, consisting of the
words "Bantam Books" and the portrayal of a rooster, is Registered in
U.S. Patent and Trademark Office and in other countries. Marca
Registrada. Bantam Books, 666 Fifth Avenue, New York, New York
10103.

PRINTED IN THE UNITED STATES OF AMERICA

RAD   0 9 8 7 6 5 4 3 2 1

For Susan Watt

Bad
Girls,
Good
Women

The music, very loud music, filled the corners of the old house.

In the big room, where the musicians in their corner were lapped by a sea of dancers, it was as solid as a wall. Overhead, where Julia stood in the shadows at the top of the stairs, it penetrated the thick stone walls and the oak-boarded floors as an insistent bass beat. She stood for a minute to listen to it.

Beneath her was the blaze of lights and the noise of people, laughter, and shouting all knitted together by the throb of the music.

Julia swayed dreamily, moving her hips inside the silky tube of her dress. She was smiling because she loved parties, and her own parties were always the best of all. She loved this particular moment, when the party was off and running on its own, and she could step back to admire it, her creation.

Somewhere behind her, in the dimness of the gallery, a door opened. A thin finger of light reached past her. Julia didn't look around, but she heard a man's voice and then a woman's low laugh before the door closed again. The man walked quickly along the gallery and stopped beside her at the head of the stairs. Turning to look now, Julia saw that it was her old friend Johnny Flowers. He had arrived hours ago in one of the packed cars that had raced one another from London to Julia's party.

She smiled, and saw the whiteness of his teeth as he smiled back at her.

"Good time, Johnny?" she whispered.

He leaned forward to kiss the corner of her mouth, and his hand rested lightly on her waist.

"Mmm. The very best time. The party to end all parties, this one."

Julia murmured, "Good. But it's early yet."

Johnny's hand slid over her hip as he passed her, and fleetingly she remembered other times. Other places, a long way from this big house beached in its dark gardens.

She tilted her head backward at the closed bedroom door.

1

"Who?"

"Shhh." The white smile came again as he put his finger to his lips. "You haven't seen me."

"I haven't seen you."

Julia watched him run downstairs and disappear into the brightness. A swirl of laughing people poured out into the hallway and the colors of the girls' dresses blurred exotically against the wood paneling.

Someone called out, "Ju-lia!" and the faces turned to look up at her. She stood on the top stair for a moment longer, surveying the scene, smiling with satisfaction. Then, with the tips of her fingers just touching the smooth, curving warmth of the banister rail, she floated down to join them.

In the doorway, someone shouted, "*Be-bop-a-lula!*"

Out of sight, in the room where the dancers surged past the huge Christmas tree, the lead guitarist mopped the sweat out of his eyes and obligingly struck the first chord.

"*She's my baby,*" Julia sang.

A chain of people formed and swayed in front of her, and arms came around her waist. She could feel the heat of the man, whoever he was, through her thin dress. Julia stumbled forward and steadied herself in the crush by flinging her arms around someone else. Everyone was singing now. "*Don't mean maybe.*"

The conga line snaked around the hallway and back into the big room. Before it jerked her away, Julia saw Johnny Flowers again. He was slipping back up the stairs, holding a champagne bottle by its gold foil neck. She looked away quickly, thinking, *I wanted this, didn't I? To be able to give parties in a big house for all my friends. To have everyone around me, enjoying themselves . . .*

Happy New Year, she wished herself. But it didn't suppress the little beat of loneliness that she had felt, in the middle of all the people.

The dancers swept her along, into the heat of the drawing room, where the carpets had been rolled back and the log fire in the huge stone fireplace crackled unnecessarily. Inside her head, all around her, the music thudded on.

Julia saw a whiskey bottle on a windowsill. As they swooped past she reached for it and tilted it to her mouth. They circled the Christmas tree. It was so tall that the silver star on the top touched the high ceiling, and there was a real candle burning on every branch. Julia had insisted on real candles, because they were so beautiful. The blaze of them and the flames in the hearth gave the only light in the packed room now.

Julia's oldest friend, Mattie, was lying along the back of the sofa, her head propped on one hand and the other waving a cigarette in a long holder. The cigarette holder was a recent affectation, adopted since Mattie had begun to be famous. The cluster of men around her was nothing new, because Mattie had attracted men effortlessly ever since Julia had known her. She waved the cigarette holder at Julia now and closed one eye in a slow wink.

"Seen Bliss?" Julia mouthed at her, and Mattie pointed the holder.

Julia's husband was on the far side of the room. He was bending over the radio in its cabinet, twiddling the knobs. Although his back was turned to her, Julia could imagine his mildly preoccupied frown, like a small boy's intent on a puzzle. Alexander Bliss was a tall, spare, elegant man. He was ten years older than his wife, and he had chosen to wear a dinner jacket for her party. Most of his country neighbors had dressed, too, but the influx of London guests wore sharp Italian suits, studded leather, evening dresses that were hardly dresses at all.

The contrast wouldn't have struck Alexander. He had seen it often enough before. If he had bothered to make any comment, he would have shrugged amiably. "Anything goes nowadays."

Julia wriggled out of the grasp of the conga man. She didn't know him but she thought that he had arrived with Johnny. There were lots of strange faces tonight mixed with the familiar ones, and she liked that because it meant that anything could happen. Julia still believed that's what parties were for.

She thought back, in an instant of painful, irresistible nostalgia. Parties in bed-sitters and parties in cellars. Crowded parties with hot jazz, and warm booze drunk out of chipped cups, and an endless, wonderful parade of new faces. It was at the time of those parties that Julia had met the aviator. Mattie had nicknamed him *your aviator*. Where was he now?

I'm twenty-one years old, she thought suddenly, *and I'm looking back like an old woman.* Julia tipped the whiskey bottle again. *Happy New Year.*

"C'mon baby. What about a dance?"

Johnny's friend, if he was Johnny's friend, had a nice face enlivened by louche sideburns. She grinned at him.

"Later," she shouted over the music. "Promise."

Then she threaded her way through the dancers to Alexander, crouched beside the radio. He looked up when she touched his shoulder and smiled at her, the corners of his eyes creasing. "It's nearly twelve. Listen."

He pressed his ear to the speaker and then leapt up, turning the volume control sharply. "It's midnight!"

The guitarists finished the number with a deafening chord and the drummer brandished his sticks in a drum roll. In the sudden silence that followed, Big Ben struck the quarters and then the hour. Twelve booming peals, and Julia imagined them echoing through the house and rolling over the trees and lawns beyond the windows. At the twelfth stroke the room erupted into shouts and cheers, kissing and clapping.

It was 1960.

Alexander turned Julia's face up to his and kissed her. "Don't look so sad. It's a new decade. Happy New Decade."

With the warmth of Alexander's kiss still on her mouth, Julia said, "I liked the old decade."

He touched her cheek, lifting the curl that lay against it. "You'll like this one too." He took her hand and drew her into the huge, smiling circle to sing "Auld Lang Syne." Julia sang with everyone else, and when the hugging and shouting was over, the music started to pound again.

"Dance with your husband?" he asked her. Alexander was a very good dancer. It was one of the first things she had noticed about him, long ago. She had been surprised, to begin with, that someone like Alexander Bliss should like rock and roll.

"Delighted."

When the number finished, so quietly that she could hardly hear him, Alexander asked her, "Are you happy?"

And Julia faced him squarely, looking straight into his eyes. "Of course I am."

Alexander turned her to face the room. "Go on, then. Enjoy your party."

The man with the sideburns was waiting. Mattie had left her sofa to dance, her long diamond earrings swinging. The house was full of friends. It was a good party. *My* party, Julia thought. Alexander wouldn't say *our* party. Nor would he invite all these people of his own accord, but he would never stop his wife from doing whatever she wanted to do.

Julia wound her way back across the room to Johnny Flowers's friend. She picked up a full glass on her way and drank the contents, not stopping to notice what she'd swallowed. The man was still waiting for her, and she accepted his admiring glance. Julia was tall, with pale, perfect skin and a mass of dark hair. Her evening dress, a satin tube cut high at the front and into a deep V at the back, showed off her figure. She smoothed the fabric over her hips, satisfied that her stomach was still flat.

"You promised me a dance," the man said.

"So here I am." When Julia smiled her face melted.

The man took her in his arms, his cheek against hers. Julia smelled cologne, whiskey, and warm skin. She closed her eyes and danced.

The house was made for parties. She had seen it as soon as Alexander had brought her to visit it, before they were engaged. She couldn't remember whether that was when she had begun to take him seriously. Bliss had begun by being a bit of a joke to Mattie and Julia. After the aviator Julia hadn't cared what she did or with whom, and if it hadn't been Bliss, it would have been someone else. Then, almost without her noticing it, he had begun to be important to her.

In London, Bliss lived in a chaotic flat in Markham Square, not noticeably different from anyone else's. But then, one weekend, he had driven her to Ladyhill. Even Julia, to whom houses were just places for sleeping in, set out in rows in city streets, even Julia could see that Ladyhill was beautiful. They rounded a curve in the drive and it faced them, a Jacobean manor house in warm brick faced with stone, the sun reflected in fiery sheets from the tall windows. Two short wings projected on either side of the arched stone doorway, and in their paved shelter were two huge yew trees, clipped into perfect ovals. It was late March, the first day of spring weather, and Julia looked at the pale blue-washed sky behind the high chimneys.

"Who lives here?" she asked.

"My father."

"And who's your father, when he's at home?"

"Sir Percy Bliss. Bart."

"Hot dog," Julia had said.

Alexander left his car slewed at an angle in the driveway and they went inside. They walked through the rooms together. Sir Percy was away, and there was no one at Ladyhill.

Julia was impressed in spite of herself. It wasn't so much by the dim rooms with their paneled walls hung with English pictures, or by the Long Gallery with views over the gardens beyond the house, or even by the great half-tester bed with its yellow brocade hangings that Alexander called the Queen's Bed, but by the difference in Alexander himself. In London he was vague, almost diffident. Julia had seen him once or twice glancing uneasily around Markham Square, or the Rocket, as if he were wondering what he was doing there. But as he showed her around Ladyhill he seemed more solid, as if the place and his love for it defined him. He did love it, she could see it in his face, and in his hands as they rested on a carved newel or measured the depth of a window embrasure.

Suddenly, startlingly, Julia liked Alexander Bliss. She liked him and envied him. She felt that she was adrift, not anchored like Alexander to this old house and its gardens. At Ladyhill, the freedom that she had set such store by seemed no more than rootlessness.

She shivered in the silent house.

"It needs people," she announced. "Lots and lots of people. Mad parties."

Alexander smiled. "Perhaps it does." He put his arms around her and kissed her, demanding. *Lots of people*, Julia remembered.

After her dance with the sideburns man someone else had claimed her, and then one of Mattie's retinue of men. She drank some more whiskey and then some champagne, and reached the elusive stage of being drunk when everything seemed warm, and simple, and deliciously funny. The crowd began to thin out a little as the staider guests left. Alexander stood at the foot of the sweep of stairs, saying good-bye. When he looked back at the dancers he realized that the stayers were going to stay all night. The music was coming from the record player now, and the group had put down their guitars to join the dancers. One of them took off his shirt to dance, bare-chested, with the sweat shining on his shoulder blades. Mattie reached out reflectively to touch the muscles in his back with her fingertips, and Julia laughed. At that moment everyone was her friend, but she loved Mattie for all the years that had just slipped out of her reach with the strokes of Big Ben. It was just New Year's Eve that was troubling her. She didn't want to celebrate the death of a year, let alone a decade.

She looked for Bliss, wanting to put her arms around him, but she couldn't see him anywhere. She turned instead, smiling back at the laughter around her, ready to plunge into the party once more.

She never knew how the next thing happened. The crush was much less than it had been at midnight, and she couldn't remember afterward who had been at that side of the room.

Someone must have stumbled, or swung an arm too wildly and reached out to steady themselves. Julia saw her Christmas tree shiver as if it were alive, and then it tilted, slowly at first, and then it fell in an arc of fire. The candle flames licked through the dark branches, and the branches crackled fragrantly as the scarlet tongues devoured them.

For an instant, still in the grip of euphoria, Julia thought how beautiful it was. The blazing tree hit the floor, its glass balls splintering around it. The dancers scattered backward and a girl screamed. The record was still playing but it seemed that there was a long moment's silence. And then the heavy velvet curtains caught fire. A sheet of flame sprang upward from the floor, blindingly bright in the dim room. A second later the dusty velvet drapes and braided tassels were blazing like the demolished tree.

There was another scream, but this one was caught and stifled by a belching pall of smoke. The horrified stillness in the room broke into a panicky scramble of bodies. Julia was carried toward the door, almost falling and then clawing her way upright again. The smoke billowed out, as acrid as her sudden terror, and she choked on it. There was a babble of shouts and screams now and a man's voice rising over them, commanding, "Don't push. Don't panic."

The joyous crackle of leaping flames was louder than anything else, drowning out the music and the shouting.

The first dancers to escape stumbled out into the hallway.

Julia saw that the man with the sideburns had wrapped himself in one of the rolled-back rugs. Under its protection he was trying to tear down the flaming curtains. They fell in a shower of vicious sparks, and the heavy wooden cornice pole crashed with them. It was already alight, and before Julia's eyes the whole of the paneled wall beside the dark gape of the window flowered into bright tendrils of flame.

She heard herself scream too. "Bliss!" The roar of the fire grew deafening as it took hold. "Bliss. Where are you?"

She couldn't see him anywhere. The room was thick with smoke now, and she coughed and gasped as it filled her lungs. The door seemed so far away. She was sure that she would never reach it, and fear spread through her as fast as the fire itself. A hand grabbed her wrist and pulled her forward. Her tight dress hobbled her, and she almost fell again, but the surge of people pushed her forward. Half-carried and half-dragged there, she lurched through the doorway into the hall. Cold fresh air bit into her lungs and she gulped at it, her eyes streaming. She rubbed the palms of her hands into her eyes and turned to look where she had come from.

The last of the dancers stumbled out after her, retching, and blinded by the smoke. A great black cloud of it licked after them. Julia could see nothing beyond it, but she could hear the fire as it leapt upward and onward. Water. She must get water to quench it. She imagined ducking through the smoke to pour water where the Christmas tree had collapsed into flame, and half-turned to run for the kitchens.

The heavy main door banged open and she smelled the frosty purity of the night air rushing past her as the fire sucked it inward. Julia felt it like a living thing now. It gave a great roar of satisfaction as the air fed it. Through the smoke she glimpsed its red heart, and sparks that cascaded downward in a mocking torrent. No one could get into that room now.

Telephone. She must telephone for help instead.

"Get everyone outside," someone shouted. "Then for Christ's sake shut the doors." Julia's guests began to stream out into the darkness. She saw Mattie, her face blackened with smoke.

"Come on," Mattie yelled at her. "Get out."

"I've got to ring for help."

Julia tried to push past her, to Bliss's little office on the right of the stairs, and the nearest telephone.

"No," Mattie screamed. "Julia!"

Then at last she saw Bliss. He ran toward her from the stone archway that led through to the back of the house. His face was the color of ice.

Julia stumbled toward him. "The fire brigade," she shouted helplessly.

"They're coming."

Alexander was methodically throwing open every door to check that the room beyond was empty. He slammed the doors shut again and the roar of the fire devoured the sound. Another obliterating blanket of smoke rolled around them, and he caught at her arm.

"Is everyone out of there?"

She nodded, and at once he was pulling her over the stone flags to the big door. She tripped in her tight dress and the thin fabric ripped, freeing her to run. The arched portico framed the night beyond, then it was overhead, and then with Alexander's arm supporting her they escaped into the darkness. The cold hit them, and Julia saw ahead of her the dark, glossy ovals of the clipped yews reflecting an ugly red glow. The crowd of people milled at the foot of the shallow flight of steps, their faces turned upward to the house. Julia and Alexander looked the same way, and understood how quickly and how terribly the fire had taken hold.

The windows of what had been the drawing room, where only a few minutes ago they had been dancing in the glow of candlelight, were now blind eyes from which the smoke coiled in thick ropes. The flames had reached the first floor, and came darting lasciviously from the windows. The crash of breaking glass and falling timber was just audible through the voice of the fire itself.

"Is everyone out?" Bliss shouted hoarsely. "Is anyone missing?"

The panic had subsided. The guests were numb with shock, and silent in awe of the fire's horrible vitality. They muttered to one another, and shook their heads. It seemed that everyone was accounted for.

Julia stood motionless, watching. Bliss's fingers were like iron hooks digging into the flesh of her arm. Looking upward at the windows in the gable end of the near wing, she thought of the magnificent beams that supported the roof of the Long Gallery, and the floor of broad oak boards that separated the gallery from the burning bedrooms beneath.

She shivered violently in the icy air. And then she remembered.

The words stuck in her throat at first. Bliss looked at her, then gripped her other arm and pulled her closer.

"What is it?"

"Flowers. Flowers was upstairs, with a girl."

They whirled apart and went blundering through the silent huddles of people. "Has anyone seen Flowers?"

No one had seen him. There were only white, shocked faces, and none of them was Johnny Flowers.

Julia remembered, with a beat of horror, what he had said in the shadows at the top of the stairs. *The party to end all parties.* She dared not look up at the lurid windows.

Fear crystalized into certainty within her. She finished her desperate circuit and collided with Bliss again.

"Not here."

Alexander turned his face to the house. Julia saw the reflected light of the fire in his eyes.

"They must be still inside."

He was already running toward the steps. Two or three other men left the shelter of the crowd and ran with him.

"No." Her scream tore Julia's throat.

"No. Don't go back in there."

Without stopping to think, she began to run, too, gathering up the ruined tail of her dress. She had gone only a half-dozen steps when more people caught up with her and pulled at her arms, dragging her backward. She struggled to break free, swearing blindly at them. They held her too tightly, and she was reduced to impotent kicking and writhing.

Her last glimpse of Bliss was as he ran back under the portico, one arm held crooked against his face in a vain attempt to shield it from the fire's fierce heat.

"Stop him," she whispered to the people holding her. "Don't let him go in there."

But he had already gone.

The men who had dashed forward with Bliss seemed to be driven back by the smoke, but Alexander was engulfed by it.

Nobody moved or spoke. The fire possessed the whole house now, and the malevolent smoke hung over it, obliterating the starry winter sky.

Julia stepped away from the restraining hands and then stood motionless. No one could do anything. Impotent anger swept over her.

"Where is the fire brigade? Why don't they come? He's going to die in there." She screamed again at the smoky mouth of the door. "Bliss!"

An arm came around her, and she saw that it was Mattie beside her. Her friend's eyes reflected the demonic red glow, as Bliss's had. Looking wildly around, Julia saw that all their faces were lit by it. The black shadows thrown by the firelight in the hollows of their cheeks and eye sockets made all of them look like skulls. She felt an instant of wild, almost exultant terror.

The fire would come for all of them. Bliss was already gone, and it was Mattie and Julia standing to face it together, as they had always done.

A bubble of hysterical laughter broke out of Julia's mouth.

Mattie held her harder, shaking her, hurting her shoulders. "Hold on. They're coming now. You've got to hold on."

Julia heard it then. Only just audible through the roar of the flames were the bells of the fire engines as they raced toward Ladyhill.

The mad laughter died in her throat, and Julia gave a long, shuddering sigh.

She stood waiting, one hand holding on to Mattie. The fingers of her other hand just rested on the concave space between her hip bones.

Julia Bliss was twelve weeks pregnant. For some reason that she didn't even understand herself, she hadn't told her husband about the baby yet.

✳ SUMMER 1955

ONE

"It's cold," Julia said.

She looked at the scuffed suitcase at her feet, but it hardly seemed worth opening it and rummaging among the grubby contents for warmer clothes. She shivered and hunched her shoulders.

Mattie didn't even answer.

They sat side by side on the bench, silently, and the pigeons that had gathered in the hope of sandwich crumbs waddled away again. Over the stone balustrade in front of them the girls could just see the flat, murky river. A barge nosed slowly upstream and they watched it slide past them. A sluggish wash fanned out in its wake.

"We could go home," Julia whispered.

Even to suggest it punctured her pride, but she wanted to be sure that Mattie's resolve was still as firm as her own. Even though their defiance had brought them here, to this.

The rumble of the evening traffic along the Embankment seemed to grow louder to fill the silence between them. It was the first time either of them had mentioned going home, but they knew that they had both been thinking about it. It was three nights since they had run away. Four nights since Mattie had appeared at Julia's parents' front door, back in Fairmile Road, with her face bruised and puffy and her homemade blouse torn off her shoulder.

Julia's father had stared past Mattie at the police car waiting in the road. Then his eyes had flicked to and fro, checking to see if any of the neighbors might be witnessing the spectacle. He had opened the door by another inch as Julia watched from the top of the stairs.

"Don't you know that it's one o'clock in the morning?" he had asked his daughter's best friend.

"I'm sorry," Mattie said.

"I suppose you'd better come in."

Mattie stepped into the hallway. Mr. Smith looked almost unrecognizable without his stiff shirt collar, and his wife's curlers sat on her head like thin sausages. Only the house looked the same. Little slippery rugs on the slippery floor, flowery papered walls and spiky plants in pots, and a framed Coronation picture of the Queen. And then Julia was the same, looking anxiously down at her, with her hair very dark against her pink dressing gown. Mattie was so relieved to see her, and the concern in Julia's face touched her so directly, she was almost crying again.

Mattie hitched the torn pieces of her blouse together and faced Julia's parents squarely. They had always hated her, of course. They thought she led Julia astray, although that wasn't the truth. It didn't matter, she told herself. If they threw her out into the street again, at least the policeman had gone.

"Whatever's the matter?" Betty Smith asked. Julia came down the stairs, pushing past her parents, putting an arm around Mattie's shoulders. Mattie felt her comforting warmth. She would keep the story simple, she decided. Tomorrow, later today, whatever the time was, she would tell Julia what had really happened.

"I'm afraid that there was an argument at home. My father . . . my father thought that I was out too late. I'd been to see *East of Eden*, that's all. Julia didn't want to come again."

"Julia was at home, doing her homework," Mr. Smith said. "As she should have been every other night this week, instead of running around goodness knows where." *With you*, he might as well have added.

Julia is sixteen years old, Mattie thought savagely. What does bloody homework matter? And I'm seventeen. I'm not going to cry. Not after everything that's happened. Not just because of these people, with their little shut-in faces.

"There was an argument," she went on. "I came out for a walk. To keep out of the way, you see? And the policeman saw me. He thought I was up to no good." She tried to laugh, but it drained away into their stony silence. Clearly Mr. and Mrs. Smith thought she was up to no good as well. "He offered to take me to friends, or relatives. I thought of here. I thought perhaps you wouldn't mind helping me. Just for one night."

I'm not here because of you. I came to Julia. And what gives you the right to judge me?

"You'd better stay, then," Vernon Smith said brusquely. He left it unclear whether it was for Mattie's own sake, or in case of another visit from the police. Betty began to flutter about dust and boxes in the spare bedroom.

"It doesn't matter," Mattie said. She realized that she was exhausted. To go to sleep, that was all that mattered. "Anywhere will do."

Julia was shocked by Mattie's appearance. It wasn't just the bruises, and the oozing cut at the corner of her mouth. More disturbingly, Mattie's verve and defiance seemed to have drained out of her, leaving her as shapeless as a burst balloon. Julia had never seen that in all the years they had been friends.

"Come on," she whispered now. "It's all right. Tomorrow, when you wake up, it'll be all right."

She steered Mattie up the cramped stairs, with Betty fussing behind them.

Vernon still wanted to impose his own order. "I should telephone your father, at least, to say where you are. I wouldn't want him made anxious on our account." He lifted up a china doll with an orange net skirt from the hall table. The telephone sat underneath the skirt. A lot of things in the Smiths' house had covers. Even Mr. Smith's Ford Popular, parked outside, had a mackintosh coat.

"We don't have a telephone," Mattie said.

Betty made Julia go back to bed. In the white-tiled bathroom Mattie washed her face with the wholesome Pears soap laid out for her. Her distorted face in the mirror looked older under its tangle of hair. Betty knocked on the door and handed her a bottle of antiseptic.

"Put some of this on your poor mouth," she said.

The small kindness brought Mattie to the edge of tears again.

She went into the spare room and climbed under the turquoise eiderdown. She fell asleep at once.

In the morning, at six o'clock, Julia came in with a cup of tea. She opened the curtains and looked out. In the early light the row of back gardens was tidy and innocent, its squares of lawn surrounded by pink hybrid tea roses. Julia turned her back as if she hated them.

"What happened?" she asked.

Mattie looked away, and Julia climbed in at the bottom of

the bed, pulling the eiderdown around her. "What happened?" she persisted.

And then, lying there wrapped in the eiderdown and enclosed by the room's sprigged wallpaper, whispering so that Betty and Vernon wouldn't hear, Mattie told her.

Julia listened, anger and disgust and sympathy mounting inside her. Afterward, with two bright spots of color showing on her cheeks, she held Mattie's hand between both of hers.

"Why didn't you ever tell me before?"

"I don't know," Mattie said. She was crying now, tears pouring down her cheeks and making a dark patch on the turquoise cover. She had told Julia everything, the smallest details that she had kept boxed up for so long. And at once, amazingly, she had felt her guilt lifting. Julia hadn't cried out in horror or accusation, of course. Had she been afraid for all this time that it was really her own fault?

"It's all right," Julia hugged her, making inarticulate, comforting noises. "Mat, it's all right. You've got me. We've got each other."

At last the storm of crying subsided. Mattie sniffed, rubbing her eyes with the back of her hand.

"Sorry. Thanks. Look at me."

"No thanks."

They laughed shakily. Julia was relieved to see Mattie lifting her chin up again. She would be all right. Everything would come back to her once they had gotten away. Excitement, a fierce heat, was beginning to boil inside Julia, fueled by her anger. It was hard to talk calmly as the idea took hold of her.

"Listen, Mattie, this is what we'll do. You don't have to go back there to him. We'll just go. We'll leave all of this. . . ." She waved through the bedroom window, and the gesture took in the bland gardens, the grid of streets with their semi-detached houses that made up the nice part of town, and the sprawling, featurelessly brutal estate beyond, where Mattie lived. It included the High Street, with its Odeon showing *East of Eden*, and the single milk bar with half a dozen teddy boys lounging outside it, the red-brick church that Betty and Vernon belonged to and the Youth Club hall behind it, the grammar school where Mattie and Julia had met, and where they had made their first small gestures of defiance. The gestures had grown as they got older. Mattie and Julia would have been expelled if they hadn't been much cleverer than their anxious counterparts.

Julia's grand gesture took in the whole of the dull, virtuous suburb, and rejected it. "We'll go to London. We'll find ourselves jobs, and we'll find a flat. Then we can live, can't we? We always said we would, didn't we?"

Up to London was where they went when they skipped school for the day. They went up on Saturday nights now, when they had enough money to go dancing at a club. It was a glittering, covetable world, distant, but now, suddenly, within reach.

"We've talked about it so often." Sitting in the park, with their backs against the green railings. Trailing slowly home from school. Whispering, over slow cups of coffee.

Carefully, Mattie said, "I could pack in my job easily enough." Since leaving Blick Road Grammar she had worked as a filing clerk in a real estate agency, and she hated every minute of it. Mattie wanted to be an actress. She wanted it so much that Julia teased her about it. "But you're still at school."

"Bugger school," Julia said triumphantly. "Dad wants me to be a secretary. Not a typist, you know. A private secretary, to a businessman. Mum wants me to be married to a solicitor or a bank manager. I don't want to be either of those. Why should I stay at school to do typing and bookkeeping? We can go, Mattie. Out there, where we belong." She flung her arm in a dramatic gesture.

Mattie and Julia traveled in their imagination together, away from Fairmile Road and the colorless suburban landscape.

"What about your mum and dad?" Mattie persisted.

Julia clenched her fists and then let them fall open, impotent. Mattie knew some of how she felt, but it was still difficult to put it into words. Even more difficult now, because it sounded so trivial after Mattie's confession. But Julia felt that this little, tidy house wound iron bands around her chest, stopping her breathing. She was confined by her parents' love and expectations. She knew that they loved her, and she was sure that she didn't deserve it. Their disapproval of Mattie, and of Julia's own passions, masked their frightened anxiety for her. Perhaps they were right to be anxious, Julia thought. She knew that she couldn't meet their expectations. Vernon and Betty wanted a replica of themselves. Julia wanted other, vaguer, more violent things for herself. Not a life like Betty's, she was sure of that.

"I'm like a cuckoo in this house," Julia said.

They looked around the spare bedroom and smiled at each other.

"If I go now, with you, they'll be shocked, but perhaps it'll be better in the end. Better than staying here, getting worse. And when we're settled, when we've made it, it will be different. We'll all be equal. They won't have to fight me all the time.''

It was all *when*, Julia remembered, sitting on the Embankment with all her possessions at her feet, and afterward, years afterward. We never thought *if*, in those days, Mattie and me.

Mattie had smiled suddenly, a crooked smile at first because of her broken lip, but then it broadened recklessly. ''When shall we go?''

''Today,'' Julia said. ''Today, of course.''

Later, when Vernon was at work and Betty had gone shopping, Julia gathered her belongings together and flung them into two suitcases. Mattie wouldn't go home even long enough to collect her clothes, so Julia's would have to do for both of them.

There was no time to spare. Betty was seldom out of the house for more than an hour. In the frantic last minute, Julia scribbled a note to her. There was no time to choose the words, no time to think what she was saying. *I'm going*, that was all.

She remembered the carelessness of that, later.

The girls caught the train from the familiar, musty local station. On the short journey they crammed into the lavatory and made up their faces in the dim mirror.

Liverpool Street Station seemed larger and grimmer than it had looked on their earlier adventures. Mattie flung out her arms.

''The Big City welcomes us.'' But she was looking at Julia with faint anxiety. Julia smiled determinedly back.

''Not only does it welcome us,'' she announced, ''it belongs to us.''

To make their claim on it, they rode to Oxford Circus on the underground. When they emerged, Oxford Street stretched invitingly on either side of them.

In the beginning it had been a huge adventure, and they had felt delighted with themselves. They started by looking for work, and they both found jobs at once. Mattie camouflaged her bruises with Pan-Stik makeup and was taken on as a junior assistant in a shoe shop. Julia had learned to type as part of her commercial course at school, and she presented herself for an interview as a typist in the accounts department of a big store. The supervisor gave her a spelling and comprehension test that seemed ridiculously simple.

"That's very good," the woman told her, looking surprised. "I'm sure you would be useful here. When would you like to start?"

"Tomorrow," Julia said promptly.

The words *accounts department* made her think of her father. She had often looked at him and wondered how he could go off every day, year after year, to the same dull, meaningless job. It's only for a little while for me, she told herself. Everything is going to happen soon. After the interview Julia walked out into the street, and she saw the sunshine reflecting off the shop windows like a greeting. *I can work,* she was thinking. *I can keep myself. I don't have to ask for anything.*

It was a moment of intense pleasure.

Julia could feel her freedom, like expensive scent or floating chiffon, drifting around her as she walked. It was as though she had already traveled a long, long way from home.

When she met Mattie later, they were both almost dancing with triumph.

"How much?" Mattie demanded.

"Eight pounds a week."

"And I get seven pounds, ten shillings. Thirty bob more than the last place. We'll be rich."

It was more money than either of them had ever had before, and they told each other incredulously that they would have that much to spend every week. They bought some sandwiches and a bottle of cider to celebrate, and picnicked in Trafalgar Square. When they had drunk the cider, they sat and beamed vaguely at the tourists photographing the fountains.

"The next thing is somewhere to live," Mattie said.

"A flat," Julia agreed, tipping the bottle to make sure it was empty. "Simple but elegant. Mattie Banner and Julia Smith, at home."

The difficulties began after that.

They had found jobs, but the days until they could expect to be paid stretched awkwardly ahead of them. The landlords of all the flats they went to see demanded rent in advance, and deposits, and the girls couldn't muster even a fraction of the money. The ones who didn't ask for money eyed the two of them suspiciously, and asked how old they were. Mattie always answered defiantly, "Twenty," but even so the rooms turned out to be let already.

They stayed in the cheapest hotel they could find, and scoured the *To Let* columns of the *Evening Standard* every morning as soon as the paper came on the streets, but by the third day they still hadn't found anywhere they could afford. The first euphoria began to evaporate. Friday morning came, and as they were leaving the grubby hotel on their way to work, the manager waylaid them. He announced that it was time for them to settle their bill to date, handing the folded slip of paper over to them. It came to much more than they had reckoned for, and even by pooling all their resources they were only just able to meet it. They were left with a few shillings between them. Julia smiled brightly at the manager to hide her concern.

"And how much longer are you planning to stay with us?" the man asked.

"Oh. Two, perhaps three more nights. Just until we've found ourselves a nice flat."

"I see." The manager examined his nails, and then he said, "I'm afraid that I shall have to ask you for a deposit on your room. The weekend is our busy time, you see. We do have to be quite sure—" He broke off, the picture of regret.

"How much?"

"Five pounds. That will cover both of you, of course."

"Oh, of course."

There was a pause. At last Mattie said desperately, "We'll let you know this evening."

"No later than this evening, then."

As they scurried away to the tube station, Mattie burst out furiously, "He knows we haven't got it. The miserable bugger."

"You can't blame him." Julia was practical. "We'll have to ask them at work to pay us for these two days."

"It still won't be enough."

"It'll be better than nothing, won't it?"

Mattie grinned at her suddenly. Her bruises were fading, and it no longer hurt her to smile. "Don't worry. Something'll turn up."

They parted at Oxford Circus and went their separate ways.

Julia waited until her supervisor came back from her dinner break, and then mumbled her request.

"Oh, no, dear, I don't think we can do that. You have to work a full week first. Your money will come next Friday, with the three extra days, which will be nice, won't it? Otherwise it makes it too complicated for the payroll people, you know. Is there some trouble, dear?"

Julia hesitated, but she was too proud to confide in this wispy, middle-aged stranger.

"Oh, no, I just wanted to buy something, that's all."

"Well. I'm sure your parents will be glad to help if it's something important. Ask your mother tonight."

Julia had told them at the interview that she still lived at home. It had seemed that kind of job.

She went back to the typewriter, which she was already beginning to hate, and started to thump at the keys.

"What did they say?" Mattie asked when they met.

"Nothing until next Friday."

"Oh, shit. Mine'll pay me tomorrow afternoon, though."

A whole night and a day to get through until then.

They collected their luggage from the hotel.

"We've found the perfect flat," Julia told the manager, who came out of his lair to see them off. "Absolutely huge, and terribly cheap."

The truth couldn't have been more different. They had divided their remaining change between them that morning, and they agreed that they would allow themselves one cup of coffee and a sandwich for lunch. When they found themselves outside the hotel with their luggage, they were at a loss, and achingly hungry. They took a bus, the first one that came along because the manager was standing in the doorway watching them, and rode as far as a fourpenny fare would take them. When they reached the Embankment, they had just three shillings left.

They sat on their bench for a long time, just watching the river. The sky faded from blue to pearl gray, with a green glow that deepened to rose pink behind the chimneys of Battersea Power Station. It would have been beautiful if they had had the heart to look at it.

At last, the sky and water were completely dark.

"We could go home," Julia whispered.

Mattie turned her head to look at her. "No," she said at last. "We can't go back. I can't." She drew her knees up and rested her chin on them, looking out over the river again. Julia wished that she had never said it, even if it was only to test Mattie's resolve.

"Something will turn up." Julia tried to be comforting, but their rallying cry had no effect this time.

After another long silence Mattie said, "We'll have to find somewhere to sleep outside."

"What about that park we walked through last night?"

They had eaten fish and chips sitting on the grass in Hyde Park. The idea of lying in the soft grass under the shelter of rustling trees seemed almost inviting. "How far is it?"

"Quite a long way."

They turned away from the black river and the necklace of lights lacing its banks and started to walk. After a few hundred yards they realized that the suitcases were impossibly heavy.

"All this junk," Mattie grumbled. "We don't need it. We should throw it away, and then we'd really be free."

"You could throw it away if it was yours," Julia pointed out. They went on in silence, irritable with each other, and then stopped again. A huge building blazed in front of them, its tiers of windows opulently draped. Julia peered at the big silvery letters on the sweep of canopy that faced the river.

"It's the Savoy Hotel," she whispered.

"Oh, that's perfect. Let's take a suite."

For no particular reason they turned their backs on the river and walked up a tiny, steep side alley. There was a big, recessed doorway in the wall of the hotel, with heavy padlocked bars holding the doors shut. A ventilator grille was set high up and warm air that smelled of cooking pulsed out of it.

"I'm not going any farther," Mattie said. "We can lie down here."

The alley was lit by one old-fashioned streetlamp, and it was completely deserted. Mattie sank down on the step and drew her legs up. She curled up sideways and closed her eyes.

To Julia, she looked suddenly as if she were dead, a body abandoned in a huddle of clothes.

"Mattie! Don't do that."

The sharp note of fear in her voice brought Mattie struggling upright again.

"What's the matter? It's all right. Look, there's room for us both. Come in here behind me and I'll shield you."

Julia looked up and down the alley. The city waiting beyond its dark mouths seemed threatening now. Reluctantly, she stepped past Mattie and hauled the suitcases into the grimy space. She opened one and took out some of the least essential clothes, bunching them up to make pillows and a scrap of a bed. She lay down with the suitcases wedged behind her for safety, and Mattie squeezed herself in too. Julia tucked her knees into the crook of Mattie's and hunched up to her warm back. Mattie's mass of curls, still surprisingly scented with her Coty perfume, fell over her face.

"I'm so glad you're here," Julia whispered.

"You helped me to get away," Mattie said simply. And then, "We'll be all right, you know."

"I know we will," Julia answered.

They lay quietly, hoping to sleep. After a little while a smartly dressed couple came up the alley. The yellow light from the streetlamp glittered briefly on the woman's necklace. They glanced at the figures in the doorway as they passed, and looked quickly away again, separating themselves.

"I've done that," Mattie whispered, when they had gone.

"Me too."

It seemed such a small step, now, from that world, padded with food and insulated with little tokens of security, to this doorway.

"I'm so hungry."

"We must save the money for breakfast."

The smell of food wafting from the ventilator made them feel ravenous and sick at the same time. There were other smells lingering in the doorway too. Mattie and Julia clung together, and after a while they drifted into an uncomfortable sleep.

Mattie had no idea how long she had been dozing. She woke up, confused and aching, with the panicky certainty that someone was watching them. She lifted her head from the nest of clothes, and a gasp of terror shook her. A man was leaning over her. His face was covered with gray whiskers and his matted gray hair hung down to his shoulders. He was grinning, his lips drawn back to reveal black stumps of teeth. It was his breath that frightened Mattie most. It smelled rawly of drink and she recoiled, trying to escape from the memories that that close, fetid smell stirred in her. She felt Julia go stiff behind her, and her fingers digging into her arms.

"Two lassies," the apparition mumbled, and then cackled with laughter. "Two lassies, is it? Ma pitch, ye know, this is. Mine." He thrust his face closer and they tried to edge backward.

"Please go away," Julia whispered. "We're not doing any harm. We've nowhere else."

"Ah can see that." He cackled more raucously still. "Well, seein' it's you, ye can be ma guests. Just fer tonight. 'Tis the Savoy, ye know. Act nice. They serve breakfast just around the corner, first thing." He picked up a filthy sack and shuffled away down the hill, still hooting with laughter.

Mattie was shuddering with fright and shock. Julia put her arm over her shoulders. "He was only an old tramp. We've pinched his place, that's all. Come on, we'll change places so that I'm in the front. You can hide behind me."

"I'm sorry," Mattie mumbled.

They scrambled stiffly to their knees and lay down again. Mattie stopped shaking at last, and she let her eyes close. It wasn't the tramp who she saw at once against her eyelids. It was only his smell that had frightened her, and repelled her so deeply that all her flesh screamed and crawled in case he touched her.

He had made her think of her father, and of what she had really run away from.

She had been to see *East of Eden*, just as she had told Vernon and Betty Smith. She came blindly out of the Odeon in the High Street with the image of James Dean more real than the windows of Woolworth's across the street, more flesh and blood than the two boys from the technical college lounging in front of them. For a few minutes more, while the spell lasted, the hated suburban shopping street and the boys whistling at her were nothing to do with Mattie.

For two whole hours she had escaped from home and her younger brothers and sisters, from work, and from everything that surrounded her. It was her fourth visit. Julia had come with her three times, but even Julia had balked at a fourth visit. So Mattie had gone on her own, and afterward she drifted to the bus stop, lost inside her own head with Cal Trask.

The enchantment lasted until she reached home. She walked through the estate, where every avenue and turning was the same as the last and the next, and reached her own front gate. It creaked open, brushing over the docks and nettles sprouting across the path. She stopped for a second outside her own front door. The house was quiet. It must have thundered while she was in the cinema, Mattie thought. It had been a dusty, muggy day but the air was cool and clear now.

She put her key in the lock and opened the front door.

Ted Banner was standing in the dim hallway.

"Where the bloody hell have you been, you dirty little madam?"

Mattie smelled sweat and whiskey and the indefinable, sour scent of her father's hopeless anger. She knew what was coming. Her stomach heaved with fright, but she made herself say, calmly and clearly so that he couldn't possibly misunderstand her, "I've been to the Odeon to see a picture. It was James Dean in *East of Eden*. It finished at a quarter to ten and I came straight home." As conciliatory as she could be, with as much detail as possible, so that he might believe her. But he didn't. He came at her, and she glimpsed the patch of sweat darkening his vest as he lifted his fist.

"Bloody little liar."

He swiped viciously at her. Mattie flung up her arm to protect her face, but the blow still jarred and she stumbled backward.

"Been out with some feller, haven't you? Taking your knickers off for anyone who asks you in the back of his car, like your sister. All the same, all of you."

"I haven't. I told you, I've been to the pictures."

"*Again*?"

Some evenings, Mattie didn't have the protection of the truth. But it made no difference anyway. Her father hit her again, hard, a double blow with the flat and then the back of his hand. Her teeth sliced into the corner of her lip, and she tasted blood, salty in her mouth. A little part of her, cold and detached and disgusted, heard the rest of herself whimpering with fear. He knocked her sideways and she fell against the rickety coatstand that stood behind the door. It collapsed with her in a humiliating tangle of clothes and limbs.

"Please," she whispered. "Please, Dad."

I hate you. The words drummed in her head. *I hate you*.

A door creaked open at the top of the stairs, and Mattie looked up to see her sister Marilyn, nine years old, looking down at them. The girl's eyes were wide with anxiety, but there was no surprise in them.

"It's all right, Marilyn," Mattie said. She pulled herself upright, pressing the palm of her hand against her throbbing lip. "Go back to bed now. Don't wake Sam up." The child melted away again.

Ted was breathing heavily through his mouth. His cheeks were blotched and threaded with broken veins, and his big mustache was beaded with sweat and spittle.

Suddenly his shoulders sagged. He rolled his head to and fro, as if he were trying to break free of something. "I'm sorry," he said at last.

Mattie tried to slip past him up the stairs. "It's all right," she murmured, pressing herself against the wall so that even her clothes need not brush against him. But his hand caught her wrist.

"Come in the kitchen," he begged her in a new, wheedling voice. "I'll make us both a nice cup of tea."

"All right," Mattie said. It was easier to acquiesce than to risk stirring up his anger again.

She watched her father warily as he lit the gas and put the kettle on. She was ready for him when he came at her again. She flinched, and slid out of his reach behind the table.

He held out his big, meaty hands.

"Mat, don't run away from me. Don't, I can't bear it."

There was a bottle of whiskey on the table, and he took a swig from it, wiping his mustache with his fingers. He had gone from anger to self-pitying drunkenness. Mattie knew what that meant too, and it made her even more afraid.

"Come here."

Her skin crawled, but she knew that she couldn't refuse him. She sidled out from the table's protection.

"Right here, I said."

Her father's hand touched her arm and then her shoulders. It weighed heavily, and the hairy skin of his forearm was hot and prickly against the nape of her neck. With his other hand he turned her face to his. He was very close, and she bit the insides of her cheeks to keep her fear and disgust hidden inside her. Ted's hand slipped downward, and his fingers touched her breast. He hesitated for a second, his expression suddenly dreamy, almost tender. Then his hand closed on her, squeezing and twisting, and she cried out in pain.

"Don't. Please, don't."

"Don't you like it? Those boys do it, don't they?"

They didn't, because Mattie wouldn't let them, but her father didn't know that. The sweat had broken out on his face again, and a thread of it trickled from his hairline, across his temple. His mouth opened and hung loosely as he rubbed his hand over her breast. He jerked her closer. Holding her so tightly that she knew she couldn't break away, he thrust his face against hers and kissed her. Wetness smeared her mouth and chin, and then his tongue forced itself between her lips.

Mattie understood how drunk he was.

For years, since she was younger than Marilyn, her father had touched her and fondled her.

"It's a little game," he used to say. "Our little game. Don't tell anyone, will you?"

Mattie hated it, and the feelings it stirred in her frightened and puzzled her. But she also discovered that it was a protection. If she let him play his game, just occasionally, he was less likely to hit her. She would stand, mute and motionless, and let him run his hands over her. That was all. Nothing else. She kept the knowledge of it in a little box, closed off from everything else, never mentioning it to her older sisters, or to her mother while she was still alive. It was just her father, after all, just the way he was. Dirty, and pathetic, and she would get away from him as soon as she could.

She had never even whispered anything to Julia.

But tonight was different. Somehow Ted had slipped beyond control. He didn't seem pathetic anymore, so she couldn't detach herself in despising him. He was dangerous now. Too close, too dangerous.

Mattie's fear paralyzed her. She couldn't move, and couldn't stop him. He was grunting now deep in his throat. He sat down heavily against the table, pulling her to him. Her legs were trapped between his. His hand went to the hem of her skirt. He wrenched at it, trying to pull it up. But it was too tight, and it caught at the tops of her thighs. He squinted at her, his eyes puffy.

"Take it off."

Mattie shuddered, struggling in his grip. "No. Leave me alone. Leave me . . ."

He tore at her blouse instead. It was a skimpy, sleeveless thing that Mattie had made herself with lopsided hand stitching. The shoulder seam ripped and Ted forced his hand inside.

"Let me do it. Just once," he begged her. His face was hidden, but she could feel his hot, wet mouth working against her neck. "I won't ask you again. Ever, Mattie. Just once, will you?"

Mattie held herself still, gathering her strength. Then she lashed at him with her hands and twisted her neck to try to bite any part of him that she could reach. He didn't even notice the blow, and he was much too quick for her. He caught both her wrists in one hand, and the other tightened around her throat. For a second they looked into each other's eyes. Slowly, his fingers unfastened from her neck. She could feel the print of them on her skin.

He fumbled with his own clothes, undoing them.

Somehow, out of her pain and terror and disgust, Mattie found the right words. "Look at yourself," she commanded in a small, clear voice. "Just look at yourself."

He saw his daughter's face, paper-white except for the black tear-trails of mascara, her torn clothes, and her swollen, bloody lip.

And then he looked down at himself.

Ted shrank, deflating as if the whiskey had found a puncture in his skin to trickle out of.

There was a long silence. Behind them, shockingly cozy, the kettle whistled.

At last he mumbled, "I'm sorry. I'm sorry I hit you. I'm jealous, see? Jealous of all those lads that hang around you. I don't mean to get angry with you, don't you understand? You've always been my girl. My special one, haven't you?"

Mattie saw big, glassy tears gather in his eyes and roll down his cheeks. She felt sick, and dirty, and she turned her face away.

"You don't know what I've been through since your mum died."

Oh, yes, Mattie thought. Feel sorry for yourself. Not for Mum, or any of the rest of us. Feel sorry for yourself, because I won't. I hate you.

With the knowledge of that, she realized that he had let go of her. She began to move, very slowly, backing away from him. His hands hung heavily at his sides, and his wet eyes stared at nothing. Mattie reached the kitchen door. In the same clear, cold voice she said, "Do yourself up. Don't sit there like that."

Then she walked through the clutter in the hall to the front door. She opened it and closed it again behind her, and walked down the path. She held herself very carefully, as if she were made of a shell that might break.

Only when the gate had creaked after her did she begin to run.

In the narrow space of the doorway her legs twitched involuntarily, and Julia stirred in front of her.

"It's all right," Julia told her. "He's gone, he really has. Are you still scared? Do you want to talk for a bit?"

"I was thinking about Marilyn, and the others," Mattie told her, half truthfully. Marilyn was only nine, and Phil, the youngest sister, was two years younger. Two boys, Ricky and Sam, came between Mattie and Marilyn. The eldest sister, Rozzie, was married to a mechanic and had a baby of her own. She lived on the estate, too, but Rozzie kept clear of the house when Ted was likely to be at home.

"The boys are all right," Mattie said, "but I don't want to leave Phil and Marilyn there with him."

Guilt folded around her again. Even if what her father had

done had not been, somehow, all her own fault, Mattie was certain that she shouldn't have abandoned her younger sisters to him. She had never seen Ted look at them in the way that he looked at her, but she couldn't be sure that he didn't touch them. Or if he hadn't, that he might not now that she was gone. Rozzie had never suspected, had she? In her shame, Mattie had kept her secret until she couldn't hold on to it any longer, but it was unthinkable that Marilyn might have to suffer in the same way. . . . Mattie rolled her head, looking up at the stained walls of her shelter. What could she do to help them from here?

"I know what we'll do," Julia said firmly. "We'll ring the council and tell them what's happened. There are people there who are supposed to see about kids, you know. They'll look after them until . . ." She was thinking quickly, improvising. "Until we can have them with us, if you like. We could all live together, couldn't we?"

Mattie smiled, in spite of herself. "Here?"

"Don't be stupid. When we're well off. It might take a year, or something, but we'll do it. Why shouldn't we?"

A year seemed like a lifetime then. When anything might happen.

"I can't tell anyone," Mattie whispered. "It was hard enough to tell you."

"It's not your fault," Julia said fiercely. Mattie and Julia hadn't spent much time at each other's homes, but Julia had seen enough of Ted Banner to imagine the rest. Sometimes he was fulsomely friendly. At other times, the times when the veins at his temples stood out in ridges and his eyes shrank to little red spots, she thought that he was terrifying. "You don't have to say who you are. Just telephone anonymously. I'll do it if you like. We've just got to make sure that someone looks after them, because it can't be you anymore. Perhaps they could go to Rozzie. As soon as we can, we'll get a really big flat. One with two or three bedrooms, plenty of room. We can play records as loud as we want, invite whoever we want in. The girls will love it. They'll be safe with us, Mattie."

Mattie nodded, grateful for Julia's generosity, letting herself accept the fantasy for now, for tonight at least. She lay still again, listening to Julia's murmured talk. The plans grew more elaborate as Julia spun the dreams to comfort herself as well as Mattie.

Cramped in the doorway, listening to her, Mattie drifted into sleep again.

Julia listened to her regular breathing. At first she was relieved that Mattie wasn't frightened anymore, but without the need to reassure her, her own bravado ebbed away. The dim streetlamp seemed only to emphasize the terrifying darkness of the alley, and the darkness seemed endless. At last she began to waver in and out of an uncomfortable dream-ridden half-sleep. The dreams were vivid, and horrible, and when she jerked awake again, the alley seemed to belong to them rather than to reality. And then, far from being eerily deserted, a slow tide of hunched figures began to wander through it. To begin with, she was sure that they were dream-figures, but then she understood that they were too real and she shrank backward against Mattie for a shred of protection.

The alley had become a kind of thoroughfare for the derelicts and tramps of the Embankment. They drifted past the doorway, muttering or singing or cursing. Some of them peered at the girls and whispered or shouted at them; others went past, oblivious of everything but their own obsessions.

To Julia, the tide of them seemed a grotesque parody of the Oxford Street shoppers in sunny daylight. *This is waiting for all of us*, she thought, the dream world half-claiming her again. *Darkness and despair.* And then, out of nowhere, the thought came to her: *Is this what Betty is so frightened of?* She was quite sure of her mother's fear, whereas in her childhood she had been puzzled by the nameless force that seemed to control her. *Darkness.* And then, like a chant repeated over and over inside her head, *I won't let it get me. Not me.*

She slept, and then woke again. She thought that the night would go on forever and then, quite suddenly, it was dawn. The spreading of dirty gray light was like a blessing.

Julia sat upright, relief easing her muscles. Leaning against the wall, with Mattie still asleep beside her, she watched the light grow stronger and stronger. In half an hour it was broad daylight once more.

Her strength flowed back again. With the return of light, she felt that the world belonged to her, and that she could take it and make what she wanted from it. They had survived the night, and the little victory made her triumphant. She shook Mattie's shoulder, and Mattie yawned herself into consciousness again.

"Look," Julia said, "it's daytime. Isn't it beautiful?"

Mattie stretched, and grumbled, and let Julia drag her to her feet. They collected their belongings and stuffed them into the suitcases, then made their way on up the alley. Neither of them looked back at the doorway.

Before they reached the corner they heard doors banging, and a metallic rumble, almost like thunder. At once there was a babble of voices and the sound of shuffling feet. The girls turned the corner and saw what was happening. Huge metal bins had been wheeled out of the hotel kitchens to wait for emptying. A dozen or so old men were clustering around them, picking out the scraps of food.

"That's what he meant about breakfast," Mattie said.

"What?"

"The old tramp, last night. Breakfast is served round the corner."

"Not for me, thanks."

They stood watching the derelicts for a moment, remembering the night's fears. Warmed and restored by the daylight, Julia felt an ache of pity for the filthy, hungry old men as they scraped up the food relics and stowed them in their tattered pockets. They weren't dark, terrifying figures waiting for her to join them. They weren't waiting for anything except their sad breakfast.

"Let's find somewhere to wash," Mattie said.

They crossed the road and walked by on the opposite side. Just like the couple in the alley last night, Julia remembered. By crossing the road she had moved from the night world back into the other. Relief and a renewed sense of her own power flowed through her, warmer than the early morning sunlight.

"I can't wait to get clean again," Julia exulted. "Water and soap, how heavenly."

Mattie eyed her. "You're more like your mother than you think," she teased. "You can't bear a bit of muck."

The public lavatories near Trafalgar Square didn't open until seven o'clock. They waited beside the green-painted railings, among the scavenging pigeons. The attendant who came to unlock the doors stared at them disapprovingly, but the girls were too busy even to notice. They ran cold, clear water out of the polished brass taps while she mopped around their feet. They drank their fill and then washed themselves with Julia's Pears soap. It smelled oddly of Fairmile Road. Julia tried to dip her head into the basin to wash her hair, but the attendant darted out of her cubbyhole.

"You can't do that in 'ere. You'll 'ave to go to the warm baths in Marshall Street for that."

The girls made faces when she turned away, and then collapsed into giggles. Their high spirits were almost fully restored.

They made do with washing as much of themselves as they could undress under the attendant's sour gaze, and picking the least crumpled of Julia's clothes out of the suitcases. Then they perched in front of the mirror and defiantly made up their faces with lots of mascara and eye liner to hide the shadows left by the night in the doorway. Then they struggled out with their suitcases to a taxi-drivers' coffee stall. They bought a mug of coffee and a ham roll each, and the simple food tasted better than anything they had ever eaten. The tide of people began to flow to work. Mattie and Julia had just enough money left between them for Mattie's bus ride to her shoe shop. It was Saturday, and Julia's accounts office was closed.

"What will you do?" Mattie asked when they had eaten the last crumb of their rolls. They hadn't nearly satisfied their hunger—Julia felt that she was even more ravenous than she had been before.

"I don't know. Sit in the park. Plan what we're going to eat when you get your money tonight. Every mouthful of it."

"Oh, I'm *so* hungry," Mattie wailed.

"Go on. Get your bus. They'll sack you if you're late, and then what'll we do?"

Neither of them mentioned the problem of where they would sleep. They didn't want to think about that, not now, when the sun was getting brighter and the day seemed full of possibilities.

"How do I look?"

Julia put her head on one side, studying Mattie carefully before she answered. Mattie struck an obligingly theatrical pose. She wasn't conventionally pretty, but she had a lively face with wide-set eyes and a pointed chin. Her expression was bold and challenging. Mattie's best features were her hair, a foaming mass of curls like a Pre-Raphaelite heroine, and her figure. She had been generously developed when Julia had first seen her, at eleven years old. Julia herself was still almost as flat as Betty's ironing board.

"You look," Julia said carefully, "as if . . . as if you've just spent a night in a doorway."

"And so do you, so there." They laughed at each other, and then Mattie ran, scrambling for the bus as it swayed toward them.

Julia felt deflated when Mattie had gone. She picked up the suitcases yet again, and began to walk, aimlessly, looking into the windows of shops and offices as she passed by.

It was going to be a hot day. She felt the sun on the back of her neck and the handles of the suitcases biting into yesterday's tender patches. She slowed down and then jumped, startled by the sound of a horn hooting at the curb beside her. She turned her head and saw a delivery van and a boy leaning out.

"Where you going?"

Julia hesitated, then put the suitcases down. Why not the truth?

"Nowhere much."

"Didn't look like it. Come on, get in. I've got to make a delivery, then I'll buy you a coffee."

Julia smiled suddenly. It was easy to be friendly in the sunshine, with the people and traffic streaming around her. Her spirits lifted higher.

"Okay." She perched in the passenger seat. They spun round Trafalgar Square, where the fountains sparkled in the bright light. The boy whistled as they wove in and out of buses and taxis, and then they turned into a network of smaller streets. Julia saw little restaurants with waiters sweeping the steps, ready for the day, and grocers' shops with goods spilling out on to the sidewalk, darker doorways, and a jumble of little shops selling everything from violins to surgical appliances. Julia had been here before, with Mattie. There were two cellar jazz clubs in the next street, the goals of their Saturday night pilgrimages from home.

"I know where we are. This is Soho."

"Right." The boy glanced at her, then jerked his head at her suitcases. "What are you doing, arriving or leaving?"

"Oh, I'm arriving," Julia said firmly.

The van skidded to a stop in front of a window hung with dusty red plush curtains. Between the glass and the red folds there were pictures of girls, most of them, as far as Julia could see, adorned with feathers and nothing else. A sign at the top read GIRLS. NONSTOP GIRLS. GIRLS. A string of colored light bulbs, unlit, added to the faintly depressing effect. The driver had jumped out, and he was heaving crates of drinks out of the back of the van. As soon as the stack was completed he began ferrying the crates in through the curtain-draped doorway. He winked at Julia. "Lots of ginger beer," he told her. "The girls drink it and charge the mugs for whiskey."

A swarthy man in a leather jacket came out and counted the crates in. The last one disappeared and Julia's new friend tucked away a roll of pound notes.

"Blue Heaven suit you?" he inquired.

Anywhere with food and drink would have suited Julia at that moment, but she knew Blue Heaven because she had squeezed in there with Mattie late at night. It looked the same as all the other coffee bars, with plastic-topped tables and spindly chairs, a long chrome-banded bar and a jungle of plants absorbing the light, but because of the crowds that packed into it it seemed the model for the rest.

"Suits me fine," Julia said. She left her suitcases in the van and crossed the street with him. It was still early, and Blue Heaven was almost empty. Julia chose a table and sat down. The Gaggia machine hissed sharply, and steam drifted between the rubber plants. The coffee came, creamy froth in a shallow glass cup, and a doughnut for Julia. She tried not to eye the glossy, sugary ball too greedily.

"Go on," he ordered her. Julia didn't need to be asked twice. Sugar stuck to her chin, and jam oozed deliciously.

"You're only a kid." He laughed, watching her.

"I'm sixteen."

"Exactly."

He stood up and leaned over the jukebox, putting a coin in and stabbing the buttons without reading the titles. The record was Johnny Ray, "Such a Night." Julia sighed happily and licked her fingers.

"I love Johnny Ray. Do you?"

"Nope. It's girls' music. I put it on for you."

"What do you like, then?"

"Jazz, of course."

"Trad?"

The bands played trad jazz in the packed clubs around the corner. Julia and Mattie could dance to it all night if they were given the chance.

"Modern, you goon. Dizzy Gillespie. Thelonius Monk."

They talked about music, testing each other, until he looked at his watch.

"Hey, I've got to get a move on."

"Who do you work for? Do they let you sit in coffee bars all morning?"

He frowned at her. "I work for myself, baby. It's my van. I specialize in supplying anything to anyone who needs it." He was on his feet now. "I'm a fixer. And I'd better get fixing." He turned to go, then a thought struck him. "Are you short of money?"

Julia murmured, "A bit. Just until tonight. My friend will . . ."

He put his hand into the pocket of his blue jeans and peeled a note off the roll. "Here."

"I couldn't. . . ."

"You could, and you will. Pay me back when you see me. I'm always around."

He had reached the door before Julia called out, "I don't even know your name."

"It's Flowers. Johnny Flowers." He winked at her. "Sounds like a queen, doesn't it? But I'm not. See you, kid. I'll leave your bags with Mickey, across the road." He left Julia sitting at the table, wishing that he'd asked her what her name was. She watched him handing over her suitcases to the swarthy man behind the red curtain. Julia had liked Johnny Flowers enough to be sure that her bags would be safe wherever he left them. The van's engine roared, and it rocketed away down the street. Julia sat still for a little while, listening to the jukebox and watching the faces passing the windows of Blue Heaven. Then, with the security of Johnny Flowers's pound note in her pocket, she ordered herself another cup of coffee and another doughnut. Later, she crossed the street again to Mickey's. He peered at her from a cubbyhole off the entry. The place was very dark, and silent except for the sound of distant vacuuming. Not quite nonstop girls, Julia thought. The strip club smelled of beer, smoke, and dust.

"Come for your stuff? It's down there." He pointed his thick finger down behind a shelf of a desk.

"Um. I wondered if I could leave it here for a bit longer? It's heavy to carry around."

He looked carefully at her, examining everything except her face. "You a new girl?"

"Er, yeah," Julia said ambiguously.

He clicked his tongue in disapproval. "Jesus, where does Monty find them? Nursery school? All right, leave your gear here. I'll keep an eye on it."

"Thanks."

Julia slipped sideways out of the door before he could change his mind or ask her anything else. The first thing she did was to head up Wardour Street into Oxford Street. Then she made her way to Mattie's shoe shop. Peering through the plate glass window, Julia saw her kneeling in front of a customer, a sea of shoes spread all around them. She was holding a shoe in one hand and the other gesticulated as she talked. The woman listened intently, then took the shoe and tried it on again. Julia saw her nodding. A minute later she was on her way to the cash register, with Mattie bearing the shoes behind her.

Julia waited until the sale was completed and then she slipped into the shop. Mattie stared. "What are you doing in here?" she whispered, and then added in a louder voice, "Black pumps, madam?"

"You look like a born saleswoman," Julia told her.

"I'm an actress," Mattie said haughtily. "I can act saleswoman, of course."

Julia took her hand and pressed something into it. Mattie looked down at the money.

"It's for your sandwiches at dinnertime."

"How . . . ?"

"Tell you later. I don't see anything I like the look of, thank you very much."

Outside, looking between the cliffs of high buildings, Julia could just see trees in the distance. She remembered that it was Hyde Park, the sanctuary that they had failed to reach last night, and the greenness drew her. She walked toward it, slipping through the skeins of traffic at Marble Arch, and then crossing on to the grass. It was brown and parched by the sun, but the softness was welcome after the hot, hard pavements. She walked on, under the shadow of the great trees, until the roar of traffic in Park Lane diminished to a muffled hum. Water glinted coolly, and Julia guessed that the wide stretch of lake must be the Serpentine. There was a scatter of green canvas deckchairs under the trees overlooking it. She sank down in one of the chairs and paid threepence to an old man with a ticket machine. Then she closed her eyes and listened to the faint rustle of leaves over her head.

It was the first comfortable, solitary moment she had had to consider what had happened since leaving home.

She found herself wondering what her mother was doing.

It was easy to picture her. Perhaps she was dusting, picking up the ornaments from the tiled mantelpiece, very carefully, dusting each souvenir and china knick-knack before putting it back in exactly the same place. It was as if the house were always being made ready, cleaned and polished, for some big occasion that never came. Even the furniture, the sofa and chairs with their cushions set at exact angles, seemed to wait tensely for inspection by guests who never materialized. Hardly anyone ever came into the house, and when she was a little girl Julia was puzzled by her mother's anxiety in the midst of their eventless lives. She was always being told not to make a mess when she played.

Don't do that, Julia, it makes such a mess.

Betty wanted her to play neatly, setting her dolls out in rows. Julia's own inclinations were to sand, and water, and poster paints that sent up plumes of brightly colored powder when she poured in the water to mix them.

Once, Julia remembered, she had come home from a birthday party with a packet of shiny colored stars. With childish cunning she had hidden them from her mother, and then one afternoon she had shut herself in her bedroom and stuck them all over the wallpaper. They looked wonderful, like fireworks, jets of cobalt blue and scarlet against the insipid pink roses. Betty had grown suspicious, and she had forced the door open just as Julia was pressing the last gummy stars into place. Betty had flown across the room and started pulling them off, but the glue was surprisingly strong and it brought little star-shaped fragments of paper with it. Those that did come away left black marks.

Betty was angrier than Julia had ever seen her.

"You little vandal," she rasped at her, and Julia recoiled in shock and surprise.

"They looked pretty," she protested. "It's my bedroom."

"Don't you ever do that. Why do you spoil everything? Why do you?" There were white flecks at the corners of her mother's mouth, Julia remembered. "It isn't *your* bedroom. Your father and I have given it to you, and you'll keep it how we want it. Look at it now." Betty pointed at the wreckage of Julia's fireworks, and then her face collapsed. She was crying helplessly. Suddenly Julia caught a glimpse of her mother's grown-up fears. She half-understood her struggle to keep everything that was lurid, and threatening, and incomprehensible, at bay with the semi-detached walls of their house. For an instant she understood what it must be like to be grown-up and still afraid, like Betty was.

She had run to her mother full of sympathy, but Betty was good at holding on to her anger and she had pushed her away. They had spent the rest of the day in silence, and when Vernon came home from work he turned Julia over his knee and smacked her with a slipper.

There must have been dozens of other times like that, Julia thought, and plenty of times when she had deserved whatever they had doled out to her. But that was the time that she remembered. Perhaps because of the embrace that Betty had rejected. Perhaps because of the glimpse of her mother's fear.

Sitting in her deckchair, with the sun warming her face and arms, Julia remembered the old men on the Embankment. In the middle of her own night terrors she had recalled her mother's too. Betty was afraid of everything, afraid that if she let any little detail out of place the long slide might begin, and leave her with nothing. Was that why she wouldn't allow her daughter anything new, or different, or dangerous?

In the night Julia had determined *I won't let it get me*. Not the darkness, nor the fear of it. And she had survived.

I won't live like Betty, Julia promised herself. I won't be afraid, and I can risk everything if I have to.

She shivered a little, trying to imagine, looking ahead, beyond herself. But the sun made coin-bright circles under her closed eyelids, and that was all she could see.

After the stars, or perhaps all along only she couldn't remember it, rebellion came naturally to Julia. As she grew older, there were more and more things to kick against. Looking back, the years seemed to stretch behind her as a long, entrenched battle against Betty's strictures. In by eight. Bed by nine. Homework done on the day it was given. Julia challenged her on everything. They disagreed about her clothes, her makeup, the music she played, the hours she came in and went out again, and the places she went to. Betty and Vernon were proud that Julia had won a place at the girls' grammar, but Mattie and Julia hated the place. They played truant and did no work, but even so Julia always came out near the top of her class.

The fights were tiring and boring, and Julia nearly always won them because she fought from strength. Betty was always forced to retrench and then capitulate.

And when Mattie came along, Julia had a natural ally. Mattie was an equally natural focus for the Smiths' disapproval. She came from the despised estate, while the Smiths clung to the middle-class isolation of Fairmile Road. She wore her skirts too short and too tightly belted so that they showed off her surprising breasts. And then there was the defiant mass of her hair. It was Mattie who produced the first Outdoor Girl cake mascara for Julia to try out, and quick-witted Mattie who yelled back at the boys who whistled at them in the High Street. But it was still Julia who was the leader. Julia had the ideas, and the determination to carry them out.

Betty had once said, with a sadness that Julia couldn't fathom, "You're not a bit like me."

She could see her so clearly, in the house that gave Julia claustrophobia. A thin, small woman with a scarf knotted around her head to keep the dust out of her hair. Always stooping to tidy something away, or smooth a crease, or straighten an edge, her head bent so that the knobs in her neck stood out, the corners of her mouth always turned down.

I'm sorry, Julia thought. I couldn't stay there with you. When Mattie came, after what Mattie had told her, the idea of escape had seemed so magnificent, so obvious, and so enticing. There had been no alternative. No question even of waiting. With a single gesture Betty and Fairmile Road and all the rest had been left behind her.

And yet, in spite of everything, Julia missed her.

I'll come back, she promised. *When I've got something worth showing you. You can be proud of me then, if you like.* The words sounded grand in her head, and she offered them to her mother in expiation.

Vernon was different. Julia had been afraid of her father, or of his slow-burning, malevolent temper. Betty was afraid of him too, she thought. She remembered how her mother cooked his tea, watching the clock all the time so that the food would be ready at exactly half past five. They ate their meal in silence while Vernon read the newspaper and Betty watched his plate, and the clock ticked far too loudly.

Julia didn't miss Vernon at all.

The sun and her comfortable chair were making her feel drowsy. Her thoughts turned from her own home to Mattie's. When she had first met her, years ago, Mattie had asked her home to tea. Julia had never ventured onto the estate before. The vast expanse of it startled her. There were thousands of houses, all the same, looking as if they had been dropped from the sky in endless lines. There were no trees to suggest that anything had existed there before the houses came, no corner shops to break the monotony. Mattie's street was identical to all the others, but her house looked more neglected. The sooty patch of front garden was cluttered with junk and rusty bits of machinery.

Mattie flung the door open. "You'd better come in. Don't take any notice of anything," she added with an odd fierceness.

Julia couldn't have avoided noticing the noise, and the smell of frying onions. There seemed to be children squirming everywhere, Mattie's four smaller brothers and sisters. Mattie picked the baby up and flung her in the air until she hiccuped with delight. In the kitchen Mattie's eldest sister was standing at the stove. Mattie didn't ask, but Rozzie announced, "He's out."

Mattie's anxious fierceness disappeared at once. "Make yourself at home," she said hospitably.

Julia looked around. Every surface in the room was piled up with broken toys and dirty clothes and open packets of food. She had a brief vision of her mother's kitchen, where every jar had its place and the floor was rinsed down every day with a solution of bleach.

"Where's your mum?" she asked. As soon as she had said it she knew that it was tactless. But Betty was such a fixture in Fairmile Road, with her dustcloths and her sewing and the Light Programme on the wireless, it was hard to understand the absence of a similar figure for Mattie.

"She's in the hospital," Mattie told her expressionlessly. "She's given up." She waved her hand at the mess as she spoke so that Julia might have thought that it was just tidiness Mrs. Banner had given up on.

"It's ready," Rozzie announced.

They took their places at the table. Mattie hoisted the baby on to her lap and fed her with spoonfuls from her own plate. The children ate ravenously, and in between mouthfuls they asked Julia dozens of inquisitive questions. Mattie made up silly names for the teachers and the other girls at their school, and Julia turned them into impromptu rhymes. Everyone laughed uproariously. The atmosphere in the steamy room was cheerful in spite of the mess and the variety of smells. The liver and onions tasted good, and the small portions were helped by piles of potatoes.

It was different from everything Julia knew about.

"I liked it at your house," she said afterward, and Mattie beamed at her, surprised and pleased. That first afternoon made a bond between the two girls that grew steadily stronger. When Mrs. Banner died a year later, Mattie turned to Julia for comfort, and it was Mattie who reinforced Julia in her depressing battles with her parents.

But she never told me about her father, Julia thought.

Not until this week.

If it had been wrong to leave Betty so abruptly, it was unquestionably right to have come away with Mattie. Julia felt a sharp pull of love and sympathy and admiration for her. That, at least, was right.

And now they were here, and there would be no going back.

Together they would make it.

Sitting in her deckchair, frowning a little, Julia fell asleep.

"I'm half dead," Mattie complained.

"You'll revive. It's Saturday night."

"Easy for you to say, when you've been snoring all after-noon in the park."

Julia met Mattie outside the shop at closing time. "I've sold fourteen pairs of shoes. The supervisor says I'll get a bonus. There's a perfect pair of black stilettos, you'll love them. Shall I put them in the back for you?"

"Don't try and sell me your shoes, kid. I don't need 'em."

They laughed, and Julia put her arm through Mattie's.

"So how much have we got?" With Mattie's three days' pay, and what was left of Johnny Flowers's pound note ("Why did you let him go?" Mattie demanded. "He sounds just what we need."), they had almost five pounds. They felt like Lady Bountiful.

"Food," Mattie said decisively.

They made straight for the nearest fish and chip shop and ordered double portions of everything.

"That," Mattie sighed later as she folded up the last trian-gle of bread and butter and bit into it, "was the best meal I have ever eaten. You're right. I have revived."

"So what shall we do?"

"We-ell. We could find somewhere to stay the night. . . ."

"Or we could go dancing, and then we needn't go to bed at all."

"You're right."

"Stick with me."

It was still early, and they dawdled arm-in-arm along Ox-ford Street, then Julia steered them south into Wardour Street.

"I've just thought. Where are the suitcases?"

"We're going to get them. This way."

The strip joint had done its best to shake off its depressing aspect ready for the night's trade. The colored bulbs were lit, and flickered bravely. The lights were on inside too, and Mickey was wedged belligerently in the doorway behind a placard read-ing THE SAUCIEST SHOW IN TOWN.

He spotted Julia at once.

"Here! Monty doesn't know nothing about no new girl."

Julia smiled, trying to dazzle him with charm.

"I'm sorry. It was a mistake. Can we just take our suitcases out of your way. . . ."

But Mickey was staring at Mattie. "Now, you," he said, "are the sort of girl Monty *always* goes for. Looking for a job, are you?"

Mattie stuck her chin out. "Not your sort of job. Thanks very much."

Julia retrieved the luggage and they retreated.

"Come back anytime you fancy," Mickey yelled after them. "You with the hair."

They turned the corner and then stopped, giggling.

"I can't leave you alone for a single day, can I?" Mattie teased. "Without you getting involved in a strip show. Fancy earning your living by taking your clothes off for a crowd of dirty men."

"Oh, I don't know," Julia answered lightheartedly. "Easier than hammering a typewriter all day. Or selling fourteen pairs of shoes."

Mattie cocked her head. "Listen."

It was music, drumming out somewhere below their feet. "Mmm." Julia tried out a few steps on the sidewalk. "And look." There was a dingy doorway sandwiched between two shops, with a temporary-looking notice pinned to the door.

NOW OPEN! THE ROCKET CLUB.

That was how they stumbled across it.

They had been heading around the corner to Cy Laurie's, but the Rocket was there and in its opening week it was offering free membership to girls. Mattie and Julia didn't need any more encouragement.

A flight of uneven steps led down to a white-painted cellar. There were tables around the walls, a bar selling soft drinks, and travel posters stuck on the walls for decoration. There was a trad jazz combo just hotting up, and people spinning and whirling in the white space.

They forgot everything, and launched themselves into the dance.

It was easy to forget in those days.

The club filled up, and the heat and the pulsing rhythm and the exhilaration of dancing swept them up and created a separate, absorbing world. They danced with anyone who asked them, not noticing whether they were young or old or white or black, and when the supply of partners temporarily dried up they danced with each other.

It was a long, hot night and it went like a flash.

At a table against the wall, from behind a stub of candle jammed into a wine bottle, Felix Lemoine was watching them.

There were lots of girls a bit like them, he thought, but there was something about these two that singled them out. They were striking enough to look at, although their clothes were grubby and looked homemade. The taller one with the dark hair had an angular, arresting face that was almost beautiful, and a thin, restless body. Her friend was plainer, but her foaming mass of hair shone in candlelight and she was a better dancer. She moved gracefully, holding her head up.

It wasn't their appearance that interested him, Felix decided. It was their vitality. He could almost feel the crackle of it from where he sat. The two girls were absorbed in themselves, in their dancing and the world they had created, and they were careless of everything else. Felix liked that carelessness. He had already identified it as style.

He took a notepad and pencil out of his inner pocket and began to draw.

When the drawing was finished he went on sitting there. It didn't occur to him to ask one of them to dance.

He just watched, as he always did.

Two

It was quiet in the studio. The Saturday afternoon life class was an unpopular option. The model was a woman, and she had been sitting for an hour. Her face was expressionless and her body looked flaccid, Felix thought, as if she had gone away somewhere and left it behind. Her long hair was pinned up on the top of her head to show the lines of her jaw and throat. He drew carefully, shading in the coils of hair. That was easy enough, but the rest of her body was more difficult. The soft heaviness of it made him feel uncomfortable, wanting to look away instead of spending another whole hour staring at it.

He glanced around at the handful of other students. They were drawing intently. The tutor strolled between them, watching. When he reached Felix's chair he stopped and murmured,

"Your execution is good, Lemoine, but there's no feeling. Loosen up."

Felix mumbled his reply, and the tutor looked at the big clock on the wall. He nodded briskly to the model. She stood up, stretching unconcernedly, and pulled on a pink wrap. Then she lit a cigarette and unfolded a newspaper. She would rest for fifteen minutes and then resume her position.

Felix put his pencil away. He waited until the tutor was on the other side of the room, and then he slipped outside. Two of the other students followed him.

"Coming outside for a cig, Felix?" one of them asked cheerfully.

"No, thanks. I think I'm going home."

"Yeah. Bit of an old dog, isn't she? See you tomorrow, then." They strolled away with their jackets over their shoulders and their hands in the pockets of their jeans.

Felix went outside. The air smelled hot and tarry, but the faint breeze was welcome after the enclosed studio. He would walk home, he decided.

Felix liked walking in London. He enjoyed the anonymity of the streets and the endless variety of faces streaming past him. He set off quickly through the afternoon crowds. When he reached Hyde Park he turned northward, his pace slowing in the cool beneath the trees. As he crossed the dirt paths, little whorls of dust lifted under his feet. He forgot the dislocation that he had felt in the life class, and after a moment he forgot the art school altogether. He wasn't close enough to home, yet, to need to focus on that either, and his thoughts slid easily, disconnected, as they always did when he was walking. Felix usually felt most comfortable in the vacuum between one place and another. It was being there, almost anywhere nowadays, that was the problem. At Marble Arch he emerged into the traffic again, and turned down the long tunnel of Oxford Street. He was within reach of home now. Another few minutes, and he reached a featureless square to the north of Oxford Street. He paused beside a row of iron railings, and emerged from the journey's limbo. He thought of home, and Jessie, as he looked across the square at their windows.

Most of the shabby Regency stucco houses in the square were occupied by offices, but a few still housed one or two flats, stranded among the solicitors and small import-export companies. Felix crossed to a gaunt, peeling house and went in through the black front door. As he climbed the stairs he could hear a typewriter clicking in one of the offices below, but otherwise the house seemed oppressively silent.

At the top of the last flight of stairs he unlocked a door and peered across the five square feet of lobby into Jessie's room. She was sitting in her chair by the window, and the sunlight beyond stamped out her dark, sybilline profile.

Then Felix's mother turned her face to look at him. "Hello, duck," she said. "You're early."

He saw at a glance that the vodka bottle was on the table beside her, and judging by the level in it, it was still early in the day for Jessie.

"Why are you home so early? Not missing classes, are you?"

Still just as if he were a little boy, even though it was Jessie who was the helpless one now.

"No," he lied, "I'm not missing classes. I'm hot, I'm just going to change my clothes."

"Go on then, be quick. Then come and talk to me. I think it might thunder. I hate thunder. Reminds me of the Blitz, with none of the fun. Oh, you wouldn't remember."

Her voice followed him into his bedroom. He took some clean clothes, neatly folded, out of his cupboard. He changed, and combed his black hair.

Jessie went on talking, but she broke off when he reappeared in the doorway. She looked at him over the rim of her glass, her eyes very bright and sharp in her shapeless face.

"God, you're a looker, all right, my boy," Jessie said. "Just like your dad. Only a better color." She laughed, her massive shoulders shaking silently.

"Have you had anything to eat?" Felix asked.

His mother shrugged.

"I'll make some soup."

Jessie didn't answer. She wasn't interested in food anymore.

The kitchen was very neat, Felix's domain. He had made the cupboards and the shelves, and painted everything white.

"I don't call that very cozy," Jessie had sniffed.

"Well, I like it," Felix told her. "And you don't cook, do you?"

He took a covered bowl out of the minute larder now and tipped the contents into a saucepan. He opened a cupboard and peered in at the tidy contents, then took a handful of dried pasta shells and dropped them into the pan. He was humming softly as he worked.

When the soup was simmering he laid a wicker tray with blue and white Provençal bowls. Felix had found the bowls in a little shop in Beak Street, and had brought them triumphantly home. More of his discoveries were dotted about the flat—a tiny still life of oranges in a basket, in an ornate gilt frame, a pair of pewter candlesticks, a batik wall hanging, contrasting oddly with the battered furniture.

"Dust collectors," muttered Jessie, not that dusting occupied her at all.

Felix finished his preparations with a twist of black pepper from a wooden peppermill and carried the tray through to Jessie. He laid the table in front of her, swinging the vodka bottle out of reach. His mother eyed the food.

"You've got to eat," he told her patiently.

Jessie ate almost nothing, but her body seemed to grow more bloated and less mobile every day. She could only shuffle around the flat with difficulty now, and she never went outside. She lived for her vodka bottle, for her occasional visitors, who stirred up her already vivid memories, and for Felix. He felt sorry for her, and loved her, and he knew that she kept him prisoner. He watched her like a mother with a child as she spooned up her soup.

"What did you do today?" she demanded. "Tell me all about it."

Felix looked out over the plane trees locked inside the railings of the square garden.

"It was life class today."

"Nude model, does that mean? A woman?"

"That's right."

Jessie chuckled coarsely. "Must make it hard for you boys to concentrate."

"Do you want some bread with your soup?"

She peered at him. "You're a funny boy sometimes. Are you all right at that college? Doing well at your drawing?"

Felix couldn't have begun to explain to Jessie that he had no idea what he was doing there. The models embarrassed him, but setting that aside, the aridity of life drawing, and the other exercises that the students were required to undertake, seemed to have no relevance at all to the kind of painting that Felix wanted to do. He needed to shout and to splash himself on to the canvases in violent colors. At the college he didn't know how to do anything of the kind. He was silent, and he worked in cramped spaces with tiny pencil strokes. He knew that he had been much happier in the year and a half after he had left school, working during the day in an Italian grocers in Soho, and going to night class. But after night class, with his teacher's encouragement, he had won his place at the Slade, and he had wanted to be a painter for as long as he could remember. Only he didn't think that any of the work he was doing now would help him with that.

He couldn't explain any of this to Jessie, who didn't even understand what painting meant.

"Of course I'm all right," he said softly.

Jessie pushed her food away. "Pour me a drop more of the good stuff, there's a duck." Felix filled her glass for her and she sat back with a sigh of relief. "That's better. God, it's nice to have a talk. I can't bear the quiet, all day long."

"You could listen to the wireless." The old-fashioned model in a Bakelite case stood in a corner of the room.

"All that rubbish? Noisy music. That's what your dad liked. Loud music, all day and all night. We used to dance, anywhere, anytime. God, we used to dance."

Felix let her reminisce. That was what Jessie enjoyed. It was almost all she had, he understood that. He had his own memories, too, as he sat watching her. They were mostly of upstairs rooms, with the sound of music and laughter, and sometimes shouting, drifting up to him. Felix used to sit for hours, drawing and waiting. When Jessie had finished work, at all sorts of strange hours, and if she was alone, she would bustle in and sweep him off somewhere to eat. In those days she had a healthy appetite, and the meals were the best of their times together. Usually they went to one of a handful of cafés, where everyone knew her and greeted her.

"Hello, Jess, my love. What's it to be tonight? Extra portion for that Felix, and we'll see if we can fill him out a bit."

They would sit down to huge platefuls of eggs and bacon, or sausages and mashed potatoes. Occasionally, when his mother was feeling flush, it would be a restaurant, and Felix learned to enjoy lasagne and tournedos Rossini and kleftiko while she told him stories of the day's work and the people who drifted endlessly in and out of the Soho clubs. In the comfortable times they were afternoon clubs, that filled the empty time for their customers between the pubs closing and opening again. Felix had a dim impression from his brief glimpses into smoky rooms of a twilight world where curtains closed out the daylight and where men sat around drinking small drinks under Jessie's benevolent, despotic eye. For a brief period, he remembered, there had been a club called Jessie's Place, and his mother had talked about sending him away to a "proper" school. He had refused to go, and one of the periodic upheavals had taken over their life, leaving them with no more Jessie's Place. She had gone to work in a nightclub then, which meant that there were no more cozy suppers together either. Felix came back from school and spent his evenings alone, in one of the succession of rented rooms that they used as home. He listened to music and drew. He painted, too, when he could get hold of the materials. One of Jessie's regular friends, a dealer of some kind who was still known to Felix as Mr. Mogridge, told him that he could be good. Sometimes he brought him paints and canvas. It was Mr. Mogridge who had introduced him to the night school, and Felix was grateful for that, even though he disliked the man. The rest of his spare time, until he left school and started work in the grocers, Felix filled up with walking in Soho. He rummaged in the strange little shops for decorative treasures and watched the people as they passed him in the streets.

There were other men of Jessie's too, of course. There were plenty of them when Felix was young, fewer as Jessie aged and her body grew more cumbersome. Felix knew for sure that his mother had once been a singer, and then, because she had not been quite good enough, she had become a club hostess. Not a prostitute. He knew most of the real girls by sight, and quite a lot of them by name, because he saw them in Old Compton Street and Frith Street, and down at the bottom end of Wardour Street. Jessie wasn't one of them. She had men friends, that was all. Felix ignored them as far as he could. He had never been able to bear the thought of what they did together. Now, looking back over the years of moving with Jessie from one set of cramped rooms to another, waiting and watching and drawing in exercise books, Felix realized that he must have been a strange, withdrawn, prim little boy. How different from Jessie herself, and how baffling for her.

She had done her best for him, he saw now, through what must often have been difficult times. He had been lonely, but he had never felt neglected. They had never had much, but he had never gone without.

Felix had no memories of his father at all.

He knew that Desmond Lemoine and Jessie Jubb had been

married, because Jessie always kept her marriage certificate with her. The wedding predated his own birthday by two and a half months. Apart from that, Felix knew only what Jessie had told him. The wedding certificate stated that he was a musician, but Jessie was unreliable about exactly what sort of musician. Sometimes he was the greatest sax player there had ever been, the forgotten star of every big band of the thirties. At other times he was a trombonist, once or twice even a trumpeter.

"He played that sax—or trombone, or trumpet—like an angel," Jessie would say mistily. And then she would snort with laughter and add, "He looked like an angel too. God, he was beautiful. A big black angel."

Desmond had come from Grenada. Felix knew that he must have been tall, because he had grown to six foot himself, towering over Jessie. But the color of his skin was only a dim reflection of his father's blackness.

What would I be? Felix wondered. *An angel the color of cold English coffee?* He also wondered if it was his half-and-halfness, the awareness of being neither one person nor the other, that gave him his sense of separation.

Desmond and Jessie had met when they were both working in a club off Shaftesbury Avenue. Within a few months Jessie was pregnant, and a few months after that her musician obligingly married her. He had also insisted on the boy's Christian name, although Jessie had preferred Brian.

"It means the lucky one, girl," he told Jessie. "We all need a bit of luck, don't we?" He disappeared for good about a year after Felix was born.

"He went on tour, with a new band, up north somewhere," Jessie said. "Going to be his big break, it was. He never came back."

"Why not?" Felix would demand. When he was a small boy his father's absence made him silently, unnervingly angry.

Jessie would only shrug. "Liked his drink, Des did. And pretty faces, especially if they were white ones. Plenty of those in Manchester, or wherever he was. Fell for someone else, I expect. He's got two or three wives to his name by now, I should think."

At sixteen, Felix had calculated, he could move away from Jessie and begin to live his own life. He dreamed of going to Rome, or Florence, to find some kind of menial job that would still give him time to paint.

Then, in the same week as the King died, Jessie fell ill.

She had double pneumonia, and for five days Felix was sure that she was going to die. He sat by her bed, waiting again, and all the waiting he had done all through the years of his childhood, seemingly for nothing, welled up out of the past and crushed the hope out of him. Later, he remembered the stillness of that week. All the music had been silenced for the King, and the faces in the street outside the hospital were somber.

He didn't believe the doctors when they told him that his mother would live. She seemed so fragile, with all the energy and liveliness that he had taken for granted drained out of her.

Jessie did recover, very slowly, but it was as if her illness had quenched some hope of her own. She struggled back to the current club as soon as she could, but the work exhausted her. The customers noticed and commented on her low spirits. They were allowed, even expected, to have their problems, but Jessie had to be cheerful for them. Not long afterward she was ill again, and missed more days of work. At last the boss, the latest in a long line of owners to whom Jessie had devoted her energy, took her aside. She would have to be more like her old self, he warned her, his special girl, our Jessie, or he couldn't promise to keep her on.

Felix was incandescent with anger when Jessie told him. He wanted to burst into the club and hit the man square in his puffy face.

"Don't upset yourself, love," Jessie advised him wearily. "It isn't worth it."

Two months later Jessie was fired. A salvo of bouquets and fulsome good wishes followed her into exile from the only world she knew.

"There are other places. Other jobs," Felix said savagely, but Jessie only shrugged. "It isn't worth it," she repeated.

Already she was drinking heavily, and her bulky body seemed more of a burden for her to propel to and fro. But Jessie had dozens of friends and they rallied round her now, almost against her will. One of them, a man like Mr. Mogridge but even shadier, owned a block of property to the north of Oxford Street. It was out of their old territory, but Jessie and Felix gratefully accepted his offer of a short tenancy, at a tiny rent, of the flat overlooking Manchester Square.

"It won't be forever," Mr. Bull said crisply. "It's due for development, all that. But you can have it for now if it's any help to you."

They moved into the flat, and Felix decorated it. He enjoyed arranging the cramped space more than he had enjoyed anything since Jessie fell ill.

"You've done a good job," Mr. Bull had said. "Made the place look like something." He looked hard at Felix, and then smirked.

By that Saturday afternoon, they had been living in the flat for two and a half years. As a temporary measure, it felt more permanent than anywhere they had ever lived before.

Felix heard his mother's chair creak, and a long, exhaled breath. He looked across at her and saw that she had fallen asleep with her chin on her chest and her glass tipped sideways in her fingers. He took it gently away and put the top back on the bottle. His face was expressionless as he lifted her swollen legs on to a low stool and slipped a cushion behind her head. Then he brought a blanket from her bed and tucked it securely around her.

Felix carried the wicker tray of dirty dishes back into the kitchen and washed up. He put each plate and bowl back in its proper place, and dried the old-fashioned wooden drainer. When everything was satisfactorily tidy he went into his bedroom and put on a dark blue sweater.

He looked at Jessie once more, and then he went out and closed the door softly behind him.

The threat of thunder had lifted, and the sky was clear. The lines of chimneys and rooftops were sharply defined against it. Felix walked for a long time, watching the darkness as it gathered softly in narrow alleyways and in the corners buttressed by high buildings. He enjoyed listening to the hum of the city changing as night came and the lights flickered and steadied.

He had been idling, not thinking, when he passed the Rocket Club. He loitered for a moment, incuriously, reading the notice on the door. Then he heard the music drifting up to him through the cellar grating at his feet. He hesitated, and then he thought that there was nothing for him to hurry home for. Jessie would certainly be still asleep, and the little flat would be quiet and dark. He could go in for an hour, to drink a Coke and listen to the music. Felix went to the door and handed over his entry money.

"Just one?" the doorman asked without interest.

Felix had to duck his head under the low ceilings as he went down the stairs into the cellar. He bought a drink and found a place at a table against the wall.

He noticed the two girls almost at once.

Felix was impressed by the club itself too. He liked the blurred distinctions of nighttime in these places, and he quite often visited the other clubs in the nearby streets. He had a loose network of acquaintances based on them, and that suited him because it didn't trespass on the rest of his privacy. There was a sprinkling of faces here that he knew, and more that he didn't. It was a pleasing mixture of beats and bohemians, ordinary kids and blacks and Soho characters packing the steaming space. He hadn't intended to stay, but the atmosphere, and the two girls, made him linger. The two of them were dancing with intent, almost fierce enjoyment. It was, Felix thought, as if they were afraid to stop.

The crowd grew thicker and wilder as the night wore on. Felix danced with a girl he knew a little. He bought her a drink and talked to a group of her friends. All the girls liked Felix, as well as admiring his looks, but they were used to his evasiveness. He glimpsed the girl with the hair laughing, through the press of people, and then he lost sight of them both. The dancers were leaping and shouting now, and the walls of the cellar itself seemed to run with sweat.

In the end it was the exhausted musicians who gave up. They played a last, storming number and then began to pack up their instruments. The crowd booed and protested, but they knew that there was going to be no more that night. They started to flow reluctantly up the stairs, and Felix went with them.

Outside it was already light, a still, pale summer morning. The air was cool and sweet after the smoky cellar. He walked a little way, and then stopped to watch the pearly light lying along the street.

Something made him look back.

The two girls were standing outside the club doorway. There were two suitcases at their feet. All the wild enjoyment had drifted away with the music. They looked tired, and dejected, and very young.

Without knowing why he did it, Felix turned and walked back to them.

"What's wrong?"

The dark one lifted her head. "We've got nowhere to sleep. We thought we'd just stay up all night. But the night didn't last quite long enough for it to be day again."

She gestured wearily at the sleeping city. The first car of the morning, or the last car of the night, purred past them. The crowd from the club was disappearing, and they began to feel as if they were the only people left between sleeping and waking. Mattie looked up too. She noticed that he was tall and slim, with black hair that curled close to his head. He looked foreign and handsome, and exotic, but she was too tired to work out whether that was threatening or not.

"Do you know anywhere we can stay?" she asked. "Just for tonight? What's left of it?" They were both watching him.

Felix thought of home, and of Jessie, who would now be prowling heavily, wakefully, in her room.

All his instincts warned him to offer nothing, but the memory of how they had looked inside the Rocket Club made him fight back his instincts. He sighed.

"There's a spare room where I live. It isn't much."

"After last night, anywhere with a roof will be a palace," the dark one said.

"Which way?" the other one demanded. Felix pointed, and they began walking. He noticed that they were both almost falling over with exhaustion. He held his hands out for one of the suitcases, then the other.

"Hey, what have you got in here?"

The dark one shrugged her shoulders. They were thin and bony, he saw, like a young boy's.

"Everything," she said.

They came into the square as the light changed from gray to gold. Felix looked up at Jessie's window. The curtains were open.

"I live with my mother," he said baldly.

The one who called herself Mattie smiled. "Mothers tend not to like us very much."

"Mine's different."

But it was Mattie's expectations that were proved right. Felix unlocked the door at the top of the stairs and they crowded together into the awkward hall. There was hardly room for the three of them and the two suitcases. There was a slow, creaking noise, and Jessie appeared from her room. Her bulk seemed to block out the light. Mattie was at the back, and she saw only an old woman, very fat, who breathed with difficulty. But Julia was closer and she saw that Felix's mother had quick, sharp eyes that were at odds with her size. Her expression was closed and hostile. Felix's heart sank. He had seen Jessie confront unwelcome customers with that face.

"Who's this?"

He told her.

"They can't stay here. This isn't a rooming house."

Jessie was suspicious, and defensive, and she didn't like strangers anymore. The little lair perched at the top of the offices was all she had, and she didn't want it to be invaded. Felix understood, and he wished that he hadn't dragged these waifs back here with him.

"It's just for one night," he soothed her. "There's not much of it left, anyway."

Jessie peered at the two girls. They were hardly more than children, and she thought that she recognized the type. And then the one with the terrible ratty tangle of curling fair hair said softly, "Please."

Jessie was angry, but she knew that she had lost. She couldn't deny that appeal. It was characteristic that she accepted her defeat and moved swiftly on.

"You'll be out of here by twelve o'clock sharp. There'll be no noise, no waste of hot water, and no funny business of any sort."

Mattie grinned at her. Their relief was like a light being turned on.

"We're the quietest sleepers in London. And we're too tired to wash or think of anything funny, I promise."

Jessie turned her massive back and shuffled away to her chair.

The room that Felix showed them into had one single mattress and a sleeping bag. He brought them some pillows and blankets, and they murmured their thanks and burrowed into them, fully clothed.

They were asleep, like small animals, even before he had draped a blanket over the dormer window.

"Well, where *do* you live?" Jessie demanded.

The girls had slept for six hours, and they woke up at midday only because Felix rapped on their door. They tried to slip into the bathroom, but Jessie was too quick for them.

"Don't sneak around," she shouted from her room. "Come in here and let me have a look at you. Then you can be off and leave us in peace."

They stood in front of her, like schoolgirls facing the headmistress. Glancing around the room, Julia saw that it was full of photographs. There were dozens of laughing faces and raised glasses, and most of the groups showed a younger version of

Felix's mother beaming somewhere in the middle. It was hard to reconcile that conviviality with this huge, formidable woman.

"You must live somewhere," Jessie was insisting. "Why d'you have to turn up at my place in the middle of the night? Although that boy's just as much to blame for bringing you."

They looked around for him, but Felix was prudently keeping out of the way. They could hear him rattling plates in the kitchen. The homely noise reminded them that they were hungry.

"Well?" Jessie demanded.

Julia decided rapidly that there was no point in attempting anything but the truth. Jessie would certainly recognize anything that wasn't.

"We haven't got anywhere to live," she said. "Just at the moment, that is. The night before last we slept on the Embankment. Last night we were going to stay up, dancing, but somehow there's a gap between night and morning, you know?"

"I remember," Jessie said a shade less grimly.

"Felix rescued us, and brought us here."

"I know that already. What I'm trying to find out is why you had to sleep on the Embankment in the first place."

Very quickly, putting in as little detail as possible, Julia told her. In Julia's version of the story, Mattie had had an argument with her father about staying out too late. That was all. But Jessie's little round eyes, sunk in the cushions of flesh, were shrewd as they darted to and fro. They lingered on Mattie for a minute longer.

When Julia had finished her speech, Jessie said, "I see. And now you've done your running away and found out how nasty it is, you'll be going back home where you belong, won't you?"

Mattie spoke for the first time. "No. We can't do that." Her voice was quiet and steady and utterly definite, and Jessie's glance flickered over her again.

"We've both got jobs," Julia told her quickly. "Well-paid jobs. As soon as we've got some money we can rent a flat. Everything will be all right then."

Jessie had seen enough. They looked so vulnerable, both of them, still sleepy, with their eyes smudged around with their unnecessary makeup, and their strange young-old clothes all rucked up with the weight of sleep. But they weren't so young, either, Jessie thought. A shadow of something, the beginning of experience perhaps, had touched both their faces and sharpened them out of the softness of childhood. And they had a defiance in them, a determination, that touched her. The way they stood, the way they looked around, stirred memories in Jessie. They reminded her of friends she hadn't seen for a long time, most of whom she would never see again. And, just a little, they reminded her of herself.

Jessie sighed. "Oh, bloody hell. You'd better have a drink and something to eat before I really do kick you out. Felix! Bring that bottle and some glasses in here."

And Felix came in, awkwardly tall in the low room, but moving as gracefully as a cat in his black sweater. The girls watched him, and he smiled at all three of them as triumphantly as if he had called the truce himself. With a flourish he took four glasses off a tray.

"There's beer or vodka," he announced. The two girls instinctively looked at Jessie for guidance, and Felix hid his smile.

"You'd better take vodka," Jessie ordered. "That beer Felix drinks tastes like piss. Dress it up with some orange for them, Felix, there's a love." Felix poured the drinks while Jessie watched impatiently, and then she raised her glass. "Here's to freedom."

It was such an incongruous toast, coming from this fat, ungainly old woman wedged in her rooftop room, and yet so apt for them, that the girls just gaped at her. Jessie broke into wheezy chuckles. "That's what you think you want, isn't it? Come on. I hate drinking alone."

So Mattie and Julia sipped at their sweet, oily-orange drinks and Jessie downed her neat vodka in a gulp. She held out her empty glass. "Come on, Felix, since we're all here. Let's have a party."

As soon as she had said the word, the four of them did become a party. The Sunday morning sun shone in through the windows and danced on the polished frames and the glass faces of the photographs, and Mattie and Julia felt the vodka warming their empty stomachs and loosening their limbs and tongues. Felix was their rescuer and their friend, and although they didn't know yet what Jessie would mean to them, they felt her warmth. After the Embankment, and what had happened before and since, that warmth was doubly welcome.

Julia stood up and wandered around the room, peering at the faces pinned in their photograph frames.

"Who are they all?" she murmured. "You've got hundreds and hundreds of friends. More people than I've ever even met."

She couldn't have struck a better note. Jessie leaned back in her chair and laced her fingers across her front.

"Used to have, dear, used to have. Dead, now, most of them. The rest are finished, like me. But we had some good times in our day, we did. Times like you wouldn't believe. See that picture there, the one you're looking at? That's Jocky Gordon with his arm around me, the boxer. I met them all in my line of business. All of 'em. You'd be surprised, some of the things I've seen."

"Tell us about it," Mattie begged her.

Jessie beamed and settled more comfortably in her seat.

Still smiling, Felix slipped out into the kitchen. It was on the shaded side of the house, cool and neat and inviting. He could make something to eat now that he had seen that Jessie was happy.

He opened the cupboard door, his movements economical in the confined space. He had planned to finish the leftovers of a knuckle of ham with Jessie, but that wouldn't stretch to four. He would make a salad and put the ham into omelettes instead. Felix unwrapped the lettuce and picked the leaves over carefully. He could hear laughter from Jessie's room. He was ready to make the omelettes when he felt eyes on his back, and turned around to see Julia leaning against the open door. He gestured uncertainly, not knowing how long she had been watching him.

"I'm sorry," she said softly. "I didn't mean to startle you. I came to say thanks."

They listened for a second to a third person's voice in Jessie's room, and then they realized that it was Mattie mimicking somebody. Mattie was a wonderful mimic, and Jessie's choking laugh rose too.

"I should thank you for listening to Mum," Felix said. "She doesn't have many people to tell her stories to."

He was moving around the kitchen again, breaking eggs into a blue pottery bowl. The yolks lay in it, a bright yellow cluster.

"I like her," Julia said simply. She was thinking how nice this kitchen was, with its bare wooden tops and white walls. No fuss, or covers, or labels, like there was at home. Felix opened the window. In the angle of the roofs outside stood four clay flowerpots. He picked a handful of parsley and some chives from them, and a few sprigs of thyme. Julia watched as he chopped the herbs and melted a knob of butter in an old copper pan.

"You're clever," she said. "I wish I could do that."

"Can't you cook?" Felix asked, surprised. He had assumed it was something all girls did automatically. It was unusual for boys to enjoy it, that was all.

"My mother tried to teach me," Julia said without enthusiasm. Betty made sponge cakes, and thin stews or flaccid pies, and looked forward to getting cleared up afterward. There had been nothing as simple and obvious and inviting as the golden puff that materialized in Felix's copper pan.

"Set the table, Julia, will you?"

It was the first time that he had called her by her name, and they smiled shyly at each other. Julia bent her head abruptly to pick the knives and forks out of a wicker tray.

Felix bent down, too, and took a dark red bottle from its resting place under the sink. "Let's drink this," he said. "Mum will stick to her vodka, so the three of us can share it."

It was a wonderful, convivial lunch.

Felix pulled out the flaps of the table and drew it into the sunny place in the window. He spread a festive white cloth over the pocked surface. Jessie sat queenly at the head of the table, with Mattie and Julia on either side.

They ate ravenously, while Jessie talked, capping and recapping her own stories. She was too engrossed even to drink more than a few tots from the glass beside her hand. The girls had never tasted wine before, and it made them talkative too. The chatter and laughter rose in the sunny room, with Felix's quiet voice prompting them all.

At last, when they had eaten all the omelette and wiped the last of the oily dressing out of the salad bowl, and Julia and Mattie had demolished the remains of a chocolate cake, Jessie tinkled her fork against her glass.

"I've thought of another toast," she declared. "A more important one."

Felix hastily drained the last of the Beaujolais into the three wineglasses and filled Jessie's to the brim with vodka. She lifted it without looking at it, not spilling even a drop.

"To friendship."

They echoed her, "To friendship," and drank again.

"And I don't imagine," Jessie went on with feigned annoyance, "that having proposed that, I'm going to be able to get rid of you quite so easily. Am I?"

The girls waited, not looking anywhere.

"So I suppose you'd better stay on here. Just till you find your own place, mind. Till then, and not a minute longer."

She shot a glance around the table, to Felix, to Julia and Mattie, and back again to Felix.

"Not a minute longer," he repeated softly. Whatever Jessie was plotting, if it made her happier, that was enough.

"Good," she said with firm satisfaction.

Suddenly they were laughing again, the four of them, drawn even closer around the table under the window.

THREE

On Monday morning, on their way to work, Mattie and Julia found a public telephone booth and squeezed into it together. They found the number they wanted, at last, through the operator.

"Do you want me to talk to them?" Julia asked, but Mattie shook her head.

"I should do it."

She dialed their local council offices and she explained to the official at the other end that she was ringing anonymously, and she had something very important to say. Speaking very slowly and carefully, she gave her father's name and address, and the names and ages of her brothers and sisters.

"They aren't safe with him," she said clearly. "I know they aren't. Please will you send someone to see them? There's no one left to look after them now."

Julia heard the man's voice crackle at the end of the line as he tried to make Mattie give him some more information.

"I'm sorry," she said. "I can't say any more."

And then she replaced the receiver with a click that made the bell jingle faintly in its casing. She pushed open the heavy door of the kiosk and the girls stepped out into the street. Mattie was shivering.

"I've abandoned them, haven't I?" she said bitterly. "I feel so bad. Like a traitor."

"You aren't a traitor." Julia tried to soothe her.

"I shouldn't have left them. Phil's only seven. What does she know? But I couldn't stay in that house with him, could I? If he did it again . . ."

My fault, Mattie began thinking, as she had done a thousand times before. It must have been my fault, some of it. But if I went back, and he did it again . . . there was the bread knife, lying beside the waxed wrapper of the sliced loaf. She heard a scream—her own or her father's?—and saw the blood. . . . Mattie shuddered, and felt Julia's hand on her arm. Warm and friendly, that was all, not twisting or cajoling.

"Mattie, it's all right."

"Is it?"

She had had to leave. After the vision of violence she thought of Ted with a queasy mixture of pity and revulsion and, still, a kind of love. She couldn't have stayed. Julia was right, of course.

Julia said, "You've done what you can for now. And you have done, ever since your mum died. It's Rozzie's turn to take some of the responsibility now." When Mattie didn't answer, she added, "You can't be everything to everyone."

Mattie stopped shivering, and her shoulders dropped.

"No, I suppose I can't. I didn't even know I was trying. I wish I saw things as clearly as you do. I wish I saw Ted clearly." It was the first time since they had left home that Mattie had spoken his name. As if it were a physical link with him, she snapped the words off and she didn't talk about him again. Mattie's face was white and taut under the heavy mass of hair.

Julia wanted to say something else, to show her that she understood, but she couldn't because she couldn't even imagine what Ted Banner must have been like. The gulf between what had happened to Mattie, and Vernon's rigid correctness, was too wide. She had the sense that she had failed Mattie, and she was reduced to mumbling, "It'll be all right. I know it will."

Mattie's expression didn't change, but in a different, warmer voice she said, "We'd better go to work, hadn't we? Sell some shoes."

"Type some accounts."

Make our way, Julia thought with a touch of wryness. *That's what we've come for, isn't it?*

"See you later, at home."

The word sprang hearteningly between them as they waved good-bye. Felix, and Jessie, and the rooftop flat stood between them and the Embankment now, and that was a good beginning. Julia saw Mattie's blond curls swallowed up by the throngs of people heading for work, and she turned around herself, more cheerfully, and began to walk briskly to the accounts office.

The thoughts of the Sunday they had enjoyed together remained with Julia as she slid into her typist's chair and started work. They had stayed sitting around the table, talking and laughing, until the vodka was all gone. Jessie had slipped by stages through excited volubility to dignified, precisely enunciated drunkenness, and then into sudden sleep.

The girls liked her more and more. She had told them the story of Desmond Lemoine. "He played the sax, dear. In all the big bands, he was. Even better-looking than him," with a wink at Felix, who was looking out of the window. "Not that Felix uses his looks to much advantage." She told them about other lovers, too, with an impartial enthusiasm that deeply impressed Mattie and Julia. At home they had cast themselves as the bad girls, although in fact neither of them had "gone all the way," as they described it in whispers. Julia had come close, in an uncomfortable, awkward grapple, with a boy from the technical college who was supposed to look like Dirk Bogarde. It was harder to tell with Mattie. Mattie was the best at sharp, suggestive repartee on the dance floor, but she was reticent about what happened outside, afterward, even to Julia.

But Jessie's stories, as the vodka slipped down, gave them an insight into a world they had never even glimpsed before. It was a salty, indoor world of smoky rooms and overflowing glasses and itinerant musicians. It was a world where, it seemed, you could do whatever you liked provided everyone was enjoying it.

While Mattie and Julia sat still, amazed and enchanted, Felix watched with an air of having heard it all before. He didn't contribute anything, but he seemed perfectly at ease.

"I've had a good life," Jessie said at last. A vast yawn stretched her face into a series of overlapping circles. "You listen to me, you girls. You make sure you enjoy yourselves. But don't act stupid, will you?"

Felix's face was almost hidden in the shadow. Mattie and Julia glanced at each other. And then they saw that Jessie's head had fallen forward on her chest. Her breathing deepened and fluttered on the edge of a snore.

Felix stood up, silently, and arranged the cushions behind his mother's head. He lifted her feet onto a stool and put a blanket over her legs. Julia picked up the bottle, empty, intending to tidy it away. She had noticed how punctiliously Felix had cleared away the plates after their meal.

"Should she drink all that?" she asked.

Felix looked at her. "No. But I'm not going to dictate to her about it, because it wouldn't do any good."

Jessie wasn't a person to dictate to, of course. They left her asleep and went outside. The three of them walked companionably through the empty Sunday streets, and Felix took them into Regent's Park. They wandered past the heady, musky roses in Queen Mary's Garden, talking about ordinary things, what they did and what they enjoyed and believed in, making the beginnings of friendship, as they had pledged over their meal.

"Miss Smith?"

Julia's supervisor was standing in front of her, looking pointedly at her fingers resting idly on the typewriter keys.

"I'm sorry," Julia muttered, and bent to her work again.

She already hated the accounts department. Her typing was good enough in short bursts, but when she had to keep at it for longer it disintegrated. By the end of the day her head and fingers throbbed and she had used a whole bottle of opaque white. The other girls at the rows of desks were the kind Mattie dismissed as "pink cardigans." They did wear cardigans, tidy ones that buttoned up to the neck over their shirtwaist dresses. They wore pink lipstick, too, and touches of pale blue eyeshadow, and most of them proudly displayed diamond engagement rings. They stared covertly at Julia in her crumpled black clothes and defiantly flat pumps. Mattie and Julia favored colorless lips and deadly pale face makeup, and they emphasized their eyes with lashings of black mascara and black eye liner painted on with an upward flick at the corners of their eyelids.

Julia stared unsmilingly back at the other typists. She knew that she stuck out among them, but she was still too young and too awkward to carry her difference off with confidence. She kept mulishly to herself, refusing to acknowledge that she felt lonely and uncomfortable.

It's only for now, she told herself over and over again. *Until I find something else.* It was not knowing what else, and the suspicion that there might not be anything, that was really frightening.

Mattie wasn't enjoying her work much more than Julia, but she had the diversion of being able to watch the women who came into the shop all day long. She watched the way they sat, and the way they looked at themselves in the mirrors, and the attitudes they adopted toward herself and the other shopgirls.

And Mattie had the consolation of a particular dream. She bought *Stage* and pored over the small ads.

> Wanted, Huddersfield. With experience. One leading
> F two M two juv one char. Start immediately.

The terse abbreviations themselves seemed to breathe a world of backstage glamour. *Experience* was the difficulty.

Before leaving home, Mattie had belonged to an amateur theatrical group that staged twice-yearly productions like *Peter Pan* and *Charley's Aunt*. The group was run by a spinster teacher who called Paris Paree and who disapproved of everything about Mattie. She kept her parts to a minimum, for all Mattie's enthusiasm. So Mattie had nothing that she could dress up as theatrical experience, even adopting the kind of wishful expanded truth that she and Julia specialized in.

So Mattie bought *Stage* and read every word, and went on dreaming of the day when she could call herself *leading F*.

The flat in Manchester Square was an oasis away from work for them both. It was too small, there was nowhere for them to sit in the evenings except with Jessie in her room or on the makeshift beds in their own tiny bedroom. But Mattie and Julia weren't particularly interested in sitting, and the flat became home in a matter of days. Jessie would wait for the girls to come home from work, and call out as soon as she heard one of them at the door.

"Come on in here, let's have a look at you. Tell me what's going on out there, and pour me a drink while you're about it."

Julia and Mattie both acquired a taste for vodka under Jessie's direction, but there was never enough to spare for them to do them much damage. With their wage packets at the end of the first full week's work they bought Jessie two bottles, and a pair of the sheerest twelve-denier nylons.

"What're you trying to do to me?" she demanded, pretending to be angry with them. But Jessie had surprisingly slim, pretty ankles. They made her put the stockings on at once and she stretched her feet out narcissistically to admire them.

"I'll do your hair for you, if you like," Mattie offered.

"What's the matter with my hair?"

"You'll see, when I've done it for you."

Jessie didn't just talk about herself, although the girls were fascinated by her stories. She talked to them about themselves, listening with genuine interest and prompting them with questions.

Julia described Betty and Vernon. She told Jessie about the colored stars that she had innocently stuck on her bedroom walls, and about another time, only two years ago, when she had gone out on her first date. She knew that Betty wouldn't allow her to go to the pictures with a boy. That sort of thing was for much older girls, Betty believed, an awkward but necessary preliminary to being presented with the diamond ring. But the boy who had asked Julia out was much admired by the girls in her class, and by Julia herself. She went, and she told her mother that she was spending the evening with a girl from school. At five minutes past the time Julia had promised to come back, Vernon telephoned the girl's mother.

And when Julia did reappear they were waiting at the front door for her. The boy had come to see her to the gate, and Vernon marched out to confront him. Julia never knew what he said to him, because Betty dragged her indoors. Vernon came in a moment later and locked and bolted the door as if he were shutting out evil itself.

Even as she described it to Jessie, Julia could smell the wet privet outside the window and feel the soft stinging of her mouth after the boy's kisses in the cinema. She could still taste the shame, too, in the back of her throat like nausea. She was too ashamed even to look at the boy the next time they met. It was a long time afterward, because Betty and Vernon had made her stay in for a month, and he never spoke to her again.

Jessie sighed and shifted her bulk in the chair. If Julia had expected Jessie to deplore her parents with her, Jessie refused to do anything of the kind.

"It's a shame, but there's plenty of boys coming your way, duck, and kisses as well. Don't tell me you don't know that. It sounds to me as if your mum and dad were trying to do their best for you, that's all, in their own way."

"What would you have done, Jessie?"

She laughed. "Asked the boy in first, so's I could have a good look at him. And smacked your backside for lying to me, as soon as I got a chance."

Mattie talked about her home too. Jessie soon knew all about Ricky and Sam, and Marilyn and Phil, and all their particular talents, and the funny things that they had done as babies and little children.

It was the things that Mattie left out that made Jessie's little dark eyes peer shrewdly at her.

"What about your ma?"

"I told you. She died, three years ago."

"Miss her still?"

"Yes. No. I don't know. She never said very much, Mum didn't. I know she loved us all, but she was ill a lot, for a long time, almost all the time I can remember. We got used to managing, Rozzie and me."

"And your dad?"

"He's all right."

Mattie looked down, or away and out of the window, or got up on some pretext and left the room. Jessie didn't ask that particular question more than two or three times. If Mattie didn't want to talk about her father, than that was her own business. When Mattie came back into the room the last time, Jessie startled her with a sudden enveloping hug.

"There's my girl," she murmured, and Mattie smiled again.

Jessie loved physical warmth, and she was demonstrative in her affection. Julia was surprised by her weighty arms around her shoulders, and the relish of her smacking, vodka-wet kisses on her cheek. It was more surprising because neither Betty nor Vernon ever touched her, nor each other, seemingly.

"Oh, I like a bit of a cuddle," Jessie beamed. "And Felix never lets me have one these days. He used to be such a lovely, affectionate little boy, but he's that touchy about himself nowadays."

It was Felix, oddly, who the girls found the more difficult to live with in those early days.

On one of the very first evenings, they found him standing at the door of their room looking in at the mess. The floor and the beds were strewn with tangled clothes and makeup and crumpled papers and discarded shoes.

"Do you always live like this?" he asked, raising one black eyebrow.

Mattie had muddled through in domestic chaos all her life, and Julia copied it as part of her rebellion against Betty.

"Always," they chorused.

"You don't here," Felix said coldly. He watched as they sheepishly picked up their belongings and folded them away, and when he was satisfied he said, "The bathroom's full of dripping stockings and things."

"Knickers and bras, you mean?" Mattie tried to tease him.

"I know what they are, thank you. Just don't leave them slopping everywhere."

They tried to make a joke between themselves about his

old-maidishness, but for some reason it didn't amuse either of them particularly. They found themselves trying to be tidier, in order to please him.

Julia found it more confusing than Mattie did. Part of her resented Felix's authority, but she submitted to it just the same. She wanted to challenge him, but she didn't quite know how to do it. She found herself watching him covertly, admiring the way that he looked and dressed, trying to adopt some of his style for herself. She would stand in the kitchen doorway when he was cooking, looking at the way his hands moved among the pots and pans.

"I wish I could do that," she said. Felix put down his boning knife and looked at her.

"Why shouldn't you be able to do it?"

He made room for her at the scrubbed work-top and she tried to copy him, but her fingers felt thick and stiff and the meat slithered awkwardly in her fist.

"No. It's like this," he said, and put his hand over hers. The knife moved, neatly severing the lean meat from the fat and glistening connective tissue. Felix's skin was tawny against Julia's whiteness, but his touch was light and dry, deliberately without significance.

Mattie and Julia speculated about him in private.

"Do you think he's queer?" Julia asked. They could usually divide men up between them. Most of them went for Mattie, with her seemingly uninhibited voluptuousness, but Julia had her share of admirers too. But Felix was mysterious, fastidious, uninterested in their messy femininity.

Mattie considered. They weren't sure, either of them, that they had ever seen a real homosexual.

"No. He can't be, can he? They're all like this." Mattie stood with one hand on her hip, the other dangling limply. Her face puckered up into a faint simper, and Julia laughed.

"Felix isn't one, then."

One afternoon he found them lolling on Mattie's bed reading. Mattie had *Stage* folded carefully so that she could read every column, and Julia, with her head propped on one hand, was reading *Gone With the Wind*. She went through phases of burying herself in books, creating her own temporary oblivion inside an imaginary world.

Felix took out his sketchpad and drew them.

When he had finished he let them look at the pencil sketch. There was a moment's silence as they looked at themselves as Felix saw them. Mattie was all loose, blowsy curves, her bare thigh showing between the flaps of her dressing gown, her hair rolling over her shoulders. Beside her Julia was angular, dark-faced, and scowling.

"You haven't made us look very pretty," Julia said at last.

"Is that what you want to be? Pretty?"

"Of course."

"Well, you aren't. You've got more than that, both of you. You've got style, although you don't know how to use it yet."

They forgot their momentary pique and scrambled at him. Mattie locked her arms around him, affectionate, just as she would have been with Ricky or Sam. Julia hung back, only a little.

"Show us, then, if you're so clever."

"I might."

Julia retrieved the drawing and smoothed the creases out of it. She pinned it carefully over the tiny black cast-iron fire grate in their bedroom.

That night, the three of them went back to the Rocket Club. Before they went out the girls presented themselves for Felix's approval.

"Too much stuff on your faces, as usual," was his verdict. So they rubbed the makeup off again and, giggling, let him reapply it. Julia kept her eyes turned down as he worked on her face, inches away.

When he had finished they stared at the result in the bathroom mirror.

"Naked. As though we've just got up," Mattie declared.

In fact they just looked younger, and less knowing. As they really were, Felix thought, instead of how they wanted to be.

"What about the clothes, then?"

They had picked through their outfits with care, but Felix only glanced at them and shrugged.

"You should buy one good, simple thing instead of five shoddy ones. That'll take time."

"That's stupid. Cheaper things mean you have more to wear," Mattie protested. But Julia suddenly saw the point. Felix himself owned hardly any clothes. He had just two sweaters, one black and one navy blue, but they were both cashmere. His trousers and jacket were well cut, on fashionable but subdued lines, and his shoes were expensive, glossy Italian slip-ons. He kept them well polished, and he put them away with shoe trees in them when he took them off instead of letting them lie where they fell on the floor. Julia thought Felix always looked wonderful, and she recognized the contrast with her own and Mattie's reckless scruffiness.

That was the beginning of Julia's longing for exquisite, expensive, unattainable luxuries.

"Enjoy yourselves," Jessie called out. "My God, I wish I had my time over again."

They headed for the Rocket, three abreast, with their arms linked.

The cellar welcomed them like a second home. The girls abandoned themselves to the music, to the frenetic jiving, to the packed mass of bodies and the overpowering heat. Felix held himself apart for a moment longer. He had spent so many solitary evenings in places like this that it was disorienting, for an instant, to find himself possessed by Mattie and Julia. He thought then of the girl who had accosted him in the street, close to here, and his sudden longing for company.

He had company now, he told himself, whether he liked it or not. He sometimes resented the invasion that these girls had made into his home, and their noisy, shrill, intrusive presence in the tidy flat. But they had done more for Jessie in a matter of days than he had been able to do himself in a year. He was grateful for that. And almost in spite of himself he liked them for themselves, too, consolidating the way that he had been drawn to them from the beginning.

"Come on, don't stand there," Mattie ordered him. "Dance with me."

Felix took hold of her, feeling the peculiar softness of her flesh under his fingers. He was glad that it was Mattie first. She was completely foreign to him, the whole scented spread of her, and in a way that was easy for him to deal with. He could treat her like Jessie, with affection that kept her at a physical distance, even in the tiny flat.

It was Julia who disturbed him.

He watched her narrow hips as she went up the stairs ahead of him, and he found himself wanting to reach out and touch the knobs of her spine when she bent her head and exposed the nape of her neck.

Felix had no idea what girls expected or understood, and he was incapable of making the movement that would bring his fingertips to rest on those fragile bones. His uncertainty made him try harder to be impersonal, to keep the space between them cool and clear and neutral.

Felix knew that he was a coward.

Across the room, with a flickering candle throwing odd shadows upward into the hollows of his face, Julia saw Johnny Flowers. He was wearing a black leather jacket over a white vest, and he saw her at the same instant. He shouldered his way across to her.

"Like I said, I'm always around."

"I'll still have to owe you your pound. I haven't got it."

Julia and Mattie spent everything they earned instantly. Everything that was left over from the much-needed rent went on clothes.

Johnny Flowers grinned. "Dance with me and we'll call it quits."

The next afternoon was Mattie's first half-day. She had had to wait her turn for a weekday afternoon off, and it had seemed a long time coming. Now it had arrived, she knew where she must go.

Without telling Jessie and Felix, without mentioning it even to Julia, she made her way back on the tube to Liverpool Street Station. At the clerk's little glass porthole she bought a ticket, a day return. She tore the ticket in half at once and she put the return portion in the pocket of her blouse, next to her heart, like a talisman. At the same time she smiled, privately and bitterly. It wasn't so easy to escape that a small oblong of green pasteboard could achieve it for her.

The estate, lying baldly under a gray sky, was exactly the same. Mattie walked the familiar route, trying to pretend that her breath was coming easily instead of in panicky gasps.

The house, when she came to it, looked the same too. The windows were closed and the stringy curtains were drawn, but that was nothing unusual. No one had remembered to open them, Mattie thought. Then she opened the front door. She smelled stale air and sour milk, and listened to the oppressive silence.

A different fear swelled up, bigger, threatening to choke her.

Ted wasn't here.

None of them was here. Where were the children, and what had he done to them?

She half-turned, not knowing whether she was going to stumble on into the house or turn and run, and then she heard a sound. It was completely familiar, a tinny rattle and then a plop. It was a record, falling from the stack poised over the turntable of Ricky's prized Dansette.

"Ricky!"

A clatter obliterated the first tinny bars of music, and Ricky appeared at the boys' bedroom door.

"Mat?"

He hurtled down the stairs, a skinny boy of fifteen with Mattie's hair, brutally cut so that it stood up in tufts all over his head.

"Are you all right?" she demanded.

He hugged her and they clung together, briefly, while Mattie stared fiercely at him.

" 'Course. Where've you been?"

Relief was making Mattie shake. "Where is he?"

Ricky knew what she meant, of course. "He's out. He's working, unloading crates at the Works. What are you shivering for?"

"Nothing. It's all right. Come on, let's have some coffee."

"Bit of a mess in there," Ricky warned her.

The kitchen was a morass of dirty pans, plates, and food. The smell of sour milk was almost overpowering.

"Ricky . . ."

"I know. Look, it doesn't matter. Me and Sam'll get around to it. It doesn't bother us, you know."

It didn't, Mattie thought. And she had left them. So she had no right to come back and fuss about details. She cleared a space and filled the kettle, rinsing out two cups from the filthy stack. There was no fresh milk, so they drank their coffee black, sitting out on the back step and looking across the hummocks of dandelions to the backs of the next row of houses. Ricky told her what had happened. A woman had come from the Council, a bossy woman with papers. Ted had refused to see her at first, telling Ricky and Sam to say that he was out, but she had come back, and then she had simply sat down to wait for him. She had looked at the house, and she had talked to Marilyn and Phil.

In the end Ted had appeared. Ricky and the others had been sent out of the room, but they had heard Ted shouting, and then mumbling. The woman had gone at last, and Ted had come to find them.

"He looked," Ricky said, groping for the words, "He looked like Phil does when someone's pinched her sweets, and then yelled at her for creating."

Mattie knew that look of her father's. Unwieldy anger, too big for him, subsiding quickly into cringing weakness. She had seen it that last time, here in the kitchen, with the kettle whistling. Only when he looked at Mattie there was something else too. That hot, anxious longing. Mattie wrapped her fingers around her coffee cup to stop the shudder.

The woman from the Council had announced to Ted that there was evidence of neglect. Either the young ones must go to live with a relative, in more suitable circumstances, or a place would be found for them in a council home.

Ricky relayed the details with matter-of-fact calmness. He had worked out a way of living for himself, Mattie understood. Ricky would be all right, and Sam too. Sam was the family survivor, happy so long as he could play football on the scuffed fields beyond the estate. The younger ones, the girls, were living with Rozzie.

"They're okay," Ricky said. "It's better than here."

"I know that," Mattie said heavily.

"The council woman asked about you. Dad said you'd done a runner. He didn't know where to, and he didn't care either."

Mattie stood up quickly and put her cup with the rest of the dirty dishes. It seemed a pointless gesture to bother to wash it out.

"I'm going to Rozzie's to see them. Walk round there with me?"

Rozzie lived a mile away, farther into the estate. They walked together, past the effortful gardens bright with zinnias and lobelia, and the rows of windows guarded by net curtains. Rozzie's house was almost identical to the one they had just left, but better kept. The window frames and the door were painted maroon and there were marigolds growing under the windows.

Rozzie opened the door to them. Her flowered nylon housecoat hardly buttoned up over her stomach. She was eight months pregnant and her two-year-old son, runny-nosed, peered out from the shelter of her skirt. She didn't smile.

"So you're back, then?"

Mattie nodded. Her sister had every right to be sullen, and Mattie had been expecting it. Rozzie was nineteen, and she had had to marry her car mechanic boyfriend two and a half years ago. The enchantment with each other had worn off almost before the wedding, and now they were confined here together with their baby. Then, suddenly, they had found themselves responsible for Rozzie's little sisters as well. "Just to see that you're all right." Mattie added awkwardly, "And to say I'm sorry."

"Sorry?"

There was a silence, and then Rozzie jerked her head. "Well. You'd better come in. Phil? Marilyn? Mat's here."

They had been in the garden at the back, and they came pelting through to leap on to Mattie. She hugged them fiercely, pulling them close and burying her face against them.

They were well, and they looked happy enough. That was something. For half an hour they took all of Mattie's attention. Then suddenly they were off, taking the little boy and Ricky with them. Mattie and Rozzie sat in the kitchen, drinking more watery coffee. The house was bleak and underfurnished, but it was clean. Mattie suddenly thought of Felix's flat, with its simple, definite style and the bright touches of pottery and exotic Soho vegetables. She had gotten away, after all, and Rozzie hadn't. Guilt dropped around her, weighty and sour with familiarity.

"Do you need money?" she blurted out. "I can send you my wages."

"We always need money, Barry and me. But Ted's giving us plenty for the girls. Guilt money, isn't it?" They both knew that it was, of course. It would last for as long as he could hold on to the job. "You keep your wages. Until things get better for you, that is." Rozzie was teasing her, and they both laughed.

It was the right time for Mattie to leave. She didn't want to stay to say difficult good-byes to the younger ones.

"Give them a kiss for me," she said abruptly. "Tell them I'll be back to see them as soon as I can."

She left Rozzie lighting another cigarette. The Orioles, *Cryin' in the Chapel*, was on the wireless.

Mattie walked quickly, with her head up. The old widower in the house on the corner was cutting his square of grass, and the scent of it mixed with the faint smell of flowers from the gardens. She looked past him as he paraded carefully with his mower, and she saw a man coming around the corner.

It was her father, and he saw her in the same instant. Mattie whirled around, looking for somewhere to run to, and he saw that too. He came toward her, past the old man and the patchy gardens. He was carrying a white paper bag, and there was a bottle under his arm. It wasn't whiskey, she saw. It was Tizer. He was bringing pop and sweets, an offering for his children.

He came closer, never taking his eyes off her, and then he stopped. He was so close that his body almost touched hers. Mattie stood rigidly.

"You were going to run off without even speaking to me. I'm still your dad, you know."

There it was, the old, cajoling mock-severity. But less sure of itself now. There was wariness in his face. He was afraid, but he was still greedy. Mattie knew, and she shrank from what she remembered. He was guilty, and too weak to stop himself from compounding the guilt.

"I've got to go," she whispered.

"Where to? You're here, aren't you? You set the welfare people on me, didn't you?"

She tried to square up to him. "I couldn't leave Marilyn and Phil with you."

"Mat, what do you think I am?"

She knew him so well. His anger fronting his pathetic desires.

"I know what you are," she said quietly.

She felt a momentary, viciously physical hatred of all men. But it was gone as quickly as it had come.

"I wanted to say I was sorry, but you haven't given me the chance," he said.

The creases in her father's face touched her, and the sight of his big hand, dirty from work, still gripping the pop bottle. She loved him, too, and she was exhausted by the obligations of love that pinioned her here among the boxy houses.

"I've got to go." She was shouting, and the old man on the corner peered toward them.

Ted stared at her stupidly. "Go where? I thought you were back. We can't manage the place without you. We . . ."

"You'll have to manage. All of you."

I'm not giving myself to you. I'm not going to sink down like Rozzie. I won't. I can't. I deserve better than that. I'm free now, aren't I? In her head she was already running, the words pounding with her. *I'm free, aren't I?* Ted hadn't touched her, but she felt as if she had to wrench herself out of his grasp.

"I'll come and see the kids when I can." Mattie was breathless with the effort.

"What about me?" Like a baby, his face puckering.

"Nothing about you. Don't you understand? Nothing."

She broke past him then, and started to run. Her legs carried her around the corner and away. She ran as far as she could and then walked, not wanting to stop and wait for a bus, all the way to the station. She took the return ticket out of her pocket and held it in her clenched fist, the torn edge of it digging into her palm. The train came almost at once and she climbed into it and stumbled to a seat. The dust puffed out from the cushion behind her head.

Sitting there, watching the backs of the houses and the factories and warehouses peel away past her, Mattie promised herself. *I will do it. I'm going to be successful, and rich, and happy, and I won't let that place pull me back again. None of the things that have happened matter at all, from now on. Only the things that are going to happen.*

She felt the resolution stiffening her, as if her spine were a steel shaft. She leaned forward to peer through the grimy window, as if she could see more clearly what was coming.

The party was originally Julia's idea, but Mattie seized on it with insistent enthusiasm. She seemed to light on everything now, Julia noticed, making whatever they did important just by concentrating very hard on it.

"Give a party for Jessie? Of course we must do it. Listen, we'll make it just like the old evenings that Jessie talks about. Squeeze everyone in, make sure everyone has a good time . . ." Mattie snatched a piece of paper and a pencil and began making a list. "Friends of ours, not too many, but enough. Felix will have to help us to round up Jessie's friends. As many as we can. We'll have singing, and vodka martinis . . ."

Mattie had been taken out once or twice by a dubious club owner, and he had introduced her to vodka martinis. Under the influence of three or four of them, Mattie had had more trouble than usual in fending him off, and she had managed the last time only by jumping out of his Ford Zephyr and running away. The girls thought that the cocktails were the height of sophistication.

Plans for the party took off with surprising speed. Slightly to their surprise, even Felix plunged into them. "We'll have to have it at home," he agreed. "Jessie won't go out anywhere else. Leave it to me to invite the people she would like to see."

They kept it a secret from her as long as they could, but they were too excited and the girls wanted to share the pleasure of anticipation with her.

"Don't be so silly," she snapped. "I'm past the age for all that nonsense." But they knew from the way that her eyes brightened that she was delighted.

Felix said that he would provide the food. Julia and Mattie, without thinking much about it, had imagined sandwiches.

"Meat paste sandwiches, I suppose?" Felix scoffed.

They realized that all the vodka martinis they could afford wouldn't go far either.

"Tell everyone to bring a bottle," Felix advised.

"And what about the music?" Felix's record player was unreliable, and there was no piano in the flat so there was no point in Mattie and Julia dreaming of the kind of pianist who thumped out the old songs in Jessie's stories.

"Don't worry," Felix answered. "Bish is coming."

Jessie had told them all about that. Freddie Bishop played the mouth organ to compete with a twenty-piece dance band.

On the day of the party, Felix went out very early to Soho. He came back with two bulging shopping baskets and shut himself in the kitchen.

Mattie and Julia contented themselves with pushing back the furniture in Jessie's room, the only decently sized space in the flat. Then they turned their attention to Jessie herself. They rummaged mercilessly in her wardrobe, exclaiming and pulling out dresses and holding them up against her.

"You're wasting everyone's time," Jessie said. "None of those things will go anywhere near me now."

"This red skirt will, look, it's loose."

"And this coat with the sequins. You'll look like Ella Fitzgerald. When did you wear all these wonderful things?"

"In my heyday, dear, in my heyday."

Mattie wound Jessie's hair up on to rollers, and they practiced painting her face with their Outdoor Girl cosmetics. By early evening she was giggling with them, as overexcited as a schoolgirl. Felix emerged from the kitchen with a blast of spicy cooking smells, and helped them to lay out the glasses and plates borrowed from a restaurant, one of Jessie's old haunts. The proprietor and his wife had promised to come to the party after closing time. Then, when everything else was ready, Julia and Mattie retired to prepare themselves.

Mattie had made herself a dress from a bolt of greeny-black shot taffeta with a bad flaw in it, picked up for a few shillings from one of the stalls at the top end of Berwick Street Market. The bodice was strapless, and she had sewn it tight to show more of her cleavage. The skirt was full, puffed out with layers of net petticoats. Using her staff discount, she had bought herself a pair of wicked black stiletto-heeled shoes. They were so high that they made her almost as tall as Julia. Mattie brushed her hair out into a froth of curls, and then spun around, admiring herself, until her skirts whirled up to show her black stocking tops.

"I just hope the top stays up," she said, hitching at it so that the creamy skin with its faint powdering of freckles bulged even more precariously over the taffeta.

Julia hated sewing. She had planned to make do with one of her own or Mattie's dancing outfits, but in Jessie's wardrobe she had discovered a red embroidered silk kimono. She wound it around herself, tighter and tighter, until it was a twisted column of scarlet splashed with fronds of abstract color. She found a black silk shawl and tied it around her waist, letting the fringed ends trail down at the back. And, with a touch of last-minute inspiration, she fastened her hair up on the top of her head and stuck the poppies from an old hat into a comb at the back.

When they emerged, Jessie was sitting in her chair, dressed up, ready to hold court. Felix had been sitting beside her, filling her glass. He looked at Mattie and Julia, his eyes traveling critically up and down, while they held their breath. And then he smiled.

"At last," he pronounced. "You're getting the idea." Mattie was like Turkish Delight, he thought. Scented and powdery and overpowering. Julia was a tall, white-skinned geisha, as clean and sappy as a peeled willow wand. His eyes slid back to her.

There was a moment's silence and then, from far down at the bottom of the house beyond the empty offices, they heard the bell ringing.

"People!" Mattie yelled, and ran to the door.

By some miracle, the party, so casually and sketchily planned, was a roaring success from the very beginning.

The people flowed in and filled Jessie's room, and overflowed into Felix's bedroom and the kitchen and even the bathroom. Freddie Bishop perched on Mattie's bed and played the mouth organ, someone else had brought a guitar, and a banjoist arrived after the pubs closed, and the guests danced and swayed and spilled down the stairs past the deserted offices. Most of them were Jessie's old friends from her club days. There were men who brought their own whiskey bottle and held firmly on to it, women who laughed a lot and shook their lacquered heads, singers and barmen and waiters and painters, and even one or two policemen. They mixed with big black men in trilby hats and colored shirts, regulars from the Rocket, Felix's student friends, and Johnny Flowers and his coterie, who devoted themselves to pursuing Mattie and Julia, all together in a big, hot, happily drunken mêlée.

That first party became the prototype, in their memories, for all the others that followed it through the short Soho years.

There was never enough food. That night Felix had made chili in a huge saucepan, with red kidney beans and chopped steak, hot chorizo sausage and chilies, and it vanished in an instant, with a great vat of rice. But there was always drink, from the bottles brought in instead of invitation cards, and noisy music, familiar faces, and beguiling new ones to focus on.

Jessie sat in state in her chair, presiding like a queen over the stream of people who came to greet her. Felix had done a wonderful job in searching them all out. Mattie and Julia danced, talked, and laughed, and drank whatever was put into their hands. Even Felix, for once, was more of a participant than an observer.

Johnny Flowers was drunk, but Julia thought she must be drunker. Everything seemed wonderfully funny and her legs kept twisting around themselves inside the tight kimono.

"I saw you first," Johnny complained, as he tried to extricate her from the arms of one of his friends. "And you still owe me a pound."

"You said we were quits. Dance with Mattie."

"Everyone else in the room is falling over Mattie."

It was true. Mattie was in the middle of a tight circle. Her face was flushed, but she was in perfect control. She was very good at keeping the onslaught at arm's length.

"Sit down here with me, then."

Julia and Johnny slid down to the floor together. They sat with their backs propped against the wall, their knees drawn up to keep their feet from being trampled on. Felix saw them, but he didn't let his attention wander from his conversation with a friend of Mr. Mogridge's.

"You two," Johnny said admiringly. "Have you always been friends?"

"Mattie and me? Yes, forever. Since I was eleven and she was twelve. Do you know where I first saw her?"

Johnny let his head fall onto her shoulder. "Mmm? Tell me."

"Blick Road Girls' Grammar School. My first day. I can see her now." At the other end of a long corridor, Mattie had turned a corner, with the sun behind her. It shone through her hair, turning it into a pale and glamorous halo. But as she came closer, Julia saw that the halo had come to rest on the wrong head. Julia's own uniform was pin-new, correct, and proud in every fold and button. Mattie's gym-slip was short and cinched in at the waist with a wide elastic belt. She had real breasts. There was no sign of the hideous bottle-green and chrome-yellow striped tie that they were all supposed to wear. Mattie's grubby shirt was open at the neck, showing a deep V of milky skin powdered with freckles. Her white socks were as dirty as her shirt, and longer than the regulation ankle length, emphasizing the swell of her calves. Her shoes were the triumph. They were bright red, with pert little heels. "I thought she was wonderful. I wanted to be her. But I just said, 'Excuse me, I'm lost.' Mattie looked me up and down, very very slowly, and then she put her head on one side and smiled at me. She said, 'You don't look lost. In fact, you look as if you were manufactured here. Made in Blick Road.' I wanted to rip off my tie and stuff it in my stupid shiny satchel and throw the whole lot into the canal."

"But I did show you the way."

They looked up and saw Mattie leaning over them. Her breasts swelled inside the black taffeta and Johnny Flowers groaned. He reached up to cup one of them, but Mattie slapped his hand down.

"Hands off the goods," she said, grinning.

"And after that there was the Christmas party," Julia reminded her. "Then I knew we had to be friends." They laughed delightedly at the memory of it. Fifty little girls in organdy dresses and white socks. And Mattie, with her hair up in a French braid, done up in a bright blue shiny low-cut dress of her mother's, with wedge-heeled open-toe shoes, and real nylons. Most of the little girls giggled at her. It didn't occur to them that Mattie might not have a party dress of her own to wear.

There was a talent contest. Most of the contributions were piano duets or recitations. And then, at the end, Mattie had jumped up on the stage to sing a song.

The song was "Ma, He's Making Eyes at Me."

Mattie's singing voice was unremarkable, but the enthusiasm of her delivery made up for that. She went through the volume range from whisper to shout, with a supporting repertoire of winks and smiles. The performance was absurd, but her confidence and a hint of real talent carried it off for her.

The last line of the song, delivered at full-throated roar, was "*Mama, he's kissing me!*" In the crescendo of chords that followed as her pianist tried for her share of the limelight, Mattie pursed her red lips and blew a lingering kiss at the girls and teachers.

There was a terrible silence.

"It was Julia," Mattie remembered, "who jumped on to her chair and clapped her hands until they nearly fell off. It was after that that we became friends."

"And slid down together all the way to here."

They looked so young, and fresh, and pleased with their loucheness, even to Johnny, who was hardly any older, that he laughed and draped his arms around their necks and kissed them.

"C'mon, you two. I can't handle you both. Let's have another drink. By the way, who won the talent contest?"

They stared at him, and then dissolved into giggles. "A girl with pigtails and glasses. Who recited Walter de la Mare."

Later, they weren't sure how much later, they saw Jessie being helped to her feet, supported by two waiters from her favorite Italian restaurant. Julia was ready to run forward to help her, thinking that she must be overcome by heat or vodka, and then she saw that Jessie was beaming with pride. She held up her hand.

"Albert's asked me to sing. I couldn't say no, could I?"

There was an instant storm of cheers. Freddie Bishop wriggled forward and cupped his hands to his mouth yet again.

Jessie sang. She loved all the old songs, of course, "We'll Meet Again," and "Tipperary," and "Pack Up Your Troubles." Everyone, all the people crowded in the smoky rooms, sang with her. Felix saw the rekindled light in her face, and he knew that in her heart she was back in her club bar, with the curtains tightly drawn, and her friends and customers around the piano. He looked across the room, and his eyes met Julia's.

"Thank you," he whispered to her through the singing, and she dipped her dark head at him.

Jessie held up her huge, pale arms. "I've got two new friends," she called out, "who made this party for me, with my Felix. Come over here, both of you, and sing with me." She beckoned to Julia and Mattie. When they reached her, Julia whispered, "I can't sing. Mattie'll do my bit for me. Jessie, do you know 'Ma, He's Making Eyes at Me'?"

"Of course I know it," Jessie roared.

They sang it together, the two of them, as if they had been rehearsing it for years. Julia saw that Mattie had grown into the ripeness that she had caricatured at Blick Road. The eyes of every man in the room were fixed on her. Of every one except Felix, because Felix was looking at Julia. Julia didn't feel even a tremor of jealousy. She closed her eyes and let the ridiculous song bridge the years back to Blick Road School. She loved Mattie. This was her family now, she thought prophetically. Mattie, and Jessie, and Felix.

"Mama, he's kissing me!"

There was no terrible silence this time. There were whistles and shouts and applause. Near Felix a small, thin man with a little thin mustache was clapping too.

"That girl packs quite a punch," he murmured to no one in particular. "She can't sing, but she must have plenty of other talents. What can I find for her to do?"

Two important things happened that evening, although at the time they seemed hardly more important than the other snatches of talk, promises, and pleas and evasions that rose with the plumes of cigarette smoke.

Mr. Mogridge's friend eased Felix into a corner. He had looked carefully around the flat, and now he said, "Did this place up yourself, didn't you? Tommy Bull told me. Made quite a nice job of it, I must say. Listen, I've got a proposition. I've got some flats, I want 'em done up and furnished for letting. Quality letting, mind. Tasteful, but nothing too fancy. Like this place. Do you want to take the job on for me? I pay well."

Felix studied the man. He didn't like him any better than he liked Mr. Mogridge or Mr. Bull, and when the man said quality letting he knew that he meant no blacks or Irish, like the signs in the landladies' windows. Then he thought about the life studio, and the art school exercises languishing in his portfolio.

"All right," he said quietly. "I'll take the job on for you."

The man with the thin mustache went over to Mattie when the storm following her song had died down. He took a card out of his wallet and handed it to her. Mattie read the name, Francis Willoughby, and the title, Manager, Headline Repertory Companies.

"I've got three companies on the road at the moment," he said grandly. "I need a girl Friday to help me out in our London offices. All aspects of theater work, on the administration side. You interested?"

"Yes," Mattie whispered. She reached out for the card as if it were the Holy Grail. "Give me a tinkle, then." The man peeled his lips back in a smile.

Jessie fell into her sudden sleep not long after that, and the crowds began to trickle away.

Julia stood with Johnny's arms around her. She wasn't sure

that she could hold herself up without his support. His mouth felt very hot on her neck, and he was excited. She could feel him pushing against her. Over his shoulder she saw Felix. He bent down to pick up an empty glass, and then he walked away.

This wasn't what she had planned for tonight, Julia realized. It shouldn't be like this. But she was too tired now, and too drunk, to change anything.

"Come on darling," Johnny begged her.

"No. I can't. Tomorrow."

"Okay." He sighed. "Not tonight. But tomorrow, or sooner. You can't keep me gasping for you like this, baby. Look. It's bad for me."

Julia shut her eyes.

Johnny picked her up and carried her to her bed. He laid her down and pulled the covers over her, kimono and all, and left her there.

Julia opened her eyes once more and saw that she was safe, although Felix wasn't there. The room was spinning around her, but she shut her eyes again anyway and plunged down into the revolving tunnel of sleep.

FOUR

It was the party that made Julia feel, *now I do belong here*. It was gratifying to have been part of a success that was still talked about in the Rocket and in Blue Heaven. Out of a new, buoyant sense of security she wrote to Betty and Vernon.

The letter said no more than *I'm here with Mattie, and I'm all right*. Betty would be worried, and even in the confusion of her feelings about her mother, Julia didn't want her to be anxious for no reason. She put the address of the flat at the top of the letter because it sounded so fixed, a long way from Fairmile Road.

Betty saw the envelope at once, lying on the rug behind the front door with a church newsletter and a bill addressed to Vernon. Her hands were shaking as she picked it up. She held on to it, crumpling it a little, while she fetched her glasses and the Brighton souvenir letter opener.

Betty read Julia's brief message, and reread it, and then sat down abruptly on the upright chair beside the telephone.

She remembered that she had done exactly the same thing when she had read the first note, the few words that Julia had scribbled before she disappeared. It had made no sense then, and she had turned the envelope over in her fingers. The gum on the flap was still damp, and she saw her daughter licking it to seal in her good-bye, her dark hair loose about her face.

"No," Betty had said aloud into the quiet of the house. "Oh, no. Julia, where are you?" The words echoed back at her. Betty had dropped the note and run up the stairs. In Julia's pretty, schoolgirl bedroom the drawers and cupboards were half empty. The neat cardigans and pinafore dresses that Betty had bought for her were still there, and the strange, defiant clothes that they had quarreled about were all gone.

Betty stood in the silent room, trying to understand what had happened. It was as if her Julia, the pretty, clever schoolgirl, were still there in the house, with all her clothes and the white furry lamb that always sat on her candlewick bedspread. It was someone else, a stranger whom she didn't know or understand, who had run away from her.

"Julia!"

Betty turned and ran frantically through the house. A series of pictures danced in front of her eyes, faster and faster, like a slide show running out of control. Her first sight of Julia, a bundle of blankets put into her arms. Julia's first steps, wobbling across the hearth rug toward her. Picnics, and an outing to the sea. Julia making her first cake, frowning solemnly over the mixing bowl. Then Julia in her new grammar school uniform, when Vernon had said, "She'll be someone, Betty. She's got a head on her shoulders."

And then, darker pictures slipping between the sunlit ones, there was another Julia who looked at Betty as if she hated her. Betty saw more and more of that Julia, a sullen, silent interloper in her skirts that were too short and too tight, her pretty face shadowed by too much makeup.

"Julia!"

Betty had searched in every room, flinging open the cupboard doors. The tidy contents displayed themselves, yielding nothing. The garden, grass and roses in the sunshine, winked emptily back at her.

Julia had gone.

She remembered all that, because it had replayed endlessly

in her head in the weeks that had gone by since then. And now there was this new message, hardly any more words, but they were headed by the reality of an address, after all Betty's imaginings. She read it again, *London W1*, fixing it in her memory in case the letter should disappear. And then, for the first time in twenty-five years, she did something important without waiting to consult Vernon first. She put on her brown coat, and the hat she always wore with it, and went up to London to look for her daughter. To look for her, and to bring her back home.

The square surprised her, when she reached it at last. People didn't live in places like this. They lived in houses set behind clipped hedges, or else they lived on the estate. She faltered for an instant, the first time since leaving Fairmile Road, but then she collected herself and marched around the railings, under the plane trees, counting the house numbers. When she reached the right door she saw that it was already standing open, revealing a hallway with a strip of shabby carpet and a shelf piled with circulars and manila envelopes.

These were offices, then, and not homes at all. She could hear typewriters, and a telephone ringing somewhere. She looked at the number on the peeling, black-painted door to make sure that she hadn't made a mistake, and then beside her left shoulder she saw a single doorbell. It was labeled *Lemoine, Top Flat*.

Julia hadn't mentioned anyone called Lemoine, but Betty pressed the bell anyway. She waited for a long time and then pressed it again, harder and longer.

Nobody came.

Jessie never answered the bell during the day when Felix was out. Even if it was someone she wanted to see, she couldn't manage to negotiate the stairs to the front door.

Betty was undeterred. She had plenty of time to wait, if that was what was needed. She looked around and saw that the iron railings sprouted from a foot-high wall with a stone coping. She wrapped her coat carefully around herself and sat down on the stone, her hands clasped over her handbag on her knees.

The occasional passing secretary or messenger looked oddly at her, but no one spoke, and the afternoon went slowly by.

It was Felix who saw her.

He had been to meet the developer, Mr. French, in the block of run-down flats, and his head was teeming with ideas and impressions as he walked through the square. He passed the small brown woman sitting quietly outside the front door with barely a glance, and he was in the dusty hallway before something, perhaps her eyes on his back, made him turn around again.

"Can I help you?" he asked.

"I'm looking for Miss Julia Smith," the woman said. "Does she live here?"

Felix's hand cupped the bell, an instinctive, shielding movement, but he said, "Yes. She lives here."

The little woman's face changed. He saw exhausted relief take the place of determination.

"I'm her mother," she said.

Felix looked at her, and then he thought of Jessie, waiting for him upstairs. The images of mothers collided hopelessly.

"You'd better come in," he said quietly. Betty followed him meekly up the stairs.

As soon as Julia came in, she felt the change in the atmosphere. She had been singing as she climbed the stairs, but the song trailed away as she opened the flat door. It was very quiet, and Jessie didn't call out *Come here. Tell me the news, and pour me a drink while you're about it.*

"Jessie?"

Julia ran the two steps to her door, and then she saw. Jessie was sitting in her chair, with her bottle at her elbow. Felix was by the window, enigmatically dark against the light pouring in. And facing Jessie, with her knees and her lips drawn together as if she were afraid of touching anything or breathing in the air, sat Betty.

She looked so incongruous among Jessie's photographs and souvenirs and Felix's objects that Julia couldn't find anything to say at all. Her first thought was, I should have known. I should have known she'd come straight here.

"Mum," she acknowledged awkwardly, at last. She bent down and her cheek brushed the brown felt crown of the hat. Betty wouldn't look straight at her but her mother's hand took hold of hers, kneading it, making sure that she was really there. To Julia's shame, the restraint of it made her want to pull away and run across the room to stand in the light, by Felix.

She realized that they were all waiting for her to say something. Jessie and Felix were waiting too. Julia's thoughts darted helplessly. What justification was there? Except what she wanted, for herself? Wasn't it just a truth of life that it was so different from what Betty dreamed, confiningly, for her?

"I'm all right, you know," Julia said. Her voice came out

sounding colder, farther away than she had meant it to. "I've got a job. In an accounts office. Just like Dad."

Betty didn't move.

"And I'm living here. With friends."

"Friends?" Betty did look up then. And her voice could be venomous when she wished it to. Julia knew all the prejudices that lurked behind the single word. She could have recited them. Dirty blacks. Drunkards and thieves. No better than a common prostitute.

That her mother could even think such things, sitting here with Jessie and Felix, ignited a sudden, violent anger. She jerked her hand away.

"Yes, friends. Good friends, who've been kind to me and Mattie. You and Dad would hardly let Mattie in the house, would you? Do you think you're better people or something?"

Anger against Betty's prejudices found a shape in the words, and they spilled out of her, regardless. "You aren't any better. You're narrow. You condemn anything you don't understand. You . . ."

"Julia." It was Jessie, warning her. "That's enough."

The hot, rancorous words dried up at once. Julia's fists had been clenched at her sides. They opened now and the fingers hung loosely.

Betty looked in bewilderment from the fat, overpainted old woman who seemed able to command her daughter in a way that she had never mastered, to Julia herself. She seemed taller, thinner than ever, and her face had lost the last blurred roundness of childhood. In the days since leaving home, Julia had grown up. Grown up here, in this horrible attic flat that smelled of drink and cigarettes, with a woman who looked like a madam, and her half-caste son. Here, instead of in the home that she and Vernon had made for her, and where they had made such plans for her for sixteen years.

Jealousy bit into Betty, and the pain of exclusion, and with them came the terrible fear that she had lost Julia. She pulled her coat tighter around her and shielded herself with her handbag.

Fear made her desperate.

"I want to talk to you, Julia."

"Here I am."

"To you, not to these people."

It was Betty's mistake to let her hostility show. Julia's face, the new, grown-up face, didn't change, but she said, "I don't have any secrets from Jessie and Felix. Or from Mattie."

"That girl . . ." Betty was sure that it was Mattie's influence that had brought Julia here, but she made herself bite back the accusation. The moment of control strengthened her, and her fear ebbed a little. She looked fiercely at Jessie and the fat woman's chair creaked as she began to labor to her feet.

"You talk to your mother," Jessie murmured to Julia. But Julia whirled across to the chair and her hands descended on Jessie's shoulders, holding her in her place.

"Please," Julia whispered. She looked across to the window, trying to see the shadowed face against the sunshine. "Please, Felix."

Jessie hovered for a moment, almost on her feet. And then she sighed. Her weight sagged backward against the cushions. She knew that Julia was fighting, and the battle clearly mattered so much to her. If Julia wanted herself and Felix to stay for it, then they would do it for her. Jessie could read the vulnerability in Julia's face, even though Betty was blind to it. She sighed again, silently aligning herself. Over by the window, Felix was looking out at the plane trees. Their leaves were beginning to curl and turn brown, the first premature autumn in August. He didn't turn, but he didn't try to leave the room either.

Julia faced Betty again.

"Go on," she said.

Betty's brown hat bobbed in front of her.

"I want you to come home."

The words dropped into the room's stillness.

Julia said nothing, and Betty, with the fear lapping up in her again, began to talk faster. "Come home. We'll forget all this. Dad and I won't mention it, if that's what you want. We'll all forget it. They'll take you back at the school, in the new term. You can finish your course, and then get a job, a real job, a good one. You needn't think that everything has gone wrong just because of this."

She was trying to say, *if it's out of pride that you won't come back, don't be proud. I'm not too proud to come here and beg you, am I?* But Betty had never been any good at words.

"You can come back. Everything is at home, waiting for you."

Julia seemed to be waiting politely for her mother to finish. But at last she said, "I'm not coming home."

Betty sprang up and ran to her. She put her hands on Julia's sleeves and twisted them, trying to move her, trying to find her. Julia thought, she's so small. Like a dry leaf. She had no memories of Betty having been the source of warmth and strength in her childhood. She couldn't remember her childhood at all. All she could focus on was this, a little, thin woman who clung to her, and whose bones felt brittle.

Suddenly all the perspectives changed.

The great battle that she had prepared herself for, the battle for her own freedom to be fought out to the sound of trumpets in front of Jessie and Felix, had never even begun. It was a nothing, a foregone conclusion, her own strength brutally crushing Betty's.

Julia wished now that she had made the small concession of letting her mother take her defeat in private.

"I'm sorry," she whispered. "I'm very sorry."

And Betty, who was just beginning to understand what her loss really was, with bitterness eating through her fear, rounded on Julia for the last time.

"Sorry? You're sorry, is that all? After what we've done for you, and given up for you, ever since you were a baby? A dirty little baby who wasn't wanted . . ."

Betty's mouth made a circle of pain, and her hand went up to cover it. She heard the warning creak as Jessie leaned forward in her chair, and out of the corner of her eye she saw the shadow move as Felix swung away from the window.

Julia didn't hear anything or see anything. There were only the words, inside her head. *A dirty little baby who wasn't wanted.*

In the close attic room she moved slowly, as if the air around her had turned solid.

"What do you mean?" The words slurred in her mouth. Like being drunk, only she knew she wasn't drunk.

Betty grown old, with all her life of fear naked in her eyes now, fear and a kind of last exultation. Power, after all. Not quite done yet.

"You're not my daughter. Not Vernon's either. We took you when you were just a few weeks old. I'd lost one of my own, couldn't have another. And the war was coming."

All Julia could think of, the only thing as she struggled to form the words, was, "My real mother? Who was she?"

Betty's face dancing in front of her eyes, aging as the seconds ticked past, a stranger's.

"I don't know. I never knew. Some silly girl, I suppose, who got herself into trouble."

That was all.

It was Felix who came forward to put his arms around Julia. Her head fell against his shoulder and she began to shiver. The sudden stripping away of it all, Fairmile Road and Betty and Vernon left her icy cold. Her teeth chattered and Felix's hands felt dangerously hot through her thin blouse. He held her close to him. For a moment even Jessie was silenced, but Julia laughed. It was a little tuneless noise that none of them recognized as laughter. She lifted her head from Felix's shoulder and said, "I'm glad you told me. It explains a lot of things, doesn't it?" She looked past Betty as if she had stopped existing and repeated, "Some silly girl."

Jessie leaned forward to Betty. "You shouldn't have told her like that," she said sharply. "Don't you know better than that?"

Betty ignored her. Her eyes were fixed on Julia, held in Felix's arms. With her last shot gone, Betty was defenseless. Felix thought painfully that she looked like a dismembered creature.

"We did our best for you," she whispered. "We loved you."

"Love?" The word sounded like an intricate puzzle to Julia, turning inward on itself until it was finally empty, without meaning. "Yes. It doesn't make any difference, you know. I won't come home."

She was more brutally certain now. Her own strength surprised her. Betty made a last effort. "We're still your parents. Your mother and father. Legal guardians. And you're only sixteen. We can make you come back if we have to."

Jessie's big gray head lifted, but she said nothing.

Julia laughed again, just recognizably now.

"You could, but what difference will it make in the end? I will be twenty-one one day, you can't stop that, and even before then you don't own me. You can't change what you've just told me." Carefully but deliberately she detached herself from Felix. She went across to the sofa and sat down, her back against the warm paisley shawl. "I'm all right," she said to Felix and Jessie. She was smiling when she turned to Betty again.

"It's funny, in a way, isn't it? Ironic, I think that's the word. I wanted to be free, and you've set me free by telling me the truth."

There was a moment of silence. Felix thought, *It isn't as simple as that.*

Then Betty stood up. Her coat seemed bigger, too loose for her frame inside it, and her handbag looked like a dead weight over her arm.

"You won't come?" she asked childishly.

"No," Julia repeated. "I live here now."

There was no more talk of guardianship, no suggestion of ownership. Betty's head nodded stiffly, just once.

Watching her, Jessie tried to promise, "We'll look after her for you. I'll see she's all right."

Betty swung around to her, bitterness only heightened by defeat.

"You? You and him?" She jerked her head at Felix. "My Julia might just as well be on the streets."

No one said anything then, not even Julia, not even though her fists clenched in her lap. She watched her mother plod slowly to the door, fumble with the catch. There was still an instant when she could have said *Wait*. Yet she didn't, and afterward she believed that she was right.

They heard Betty's footsteps going away down the stairs.

Julia had stopped shivering. To Jessie and Felix she said almost triumphantly, "I told you, didn't I? You're my family now. You and Mattie."

Mattie was at the front door when Betty passed her. She caught a glimpse of her face and automatically put her hand out, but Betty never wavered. Mattie watched her go, away under the plane trees with her brown hat held upright. She seemed to carry the smell of Fairmile Road with her, Air-Wick and polish and ironing.

Betty sat quite still all the way back on the train to the local station. She crossed the High Street, quite blind, although she nodded to the people who greeted her. Everything inside her was focused on her longing to reach home. Outside the front door she groped for her key, not even noticing that the panels of the door were coated with street dust. But when the door swung open there was none of the relief of sanctuary. She saw Vernon's mackintosh hanging from its peg on the hallstand, and his black briefcase on the floor beside it.

Of course, it was past the time for Vernon to be at home. It was strange, she realized now, that she hadn't thought about him all the way back.

He appeared in the living room doorway, at first only a dark shadow seen out of the corner of her eye, and then she looked full at him. He was wearing his navy blue office suit, shiny at the cuffs.

"Betty? Where have you been?"

She always had his tea on the table by half past five, always. Her eyes met his.

"I went up to town. To look for Julia."

His stiff face, frowning, measuring her.

"And did you find her?"

"Yes."

"Where?"

She told him, awkwardly, stumbling over the words while he frowned. "She won't come back to us, Vernon. She says she won't come home." She wanted to go to him and have him put his arms around her, as that black boy had done with Julia, but neither of them moved. That wasn't part of what happened between them.

Vernon said at last, "Well. If she won't, she won't." He turned back into the sitting room.

Betty's hand reached out to the pretty, orange-skirted lady who covered the telephone. Her fingers caressed the layers of net skirt, searching for comfort.

"I'll put the tea on," she whispered.

It was an evening like any of the others, except that Julia's room upstairs was empty. There was not even the expectation of her key in the lock. Vernon listened to the play on the Home Service and Betty sat in the armchair opposite him with her knitting coiled in her lap.

At ten o'clock exactly she asked him, "Shall I make the cocoa?"

He nodded, not even looking at her over his reading glasses. She was heating the milk in the special pan she always used when he came in behind her. His presence seemed incongruous in the tidy kitchen. Betty looked down into the still, white circle of milk.

"I told her," she said roughly. "I told her about the adoption." He almost bumped against her, but then he stepped back again.

"I wish you hadn't. She's too young yet."

"Vernon, she's grown-up. She's grown-up in that place."

"What did she say? How did she take it?"

The milk rose swiftly, and Betty lifted it off the heat.

"I think she laughed. She said . . . she said it set her free."

She couldn't understand that. Perhaps Vernon would understand it. But all he said, after a long pause, and so quietly that she could hardly hear him, was "Perhaps it's for the best. In the end."

Betty carried the cups back into the living room and they drank their cocoa in silence. When her cup was empty she said, "I'll go on up."

Vernon usually followed her, after locking the doors and winding the clock on the mantelpiece. But tonight he sat for a long time in his armchair in the quiet house, staring ahead of him at the lavender and yellow flowers that ran in garlands down the wallpaper.

Betty lay under the eiderdown upstairs with the tears wet and stinging on her cheeks.

It was Jessie who told Mattie what had happened. Julia listened with her head bent, picking at the fringe of the shawl. At the end she broke in, saying fiercely, "I'm sorry about what my . . . about what she said to you and Felix. That's the way she is. Anyone who doesn't live like she does is condemned. She did it to Mattie . . ."

Jessie said gently, "There's no need to be sorry, my duck. And she is your mother. She raised you all those years, whoever had the birth of you."

Mattie didn't say much. She was shocked, but a part of her wasn't even surprised. She put her arms around Julia's shoulders and hugged her, and then she grinned lopsidedly at Jessie and Felix.

"Here we are, the two of us. What do you think?"

"I don't think anything," Jessie declared. "I know you belong here, that's all. You can stay as long as you feel like it. Felix?"

He had gone back to his place by the window, looking down on the square. "Of course they can stay," he answered.

They had given Julia a glass of vodka and orange juice and she drank it in a gulp, and then looked around at the three of them.

"What shall we do?" she demanded.

"I've just told you," Jessie said. "Stay here with us."

Julia's face softened. "Thank you for that. But I meant now, tonight." There was a pressure in her chest, tightening, like something threatening to burst out of her. And she felt a weird, wild gaiety. When the others stared at her she laughed, a little too loudly.

"I want to go out somewhere. Have some fun."

Jessie hesitated, and then she nodded. She reached down beside her chair for her huge, cracked leather handbag and then peered inside it. From one of the powdery recesses she produced a five-pound note and waved it at Felix.

"She's right. No point moping here. Take them both out and buy them dinner. Go on with you."

Felix took charge. "Get dressed, both of you. Something decent. We'll go to Leoni's."

"Good boy," Jessie said approvingly.

When they were ready, they tried to persuade Jessie to come with them.

"We need you," Mattie said, "if we're going to have a posh dinner. Julia and me won't know which knife to use."

"Felix will tell you. He's good at all that."

Jessie seemed more firmly lodged in her chair than ever. She was afraid of the long flights of stairs outside her door, and the streets beyond them, but she tried not to let them see it.

"I'd rather stay here in peace, you know. Fill me up, Mat, will you?"

"But you belong with us." Julia knelt down in front of her, and Jessie saw her feverishly bright eyes.

"I know I do, duck. And here I am. Now, go and have your dinner, and don't make too much bloody noise when you come back."

On the way to Dean Street, passing through streets that had become familiar, even homely, Julia felt herself spinning, as if her feet might lose contact with the paving stones. The pressure inside her intensified until she had to run, her arms and legs pumping up and down. Mattie and Felix were breathless behind her, and their feet thudded faster and faster, like drumbeats.

Felix reached out and grabbed her wrist and she swung outward, her full skirt ballooning up around her legs.

"What are you running away from?" he demanded.

"I'm not running away. Toward something."

"What?"

"Oh, Felix. I don't know. Freedom."

"I'll drink to that," Mattie shouted, catching Julia's mood.

"What will you do with it, all this freedom?"

Julia had a momentary sense of space. Dark, windy emptiness, dropping away all around her. She was perched on a tiny foothold, all alone. She reached out and put her arms around Mattie and they swayed together, laughing at Felix.

"Gobble it all up," Julia said triumphantly.

At first Leoni's seemed forbidding, with its long, white-starched tablecloths and faded decor. It was full of people, all seemingly much older and richer than themselves. But when a table was found for them in the center of the room, the other

diners looked up as they sailed past in the wake of the headwaiter. The three of them held their heads up. They knew,
somehow, that tonight they were worth looking at. A spark had
ignited them.

"I'll order for you," Felix said. He studied the big white
menu and spoke rapid French to the waiter.

"How do you know French?" the girls demanded, impressed in spite of themselves.

"I know only menu French. And please and thank you. I
taught myself."

"Teach us," Julia demanded. "I want to learn everything."

He smiled at her. "I know you do." Her eagerness pleased
him, and at the same time, in a different recess of himself, it
frightened him.

When their plates came, Mattie and Julia stared disbelievingly
into the bubbling interiors of the big, amber and gold striped
shells nestled in their special dishes.

"They're snails," Mattie whispered.

"They certainly are," Felix agreed. "And you will eat
them. You can't let me down now. Look, like this." He fitted
the little silver clamp around one of his shells and winkled the
snail out. It dripped hot, buttery sauce. When the snail was
gone, Felix tipped the juice out of the shell and mopped it up
with bread from the piled-up basket.

"I'm so hungry," Julia said suddenly. "I've never been so
hungry."

Copying Felix, she extracted a snail. She opened her mouth
and it slid down her throat. She blinked, and realized that it was
delicious.

They devoured their snails and emptied the bread basket.
The waiters were fatherly, bringing more bread and beaming
their approval, all except one, who was young and hovered
around Mattie's chair.

After the *escargots*—"*Escargots*," repeated Julia—came
tournedos Rossini. The thick wedges of steak with pâté and
toasted bread were rich and utterly satisfying. Wine was brought
in a wicker cradle, the neck of the bottle wrapped in a white
napkin. Felix tasted the drop that the wine waiter poured into his
glass and nodded.

"This is Beaune," he told them.

The dessert was a puff of choux pastry oozing with dark
chocolate. Mattie loved all sweet things and she chased the last
fragments of hers around her plate, groaning with pleasure.

"Oh, how I love food. And wine." Looking across the table at Felix and Julia, she was suddenly struck by their likeness. Julia's skin was white and Felix's was milky coffee, but their faces had the same high cheekbones and strong mouths. And their expressions were the same. Appraising. Touched with arrogance but ready to dissolve into laughter as well. "And I love you two," she whispered.

They both heard it. *You two.* Julia's hand was lying loosely on the white cloth. Felix had raised his own hand, intending to cover her fingers, draw them toward him. *Now,* he thought. *It has to be now.*

But he felt the waiter behind him, leaning forward to speak in his ear. *"Excusez-moi, monsieur."*

They heard ice clinking, and a frosty silver bucket materialized beside their table. In the bucket was a bottle of champagne. Through the droplets misting the clear glass they could see the wine. Pink champagne.

"I didn't order . . ." Felix murmured, unusually disconcerted.

"No, *monsieur*. The gentleman over there ordered it. He asked me to present his compliments."

They turned their heads in unison.

"Who's that?" Julia breathed.

Joshua Flood and Harry Gilbert always met for a drink or dinner whenever Josh passed through London. Harry was an ex-RAF pilot, ten years older than Josh. The two men had met when Harry and his air charter company pilots were flying eighteen hours a day, lifting supplies to Berlin, and Josh was a skinny American teenager who was hanging around the airfield looking for work, any work, that had anything to do with flying. Harry had given him a job loading and unloading crates, and Josh stuck to it. Harry Gilbert gave the boy his first flying lesson, and they went out and got drunk together on the day Josh got his pilot's license. It was an unlikely relationship, between the upper-class Englishman and the much younger American, who, by his own admission "came from Nowhere, Colorado, but was going plenty of places," but it had persisted. They enjoyed each other's company, and they were drawn together by their mutual enthusiasm for aircraft, skiing, and women.

They had amused themselves over dinner at Leoni's that evening by speculating on the threesome at the center table. It was Mattie who had first drawn their attention.

"Look at that hair."

"And the superstructure."

"Harry, you're a dirty old man."

"Age has nothing to do with it, my boy."

"Anyway, the blonde's mine. You can have the dark one."

"I fancy it's an academic question. They're having far too good a time on their own."

"With that pantywaist?" Joshua's blond eyebrows shot up into his tanned forehead.

Harry laughed. "Appearances can be deceptive."

"Not that appearance." Josh signaled to the waiter. "But there's only one way to find out. Let's send 'em a drink."

The bubbles fizzed and burst on Julia's tongue. The champagne seemed to send currents of elation through her veins. She gripped the edge of the white cloth to anchor herself in her chair.

I'm still here, she thought. *I'm still myself. That's good. That's all that matters.* She knew that she was hurt, somewhere, but the pain, if there was going to be any, hadn't bitten into her yet. There was only the strange, tight, bursting feeling buried inside her. "We can't just drink their champagne," she said aloud. "We'll have to invite them to join us."

A moment later Joshua Flood leaned between Mattie and Julia.

"I thought you were never going to ask."

He had green eyes, and his hair was bleached by the wind or the sun. He positioned his chair between Julia and Mattie, and his good-humored, appraising glance slid from one to the other.

"Thank you for the champagne," Julia said.

He bowed, mock-formally. "It was my pleasure." When he held out his hand, it was to Julia first.

"I'm Joshua Flood. Josh. And this is my buddy, Harry Gilbert."

"We'd better have another bottle." Harry smiled.

Even Felix liked them. They were breezy, and funny, and attractive, especially Josh. He saw Julia looking at Josh, watching the way he put his glass to his mouth, the way he flicked his Zippo lighter to his cigarette. He was glad that his hand hadn't reached her fingers. Not tonight.

Julia had drawn Josh closer, almost cutting him out of the circle. It wasn't deliberate but she couldn't stop looking at him. Joshua caught Harry's eye and grinned, shrugging faintly. The blond one was sexier, but he didn't mind. Harry didn't mind either. With his developed English nose for who was what, he had spotted at once that these girls and their friend weren't his own kind. They were very pretty, and they were lively and interesting, but it was only an evening's diversion, no more than that. He glanced at Josh again. Josh had no time for the English class system, and Harry could see already that the dark girl promised more than an evening's diversion for Joshua. Good luck to him, Harry thought cheerfully, and he refilled Mattie's glass with pink Louis Roederer.

Later, when Mattie and Julia retired to the ladies' room to repair their makeup, Julia asked breathlessly, "Isn't he beautiful?"

"He's that all right," Mattie answered. "Nice too."

"Mattie?"

"Mmm?" She was painting her lips with pink lipstick, but their eyes met in the mirror.

"Mattie . . . do you want him? I saw him looking at you first." Julia was cold with fear of her answer, but she had to ask.

Mattie smiled. "You go ahead. I like his friend." His friend was older and somehow safer, Mattie added silently. Joshua Flood was someone special, but Mattie wouldn't stand in Julia's way tonight.

"Julia, are you all right?" she asked abruptly.

Julia stood still for a moment.

"I meant about your mum. About what's happened."

A dirty little baby who wasn't wanted, Julia heard again. But I am wanted. Josh wants me, I can see it in his face. She laughed a little shakily. "Yes, I'm all right." Mattie hugged her and then smoothed her dress.

"Come on, then. Let's get back to your aviator."

When they reached the table the second bottle of champagne was empty, and Felix was standing up ready to leave.

"I'm sure I'm leaving you in good hands," he said lightly.

The girls kissed him, one on each cheek. "Thank you for a wonderful dinner," they told him. "You and Jessie."

Felix's black eyes flickered, not quite to Julia's face. Then he lifted his hand, almost into a salute, and turned away.

After that there was a taxi, and a nightclub, a proper one with tables in alcoves and girls in evening dresses to serve drinks. Mattie and Julia tried to look as if they came to such places every night, and Harry and Josh played along with the fantasy.

A crooner came out onto the little stage close to their table and addressed his songs to Mattie. She snorted with laughter, and told Harry, "I can do better than that. Julia, shall I get up there and give them 'Ma He's Making Eyes at Me'?"

"Oh, no, please," Julia murmured faintly.

"You stay right here with me," Harry ordered. His arm was around Mattie's shoulders and his hand rested on her breast. Mattie, fueled by champagne, was at her best, teasing and flirtatious and quick-tongued. She knew that she was safe, here in this nightclub surrounded by people. She had also guessed, accurately enough, that Harry Gilbert would have a steady girl, perhaps even a wife, who rode horses somewhere in the country. And so he wasn't likely to be a long-term threat either. She could sit back and enjoy sparring good-naturedly with him.

Josh was different. Even when he was sitting at their table telling Julia about flying he was moving, restless, confined by the nightclub's smoky ceilings. His hands moved, making shapes in the air, and he leaned closer so that she saw his white, even teeth and the play of the muscles around his mouth. He had long eyelashes, bleached gold at the tips like his hair. She wanted to touch the backs of his hands, where the taut sinews showed.

"Why are you so brown?" she asked him.

"I'm a traveler. I work where I can, flying, and if it's in the sun, so much the better. Then, when I've put enough money together, I ski until it runs out."

Julia thought of languorous silver beaches, and then snow under a brittle blue sky. A long way from the attic flat, and from the rows of desks in the accounts office. Her freedom seemed suddenly tame. Josh's glittering energy fired her own, making it blaze up inside her. It was impossible to sit still any longer.

The singer finished his spot.

"I want to dance. Can we?" she asked Josh.

He smiled at her. "Sure we can."

On the little dance floor he held out his arms to her. She stepped forward, a small, deliberate step. His hand on her waist felt light and warm.

Dancing at the Rocket was nothing like this. Usually Julia knew what tune the band was playing, what the other girls were wearing, who was dancing nearby, and what steps they were doing.

Tonight she didn't notice anything except Josh. She forgot how to dance, and learned all over again through Josh. She felt lighter than she ever had, part of the music itself.

From across the room Mattie saw them smiling at each other, hypnotized. She was dancing with Harry, whose stiff

English bearing was such a contrast to Josh's. Harry danced like a poker. Harry Gilbert wouldn't look at her like Josh was looking at Julia. She was glad of that, because she knew what that look meant. But she was touched by a tiny, unfamiliar shiver of jealousy. Mattie wanted to be overtaken too.

Julia and Josh danced for a long time. They hardly spoke but they were still listening to each other, to the sound of each other's breathing, the unspoken words.

At last, reluctantly, Harry let his arm fall from around Mattie's waist. He was still standing close enough to see down her blouse, into the blue shadow between the creamy, gold-freckled breasts. But Harry had to work the next day. There was an old Lancaster, converted for freight carrying, waiting to be flown. Not like Josh Flood, who seemed to have the knack of working only when he felt like it. Harry touched Mattie's cheek, pushing back the blond waves. The pair of them were not much more than children anyway, he thought. It was tempting, but impossible.

"I must get to bed," he told her sadly.

"And me too." Mattie's eyes held him. "My own bed."

She had been perfectly honest with him. And Harry was always dogged by his own gentlemanly code. "Of course," he said.

Julia and Josh followed them. They held themselves apart by a little artificial space. Outside in the cool darkness Josh turned suddenly.

"It's too early to go home. Do you want to go home?" he asked Julia.

Slowly, she shook her head.

"Josh never sleeps," Harry said. He flung out his arm to a passing taxi. "I'll see Mattie home."

He held open the door for her. Mattie's knuckles brushed against Julia's, hidden in the folds of their full skirts. She took her hand quickly and squeezed it. Julia watched her friend subside into the taxi with Harry beside her, but she didn't look around. The cab chugged away into the night.

I love you, Mattie, she thought.

"Julia Smith," Josh said softly. "What shall we do now?"

Julia looked up. The sky was powdered with faint stars. "Let's walk a little way."

He took her hand, drawing it close against him. They began to walk, not noticing which way, perfectly in step.

"I've talked all night about aircraft and ski slopes," Josh

complained. "I'm surprised you're not asleep. I don't know anything about you, except how pretty you are."

Julia laughed. There was nothing to tell Josh, she thought. She was a blank canvas, like one of Felix's, waiting. The idea was intoxicating. She felt electrically alive, charged with an astonishing happiness. It made her want to take hold of everything, that lamppost and these shop windows and the newspapers crumpled in the gutter and hold them, here and now, because they were part of Josh and part of tonight. Nothing could go wrong tonight. Nothing could touch her now.

"I can't fly. I can't ski." She heard herself laughing.

Josh lifted her hand and kissed the knuckles where they had brushed against Mattie's. "I'll teach you."

So much to learn.

"There's one thing," Julia said softly. She would tell Josh, of course. "It's why this evening happened, in a way. My mother told me today that I'm adopted." She lifted her chin, looking at him. "I didn't know. I'm on my own now." It was easy to say that because she knew that she wasn't.

Josh stopped and put his hands on her shoulders. He looked into her upturned face for a minute, a long time. Julia felt his concern like the sun, warming her.

"That's tough," he said at last. He didn't try anything else and she loved him for that, for not flooding her with words.

Josh was watching her under the light of the streetlamp. The attempted sophistication of Leoni's and the nightclub had dropped away from her. She wasn't just another girl now. She was this girl, looking back at him with wide eyes that reflected the light. He cupped her face in his hands. Her neck and throat were fragile, and her skin was luminous. He kissed her, twisting her around against him, tasting the sweetness of her mouth and tongue. She held on to him, answering him, but Josh lifted his head again.

"How old are you?" he asked harshly.

"Seventeen," Julia said, and then she whispered, "Almost." That was the truth. She wouldn't lie to Josh.

"Jesus." He turned her face again, so that he could see her more clearly. "That's jailbait."

"Josh. I'm older than you think."

He remembered her in the restaurant. She had laid her claim on him then, as coolly as a woman twice her age. And she had danced with him, keeping nothing back. They had been making love, upright and fully clothed. Children didn't dance like that. And he couldn't relinquish her now. It was already too late.

"Are you?" he demanded roughly. "Are you?"

Julia only smiled. When he kissed her again he could feel the outline of her body under her thin clothes. She had long legs and narrow hips, and small, hard breasts. She felt hot, and her head tilted back under the weight of his.

"Come on," Josh said. "Julia Smith, this is a public street." He was grinning but he wasn't quite in control of himself, and he didn't want Julia to see that. "Let's walk on a way, or there'll be real trouble."

They went on under the streetlights, walking very slowly, their hands still touching. Telling Josh about her mother had breached a dam inside Julia. The words poured out of her now, and she told him about home, and the High Street, and Blick Road, and about Mattie and the Embankment and ending up with Jessie and Felix in the square. They sounded such small doings compared with Josh's, but Julia didn't care about that. It was important that he should know everything, that was all.

He listened gravely, nodding his blond head.

"Now you know," she said at last.

"Now I know."

He was touched by her offering it all to him. It was very different, this walk in the deserted streets, from the conventional overture to the evening. Nor was this girl anything like one of the pair of pretty, giggling women he had ordered pink champagne for. Josh sighed. He touched Julia's face with the tips of his fingers before he kissed her again.

"It's very late," he said.

"I know." Time didn't mean anything to Julia then.

Josh had been thinking. He had been staying with a girl, an ex-girlfriend, but even so he didn't think that Carol would be happy to see him at three in the morning with Julia in tow. He knew that Julia shared a room with Mattie, back in their friend's apartment. And it was far too late for a hotel, without any luggage.

"I'd better take you home," he said gently.

Her hand tightened on his, but she only said, "It isn't very far from here. I know the way." Julia smiled at him, and he saw the happiness in her face. "Tonight has been the most perfect evening I've ever had," she said simply.

Josh wanted to pick her up and hold her, and he knew that he was crazy, and that there was nothing to be done because it had happened now.

"I kind of enjoyed it too," he said.

Outside the black-painted door in the square he held her again. Julia let her head fall against his shoulder, thinking, *I don't care what happens*.

"Can I see you again?" Josh asked, and as soon as he had said it she knew how much she did care.

"Oh, yes. Yes, please."

Joshua couldn't help smiling. "Give me your phone number, then."

"There isn't a telephone here."

He looked up at the numerals on the shabby black door. "Okay. I know where you are." His hand touched her shoulder lightly, like a friend's. "So I'll be back."

He walked away quickly, his hair a spot of brightness under the dark trees.

Julia let herself in and climbed the stairs. She couldn't feel their dusty solidity under her feet. She was light, as if she could float, and the tight feeling inside her was all gone. It was a stream now, washing freely. She wanted to lie down in the warmth of it, with Josh, and let the current pour over them. Was that what love was? Julia was laughing. She could see Josh's face so clearly. *Your aviator*, Mattie had said. The word was as beautiful as Josh himself. Julia tried the words aloud.

"I love you," she said. "God help me, I love you."

FIVE

Julia waited for a week. Every evening she ran through the homegoing crowds and into the square, certain that Josh would be there. But every evening at the top of the stairs there was only Jessie in her chair.

"I know he'll come," Julia said with the light still in her face.

Jessie scowled. "What do you mean, you know? The only thing to know about men is that you can't trust them. You listen to me."

"Josh is different," Julia said simply. It was unthinkable that he might not come. Another week went by.

Julia stopped talking about her aviator, but Mattie could see from the way that she sat with her head cocked that she was listening to the street noises below their window, willing the buzz of the doorbell to cut through their aimless conversation. Julia wouldn't go out anymore, however hard Mattie tried to persuade her. She sat on her bed, apparently absorbed in a book, but the pages either flicked over too quickly or else they didn't turn at all.

"Do you think he'll come?" Mattie whispered to Felix one night, but Felix only shrugged and turned away.

Mattie had her own preoccupations. After the party she had dialed the number on the card that Francis Willoughby had given her. She had imagined that such an important man would be shielded by secretaries, and she was faintly surprised when he answered the telephone himself.

"Come and see me in my office," Mr. Willoughby said. "Shaftesbury Avenue, of course. Address on the card I gave you. Top floor. Tuesday at three sharp."

On the Tuesday afternoon Mattie told her shoe shop manageress that she had a headache and would have to go home.

"You can't do that," the woman said. "What if we all went home on the slightest excuse?" Mattie made her face sag, and swallowed very hard. "I feel sick. I might be sick near a customer. Or on some stock."

"Oh, go on then," the manageress said hastily.

Mattie caught a bus to Piccadilly Circus and began the walk up the enchanted curve of Shaftesbury Avenue. She didn't see the dusty shop windows, or the advertisement billboards, or the city-sharpened faces of the ordinary people passing her. She saw only the majestic fronts of the theaters and the names up in lights. She dawdled for a moment, staring greedily at the production stills in their glass cases. She had seen two or three of the plays, perched up in the cheapest seats, but with the talisman of Mr. Willoughby's card in her hand, Headline Repertory Companies, she felt closer to the stage than she had ever in any audience.

It was farther than she thought. She found the Victorian red-brick block housing the Headline company at the northernmost end of the avenue, set among a cluster of tiny shops and Italian cafés. She took the ancient lift to the top floor, panting from having run the last hundred yards.

Mr. Willoughby was sitting alone behind the glass-paneled door of his office. The door announced his name, and the name of his company in full, in not quite evenly-painted white letters.

Mattie saw at a glance that the office was a green-painted cell, furnished with two pine desks and a pair of battered metal filing cabinets, a telephone and an electric kettle, and a dog-eared copy of *Spotlight*. It smelled of linoleum and cigarette smoke and, rather strongly, of Mr. Willoughby himself.

"Come in, dear, come in," he said. "Make yourself comfortable."

He was looking at Mattie's flushed cheeks and the cork-screws of blond hair sticking to her forehead. Then his glance traveled downward. Mattie was wearing a new circle-stitched bra and her sweater fit tightly. She stumbled to the empty desk and perched on a typist's chair with a broken back.

"What I need, dear," Francis Willoughby announced with a show of briskness, "is a really efficient girl to help me with all aspects of this business." He waved his hand around the office. "Bookings. Contracts. Auditions. I'm a very busy man." He glanced at the telephone, but it remained silent. "There's answering that thing for me. Are you used to the telephone?"

"Oh, yes," Mattie assured him.

"Typing, of course . . ."

"I'm afraid I can't type." *I can't pretend about that,* Mattie thought desperately. Mr. Willoughby glanced at her sweater again and ran his thumb to and fro over his thin mustache.

"Well. Perhaps you could pick it up as you go along?"

"I'm sure I could."

"The job pays six pounds ten a week."

Less than at the shoe shop. Mattie looked over Mr. Willoughby's shoulder and through the sweaty green walls. Beyond them was the stage.

"Could you make it seven pounds?"

Mr. Willoughby's smile showed his teeth, too white and even to be real.

"Lots of girls want to do theater management, dear. It's not like ordinary office work, is it?"

"All right," Mattie said quickly. "Six pounds ten."

She started work with Headline Repertory Companies the following Monday, leaving the shoe shop without a backward glance.

While Julia listened to the clamor inside herself and waited, trying to contain it, Mattie went out to explore the limits of her new job. It seemed to consist mostly of explaining to angry-sounding voices on the telephone that Mr. Willoughby was auditioning and couldn't speak to anyone now.

Mattie quickly understood that most of the anger related to the nonappearance of money. Francis would look up from his desk, squinting against the smoke from his cigarette, and hiss, "Check's in the mail, tell 'em."

Mattie knew that there was nothing of the kind in the post, because she did Francis's few letters, too, but she made a convincing job of lying for him, and he grinned approvingly at her.

One caller was particularly insistent. His voice was deep and resonant, the perfect actor's voice as far as Mattie was concerned. His name was John Douglas, he told her, and he was the manager of Francis's number one company, currently on tour in the north of England.

"Tell fucking Francis," the rich voice issued from the telephone mouthpiece, "that unless I get fucking paid in full and unless I get cash in hand to pay the fucking company every Friday night as well, I don't take them or sodding *Saint Joan* to fucking Gateshead next week. Got that?"

"I think so," Mattie murmured.

Wincing as if it hurt him, Francis at last unlocked the big company checkbook from the safe.

"It's all cash flow, dear," he told her as he wrote a check. "If you don't get the takings during the week, it isn't there to pay the actors at the end of the week, is it?"

When she bent down to find the company's current address in the filing cabinet, Francis put his hand up her skirt. His fingers squeezed her thigh and then slid up over her stocking top. Mattie jerked away from him.

"Six pounds ten a week doesn't cover that, Francis," she told him wearily, and he chuckled. A large proportion of Mattie's time was spent dodging his hands, but the more brusquely she shook him off the more Francis seemed to enjoy it. Sometimes, especially after one of his lengthy lunches, the atmosphere in the little office was so highly charged with his erotic tension that Mattie was half-afraid the spurt of flame from his cigarette lighter would set fire to it. But most of the time she felt sorry for Francis and his beleaguered existence. Were all men pathetic, she wondered, under the armor plate of their aggression?

Mattie sighed and directed her attention back to whatever nontask Francis had set her between fumbles and phone calls. This was the Theater, that was the thing to remember. However marginally, she was involved in the magic world at last.

At the end of the third week Josh came. Mattie opened the door to him, and Felix saw Julia's face when she heard his voice. It was as though a soft light had been turned on under the skin of her face. It shone out of her eyes and glowed through her bones. The blurring of familiarity lifted for an instant, and Felix saw her as if she were a stranger again. *She's beautiful,* he thought.

He went on calmly slicing the eggplants he had been preparing for their meal. Their rich color made the backs of his hands look ashy by contrast.

"You see?" Julia whispered to nobody. "I knew he would come."

A moment later Josh stood in the kitchen doorway with his arm around Julia's shoulder. He seemed to fill the space with his height and the breadth of his shoulders, although in reality he was no taller than Felix. Julia was laughing at something he had said to her in the hallway, gasping a little, as if she were short of breath.

"Hi there, Felix," Josh said easily. "What's new with you?"

The kitchen was so tiny that Felix noticed the sun-bleached tips of his eyelashes. He looked down at the work-top and saw the dark moon of his own face reflected in the blade of the knife.

"Hullo. Nothing new." He sounded stiff, but Julia and Josh were too engrossed in each other. Josh swung her around so that he could look at her.

"I've come to take you out. Is that okay? Or have you got a date already?"

"If I did, I'd stand him up for you. Shall I change?"

Julia had learned from Felix. Her clothes were simpler now, and she took more care with them. She was wearing a vivid green crew-necked sweater and tight black matador pants with flat black pumps. Jessie had lent her a pair of jet earrings that Julia coveted, and they swung when she turned her head.

Josh touched one of them with the tip of his finger. "Don't change," he said softly.

Felix felt their intimacy like an electric charge. In the second's silence he leaned against the sink, hating the scummy detritus of potato peelings, hating his own jealousy.

"Let's go, then," Julia said.

Felix went on standing at the sink after they were gone. He saw that the enamel was badly chipped, and the shelf above it where he kept his saucepans was speckled with city soot. Suddenly he swept the potatoes and the eggplants and the chopping knife in a pile on top of the peelings in the sink. The clatter of the knife against the enamel didn't change his feelings.

"What the bloody hell's the matter with you?" Jessie shouted from her room.

"I don't feel like cooking tonight, that's all."

"Don't cook, then. Mat and I don't care, do we, duck? And I don't suppose Julia and that young man have got their dinners on their minds right now either." Jessie laughed, her deep, coarse laugh, and Felix smiled in spite of himself and went through into her room. She was sitting with her bottle, and Mattie beside her with her nose in a film magazine.

"Don't be a dog in the manger, son," Jessie ordered. "If you were going to do anything with Julia, you'd have done it by now, wouldn't you?"

Yes, Felix thought. *Yes, I would. Jessie's right, as usual.*

"So you let her go off and enjoy herself while she can, without pulling a long face."

Mattie lowered the magazine. "While she can?"

"That's right. What did you think I said? That boy's big and beautiful, but he's not a stayer. Any more than your old man, Felix Lemoine. Let Julia go while he's here, that's all."

Mattie and Felix didn't look at each other. Mattie stood up and said, "I'll do the tea if you like. You'll have to tell me what needs doing, Felix."

"Supper," he corrected her automatically.

Josh took Julia to an Italian restaurant, where they sat and let their plates of fettuccine go cold in front of them. They drank Chianti from a bottle with a raffia case, and stared at each other, sometimes not even talking.

When the bottle was empty Julia said daringly, "I was afraid that you weren't going to come. Three weeks is a long time."

Josh's face changed, darkening a little, and she wished immediately that she hadn't said anything.

"I was flying," he said. "For Harry Gilbert. I needed the money, but Harry expects good value for it."

It was partly true. Harry's air-freight business was doing well, and Josh had flown several trips to the Mediterranean for him, lifting materials for a hotel development in Malta. But the real reason was that Josh had been disturbed by the strength of the attraction he had felt to the thin, dark girl he had watched in Leoni's. Josh liked his girls to be willing, decorative accessories who didn't ask too much of him. By choosing carefully, Josh could be sure of a warm welcome when he needed it, and no fuss when he didn't. Julia clearly didn't belong to the right category. She was hungry, and eager, and too vulnerable. Julia meant trouble for both of them, and Josh thought that she was too young for it.

But he had thought about her as he watched the instruments in the Lancaster's cockpit. He had decided that he wouldn't go looking for her, but he still hadn't forgotten her. Harry Gilbert asked him, and he shrugged. "She's only a kid. When I need a kid of my own I'll get one the interesting way."

And then, without letting himself think about it, he had found himself at the door in the square. It was the first night he had been back in London since the dinner at Leoni's.

As soon as he saw Julia, Josh didn't want to think anyway. He wanted to look at her, and listen to her voice, and smile at her mixture of naïveté and willful, calculated knowingness.

He lifted her hand from the tablecloth and kissed the knuckles.

"I'm here now."

"Yes. I don't care about anything else."

She looked at him, her head on one side, the absurd earrings winking in the candlelight. Josh imagined how he would lift the green sweater over her head and fit his hands around the narrow ridges of her rib cage. He would taste her skin, quartering it inch by inch with his tongue. Josh shifted in his chair and let go of her hand again. She was sixteen, he reminded himself.

After their dinner he took her to a party. It was in a flat in Bayswater, and the high-ceilinged rooms with their peeling cornices were packed with people. Everyone seemed to know Josh. He cut an avenue of welcome through the crowd.

"Hey, Josh. How ya doing, man?"

"Josh, darling. Why so long?"

Julia might have been shy among so many smart strangers, but with Josh she felt that they were all friends.

"Who's this? Your kid sister?"

"I'm nobody's sister," Julia said briskly, and a man laughed and put a drink into her hand. She floated through the party, made invulnerable by her happiness. Sometimes the crowd carried her away from Josh and she talked, or danced, and then across the room she saw his blond head turning to look for her.

I love you, Julia thought again. The happiness was so perfect that she didn't question it. It fit around her as if it had always been there.

She had no idea what time it was when the party ended. Josh took her home and she watched the streetlamps flick past the taxi window, shining their brief nimbus of gold light through the glass, with her head against his shoulder. Outside the door in the square Josh put his arms around her. They stood without moving, their faces not quite touching. They seemed already to have traveled a long way from the nightclub, from the streets where they had walked and talked on the first evening.

Julia knew where they were going. She felt certain of it, her certainty like a warm, pleasurable weight under her ribs.

"Can I see you tomorrow?" Josh asked formally.

She nodded, smiling at him.

"Be ready early, and wear warm clothes. We'll be away until Sunday."

A night, away with Josh.

"Where are we going?"

"Flying."

He kissed her, his mouth very warm against hers.

"Until tomorrow."

Julia went slowly up the stairs. The flat was in darkness, but the blackness seemed full of stars.

Felix's door was closed, and when Julia turned the light on in her bedroom she saw Mattie curled up under her bedclothes with her arm up over her face. Julia watched her, trying to imagine going to sleep herself. It seemed impossible, the surrender of what she felt now to wasteful unconsciousness. She turned off the light and went out, closing the door with a soft click behind her. She stood in the hallway, hesitating, wondering whether to perch in the kitchen or to go down and walk under the trees in the square. Then she heard Jessie, calling out to her.

Jessie was sitting up in bed. She had slept for a few hours, numbed by vodka, but now she was awake again, facing the empty time until daylight. Until recently she would have levered herself out of bed and shuffled up and down the room to ease the restlessness, but now she felt too heavy and too exhausted to get up. Insomnia was like a grub inside her, gnawing, exposing her tiredness. This was the time when her memories assailed her, so vividly that it was hard to distinguish between what was real and what was remembered.

"Julia?" she begged. "Is that you? Come in here to me, will you?"

Or was it Felix, a little boy pattering in the night, or Desmond, creeping in from she didn't know where. . . .

Julia slipped into the room. Of course it was Julia. Back from her night out. She brought the old scent of cigarettes and closed rooms and perfume with her, and Jessie felt the past stirring like a massive body in the bed beside her.

"Can't you sleep?" Julia whispered. She saw that Jessie's huge face was gray, mottled with mauve, and her scalp showed through the strands of gray hair. In the daytime, with her face painted and her glass in her hand, Jessie was like a rock. It was a shock to see her so clearly at the night's mercy. "Do you want a cup of tea?"

Jessie shook her head. "Just sit with me for a bit."

Julia sat down on the edge of the bed. She felt the mattress dip sharply away from her, sagging under Jessie's weight.

"Well? How was it?" Jessie demanded. That was more like her, and Julia's anxiety ebbed a little.

"I had a wonderful time," she said simply.

"Dear God, I can see that. Tell us about it."

Julia told her and Jessie listened, Julia's talk interweaving with her own times, the fair-haired American boy with his ready smile and his manlike evasions all mixed up with a big black man who played the saxophone under a blue light and a boy from a long time ago who came knocking on a terrace-house door in Hoxton with a bunch of marigolds in his hands. . . .

Jessie's eyelids had dropped, but they opened again as soon as Julia leaned forward.

"I thought you'd gone to sleep."

"No. Go on."

"That's all. Jessie, he's going to take me flying tomorrow."

Just like a little girl, promised a treat. The seaside, or a film show. Jessie looked at her face. Her mouth, and her eyes, belonged to a woman. But the way her arms wrapped around her chest, to keep the excitement in, that was what a child did. Jessie thought of the little woman in her brown coat and hat who had come to look for a child and had found Julia.

"D'you ever think about your ma?" she demanded roughly.

Julia stared at her, and then she said, "Yes, I think about her."

In the silent, feverish weeks that had gone by since meeting Josh, Julia had tried to imagine her mother. Why had she made her a dirty little baby? Why hadn't she wanted her? Perhaps she had been in trouble, not just that ordinary trouble. Or in some kind of danger, and so had given up her baby rather than let her inherit that. Perhaps she was someone special, nothing to do with the world of Fairmile Road. How much had it cost her to give her daughter away to Betty and Vernon? Julia had let herself imagine a big house at the end of a curving avenue of trees. Even a face at one of the windows, a pale but exact replica of her own. She wondered if her mother was looking out, praying for a sight of the child she had lost.

"I wonder about what she's like. Why she had to give me away."

"I didn't mean her," Jessie said.

Julia bent her head and picked at a loose thread in the bedcover. "My adopted mother?"

"Of course. She counts as your mother, my girl, whatever other nonsense you're letting yourself run away with."

Julia flared back at her. "They've tried to turn me into someone else. Tried to turn me into themselves. A reflection of themselves. They didn't want me. If they'd just loved what they got, it would have been different. Wouldn't it?"

Jessie saw the hurt then. Julia had kept it to herself, but it was there. They had rejected each other, the mother and the daughter. No one's fault, and everyone's fault. She felt sorry for the little brown woman with her pulled-in mouth, and she felt a different sadness for Julia, who was just beginning everything.

The weight of Jessie's memories heaved again beside her, pulling her down. She wanted to cry, for herself and Felix, and for the two silly, fresh, blank young women who had been washed up here.

The tears felt greasy under her eyelids, and then on her cheeks.

"Jessie, I'm sorry. I didn't mean to upset you." Julia moved quickly, putting her arm around Jessie's big, doughy shoulders, hugging her. "I've got you. I don't need Betty or the other one. Don't cry, do you hear? You've got us, too, me and Mattie as well as Felix. What else do you need?"

Jessie wiped her face with the corner of the sheet, an angry scrubbing movement. "Need? Nothing. Everything. Oh, don't listen. I'm just an old windbag with indigestion and insomnia. And you can't sleep because you're too happy. Funny, isn't it?"

They sat and looked at each other, and then suddenly they laughed. The daytime Jessie was there again.

"Look at the time," she said sharply. "If you're going flying with that boy tomorrow, and I'm glad I'm not, you'd better go to bed for a few hours first. Go on. Do what I tell you."

Julia leaned over her first and kissed her cheek. Jessie's skin was cold and dry. "Good night. Jessie . . . ?"

"What is it now?"

"Thank you for letting Mattie and me, you know, do what we want."

"Go to the bad, you mean? That's up to you. Nothing to do with me. Go on."

Julia went, and Jessie lay back against her flattened pillows to watch the window, where the light would begin again.

Josh came in the morning. Julia ran down the stairs to meet him, the bag containing her overnight things bumping a tattoo against her legs. There was a little black open MG parked in the square, and Josh held the passenger door open for her with a flourish.

They climbed in, and the car roared through the Saturday morning traffic. Julia looked up at the red buses looming over them, the pigeons strutting on ledges, and the boys on Vespas trying to outpace the MG, and sank back into her leather bucket seat with a sigh of satisfaction. It was like being in an Audrey Hepburn film.

They left London behind and wound out through the neat suburbs that reminded Julia of Fairmile Road. It was an added satisfaction to be zipping past the identical semi-detached houses where men were sweeping the fallen leaves off the paths. Josh was beside her in his brown leather jacket with the worn sheepskin collar turned up around his chin. The wind blew his hair back off his forehead and sharpened the handsome lines of his face. He was whistling as he drove.

"I'm so happy," Julia said.

Josh looked sideways at her. "I'm happy too." Then he glanced up into the thin autumn blueness of the sky. "It's a great day for flying."

Happy because of me, Julia wondered, or because of the sunshine?

They drove on through the Kentish lanes, and then at last they swung through a pair of tall gates and out on to an airfield. There was a cluster of low huts, and a row of light aircraft drawn up with the sun reflecting off their windshields. A wind sock hung limp in the mild air. There were men in overalls moving between the huts, and one of them lifted his arm in a half-salute as the MG stopped. In the sudden quiet that followed, Julia could hear a plane somewhere overhead. The ones on the ground looked very small and fragile.

Josh was already out of the car, calling out greetings and shaking hands and joking with the men. Julia followed him shyly, not looking at the waiting planes.

Josh put his arm around her shoulders. ". . . And this is Julia. Making her first flight today. I can tell she's going to be a flier, just by looking at her."

Julia shook hands. Her knees were going wobbly with fear.

"Welcome to the Kent Aero Club," a man with a handlebar mustache boomed at her.

"It's an amateur club," Josh explained. "I like this kind of flying as well as the stuff I do for Harry. I started out on planes like these."

"Is it safe?" Julia asked. She hadn't meant to, but the words just escaped.

The mustache man roared with laughter. "You'll be safer in the air with Josh Flood than you are on the ground with him. She's all ready for you, Josh." He laughed so much at that that his face turned crimson.

"Let's go." Julia could feel Josh's eagerness crackling beside her. She turned and followed him over the wide concreted space of the apron. Josh's strides in his baseball boots seemed to cover yards at a time. Her own legs were leaden.

They reached a plane parked to one side of the line. It was white with spruce-red lines along the fuselage, and the letters G-AERO near the tail. Josh ducked under the wing and opened the cockpit door. The whole airplane looked no bigger than the MG.

"Jump in." He smiled at her. "Are you excited?"

"Oh, yes." Julia's voice was faint.

She climbed into the tiny space and settled herself into her seat. Josh swung in on the other side. He leaned across her and pulled the webbing straps over Julia's shoulders.

"This is the quick-release catch, look." He showed her the lever on her lap buckle.

Julia looked at the hump of the instrument panel, and then over the plane's tilted nose to the stationary tip of the propeller. "Don't I get a parachute?" She tried to make it sound like a joke.

He looked at her properly then. "You don't need a chute in a crate like this. Didn't you believe what Jimbo said? You're quite safe." He kissed her on the corner of her mouth and Julia thought, *If I'm going to die I'm glad it's with Josh.*

Josh gave the thumbs-up sign to a mechanic waiting at the nose of the plane. The engine coughed and the propeller turned, then spun into a blur as the engine note rose and settled into a steady roar.

"What kind of plane is this?" Julia tried to focus on something, anything other than the thought of pitching into the air in this little shell.

"Auster Autocrat. Powered by a one-hundred h.p. Cirrus Minor Two engine. Okay?"

Josh was busy. He touched the rows of switches and watched the dials, turning his head to look at the tail flap and the wing tips. Julia sat and waited, hoping that he couldn't hear her heart banging. She hadn't expected to be afraid, and the surprising fact of her terror somehow made it worse.

Josh gave another thumbs-up to the mechanic. He stood to one side and beckoned them on and the Auster taxied forward. Josh was whistling again, the same tune as behind the wheel of his MG. They reached the end of the tarmac runway.

"Here we go, baby. Hold tight."

The plane darted forward and then skipped into the air.

Julia saw the tarmac lurch and drop away beneath them, and then she saw the roofs of the huts and the treetops beyond the perimeter fence, swaying drunkenly, then a scatter of houses and the scarlet blob of a telephone kiosk. The ground seemed to swoop sideways and upward, pushing the horizon into the wrong place, terrifyingly wrong, so that the empty space of sky was beside her instead of over her head. Julia lurched sideways, wanting to grab hold of Josh, but her seat straps held her down. She was amazed to see that he was still smiling.

The horizon swung again, and then tilted into its proper place. The brown and gold and pale green squares of fields unrolled toward it, and Julia looked down to see white threads of roads, thick dark curls of woodland, and a village laid out around a church. She could even see the pale flecks of gravestones under the shadow of the spire.

Above the Plexiglas cockpit bubble the air shimmered. The air felt solid all around them, bumping against the plane's skin, lifting them up. They were flying.

Julia opened her clenched fists. Her fingernails had left red arcs in the skin of her palms and she was sweaty between her shoulder blades, but she felt her fear loosening its grip.

Josh took his hands off the controls and casually unfolded a map. The plane hummed on, pointing its nose into the blue haze.

"I thought we'd head out over the Channel," Josh announced, "and then take a look at the French coast."

"That sounds fine," Julia murmured. She thought, *France.*

She had never left England in her life. Fascination overcame Julia's fear.

The Channel appeared beneath them, the sheeny water dotted with tiny ships that drew a white gull's feather of wake behind them.

Josh pointed ahead and said, "Look, there's France. Cap Gris Nez."

A headland pointing into the sea, with brackets of beaches on either side of it. Then came the French countryside, bigger fields lined with poplars instead of fleecy elms, whitewashed villages instead of gray ones. When Josh said that it was time to turn back, Julia was ready, and the roll of the horizon and giddy veering of the landscape didn't bring the sweat out on her skin.

"Do you like it?" Josh asked her.

She nodded carefully. "It makes everything look so beautiful."

"We're almost home," he told her at last. Julia was wondering how he would find the strip of tarmac among the little domestic jungle of the English countryside when she heard Josh say, "Shall we have five minutes' fun first?"

She just caught sight of his face, his white smile and a new glint in his eye, before everything overturned.

The wing tip beside her flipped up, and the blue, innocent dome of the sky revolved and disappeared under the earth, where fields and trees leapt up at her and she fell helplessly toward them so that her stomach sprang suffocatingly into her mouth, and her mouth opened, gagged by terror. She felt her seat straps bite into her shoulders and she was pressed into the hard contours of her seat, and then they were over and the sky was coming up again to take its place over her head.

She heard Josh laughing. "Better than the fairground, any day. That's a sideways roll. Now the other way, and over she goes."

The same terrifying plunge, the same displacement of earth and sky. Julia closed her eyes and she heard herself whispering, *Stop. Please, stop.*

"Those are the simplest aerobatic maneuvers," Josh was saying, as if they were strolling safely with their feet on a London sidewalk. "Now let's try this one."

Tipping forward now, so that the ground leapt for them again, greedy beneath them and then over their heads. There was a cough, like the engine's apology. Then nothing but awesome, whistling silence. Julia saw a blade of the propeller motionless with the exquisite, remote safety of the Kent countryside etched behind it. They swooped downward in the silence.

Julia screamed, just once. "Josh!"

The engine started up again at once. The white wing tip steadied itself at the edge of her field of vision, and they were flying again instead of falling. Julia's head fell back against her seat. She was cold now, and wet down the length of her back and between her thighs. Josh's hand touched her fist. How could he be so warm, so sure of what he was doing?

"The engine . . ." she whispered.

"I cut it out. We were gliding. It's nothing. I'm sorry to frighten you. Look, I'll take us down now."

When Julia opened her eyes again, the airstrip was ahead and below, and she could see the Nissen huts and the mechanics in a group, and the MG waiting for them beyond. The ground came closer, and the perspectives were almost right again; she felt a gentle bump as the wheels made contact with solid earth and the huts and trees whisked past them as they slowed, ran to the edge of the strip, and then swung around and taxied back to the line of aircraft.

Julia sat very still, trying to swallow against the pressure that was rising in her throat. Josh cut the engine again and undid her seat buckle for her. Another mechanic opened the cabin door and held out his hand to help her out. The fresh air blew in her face. Julia stood on the tarmac but it swayed under her feet and then tilted upward. Her knees were buckling.

"Josh. Where's the . . ."

He took one look at her face. "Over there. Near door in the nearest hut."

Julia couldn't run, but she reached the hut somehow. She pushed the door open and saw a roller towel, a cracked mirror, and a washbasin.

She ran the last steps, and was sick into the basin.

She was leaning against the wall, empty and shaking, when Josh came in.

"Oh, darling," he said. "I'm sorry."

He put one arm around her waist, and with his free hand he ran the taps in the basin. He took a handkerchief out of the pocket of his leather jacket and soaked it in cold water. Then he wiped her mouth with it and held it against her forehead.

Julia closed her eyes. If the linoleum floor would just open up and swallow her, that would be enough.

Josh smoothed the strands of hair back from her face. "Will

you forgive me? I was just showing off to you like some dumb kid. And you were being so brave."

She laughed shakily. "Brave? That's not what I'd call it."

"Sure you were. Everyone's scared the first time. I was sick the first time too."

"Did Harry Gilbert sponge your face?"

Joshua grinned. "He was nowhere around, thank God. Or else I'd still be hearing about it."

He's kind, Julia thought. As well as everything else. Oh, Josh.

"Do you feel better now?"

"Yes."

"I was going to go up again, but now I won't, as a penance. Is that good enough?"

"Go up if you want to." Julia would have given him anything if only she could.

"No, we'll go walking instead."

He took her arm and led her out to the little black car. The spring came back to Julia's step, matching itself to Josh's.

It was an idyllic afternoon. They walked through a beech wood, where the falling leaves made ochre and gold tapestries under their feet and the sun slanted in fretted bars through the trees. Josh didn't talk about airplanes or ski slopes now. He told her about the little town in Colorado where he had grown up, and his mother and father, and the men who worked in his father's timber business, and their wives and the children who had gone to school with him. Julia imagined the place as a huddle of wooden-framed houses under a mountain ridge, set among black pines and empty snowfields. The lights spilling from the windows would look very warm on the snow.

"Were you happy?" she asked.

He thought for a moment. "I guess so. It was a good life. But I always had itchy feet."

"Why?"

He put his arm around her shoulders, and the leather sleeve creaked against her ear.

"I don't know why," he said softly, "but I have to keep moving on."

Julia knew that it was a warning. And it was a warning he had delivered often before. She jerked her head up and looked at the sky through the canopy of beeches. It was fading to pearly gray as the light went. She didn't need a warning, and she would take whatever came. A fierce determination took hold of her. She would spend tonight with Josh. She would make him hers somehow. She could do it because she wanted it so badly.

She listened carefully to the sound of their feet brushing through the leaves. She had the sense of crossing some divide, here, under the beech trees. *I've grown up,* she thought simply.

Josh felt the set of her shoulders. He was looking at the angle of her face, turned away from him. The skin of her cheek and throat was silky white under her dark hair. Josh knew that he had frightened her and made her ill, and he felt protective as well as drawn to her.

His arm tightened. "Come on," he ordered her. "Let's go home now."

They drove a short distance through the lanes and came to a field gate. Josh heaved it open and the car bumped into a rutted track. Peering into the dimness ahead, Julia saw a little house at the end of the track, fitted into a corner of woodland. It had two windows below and two gables above, and a door in the middle.

"It's like the three bears' house."

Josh laughed. "It isn't big enough for three of anything."

Outside the front door it was cold, and the air smelled of frost and smoke. Julia shivered, but it was a shiver of anticipation. She was certain of what she was doing, and she was exhilarated by it.

Inside, the little house was less like a fairy tale. It was furnished with utilitarian modern furniture and there were contemporary print curtains, a telephone and a gramophone, and a scatter of books and papers. Julia wandered around, trying to gain an impression of Josh's life from the thin layer of his possessions.

"Is it your house?" she called. Josh had gone through into the kitchen.

"Nope. It's rented, for as long as I need to be here."

No roots, of course. How long would be as long as he needed?

Josh was making tea, whistling and moving briskly from the cupboards to the stove. "Let's have anchovy toast. I love it, it's so British."

"Is it? I've never had it in my life." Julia remembered Betty's teas. Betty favored Robertson's jams and thin, sweetish lemon curd. She seemed a very long way away from here and what was going to happen.

"Don't disappoint me."

Josh lit the fire. It was already laid, and the flames shot up through the dry kindling. The room looked more homely in the firelight, with the tea tray on the coffee table. Julia perched on the red and black sofa.

"Shall I pour the tea?"

She was reminded of Betty and Vernon again, Betty pouring out the tea and handing Vernon his special cup.

Now Julia was pouring the tea herself, and she would give herself to Josh. She felt her own power, and fear and anticipation and excitement dissolving deliciously inside her. The anchovy toast tasted salty and exotic on her tongue. And she knew that Josh was watching her. She felt beautiful, and a little in awe of herself.

Josh took her plate away, and her cup. The fire had settled into a red glow. He knelt in front of her for a moment, and they looked at each other. Then Josh took her hand, turning it over very gently, as if to ask, *Well?*

Julia leaned forward and kissed his mouth.

"Julia," he said softly. "Do you know what you're doing?"

There was no need for her to answer. In the fireplace a log fell, sending up a scarlet fountain of sparks.

Josh was very gentle, and very deliberate. He unbuttoned her clothes, understanding the hooks and fasteners, and laid them gently aside. In the past, in her awkward grapples with boys, Julia had wondered why it was all so uncomfortable and undignified. It was different with Josh, of course. He made undressing seem simple and natural. Yet when she felt the cool air on her skin, she was suddenly embarrassed. She wrapped her arms around herself, to defend her nakedness.

"I would like to look at you," Josh whispered. "May I do that?"

Slowly, Julia let her arms drop. She faced him, innocence overlaid with boldness. The firelight brought a glow of color to her pale skin. Josh heard his own breathing in the stillness.

He looked at her, greedy, but holding himself back.

Josh loved women, but Julia wasn't like the girls he usually chose. He liked full-breasted girls with rounded hips and peachy flesh that he could bury himself in. For Josh, ever since he had turned twelve, the varied appeal of women's bodies had depended on their utter difference from his own. But Julia had no opulent curves, and her hips and stomach were as flat as a boy's. She was tall and he was surprised now, seeing her naked, by her fragility. Her bones looked fine enough to snap under his hands, and her breasts were tiny, with pale pink nipples. The separate parts of her were like a boy's, and yet they added up to nothing like a boy at all. Just in the way that her legs crooked, in the way that her shoulders sloped, and the way she looked at him under her dark eyelashes, she was more female than any woman he had ever seen.

And just as knowing. She had picked him out, after all, with total conviction. There was an added charge in that.

Josh breathed out, a long breath. He couldn't hold himself back from her any longer. He put his mouth to one of her small, hard breasts. Her skin tasted faintly sweet, like honey. He felt her breath warm in his hair, and then he pulled her against him. She was supple, like a sappy willow wand.

Josh took her hand, guiding it.

"You could take off my clothes too."

Julia drew back a little, and undid the buttons of his plaid shirt. She saw the curling blond hair on his chest, the sun-reddened hollow at the base of his throat, and then the developed muscles of his shoulders and arms.

"Go on," Josh ordered her.

She undid the buckle of his belt.

When Josh was naked, too, he laid her against the sofa cushions, very carefully, as if she were precious. Over his shoulder, through half-closed eyes, Julia watched the fire's glow. The silky feel of bare flesh against her own was surprising, exciting. She had thought that when the moment came she might be afraid. She wasn't afraid at all. She felt hot and clear-headed at the same time, and there was a pleasurable, painful knot inside her.

"Julia," Josh said.

On the table beside the door, the telephone began to ring.

Under his breath Josh swore, very comprehensively. He wrapped his shirt around himself and went to answer it. At the other end a girl said. "Josh? It's Stella."

"Uh, hullo. Hi there."

He glanced around. Julia was lying where he had left her, hidden from him now by the sofa back.

"Josh, I've got something to tell you. You won't like it much. I'm pregnant."

He stared down at the angular black lines of the receiver, blinking, trying to take the words in. "You're what?"

"I'm pregnant. I've been to the doctor. It's all quite certain. I'm sorry, Josh."

Josh was usually very careful. His boyhood hero, Bim Hassell, the sawmill manager's son, had told him always to carry rubbers in his wallet. That was long before Josh had needed anything of the kind, but Bim's muttered warnings had sunk in. Josh had developed his own code in the years since then. He wasn't faithful, or reliable, but he wasn't callous either. And yet, in the bed upstairs with Stella's legs around his waist, he had let her whisper, "Don't use that thing. I want to feel you inside me. It'll be all right. It's my safe time."

Josh remembered. He had come like a dive from thirty thousand feet.

He rubbed his hand over his face. "Oh, Jesus. I'm sorry. Look, don't worry. We can fix things up. It happens, you know."

"You don't understand, do you? You don't know what it's like." She was almost screaming now. "Ring me, Josh. Ring me with a doctor's name."

Stella hung up.

Joshua put the receiver back in its cradle. He unwrapped his shirt and put it on properly, buttoning the cuffs. He was thinking about a baby. Not a baby yet. A mysterious sliver of life, like a tadpole, inside Stella. He had put it there, on an evening like this.

He saw that Julia was sitting up, her arms folded on the back of the sofa and her chin resting on them. "What's the matter?"

"Nothing. Some bad news." It wasn't nothing. Only nothing to do with this, Julia. He walked around the end of the sofa and stood looking down at her. Her arms and legs suddenly seemed childlike and her face had lost its dreamy, feminine mystery. She was hardly more than a baby herself.

What had he been doing?

Josh bent down and picked up the tidy pile of her clothes. He held them out to her. "Here you are," he said gently. "Put them on."

Julia was bewildered. Surely a telephone call couldn't change everything so disastrously?

"What's wrong? What have I done?"

You asshole, Josh told himself. *You stupid jerk.*

"You haven't done anything." He stooped down so that their faces were level. "Listen. You're a virgin, aren't you?"

She nodded, biting her lip. "Does it matter?"

"It matters. Don't give yourself to me. Stay the way you are for a bit longer, okay?"

"I want you. Josh, I . . ." She held her hand out to him. He took it, and replaced it in the shadowed fold of her lap.

"Do what I say."

There was a note in his voice that stopped her even trying to argue. Julia stood up with her cheeks burning. She turned away from him and dressed herself, her fingers stiffly fumbling with the buttons that Josh had undone so deftly.

When they were both ready, he said lightly, "Good girl. Now I'll take you out and buy you some dinner. You must be hungry after losing your breakfast on the airfield."

Julia fought back her humiliation. Obediently, she followed him out to dinner.

They went to a pub, with oak settles and beams and another log fire in the welcoming dining room, but the spontaneous happiness of their day together was gone. Julia talked as brightly as she could, but she felt awkward and miserable, afraid that she had disappointed him in some way that she didn't understand.

And Josh was preoccupied with thoughts that didn't concern her.

At the end of the evening Josh took her back to the cottage at the end of the track. Courteously, he showed her the bathroom, and the bedroom opposite his at the top of the stairs. There was a single bed in it that looked as if it had never been slept in.

He kissed her good night as if he were her uncle.

"Josh, please . . ."

"Don't." He was warning her off again. "I was a jerk to bring you here. It's not your fault, it's all mine. You're so nice, Julia. Don't get things all wrong, like I do."

He turned abruptly and went into his own room, closing the door on her.

Julia lay down on her bed. She was crying, hot tears of hurt, and frustration, and love.

But she did know that she wanted Josh Flood, her aviator, more than she had ever wanted anything and more than she could imagine ever wanting anything else in the world. She promised herself that she would get him, somehow.

SIX

John Douglas was on the telephone again.

Mattie listened to his wonderful voice. She was doodling on
her notepad with her free hand, a proscenium arch and curtains,
a single spot shining on the empty boards. . . .

"Tell him what I said, won't you?" John Douglas finished.

"As soon as he comes in," Mattie promised.

"Good girl. Be seeing you."

If only, Mattie thought wistfully. Did he look like he sounded?
She went back to her one-fingered typing, frowning at the keyboard in search of elusive characters.

Francis appeared a few minutes later. He looked cheerful,
and he was smoking a cigar so big that it threatened to overbal-
ance him.

"It's a cruel world, my love," he told her. "A big cruel
world, and you have to go with it or go under."

Mattie deduced that he had satisfactorily done somebody
down. His instincts were predatory and self-seeking, but Mattie
didn't condemn him for that. She was beginning to like Francis,
and through him to see a picture of the theater that wasn't all
glitter. She was glad of it.

She ripped a completed letter to a theater manager in Dur-
ham out of her machine and pushed it across for Francis's
signature. "What have you done? Stabbed your grandmother in
an alley for two percent of the takings?" She had discovered that
Francis loved to be teased about his ruthlessness.

"That's enough cheek from you. Look at your bloody
spelling. Is this supposed to be 'commencing'? Any phone
messages?"

"My spelling's as good as yours. Just different." They
smiled appreciatively at each other. "Just one message. From
John Douglas. He says that Jennifer Edge has left the company.
He also said, as far as I can remember, that she's gone off with
the fucking Italian chef from some poncy caff, and you'd better
send him up someone else who isn't going to fall on her back
every time some fucking dago unbuttons his equipment and

120

waves it at her. And you'd better do it right off, or he's wrapping the whole fucking show and sod 'em. And sod you.''

Francis sat down behind his desk and rubbed his hand over his face. "Language, language."

"I quote," Mattie said crisply, and rolled a fresh sheet of paper into her typewriter.

"That fat bitch," Francis sighed. "I should have known better than to send Douglas off with a middle-aged nympho for a stage manager. Once she'd had him and everything else in the company in trousers, she'd be bound to be looking elsewhere. Gone off, you said?"

"Gone off, left the company. Took the half a week's wages owing to her out of the night's takings and went without a forwarding address. That's loosely what Mr. Douglas said, if you prefer it that way."

"Oh, Christ," sighed Francis. He took his cigar out of his mouth and stared gloomily at the shiny, wet end of it. "Let's think. No use hoping that they could do without anyone. The company's stripped to the bone as it is, and Douglas wouldn't stand for it. Who can I send up there halfway through a tour?"

Mattie knew. She saw her chance shining at her like a beacon through the banks of cigar smoke. "I'll go."

Francis snorted. "You? What do you know about stage management? Edge knew what she was doing, if she could get herself off the horizontal for long enough. We'll have to advertise."

Mattie jumped up and went around to his chair. She perched on his desk, gripping the splintered wood with her fingers to contain her eagerness. "I can do it. I've got experience. It's only amateur, but I know what to do. Let me, Francis."

He was silent for a second, and her heart jumped in her chest. She pressed on recklessly. "I could go straight away. Tomorrow, if you like. You won't get anyone else that quickly." When he still said nothing, she begged him. "Please, Francis. Send me."

Francis looked down at her knees. They were smooth and nylon shiny. He put his hand over one of them and squeezed it. For once Mattie didn't pull away. He was remembering the first time he saw her, singing with old Jessie. She can't sing, he had thought, but she's got plenty of other talents.

A rare generous impulse took hold of Francis. He liked her, and she deserved her chance. She was also the worst typist he had ever known. "You can go as a fill-in. Just until I find a proper replacement."

Mattie put her arms around him and kissed the top of his head. Francis leaned back, resting against her breasts, glowing with the pleasure of being rewarded, for once, for having done the right thing. "You're not going for good," he reminded her hastily. "Just for half of a six-month tour. I need you here."

"Not for good, of course," Mattie agreed. *Just for as long as it takes.*

Three days later, Julia and Felix were seeing her off from Euston Station. There had been a surprise addition to the send-off party—at the last minute Josh had turned up too.

Mattie leaned out of the carriage window. Spouts of wet, stale steam separated her from Julia and Felix, and now that the time had come she didn't want to leave them. In the last weeks in the square they had become a family. But Felix had heaved her one suitcase into the rack over her seat, and her one-way ticket was stowed in her purse.

"Good-bye," she called. "I'll write, lots and lots." As if she were going to Australia. It felt like it, suddenly. She wanted to whisper to Julia, "Be as happy with him as you like. Just don't make him *be* your happiness." There was no chance of saying anything of the kind now, even if she could have found words precise enough to express her uneasiness. Julia was smiling, waving, with Josh's arm around her shoulder.

Mattie wanted to whisper to Felix, too, but she had even less idea of what she might have said. There was just something in his face, behind his smile. Perhaps bewilderment. Josh's other arm rested on Felix's shoulder, drawing the three of them together into a little circle of light. Josh's vitality and charm had that effect, Mattie thought.

They might have been a picture, the three of them on the platform. Called something like *Au Revoir,* or *We'll Meet Again.* That was another effect of Josh's. He didn't seem to belong, quite, to reality.

The guard's whistle blew. Steam was thickened with smoke, and the train jolted forward. She was going, anyway. She would miss them, but she wouldn't miss her chance.

"Good-bye! Good luck!"

"Be a good girl, Mattie!"

She leaned out as far as she could, and blew kisses. "Not if I can help it!" Julia and Felix stood waving, linked by Josh, until Mattie's train swayed out of sight.

"I wish she hadn't gone," Julia said, but she could only

make herself aware of Josh. When he was with her everything else faded into insignificance, even the bleakness that she suffered when he wasn't.

Since the flying weekend he had come to see her two or three times, appearing as if he had just thought of the idea five minutes earlier. His seeming casualness hurt Julia, but she accepted it because there was nothing else she could do.

Josh fit well into the family in the square. Jessie always had time for good-looking young men, and although Mattie was wary of him for Julia's sake, her touchiness disappeared when he brought a pile of American records in their paper sleeves and lay on the floor beside her to play them. One of the records was by Bill Haley, and that was the first that Mattie and Julia heard of rock and roll. From that time on, the sound of it belonged to their bedroom over the square, and to Josh.

Julia watched him with admiration, and pride, and unmistakable love that made Jessie sigh for her. Only Felix held himself apart. He almost never looked straight at Josh. Whenever he was there, Felix was busy in the kitchen or in his own room. If Jessie insisted that he join them, he spread his work out on the table so that he could keep his head bent over that. He did one drawing, of Julia and Josh and Mattie listening to "Rock Around the Clock," and he kept it pinned to the wall in his room.

Felix walked all the way from Euston to the block of flats in Ladbroke Grove. He walked quickly, with his head bent, and the rhythm helped to drum some of the impatience out of him. He didn't enjoy being with Julia and Josh, but when he was apart from them he found himself thinking about them.

Felix shrugged so angrily that two girls who were passing giggled and stared. He didn't suppose that Julia and Josh thought about him. He didn't have any reason to suppose that Joshua Flood thought about anything at all except his various appetites. So why did he occupy Felix's own consciousness like a splinter under a ball of flesh?

Deliberately, with an effort of will, Felix turned the thought away. He was going to work, and he would concentrate on that.

Felix had given up the pretense of studying art on a formal basis. The building work on the flats belonging to Mr. Mogridge's friend was almost complete, and there were six empty shells waiting to be fitted. Felix discovered that he was expected to be designer and decorator, and he was enjoying the challenge. On a tiny budget, and with his employer's instructions to make the flats look "classy, you know the kind of thing, but not overpowering," he was struggling to turn his ideas into cupboards and curtains.

Felix hated almost everything to do with modern design. He disliked splashy prints in harsh colors, and spindle-legged furniture, and synthetic materials. Felix dreamed of country houses and acres of brocade, Aubusson carpets and crystal chandeliers, and the faded splendors of inherited treasures. It was hard to know how to translate that yearning into the reality of six speculator renovations in Ladbroke Grove, or even how to recreate the particular atmosphere of the flat above the square, but Felix was going to do his best. By the time he reached the site he had almost forgotten Julia and Josh. On a Saturday afternoon the flats would be empty of builders and their sneering foreman, and he could walk around and think in peace.

So long as he was working, he could keep the darker anxieties at bay.

It was dark, with the sudden depressing weight of a northern November, when Mattie reached Leeds. She stood beside the ticket barrier with her suitcase, peering around her. Even under the station lights, fog thickened the air and her breath hung in a cloud in front of her.

There was no one to meet her.

Mattie squared her shoulders and went out to the taxi rank beyond the station. She gave the taxi driver the address of the theater and they started off into the murk. The driver called something to her over his shoulder, in an accent so impenetrable that Mattie could hardly understand him. She felt as if she were in a foreign land.

But the theater, when they reached it, reassured her a little. It was a huge gray edifice, seemingly big enough to seat a thousand playgoers. Lights streamed out and the taxi slid forward into the yellow glow. Mattie paid the driver and went up the semi-circle of shallow steps into the foyer. It was hung with playbills from past shows, and with grainy photographs of the two Headline productions.

It was completely deserted except for a bored girl staring vacantly out of a glass-fronted booth. Mattie strode up to her.

"I'm here to see Mr. Douglas. I'm the new stage manager for Headline." It was the proudest sentence that Mattie had ever uttered, but the girl's face didn't even flicker.

"They're halfway through t'second act. You want stage door. Or mebbe e'll be oopstairs. You can tek that door."

She nodded across the expanse of darned carpet to a door marked Staff.

"Can I leave my things here?"

"Suit yersen."

Behind the door was a narrow staircase of bare boards. It was almost pitch dark. Mattie groped her way upward, with no idea where she was heading.

Then she heard the voice. It was unmistakably John Douglas, and he was shouting. While Mattie hesitated, a woman's voice screamed back. She couldn't make out the words, but it was clearly a full-blown row. Making her way toward the noise, Mattie came to a dingy corridor lit by a bare bulb, and a door marked Office. The door banged open and a woman stumbled out. Her graying hair was falling out of a bun and she was crying.

"You're a monster," she sobbed. "No less than a monster. Not a human being at all." Then she pushed past Mattie without glancing at her and ran down the stairs.

"Yes, yes," said John Douglas from inside the office. "Tell me something new, Vera."

Mattie tiptoed forward and tapped on the open door.

"I thought you'd bloody gone," John Douglas said.

"She has," Mattie answered. "I'm Mattie Banner."

John Douglas looked up from the one chair in the room. There was a long pause, and then he said, "Is that supposed to mean anything to me?"

Mattie quailed. He was a big man with a lion's head of shaggy gray hair. Mattie saw a rubber-tipped walking stick leaning against his chair.

"I'm your new stage manager."

His sudden shout of laughter was even more disconcerting. "Oh, sweet Jesus Christ."

It was the same rich voice that she had admired, but how could such a voice belong to this creased, belligerent man?

"What's funny about it?" Mattie asked, stung by his rudeness.

"Just that Willoughby said he was sending me his own personal assistant, as a great favor."

"I am—I was—Francis's assistant."

John was still laughing as he looked her up and down. It made Mattie feel hot and angry.

"Yes, of course. It's just that I was expecting a lady of a certain age and certain capabilities. Given that we're talking about Francis, I should have known better. I'm sure you've got your own talents, love, but I doubt that they'll be the ones I need for eight shows a week. How old are you?"

"Twenty-two."

John Douglas's mouth twisted. "Of course you are. Kids and cripples, that's what we are in this company. They should give us special billing." He took hold of his stick and stood up. He was tall, but his body screwed over to one side. "I provide the cripple element, in case you were wondering. Usually I tell pretty girls it's a war wound, but I can't be bothered tonight. It's osteoarthritis, and I blame my vile temper on it."

"I thought there must be a reason for it," Mattie murmured.

He looked at her then, with the corners of his mouth drawn down. "What do you know about stage management?" he snapped at her.

"Enough."

"Oh, that's very good. You can do the get-out tonight, and I'll go home to bed."

Mattie felt her face go stiff. "Do the . . . ?"

"This is wonderful." He laughed again, without any warmth. "Francis may not have explained to you that this is a touring company. This lovely Saturday evening is our last night in Leeds, and on Monday we open a week in Doncaster. We have two shows on this tour, George Bernard Shaw's *Arms and the Man*, and *Welcome Home*, which is a three-act drawing-room comedy complete with maid, of the sort beloved by mystified northern audiences. After the curtain tonight both sets have to be struck and loaded, with props and costumes, on to trucks. This leaves room for the next company to bring in *Rookery Nook*, or *Ghost Train*, or whatever bloody masterpiece the manager imagines will appeal to the citizens of Leeds. On Monday the procedure is reversed, in the next theater. The get-in, as we theater folk call it. That's your job, dear, among other things. I'm afraid you'll have Leonard to help you too."

"Leonard?"

"Your ASM. One of the kids, and half-witted as well. You'd better come backstage now, in the interval, and I'll introduce you. You've already seen Vera. She's the deputy manager." He was walking away down the dingy corridor, moving awkwardly but surprisingly quickly.

"What was the matter with her?"

His voice boomed back, amplified by the funnel of the passage. "Apart from incompetence? Time of the month, I should think. All women are the same, from our lovely leading lady to yourself, no doubt. No, that's not quite true. Our lamented Jennifer Edge didn't seem to suffer, but then, she took plenty of exercise."

She heard him laughing.

Mattie contented herself with making a face at the director's distorted shadow as she scuttled after him down to the stage.

An hour later the curtain had come down. It was a thin house for a Saturday night, and the audience dispersed quickly. The actors vanished in their wake, heading for the pub or the landlady's cooking at their digs. Nobody paid the slightest attention to Mattie. John Douglas had gone, and she found herself standing in front of the *Welcome Home* set, frozen by the certainty that she could do nothing with it. She would still be standing there when *Rookery Nook* arrived on Monday.

"You're in charge, then. Where shall we start?"

It was Leonard, a spindly youth in tight trousers, and the theater's two stagehands. They were staring blankly at her, without hostility, but with no hint of friendship either.

Mattie wanted to cry, or to run away, but the three of them were blocking her way, and she hated anyone to see her in tears. She breathed in instead, and said sharply, "I'm new here, Leonard, and you know the show. Do what you usually do, and I'll get started on the hampers."

To her relief, they turned away and began dismantling the flats. The heavy weights thumped and the metal poles clanked. That, at least, was familiar.

Mattie found the big wicker costume and prop baskets stacked up backstage. She trailed around the deserted dressing rooms collecting discarded costumes and props, praying that she was finding everything, and began packing them up.

It took one and a half back-breaking hours to clear the theater. Mattie and Leonard heaved the last wicker basket into the waiting truck, and the two stagehands melted away. The theater janitor was locking the doors within five minutes, and Mattie only just retrieved her suitcase. She found herself out in the foggy street again, without even the glow of the theater lights for reassurance.

"You got any digs?" Leonard asked her. He was about Mattie's own age, an undernourished-looking boy with a bad skin and sparse, greasy hair.

She shook her head, and Leonard sighed.

"They never think, do they? You'd better come to mine. They're nothing special because the cast always pinch the best ones. But it'll be better than nothing."

He held out his hand for her suitcase, smiling at her. Mattie was so tired that she let him take it. Leonard might easily have resented her arrival, she reflected, except that he didn't seem to have the necessary spirit. He didn't look like much of an ally as he loped along beside her, but Mattie needed a friend that night. She was grateful to him.

"Thanks, Leonard," she said.

"You can call me Lenny, if you like."

His landlady served them a late supper in the front room. Eggs and bacon and fried bread, two bottles of Guinness, and a choice from the bottles of sauce that stood on a wooden tray on the sideboard. Lenny ate in silence, with his mouth open, and Mattie tried to keep her eyes fixed on the Victorian oleograph hung over the chilly grate.

She wanted to talk, to say, *This is it. I'm here,* but there was no one to share her mystified triumph with. Not Lenny, with his churning mouthfuls of food, and certainly not the brick-jawed landlady.

"No funny business, is it?" the landlady had snapped when Lenny presented her.

"Of course not," they had said.

Mattie thought of Jessie, on their first night in the square. *Nothing funny at all,* Mattie repeated as she prepared for bed in the icy back bedroom. *I'd give anything for something to laugh at.*

Her first night in the professional theater ended with her shivering between damp sheets, and longing for Julia and Jessie and Felix at home in the cluttered warmth of the flat.

Through the lumpy wallpaper she could hear Lenny snoring.

It was the hardest week that Mattie had ever lived through, but when the time came for her second get-out she was beginning to believe that she might survive as stage manager of the Headline number-one company.

By sitting up late in her digs, and by working early when the rest of the company were comfortably asleep, she had learned the two scripts. She had mastered the props list and the calls. She knew that she could avoid any more of Sheila Firth's tantrums by always calling her at the correct second, and always waiting meekly in her dressing room doorway for her languid acknowledgment. Sheila Firth was the actress playing Raina, and the fiancée in *Welcome Home*. She was temperamental and sickly, and not at all convincing as Shaw's heroine, but Mattie watched her with intrigued intensity. She was the *leading F* that Mattie had sighed over in *Stage*.

Sheila's technique for dealing with John Douglas was to ignore him. His abuses seemed to roll off her tilted head, and Mattie thought it was a very effective technique indeed. She adopted a mild version of it herself, and it helped her to survive the first week's exposure to the director-manager's fury. Mattie also had the comfort of recognizing that even a hopeless stage manager was better than no one at all, and if John Douglas threw her out, Francis was unlikely to replace her at any great speed.

The company moved from Doncaster to Scarborough, and from Scarborough to Nottingham, and Mattie's new life began to develop a pattern.

On Saturday night, after the last curtain, there was the get-out. When it was done, two trucks took the flats and the props and the hampers of costumes away. The people were all gone, and the two-dimensional bric-a-brac that created the illusions, and the stage was left. Mattie liked it best then. It was easier to recapture some of her illusions about it in the absence of Francis Willoughby's touring productions.

When the theater was finally dark, Mattie could limp home to her digs for the last evening's supper and bed. The digs improved after the first week. Vera took her under her wing, and introduced her to the network of theatrical landladies. They were there, in all the foggy northern towns that the company visited. Some of them were ex-professionals themselves; all of them were in love with the theater. They always saw all the shows, and the actors waited politely for their verdicts. They treated their weekly regulars like members of the family, feeding them huge, fatty, late meals in gasfire-heated parlors, and sitting with them afterward for long sessions of gossip and discreet tippling.

Mattie suspected that the digs patronized by company members less genteel than Vera must be even livelier. There were two middle-aged actors in particular who had been working the circuit for years and years and who always stayed in the same place in each town. At the end of the week they would murmur something like, "Old Nellie's still got the stamina, dear, but I don't know that I have. Just look at my skin. Early bed for me every night in Middlesbrough, whatever Phyllis says."

Their names were Fergus and Alan, but they always referred to each other as Ada and Doris. They were the first homosexuals that Mattie had ever seen at close quarters, and her first introduction to theatrical camp. Doris and Ada convinced her that Felix couldn't be queer. The thought of Felix pursing his lips and whispering, "She's nice, *and* she knows it" behind the back of some stagehand made her laugh, and long for Julia.

On Sundays they did the transfer. Usually that meant a long, cold train journey with awkward connections. John Douglas drove himself in his filthy black Standard Vanguard, but the rest of the company huddled into the train with thermos flasks and sandwiches and the Sunday papers. The actors read the reviews of the West End productions aloud to each other. Mattie enjoyed the acrimony of that, listening in her corner. Most of the company was too old or too defeated for anything more challenging than Francis's seedy productions, and one or two of them were grateful to be working at all. But the younger ones like Sheila Firth believed that they deserved better, and used the close captivity of the train to tell everyone else. There were uninhibited rows, and shouting, and tears. Mattie watched everything, from behind the shelter of the *News of the World*.

In the Sunday twilight of the new town, smelling of fish and chips, and canal water, and coal-smoke, there would be the new digs, perhaps a cinema with Vera or Lenny or Alan and Fergus, and then bed in another back bedroom with a brass bedstead, and a china bowl and ewer on the washstand.

Monday was a hard day. There was the physical struggle with recalcitrant flats as they came off the trucks, the unpacking of costumes in various dressing rooms, and then a long trail of visits to unsympathetic shopkeepers to beg for the loan of furniture or supplies in exchange for a mention in a program slip. The cast hated Mondays, too, and they complained about their dressing rooms, the lack of their pet props, their unmended or uncleaned costumes, and Mattie had to try to soothe them all. At the end of the day there was the show itself, with the calls to be made, the backstage business to handle, and her turn to be taken with Lenny in the prompt box.

Mattie had promised that she would write down everything she was seeing and doing, like a diary, and send it to Julia. It was Julia herself, greedy even for someone else's experience, who had begged her to do it. But by the end of the day Mattie was too bleary with exhaustion and suppertime Guinness to do anything but roll into bed.

Julia wrote two or three letters, thin little notes with news of Jessie and Felix, but none of herself. *Josh has been here*, she told Mattie dully. *Nothing happened.* Mattie sighed over the letters in her backstage corner, not even needing to read between the lines.

After Mondays the week grew easier. Even Mattie could lie in bed late and take time over her breakfast before scurrying back to the theater and her day's work. Before the early evening preparations she mended scenery, repaired costumes or sewed curtains, developing talents she had never dreamed she possessed. On Wednesdays there was a matinee, treasury call on Friday, and then it was Saturday once more, and everything was ready to begin all over again. She watched every performance, from the wings or from the shelter of the prompt box, thinking, *I could do that*. She listened to Sheila Firth's high, consciously musical voice and mouthed her lines. *If it was me*, Mattie thought.

Her real position was much humbler. By the end of her first month on tour Mattie had found her niche in the company. Vera mothered her, and Lenny was her regular companion. Mattie was relieved that he at least didn't try to be more than that. The younger men in the company regarded her as one of the props, and were surprised when she refused to let them try her on like a new costume. She joked with them and fended them off, secretly not liking any of them very much. She enjoyed the company of Alan and Fergus because they made her laugh, and they clearly preferred her to Miss Edge.

Fergus's sandy eyebrows would go up. "Some of the things I could tell you about that one," he whispered.

"Do tell me."

"I wouldn't dream. You're too innocent, love."

The actresses mostly ignored her, except to complain about each other. Mattie particularly disliked Sheila's breathless girlishness, but she did try to copy her posh-sounding elocuted accent. "What's the matter with you?" John Douglas asked her. "Got a gumboil?"

Mattie watched him too. She was intrigued by his theatrical standards, and by the way he cajoled or insulted his lackluster company into meeting them. *He must have been a good director, once*, she thought. He was also realistic. He couldn't give much stature to Raina and her Bluntschli, played by a hollow-chested, languidly poetic young actor called Hugh, so he made them tender instead. And he sent the hackneyed drawing-room comedy humming along at a snappy pace that disguised its predict-ability. The audiences always enjoyed it much more than the Shaw classic. John didn't ask too much of his actors, but he expected a certain amount and he made certain that they delivered it. Most of the company hated him, but they were careful enough to be civil to his face. Vera lived in terror of him. Mattie didn't know what she thought. There was still the potent appeal of his voice. Sometimes when she heard it she would turn around and look covertly at him.

Mattie had suffered from his temper more than any of the others at the beginning. On her third night she had failed to deliver a tray of glasses to the wings for the maid to walk on with. The actors onstage had been forced to drink the engaged couple's health in thin air, and John Douglas had rounded on Mattie in the interval as if he wanted to tear her arms off.

"I won't tolerate incompetence," the voice boomed at her. "You can't help your ignorance or your crassness, and the rest of us must put up with you. But you do have a marked script in your hands and it tells you in plain English what to do, and when. None of it is very difficult, even for you. Don't make another fucking mess-up like that."

"I won't," Mattie made the mistake of saying.

The voice attacked her all over again. "Don't assure me of that as though you're giving me a fucking present. Just remember what I say."

How could I forget? Mattie retorted silently as she backed away. It was after that that she learned to listen and say nothing, like Sheila Firth did. Wisely, she didn't copy Sheila's pained, innocent, I-will-forgive-you expression. She was only the stage manager, not *leading F*.

Gradually, as she grew more confident and more capable, John Douglas turned his attention elsewhere.

One Friday evening John and Vera were sitting in the office before the six o'clock treasury call. In very poor weeks the box office receipts didn't even cover the company's wages, and those were the times when John had to telephone Francis Willoughby. This time, however, the takings were good and John and Vera were working on the wage packets. It was a complicated process because some actors received a percentage of the take above a certain figure, so their cuts had to be calculated and deducted from the total before the profits could be grudgingly sent off to Francis. It was Mattie's job to keep Vera supplied with tea and John with whiskey while they worked.

She was filling the kettle in the grubby kitchen cubbyhole when Sheila Firth brushed past. Sheila was wearing her street clothes, complete with a soft black felt hat pulled down over her eyes. That was unusual, because Sheila liked to be in her dressing room in good time so that she could drift soulfully around in her robe, dabbing at her wig and makeup. Mattie heard her stop at the office door. Sheila opened it, and when John and Vera looked up she half-fell against the frame.

"I can't go on tonight," she said. Her voice quivered with emotion.

Vera got up from her seat and scuttled away like a rabbit, ducking around the tragic Sheila. She left the door considerately open, so that Mattie could hear everything.

"Why not?" John's voice was expressionless by comparison.

There was a long, palpitating pause, and then Sheila said, "You don't really understand about love, John, do you?"

Hugging herself with pleasure, Mattie crept closer.

Sheila's story came spilling out without any further prompting. Everyone knew that she was in love with the leading man of another of Francis's companies. It was a love conducted on a higher plane, a rarefied and special thing. Sheila was fond of elaborating on the themes of it. Now, Mattie gathered from between the racking sobs, her leading man had abandoned Sheila for a thirty-five-year-old character actress.

"I worked with her in *Peter Pan*," Sheila wailed. "She's a woman completely without talent or refinement."

Mattie stifled her laughter. She was thinking. Sheila was understudied by a mousy girl who took the part of the maid and two other walk-ons. The mouse had a heavy cold. She was practically voiceless, and her nose was swollen and bright scarlet.

"I'm so very, very hurt, John. So crushed, and broken. I can't work when I feel like this. I can't . . ." The sobs broke out again.

Mattie waited gleefully for John's outburst. But if she had been thinking, he had been thinking quicker. She heard his chair creak, then the thump of his stick as he took two steps.

"My poor girl," the rich voice murmured. "You poor, brave girl. And now you must learn about pain."

Mattie was transfixed. She slipped closer, to the spot where she could peer through the crack in the door and watch.

John was towering over Sheila. He had taken her face between his hands and he was looking deep into her eyes.

"You will suffer, my dear. But you can, and you must,

cling to your art. Only by making that sacrifice can you grow, and it will reward you by growing with you.''

Sheila let out a low moan and her head fell forward against John's shoulder.

Mattie gaped. *You clever old bugger,* she thought. Admiration flooded through her, and swept away her short-lived dream of stepping onto the stage in Raina's opening-scene nightgown and fur wraps.

She slipped back to the cubbyhole and clattered noisily with the kettle and cups. When the tea was ready she laid a tray and carried it back to the office. Sheila was nodding bravely, with her hands folded between John's.

Mattie knelt beside her and poured her a cup of tea. When Sheila took the cup, Mattie put her arm around her shoulder and gave her a hug of sisterly solidarity.

"Oh, Mattie," Sheila broke out again. "It takes a terrible shock like this to make one realize how valuable friends are."

"I know, I know," Mattie said warmly. "The door was open, and I couldn't help hearing a little. Just remember that we all love you, and admire you." Not wanting to risk overdoing it, she tiptoed away again.

Ten minutes later, her face set in lines of sorrowful courage, Sheila was on her way to her dressing room.

Mattie went back for the tray. John was sprawled in his chair with his hands over his face, but he looked up when he heard her come in, and smiled at her.

"Good," he said. "Thank you."

It was so rare for him to praise, and it was such an odd, conspiratorial moment, that Mattie didn't know what to say.

"I need a drink," John grumbled. He poured whiskey into two glasses and handed one to Mattie. "Will you join me? To celebrate our success in going forward into another evening of theatrical mediocrity?"

They raised their glasses and drank.

With the spirits burning the back of her throat, Mattie blurted out, "What are you doing here?"

He turned his molten glare on her. His eyes were the color of syrup, and because of their surprising glow they were the only part of him that looked healthy. His skin was gray, and the front of his ash-colored hair was yellow with nicotine. Mattie noticed that his hands on the arms of his chair were knotty with pain. She might have felt sorry for him if she hadn't felt more afraid.

"Doing?" He laughed throatily and she relaxed a little.

"Isn't that obvious? Earning a few quid. A very few, I should say, thanks to your friend Francis. One has to live, and I do have a wife to support."

"You're married?"

The laugh again. "Of course I'm married. I'm fifty-four years old, and one would have to be very clever, or very determined to escape the net, to survive as a bachelor for this long."

Mattie thought back over the grinding weeks that had just passed. Her own time was fully occupied, but John Douglas was hardly less busy. How did he fit in a wife, unless he glimpsed her on Sundays when he drove off in his Standard Vanguard?

"Where does she live?"

"You're an inquisitive little girl, aren't you? Helen lives in our house, an attractive if chilly Cotswold stone edifice outside Burford, in Oxfordshire. To forestall your next question, she loathes and despises everything to do with the theater, and prefers to live her own life while I pursue my spectacular career. It is a perfectly agreeable and amicable arrangement, and I return to Burford and to my wife whenever I can."

If Mattie had had time to analyze it, she would have realized that the vaguely unhappy feeling that took hold of her now was disappointment. But John turned sharply to her.

"And what are *you* doing here?"

"I want to be an actress."

She said it automatically, and she regretted it at once. His shout of laughter was hurtful, but it made her angry too. John Douglas saw both reactions.

"Of course you do. Of course you do. Do you have any experience?"

"Only amateur. But I'm good." She was stiff and red-faced now, like an offended child.

He nodded. "Tell me, did you think your big chance was coming tonight? With Sheila's broken heart and whatshername's laryngitis? I bet you know all the lines."

Mattie shrugged. She felt too angry to give him the satisfaction of an answer. He waited for a moment, and then he drawled, "Well, then. Thank you."

Both whiskey glasses were empty. John glanced at the half-bottle on the table, and then snapped at her, "Haven't you got work to do?"

Mattie swung around to the door, but he called after her. "Mattie?"

It was the first time she could remember that he had called her anything except *You*.

"Yes?"

"You're not quite the worst stage manager I've ever had."

She had to content herself with that.

The company moved on again. Two weeks before the Christmas of 1955 they were in Great Yarmouth. There was a sudden spell of clear, mild weather and through the usual smells of chips and sweaty costumes and smoke, Mattie caught the fresh salt tang of the sea. Early one morning she went for a walk along the beach. The world was an empty expanse of gray water and gray, glittering pebbles and sand. There wasn't a sound except the sucking water and the shingle crunching under her unsuitable shoes. The air tore at Mattie's lungs.

She remembered that day, afterward, and the scrubbed gray light of winter seascapes always brought the after-memories flooding back.

It was an ordinary evening, to begin with. It was a Shaw night, and Mattie noticed that John Douglas was hovering in the wings, watching the performance more closely than he usually did. Sheila was suffering an emotional relapse, and at the end of the first act she rushed offstage and flung herself against John.

"I can't," she whispered loudly enough for everyone backstage to hear her. "I can't do it. Why is it so hard? What have I done to be made to suffer like this?"

It was obvious to everyone except Sheila that the manager was only just keeping his temper. The edges of his nostrils went white with the effort.

"You can't? But your performance is only a little bit worse than fucking well usual."

Sheila's head tilted sideways, and her eyelashes made a dark crescent on her Leichner-pink skin. John looked down at her and hoisted himself with the support of his stick. He took a deep breath that clearly hurt, and tried again.

"My darling. Do it for me if you can't do it for yourself. It's important for me tonight."

"Is it?" she breathed. "If it's for you, John. I need to know that."

She went on again for the second act, but watching her from the wings Mattie thought that the performance could hardly have been any more terrible without her. Sheila fluffed almost every line, and Lenny struggled to help her from the box. Hugh's

Bluntschli turned sulky and then perfunctory, while Fergus and Alan as Petkoff and Saranoff battled on with weary determination.

The final curtain came as a release for everyone. The applause was no more than a dry patter, extinguished by the banging of seats. John Douglas limped away without saying a word, and Sheila fled to her dressing room with her handkerchief pressed to her face.

I've seen worse performances, Mattie thought philosophically. *Why the fuss? I wonder.* She did her clearing up with the mechanical ease of familiarity, then went around the dressing rooms for the last time to turn off the lights. She was on her way down to the stage door, imagining she was the last person in the building, when she saw threads of light framing the closed door of the office. She tapped on the door, and when no answer came she opened it.

John was there, alone, although there were two other glasses on the table beside his. "I'm sorry," Mattie mumbled. "I was just doing the lights."

He waved his arm at her, beckoning her in with a big, ironically florid gesture. The knuckles of his hand cracked against the wall of the poky room, but he didn't seem to notice.

"Come in, come in. I'm drowning. Oh, don't look so fucking nervous. Just my sorrows. Nothing more dramatic than that. Oh, shit. Dramatic's not the best bloody word this evening, is it? Here, come and join me." He held up one of the two empty glasses. "Don't mind a dirty one, do you? That stupid bloody bastard had it first, but I don't suppose that's catching. Here." He pushed the drink across to Mattie and turned back to his own. He drank the three fingers of it in one gulp.

"What's the matter?" Mattie asked. "Not Sheila, surely?"

"Silly premenstrual bitch." He chuckled sourly. "If I could personally insure that she never works again, I'd do it with the greatest pleasure. No, not Sheila specifically, although she contributed in her special way." He poured himself another measure and drank again. "We both have our ridiculous ambitions, Mattie, you see. No, I don't mean that. Yours is less risible than mine. After all, we have Miss Firth as our leading lady, don't we? Why not Miss . . . ah, Miss . . . ?"

"Banner."

"Exactly. Well, since you asked what's wrong, I'll tell you. My little dream is to start up a company of my own. No more *Welcome Home*. No more pig-ignorant Willoughby. To this magnificent end I have been saving up my hard-won wages, and looking around for some financial backing. Tonight two dear old theater cronies of mine, who have been more successful in lining their pockets than I, traveled all the way up here from town to see my show. My Shaw. Miss Firth's shitty Shaw show, ha-ha. I'm sure you can guess the rest?''

There have been worse performances, Mattie thought again. But not very many.

"No money?"

"Quite right. And not only no money, but suddenly no time either. Not even for an hour or so of food and wine and conversation. A pressing need to drive back to town developed after just one small whiskey apiece. As if I smelled bad. But nothing stinks quite like failure, does it? What *am* I doing here, to take your own question from you?''

Mattie went over and stood by him, looking down into the thin patch in the hair at the top of his head. She had never noticed it before. She thought, *He's lonely too; how cut off we all are, living so close together*.

She leaned down, very gently, and let her cheek rest against the top of his head for a second. He didn't move, either to shake her off or draw her closer, and Mattie's courage deserted her. She was hardly in a position to comfort John Douglas as if he were Ricky or Sam. She went back around the table and picked up her drink.

John drank in silence for another moment or two, and then he roused himself. "Come and have some dinner," he boomed at her. "Would you like that?"

"Yes, please," Mattie said simply.

He looked surprised, but he heaved himself out of his chair and shuffled around with his stick. He put on an outsized overcoat and a khaki muffler, and a hat pulled down over his eyebrows. Immediately, he looked like an old man.

They went down the stairs to the stage door. Mattie turned the lights off behind them and John produced a bunch of keys from his inner pocket and locked the door. Outside in the street, with the wind slicing off the sea into their faces, he asked her, "Where are your outdoor things?"

"I'm wearing them."

It was much colder in the bleak northern towns than in the cocoon of London streets. Mattie had discovered that very early on. But she needed every penny of her wages to keep herself sheltered and fed, and there was nothing left over for thick winter coats.

John Douglas exhaled, and Mattie saw his cloudy breath dispelled by the wind. "You'd better see Vera at the end of the week, then. Get a loan before you get pneumonia."

Mattie raised her eyebrows, but he was already walking away and she had to move quickly to keep pace with his fast, lopsided steps.

They went to a little French restaurant, tucked away in the angle of two streets behind the sea front. It was the kind of place that Mattie and Lenny and Vera would have passed without a second glance, knowing that it was out of their league. The headwaiter showed them to a table laid for three. The third setting was quickly removed and Mattie pretended not to have noticed it. She looked around instead at the flocked red wallpaper and the little wall lamps with pink-fringed shades. The handful of other diners, red-faced men and permed women, were already finishing their meals. A waiter brought the menus. They were bound in red leather and hung with gold tassels.

"What do you want to eat?" John asked her.

"Steak," Mattie said at once. "And chips. And soup to start with." She was always hungry, and she wasn't going to hold back in ordering a free meal in a place like this.

John frowned. "And ice cream to follow, I suppose." He ordered the food rapidly. "And bring me the best bottle of burgundy you've got. Do you like wine, Mattie?"

She thought of Felix and his careful bottles of Beaujolais and Chianti stored under the kitchen sink. "I love wine."

It wasn't an easy meal, to begin with.

Mattie was sharply conscious that her company failed to compensate for John's missing friends. He leaned back in his chair, watching her without seeing her, turning his glass in his fingers in between drafts of wine.

"Tell me about yourself," he ordered. "Isn't that what usually happens on these occasions?"

"I haven't experienced an occasion quite like this," Mattie said. She wouldn't let John Douglas browbeat her. But she talked anyway, to fill the silence, to distract him. She glossed over her childhood, but she embroidered her escapades with Julia and she described Jessie and Felix in lengthy detail. The bottle of burgundy was emptied and John called for another. Once or twice he laughed, the loudness of it making the other diners peer covertly at him.

Their food came. John barely touched the cutlets he had ordered, but he drank steadily. Mattie ate because she was ravenous, but she thought privately that this food was nothing near as good as the meals that Felix cooked at home.

"It's your turn now," she said with her red meat cooling on the plate in front of her. "You talk while I eat."

John Douglas's thick gray eyebrows drew together. "I was an ac-tor," he said. The dark, resonant voice seemed to fill the room. Mattie resolutely didn't glance at the surrounding tables. John picked up his stick and thumped it on the floor. "But there aren't many parts for cripples. You can't play Dick the Bad forever. I did have five or six good years, after the war. I was at Bristol Old Vic, Stratford for a couple of seasons."

"Tell me," Mattie implored.

"Ah, it's all bollocks. All of it. That's my consolation. But I'll tell you if you want to hear."

Mattie chewed her way through her tough steak and the floury chocolate pudding that followed, listening, entranced. He told her stories of Alec, and Sybil, and Larry, stories of first nights and tours and tryouts, triumphs and disasters.

When the burgundy was all gone he started on brandy, in a fat balloon glass. He had become briefly animated, embellishing his stories with comic accents and breaking into his thunderous belly-laugh, but the brandy seemed to puncture his euphoria. He sank back into his chair again, staring over Mattie's head.

"And now here we are. Washed up in fucking Yarmouth, dining out with a little girl stage manager."

"I'm not a little girl," Mattie said softly.

After a moment he said, "I know that. I'm sorry."

Their eyes met, and it was Mattie who looked away first. She saw the waiters standing impatiently by the door. The chairs were stacked on all the other tables.

"I think they want us to go."

"Who gives a fuck what they want?"

But he fumbled for the bill that had been placed at his elbow an hour before. He slapped the pound notes onto the plate, and they stood up together. The waiter opened the door for them with an ironic bow.

Outside, the air broke over them like an icy sea wave. Even Mattie gasped, and John lurched sideways. His legs seemed to buckle under him and he clawed at Mattie for support. She leaned into him, trying to support his weight.

"Oh, Christ," he murmured. "A cripple. A fucking legless cripple."

They tottered together to the nearest lamppost and leaned

against it, washed by the impartial yellow light. John stared into the gloom. The waves crashed dully in the distance, but there was no other sound. They were alone, cut off by the lateness, the dark, and the muffled sea.

Fear turned over like a sick lump in John Douglas's stomach. He was afraid of everything, of the entirety of life beyond this circle of light. And the girl's hair was close to his mouth, a metallic-shining mass of curls. He shuddered, and then he bent his head and buried his face in it.

She stood still, sturdy, holding him up.

"Come home with me, Mattie." He begged her, knowing that he couldn't bear it if she refused. She was so warm, so full of bloody life.

"All right."

It was as simple as that.

They began to walk, zigzagging, with Mattie's arm around his waist. He was too heavy for her, too drunk to be controllable. They reached the sea front, and the wind flattened them against the wall. A ball of screwed-up chip papers scudded past their feet.

"This way," John said grandly, and they leaned forward into the salty blast.

He was staying not in digs but in a small hotel at the far end of the front. They stumbled up the steps, and Mattie caught a glimpse of a sign in the front window announcing *Vacancies*. The doors were locked, and John pressed his fist against the bell, mumbling.

After a very long time a dim light blinked on over their heads. A yawning boy opened the door and gaped at them.

"Where is the night porter?" thundered John. "Why should my friend and I be kept waiting on the front steps?"

"I'm sorry . . ." Mattie began, and then with a flutter of relief she realized that the boy wasn't interested in anything except getting back to his bed.

He bolted the door behind them and disappeared. John took a key from a row of wooden pigeonholes and held it up for Mattie to see. "Number thirteen. Not a difficult one to remember, luckily."

She followed him in silence. The hotel smelled pungently of air freshener and boiled vegetables, and then they passed the bar, and the hoppy stink of beer was momentarily dominant. Mattie thought of the traveling salesmen congregated in there in the empty evenings. Past the bar they negotiated a flight of stairs, and reached John's room. After several stabs with the key he found the door and opened it. Mattie looked back down the bare hallway, and then she followed John Douglas into room number thirteen. The ceiling light was very high up, a fringed and bobbled shade pendant in a gray, shadowy space. The room seemed full of shiny brown furniture, ranks of unmatching wardrobes and glass-topped dressing tables. The double bed had shiny wooden head- and footboards, and a green candlewick cover. The curtains were faded green velour and the carpet was a third shade of green.

Mattie wondered, *Am I going to do this, here?*

John Douglas took off his overcoat and put his hat and scarf on one of the dressing tables.

"Excuse me a minute," he muttered. He went out of the room, and Mattie heard the clank and flush of a lavatory. She stood motionless, still in her thin coat, waiting. John came back and closed the door. He came to her, and with his big hands began to undo her buttons. When he saw her bare shoulders he was breathing heavily, with his mouth open. He touched the scattered golden freckles with his fingers.

Mattie felt nothing except the cold air of the room on her skin.

With a sudden blundering movement John pushed her backward onto the bed. He fell on top of her, squashing her with his weight. Experimentally, Mattie reached up and put her arms around his neck. He kissed her face and told her, puzzled, "You taste of salt."

The wind had blown the sea spray into her face.

He licked her cheek gently. There was tenderness in it, and it touched her. She turned her head to find his mouth, but he had drawn back a little. He was lying with his eyes closed, and she listened to his breathing. It was a moment or two before she noticed that he had fallen asleep.

Mattie looked up at the tiny light above them. Even the feeble speck of it seemed to hurt her eyes, and she realized that she was exhausted. Slowly and gently, inching herself sideways, she extricated herself from John Douglas's heavy limbs. She went across to the bathroom and washed herself in cold water, then crept back into the bedroom. John hadn't moved. He looked like a big, crestfallen child. Mattie struggled to pull off his trousers and jacket, and he grunted and pitched away from her. Under his clothes he was wearing long underwear, his big hands and feet protruding from the ribbed cuffs of it. She felt hot with her efforts, and with sadness, and with the burgundy fuming in her head.

Mattie half-undressed herself and pulled the covers up over both of them. The weight of him in the bed beside her felt strange, but it comforted her. She fell asleep at once.

When she woke up again it was daylight. She frowned at the tall rectangle of light in front of her, and then it resolved itself into a window, with thin sunshine filtering through grayish net curtains. There were green velour curtains framing the net. She remembered, and turned under the bedcovers to look for him.

The bed was empty, although the pillows on the other side were dented and creased. He had been here, then.

Not a dream.

The room was empty, too, for all the lowering, shiny furniture. Mattie drew her knees up to her chest and wrapped her arms around them. She lay and listened to the sounds of doors opening and closing, distant vacuuming, a car passing outside. She was thirsty and her head felt muzzy.

The door opened. John came in and closed it with a gentle click before he looked and saw that she was awake. He stood at the side of the bed, peering down at her. Then he sat down heavily on his own side. He was wearing a startling red paisley dressing gown.

"I'm sorry," he offered at last. "That wasn't a very attractive display, was it? I don't often drink like that, although it may surprise you to hear it. Can't afford it, for one thing. And when I did I used to be able to hold it. But I'm an old man now. Failing in every direction."

Mattie broke into his monologue. "Fifty-four isn't old. Not if you don't let it be."

She remembered how he had looked last night, in his underclothes. She felt pain for both of them, but John laughed. He was snorting a little, running his fingers through his hair so that it lay back flat, like a badger's. He stood up again and walked restlessly around the room, then stopped at the window to stare through the mist of gray net toward the sea.

In a low voice he asked her, "Do you want to try again?"

Mattie tried to blot out the room and its depressing furnishings, and the dusty, heavy green folds of fabric shrouding them.

The room didn't matter. They were here, that was all.

She was troubled more by the sense that nothing else mattered either. Whether John Douglas made love to her against this

shiny wooden headboard, or not. It wouldn't make any difference. It wouldn't be a cataclysmic moment, not like in the
stories. Except that there had been that moment of tenderness
last night. That stayed with her, like warmth and wetness still on
her cheek.

Afterward she had undressed him and he had been vulnerable.

In the restaurant's sickly warmth, with the wine in her head,
she had wanted to come here to his bedroom. This morning she
knew only that she liked John Douglas, rumpled and hung over
in his cherry-colored dressing gown. Liking unclouded by longing or lust.

Mattie thought fleetingly of Julia's aviator. With his broad
back and strong arms and blond head, his potency like a spell
cast over Julia. Mattie's mouth curved. She didn't long for Josh
Flood either.

What difference, then?

Without speaking she lifted her bare arm from the musty
shelter of the blankets and held it out to him.

He came to her quickly, pulling at the paisley cloth. He was
naked underneath it and Mattie saw white corded flesh and
thickly matted gray hair. Then he was beside her, on top of her,
his tongue in her hair and in her ears and in her mouth. He
pulled at the layer of clothes she had slept in and she helped him
where she could, wriggling awkwardly beneath him. He hoisted
himself up so that he could see her.

"Oh, God, you've got a beautiful body."

He seized her breasts, kneading and squeezing and bumping
them, and then taking them in his mouth with the nipples between his teeth. Mattie lay perfectly still and let him do what he
wanted to her. For a moment everything seemed simple. *He just
does it*, she thought with relief. But it wasn't enough.

"Hold me," he ordered her. He fixed her fist over himself.
She felt thin, shiny skin stretched perilously tight over hard
flesh. Mattie moved her hand tentatively up and down, wanting
to do it right for him. He hissed hotly in her ear, "Hold it
tighter. And do it harder, like this." His hand pumped with hers,
big, long strokes that he thrust into.

Is that right? she wanted to ask. Is that right?

His fingers tweaked at her, rubbing and probing. "You like
that, don't you?"

"Yes." Her breath came in a suffocating gasp, and she felt
him smile.

"Good. Yes. There's nothing bloody like it."

Mattie felt nothing. She had never felt anything with the boys outside the dance halls, or in the back row of the cinema either.

Suddenly John pulled the pillows down from behind their heads. He thrust them under Mattie's hips, lifting her into the air. She felt stripped and exposed and tried to roll aside, but he bent his head over her, probing with his tongue. Mattie tried to respond. She screwed her eyes up so tightly that stars exploded behind her eyelids. John leaned over the side of the bed and fumbled in his dressing gown pocket. He unrolled the rubber over himself and balanced over her on all fours.

You can do what you want, Mattie repeated childishly inside her starry head. *I don't mind. You can do what you want.*

He pushed her legs so far apart that the tendons strained in her groin. Then he took hold of himself with his fist and guided it into her. He did it quite gently, but Mattie felt the resistance inside her, and the pressure of him jabbing in and down. There was a sharp tear and she yelled out, an aggrieved shout of pain.

John held himself still.

"Jesus Christ. Is this your first time?"

She nodded blindly. "I'm sorry."

He took her face in his hands and kissed it, rubbing her mouth with his lips. "You should have told me, you bloody silly girl. Oh, Mattie."

His gentleness salved her a little, but he seemed to forget it quite quickly. He began to saw up and down inside her, all the way in and then almost out again. Mattie felt nothing. The soft, melting, warm-watery sensations that her father gave her when they were alone in the house together were all that Mattie knew. And she had buried those feelings so deeply and defensively that it would take more than John Douglas to disinter them.

It seemed to go on for a long time. The weight of him ground against her hip bones, and her soft membranes felt bruised and assaulted. Mattie concentrated on his thick white shoulders sheeny with sweat, on the creases in his neck, and the tufts of gray hair that sprouted from his ears.

He began to move faster, his breath coming in hoarse gasps. He went rigid and shouted out, "Jesus," and then gave a long, wailing cry. Mattie was afraid for him, and then she realized that it was all over. She held his head between her hands, supporting him until he stopped thrashing over her.

Milky silence folded over the room, and they lay limply in the knotted blankets.

There, Mattie thought. *I was right. It didn't matter.*

She thought that John had fallen asleep again, but he lifted his head to look at her. "I wish you'd told me that you were a virgin."

"It doesn't matter," she whispered.

His face looked different, she noticed. Softer, perhaps.

"You made me very happy this morning, Mattie Banner," John said.

She smiled then, a quick flickering smile, but she felt warmer inside.

"Good," Mattie said.

They lay comfortably together, listening to the world moving outside. It was nice, Mattie thought, to share a moment like this. Private, just to themselves. John reached for his cigarettes and lit one for each of them, fitting Mattie's between her fingers for her. She inhaled deeply, knowingly. She felt wiser, almost happy.

"John?" she asked suddenly.

"Mmm?"

"Did you go to bed with Jennifer Edge?"

A laugh rumbled in his chest, under her ear. "Yes. Everyone did, it was more or less obligatory. I'm not sure about Doris and Ada."

Mattie laughed, too, but the little glow of warmth faded. She could cope with his Burford wife. But Jennifer Edge, whom she had never seen and cared nothing about, she made a difference. She put Mattie herself into perspective. One in a line. It probably went with the job.

She tried to banter. "What? Lenny too?"

"Almost certainly."

It was hard to laugh. Mattie saw the room again. Green and brown, hideous in the livid winter daylight. She butted out her cigarette in the tin ashtray beside the bed.

"I should be at the theater now."

"Come here for one more minute."

He put his thick arms around her and pulled her closer. The woolly hairs on his chest crinkled against her skin.

"Jennifer's nothing like you, you know. You're a nice girl, Mattie." He kissed her thoroughly, and when he let her go again Mattie said softly, "I used to be a nice girl."

They both laughed then. Mattie took the opportunity to slide out of bed. She put her crumpled clothes on and combed her hair in front of the greenish mirror.

"I'll see you later, my love, at the theater," John said.

"Of course."

Mattie walked down through the Air-Wick-pungent hotel and out through the front door. Nobody shouted an accusation after her. The sea was puckered and steel-gray, but she didn't stop to look at it. She turned into the town toward the theater. Women with shopping bags passed her, and errand boys on bicycles.

They must all be able to see, Mattie thought. I know they can tell what I've been doing. She held her head up. It doesn't matter. It's happened, that's all. She felt very lonely, and she longed to tell Julia. Not in a letter. Not after the weeks of silence that she had allowed to slip by.

She would have to wait until Christmas. Two weeks until the company disbanded for the Christmas break.

Everyone in the company knew at once. Vera took her aside when she reached the theater. "Where were you last night? I was so worried."

"Were you? I went out to dinner with John," Mattie said deliberately. "Someone else stood him up."

Vera's eyes and mouth made three amazed circles. She scuttled away as soon as she could to spread the news.

It turned out to be a short-lived sensation. Everyone was used to the permutations of company lovers, and when the brief flurry of interest died down, Mattie discovered the effects were that the actors treated her more circumspectly and Sheila Firth adopted her as a kind of ally. Only Fergus and Alan didn't share their jokes quite as generously, and Lenny didn't expect her to be a friend now that she had John Douglas.

At the next treasury call Vera handed her a separate envelope with her wages. It contained exactly seven guineas in notes and silver and Mattie was puzzled until she remembered that it was the price of a coat in the middle display window of the High Street department store. John Douglas must have seen it too. Mattie went to look at it again before the Saturday matinee. It was green tweed with big flaps and pockets, and when she tried it on she looked like a farmer. She chose a black cloth coat instead. It had a big black fake-fur collar that framed her face, and a wide black patent belt. It was cheaper than the green tweed, and she spent the rest of the money on a pair of black suede gloves.

Mattie put on her new finery and went in to the theater

office to see John. He frowned at her through the smoke of his cigarette and muttered, "You look like a bloody tart. But that's your business, I suppose. Is it warm enough?"

"It's lovely and warm. Thank you."

"Vera'll take ten bob a week out of your wages until it's paid for."

Mattie couldn't help laughing.

The two weeks went by and there were carol singers outside the shops, and strings of colored light bulbs hung bravely from the streetlamps. Mattie had warned herself not to expect anything from John Douglas, but she was softened by his brusque affection. Sometimes he put his arm around her, almost absentmindedly, or touched her hair, as if he liked the feel of her for herself and not just for sex. He took her to bed in his salesman's hotels, too, of course, and she submitted to it because it mattered to him.

The best thing was the way that he talked to her, about books and opera as well as the theater. Mattie listened thirstily.

The last week ended and she did the get-out with a mixture of relief and regret. The scenery and props were going into storage until the tour started up again. There was an impromptu Christmas party for the whole company in the corner pub beyond the theater. Mattie played darts and drank Guinness, and laughed at John's stories, which he performed for the benefit of everyone in the bar.

She felt that she had come a long way.

She had bought and wrapped a Christmas present for John. It was a book about opera, and she was hoping to impress him with her clever choice. But the afternoon ended, the company separated on a wave of boozy comradeship, and John drove her to the station in the Vanguard without producing a present for her. Mattie kept the book hidden.

He said good-bye absently. Mattie knew that he already belonged to Burford and not to her at all, and she accepted the knowledge uncomplainingly. John kissed her and opened the car door.

There was one thing, a kind of present.

"When you get back," he said, "we'll look at a bit part for you."

The black car bucked away and Mattie went smiling to the London train.

SEVEN

Julia was waiting at Euston.

Before the train pulled in she stood in front of the bookstall staring at the models' faces on the magazine covers. They were shined up for Christmas with glossy lipstick and bouffant hair, and as she looked at them and heard a Salvation Army band playing carols she felt that everyone was full of excitement and expectation, and that everything was in motion, except herself.

Josh had gone somewhere for Christmas, only promising "See you in the new year." Julia turned irritably away from the magazines and paced up and down the station concourse. Sometimes she thought she hated Josh, but even when she hated him she longed for him so intensely that her stomach writhed and she twisted her head to and fro to escape the pain of it.

Mattie's train pulled in and Julia turned in relief to the barrier. The passengers poured out, their faces bobbing as they jostled toward the ticket collector. Julia didn't recognize Mattie at first, and then when she glanced back at her face, and it sharpened, coming into focus, she thought, *Mattie's changed too.* She had been looking forward to her company almost desperately, and she felt an instant of resentful disappointment. Then the crowd surged forward and deposited Mattie in front of her. Mattie dropped her suitcase and flung her arms out, and then they were hugging each other, hopping and swaying and laughing. Mattie still smelled the same. Coty perfume and a faint whiff of cigarette smoke.

"You look different," Julia accused her, and Mattie grinned and fluffed up her fake fur collar.

"Must be the new coat. Do you like it?"

"I don't know." She grabbed her arm and pulled. "Come on, let's get the bus. Then we can talk."

They ran, and when they reached the bus they clambered up to the top deck. They squashed into the front seat and lit cigarettes, exactly as they had hundreds of times on the way home from school. The familiarity of it, and the pleasure of seeing each other, dissolved Julia's resentment and the new worldliness that Mattie was rather proud of. At once they were back on the old footing.

"What has happened?" Julia asked.

"Guess." Mattie's eyes were wickedly sparkling.

"You . . ."

"Yes, I have."

"Mattie." Julia's head jerked around to see who was listening. She pressed even closer and then implored her, "Tell me. Tell me what it was like."

Mattie tilted her head against the black fur and pursed her lips, as if she were considering it. At last, judiciously, she said, "It was all right."

Julia thought of Josh, and the cottage, and the brief, blurred glimpse she had been allowed of something that was momentously strange, and different, and important. And then she exploded. "All right?"

Mattie was half-laughing, but she was serious too. "Exactly. It wasn't wonderful. But it wasn't awful either."

Julia took her hand in the black suede glove and held it tightly. "Tell me. Tell me about him, for a start."

Mattie smiled. "He's nothing like Josh," she began.

Then, while the bus jolted and swayed down Gower Street, Mattie told her. She described Room Thirteen and the tall brown furniture, and the smell of Air-Wick. She told Julia about the theater office and Sheila Firth and the burgundy in the restaurant, and about John Douglas's rubber-tipped stick and the moment of tenderness when he had licked the sea salt off her face. She also described the warmth and comfort she had felt the next morning, afterward, when they lay quietly together. She didn't say anything about how she had felt when she had asked about Jennifer Edge.

Julia nodded at everything, but she was clearly still waiting. "But what did it feel like?" she ventured at last, when Mattie didn't volunteer it.

Mattie tried for the words. She knew what Julia was expecting. Like fireworks going off. Like a waterfall. Waves breaking. Something like that. What she had really felt was so far from any of those things that she couldn't even manage to make it up.

"I told you," she said softly. "It was all right."

They stared at each other for a minute, resignation confronting disbelief.

Julia whispered anxiously, "Is he . . . is he nice to you?"

Mattie held up the hem of her coat. "Sometimes. But do

you know what? He's going to give me a part. That's what I really want. . . ."

Julia snorted with laughter and put her arm around Mattie's shoulder. Mattie laughed too.

"Oh, Mat, I'm so happy you're home."

"I'm happy to be home."

"I thought you were different. But you aren't."

"Do you know, on the first morning I thought it must be written on my face. I walked past everyone thinking, *They all know. They can see.*"

They laughed so much then that all the other passengers stared at them. Julia rubbed the condensation off the window with her sleeve and peered out.

"Oxford Street. Hurry up, Felix is making you a wonderful dinner."

The flat over the square was warm and welcoming.

"Home," Mattie murmured.

Jessie was immobile in her corner, and her clothes compressed the flesh beneath into swollen ridges. It was an effort for her to reach up and plant one of her resounding kisses on Mattie's cheek, but the Christmas tree that Julia and Felix had bought and decorated glowed beside her, and the soft light made her look rosy.

"Are you all right, Jessie?"

"As right as I'll ever be. Give us another kiss. What's your news, then?"

"Lots of news. I'm going to be an actress."

"That's what they call it?"

Felix materialized from his room, like a shadow in his black jersey. He kissed Mattie, too, brushing her cheek with his mouth. She looked older, he thought, as if some experience had rubbed off on her. That made him glance at Julia, and for the hundredth time he noticed her gnawing impatience. Julia hadn't had Mattie's luck, whatever that was.

"Felix? Get some glasses, there's a duck. It's Christmas."

Felix went into the kitchen for a bottle of wine and a corkscrew. At least it was easier to live here with Julia when her aviator was away. *He isn't mine,* Julia had once snapped viciously when Felix said that. *Why do you call him mine?*

He isn't mine either, Felix might have answered. But he said nothing and Julia had stood up, walking to the door and then twisting back again in the confined space. It was better at times like this when Josh wasn't here, although Felix still thought about him. He thought about airplanes too, imagining flying at night and the pilot's face lit up by the red glow of the instrument panel.

As he tore the cap off the wine and twisted the point of the corkscrew downward, Felix heard the women laughing. Jessie wheezed and coughed delightedly, and then Mattie said something that set off a fresh burst of laughter.

Carefully, Felix eased the cork out and wiped the neck of the bottle with a clean cloth. He felt the women's mysterious femininity as solid as a wall.

The next day, Christmas Eve, Mattie put the presents she had bought for Ricky and Sam and Marilyn and Phil into a string bag. There were presents for Rozzie and her husband and the babies, too, even something for Ted, and the red and gold paper bulged cheerfully through the netting.

"I'm going home to see them all," Mattie told Julia. "Are you coming?"

"I have to work today. The bloody office doesn't close until four o'clock."

There would be mince pies, and the managers would come into the typing pool to wish them all a Merry Christmas. Julia was dreading it.

"We could go after you finish."

Julia had been thinking about Fairmile Road. Christmases there were easy enough to remember, although she couldn't distinguish between any of them once she had stopped believing in Father Christmas. Betty and Vernon didn't have close relatives or friends, and the celebrations had only ever involved the three of them. Julia had opened her presents beside the tree, with Betty and Vernon watching her. Once that was done, it was hard to know how to keep the festive atmosphere going right through into evening. There was church, and Christmas dinner afterward. Vernon always put on the paper hat out of his cracker and read the mottoes and riddles aloud. After Christmas tea, when the red and brown plaster robin and the tiny metal-spined Christmas tree had been taken off the cake and stored away until next year, it felt like any other day. Julia went up to her bedroom and read her new Bunty annual, and dreamed of lavish, exotically scented, faintly Victorian family Christmases with plump mothers and twinkling fathers and broods of children who played charades after supper. Later there would be dancing around a towering tree decorated with real candles.

Sentimentally now, Julia wondered if she had a real family somewhere, preparing for the kind of Christmas she had dreamed of as a child. Did her real mother think of the daughter who should have been there, as she watched the dancers around the tree?

"It's all right," she said to Mattie. "You go."

Julia had bought a pretty blouse for Betty using her staff discount at the store, and a camel-colored cashmere scarf for Vernon, and she had wrapped and posted them in good time.

She had written to Betty, too, in the weeks since Mattie had gone away, almost as many times as she had written to Mattie herself. But she didn't want to go back to Fairmile Road. Not yet. Certainly not for Christmas. She remembered the silence in the house, that heavy silence that was unlike quietness anywhere else, and Vernon wearing a purple paper crown.

Julia leaned over quickly to turn the wireless up louder. The music was Dickie Valentine's "Christmas Alphabet." She whistled the tune and ran to finish getting ready for work.

Mattie went home by herself. It was a relief to find that although the house on the estate was cold and chaotically filthy, the boys seemed to be living safely enough with their father. Ricky looked taller. He talked about when he would leave school and find a job, and he told Mattie that Ted had fallen down drunk on the path late one night, and he and Sam had hauled him in and put him to bed between them.

"Ricky . . ." Mattie began, wanting to say something as an excuse for their father and as a warning, but Ricky cut her short.

"Stupid bugger, isn't he? That's all. But he can't help it. And we couldn't leave him out there to freeze to death, could we?"

Mattie nodded, and then laughed. "I don't think I need to worry about you, Rick."

" 'Course you don't. I need to worry about you, more like. How are you doing?"

"Getting along. So slowly you'd hardly notice, but I think I can see the way now." John Douglas seemed surprisingly distant. Mattie told herself that that was all right because he certainly wasn't thinking much about her either. "You'll see my name in lights in the end."

"When I do, I'll expect you to buy me a guitar."

"Pleasure. In the meantime, you'll have to make do with a Billy Haley record."

Mattie went on to see Roz.

The children swarmed ecstatically over her, and Rozzie eyed the black coat. The new baby lay in his pram and Mattie hung over it, slotting her finger into his minute fist to feel the surprising strength of his grip. The baby's unwinking dark eyes stared up into hers. Mattie wanted to scoop him up and wrap him against her body.

"He's so lovely. Can I pick him up?"

Rozzie shrugged. "If you want. Mind he's not sick on your fur. Feeling broody, are you?"

"I love babies. Just smell him." She rubbed her face against his downy head.

Rozzie lit a cigarette. "You could have one. All you need is a man."

The baby kicked in Mattie's arms and nuzzled against her breast. Mattie felt the pull of it, underneath her stomach. "They're easy enough to come by," she said flippantly, hiding her feelings.

Rozzie turned her attention to the coat again. "I can see that."

Mattie stayed for tea, and saw that Marilyn and Phil were as uncontrollable as any children on Christmas Eve. They looked taller too. They bathed the baby between them, demonstrating self-importantly to Mattie, and Marilyn gave him his bottle.

"Bed," Rozzie said, and they went, wanting the morning to come quicker. They included Mattie in the general good nights, just. She saw that they didn't need her, or miss her very much.

"I thought I'd go and have a Christmas drink with Dad," she said to Rozzie.

"Good luck to you."

Mattie found her father in the nearest of the four barnlike pubs that served the estate. There were colored-paper streamers and tinsel shapes suspended everywhere, and a pianist was playing "Rudolph the Red-Nosed Reindeer," but the crowded room seemed bleak after the cozy, firelit corner pubs that Mattie had frequented in the last weeks with John and the others.

I've gotten away, Mattie thought exultantly. *I've done it.*

Ted was sitting at a beer-ringed table near the piano. He greeted her with a mixture of surprise and awkward familiarity. He was only half-drunk. Mattie bought him a pint of beer with the money that Vera had handed her at the last treasury call—minus the ten shillings that she owed for the coat. She sat beside Ted and told him about what she was doing, watching his face as he drank. She wasn't afraid of him anymore, she realized. Even when she talked about John Douglas, the old, terrifying, bleary jealousy didn't swell up at her. She thought that it must be because she had walked clean out of his world. Her father's view was limited. He couldn't be jealous or angry about what he didn't know or understand.

They had another drink, and Ted's eyes lost their wandering focus. A man pushed up to the table, and Ted pulled at his sleeve. They hardly knew each other, but they fell on each other like old friends. Five minutes later their arms were around each other's shoulders and they were reminiscing about the best days of the war. Mattie listened for a little longer, and then she stood up. She bent down and kissed her father on the gray stubble that masked his mottled cheeks. His head sawed up and down and he proclaimed to his friend, "Kids today. They know nothing."

"You're right, Teddy," the friend answered.

Mattie walked to the station and caught the last train back to London.

It was a warm, cramped, happy Christmas in the flat over the square. Felix had money from his decorating work, and he had bought smoked salmon and crystallized fruits and baskets of nuts as well as a goose. He had also made red felt Christmas stockings for Jessie and Mattie and Julia, and in the morning they found them at the end of their beds. Inside the stockings there were tiny bottles of scent and little tablets of soap, and sheer nylons and fanciful earrings that he had made himself from beads and feathers bought from the little haberdashers down Berwick Street Market.

Julia fixed her earrings on and turned her head to and fro.

"You are clever, Felix. How do you know about so many things?"

"I use my eyes," Felix said mildly. "Those earrings suit you."

He was pleased with the plain silk handkerchiefs that Julia had bought him from Liberty's. The electric-blue Teddy-boy socks from Mattie were less well received.

"Have you ever seen me wearing anything of the kind? You don't use your eyes, Mattie."

"They're supposed to be a joke."

Felix looked amazed. "Who wants to look like a joke? And while we're on the subject, that coat of yours . . ."

"I like it," Mattie said in a voice that invited no argument.

"Your present's the best of the lot, my duck," Jessie said,

putting it on to prove her point. Mattie had found it in a crumbling second-hand clothes shop in Nottingham. It was a hat, and when she bought it it was still enveloped in yellowing tissue paper in its round black hatbox. It was a little shell of black velvet with sequined wings and quivering ostrich feathers, the whole creation swathed around and around with spotted veiling and skewered with an enormous pearl-handled hatpin. As soon as Jessie put it on, tilting it instinctively over one eye, she was transformed into a risqué Edwardian grande dame.

Julia and Mattie clapped with delight, and Felix murmured, "That was a better choice."

Later, Felix retired to the kitchen to cook. Julia put her head around the door and asked, "Can I help?"

Felix nodded, and they worked side by side, enjoying a silent companionship that had been missing since the arrival of Josh. In Jessie's room, Mattie and Jessie began by singing carols, and under the influence of Jessie's vodka soon moved on to the old music hall favorites. The two voices competed gleefully for the top notes. It was already dark outside when they sat down to their Christmas dinner. Jessie ate only one or two mouthfuls of goose, but she presided majestically over the table, lifting her glass and setting the wings and feathers of her hat quivering with her wheezy laughter.

Felix brought the pudding in, set in a nimbus of blue flame. They pulled crackers and unwrapped their paper hats. Watching Felix with his yellow crown pulled down over his dark olive forehead, Julia thought that he looked like a real king. He would never look ridiculous, like Vernon, even in a paper hat. Narrowing her eyes so that the candlelight softened into a golden blur over Jessie's hat and Mattie's anarchic hair, Julia breathed in the scents of tangerines and brandy and candle wax. At last she had come close to the Christmases she dreamed of in Fairmile Road.

Only Jessie had drunk too much.

Sometimes, when she was drinking, Jessie drifted away until her memories became more real than her solid room around her.

"I was thinking about *my* first time. I was just as old as you. Like Mattie here, with her theater man. I don't like the sound of him, dear. I told you, didn't I?"

"You told me," Mattie repeated, but Jessie ignored her.

"Your first one should be young, and handsome. Prince Charming, for you to dream about afterward when they've all turned old and useless, like yourself. Julia's boy is one, isn't he?

And if not him, then somebody else. There's plenty of them. Like my Felix.''

Felix stood up, as silent and elegant as a black cat.

"I'm going for a walk," he said softly. "I need some air. Julia and Mattie will look after you." As he slipped out of the door, they heard him say "Happy Christmas."

"I remember the day," Jessie repeated. "I was still living with my ma and pa. It was Hartscombe Terrace, Hoxton. I was working in the market, singing at nights in the clubs. They were good days. I met Tommy Last and we started walking out together. He took me to the Empire. Up west, on the train. Walking, under the trees in the park. Black hair, he had, smooth as glass. Black eyes, too, and a little mustache that tickled your skin when you kissed. This day, he came for me, and he'd brought me a bunch of marigolds in white paper. They were so bright and hot, like the day itself. We walked down by the canal, and Tommy was in his shirt-sleeves with his arm around my waist. I remember how hard his arm seemed, and the black hairs on it. We walked under a bridge and it was cool, all shadowy, and then we came out into the sunshine again. We climbed up the bank a little way and sat down, and there were bushes and tall grass all around us. No one could see we were there. There was only the grass stalks, and the sun over our heads. Tommy pushed my skirt up. I helped him. I was wearing white drawers with blue satin ribbon that I'd threaded myself. I thought I was the Queen of England, and I lay down in the grass with Tommy Last on top of me. That mustache. It felt like silk against my neck."

Mattie was looking away, into the candlelight. She said nothing, and it was Julia who asked, "What was it like?"

Jessie laughed, her old rich chuckle. "It only lasted about two minutes. Tommy Last wasn't much more than a boy, even though he seemed a man to me. But I knew then that there would be nothing else like it. Nothing like that day, even though the best times came afterward."

They were quiet for a moment. Jessie was staring ahead of her, and Julia and Mattie knew that she was seeing the grass shelter and the blue sky, and Tommy Last's face, darkened by the sun behind his head, bending over her.

"What happened to him?" Mattie asked.

Jessie shook her head. "What happened to any of them? Like that bunch of marigolds. I can see them now, orange petals in the white paper. But they're gone, aren't they?" Her eyelids drooped and then closed. "I had so many good times. So many." They thought she had gone to sleep, but after a moment her eyes flicked open again and she pointed at Julia. "Make sure you enjoy your own times."

"I will," Julia said, but Jessie frowned.

"All your talk about freedom. Then you go and make your own bars for yourself. Shutting yourself in for that boy. He's almost the first one you've seen, so don't mope for him. Enjoy him and then forget him, or just forget him. Like I did." She smiled then, lacing her fingers over her stomach.

Mattie looked sideways at Julia. Her face was hollowed with shadows, and the bones sharp with hunger. *Jessie's right,* Mattie thought. *Bloody Josh.*

But Julia didn't move. "I can't help it," she said sadly.

Mattie reached out for her hand and held it. They sat silently beside Jessie's chair, listening to her breathing thicken into snores and with the glassed-in faces of her photographs staring down at them. Much later, when the candles had burned out, they lifted her up between them and settled her in her bed.

In Fairmile Road Vernon had locked the doors and closed the windows. He stood in the doorway waiting, but Betty still sat in her armchair.

"I'll go on up, then," Vernon said, fingering the bookmark in his library book.

She listened to his footsteps going up the stairs, and heard the floorboards creak as he passed overhead. Betty was staring at the Christmas tree. It was an artificial one that she brought out every year and decorated with fairy lights in the shape of Chinese lanterns. It stood on the table in front of the window, and Betty knew that if she half-closed her eyes, the lights would blur prettily and the tree would look almost real. She remembered Julia kneeling beside it to tear the paper off her doll's house. They had given it to her the year the war ended, so Julia would have been six then.

It was so quiet.

The kitchen was clean and tidy after their meal, Betty had seen to that. Behind the wire-mesh door of the meat safe, the remains of the turkey sat waiting for her. It was too big, of course. They had made hardly any impression on the splintery white meat. There would be cold for tomorrow, and a pie for the day after. Then rissoles, and soup from the bones.

Meals, Betty thought. To be cooked, and eaten with Ver-

non's newspaper folded beside his plate, and cleared up afterward. She saw herself, suddenly, as a caged rodent pattering a
circuit between the cupboards, the table, the sink, and back to
the cupboards again. The thought made her flush with quick,
uncomfortable anger. She stood up and went to the window
behind the Christmas tree, pulling the curtain aside to look out.
The rooftops of the other houses, identical to her own, just
showed against the sky. Some of the windows stood out as
patches of orangy light, but most of them were already dark.
Behind the dark windows people were asleep. The last steps of
her own circuit for the day remained to be taken. She would pull
the plugs from the sockets, as Vernon liked her to do, and turn
off the lights. Wash her face in the clean bathroom, and lie down
beside her husband in their bed. He wouldn't reach out to touch
her, nor would she reach her hand out and let it rest against his
solid, obdurate warmth.

Betty's face was still burning with her anger.

If she were to walk out of the house now, in the middle of
this quiet darkness, she wouldn't have to go on making her
worthless circular loops through the days. She leaned forward
and let her forehead rest against the glass. It was wet with
condensation and the coldness soothed her, and then sobered her.
Betty had the impression of roads radiating away from her,
crossing and recrossing, spreading into a vast unmapped and
unknowable territory.

There was nowhere for her to go, of course. She knew that
at once. She was Betty Smith, almost fifty, a wife and mother,
and that was all. Not even those things anymore, in truth.

She put her hand up to her throat, easing the collar of her
new blouse. It was pretty, but Julia had bought a very small size,
as if her mother had already shrunk in her recollection.

But Julia had gotten away, Betty thought. She straightened
up and let the curtain fall back into place. For the first time since
Julia had gone, the weight of Betty's bitterness and loss shifted a
little. Julia had gone because she was young and careless, and
because she needed to. Suddenly, oddly, standing there beside
the artificial tree that Julia had always complained about, Betty
felt the comfort of pride, and relief. Julia's life would be different, at least. Betty saw the bizarre flat over the square, the fat
woman and her half-caste son, and even Mattie Banner, in a new
perspective.

The unexpectedness of it made her smile.

Betty sniffed sharply and turned away from the Christmas

tree. She went carefully around the room unplugging the tree lights and the wireless, and then she turned off the main light and went up the stairs to bed.

Mattie and Julia, for their different reasons, devoted themselves to having a good time during the rest of Mattie's holiday. They went out every night, to the Rocket or to a party or to jazz pubs, sometimes with Felix but more often just the two of them. In the second week Julia faked a stomach complaint and didn't go to work at all. They sat in Blue Heaven watching the people go by, or wandered through the Oxford Street shops looking at clothes and wishing they were rich. At Jessie's suggestion they made an early-morning excursion to Brick Lane Market. They sifted through the heaps of secondhand clothes and came triumphantly back with ratty fox furs and stained silk blouses and boxy tweed jackets. They dressed up, painted their faces, and pretended they were Marlene Dietrich, and made Felix take them out. They laughed a lot and drank as much as they could afford to, and people turned around in the street to stare after them.

For a few days they were just as they had been before Josh and John Douglas came between them. With Mattie, Julia thought, with Mattie's laughter and mimicry and boldness to arm her, she could even bear to be without Josh.

But then the time came for the Headline company to reassemble. Julia had treacherously been praying that he would not, but Francis Willoughby had agreed to let Mattie continue with the company. The tour was to restart in Chester, and there was a second enactment of the Euston departure. This time Josh wasn't there. Julia waved Mattie off on her way to become an actress and went back to her typing.

Julia would have felt less sharply jealous if she could have witnessed Mattie's return to the theater. John Douglas was liverish after his holiday and he berated Mattie, along with everyone else, for bloody unprofessionalism.

It was two days before she dared to remind him of his promise, and his response was withering.

But then, slowly, routine reestablished itself and the company temper improved. One afternoon, sitting in the chilly theater, Mattie felt the weight of his arm drop around her shoulder. He pushed the weight of her hair back from her neck and mumbled, "I'm sorry to bawl at you, love. This company's a damned shambles, but it's not your fault."

Mattie went to bed with him because he seemed to expect it

of her and because she didn't know what else to do. He did it very thoroughly but without the tenderness that had touched her at the beginning. It occurred to her that it was just something else that she did for him now, like bringing him whiskey when he did the money on Friday afternoons.

But he gave her a part.

It was ten lines as a daffy debutante in *Welcome Home*. The actress who had been doubling it made a fuss, but to Mattie's relief John Douglas stood firm.

"Give her a chance, or she'll go on nagging the balls off everyone."

She learned the lines and worked for hours on what she imagined was a cut-glass accent.

In Blackpool, a week later, she went on for the first time.

When she came off she was shaking and the palms of her hands were hot and wet.

Fergus and Alan kissed her and congratulated her, but it was John's approval she wanted. By a great effort of will she stopped herself from searching him out there and then, but when she saw him leaning against the bar in the pub afterward, she couldn't help herself. She pushed through the crowd to him and blurted out, "John? Did you see me? Was I all right?"

His gray eyes appraised her. "You were just that. All right."

Mattie flushed. What more had she expected? She nodded, and went back to her place. But she had done it. She had made her professional debut, and she could live without praise if she had to.

EIGHT

The February rain fell like a thick, cold veil. Julia stepped outside reluctantly with a group of other homeward-bound typists who giggled and turned up their collars and skittered away toward the bus stop. The gutters were gray, pock-marked lakes, and the traffic plowed through them to send plumes of water over the crowded sidewalks. The rain immediately pasted Julia's bangs flat to her forehead and poked intrusively into her face.

She had no umbrella and she turned sharply away from the streaming, dun-colored mess of Oxford Street and began the walk home.

The little streets along her route were already taking on the closed-up, sullen air of winter nights. As she passed the corner greengrocers where she sometimes bought vegetables, the green wooden shutters rolled down with a clatter. The shopkeeper ducked out to lock them and the rain made dark spots on the shoulder of his smock. He rushed back into the shop without glancing at Julia. Her shoes were filling with water, and she walked faster, trying to dodge the biggest puddles.

The shop on the next corner was still open, and in the steamy neon brightness inside she bought milk and bread and cheese, and felt her spirits lifting. She thought of reaching home and putting on dry clothes, making a pot of tea and taking a cup in to Jessie. Perhaps Felix would be home, and she would lean against the kitchen cupboard to watch him prepare a meal. Julia came out with her bag of shopping and saw that the liquor store opposite was just opening for the evening. It seemed to contradict the soaking, shrinking mood of the night so positively that she marched across and bought a bottle of red wine for Felix. She chose at random from the shelves and paid over her shillings cheerfully. She hurried the length of the last streets and into the square, humming to defy the cold and the rain.

She thought of Josh as she passed under the dripping trees, but all her longings were fixed on being warm and dry and the yearning slipped away again.

On the dingy stairs she met the last office worker on the way out. She was an anxious-looking middle-aged woman, always the last to go. Julia brushed past her, nodding, and heard her locking doors on her way down.

The black door of the flat loomed on the landing above her. With a grateful rush she took the last stairs two at a time and reached it, panting, raindrops rolling from her hair and coat and spattering unseen on the dusty floor.

Julia unlocked the door and pushed it open.

It was dark and quiet inside. Jessie didn't usually sleep in the early evening. Julia wasn't afraid of disturbing her.

She called out, "I'm home. Hello, I'm home."

Jessie's room was in darkness, and the streetlight from the square seeped into a dull, orange glow on the cracked ceiling. As she turned in the doorway Julia heard water running. Jessie was in the bathroom. A line of light showed under the door. Julia went into the kitchen and unpacked her shopping, then crossed to her own room and stripped off her wet clothes. She turned on the electric fire and warmed her feet, then leaned forward to rub her hair dry. It steamed as she combed her fingers through it, and the brittle heat from the red bar made her cheeks smart. When she was warm all through, Julia pulled on slacks and a sweater, and stuck her feet into her slippers.

The flat was still quiet except for the sound of running water.

She had almost reached the kitchen when it struck her that it had been running for a long time.

If Jessie was taking a bath, it would be full by now. Julia turned back and put her hand out to the bathroom door. She felt the grainy wood of the panels under her fingertips. The bath water was running, but it had a peculiar double resonance. It took Julia a second to realize that it was splashing too. Spilling over the side of something.

"Jessie?"

The water noise seemed to have grown louder. It drowned her voice.

"Jessie, are you all right?"

Julia thumped on the door. There was no answer, except the water.

"Jessie."

Julia went on shouting, but her shoulder was already against the door. Inside her head she could see the other side of it. The door was painted white, Felix must have done that. There was a little chrome-plated bolt screwed to it. Only four tiny screws holding it in place. Nothing substantial. The door creaked under her weight, protesting, but the lock didn't give. Why had Jessie locked it, alone in the flat? Julia rattled the knob, turning it to and fro. Then she looked down. She saw the dark finger run out beneath the door, then spread into a fist shape. The water was reaching out to her. The sight of it gave her terrified strength. She leaned away from the door and then flung all her weight against it. There was a shudder as the screws were torn out of the wooden frame and the door collapsed inward. Julia fell into the bathroom, where the water was running from the taps, spilling over the side of the tub and washing over the floor.

Jessie was in the tub. Julia saw mountainous, veined flesh and floating sparse gray hair. Her face was gray and purple, and it was under the moving skin of water. The noise of the water was deafening, like a terrible waterfall, thundering in the wet white space.

Julia stumbled backward, a single step. Her eyes clenched themselves shut and her knuckles were crammed against her teeth, stifling a scream. It was no more than a second before she opened her eyes again; Jessie was still lying there, under the water, her hair moving tranquilly around her head like seaweed fronds.

Julia began to move at last through the waves of shock. She stooped to the taps and turned them off. Water still slopped over the side of the bath, soaking her legs. She plunged her arms into the tub, locking her hands behind Jessie's shoulders, straining to lift her up. Julia grunted and her feet slid on the slippery floor. She could hear herself whispering, "Come on, Jessie. Sit up, Jessie. Sit up, please, won't you?"

The huge weight shifted a little with her efforts and the bath plug on its chain was wrenched out of the plughole. The water gurgled and drained quickly away, and Jessie was left supported in Julia's arms. Julia heaved at her, imagining that she would lift her out of the bath and lay her on the floor so that she could tend to her. But Jessie's wet skin only sucked against hers, and the weight of her didn't move again.

Gasping and sobbing with fear and panic and exertion, Julia let her fall backward again against the slope of the bath. Jessie's face turned upward with tendrils of hair stuck to her cheeks. Her mouth hung open a little, like a yawn.

Without looking into the eyes Julia understood that she was dead.

She knelt down helplessly in the wet and groped for Jessie's hand. Her skin already felt cold, and Julia's tears that ran down her face and on to Jessie seemed hot enough to burn.

"Oh, Jessie. I'm sorry. I'm so sorry."

She knelt there, holding the cold hand and crying.

After what seemed like a long time, Julia replaced Jessie's hand by her side and stood up stiffly.

"I'll have to go for some help," she whispered.

She turned then, and ran. The movement thawed her and made her heart thump in her chest, and she cursed her own slowness, even though she was dully certain that Jessie was dead and nothing or no one could help her however fast she ran.

The floors of offices were silent, and their telephones were securely locked behind unyielding doors. Julia ran out into the rain again, her sodden clothes flapping as she ran. There were people in the square, but she ran past them, unseeing. She reached the scarlet rectangle of the telephone kiosk on the corner and listened to the quiet burr of the dial tone.

When she had given the details and she knew that the ambulance was coming, she let her head fall sideways and rest against the streaming glass. There was a pain in her chest and her breath was ragged and her legs felt as if they would dissolve beneath her.

So much running and shouting and struggling, and yet Jessie was dead. As the first dim understanding of finality touched her, Julia thought of Felix. She didn't want him to come in and find his mother lying like that in the bath, in all her huge and painful vulnerability. Julia was running again, back across the square and up the dark, gaping flights of empty stairs. There was no one there, still, except Jessie.

Julia gathered up towels and brought them in a heap to the side of the bath. She folded one and put it behind the wet, heavy head like a pillow. She draped the others over Jessie's body, tucking them in like a mother with a child. The tears ran down her face, but she went on working without stopping to wipe them away.

Jessie's face wasn't like Jessie now, but Julia left it uncovered. She couldn't hide her, as though she weren't a part of the world any longer.

When the job was done, Julia sat down to wait. She was wet to the skin and shivering, but she felt that she couldn't leave Jessie alone, not now. She thought about the boy with a bunch of marigolds who had come looking for Jessie on a hot summer's afternoon.

At last the doorbell rang. She stood up stiffly and went to open the door to help that was much too late. The men came up the stairs in their uniforms and Julia showed them where Jessie was lying. They bent over her and Julia turned away. She went and stood in the kitchen, still in her wet clothes, looking out at Felix's earthenware flowerpots in the angle of the roof. He would be home soon. Julia closed her eyes and clenched her fists, thinking about him, and then she heard his light, quick footsteps on the stairs.

She met him at the door, and saw his face. "The ambulance?" he asked.

Julia put out her hands and he gripped her arms, frowning at the clammy coldness of her sleeves.

"It's Jessie," she said. He was already looking past her, but into the darkness of Jessie's room. "Felix. She's dead."

There was nothing to soften that. No time for it, no words

that could change anything. Julia wanted to put her arms around him, to comfort him somehow from her own meager stock of comfort, but he put her gently aside.

The ambulance men stood awkwardly in the bathroom doorway. Felix walked past them, going in to his mother, and shut the door behind him.

Jessie had died of a heart attack in the bath. Her weight and the bottles of vodka she had come to depend on had contributed to it, of course. The doctor explained carefully to Julia and Felix when he came to sign the death certificate. They listened, without looking at each other.

Felix made the funeral arrangements. Jessie had left no instructions, but she had once said to Felix, only half-joking, "Make sure there's a party when I go. All the old faces, if there are any left by then."

They buried Jessie in a bleak, windswept north London cemetery. A little group of people, Mr. Mogridge and a handful of others like him, came to the funeral. Mr. French, the property developer, turned up and watched Felix covertly across the heap of raw earth. Felix's face was as expressionless as if it were carved out of wood. Mattie arrived just before the brief ceremony began. John Douglas had given her one day off.

"Do your friends and relatives die regularly?" he had asked her.

"I'm not asking for sympathy because Jessie's dead," Mattie said quietly. It occurred to her at that moment that she was making a mistake in wanting, or needing, to love John Douglas. "I'm just telling you that I'm going to her funeral, whether you say I can or not."

He had looked ashamed just for a moment. "We need you here, that's all," he mumbled. Mattie stood at the graveside, the black fur of her coat collar blowing around her face, holding Julia's hand tightly.

"I'm sorry I wasn't here," she whispered.

"What could you have done?"

"Is Felix all right?"

They didn't look at him.

"I don't know."

The vicar arrived at the graveside, the wind whipping his surplice. The little knot of people bent their heads.

Afterward they went back to the square, leaving the mound of earth in the graveyard fluttering with wet flower petals. More people came to the flat to remember Jessie. Felix had made some food and bought whiskey, and Julia laid out plates and glasses in Jessie's room. The photographs and mementoes crowding the walls already looked faded, as though they belonged to a sad past, although Julia had tidied and polished them.

It was a subdued gathering. They missed Jessie's talk, and her lewd laugh. Too many of them were remembering the other party, the unexpected, joyous one that Mattie and Julia had given for her. Jessie had sung the old favorites, and "Ma, He's Making Eyes at Me." No one tried to sing tonight, even though Freddie Bishop was sitting in the corner with his mouth organ in the pocket of his black coat.

It was very early when people began to leave, in twos and threes, gravely shaking Felix's hand at the door.

At last it was time for Mattie to go and catch the last train north. She hugged them both, wordlessly, and they let her go.

Alone in the flat, Felix and Julia went around picking up empty glasses and clearing dirty plates. They moved past each other considerately, in almost complete silence, as they had been doing ever since Jessie died. It was as if they didn't know what to say to each other now, and were afraid that if they said anything, it might hurt in some way.

Felix picked up an empty whiskey bottle. He stared blindly at the label, and then he groaned and hurled it against the wall. It smashed and glass scattered among Jessie's possessions.

Julia reached out to him, but he evaded her.

"I couldn't even give her the good-bye party she wanted."

Julia heard the bitterness in his voice. "You can't make people behave to order," she said gently. "Jessie could make people want to celebrate just by telling them to have a party. That's what she was good at, not you. We all missed her too much tonight."

"Do you think she knows that?"

Felix had been so controlled up to this moment, but now his loss and bewilderment were clear to Julia.

"Of course she does," she whispered.

Jessie seemed very close, then, in her overfilled room.

Felix nodded, and bent down to pick up the pieces of broken glass. He found another empty bottle on the floor beside Jessie's armchair.

"There's nothing left to drink," he said. "I'd have liked a drink now."

Julia went into the kitchen and took out the bottle of wine

she had bought for him. She carried it back into Jessie's room and held it out, an offering.

"Let's drink this. We'll make our own celebration for her." She saw that Felix was looking at her, a long, careful look.

"Jessie would like that," he said at last.

Wouldn't you? Julia wanted to ask him. *Wouldn't you like it too?* She remembered how she had wanted to comfort him when he came home on that terrible evening. She had been aware then that she had few enough resources to offer him, and she thought now that she didn't know what they needed or wanted from each other.

Julia pushed the confusion of her feelings aside and held out the bottle. "Open it."

They couldn't sit in Jessie's room. They went into Felix's bedroom and perched on the bed. Julia had been in there only rarely, and she was surprised to see the drawings pinned over the mantelpiece. There were the pictures of herself and Mattie that Felix had done when they first moved in, and beside them was the one of the two of them, with Josh, listening to Bill Haley. Felix didn't look at it, and after the first glance Julia kept her head turned away from Josh's.

They both discovered, suddenly, that they were ravenously hungry. Felix went to the kitchen for a loaf of bread and some ham, and they made thick, crumbly sandwiches. The first bottle of wine emptied rapidly, and Felix produced another. The bottle was dusty.

"This is a first-growth claret," he told her. "I was saving it." Then he smiled, one of his rare complete smiles that made the austere angles of his face dissolve. "What better occasion is there than this one?"

Julia smiled back at him. He poured the dark wine into their glasses. Copying him, Julia sniffed it. At first there was nothing, but as the glass warmed in her hand she caught the scent of black currants. They drank, looking at each other. Felix settled the pillows behind them, and they leaned back, their shoulders touching.

"I miss her," he said softly.

"I know."

They didn't talk about Jessie after that.

Julia lay back with her head almost against Felix's shoulder. She looked around his room, at the worktable with papers and drawings spread out under the desk light, at the bookshelves with their art and architecture books. She was thinking how separate he had managed to keep himself, detached from herself and Mattie, even in the confined space of the flat. This sudden closeness would have alarmed her, but for the drowsy elation lent by the wine. She sighed and let her eyes close. A strand of dark hair brushed Felix's mouth.

She seemed very warm, so close to him. He could imagine the weight of her in his arms. The warmth, the solidity of another human being. His loneliness made him feel dry and papery beside Julia's breathing, scented warmth. He took the lock of hair in his fingers and put it between his lips.

They lay very still then.

Until Felix turned his head, almost against his own will. He saw the dark line of her eyelashes, and the fine down on her cheekbone. He leaned down and kissed the corner of her mouth. She lifted her hand, very slowly, and touched his face. The thin skin over his temple was almost the color of violets. The color, and the scent of the wine, blurred in her head. A strand of her own hair still clung to his lip and she smoothed it carefully away. Felix was shaking.

A second later they were clinging together. He held her tightly, too tightly, and the kisses he planted all over her face were feverishly hot. Julia closed her eyes and Felix rolled awkwardly on top of her. Their faces pressed together as they searched for each other, huddling closer to obliterate their sadness. Felix saw how Julia buried her face against his shoulder, trying to shut out everything else, and he knew that she was lonely too. A little of his desperation slipped away, replaced by a kind of wondering tenderness. He wanted to hold her, and warm her, and make her happy.

Was this how to do it? He didn't know this way, but he didn't know any other way either. Josh would know all the ways, Felix thought. The image of Josh rose up at once to taunt him, and Felix lay still, trying to stare it down. Julia's eyes opened at once, watching him.

Not Joshua Flood, not now.

Clumsily, he began to undo Julia's clothes. She helped him, smiling a little, letting him examine her white skin. It was so pale that it was translucent. Over the points of her hip bones he could see the blue net of veins. He bent his head to kiss her there, over the hard ridge of bone, and her fingers knotted imperiously in his hair.

When he looked at her again he saw that her face was soft, her expression remote. She was unfathomable. Fear stirred inside him.

"Now you," she whispered. Her hands with their inexpertly varnished fingernails touched the neck of his white shirt. He undid the buttons one by one as Julia watched him. The black, springy hair on his chest made the skin beneath look milky. Julia saw that his arms and shoulders were surprisingly muscular for the slightness of his build, and she smelled his clean sweat as he lifted his arms to stroke her cheek and then her breast. His wonderful color made her feel pallid.

She whispered, "Felix."

She had forgotten Josh, in that moment.

Felix knew what he must do.

He swung his legs abruptly over the side of the bed, and it struck him that it must look to Julia as if he were about to run away. He unbuckled his belt instead. He took off his trousers and socks, sitting with his back turned to her. Julia lay with her head pillowed on her hand, watching the way the bones of his spine moved smoothly under the skin.

Almost defiantly he turned to face her again, and lay down along the length of her. He pressed himself closer, and the touch of her bare skin against his own, with all its sameness and difference, was utterly disconcerting.

Julia kissed him, and then with the tip of her tongue she outlined his mouth. It was a darting, mischievous flicker that he felt almost as a taunt. His hand settled uncertainly in the hollow of her waist.

"Felix," she whispered again.

"Wait," he said softly. He reached up and turned off the light. The darkness settled comfortably around them. Under its protection he began to stroke her, letting his hands cover her thin shoulders and the ripple of her rib cage, her little, hard breasts and the concave space between her hip bones. He could feel that she was perfectly beautiful, a flawless and completely contained entity, like a painting or a sculpture. The recognition excited him, and he felt himself grow harder. His hands seemed clumsy now, and he bent his head so that he could explore the beguiling shape of her with his mouth. She gave herself up to him, but he could hear her jagged breaths. Felix had mistrusted her knowingness, but now he was sure she was as innocent as himself. He wanted to say something loving, but he could only summon up her name, whispered over and over against her cheek.

"It's all right," she murmured, holding him in her arms. "It's all, all right."

He took her hand then and guided it, showing her how to

move her fist around him. He groaned with sudden surprising pleasure as she grasped him, as unerringly as he would have done it himself.

Julia knew only how much she wanted him. The simplicity of it amazed her.

She turned to him, offering herself. He touched her, very gently, and she lifted her hips to him. Felix felt the complicated folds, seemingly countless layers turning in on themselves, utterly foreign. The flesh was so soft and moist that it seemed to dissolve under his fingertips. Julia stirred restlessly in his arms and he felt fear renew itself. The darkness grew threatening instead of reassuring. Felix jerked himself onto all fours and knelt over her. He was certain only of the need to do it now, at once, if he was going to do it at all.

Julia drew her lip between her teeth, sensing the weight of him hanging over her. She thought briefly of what would happen if he made her pregnant, because she was sure that Felix wouldn't take precautions in the middle of this feverish, whispered intimacy. She knew at once that she was going to risk it anyway, because she wanted to give him something simple, and because he was making her feel happy, and wanted, and perfectly desirable.

Without warning Felix's weight seemed to collapse on top of her. The angle of his jaw caught her lip, but the pain of that was obliterated by the other pain. He jabbed at her and she bit her swelling lip and spread her legs wider, trying to help him. Felix kept his eyes tightly closed, as if even the darkness weren't enough. The folds of flesh seemed impenetrable, but he pressed himself into them, willing himself to be able to enter her now, quickly, before he could think of anything else.

Julia had opened her mouth to beg him, "Stop, please stop," but suddenly their mutual struggle brought them to the right place. She felt him bury himself inside her. It was a long, deep way. A second or two ticked by before she realized that the shock it gave her was more pleasure than pain.

They lay still, fitted together, their breathing slowing a little. Julia smiled, and rolled her head so that her cheek touched his.

Slowly, experimentally, Felix began to move.

Everything was wrong, he knew that at once. This softness, the spongy, alien warmth. Even the scent of her. Coldness touched the base of his spine, spreading through his pelvis, shriveling him. He screwed his face up and drove himself harder, willing himself to make it right for her. He could sense her puzzlement now, her hands fluttering helplessly at his back. It was too late. He was shrinking, away from her, and then slipping away entirely.

Abruptly, Felix rolled onto his back and stared icily up into the darkness. Julia swallowed, and the muscles in her throat contracted painfully. In her bewilderment she put out her hand and touched him again. There were only limp, moist touches and whorls of flesh. She snatched her hand back as if it were burned, and pressed the knuckles into her eye socket.

They lay in silence for a long time. Even though she pressed her hands into her eyes, Julia couldn't stop the tears coming. They ran down her cheeks and into the pillow. Felix didn't move, or make a sound, but she had the impression that he was crying too. *Let him*, she thought with deliberate bitterness. And then, *There must be something the matter with me. Some reason why they don't want me. Josh, and then Felix.* She fought to stifle a sob.

At last Felix rolled toward her and tried to pull her into his arms.

Julia held herself stiff. "Don't," she ordered. She knew that he had been crying because his face was wet.

"It was my fault," he said. "Everything. All of that. You're so beautiful. I'm sorry, I'm so sorry."

"It doesn't matter."

It mattered so much that she was ashamed of the words as soon as she had spoken them. After today, after everything today, at least they could try to comfort each other. She turned to Felix now, and he wrapped his arms around her.

Clinging together, they cried for Jessie, and for themselves.

And then, when they couldn't cry anymore, with their wet faces still touching, they lay in the darkness and held each other.

"What will happen?" Julia asked childishly at last. She had meant, *to everything. To all of us, because we are so fragile.*

But Felix answered her carefully, deliberately. "To you and me? We'll go on being friends. Will you let us?"

After the rush of grief he felt peeled bare, clearsighted, and precise. He loved Julia, and he wanted there to be no hope of anything else for them. No reopening of the murky, fetid labyrinth that had almost lost them tonight.

He felt her nod her head slowly. There was a moment when she might have asked, *Why? Why is it like this?* He sensed her turning the words over in her mind, and then delicately rejecting them.

Thank you, Felix thought.

"Of course we will," she answered. She was imagining how it would be. As simple and as comfortable as before, but with a new measure of understanding, bred from tonight. They would got out to work and come home again. Felix would cook in the white kitchen and she would learn how to chop an onion with the same deft movements, how to bone and sauté and braise. What could she teach Felix in return? Julia felt the burden of her own ignorance. But if she didn't know anything now, then she could learn. Resolve and determination and a sudden optimism stiffened her. Mattie would come home again, and the three of them could be together. They couldn't fill the abyss that Jessie had left, but they could remember her. The thought eased the painful memory of the raw graveyard earth and the rain-sodden flowers.

"We'll live here together," Julia said softly. "Just like a family."

Felix hesitated, but the need for precision impelled him. "I won't be here for much longer. I wish I could be."

Julia didn't move. "Why won't you be?"

"I've been called up. I've got to go for the medical in three weeks time."

The idea of Felix as a national serviceman was so incongruous that Julia laughed. It sounded shrill, and she swallowed it quickly.

"But . . ."

"It was deferred while I was at the art school. But I'm not anymore, am I? I notified them before Christmas and the letter came last week."

He had set the wheels in motion gloomily, knowing that he would have to get it over with. But now the time was coming closer, the prospect almost attracted him. The army would lift him up from here and drop him down somewhere else, somewhere utterly different. And that could only help, after all, Felix thought.

"Poor Felix," Julia said bleakly. She couldn't help thinking, *Poor me. Now there's only me left. Of course there won't be any family. Jessie's dead, and Mattie's gone. And now Felix will go too.*

Felix heard her as clearly as if she had spoken the words aloud. "I'll survive," he said gently. "And so will you. You're better equipped for it than any of us. Look at you. You're clever, much cleverer than Mattie and me. You see things clearly, and you feel them more strongly. That makes it hard for you. But you're brave, and you're determined as well. You must be, or you wouldn't have got even this far.''

I'd still be in Fairmile Road, Julia thought. *Perhaps that would have been better*. But she answered herself. *No, it wouldn't. Whatever happens is better than that*. She felt Felix's fingers brush her cheek, and then stroke her hair.

"And you're beautiful, you know. That always helps.''

"Does it?''

He had told her that she was beautiful in that ugly moment afterward. Fending her off with assurances. Once again the questions quivered between them, but neither of them spoke. Julia understood that they would never be asked now. So close, but no closer.

"Yes, it does," Felix said firmly.

"Can I stay in the flat?''

"Of course you can. I don't suppose old Mr. Bull will pitch us out, for Jessie's sake. You could always share with someone if Mattie isn't here to help with the rent.''

"Oh, yes," Julia said. "I could always do that.''

There didn't seem to be anything else to add. She reached up and clicked on the light. She saw Felix's coffee skin and her own, touching it. In the light it was somehow shocking, and she sat up abruptly. Looking down at the space between them she saw a thin smear of blood.

She had wanted the first time to be with Josh. She had planned it, dreamed it. Instead, it had been here, on this sad night with its secrets and empty spaces. What was it Mattie had said? *It was all right*, that was it. Only it wasn't all right. Julia didn't want to cry again. She swung her legs out of bed and stood up, holding her discarded sweater against herself. Felix's hand caught her wrist and held her. She looked down and saw his black eyes fixed on her.

"Stay here," he whispered. "Sleep here with me. Just for tonight.''

She smiled at him then, an awkward, crooked smile. "I'll come back," she promised.

She went across to the bathroom. It smelled threateningly damp from where the water had washed under the floorboards and into the joists.

Julia stood in front of the mirror for a long time. She rubbed cream into her face and brushed her hair until it crackled with static. She cleaned her teeth, then took her nightdress off the hook behind the door and put it on.

She stared solemnly at her reflection in the mirror. She told herself, *You will have to make your life for yourself. You can. Felix believes it too. You can't expect anyone else to help you, because they have to help themselves. Mattie. Felix. Josh. Betty and Vernon even. That's the truth, isn't it?* She had almost turned away, but she added, *If what you want is Josh Flood, he won't come to you. You will have to go to him. That's also the truth.*

She went back to Felix's room and she was smiling properly now. He smiled back at her and lifted the covers. She lay down beside him and he fitted himself neatly against the curve of her back. It was comforting to have him there. She felt that she had reached the end of a complicated journey.

"Thank you," Felix said with his mouth against her ear. And then, "I love you."

"I love you too," Julia answered.

They fell asleep together, the first and last time.

NINE

There was the cottage, in the angle of the wood. Julia stood with the frosty grass crackling under her feet and looked at the lights in the windows. It had taken her almost a month to decide to come. In the end she had left the square on impulse, caught a train to the country station, and walked from there along the icy lanes. It was almost dark, and she had fixed all her attention on finding the way. Only when she saw the lights did she wonder what she would have done if there had been no one there.

She wrapped her coat tighter around her and ran the last few yards. She knocked so hard on the door that her knuckles stung.

Josh opened it. Yellow light spilled out from behind him and lit up her face.

"I'm here," she said unnecessarily. "Can I come in?"

Josh laughed, and his breath sent up a smoky plume between them.

"Julia, Julia. Yes, you'd better come in."

Across the room behind him Julia saw two pairs of skis propped against the wall, ski poles, and heavy laced boots, a scatter of other equipment she didn't recognize. Josh was busy. Now that she was here, she was suddenly furiously angry.

"Why haven't you been to see me? Do you think I don't matter? That you can appear and disappear just as you like?" The words hurt her throat as they came out.

He stared at her then. Julia's eyes glittered and her cheeks were reddened by the cold.

Slowly, he said, "No, I don't think you don't matter."

Julia stared at the long, sharp blades of the skis, and her taut shoulders suddenly dropped. In a different voice she said, "I suppose I shouldn't have come here. Girls don't do things like that, do they? But I wanted to see you so much, and I didn't think you'd ever come, so what else could I do? I know you think I'm too young. I came to tell you I'm not. I'm old enough to know my own mind."

Her face was turned away from him, her eyes still fixed on his skis. Gently, Josh held out his hand. She ignored it, and he fitted his fingers around her wrist. "I think you do know your own mind," he whispered. "The question is whether I know mine."

She turned to look at him then. They watched each other, wary.

Josh was thinking that ten minutes ago, with his Long Lanyard ski bindings and his new Subito boots, everything had been simple. It wasn't simple now, and it would grow steadily more complicated. All the risks that he had sensed and shied away from in Julia Smith were intensified now, and Josh was elated to realize that he didn't care. He looked at Julia's rosy cheeks and burning eyes. It was right that she was here. Better than right, much, much better. It was perfect.

"You know I love you," Julia said.

Josh took her other hand. "I think I must love you too. Just a bit. A little, tiny bit."

She jerked her chin up. "That's enough. To begin with, of course."

He pulled her closer and kissed her. She smelled of cold air, clean and delicious. He wanted to go on smelling and tasting her, but Julia drew away from him.

"Are you going away?" She pointed at the ski gear and an open canvas grip on the floor.

He nodded. "Into the Inferno."

Julia rounded on him. "Don't talk in riddles. I was plain and honest with you, wasn't I?"

Josh laughed, still holding her hands in his. Julia was completely and beguilingly unlike any of the other women he knew. He admired her sharpness. He really did love her, he thought. Perhaps even more than a little bit.

"It wasn't a riddle. The Inferno is a ski race. In Mürren, Switzerland. This Sunday." Switzerland. Saw-toothed mountains against the blue sky, and Josh.

Julia remembered the square, and her fear of the silence that would choke it as soon as Felix left. And her typewriter, crouching under its black hood, waiting to recapture her on Monday morning.

She didn't hesitate any longer. "Take me with you," she begged him.

With anyone else, Josh would have snorted with laughter. No one took any diversions to the Inferno, he would have said. But simple responses like that had slipped out of his reach now. He sighed.

"Yes, you can come with me," Josh said. "We leave on Wednesday morning."

He saw the delight and disbelief leap together in her face, and he thought how lovely she was. It would be his pleasure to show her the mountains.

"I'll be ready," she promised him.

"What about your work?"

"There are thousands of jobs," Julia answered. "But only one chance to do this."

At last, she thought. She was in motion too. *You have to make your life for yourself.*

"I haven't got very much money," she said awkwardly. "Just a bit that I've saved. How much will I need?"

"Oh, Jesus, I'm not a millionaire," Josh groaned, "but I guess you can come along at my expense."

She smiled at him, a brilliant smile. "Thank you."

They went to the timbered pub for a celebratory drink, and afterward Julia insisted on being driven to the station in the black MG. Josh protested, but she was adamant that she wouldn't stay. Julia was intrigued to discover that suddenly she wielded power too.

"Wednesday morning." She beamed at him, and reluctantly he let her go.

On Thursday morning they were in Switzerland.

*   *   *

At the little station at Lauterbrunnen Julia gazed upward. The peaks of the Bernese Oberland reared massively into the sky. In the course of the long train journey the world had lost its familiar shades of earth and mud and winter grass and had turned monochrome. Everything here was spidery black, or gray, or glittering white, and the air tasted thin and sharp.

She waited quietly, breathing it in.

Josh was across the platform beside the mountain train. He was tenderly stowing his ski bag into a little open wagon already bristling with skis. If he could have slept with them beside him in the couchette berth last night, Julia thought with amusement, he would gladly have done so. Since yesterday morning she had discovered that she was as bad a traveler as Josh was a good one. As the boat train rumbled across the river from Victoria Station and into the shadow of Battersea Power Station, Julia had delightedly told Josh, "This is the most exciting thing that's ever happened to me."

He had grinned back and drawled, "Wait till you see the Inferno."

But in the long progress over the Channel and across France impatience had replaced the first exhilaration. She paced up and down the corridor, eager for the new experience to begin now, at once, while Josh dozed in his corner seat. She stared at him, baffled. They were here together, but this interminable journey held them apart. The train slowed and stopped in the middle of a wide, empty field.

Josh opened one eye to look at her. "Relax," he murmured.

But Julia lay awake for most of the night in her couchette berth, listening to Josh and the other passengers breathing through the unhypnotic rattle of the wheels. And now they were almost there.

Josh turned and hoisted the rest of their bags into the train. "Let's go," he called to her.

They climbed in and skiers in knitted caps and nylon parkas crowded in after them. The train jerked forward, nosing the ski wagon ahead of it. It reared upward, climbing at a sharp angle.

Julia leaned forward, pressing her face against the window. Black-limbed trees poked up out of folds and curls of snow along the track. The trees slid past and fell away behind them. Julia watched, mesmerized, only half-hearing the babble of French and German around her. The train climbed on, higher and higher.

As it shuddered to a halt at the upper station the sun came

out. Black and white changed instantly to blue and silver. Julia looked up, through air that seemed to glitter with crystalline specks, and saw the Eiger pointing over her. She stumbled down the steps of the train into the snow.

"Wengen," Josh announced unnecessarily.

Julia looked at the little wooden houses, each with its three-cornered hat of snow. It was like a toy village handed to a child. She thought she had never seen anywhere so pretty, or so unreal. It was enchanting to have arrived here, of all places, with Josh.

Julia's everlasting memory of her first days in Wengen was of being wrong, conclusively wrong in the big things and on down to the smallest detail. Her appearance was wrong, her voice and her manners were wrong, her clothes and her opinions and her inability to ski were laughable, but most unforgivable of all was the fact that she was with Joshua Flood.

Frau Uberl was a square, motherly Swiss widow who ran her chalet as an informal guesthouse for English girls race-training with the British-run Downhill Only club. Frau Uberl and a flinty Scots matron inappropriately named Joy chaperoned the girls between them. On that first morning Frau Uberl showed Julia to her bed in a wooden-floored four-bedded room under the sloping eaves. The window looked over its balcony to the Eiger. Julia wanted to rush across and fling it open to gulp in the air and the view, but her roommates were eyeing her suspiciously. They had names like Belinda and Sophia, and they wore thick patterned sweaters that clung to their bosoms, and tight Helanca ski pants. Julia noticed that they all had enormous bottoms, and she told herself in an effort at superiority that she wouldn't wear pants like that if she were half their size.

Belinda perched on the end of Julia's bed to watch her unpack. Out came the silk blouses and tweed jackets from Brick Lane, homemade evening dresses and Jessie's scarlet kimono, her adored jet jewelry. Julia picked up the long earrings and fixed them in her ears, tossing her head to make them swing.

There was nudging and muffled giggling behind her back. If only Mattie were here, she thought grimly.

She turned around sharply and caught them at it. The youngest pinched her nose to stop the laughter exploding.

"I don't ski, you know," Julia said loftily to forestall them. "I've come out here only to see Josh win the Inferno."

That silenced them for a moment, but Sophia announced,

"He won't win, of course. He's only an amateur, even though he's pretty good. Really good, actually, for an American. He might scrape in tenth or twelfth if he skis brilliantly. What was his place last year, Bel? Twentieth?"

Julia shrugged, and went back to unpacking. She knew they wouldn't be able to resist asking, and sure enough Belinda was the one who came out with it. "How long have you known Josh?"

"Oh, months now. Let's see, he took me flying for the first time in the autumn . . . yes, it's ages. It's getting quite serious, I'm afraid." She laughed apologetically. They stared at her enviously.

"How funny that you don't ski," Sophia murmured. "When it's so important to him."

"Is it?" Julia shook out the last blouse and hung it up in the communal wardrobe. It was full of large, sensible tweed skirts and three almost identical taffeta dance dresses. "Do you all ski?"

It was as if she had asked, *Do you all breathe?*

"You don't need taffeta dresses to ski in."

"Oh, no. Those are for the Swann Ball. *Everyone* goes."

Julia didn't inquire any further.

Julia went slowly downstairs to the kitchen, where she found Frau Uberl. The Swiss woman beamed at her, and Julia, with relief, recognized foreign impartiality to class and probably ski competence as well.

"You will be wanting something to eat, no?"

"Yes, please."

The plate that was put in front of her was piled up with meatballs and sauce and potatoes smothered in cheese. Julia stared at it in amazement. "Frau Uberl? Thank you, but I can't possibly eat all this."

"Ach, you will. You are as thin as a pin. You will need it if you ski this afternoon."

I doubt it, Julia thought, but she struggled with it as best she could. The frau clucked over her leftovers, but then Josh arrived to rescue her.

He was wearing navy ski pants and a light blue quilted jacket with a knitted collar and cuffs. He had laced ski boots and a navy knitted cap with a tiny US flag stitched to it. He held his skis over his shoulder with one arm curled lightly around them, and he looked absurdly handsome. Julia followed him down the path.

"Let's go and rent you some skis." He looked her up and down. She had changed into the nearest approximation of ski wear that her wardrobe would yield, and Josh nodded briskly. "That'll do for the nursery slopes. Are you going to ski in those earrings?"

"Bloody nursery slopes," Julia snarled under her breath. "Yes, I'm going to ski in these earrings. I'm probably going to die in them as well."

Josh grinned. "You won't die. You'll enjoy it."

He set off with Julia panting along beside him. She felt possessive and greedy and afraid and inadequate all together, and it was galling that she could hardly even keep pace with him through the slippery snow.

"Josh! Why have I got to stay with these girls? I can't bear them. I want to be with you."

He looked faintly surprised. "I told you why. It's important to appear to behave, at least. Look, when I first came out here I thought the English and their little clubs were so goddamn snooty that I skied alone for a month. But once you get to know them, they're okay. Obey their rules, that's all, and they'll be your friends."

As if to prove his point, they came down to the railway track, where another fussy little train was waiting to climb on upward. People leaned out of its windows and shouted, "Coo-eee! Josh, we heard you'd arrived. We're going up to Black Rock. Are you coming?"

He waved back, grinning. "No, I'm going to the nursery slopes."

"Ha-ha-ha. What's the secret? Hiding yourself until Sunday?"

"Wait and see."

Julia plodded on, thoroughly disheartened. "I'm cramping your style," she said. "I shouldn't have come."

He put his free arm around her shoulders. Julia managed to stop herself burying her head against his parka. "I'm glad you're here. We'll have a good time, you'll see. Sophia Bliss and the others are nice girls. Just not very much like you."

"Not much," Julia agreed, thinking, *Swann Ball indeed! Taffeta dress and all.*

"Why don't you give them a chance? Watch them. You might even learn something."

"I might," she conceded, doubting whether it was anything she would want to know. Then she thought of Felix. They had been gentle with each other since the night of the funeral.

Jessie's death and their failure in bed had drawn them close. Felix had made her critical of her own clothes, taught her the difference between good food and bad food, made her aware of the existence of style. Felix was always telling her to use her eyes and ears. Perhaps Josh was right. Perhaps the Belindas could teach her something, even if it was only never to wear tight pants over thirty-eight-inch hips. And some breathless upper-class argot. *Might come in useful someday,* Julia thought philosophically.

They reached the ski shop and Julia submitted herself to having boots strapped to her feet and poles thrust into her hands.

After that, everything was awful.

Josh came to the beginners' slope, but Julia soon begged him to go away and leave her to her humiliation. He went, bestowing her on the Swiss ski-school instructor and a gaggle of tiny Dutch and German children. For the first time in her adult life Julia discovered that her rangy height was a disadvantage. She had farther to fall than the little children, and every puff of wind seemed enough to blow her over. She fell so often that it began to seem simpler just to lie in the snow, only Heini the instructor came and hauled her to her feet again.

Snow filled her mouth and ears and slid down her neck. Her hands froze to her poles and her legs ached so that she could hardly lift her skis. She wobbled and slithered and Heini yelled, "Bend your knees," and the children sliced cheekily past her.

At the end of the afternoon, when the snow had turned blue in the fading light, half a dozen skiers appeared at the top of the slope. They swooped down together, their immaculate, pure christies carving a sinuous line down to the village. They were whooping and calling to one another, and Julia recognized Belinda and her friends. They were as graceful as swans on their skis. She ducked her head and shrank behind Heini and the children, impressed in spite of herself.

Julia didn't see anything of Josh while there was enough light to ski by. She knew that he went across to Mürren and climbed the Schilthorn to ski the Inferno route, but when she asked him about it he shook his head and didn't answer.

In the evenings they went out together, but never alone. They ate in candlelit restaurants and drank glühwein in tiny cozy bars crowded around tables with the other skiers. As well as Joy and her girls and the other DHO regulars, there were Inferno competitors who eyed Josh surreptitiously and tried to make him talk about his practice. Among them were the members of the military teams competing for the Montgomery Cup. Sophia and her friends found the British and American soldiers particularly fascinating, although Julia was secretly gratified to notice that they looked at her far oftener than they did at the other girls in their reindeer-patterned sweaters.

Josh saw it too. He winked and squeezed her hand.

The only other skier who Julia liked was a sandy-haired tough-looking Scot called Alex. She mentioned him to Sophia as they scrambled home through the silent, biting dark before Frau Uberl's midnight curfew.

"Oh, no, not him. You can't," Sophia shrieked. "He's utterly non-sku. He wears his socks outside his ski pants."

Julia smiled in the blue dark. Felix would like that.

By Sunday morning, the day of the race, Julia was so stiff and bruised that she could hardly walk. She lowered herself out of bed and groaned on all fours on the shiny floorboards.

Belinda was infuriatingly doing kneebends by the window. She came over to the end of Julia's bed and peered down at her. Then she held out her hand. Julia glared at it, but she needed help. She took the hand and Belinda pulled her upright.

"Ouch. Oh, God. I can't walk. I'm crippled."

Belinda giggled. "It'll get better after today. Promise. You'll start to loosen up. You know, I saw you with Heini yesterday."

"How embarrassing."

"Not a bit. You're doing really well. Isn't she, Felicity?"

"Brilliantly."

To her surprise, Julia felt herself turning crimson with pleasure. Their praise was unexpected and welcome, but it was also a gesture of friendship. She had turned into enough of a skier for a truce to be called.

She smiled at them. "Thanks."

"Are you going to watch the race?" Belinda asked.

"I don't know where to go," Julia admitted. Josh had told her airily to go with the girls. She did know how desperately she wanted to see him compete.

"Come with us. We're going up the Alibubble."

"I will, then. Thanks again."

Josh had set out while it was still dark.

He reached the top of the Allmendhubel funicular at eight-thirty, and with his skis over his shoulder he started to climb. He set himself a careful, steady pace. There were almost four hours of climbing ahead of him. The race would begin at midday, and the thirty-two competitors would be started at thirty-second intervals. Josh knew from experience that it required perfect timing not to arrive hurried and winded, and not to have to wait for too long on the summit of the freezing mountain.

He frowned at the snow as he climbed steadily beside the downhill route. It had been unseasonably warm and wet at the beginning of February, but fresh heavy snow had fallen on the slippery base in the last week. He prodded his long pole into the glistening powder as he tramped upward. When he glanced toward the heights above, he could pick out the figures of other competitors, black and gray specks against the snow.

Julia and the others clambered out of the funicular just before midday. A handful of spectators was already clustered in the lee of the station hut, cheerfully passing flasks among them. Belinda produced the provisions Frau Uberl had sent, and they gulped thankfully at hot chocolate laced with plum brandy.

Sophia looked at her watch. "Exactly twelve."

Josh was number fifteen. In seven minutes he would be on his way down. Julia felt her heart knocking painfully in her chest.

Josh was waiting in a silent line of skiers. He knew most of them, although they were barely recognizable beneath their caps and yellow-lensed goggles. No one spoke. The Swiss official at the head of the line raised his arm and then dropped it. The first competitor plunged away. Josh heard the thrilling swish of skis through the powder, but he didn't look. He was breathing slowly and evenly. His fingers flexed in the loops of his poles. He was following the course in his head, every twist and dive of the endless, treacherous fourteen kilometers.

Swish. Swish. Starter after starter.

Josh moved forward in the line. Swish. Two people ahead of him. He eased his goggles over his eyes. In a little more than thirty minutes, with luck, he would be at Lauterbrunnen, nearly three thousand feet below.

Next but one. The Scot, Alex Mackintosh, was just ahead at number fourteen. The raised arm fell again, and Josh was at the head of the line. He had taught himself never to feel nerves. Fear was one thing, it was a safeguard, but nerves were simply destructive. The seconds ticked off. In the last two or three, as he crouched ready for the arm signal, he wondered where Julia would be watching.

Swish.

Josh didn't hear the rasp of his own skis. He was off,

traversing the opening slope that was as steep as a roof. Down, and down, with the powder spurting up behind him. So fast that it was gone while the starter's arm still flickered in his head. At the bottom, a sweeping left turn and into the Engetal, the Happy Valley. Ahead lay a great schuss, a huge S-shaped sweep that dropped more than a thousand feet.

Josh was traveling like a bullet. The speed pinned the flesh of his face to the bones, carving a white smile beneath the blank goggles. But behind the yellow shields his eyes were like an eagle's. They saw every bump and turn and carved out a path for him before his skis sliced over it. He had become a machine, as he always did when he skied at his best. His blood froze and his body fused to the skis.

Down. The wind and the snow plumes and the sweet slicing turns.

On down. Like flying, but rawer. Like diving, but faster and fiercer. Like sex. Like death itself.

Almost the bottom of the Happy Valley. A right-hand turn and ahead a flat traverse, then a rise to the Mürren ski hut, and the control point.

Josh's head jerked up.

He heard the roll of thunder before he saw anything. But he knew that it wasn't thunder. It was a crack and a spreading roar that came from the Schwarzgrat, high overhead. The noise rose up to choke him, indistinguishable from his own fear. Then he saw the snow falling off the cliffs. Only it wasn't snow anymore. Vast white monuments dropped and sent up billowing clouds and brought rocks and trees and churning debris racing toward him.

Josh turned with such violence that spraying snow lashed his face. He shot away at an angle with the avalanche clawing at him like a nightmare. And out of the corner of his eye, in one split second, Josh saw Alex Mackintosh. The ragged white wall swept him up and threw him over and over like a twig, and then he was gone.

The leading edge of the avalanche caught Josh at the same instant. It smashed him down and punched the breath out of his body. He folded his arms helplessly around his head as the snow gagged him, blinded him, and sucked him down. His skis were torn off and he was pitched into blackness, uselessly clawing and fighting against its brutal strength.

Then, after what seemed like an eternity of suffocating terror, it was suddenly quiet. Josh opened his eyes very slowly, as if his eyelids were weighted. There was blue sky above him.

He was gasping for breath and whimpering like an animal, but even as he lay there he knew that he had never seen anything so beautiful as that pure ice-blue sky.

He stared at it, fighting for his breath, with the euphoric realization *I'm not buried* singing in his head. For a long moment he couldn't move, and he looked up into the wonderful space above him as content as a baby. And then he remembered Mackintosh. He sucked more air into his burning lungs and tried to struggle on to all fours. Pain throbbed down his left side and Josh swung his head from side to side, trying to clear the mist of it. He saw then that the snow had engulfed him up to his thighs. He kicked and writhed, hauling at the debris with his hands to pull himself free. At last he lurched to his feet and saw his skis sticking out of the snow behind him. Josh lunged toward them, one hand pressed to his side, jerking like a clumsy marionette over the snow blocks.

It seemed to take hours.

With each step Josh was trying to work out where in the hideously changed landscape he had last seen Mackintosh.

At last the skis were within his grasp. He wrenched them out of the snow and jammed his boots into the bindings. The way ahead looked almost impassable, but he pushed forward, staring into the hollows for any sign of the other skier.

He fell and fell again as he plunged down the slope, and then as he scrambled up again he saw the aluminium basket of a Tonkin pole identical to his own sticking up out of the tumbled mass. Josh hurled himself down next to it, kicking off his skis. He scrabbled at the snow, cursing his hands which seemed so ineffectual against the avalanche debris. He began to gasp with the effort as he worked, and sweat ran down behind his goggles, almost blinding him. He glanced up once in desperation and saw black figures bouncing and sprawling over the snow. Help was on the way from the control point at the Mürren hut. He bent down again, working faster, and the ice tore through his knitted gloves.

Then, suddenly, his hand broke through into space. His bare, frozen fingers felt the smooth canvas of a ski jacket. Josh hauled at the snow, dragging it in chunks away from the man's body. He was shouting without knowing what he said. "It's all right. You're clear. You're okay."

And then, like a miracle, the body was moving too. It shuddered convulsively and one shoulder appeared. Mackintosh was lying curled on his side, his arms raised in front of his face to make an air pocket, and his Tonkin pole thrust vertically over him.

Josh stuck his hands under the man's armpits and hauled at him. The Scotsman's head broke out of the snow and ice as the first of the rescuers reached them. His face was gray, and ridges of snow and ice clung to his hair and eyebrows. His blue lips hung open, and he was breathing.

"He's alive," Josh yelled. His shout rolled over their heads, echoing briefly, and then was swallowed up by the heights. The rescuers flung themselves forward. There were shovels and ropes now in place of Josh's hands. He stood back, shivering a little, looking at Mackintosh's face.

One of the Swiss officials was shouting something at Josh. He waved and pointed on down the slope. Josh gaped at him, understanding at last that the man was telling him to go on. He had forgotten all about the Inferno. He shook his head impatiently. Mackintosh was all but free now. They were reaching gently to lift him onto a canvas stretcher. Somehow, on their backs or on a sledge, they would carry him up to the hut. They had done it often enough before.

"He is *gut*," one of the officials said. Josh lifted his head then. Racing away, out of his control, his imagination swept to the route down, beyond the avalanche. Mackintosh's face had been hidden by the backs of the rescuers, but as they moved him Josh saw it again. His eyes were open, incongruously as blue as the sky. He was looking at Josh, and his lips moved.

Go on.

"*Ja, ja.*" They were shouting and pointing again. They were telling Josh that he was to climb back up and walk along the flat to the control point, in order to restart his race from there.

Suddenly, Josh was moving. He snatched up his poles and hoisted his skis over his shoulder. He glanced at Mackintosh for the last time, and saw the flicker of a painful smile.

"I'll have to finish for us both, Alex," he shouted. "You do the same for me some other time."

He was already on his way when one of the rescuers grabbed his arm. He was holding out his own gloves. Josh tore off his ruined pair and waved the good ones in a salute. Then he was off, up over the debris, his legs pumping like pistons.

At the control hut Tuffy Brockway had materialized. He clapped Josh on the back and Josh staggered.

"They'll credit you with the time you've lost," Tuffy

roared. "It's happened before. Esme Mackinnon stopped down at Grütsch to let a funeral go by. Took off his cap and stood at attention, of course. They gave him the time back."

Josh barely heard him. He leaned on his poles for a second, gulping air and trying to steady his shaking legs. He looked down and was amazed to see other skiers skirting the worst of the avalanche. They were sliding and falling, but the race was still in progress.

A stopwatch clicked decisively beside him. Josh's grip tightened on his poles and he flashed away. Ahead lay a steep drop, a rise up to Castle Ridge, and then the hideous Inferno slope itself. Josh tried to shut off the pain that wrenched at his side, the memory of the thundering snow and Mackintosh's deathly gray face. Alex was alive, and he wanted to stay alive himself. That was all there was room to know now. He was skiing again. A second later there was nothing in Josh's mind but the way down, unfurling like a treacherous ribbon ahead of him.

At the Allmendhubel, Sophia looked at her wristwatch again. She was frowning. "He should have come through by now. And the man before him. If he's going to stand any chance, he should be here by now."

They stared up at the route until their eyes stung, searching for another of the black specks that would fly down to them and grow, faster and closer, until it became a man who swooped past them in a glittering plume of speed and ice.

The mountain was empty.

They stood in a huddle, not speaking. Julia's hands and feet were numb, but she was watching too intently to stamp and clap to try to warm them.

Another minute went by, and stretched into five. No one came, and the other spectators began to mutter at one another, eyebrows raised.

Sophia murmured, "Something has happened."

Looking up, Julia suddenly saw that the mountains were hostile. Josh was somewhere up in that high white space. She was afraid, and she shivered. Without taking her eyes off the route, Belinda put her arm around her. Gratefully, Julia huddled closer. The four girls drew together, waiting.

Then Felicity shouted, "Look!"

At last, a black speck appeared on the lip of a col high above them. The skier seemed to hang there motionless for a second, and then he came twisting down the huge slope.

No one spoke. "Is it him?" Julia almost screamed.

Sophia shook her head. "Josh doesn't ski like that."

Another skier appeared over the col, and then another. The leader came closer, and Julia heard that he was shouting something at them. They crowded forward and she saw his mouth open, a black shape under his blank goggles.

"Av-a-lanche!"

He was French and the syllables of the word sounded too soft for the images that exploded with it. He lifted his pole and waved it backward at the white walls. And then he hurtled past them, on and down toward Winteregg below.

Julia did scream now. "What does he mean? Where is the avalanche?"

The other skiers passed, unrecognizable, but not Josh. Sophia's ruddy face had turned gray-white. Julia understood that *avalanche* was something terrible. She shrank back against the wooden wall of the funicular station, feeling the splintery planks give a little at her back. They waited, still in silence, their faces all turned upward.

And then, again, Felicity shouted, "Look!"

Julia knew at once that this one was Josh. He came, seemingly, straight as an arrow down the dizzying slope. Crouching low over his skis, he didn't swoop, birdlike, as the others had. Josh had power, not grace. A wordless cry burst out of the girls, and before the echo of it had gone, Josh was whirling down to them. Julia glimpsed the red silk scarf wound around his neck, the white flash of his smile, and his pole lifted in a brief salute. An instant later he was past and they swung around to watch him carving a straight path down the fall of the slope.

Julia realized that they were all cheering and whooping. The icy air tore at her throat, and there were tears of relief and excitement pouring down her face. She clasped Belinda in a bear hug, and they capered in a circle, laughing and gasping.

"He's not there yet," Felicity warned.

"But skiing like that," Belinda answered, "he'll not only get there, he'll bloody well win."

Down again, after the Allmendhubel. Josh had glimpsed Julia at the funicular station, but the thought of her had vanished from his head just as quickly. He was tiring rapidly and he was skiing through open country, over and down treacherous humps, and every atom of concentration and muscle power was needed to find the right route, the fast route. But he had come this far, and determination was like a tight wire inside him.

At Winteregg he came to the railway line. A bigger knot of spectators waited beside a little tea hut, and as he reached them a storm of questions in three languages broke around him. "Happy Valley," he panted. "Alex Mackintosh was hurt, but they've got him away now."

Someone tried to pat him on the back, but he ducked away and pushed on again. Beyond Winteregg was a kilometer and a half of flat country. His body felt like lead, but he clenched his teeth and poled on. He thought of Alex Mackintosh's faint encouraging smile.

And then, at Grütsch station, the route dived downward again. Josh took one gasping breath and pointed his skis down the slope. Beneath him, beyond the dense fir forests, was Lauterbrunnen.

Down.

The pain had spread to his chest now, and there was burning from his armpit to the top of his thigh. But still, there was the kiss of fresh powder under his skis, too, and the clearings between the black trees opening like soft white mouths.

If he was going to make time, he must do it now. Josh flexed his knees, lower, crouched into an egg shape. The trees and the snow and the clearings flickered by, but suddenly they were no threat. Miraculously, forgetting everything that had happened, he was part of them. He was inviolable, spawned by the snow itself. The wind of his speed sliced into his cheeks. Josh could hear his own breath rasping in his chest. He was skiing faster and better than he had ever in his life, and he was drunk on it. In that moment he was all-powerful.

The arches of the funicular loomed and flashed overhead. Still down, crossing and recrossing under the pylons. Then he was out of the trees, and open grazing fields lay below him. Swooping across them, the seconds began to beat in his head. How long? How much farther? He caught the warm lowland smell of animal dung. He saw Lauterbrunnen, a frozen sea of snowy roofs. There was the station to one side, and a little road leading to it. The finishing line. Josh's poles bit into the snow, and he flung himself forward for the last time. He knew that he was exhausted now.

A dark knot of people spread across the snowy track ahead of him. He heard them cheering and half-turned his head to look for the reason. As he swished over the finishing line he understood that they were cheering for him. The Swiss timekeeper clicked his stopwatch and Josh collapsed against a wooden fence.

It sagged beneath his weight but it held him. It was just as well, because Josh couldn't stand up.

The prize-giving for the 1956 Inferno was held at the Palace Hotel, Mürren. The room was packed with competitors, finishers, and nonfinishers, organizers and supporters. When Julia saw Josh she felt almost shy. She couldn't manage to struggle across the room to him before silence was called for the results.

Twelve skiers had finished the course.

Julia clenched her fists, struggling to hear. She couldn't understand any German, and barely a word of the rapid French. There was a lot of cheering and laughing. The Swiss race chairman peered at a sheet of paper. As he read out a name and a number, there was a burst of clapping. The winner was the Frenchman, Gaçon.

Beside Julia, Sophia whistled. "Twenty-seven minutes, thirty-seven seconds. Bloody fast. But then, he was through before the avalanche."

Everyone knew about the avalanche. On their way up, the girls had heard that someone had stopped to dig someone else out.

Amid calls for silence, the second and third placings were read out. Neither of them was Josh. Julia stared with dull disappointment at the back of the head in front of her. She had been sure that Josh would win, whatever Belinda and the others said. She didn't see Tuffy Brockway stand up, but as soon as he started speaking her skin prickled.

"In announcing the fourth, and incidentally the highest amateur placing, we have a special commendation to make. This competitor was caught by the avalanche in Happy Valley. Nevertheless, he freed himself and went to the rescue of Alex Mackintosh. Alex is now in the hospital in Berne. He has a broken leg, some concussion, other uncomfortable but fortunately minor damages. His fellow competitor reached him very quickly, and there is no doubt that he was instrumental in saving his life."

Julia's heart began to thump in her chest. "Once he was assured that Mr. Mackintosh was safe, he continued the race. And finished the course in the remarkable time, once credited with the minutes he had lost in helping another man, of thirty-one minutes and seventeen seconds. Ladies and gentlemen, I ask you to applaud the courage and spirit of Mr. Joshua Flood."

Sophia and Belinda and Felicity cheered wildly with everyone else. Julia sat silent, stock still, hardly able to see for pride.

Josh was presented with a commemorative Inferno medal. Tuffy Brockway pinned it to his dark blue sweater for him. In the hubbub afterward, it was Josh who elbowed his way through the crowd to Julia. Belinda clung to his arm and Sophia and Felicity kissed a cheek each. Julia just looked up at him.

"Well done," she said quietly.

Josh held out his hand and she stood up. The room might have been empty as they looked at each other.

"Will you do me the honor, ma'am," Josh drawled, "of accompanying me to the Swann Ball tonight?"

Julia pretended to consider.

"I might," she said at last. "I just might, at that."

He nodded gravely, and offered her his arm. They swept out together.

There was a string orchestra that played Strauss waltzes, and polkas, and fox-trots and a wide, shining dance floor. Julia had giggled as Josh led her out onto it. There was no bebop and certainly no rock and roll, but Josh had been properly brought up and he knew the right steps to the right dances. Julia had only to let him whirl her in grandiose circles.

She felt that she had stepped, satisfyingly, into one of her own dreams.

There had been a wonderful banquet at the hotel. They had sat down at long white tables glowing with candles in branched candelabra. After the food and wine there had been speeches, speeches that had seemed funny even to Julia. There had been a toast to the race winners, a special toast to Josh that had made her glow with pride all over again. Julia was wearing Mattie's greeny-black party dress, far too big for her around the hips and bosom, but Belinda and Sophia had pinned and stitched her into it in the latest demonstration of their newfound friendship. Julia had received enough flattering glances and invitations to dance to make her feel that even if she didn't belong she could at least cope on her own terms. The champagne was flowing, but Julia was used to drinking at Jessie's and Mattie's pace, and the wine simply made her feel that she was floating on a warm tide of happiness.

And there was Josh. Josh, with his black bow tie and his white starched shirt, his blond hair watered so that it lay smooth and dark, as correct as any of the Englishmen. Yet somehow wicked as well. The hero and the villain, infinitely more intriguing, all at once.

Julia laid her head against his black shoulder and sighed.

She knew that it was the most perfect evening of her life.

Josh lifted her chin with one finger so that he could look at her. "Are you tired?"

"No. I want to go on dancing forever."

"Mmm. Not quite forever, perhaps. D'you remember that place that Harry took us to? The night we met?"

Julia remembered it, and she remembered how they had danced then, fused together, making a promise that was still unfulfilled.

The thought struck a white-hot bolt of longing straight through her.

Her feet tangled with Josh's, and they stood still in the swirling sea of dancers.

"I think we should go upstairs now," Josh whispered.

Julia bent her head, unable to say, *yes please,* and he kissed the thin, warm skin over her temple before they slipped out of the crowded room and left the music soaring behind them.

They ran up the stairs and along the shadowy corridor to Josh's room, laughing and whispering like children playing truant. But when he had unlocked his door and locked it again behind them, the stillness and quiet stifled their laughter. There was a bright white moon in the star-prickled sky, and pale silver-gray squares lay over the floor in front of them. With Josh's fingers wound in hers, Julia went to the window and looked down. She saw the shallow roofs of the little wooden houses under their thick folds of snow. The streets were empty and the village lay in its silver cup with the mountains raising their heads against the stars.

"It's so beautiful," Julia said. And then, reaching awkwardly for the words, "I'm so happy tonight. It feels strange."

"It shouldn't be so strange," Josh told her.

They turned away from the window and faced each other. They kissed, tasting each other out of hunger, suddenly greedy. It seemed a long time, infinitely too long, since the nightclub in London with Mattie and Harry Gilbert.

Josh's hand touched the bodice of her dress.

"May I?" he asked, and she nodded. He couldn't find how to undo it and she told him, "I'm stitched into it."

Josh groaned and they were laughing all over again as they pulled at the dress. In the end they tore it off her. Julia stood in her stockings and garter belt while Josh looked at her. They had forgotten the cottage in the woods, and everything else except the gray and silver room, and this moment. Josh unhooked her stockings and rolled them down, and kissed the exposed white skin of her thighs. He kissed her belly, slowly tracing downward with his tongue, and then he turned her around and touched his mouth to her shoulders and the long furrow of her spine.

Julia's back arched. "Josh."

He picked her up and put her on his bed. She sank down into the feathery Swiss mattress, and the feather coverlet billowed luxuriously around her. She lay in her white nest, watching as Josh undid the ribbon of his black tie. He took the studs out of his shirtfront and the starched wings crackled. As he turned, bare-chested, Julia saw the vicious dark bruises down one side of his body. She jerked upright, her hair falling around her face, and he looked back at her. His face changed at the sight of her, and she was suddenly almost frightened.

"You're hurt," she whispered.

He was beside her, leaning over her, and she felt the heat of him.

"The snow fell on me," he told her. His mouth closed on her breast. Julia's head dropped back and she shuddered. Josh struggled out of the rest of his clothes.

"Isn't it painful?" Julia asked innocently. He leaned over her now, and she glimpsed the old, mocking Josh.

"Tomorrow I won't be able to move. But tonight who gives a goddamn?"

He lay down beside her, and they reached out for each other, smiling. It seemed very simple to Julia. There was only Josh, and Josh was all she wanted. Her arms locked triumphantly around his neck.

"Are you sure you want to?" Josh whispered. "The first time . . ."

"It isn't the first time. I went to bed with Felix. The day of Jessie's funeral."

He lifted his head to look at her. "Is that so? That surprises me a little."

"We were both so sad. It was very sad too. It didn't work very well." She thought of Felix, left alone in the flat waiting for his call-up. He seemed close, important. "But it made us better friends."

"I'm glad," Josh said.

She knew that he meant he was glad she was friends with Felix, that he didn't have to take the responsibility for the first time, that she was here with him now. If there was anything missing, Julia willed herself not to notice it.

"I think it will be better for you and me," Josh murmured.

His hands stroked her, teasing her, and there was no need to say any more. Julia closed her eyes, and this time there was no interruption, nothing except the muffled, unheard music of the little string orchestra and the unseen silver light.

Josh was as thorough and as expert at lovemaking as at everything else. He was generous, too, and he found that his gentleness drew from Julia's narrow body an intensity that he had never dreamed of.

Julia hardly knew her own body. Betty's influence had been strong enough to make sure of that. But what Josh did seemed so natural, surprising at first and then essential. She was amazed to discover that he did it without embarrassment, only humor and tenderness, and she responded to him as he guided her. Their bodies wound together, shiny and supple, and the squares of moonlight crept over the floor.

In the Swann Hotel ballroom the violins played the last waltz and the English skiers joined hands for "Auld Lang Syne." Julia and Josh didn't hear the singing or the cheering.

At last, when he could lead her no further, Julia's head fell back and she cried out, one long, silent cry. The discovery was made. The enormous simplicity of it, the depth of satisfaction, left her peacefully rocking like a boat on a wide, spangled sea. She turned and looked into Josh's eyes. Her mouth curved and he touched it with the tips of his fingers.

Beneath their window the dancers were streaming out of the hotel and lights glimmered on the snow. Julia and Josh lay quite still in each other's arms, almost shy now, faintly awed by what they had created between them.

"Thank you," Josh said gravely.

Julia was so happy that she wanted to laugh. The feathers from the white coverlet tickled her throat and suddenly she was shaking with it. Josh laughed, too, rolling her over and over in the mounds of the mattress and kissing her face and her neck and her breasts. They clung together and Julia rested her head on his chest.

"I didn't think it would be like that," she admitted. "I didn't think it would be so . . . important. I love you, Josh." Her eyes shone and her face was suddenly wet with tears. Josh stroked her hair. He was looking at the navy blue square of the window, and he didn't see her face.

There was snow outside the window, and he remembered

the race. The Inferno medal was still pinned to his ski sweater. Josh grinned in the darkness. Julia was in his bed, with her long legs wound around him and the fresh apple scent of her skin caught in the feather folds. He had enjoyed making love to Julia more than anyone else he could remember. Her pleasure, the surprising strength of it, had made his own much keener. Josh felt himself harden again at the thought of it.

He turned and buried his face in her hair.

"I love you too," Josh said.

Later, Julia asked him, "No Frau Uberl's?"

Drowsily, Josh said, "Nope. No Frau Uberl's. I guess I'm popular enough tonight for even Tuffy Brockway to turn a blind eye to immorality. So you see, honey, ski racing does have its uses after all."

In the morning, Julia woke up first. She lay looking at the duck-egg-blue sky and thinking, This is being happy. Here and now. If I could take hold of this moment, and keep it . . .

Josh stirred beside her, and groaned. He opened his eyes and saw Julia leaning over him. Her dark hair brushed his face.

"I told you I wouldn't be able to move."

Julia lifted the covers and inspected his bruises.

"Hmm. Looks nasty. But you don't seem to be too badly damaged elsewhere."

"That's luck."

Julia grinned. Then she lifted her hips and gently slid her body over his.

"Would you like me to move for you?"

"Yes, please," Josh said.

It was long past breakfast time at Frau Uberl's when Julia skidded back through the snow to the chalet. The hem of Mattie's dress was bunched up under her coat, but Julia felt that her evening slippers were painfully conspicuous to the ski-booted crowds. She reached the gate of the chalet and slipped in through the front door and up the stairs. In her room all four beds looked identically slept in, and Frau Uberl's maid was polishing the floor under Felicity's. Julia shot her a dazzling smile, grabbed her ski clothes, and fled to the bathroom to change. Sophia was hovering there, white-faced after her evening of champagne and army officers. They eyed each other, and then Julia held out her hand.

None of them was like Mattie, but Josh was right. They were nice, friendly girls.

"Thanks," Julia said.

Sophia nodded and weakly shook hands. "We guessed you wouldn't be in. We rolled in your bed and told the frau you'd gone out early to the slopes. She looked so pleased that you were getting keen at last, it was quite touching." Sophia peered at her, but she was clearly feeling too ill to be envious. "What about you? Are you all right?"

"Never better."

Sophia shuddered and gripped the edge of the basin. "Wish I could say the same."

Julia patted her back. "What you need is Mattie Banner's patent hangover cure. I'll get you a glass."

Innocent in her ski clothes, Julia ran downstairs to the girls' sitting room. A tray of drinks was kept on the sideboard for them to offer to their visitors, and Julia had seen a bottle of vodka lurking behind the sherry. She sloshed tomato juice on top of a generous slug of it and bore the glass into the kitchen. Assuring Frau Uberl that the English often resorted to it when they required a really nourishing snack after violent exercise, she added a beaten egg. Under Felix's tutelage, Mattie insisted on celery salt for her own concoction. There was nothing of the kind in Frau Uberl's cupboard, so Julia put in a liberal dash of Tabasco sauce and carried the result up to Sophia.

She put the glass into her shaking hand.

"Here you are. It's kill or cure, actually."

Sophia gulped it down. "Oh, God." In Sophia's case it was cure. Fifteen minutes later the girls were in a café, facing each other over mugs of hot chocolate.

"So you stayed the night with Josh?" Sophia narrowed her eyes against her cigarette smoke, a woman of the world.

Julia nodded. It was snug in the café, and missing Mattie to confide in, she blurted out, "It was the first time."

Sophia stared at her, unable to keep hold of her veneer of knowingness. "What was it like?"

Julia remembered asking Mattie, in the same words, on top of the bus from Euston Station. *It was all right,* Mattie had said. Only that. Because of the dreadful-sounding man she had chosen? *Oh, Mattie,* Julia thought. And then she looked over the rim of her cup into Sophia's prominent pale blue eyes.

"It was wonderful," she said, with perfect honesty.

After that, Julia found that she enjoyed Wengen as much as Josh had promised her she would. With the Inferno safely behind him he was free to ski with her, and under Josh's instruction Julia blossomed. It was as if something profound had happened to her body. Her knees flexed of their own accord, and her rigid spine melted. Her skis were no longer flat, heavy boards that tangled and crossed and willfully tripped her up. They grew sharp edges that hissed delightfully through the snow and even, one magical afternoon, carried her all the way down the hated nursery slope in a series of elegant arcs.

"Hey." Josh caught her cheeks between his gloved hands. "You can do it."

Julia beamed back at him. "You're right. I can do it."

In that successful instant she had caught a glimpse, at last, of what they were all so mad about.

Josh took her on the little train, on upward from Wengen to Kleine Scheidegg, right under the blue and gray pyramid of the Eiger. With Josh's broad blue shoulders reassuringly just ahead of her, she skied all the way down again.

"You can ski," he told her. "You may not make a flier, but you can damn well ski."

Julia was so glowingly proud of herself, and so pretty, that he wanted to undo her ridiculous parka and make love to her there and then on the icy piste that led down into Inner Wengen.

There were no more nights in the Swann Hotel, but there were afternoons as the skiers crossed through the snow under their window, calling to one another, and the white light faded gently to blue and then to gray as soft as the duck feathers that escaped from their covers.

Their evenings were noisy with music and skiing jokes and the giggly company of Belinda and the others.

"We didn't like you much to start with," Sophia confided as they downed another glühwein. "We thought you were, you know . . ."

"Non-sku? Like Sandy Mackintosh?" Julia asked innocently.

Sophia blushed and giggled. "But you're good fun. And you've got guts as well. That's what counts."

Julia widened her eyes. "Guts? Is that really it?" But there was no point in teasing Sophia, because she was never aware of it. "I thought you were all stupid and snobbish. But you're okay, really, all of you. *And* you can ski."

They raised their glasses and toasted each other.

Julia had been in Switzerland for almost two weeks when she

looked out of the window of the Swann Hotel and sighed at the sight of a fresh fall of snow.

"Grass," she said softly. "Leaves and bare earth. Flowers. They're there, underneath it all, aren't they?"

Josh came up behind her and put his arms around her waist. "Restless? It'll be time to move on, pretty soon."

Julia had known that the sentence must be pronounced, but she was angry with herself for being the instigator of it.

"I'm not restless. I'd like to stay here forever."

Josh laughed. "Well, I've got to get back and rake together some dollars to pay for our pleasures. But what would you say to going south just for a few days first?"

She looked at him, knowing that she would follow him anywhere. "South of what?"

"Italy. I've never seen much of it."

"I'd say yes."

Josh's energy was impressive. Once anything was decided, arrangements were made at whirlwind speed. Maps were consulted and tickets were bought, a farewell party was held in the Swann Bar, and they were on their way, all in the space of twenty-four hours. Belinda and Sophia and Felicity came down to Lauterbrunnen to wave them off.

"Bye-ee! See you next year? Promise? Really and truly?" They meant Julia as well as Josh. Josh only grinned at them, but Julia murmured, "I'll try." A year with Josh was unimaginable, but it was unthinkable without him.

She felt cold as she sat down opposite him.

The train journey took them from Berne to Turin, from Turin to Rome, and from Rome to Naples. The landscapes sliding past the smeared windows of the hard-seated Italian railway carriages conquered even Julia's impatience with long journeys. She watched entranced as the world changed from white to brown, and from brown to rich, succulent green. South of Rome there were silvery olive groves and vines that had put out fresh leaves, men working in the fields and wildflowers scrambling over the banks beside the track. After the hard white Alps the fecundity made Julia feel drunk. The train slowed beside a country road, and there was an old woman in a black dress trudging beside a donkey, its wicker panniers full of yellow flowers.

"Look." Julia pointed, her eyes shining.

Josh took her hand. "I like traveling with you. Everything hits you square in the face."

"It's because I've never seen anything before," Julia told

him. She wanted to fix everything inside her head so that she could remember it when it was all gone. They reached Naples, and found a crumbling hotel to stay in. Julia made Josh buy a guidebook, and led him through tiny, teeming streets into musty churches, down rancid alleyways into food markets, up steps and around corners into dead ends. The smells and the crowds and the color and sudden violence of street life fascinated her. She was alternately shocked by the poverty and charged by the pure vitality of the people. Josh was less drawn to it all. He had an American distaste for their unsanitary hotel, and a positive mania about the Neapolitan ingenuity at relieving him of his money.

"Damn cities," he grumbled. "I didn't come to see places like this, and one old church is pretty much the same as the next one. Let's get out of here and find a country place."

They went on southward to Salerno, and from Salerno they rode on country buses through wide green fields dotted with herds of slow-moving buffalo. The sea glittered at the end of empty roads, bluer than the postcard cliché that Julia had envisaged. In the end it was Julia who saw the perfect stopping place. A steep hill reared out of the coastal plain, and thick stone walls and a skirt of houses clung to the top of it, looking down over a blanket of scrubby trees and bare outcrops of rock to the Gulf of Policastro at its foot.

She knew only three words of Italian, but somehow she made the bus driver understand what she wanted. *"Questo è Montebellate,"* he told her.

Obligingly, he stopped to let them off. They climbed down with their heavy suitcases and stood blinking in the sunshine, much too hot in their thick clothes. The bus trundled away and left Julia and Josh staring at the tortuously steep road that led up to Montebellate.

They were lucky. A dusty pickup truck driven by a nut-faced man stopped, and they climbed into the back. They wound upward, the ancient engine laboring, and slowly the Campania countryside and the shimmering sea spread out beneath them. Julia saw that the rough grass between the rocks was starred with wildflowers, flowers that looked like English harebells and ladies' smock, but bigger and brighter. The pungent scent of herbs was everywhere, reminding her sharply of Felix, cooking at home.

"Italy," Julia murmured voluptuously.

If only Felix could see this. In the square, in London, it was mid-March and the bare plane trees would be shiny-black with rain.

When they reached the little houses clinging under the shelter of the stone walls, their driver shouted a torrent of Italian and stopped with a jerk outside a little pink-washed house. The door was painted the same blue as the harebells, and above it was a hand-painted sign, PENSIONE FLORA.

"Can we stay here?" Julia breathed.

Josh hauled cheerfully at the luggage. "Why not?"

A woman in an apron came out of the pensione and stared at them. Josh opened the phrase book they had bought in Naples and began to ask.

Julia couldn't bear to listen in case the woman said no. She crossed the road and folded her arms on the top of the warm stone wall. The hill rolled precipitously from its foot. Below her was the sea, fringed with white and gold, and the ochre and spring-green and amber squares of the land.

Josh came back and leaned beside her. The sun laid a buttery light on his head.

"She says they've got only one room. I couldn't pretend we're married, because she's quite likely to ask for our passports." Julia's heart dropped like a stone, and she wondered why he was smiling. "But she says that there are two beds. I explained that in that case we would be happy to take the one room."

"Oh, Josh."

The signora took them upstairs.

There were two beds with elaborately wrought iron bedheads, bare floorboards and a massive wardrobe, and a marble-topped washstand with a tin jug and basin on it. When the blue shutters were opened they framed the incomparable view.

When Julia remembered the few days that she spent in Montebellate with Josh, the same sharp mixture of delight and agony always came back to her.

She had never imagined anywhere so perfectly beautiful. There was nothing jarring, nothing ugly at all, not even a tablecloth with a strident pattern, a shiny car or a phonograph to remind her of her own world. Everything in Montebellate looked as if it had occupied its own place, exactly as it was meant to do, for hundreds of years. Behind the stone walls at the top of the hill was a pink-walled medieval palazzo, now housing a nunnery. The chapel bell rang the hours over the roofs of the village, and Julia and Josh kept their time by it, leaving Josh's watch on the marble washstand in the bedroom. They walked through the twisting streets until they knew every doorway, and they climbed over the rocks on the hill to look at the flowers. They sat for hours on the low walls and looked out over the sea on one side and the land on the other. They ate the platefuls of pasta that the signora put in front of them, and struggled to understand her jovial husband's well-meaning conversation. At night they made love, over and over again, with appetites that seemed to grow steadily sharper. They were as quiet as they knew how to be, but Julia was afraid that their hosts must hear them. In the mornings the signora impassively served them warm bread and local honey, and coffee with a steaming jug of hot milk.

But the beauty and the calm of Montebellate stabbed at her. Montebellate had all the time, and Julia was afraid that she had only a few days. She wanted to fix herself and Josh as Montebellate was fixed, but with Josh there was nothing to hold on to. He was wonderful company and he was generous and kind to her, but he gave nothing away. No promises, not even any talk of next week, next month. Julia longed to be satisfied with as much as they had, but she was greedy for more, and she was helpless. Every time she heard the flat notes of the chapel bell and imagined the nuns' habits sweeping over the hollowed steps, she was dreading that Josh would say, "Time to move on, pretty soon."

The peace grew threatening and their unbroken intimacy only reminded her that it must end soon.

On the fourth morning, as they sat drinking their coffee at the table in the window of the Pensione Flora, Julia knew that she would have to burst the bubble for herself before Josh could do it.

Her hands shook and her cup rattled against her plate.

"What's wrong?" Josh asked quietly.

It occurred to her that they had lived through all these hours together, and Josh had grown to matter more to her than herself, but still they seemed hardly to know each other. She was afraid of the detachment that might lie behind his eyes. The tears stung in her own eyes, but she stared hotly through them.

"We have to go soon, don't we?"

He nodded.

The tears ran slowly down her cheeks now. Josh wasn't looking at her.

"I don't want to go. I want to stay with you. Josh, what will happen to us?"

He looked down at the tablecloth. It was scattered with fragments of broken bread. Josh marshalled the crumbs with his forefinger.

At length he said, "We had a good time, didn't we?"

Julia wanted him to say, *Come with me. Live with me. Be my woman, or my wife.* She knew that he wouldn't, but she had clung absurdly to the hope. But what he said was, *We had.*

She nodded, wiping the tears away with the flat of her hand. "Yes. I never thanked you properly."

Josh sighed, and closed his fingers around her wrist. "You did."

The chapel bell was ringing again. With a separate, chilly part of herself Julia wondered if it was for refectory, or prayers, or work in the kitchens and garden. She stood up, not looking at him.

"I'm sorry. I wish I could make things easy. You'd like that, wouldn't you?"

"Julia . . ."

"Don't. Just don't." She shook her hand free of his. "I'm going for a walk."

After she had gone Josh sat staring at the tablecloth, still heaping the fragments of bread with his finger. For a moment he wasn't thinking of Julia. Her words, or perhaps the way she had pulled away and run out of the room, had reminded him of something else. In place of the Pensione Flora he saw the kitchen table back at home, even the loaf of bread and the jar of jelly next to his plate. He had been having his tea. The porch door opposite him still rattled in its frame. His mother had run out, banging it behind her, and the silence that had descended when she was gone was doubly ominous because of the noise that had gone before. Shouting. They were always shouting at each other, at least his mother shouted and his father sat, numbed by it. It had been the worst of all that time.

In the quiet afterward his father sat perfectly still, looking nowhere, rubbing his big hand up and down his face.

That was the last of those times, of course. She hadn't lived in the timber house with them, after that.

Josh made two concentric circles with his heap of crumbs. He was wondering why the net of memories had come back to him here, on a hilltop overlooking the Mediterranean. It wasn't just a door banging, of course, or a cloth scattered with crumbs. Josh frowned. In a life consciously dedicated to enjoyment, plain thinking didn't give much comfort. But he had seen Julia's face smeared with tears and he wanted to make the way straight, now, for her sake.

He thought of high school, and the year at the University of

Colorado, mostly spent on skis, before he had set off for Europe and drifted finally to Harry Gilbert's air-freight base. All through that time, popularity had followed him like a shadow in sunlight. And Josh was shrewd enough to know why men and women liked him. Not always for the right reasons, but it was more comfortable to be liked than otherwise. He had loved some of them in return, of course. But with circumspection, and only for as long as it did stay comfortable. Josh didn't like scenes. Scenes were naked displays of anger or passion or despair, and he recoiled from them. Perhaps, he thought with a touch of bitterness now, that was why he and his father had lived together so safely for so long. By backing away from any more danger. By pretending nothing dangerous existed.

With a sudden savage movement Josh swept the crumbs off the table and onto the floor.

Julia was different. He had taken her up because he had wanted her, more keenly than usual, but it had happened a dozen times before. He had done it with misgivings, but he had found that he had already gone too far to step backward again. And he had discovered, comparing her with Sophia Bliss and all the others at Wengen, even here in the last days in their Italian paradise, how dangerous Julia was. She wanted everything, all of life and not just himself. She was raw and hungry and contemptuous, but she was more eager to give than anyone he had ever encountered. Josh knew that he had always found it easier to take. He looked out of the little window into the sunshine without any liking for himself, but with a certain knowledge of what he must do.

He got up slowly and ducked through the low doorway. Then he walked across the road and sat down on the wall to wait for Julia.

She had lingered outside for a moment, looking at the blue haze hanging in the sky. It was like a veil over the land.

Suddenly Julia didn't want to look at the view anymore. She walked quickly up the hill, hugging the high stone wall that enclosed the palazzo grounds. It was so steep that she was panting when she reached the top. There was a little square with plane trees just coming into leaf, and a seat built around the trunk of one of them. Julia sat down, painfully picking at the tree bark. It made her think of the London square, and going unwillingly back to it.

There was a beating need inside her, and she knew that there was no outlet for it. She jumped up, trying to contain the pressure, and ran across to the palazzo gates. The iron curlicues were rusty. Beyond the pink walls she could see the corner of a garden. There were dark trees and hedges, breathing neglect. The nuns didn't work the gardens after all.

Julia's fingers wound around the metal bars, and she stared through, trying to catch her breath in even gasps that would half-fill her lungs.

She stood for a long time, looking in at the glimpse of overgrown garden.

When she turned back to the square again she saw that one of Montebellate's black-clad old women had appeared. She had driven a goat up with her, and now she tethered it to a post driven into a tiny square of grass. The goat put its head down at once. The old woman nodded to Julia and shuffled to the seat. She fumbled in her black pouch bag and produced her crochet work. Julia saw that it was a tiny, lacy diamond. The white thread was as fine as a cobweb. The crochet hook flickered and the old woman stared with milky eyes over the goat's back to the blue line beyond the roofs.

Very slowly Julia let her head fall back against the gates. Nothing moved, and there was no sound except the goat's rhythmic cropping.

She had a sense of years, stretching away, waiting for her. The enormity of it frightened and frustrated her, because it lay out of her grasp. Yet the prospect soothed her. It was all far distant, immense and hazy, like the view from the hill. Julia wondered for how many years the old woman and her goat had looked at their own view before achieving their postures of perfect mutual calm.

She watched them for a little while longer until her breath came smoothly. The hammering inside her body had stopped. The tears still lay behind her eyes, but she knew that she could go back to the Flora and face whatever Josh would tell her.

She went back down the hill, listening to the steady clopping of her shoes over the cobbles. Josh was sitting on the wall opposite the pensione, looking down, and Julia went and stood beside him. They watched the view in silence for a moment, but it was just a view again, opaque, almost overfamiliar now.

In a clear voice Josh said, "I can't give you what you want. There isn't anything of me. Nothing that you should want, or need, anyway. You'll see that for yourself before long, but I don't want you to be hurt while it happens."

Clumsy, inept words, Josh thought. But for once he meant them.

Julia's answer came at once, violent, spilling out of her. "How could you hurt me except by not letting me be with you? I do want you. I love you and I need you. No one has ever made me happy like you, and I don't want anything else. Nothing at all, nothing out of life if you aren't there. Don't you understand?"

It helped, to abase herself. It made her feel that there was no more she could do. She had held out the offering for Josh to take. *Take it,* she implored him. *Don't say what I'm afraid of.*

"No," Josh said, very gently.

There.

Julia nodded her head, just once. The words had been said, all their words. She discovered that she had pride too.

"What will happen?" she asked.

Josh said, "I'll take you to Agropoli and put you safely on the train."

"The train to where?"

"To London."

London. There was nothing in London. Julia's eyes were dry and hard. She wouldn't cry now. There would be enough time for crying later.

"And what about you? What will you do?"

"I don't know yet. Some flying. Something."

Julia lifted her hands from the crumbling stonework of the wall. "I'd better go and pack my things up."

They turned to each other then. She buried her face against his shoulder and he held her, and then he lifted her face between his hands and kissed her eyes and her mouth. They knew that the signora could see them out of her lace-hung window, and they stepped awkwardly apart again.

"Will we . . . will I see you anymore?"

"I hope so," Josh whispered. Faltering, at the end.

Julia looked at him. She was remembering that way his hair fell over his forehead, the lines that his eyes made with his mouth and cheekbones. The same as the first time she had seen him.

"I hope so," she echoed. Her longing was already touched with bitterness. "I hope so, too, my aviator."

TEN

"What other work d'you suggest I do?" Mattie demanded.

Without looking at Julia she opened a leatherette holdall and threw a red satin slip into it. On top of the slip went a red bra and a red G-string stitched with a trail of sequins. A shapeless billow of red feathers was thrust in on top of that, and then some folds of dusty black stuff and a thin, whippy cane.

Julia looked sourly at the cane. "Miss Matilda, indeed."

Mattie zipped the bag up and leaned over to look at herself in the mirror. She licked her forefinger and brushed her eyebrows into shape before finally turning to Julia.

"Listen, love. If they were begging me to give my Ophelia at the Old Vic, it would be different. In fact, if anyone offered me so much as a two-line walk-on in a kids' show in Wigan, I'd go down on my knees and give thanks. But no one has, have they? If I go to one more audition and the fat slobs say 'Thank you, dear, we'll let you know,' I'll push their scripts down their throats."

Julia said nothing and Mattie sighed patiently. "An even more important fact is that Miss Matilda earns me nearly thirty quid a week, cash, and it's not exactly the hardest work I've ever done. It's easier than selling shoes. It's easier than working for John Douglas, too, most days of the week."

"Taking your clothes off for a lot of dirty old men?"

Mattie laughed then and sat down on the bed beside her. "I'm an *artiste*, remember. I don't just take my clothes off. I do a dance routine, very tasteful. I act as well. I become a schoolmistress, with the heart and soul of a courtesan trapped within her."

Julia was laughing now. They sat side by side with their arms around each other's shoulders, shaking with it.

Mattie stood up. "Oh, what the hell. Let's have a drink before I go."

Julia sighed and took the glass of gin Mattie gave her. She looked around the bedroom at the twisted stockings and heaps of discarded clothes with sudden distaste. Without Felix, Mattie and Julia had reverted to their old ways. She frowned, annoyed with herself.

"Hey." Mattie touched her arm. "Who are you really worrying about?"

"Both of us, Mat. Both of us."

The gin had warmed Mattie up and she leaned forward confidingly. Julia was reminded of Jessie. They missed Jessie every day, even now.

"Don't worry. I'm a brilliant actress, temporarily filling in as a stripper. My turn will come. You are rather smartly employed at George Tressider Designs, and you also have the chance of a modeling contract. . . ."

"Some pervert wants to photograph me. They always call it a modeling contract, didn't you know?"

"Don't be cynical. And you've got lovers, admirers, and friends. What more could you ask?"

Julia opened her mouth, but Mattie dived forward and clapped her hand over it.

"I know, I know. But until he flies back again you'll just have to make do with what you've got. Who is it tonight, by the way?"

Julia acknowledged the interruption with a twisted smile. "Flowers."

"Flowers, faithfully unfaithful Flowers." Mattie was springing around the room, gathering up the last pieces of her costume. "D'you know, it's your fault, and Flowers's, that I'm working for Monty now? You were the ones who left our luggage at The Showbox. *I* was the one who was shocked, remember?"

"Right at the beginning. The day Flowers bought me a coffee and a doughnut in Blue Heaven. We met Felix that night, and Jessie. More than three years ago."

Mattie straightened up slowly and they looked at each other. "Do you feel old?" Mattie asked.

They were twenty and twenty-one.

"Very, very old."

They didn't laugh, for some reason.

Mattie hoisted her holdall over her shoulder and made for the door. Julia watched her go and then called after her. "You missed something off your list. We've got each other."

Mattie's head reappeared, a mass of waves, now bleached white-blond. "And always will have. Listen, I finish at twelve on the dot tonight. I'll meet you and Flowers at the Rocket."

Julia listened to her thumping away down the stairs. Flowers and the Rocket. The Showbox and Monty. Saturday afternoon in the flat stretching ahead of her, then Sunday, and Monday morning again at Tressider's scented premises in the King's Road. Julia's fists clenched until her fingernails dug into the palms of her hands. Her impatience was no easier to control than it had ever been. A sense of her own purposelessness rose stiflingly around her, and she jumped up and went to the window. Mattie was crossing the square on her way to Old Compton Street, and Julia watched her until she was out of sight. It was November, and the last yellow leaves lay in archipelagoes on the wet sidewalks. Three years ago, she was thinking, Josh had come. And in the spring he had sent her home from Italy. A little time in weeks and months, but it seemed much longer in her memory. Twisted up with what Betty had told her on the day she first saw Josh, with Jessie's death, and with Felix.

After Montebellate she had crept back to London. There had been office jobs, a succession of them that she could hardly remember now. Josh had come back and gone away again, then come back once more. Julia knew that he should have had the determination to stay away altogether, but she clung to the hope that he couldn't, and gratefully took the crumbs of time that he bestowed on her. She had been very lonely in those days, without Mattie or Felix at home.

With one finger Julia drew a deliberate circle in the condensation on the window. Drops like tears gathered around the clear margin and slid downward.

Two years ago, November 1956. There had been a convulsion then. Julia had read the newspapers and listened to the radio reports with fierce concentration, as if her attention would make some difference to the world. Josh flew refugees from the Russian tanks out over the Austro-Hungarian border, and Felix was one of the few national servicemen to be sent out to Suez. She was intensely proud of both of them, and she knew equally that the remainder of her feelings were perfectly selfish. But she couldn't escape the conclusion, or fail to resent it, that it was men who had the chance of action. They could make the choices, bestow or deprive, whether the gift was simply happiness or even, that November, seemingly life itself. Her freedom, women's freedom, that totem she had upheld with Mattie, enabled her to go to work, to earn enough money to buy herself nylons and fashionable clothes, and to wait.

I have waited, Julia thought bitterly.

Another year, and then a time came when Josh told her that

he was going back to Colorado. Vail was beginning to open up as a ski resort and Josh, businesslike, saw his chance. The parting had been painful for both of them, but it hadn't hurt Josh enough to hold him back. Julia had tried to believe that she couldn't survive without him, but she had survived with dreary adequacy.

It was twelve months since she had last seen him. He wrote, sometimes. Julia turned away from the window again and began picking clothes up from the floor, unseeingly turning them the right way out, then laying them down again.

At about the same time Mattie had been spotted in one of her roles for John Douglas by a Binkie Beaumont scout. On the strength of it she had been offered a part in an ephemeral new play at the Lyric, Hammersmith. Julia had welcomed her back to the flat with relief, and they had fallen back into their old inseparability. But after the play had closed no more parts came up, and Mattie was philosophically performing as Miss Matilda for eight hours a day, six days a week.

Julia drifted into a more permanent job. She had gone to George Tressider Designs as a temporary secretary and stayed there partly because it interested her more than any of the other jobs she had had, partly because she had no ideas about what else she might do with her time.

George Tressider's sharp eyes noted and approved of her appearance, and he made her his receptionist. He was a velvety man of about fifty, an interior decorator with a list of prosperous or aristocratic clients and what Julia privately considered to be an overblown fondness for the grand English style. No chintzes were chintzier than George's, no gilt more gilted.

Julia sat at an Empire desk toward the rear of his small shop, surrounded by George's small selection of hand-picked antique pieces, and guarded the door through to the design offices where George and a handful of young men worked on the clients' requirements.

In a week when one of the young men was on holiday and two of the others had flu, Julia did some letters for George's signature. She also put together a selection of silks for a less important customer and interviewed an out-of-town dealer who had a pair of old mirrors to sell, fast. She looked at the photographs and made the man promise to see no one else before Mr. Tressider came back from the country that afternoon. She let the man take her to lunch, just to be sure.

At the end of the week George Tressider strolled past her

desk and rested one lavender-gray cuff on the back of her chair. "You're quite a clever creature, aren't you?" His smooth head tilted to one side as he studied her. "A decided asset. Pretty girls don't usually have as much brain as you do."

"Don't they?" Julia murmured. *How do you know anything about girls, pretty or not?* she added in silence.

"Mmm. I can offer you another two pounds a week. We could make your work more interesting. Flexible."

Julia was confident enough that George wouldn't make demands that were too interesting or called for too much flexibility.

"Thank you," she said meekly.

She wasn't elevated to the same status as the young men, of course, but for the first time in her working life she didn't dread Monday mornings as a return to slavery. Betty called it "a real job."

Very gradually over the last year Julia had started visiting Fairmile Road again. It was the finality of Josh's disappearance that had made her feel she was being too harsh in cutting herself off altogether from Betty and Vernon. It seemed a long time since she had run away, and in those years the house, and her parents' strictures, and the threat of both, seemed to have shrunk sadly in importance. When she saw it again the house seemed to have shrunk too. It was poky, and shabbier than she remembered, in spite of Betty's protracted polishings. Even the Smiths themselves seemed smaller, and older.

The first two or three visits were awkward, but slowly a pattern was established. Julia went home about once a month, always on a Sunday, arriving after Betty and Vernon came home from church and staying for dinner and tea. Once, unthinkingly, she called their midday meal *lunch*. She saw Betty look at her with a new expression and recognized respect in it, with resignation, and timid approval. After that it was always *lunch* that Betty invited her to. The way that they had both noticed the little distinction and resolutely left it uncommented on underlined the speed with which Julia was marching away from Fairmile Road. The fact that Julia imagined she despised class distinction, and used the words she did only because she was more used to hearing them from George and his people, seemed only to emphasize the difference.

But it was just enough, for all of them, that Betty had found a way to be proud of her daughter again. After all, Julia worked with a smart decorator in Chelsea, and she talked to people with titles. Betty was always eager to hear about that, and it provided a safe topic of conversation while Vernon sat behind the *Sunday People*. "Thirty square yards of pure white Carrera marble," Julia would say, "in the master bathroom."

"Imagine," Betty would breathe. "The master bathroom."

Julia was oddly touched by the simplicity of her mother's pride, and her view of her mother's life was softened by her own experiences. The two women would never be friends, that was understood, but they were polite and considerate to each other for the few hours of their Sunday visits. Vernon mattered less to Julia. She had never understood her father and she doubted that she ever would.

The fact of her adoption was never, ever mentioned.

On Sunday evenings Julia took the train back to Liverpool Street with composed relief. She was far enough away, now, not to feel the old, frightened jubilation. On those short, familiar journeys she often thought of Jessie. If Betty Smith had possessed any of Jessie's qualities, what would the difference have been? Julia did know that Jessie would have approved of the bloodless truce that had been called.

Between the opposite poles of Tressider's and Fairmile Road, there was the square, and Mattie. Julia wondered if this was real life, if this was what she should be living instead of waiting through. In the year since Josh had left for good, Julia had done her best to distract herself. She existed at a pace that raised even Mattie's eyebrows. There was usually a party, and when there wasn't, Julia set out to create one. At a party, or at the Rocket, or wherever else she went that was crowded enough, there was always the chance of meeting someone new, someone who would survive the comparison.

The ripples of meetings spread wider and wider. Mattie and Julia had installed a telephone in Jessie's room, and it rang constantly. The men they met as they sliced their way through the parties still looked at Mattie first, but more often it was Julia who finally commanded their attention. Her hunger was indefinable but potent. She could look at the latest possibility as if there were no one else in the world, and then sooner or later she would look through him as if he didn't exist. Many of them found the treatment irresistible, but Julia seemed hardly to notice. She went to bed with two or three of them, but she did it more because Josh had stirred her sexual needs than because she particularly wanted any of his successors. She took her sharp physical pleasure, and then felt painfully guilty.

She was always comparing. But no one ever came close to

Josh. Josh had made her feel alive, as though thick, dead layers of skin had been peeled back to leave all her senses sharpened. She missed him every hour of the day, every night.

Mattie despaired of her. "No man is worth loving to distraction," she insisted.

"Josh is," Julia said simply.

"So what will happen?"

Julia shook her head slowly from side to side. "I don't know. But something will. It must."

The flat was quiet without Mattie.

Julia finished picking up the discarded clothes and went through into Jessie's room. The old bed had been exchanged for a third-hand plush-covered sofa, but everything else was almost the same. Julia walked slowly around, picking up the framed photographs and looking down into the mysterious faces, running her fingers over Felix's eclectic arrangements of bits and pieces. Dust collectors, Jessie had always called them. They were certainly thick with dust now. The paisley shawl on the sofa back was wrinkled and creased, and the water in a vase of long-dead flowers brought by one of Julia's friends smelled stagnant. The room was stale and neglected. Mattie and Julia hardly ever touched down for long enough to sit in it. Felix would be disgusted, Julia thought, smiling a little.

Felix had completed his national service. He had seemed even more self-contained afterward, restrained and economical in his relationship with Mattie and even with Julia. But they had had little enough time to judge. He had gone almost straight to Florence. "I always wanted to," he told them. "Before Ma got ill."

He supported himself by working as a hotel cleaner, and studied art history. Thinking about him, Julia found a sudden focus for her restlessness. She would fill the afternoon by restoring the murky flat to the pristine condition that Felix would have approved of. She was whistling as she tied her hair up in a scarf and wrapped herself in a faded smock that must have belonged to Jessie. The kitchen sink was full of dishes, and Julia set to work.

When she finished it had been dark outside for more than an hour. The rooms smelled of polish and fresh air, and there was no more dust or dishes to be done. Julia's back ached, but she was satisfied as she emptied her bucket of water and wrung out her cloths. Felix would approve. She was just putting the kettle on the stove when the doorbell rang. Julia ran downstairs past the locked offices to the front door.

A man was standing on the step. He had thick gray hair and a lined face, and he leaned heavily on a stick. Julia had no idea who he was. He looked at her without interest, and then peered past her.

"I'm looking for Mattie Banner," he announced.

His voice told Julia what his appearance had failed to.

"Um. I'm afraid Mattie isn't here. She's working this evening."

"In the theater?"

"Not . . . not exactly."

The man frowned irritably at her. "What?"

It just finished, Mattie had said. *We ran out of things to need from each other. Or just didn't find enough of them.* That was all she would say.

Julia held the door open wider. "You'd better come in."

"Thank you. My name's John Douglas."

Upstairs, Julia turned on the lamp in Jessie's newly glowing room. John Douglas was breathing hard after the long climb up the stairs, but he looked around in clear surprise.

"Hmm. Not what I imagined."

Julia smiled innocently. "What did you imagine?"

"Less domestic order, knowing Mattie as well as I do."

"Ah." Julia untied her scarf and shook out her hair, then took off Jessie's baggy smock. John Douglas stared again, but this time Julia hid her smile.

"I'm Mattie's friend, Julia."

"I'm sorry, I thought you were the bloody cleaning woman."

"I'm both today. Why do you want to see Mattie?"

John Douglas reached inside his overcoat and took out a big, thick brown envelope. He laid it carefully on the table.

"I want her to do something. Don't look at me like that. Not for me, for once. For herself. Where is she?"

Julia sighed. "Let me make us both a cup of tea. Then I'll tell you."

Mattie leaned against the grimy wall in the tiny changing cubicle behind the stage at the Showbox. It was eleven-thirty P.M. and she was waiting to do her last spot of the night. It would be her fifteenth of the day. The music playing for the girl onstage stabbed monotonously through her skull.

Monty owned four other little clubs in the surrounding streets, and like all his other girls Mattie spent her day working a circuit of them. When one act was over she would pull her clothes on again backstage and haul her bag with her costume in it through the streets to the next club, and the next invisible audience hunched in the dark beyond the footlights. When her music started, a crackly version of "Teach Me Tonight" that had dinned itself sickeningly into her head, it was time to bundle her hair up under the tasseled mortarboard and sweep through the curtains and onto the stage. Into the cubicle afterward and dress again. Round and round. Sometimes Monty's schedule gave her enough time to down a gin in one of the pubs, or to share a sandwich with the other girls. There was a camaraderie between them that was nothing to do with friendship, everything to do with mutually surviving the physical demands and mental stultification of the job. Mattie's way of getting through the day was to treat each spot as a theatrical performance. She concentrated on injecting fresh nuances into the process of stripping down to her G-string and flinging it triumphantly offstage in the second before the lights went down.

The punters appreciated her work, and Monty loved it.

"You're a natural, pet. Born to it."

He even paid her a pound or two more than the other girls, swearing her to secrecy first.

The music stopped and the girl before Mattie came offstage and slouched into the cubicle. She had big blue-veined breasts. Neither the girl nor Mattie even glanced around when the boy who worked as backstage factotum dumped her discarded stage costume inside after her. Mattie didn't think she would ever care again who saw or didn't see her body. She had told Julia the truth when she said that stripping didn't bother her. It simply numbed her, somewhere inside herself, where she already felt cold. She yawned now, and wished there were somewhere to sit down and wait that wasn't the floor.

"One more tonight," she muttered. "I'm half dead."

The other girl was wriggling into her tight skirt. The zipper dragged at her flesh as she pulled it up. She glanced at Mattie and reached for her handbag.

"Here. Have a blue."

She held out a crumpled paper cone, just like the ones Mattie used to buy pennyworths of sweets in. Mattie dipped into it. She cupped the amphetamine in the palm of her hand and gulped it straight down.

"Thanks, Vee. Saved my life."

There had been some shuffling beyond the stage that meant new customers had arrived, but it had settled now into impatient creaking. The audience didn't like to be kept waiting for too long between turns.

The first bars of Mattie's music suddenly blared out and the backstage boy jerked his thumb at her. Mattie picked up her cane, made a resigned face at Vee, and pushed through the dusty curtains and onto the stage.

Julia sat between Flowers and John Douglas. The wooden chairs were very small, very hard and upright. She couldn't see much of the room because it was so dark, but she had the impression that she was the only woman. She folded her hands in her lap, aware of the laughable primness of her posture, and waited. She had never thought of coming to one of Mattie's performances before this, and Mattie had never suggested it. She wondered now if Mattie would mind.

The music was very loud and distorted. A black-gowned figure materialized on the stage. It was wearing a teacher's mortarboard and heavy spectacles with no glass in the frames, and it was just recognizably Mattie.

At first Julia wanted to laugh. The pantomime strictness, frowning, and cane-waving, were almost irresistibly funny. But then Mattie reached up and swept off her cap. Her wonderful hair fell over her face and down over her shoulders. There was a sigh of indrawn breath, and every man in the stuffy basement room leaned forward on his upright chair. Mattie smiled. She swung the point of her cane down to the stage and balanced it with the tip of one finger. With the other hand, lazily, she opened the front of her gown. Red satin flashed underneath it. With one movement Mattie slid the black stuff off her shoulders and let it fall at her feet. Her skin was so white that it looked blue under the lights.

She took her glasses off, touching them to her mouth before letting them drop. Miss Matilda was completely gone and it was Mattie on the stage, the shape of her only just veiled by her red slip. Mattie danced, moving as gracefully as she always did. Julia could hear John Douglas's breathing. Johnny Flowers was leaning forward, too, watching motionlessly. The straps of the flimsy thing eased off her shoulders. Under the red slip was the sequined bra and G-string that Julia had made fun of. The dance went on, and the lights caught on the sequins, twinkling points under the bald light. Mattie took the bra off. She stood still for a moment, her back half-turned, black shadows emphasizing her curves and hollows. The horrible music reached a crescendo.

Mattie unhooked the G-string and threw it aside. She turned completely around, her pretty body fully revealed.

Her expression was defiant, almost taunting.

Julia didn't feel the remotest desire to laugh now. Mattie's striptease had touched her, and she shivered. She also thought that it was painfully erotic.

A second later Mattie had disappeared. There was a wave of clapping, some foot-stamping and catcalling.

Beside Julia, John Douglas murmured, "Sweet Jesus Christ." Flowers took Julia's hand and held it tightly. They stood up in unison and pushed their way out through the darkness.

They waited for Mattie beside the row of trash cans outside the back door of the club. She emerged hardly a minute later, her hair wound up in a knot, ordinary Mattie again in her stovepipe trousers, except for a teacher's cane gripped in one fist.

She stared blankly at John Douglas.

Then she pointed back over her shoulder. "Were you in there tonight? All of you?" It was Julia who nodded.

Mattie suddenly grinned, surprisingly childlike. "It wasn't much cop, was it? I usually put more effort into it than that. I was too tired tonight." Her eyes looked very bright in the dingy light. "But I'm livening up now. Are we all going to the Rocket? You, too, John, whatever you're doing here."

His hand shot out and snatched at her wrist. "What in God's name do you think you're doing? In that place?"

Mattie stared at him for a second and then she shrugged wearily. "Don't you start. It isn't all that different from the theater, is it? One way or another?"

There was a silence. They stood there, in an awkward circle, until John Douglas said, "I want you to come home now. I want you to read something."

"To read? It's Saturday night. I want to go dancing. Julia?" She looked around to her for support, and the girls' eyes met.

"Go on," Julia said softly. "Go with him." So that Mattie couldn't protest anymore, she turned and let Johnny Flowers lead her away down the alley. She rested her head for a second against his black-leather shoulder.

"Come on, baby," he murmured. "You're big girls now. Both of you."

They came out into Wardour Street and began to walk northward toward the Rocket.

"Are we? Yes, I suppose we are." It was cold and the few

other shadowy figures in the street looked menacing. Julia shivered again. "I'm glad you're here, Johnny."

Cheerfully, he said, "I'm always here when I'm wanted."

Mattie turned the light on and glanced disparagingly around the room. "Julia's been at the polish again. Well, where is it? Whatever it is you want me to read?"

John Douglas picked the envelope up from its place on the table. Mattie opened it and took out a script in a blue binding.

"This?" The title was set in a little window cut out of the blue paper, and Mattie read it aloud. "*One More Day*. I've never heard of it."

"Why should you have?" John Douglas said sharply. "I more or less stole it, and I've left the company to bring it down here to you. Now, sit down in that chair and bloody well read it. Have you got any whiskey?"

Mattie opened the blue cover. "There's a bottle of gin in the kitchen."

"I never drink gin."

Mattie didn't answer. She was sitting in Jessie's old armchair with her legs drawn up underneath her, reading the play.

It took her an hour, and the only movement she made was to turn the pages.

When she did look up again she couldn't speak for a minute. When she did manage to ask the question, breathlessness caught at the words.

"Have they cast it yet?"

John Douglas shook his heavy gray head. "Auditions on Monday."

Mattie could hardly bear to look at him. "Can you get me in?"

"You're on the list, love. I've managed to do that much for you."

She got up then and went to him. She laid her cheek against his hair. "Why?"

"Because I think you can play the part. It might have been written for you."

Mattie waited, and then rubbed her cheek sadly against his head. Of course, John Douglas wouldn't say, *Because I love you. A little.* Even if he felt it, he wouldn't say it. He hadn't ever said anything of the kind. He had kept his irascible distance, and Mattie understood that there wouldn't be anything more between them. But he had come down here to give her this wonderful, terrifying play, and he had secured her an audition. He must believe, after all, that she could act. That was as good as being loved, wasn't it? Sometimes Mattie despised her own needs.

Very softly she said, "I can play it. I know I can."

"Good girl. And now, if there isn't anything else except bloody gin, perhaps we could have a cup of tea?"

Mattie went into the kitchen and came back with a tray after a few moments. She put it down on a low table in front of the hissing gasfire. The red glow of it shone through the tips of her hair, lending her a bronze halo. John Douglas was irresistibly reminded of the Showbox. Mattie up on the tiny, tawdry stage, with her hair spilling out from under the black cap. The worthless glitter of sequins and then her body, taunting and innocent at the same time.

Of all the ways she might have chosen to support herself. He was angry with her, and touched, and titillated. Yet if Mattie could do that, he thought, she had the toughness he had doubted in her. And she would need to be tough if she were to go the way she wanted. There might well be times when she would have to go further than stripping.

He stood up, ignoring his cup of tea, balancing awkwardly without the aid of his stick. He put his arm around her and pulled her body against his. "Do you remember the night in Yarmouth?"

"I remember."

He started kissing her and then rubbed his hands over her breasts, grunting softly. Mattie stood very still until he lifted his head again.

He saw her face, but he asked, "Shall we go to bed, then?"

"I don't think so," Mattie said as gently as she could. She was surprised to find that she had acquired a kind of resolve. "It didn't have very much value when we did it before. It seems a . . . meaningless transaction now."

He looked sharply at her, and then he thought of the men in the darkness at the Showbox, leaning forward to peer at her white skin. "I'm not surprised," was all John Douglas said.

Mattie exhaled with relief and immediately insisted, "But you must stay here tonight; there's Felix's room. You will, won't you?"

"Thank you," he said gravely. His arms had dropped to his sides and Mattie went away mumbling about sheets and blankets.

For a long time after John Douglas had gone to sleep in his room across the hallway, Mattie lay wide-eyed in her own bed. She was thinking about the audition. There was already a knot of longing and fear and determination in the pit of her stomach. The time when the Rocket would be closing came and went, but Julia didn't come home. Mattie guessed that she must have gone back to Bayswater, or Paddington, or wherever Flowers was currently living, tactfully leaving her on her own with John Douglas. Mattie's mouth twisted in the darkness, but the thought slipped away as quickly as it had come. She didn't sleep, or even close her eyes. She was thinking about *One More Day*. Her play. Her part.

"Name?"

"Mattie Banner."

The man in the middle of the row of chairs nodded, and drew a line through an item on a list in front of him. There were two other middle-aged men in the cold, bare rehearsal room, a woman with gray hair and a much younger girl who looked like someone's assistant. She had just brought coffee in mugs for everyone, except Mattie, of course. A young man with tufty black hair and a hungry, hollow face sat a little apart from them. Mattie thought he must be the playwright, Jimmy Proffitt. She stared covertly at him, wondering how someone she wouldn't have glanced at in the Rocket might have written such a play. He felt her eyes on him and looked up. Mattie stared at the room instead. It was in the Angel Theatre, a Victorian building of faded grandeur that had once been a music hall. It was in an unfashionable inner suburb, and it looked much the same as any of the northern theaters that Mattie had trailed through with Francis Willoughby's company. It existed just as precariously on the brink of financial collapse, but the Angel Company was distinguished by its willingness to stage new and experimental plays, to displease the lord chamberlain, and to give directors a free rein. Mattie recognized two of the men facing her by sight and by reputation. She swallowed and rolled the blue-covered script in damp hands.

"And you're going to read for the part of Mary?"

"Yes."

I want this part.

She had read it so many times since John Douglas had given it to her on Saturday night that she almost knew the lines already. The play was a tragedy, so raw and strident that it hurt Mattie's throat to whisper some of the words. But when she thought of other new pieces, three-act pieces of fluff that dealt with engagements and tea parties and family misunderstandings, as two-dimensional as the painted flat behind the French windows, Mattie wanted to laugh in the same harsh voice as Jimmy Proffitt's play.

"At the top of page seventeen, then. Mr. Curtis will read the part of Dennis for you. When you're ready, Miss Banner."

Mattie read.

At first her hands shook so much that the typed speeches jumped in front of her eyes and she faltered over the words. But then, as the lines worked inside her, Mary became more important than Mattie.

Jimmy Proffitt's Mary was a nineteen-year-old girl. Her husband was a boy even younger than herself, and they had a baby of five months. They lived in one room, and Mattie knew how it would be. The wallpaper would hang down in soaking strips and there would be foul blue-gray patches spreading behind it. Mattie also knew how life would be for Mary and Dennis. They would claw at each other while the baby cried, the way Jimmy Proffitt had made them do. There would be desperation, and the compensation of tenderness and savage laughter that he had also given them. The opening of the play was viciously comic, and then the seams of it split open. One night, after a quarrel with Mary, Dennis took their week's money and spent it on whiskey. Then, outside a bar, he met a man he owed money to. There was a fight, and Dennis killed him.

The stage was split for the rest of the play. On one side, Dennis was marched toward life imprisonment. On the other, Mary slowly lost her insignificant battle. In the last scene she gave her baby away to a childless woman. The woman paid her fifty pounds. Mary went home and burned the money, and then she blew out the flame and knelt down in front of the square mouth of the oven.

When Mattie finished her reading there was a brief silence, no more than a second or two. The director looked up from his lists. "Thank you. Have you prepared another piece for us? Anything you like."

"Umm. One of Rosalind's speeches. From *As You Like It*." Mattie wasn't sure why she had chosen it, except in the vague hope that if she did Shakespeare they might mistake her for a proper actress. She was hardly half a dozen lines into the speech before the man held up his hand.

"Right, right. Not thoroughly at home with the classics, eh?"

Mattie waited, her arms limp at her sides. They were mumbling with their heads together now. Then the gray-haired woman said, "Thank you, Miss—ah—Banner. We'll let you know."

She made her way, somehow, across the apparent miles of dusty floor to the door. She was only dimly aware, through her misery, of Jimmy Proffitt moving behind her, more mumbled talk. The door was already open when the director called, "Could you wait outside, please?"

She wanted to let her head fall forward, to rest her forehead against the cool, hard door.

"What?"

"Could you take a seat outside. We'll try not to keep you waiting for too long."

She stumbled out into the corridor. There was a row of hard chairs, reminiscent of the Showbox. Mattie sat down at the end of the row. Three other girls were waiting for their turns, and one of them was called in after Mattie. The other two went on talking about RADA. They had elocuted voices like Sheila Firth's. Mattie sat with her head turned away from them, staring at the wall, resolutely not thinking.

Certainly not hoping.

But she was still here, wasn't she?

The first girl came out and went straight down the stairs without speaking. The others followed her in their turn. It was cold in the unheated corridor and Mattie was shivering. At last the girl assistant put her head around the door. "Mr. Brand would like you to read again, Miss Banner."

Once again Mattie faced the row of chairs. She felt so stiff with cold and fear that she was sure her jaw would crack as soon as she opened it.

"The last scene this time, if you wouldn't mind, Miss Banner."

Jimmy Proffitt was watching her, and so were Brand and the gray-haired woman, and the girl assistant had stopped winding her finger through her back-combing. Curtis's voice was uninflected as he read Dennis's corresponding lines.

Mattie was aware of everything, and nothing.

Afterward, all they said was "We'll be in touch with you."

At the door the assistant asked her, "Who is your agent, Miss Banner? We don't seem to have a note of it here . . ."

"Mr. Francis Willoughby," Mattie improvised quickly. Francis would do it for her, of course. For a percentage, if there ever were to be anything for him to take his percentage of.

She felt so shaky that she was almost sick on the bus on the way home.

Four days later they called her back for a second audition. Monty was angry at her request for another afternoon off and even threatened her with the sack, but one of the other girls offered to stand in for her.

"Just this once, Monty," Mattie soothed him. "I won't ask again."

She wouldn't need to. It was this part or nothing at all.

This time there were more faces in the line opposite her. Mattie had no idea whether she read well or badly. They dismissed her just as noncommittally, but this time there was only one other girl waiting on the hard chairs. Mattie recognized her. She had had a success in a play at the Lyric.

When Mattie reached home Julia saw her white face and poured two inches of gin into a tumbler for her. "They want their money's worth, don't they?" Julia said fiercely. "How much longer are they going to take?"

"I don't know," Mattie said. "I just don't know."

It was three more days before the telephone rang.

Julia heard Mattie answer it. "Hello, Francis. Yes. Yes." There was a long silence, and then Mattie's voice again. "What did you say?"

Julia put her hands over her ears.

But seemingly five seconds later Mattie whirled into the room and tore them away. "I got the part."

"You got the part?"

Their combined shriek rattled Jessie's ornaments on the tables. They flung their arms around each other and hopped and danced until they were gasping for breath. When they staggered to a standstill, Mattie rubbed the tears from her cheeks and panted, "I wasn't even hoping. But I know I can play this part better than any of those RADA girls. I can do it better than anybody. Oh, God, I'm frightened."

Julia shook her and kissed her and held her by the wrists. "You won't be any good if you aren't frightened. And you will be good. I can feel it. *Mattie Banner, the actress.*"

They laughed, looking at each other, slightly awestruck.

"When do you start?"

"We go into rehearsal in two weeks' time."

"Monty will miss you."

"I don't think I'll miss Monty."

Julia was rummaging in her handbag. "Hey, how much money have you got? I've got some. Let's go out and celebrate. A real, proper celebration."

Mattie's face shone like a beacon. "Just the two of us?"

"The two of us. No Flowers, or Francis, or anybody else. Just you and me."

"You're on," Mattie said.

And so they went out on the town, already half-drunk on the exhilaration of Mattie's success, on their precarious independence and on the invincibility of their friendship.

Mattie telephoned Monty from the first Soho pub. Julia could hear his voice crackling indignantly out of the earpiece as Mattie held it away from her face. She raised her gin and tonic aloft in a silent toast to him.

"I'm an actress, Monty."

Julia didn't hear his response, but it made Mattie snort with ribald laughter. There were more drinks at another pub after that, and then they decided that they must eat dinner at Leoni's. The headwaiter looked suspiciously at them, but Mattie gave him her best smile, and some faint recognition must have stirred in him because he found them a table in a discreet corner. Mattie ordered champagne, and they worked their way methodically through the menu. Often, still, they were as appreciatively hungry as children. Julia sat with her back to the room. It wasn't the time to think of Josh. Tonight was Mattie's night. . . . It was Mattie's success. . . . She lifted her champagne glass, spilling a little of the silver froth onto the tablecloth.

"Here's to you, Mattie. May every bart pee—dammit, may every part be what you wish for, may every line you utter be a triumph."

They drank, and then Mattie squared herself in her chair. " 'Nother toast. To Felix, whatever the hell he's doing, and to Jessie."

Julia echoed it. "Jessie and Felix. Jessie'd be proud of you. And Felix will."

"Tha's good. Got nobody else to be, except you." Ted Banner wasn't fit enough any longer to know what was happening to any of his family, or even to himself. Rozzie and Marilyn and the others were still living on the estate. A long way away.

Mattie's head jerked up. "Hey. This's a celebration. Less have some more toasts. To Francis Willoughby."

"May his percentages multiply."

"And to John Douglas."

"And to Monty, bless his dirty heart."

"We're going to need some more champa-agne."

They went on through the list of their friends and then acquaintances, drinking lavish toasts to everyone they could think of.

Except for Josh.

Julia kept her back turned to the specter of him watching her from across the room. But she could still see him as clearly as she could see Mattie, the waiters covertly peeping at them, the headwaiter's frown. For all her gaiety, Julia's eyes felt hot, and she knew how dangerously close she was to tears. Selfish tears, mustn't let anyone see. It's Mattie's night . . . can't spoil it with crying . . . smile, and drink some more.

Mattie yanked the bottle out of the ice bucket for the last time and peered into the beaded glass. "There's one las' toast. The most important one of all. Just enough bubbles left. Here, give me your glass."

They faced each other, mistily now.

"To you and me," Mattie proposed. "The two of us, whatever comes."

"Whatever," Julia answered. She tried to imagine it, but the future was as opaque as it had been from the height of Montebellate, presided over by the old woman and her goat. They drank the last of the champagne. It tasted a little flat now.

"I'll tell you what." Mattie leaned forward and cupped her hand over Julia's, as though reading her thoughts. "I'll be Vivien Leigh and Peggy Ashcroft and Grace Kelly all rolled into one, the biggest star in the firmament, but we've heard enough 'bout that for one night. You'll be a top model—I know—you'll invent something wonderful."

"The zip fastener? Nylon? Sliced bread?"

"Yeah, something like that. You've just got to decide what. You'll make a million pounds out of it, and then . . ."

"Oh, and then I'll marry a duke, and I'll have twelve beautiful children, six of each, and a garden where the cherry trees flower all the year round, and I'll live happily ever after."

Their hands gripped one another across the table.

"Julia, it doesn't matter what you do," Mattie whispered. "Because you're wonderful. You're the best friend, the best person, and I love you."

Julia was crying now. She sniffed savagely, feeling the waiters' eyes on her. "I love you too. I know it doesn't matter. If I wanted to do something worthwhile, the way you do, I'd be doing it, wouldn't I?" *I would be with Josh, except I can't be.* "Mattie, listen. I'm so pleased about your play. I'm more pleased than I could be about anything else in the world. It's all that matters tonight. Why'm I bloody well crying? Come on." She sniffed again, more successfully. "Let's get out of here before they throw us out. Let's go somewhere different, not the Rocket. Let's go and dance."

Mattie held up one finger to the nearest waiter. "The bill, please, young man."

With champagne swiftness their mood changed again and they were giggling as they tried to add the figures up, making a different total each time. They abandoned the struggle and paid what seemed an enormous sum, counting out a scruffy pile of notes and silver. The waiter bore swiftly down and carried it away before they could change their minds. They were escorted to the door with affable bows and almost audible sighs of relief.

"What a charming place," Mattie fluted. "We must certainly come again very soon."

Outside the restaurant the cold night air hit them.

"Whoops." Mattie's feet wavered and they propped each other up, breathless with laughter. Mattie caught her breath at last and opened her bag with a flourish. There was a little brown bottle tucked inside it, and she turned into an angle of some buildings and shook out the pills. Mattie had laid in her own supply of blues to get her through the auditions, and the last days of Miss Matilda.

"Go on," she ordered Julia. "Otherwise you'll fall asleep, won't you?"

A second later they had turned back to the street and flagged down a passing taxi.

After that there was a club, an unfamiliar one, and a great deal of music and dozens of new faces. For a little while Julia thought she was having the time of her life. Everyone was warm and attractive, and she wanted to dance forever. She drank the several drinks that her new circle of best friends bought for her, and danced some more, and then through a gap in the crowd, very hazily, she caught a glimpse of Mattie. Her eyes were closed, her arms were locked around her partner's neck, and she had gone completely limp. Julia blinked and opened her eyes again, but the view was just the same.

She broke away from her own partner and walked carefully across to the ladies' room. She ran a basin full of cold water and plunged her face into it, then came up gasping.

A little bit better, but not much.

She rubbed her face on the roller towel and went back to the dance floor. The man had steered Mattie to a corner and propped her against the wall.

"Will you help me to get her outside, please?" Julia said crisply.

The man was only too pleased to delegate responsibility. The crowds parted briefly as they half-carried her out and deposited her on the sidewalk.

"Wha' now?" Mattie asked.

"Bed," Julia said. Mercifully, another taxi materialized and they hoisted her inside it. Mattie snuffled contentedly and fell sleep in her corner.

When they reached the square the disgruntled cab driver had to help Julia to pull her out. They left her leaning against the railings while Julia paid the fare with the very last of their money, no tip.

"And a very good night to you too," the driver muttered as he chugged off.

"Mattie," Julia said sternly. "Walk."

Inside the dark hallway she saw that there was a letter in the wire basket where the office tenants left their mail. She stuffed it unthinkingly into her pocket. "Stairs, Mattie. Unless you can climb them, you'll have to sleep here in the hall. Now, let's get going."

It took a long time and Julia was sweating by the first landing, but at last they reached the top. She coaxed Mattie into their bedroom and rolled her into her bed. "Mmmmmmmmmm." Mattie sighed blissfully. Julia took off her high heels and dragged the covers over her. Julia was grinning triumphantly.

"We made it. Just for a minute I thought we weren't going to."

Mattie was already sound asleep.

Julia went into the kitchen and put the kettle on. Tea would be her reward. Her mouth was as dry as sand and the bright light hurt her eyes. While the gas whispered under the kettle she took the crumpled letter out of her pocket.

It was from Felix.

He had written on thin blue paper, crackly and foreign. It made her think of Italy, warmth and the scent of herbs, and the Pensione Flora. Julia stared deliberately hard at Felix's neat black handwriting.

I'm coming home, he had written. Back to London.

She lifted her head then. "Mattie?" she said softly. "Guess what? Felix is coming home."

The kettle's sibilant whistle sharpened to a blast that pierced the silence. Julia lifted it up, smiling, and made herself some tea.

ELEVEN

"It is Julia, isn't it?"

Julia looked up from her desk. The plump young woman had come to see George, and Julia knew from his appointments diary that she was Mrs. Horton. Mrs. Horton was wearing a covetably smart Chanel-style suit in raspberry-pink wool, but as Julia looked at her, a different outfit popped into her head. The recollection featured too-tight ski pants and a pair of fluffy angora earmuffs. But on closer inspection the pink cheeks and slightly protuberant china-blue eyes were exactly the same.

"Sophia."

Sophia crowed with innocent delight. "You do remember. Dear old Wengen. I haven't skied for the last two seasons, can you believe? Such bad planning to be in pod two winters running. You never came back the next year, did you? Nor lovely Josh Flood either. We were all so in love with him. But as soon as you appeared we knew none of us stood a chance, you were so pretty. I hated you for at least a week. What happened to him? You're not Mrs. Flood, are you? Everyone seems to be married these days."

"No," Julia managed. "He went back home. He's making lots and lots of money out of turning Colorado into a ski resort."

"God, how heavenly. Lucky Josh. What are you doing? You look wonderful, I must say."

Julia smoothed the lapels of her black barathea jacket. She earned hardly more than a pittance at Tressider's, and most of it was spent on clothes. The longing for elegant things that Felix had stirred in her was undiminished, although she was hardly any better able to satisfy it. But she had learned to buy one good item rather than half a dozen shoddy ones. Mattie stuck to the old philosophy of cheap and colorful.

"I'm working here for George," Julia said. "Just for the time being." She was wondering with faint irritation why she should have to hint at being on the brink of something much more fascinating just for Sophia's sake, when the inner door opened and George himself appeared. Sophia whirled around to him.

"Hello, Mr. Tressider. Isn't it amazing? Julia and I are old friends."

George raised one eyebrow by a sceptical fraction of an inch, but the implication was lost on Sophia. Julia smothered a grin. "Julia, I've got to look at some drawings with Mr. Tressider, but it won't take long. Toby's bought us a sweet little house, but he is rather leaving me to see to everything. Say you'll have lunch afterward, and we can have a good old gossip."

"I have only an hour," Julia said mildly.

Sophia called over her shoulder as she followed George, "Actually, I'm supposed to be lunching with my brother. He'd love to meet you, but perhaps you'll be glad to get away after an hour. We can make him pay, can't we? And then we can have a girls' lunch another day."

Julia smiled. "All right. I'd like that."

Someone new, someone different, to assuage the restlessness for an hour. And if there wasn't a party, it was important to make one.

So Julia met Alexander Bliss.

When he stood up behind the table in the new Italian trattoria to shake her hand, Julia thought she could easily place him. He didn't look like Sophia. He was tall and spare, and the slight beakiness of his face was emphasized by very well-brushed hair. He was wearing a gray suit and a soberly striped tie, and Julia concluded that he must be a banker, as Sophia had told her Toby Horton was, or something almost as boring. Julia and Alexander sat down and looked at their menus while Sophia talked. There was one thing in Alexander Bliss's favor, she thought—he was as economical with words as his sister was profligate.

"Actually, we're only half brother and sister," she confided at full volume. "Our father and Alexander's mother were divorced when Alexander was six, terrible for them and a bit of a scandal in those days, not like now, when everyone does it, although you still can't get into the Royal Enclosure when you've done the deed, can you? Anyway, Daddy married my mother and I came along later. You remember Tuffy Brockway, of course? My mother's a Brockway."

"Is she?" Julia said faintly. She thought she caught Alexander out in a half-smile, but he bent his head again over his cannelloni.

"What's Alexander's mother, if yours is a Brockway?" Julia asked, driven by some mischievous impulse. Sophia's eyes went even rounder.

"Utterly wonderful, but ra-ther eccentric. If she walked into this restaurant now, everyone would turn around and look at her. Wouldn't they, Alex? She wouldn't care either. She'd enjoy it."

"There are people who attract attention wherever they go without necessarily intending to do it, Sophia. And there are also people who enjoy the effect they have on others. It isn't uniquely China's disability." Alexander's manner was dry. "China is my mother," he explained courteously to Julia.

Julia played a game, sometimes, of summing up the new faces that floated past her and slotting them into categories. *One,* she thought, *Alexander admires his mother but isn't influenced by her. Two, he's not nearly as dim as his sister. And three, he's a bit of a stuffed shirt, even so.*

"Oh, I know, darling," Sophia said, noticing none of the undercurrents. To Julia, she explained, "China never cared for Ladyhill, that was the problem. And Daddy adores it. It's his real love. Mummy comes only second."

"What's Ladyhill?" Julia asked, wondering what could possibly outrank a Brockway in Mr. Bliss's affections.

"Ladyhill is home." Sophia sighed. "It's where we come from—Daddy, Alexander, me . . . the most beautiful place in the world."

Alexander interrupted her. "That doesn't tell Julia anything. Ladyhill is a crumbling Jacobean house and a patch of land in Dorset. My father farms the land and spends the proceeds on shoring the house up."

Oh God, Julia thought. *The manor house. The bloody country acres.*

Sophia attacked her *petto di pollo* with relish. Two glasses of Frascati had turned her cheeks deeper pink.

"I can't think why we're rabbiting on about our family history. I want to hear all the glamorous things you've been doing, Julia. Alexander, when I met her in Wengen—how long? three and a half years ago?—she was with the most divine American. He was perfectly reckless. He flew airplanes for a living. He could ski faster than anyone else, and he dug someone out of an avalanche during the Inferno and then picked up his skis and finished the race."

"He sounds like a character out of a boys' adventure comic," Alexander murmured. If he had been dry before, he was arid now.

"He was. But handsomer. Belinda and I and all the rest of us adored him for years. Then he turned up with Julia. She didn't ski, and she didn't have clothes like any of the rest of us, and we thought she was so glamorously racy. She used to sneak out of Frau Überl's to stay with him at the Swann Hotel. . . ."

"Sophia." It was Alexander who interrupted her lubricated babble. He had been watching his sister's friend. He liked the way that she had said almost nothing, listening and looking instead, but still gave the impression of energy and strength. He thought she looked clever, and contained, but with an edge of vulnerability that he found powerfully attractive. Alexander knew hundreds of women like his sister Sophia, but he couldn't remember ever meeting anyone who intrigued him like Julia Smith. He wanted to know her better, and because he rarely wanted anything particularly seriously, Alexander usually got his way.

Julia was hardly aware of him. She was staring at the tablecloth. Sophia's prattle had unlocked the memories, too sharp, startlingly vivid. The white feathery bed and the ice-blue sky beyond the window. Skiers laughing and calling to one another in the snowy streets below. And Josh, with his breath warm on her face. She could see him and feel him. Hear his heart beating.

Julia crumbled the last of her roll into fragments and pushed it off the edge of her plate.

"I'm sorry, I talk too much." Sophia was clearly contrite. "I never learn."

"It doesn't matter," Julia said.

"So what do you do nowadays?" Alexander asked, filling a small silence.

Julia's head jerked up. Suddenly she wanted to make Sophia's eyes open really wide and to shake her brother out of his complacent quiet. She felt stifled by the restaurant's self-conscious smartness, and by the Blisses' company, and by the thought of the secure green acres of their Dorset manor. She smiled a little. Mattie would have recognized the smile, but Sophia and Alexander simply sat, listening. Julia didn't notice how much Alexander was taking in.

"I've done all kinds of things since I was sixteen." Julia leaned comfortably back in her chair, keeping her voice soft. "Since I ran away from home with my friend Mattie. Before I met Josh, you know. We started by finding ourselves jobs. But we had nowhere to live, and we had to sleep rough. On the Embankment, actually."

With relish, Julia went on to tell them everything, not glossing over any of the riskier parts, and embroidering wherever she felt like it. She told them about the square, digressing to Felix, and Jessie's career in the clubs, about the parties and the Rocket and Flowers and Mr. Mogridge and Francis Willoughby. She went to town on Mattie and the Showbox, on how Mattie had landed the lead in the most important play of the decade, and on their night's celebration at Leoni's and after. She dressed up her own importance to George Tressider, not too subtly considering Sophia was already a client and likely to notice any major exaggerations. But then, being Sophia, Julia thought, she probably wouldn't notice anything of the kind. But she passed quickly anyway from Tressider's to her position on the brink of a career in international fashion modeling. The shadow of truth behind the story was that a photographer friend had taken her pictures, and claimed that he could get her some work for one of the magazines.

"And that's about it, really," Julia concluded. She made a dismissive gesture with the hand that wasn't holding her glass.

Sophia made a little sound that was half a laugh, half a gulp.

"And I thought I had a busy life with a husband and two infants. Golly, how tame it is."

Alexander's expression was unfathomable.

Sophia looked at her watch. "Oh, dear, and I'm supposed to be at the hairdresser at this very instant. I must fly."

A minute later they were out on the street. Sophia kissed the air on either side of Julia's cheeks and insisted that they must do it again, very soon. Then she was gone.

Julia looked at Alexander. She had been intending defiance, but to her amazement she saw that he was smiling properly now. It made his face look quite different, younger, with the sharpness smoothed out of it.

"I'm very fond of her, you know."

It was so unexpected that Julia answered in the same spirit. "So am I. She was very kind to me in Switzerland. I was having a bloody time because I couldn't ski."

"Didn't the cartoon hero teach you?" His dryness had dissolved into mockery. Julia tried to find some lighthearted words, but her mouth felt frozen.

"Hmm. Have you got to go back to work at once?" Alexander asked.

Julia should have been at her desk half an hour earlier. She thought of George and the telephone and the afternoon's clients, and sighed. The Frascati and too much talk had fuddled her head as well as Sophia's.

"No," she answered with a touch of weariness. "I don't suppose I do."

Alexander drew her arm through his. "Then let's go and take a look at the river."

They walked mostly in silence. He asked her just one question, still smiling, when they could see the tracery of the Albert Bridge ahead of them.

"Was any of that story true, by the way?"

Julia kept her eyes fixed on the airy lines of the bridge. "Bits of it. But I shouldn't have told you any of it."

"Oh, I enjoyed it," protested Alexander.

They leaned against the wall and looked down at the river. The water was the same color as the green olives presented with their lunch, and a deep, muddy reek drifted off it. A barge came sluggishly upstream and Julia was reminded of herself and Mattie, stranded, with their belongings in two suitcases at their feet. Alexander appeared to read her thoughts.

"Was it this part of the Embankment where you slept rough?"

"That bit was true. We slept in a doorway beside the Savoy." She shivered at the memory. "I never want to have to do it again."

"You shouldn't have to. You don't see many top models dossing in doorways, do you?"

Julia went faintly pink. "All right, you tell me something about yourself. Do you work in the City?"

Alexander snorted. "I most certainly do not."

Alexander Bliss was a musician. What he liked doing best, he said, was playing the trumpet, but he wasn't good enough at it to be any use to anyone. He earned his living as a freelance composer. Julia looked suspiciously at him, but he drew his finger across his throat with a flourish.

"Honest. The twiddly bits in films. Advertising jingles, that sort of thing."

The fresh air was clearing Julia's head. They turned and walked toward the bridge, admiring its grace. They talked a little about his work, and then films that they had seen. Alexander was easy to talk to once the dryness was penetrated, and Julia felt faintly regretful as she told him, "I must go back to work now. George will be in a pet as it is."

Alexander faced her. "May I see you again?" Formal, very English. She saw his clothes again and remembered that she had categorized him as a stuffed shirt. He was probably just that, however profoundly he admired Bix Beiderbecke.

Suddenly Julia smiled. She had a private system of tests for the men who took her out. She would make Bliss take her to the Rocket and see how he stood up to that.

"Yes," she said meekly. "That would be very nice."

He took her to the Rocket without demur, and he passed the test with top marks.

He wore unexceptionable jeans and a turtleneck sweater, and he was a better dancer than Johnny Flowers. Julia watched him jiving with Mattie. She was impressed, in spite of herself. Mattie looked over her shoulder, and winked.

After that, Bliss took Julia out quite regularly. They went to the cinema or the theater, or to a restaurant. Sometimes Julia cooked a meal at his untidy flat in Markham Square, and once Sophia and her pedantic husband joined them.

"Is this a serious romance?" Sophia whispered eagerly.

"Of course not," Julia told her. "We just get on well together."

Bliss simply became a looked-for part of Julia's life. He put his arms around her and kissed her, leaving her in no doubt that he found her attractive. But he didn't ask for any more than that, and Julia didn't volunteer anything. It didn't occur to her that Alexander was playing a more subtle game than her own. Nor did she look closely enough at him, in their round of jazz clubs and parties and Chelsea pubs, to discern that his irony and his vagueness had long ago been assumed as protective camouflage. She enjoyed his company without feeling threatened by it, and she never guessed that that was exactly what he intended.

As the weeks went by he passed all her tests except one.

And the last one was impossible because it required him to be Joshua Flood.

Julia saw less of Mattie. She was engrossed in rehearsals for *One More Day*. The play was to open after Christmas, and Mattie said that she was working harder than she had ever worked in her life and enjoying herself more. She was drinking noticeably less, and there was a glow about her that wasn't all professional. She also mentioned Jimmy Proffitt more often than was strictly necessary, Julia thought sagely.

Christmas came, and Felix arrived home just in time for it.

He came up the stairs one evening, without warning, when Julia was trying to fix the Christmas tree in its pot in front of the window in Jessie's room. She looked up and saw him, dropped the hammer, and ran to fling her arms around his neck. "Felix! Oh, Felix, I'm so happy you're back. Just wait till Mattie hears . . ."

"I'm glad to be home. It's been too long."

They stood back to admire each other. Felix nodded at her black jacket and slim skirt. "You look wonderful. You must have learned something while I've been away. But that tree's crooked."

They laughed, delighted to have slipped into the old idiom so easily. Julia looked carefully at him. Felix was too thin, and that made him seem even taller. But his expression was different. He looked older, and better. As if the parts of him fit together more comfortably.

"Welcome home." She smiled at him. She reached up and kissed the corner of his mouth. The color of his skin was richer, warmed by the Italian sun. He smelled of lemony cologne.

"Let me go and get my bags. I've got presents."

Having Felix back at the square again, especially this Felix, who was both more relaxed and more sociable, made Julia and Mattie realize how much they had missed his company. They shared the happiest Christmas together, just the three of them. Mattie's rehearsals were suspended for three whole days, George Tressider's closed down for a week, and Bliss had gone home to Ladyhill, explaining that it was a family imperative. Felix happily spent most of the holiday in the kitchen. Julia was his assistant once again.

"I had nowhere to cook in Florence," he explained. "Just a room to sleep in. I used to make meals in my head." Julia laughed, but Felix was suddenly somber. "Oh, dear, what a pointless exercise. After Christmas I'll find myself a job. What shall I do, Julia?"

"You can do anything," Julia said, meaning it.

The day of the dress rehearsal came. Mattie was suffering badly after her early confidence.

"I'm going to bomb," she whispered. "I don't know what I'm doing anymore. I was so sure I had her . . ." Her voice trailed away. Her face was as white as paper. "Can I have a drink?" she begged.

Julia brought her some gin, no more than a mouthful, but as soon as she had drunk it Mattie was sick. Julia held her head and then wiped her face with a warm cloth.

"Are you ill? Shall I call them and say you're ill?"

Mattie shook her head as if it hurt her. "I'm not ill. I'm just frightened. I'm so frightened I can't do anything. It's like being paralyzed."

Julia soothed her. "You're going to be all right. You're going to be a big success. A sensation."

"Please, no," Mattie moaned.

"Shall I come and watch the dress rehearsal? If you know I'm there . . ."

Mattie's fingers tightened around her wrist like iron rings. "No. I don't want you to see it. I don't want anyone I care about to see it."

The tickets for the first night were in Julia's drawer. Everyone they knew was coming, and Bliss was even bringing China. Julia hadn't met his mother yet.

Julia stroked the bright mass of Mattie's hair. "All right. That's all right. If you don't want us to be there, we won't be. Look, Mattie, it's time for you to go now. It's only the dress rehearsal today. You can get through that, can't you? Isn't it supposed to be terrible? Just think of one thing at a time."

Mattie nodded. Her face was so pale it seemed transparent.

Julia helped her into her coat and Felix came down the stairs with them. He found her a taxi and put her into it. They had a last glimpse of her wan face as they watched it drive away. Julia exhaled a long breath. They were like fond, anxious parents waving a child off to take an exam. Felix felt it, too, and they both laughed.

"She'll do it, won't she?"

"Of course she will."

Companionably, they walked once around the square. The day was frost-sharp and the noise of the traffic was amplified in the stillness. The grass inside the railings of the square garden was still silvered in the hollows, and there were tufts of startling wet emerald where the weak sun touched it. When Julia gripped the iron railings, looking through them at the green and silver, her bare hands seemed to freeze to the metal. With her senses sharpened by her anxiety for Mattie, she had a sudden sense of the exquisite, orderly power of the physical world.

Felix's hand brushed her shoulder. "Sensualist," he said.

Not really, she might have answered. *I would have been, but not without Josh.* It occurred to Julia again that she was getting older. She felt it in her heart, and in her cold hands.

They went inside again, up the familiar stairs.

In Jessie's room Felix prowled silently to and fro, turning a picture to catch the light, lifting the heavy folds of the curtains and letting them fall again in looser ripples. Watching him, Julia felt her forlorn longing relax its hold a little. She had missed Felix, too, and now he was home. She sat down on the plush sofa and drew her knees up so that she could rest her chin on them. She wanted to draw him closer, to fill in the space between them. Felix was easier company now, but Julia was clearly aware that he guarded his feelings even more carefully.

"Tell me about when you were away," she asked.

Felix turned abruptly. In the silence she heard the whisper of dry needles falling from their Christmas tree. Julia wouldn't allow it to be taken down before Twelfth Night.

He had been waiting for a question that he could put an answer to. He had never done so for Jessie, and in a sense what he wanted to tell Julia was for Jessie too.

"Julia. You know that I'm a homosexual, don't you?"

Her head didn't jerk up. She didn't even catch her breath. She went on looking at him, her expression not changing. He loved her then.

Julia said, "Yes. Yes, I suppose I did know. Without really knowing it."

"I wanted to be sure." His voice was expressionless. "Because of what happened between us."

She nodded quickly. They were remembering the day of the funeral, and the wet petals glued to the soaking earth. The party that Felix had wanted to give for Jessie afterward, and the quiet grief that the bottles of whiskey had failed to dispel. And after that. Felix's bedroom with the pictures of Mattie and herself and Josh pinned over the mantelpiece. Felix had turned off the light, leaving the darkness full of silence and empty spaces.

What would Jessie say now? Julia thought. It was imperative to make the response that Jessie would have made, to be able to offer Felix some of his mother's broad understanding. She was afraid of her own inadequacy, but it occurred to her that it was easier for her than it would be if she really were Felix's mother. She smiled faintly. Felix saw it and came to sit beside her, the old plush sofa creaking in protest. Julia held out her hand, palm up, and Felix covered it with his own. Their hands clasped.

"Did you always know?" she asked simply.

"No." And then, "If I did, I didn't admit it for a long time." Felix was thinking, *That doesn't change. I can't admit to you now that when I took you to bed, all that time ago, I was thinking of Josh. Wanting to think of Josh, and then despising myself for it. Subterfuges, and learning to live with the need for them.*

Julia couldn't decipher what he must feel. She was aware only of wanting to offer him what he needed, as Jessie would have. "Tell me," she said awkwardly. "Only if you want to."

They had both changed, Felix realized, Mattie and Julia. They had acquired reticence, even with each other. Their exchange of confidences was less raucous, the atmosphere of femaleness surrounding them less exclusive. They had turned into women, Felix thought. The realization touched him.

He told her what had happened. Not everything, not even most of it, but at least the truth at the heart of it.

Felix had survived his national service, had almost, perversely, enjoyed it. He soon discovered, however, that he was better equipped for the struggle to survive each day than most of the other recruits in his squad. He was older, he was self-contained and used to the necessity of being so, and he was dexterous and efficient. It was Felix who discovered that the thick, shapeless khaki uniform trousers that they had all been issued with could be made to hold creases that would satisfy the NCOs if the nap was shaved off along the crease line with a razor blade. He could mix Green Blanco to just the right consistency and apply it to his webbing in the correct quantity so the smooth surface didn't crack. He could polish his brasses to a mirror shine, and he was the barracks champion with the heated spoon that was the only way of removing pimples from the leather surface of standard-issue boots. He could also execute the intricate regulation folds in the rest of his kit when laying it out on his bed for the daily inspection, and he learned to stuff the empty pockets of his laid-out kitbag with newspaper to give it the correct square proportions.

Almost all of their nonsoldiering interest and conversation centered on sex. As soon as they were allowed Saturday-night off-barracks passes, the squad's two loudest studs had fresh encounters to boast about. Almost all of the others had their own stories to tell, true or—as Felix suspected—mostly invented. Not a detail was spared. Only the grammar-school boy with glasses blushingly admitted his virginity.

"Get in the boozer with us Saturday night and we'll find yer a tart," one of the others roared. "We'll lose yer cherry for yer, won't we, lads? Just as long as we can watch, mind."

Felix had nothing to contribute. He was popular enough for no one to rib him about it, anymore than they would have joked mildly about his color, but one evening around the Blanco tins someone asked him, "You got a girl, Lemoine? Must have, a looker like you."

"Bet they get their knickers off and wave them at you, don't they? All those old wives' tales about what your lot can offer . . ."

"There's a girl, yes," Felix said, to cut off the flow.

"What's her name, then?"

"Julia."

Sitting beside him on the sofa, watching the incandescent crimson of the gasfire, Julia laughed.

"I should have sent a photograph for your locker."

"One of Miss Matilda in full regalia would have been more impressive."

The worst, the very worst social crime that stalked the barrack rooms, was to be queer. It was the most pointed accusation, the direst insult in the soldiers' extensive repertoire of abuse. "Fucking queer" was the last epithet in a confrontation before the fighting broke out.

Felix heard it all. He also knew that most of his colleagues adopted their attitudes of swaggering potency more for fear of being thought effeminate than from real sexuality. There was rumored to be enough bromide in the NAAFI tea to dampen any genuine ardor. He thought, with relieved amusement, that he certainly felt none himself.

Among the regular NCOs there was a stores corporal referred to by everyone as Maisie. Maisie was very slightly camp, but he also had a sharp enough tongue and enough authority for the nickname only ever to be used out of his earshot. Felix had looked at Maisie once or twice, but only for long enough to speculate on how the corporal managed to exist in this society if he really was queer. He was an ungainly little man with a red, lumpy face and hair cut so short that it shadowed his skull with colorless bristles.

One Saturday evening Felix was in the bathroom, shaving.

On Saturday nights almost every soldier had an off-barracks pass, and the camp emptied itself for several hours. Felix preferred to stay put. Solitude was a rare luxury in the overcrowded huts, and he used the little, precious time to read or to draw. On this Saturday he had cadged a tin of boiling water from the mess and carried it over to the ablutions. The water there was almost always tepid or cold, and tonight he was looking forward to the comfortable ritual of a peaceful shave. He was whistling softly as he rubbed the soap into a lather over his cheeks. Water hissed and dripped in the overhead pipes, and the steam from his can of hot water clouded the dim fragment of mirror. He rubbed it clear with his wrist, and reflected over his shoulder he saw Maisie. The corporal was standing in the doorway. As Felix watched him he closed the door quietly and looked up and down the length of the ablutions room. The doors of all the cubicles stood open, and there was silence except for the amplified dripping of water. He came across and stood at the next basin, looking at Felix's soapy face in the mirror.

"Best bloody time of the week, eh?" Maisie chuckled.

Felix nodded and deliberately carved the first path through the white foam with his razor.

Then Maisie reached out and put his hand on Felix's backside.

It was a gesture so completely natural and direct that Felix almost responded to it. He put his razor down and it clanked awkwardly against the tin basin. He looked into Maisie's eyes in the mirror. Their expression was imploring, shaded with defiance. The man's hand moved appreciatively, cupping Felix's buttock under the thick khaki. Felix looked down. He knew every crack and pockmark in the brick floor. He had scrubbed each brick, his shadow lengthened by the naked bulbs overhead as he worked, ready for inspections. He followed one particular crack that ran right across the floor to the urinals. As his eyes reached the wall, without warning, fear spilled and washed all through his body. It gripped and twisted in the pit of his stomach and it cut off the breath in his chest. He tore the towel from around his neck and rubbed the soap off his face. As he reached the door he heard Maisie say coldly, "Who are you trying to fool? It's as plain as the nose on your fucking face, laddie."

Felix didn't look around.

He reached his own section of the hut and sat down on his

bed. He rubbed his face mechanically with the towel. He was thinking, *Is it so obvious, then?*

And as he grappled with the question he realized that for the first time, in full consciousness, he was admitting the whole truth to himself.

Felix sat on his bed for a long time, unmoving. He knew that Maisie wouldn't come looking for him here. When his thoughts were orderly again and the fear had gone, Felix was left with a last, unwelcome realization. The red-faced corporal's touch had aroused him physically. Felix stood up. He went quickly across to the recreation block and into the washroom there. He locked himself into one of the stalls and dealt with himself, using short, vicious strokes.

Afterward, he went into the recreation hall and found a group of men who were confined to barracks, playing cards. They greeted him cheerfully, and Felix sat down to join in the game.

Maisie didn't single Felix out again, but whenever he saw the corporal he asked himself the silent question. *Is it so obvious?*

By the second half of their sixteen-week basic training program, Felix and the rest of his intake were more skilled at getting through the work assigned to them, and the NCOs' withering attention had passed to the new recruits coming up behind them. There was more time for off-duty pursuits, and the possibility of friendships outside the immediate barrack-room circle.

Felix met David Mander because they both used a little box in the recreation block officially known as the hobbies room, although it contained no hobbies equipment except for a crumbling dartboard fixed to one wall. The light in the room was good because it had windows all down one side, and on Saturday and Sunday afternoons Felix used to sit and draw at a metal table. In camp he mostly drew London scenes, from memory, filling them with obsessive detail. He drew Berwick Street Market and Shaftesbury Avenue, and the square shaded by plane trees with the windows of the flat showing over the tops of the trees. Drawing the places seemed to bring him closer to being there.

In the swarming world of the camp Felix had never even seen Mander before. He was just a silent figure at a table at the other side of the room, someone who made accurate but uninteresting models of famous buildings out of scraps of balsa wood. They began to nod to each other, and one afternoon Mander strolled over and stared at Felix's drawing.

"That's very good," he said, sounding surprised. He had a drawling, affected voice that sounded almost shocking after the rough obscenities of the other conscripts. Felix glanced at him, irritated. Mander had black hair and a red mouth. "Better than that rubbish anyway," he added, nodding at his own model.

"Why do you do it?" Felix asked. Mander grinned, showing his teeth. He looked pleased with himself.

"I started doing it at school. Important to have something to concentrate on besides rugger. Model-making was the least taxing option. But it's curiously compulsive, you know. I'll probably be doing it into my dotage. God, what a prospect."

He stuck his hands in his pockets and wandered over to the window. The Saturday afternoon interunit football matches were in progress.

"Look at 'em all." Mander sighed. "Mud and blood. Shall we go across and get a cup of tea?"

Felix closed up his sketchpad. "I suppose so," he said without enthusiasm.

That afternoon he learned that David Mander was a public-school boy from Highgate in north London. His mother was a doctor and his father was a criminal barrister. Their son was a clever and precocious only child. Felix hadn't intended to like him, but the company of someone as sophisticated and subtle-minded as David was an undeniable pleasure after the four-letter interests of his own squad.

"Going for a pint tonight?" David asked casually.

"Could do," Felix responded.

They fell into the habit, after the first evening, of spending their off-duty hours together. They talked about books and films and music, about their own lives and about London. It was glaringly obvious to Felix that they never talked about girls, and the common-currency topic of sex was never raised. It was equally obvious that neither of them ever commented, either, on their lack of interest in everyone else's obsession.

May turned into June, and they were in the last month of their basic training. The north-country evenings were long and light, and it was a pleasure instead of a routine punishment to be outside. The shaggy majesty of the Yorkshire moorlands and the milky sweetness of the air were a revelation to Felix, brought up a city child. David's parents had a weekend cottage in Suffolk.

David announced that he was saving his pay for the leave that came at the end of basic training, so instead of going to pubs they took buses up onto the moors and walked, following the ordnance survey maps borrowed from the barracks library.

One evening they came down a long hill to a stone bridge over a stream. Felix took off his pack and they leaned over the stone parapet. Brown water curled and slid underneath them, the ripple of it making the only sound. There was a stone barn on the other side of the stream. As they watched, the sun slid behind it, a coppery disc flattened by the black line of the roof, and then a semi-circle, then no more than a flare of gold. The shadow of the barn turned violet and Felix was thinking, *If I could paint that*. He turned to look at David and saw his red mouth. David opened his mouth, perhaps to say something, and a tiny glint of light caught on the moist lining. Instantly, Felix felt his otherness. It seemed magical that a separate, moving, breathing individual was here in the faint purple dusk. It was the most perfectly erotic moment he had ever experienced.

David was frozen into stillness. It was Felix who put his hand out. He curled it around the nape of David's neck and felt the stubble of cropped hair under his fingers. Somewhere, no more than a flicker over their heads, a bat rose and fell like a black leaf. Felix bent his head to David's. They kissed, and Felix tasted the conjunction of coarseness and softness, dissolving moisture, familiarity and perfect difference. David's face against his own and his tongue, searching Felix out. Felix lifted his head and groaned. It came from his heart and his bowels, a sound he had never thought that he could make.

It was David who said, "Let's go into the barn."

He unlatched the door and it opened without protest. It was gray inside the barn, with twilight and a thick ruff of dust. But against one raw stone wall there was a heap of hay, left over from the winter feeding of the moorland sheep. David and Felix lay down in the hay.

It was dark outside when Felix groaned again, and he called out, too, shouting David's name. David put his hands over his mouth, silencing him. There might have been ears in the darkness.

Afterward, in an odd silence, they brushed the hay from their clothes and hair. They dressed themselves and went out, glancing up at the first star. They sat on the parapet of the bridge and smoked. Felix was calm, and he felt as invincible as the stars.

David broke the silence. "Have you done that before?" he asked.

Felix remembered that at the beginning he had been sure

that he wouldn't like him. He didn't know what he felt now, except relief, like a wide, flat sea. "No," Felix said. "Maisie tried it, once, in the showers. I ran away." David laughed. "Have you?"

"At school," David answered slowly. "Everyone did. But I had the impression I was more serious than most of them. I fell in love, with captains of the Eleven and with angelic, dirty little boys. But not like that. Not like what we've just done."

Don't fall in love with me, Felix silently warned him. Aloud, he said, "I wondered, when Maisie tried it, how obvious I seemed to him. I didn't even really know. Bloody stupid, isn't it?"

David looked at him, his heavy-lidded eyes wide open.

"As obvious as I was to you."

That was the only answer he would get, Felix understood. It was invisible, and yet as clear as the features of his face. He looked at his watch.

"Christ. We're going to be late back."

They threw their cigarette butts away. Felix always remembered that they made two crimson arcs before they fell into the water. They half-ran down over the next fold of moorland to the main road. They thumbed a ride from a farmer in a pickup, who obligingly made a detour and dropped them at the camp gates with time to spare.

A week later David Mander was notified that he had been selected as a potential officer. After basic training he and the other POs would enter a special course, and if he passed he would progress to a war office selection board. Successful candidates passed on to the officer training school at Eaton Hall.

Felix, with most of the rest of his squad, was bound for the Royal Tank Regiment. David was moved out of the squaddies' barracks into more comfortable accommodation with the rest of the intake's officer material. His air of being pleased with himself intensified, but he also seemed embarrassed by the divide that had opened between Felix and himself.

"You'd make a bloody sight better officer than me," he remarked.

Felix didn't bother to disagree. "But you don't see many black officers in the British Army, old boy, do you?"

David chewed one corner of his full lip. "Do you mind that?"

Felix laughed. "I couldn't care less."

It was the truth. He had no desire to be an officer, whereas

David clearly did. He had no feeling for the army except a desire to survive it, and he thought that survival would probably be easier in the undemanding company of his barrack-room mates.

Abruptly, David said, "I thought I'd use my leave for a few days' camping and fishing in Scotland. D'you want to come?"

Felix thought about it. He had planned to go back to London, to the flat, because he had nothing else to do. Back to Julia and Mattie. Suddenly the memory of their clannish femaleness seemed thoroughly alien. He didn't want to go there, not yet. "Thank you," he said to David.

They took David's pup tent and a few clothes in rucksacks, and hitchhiked to the west of Scotland. It was the beginning of July and every day was cloudless and still. Felix lay in a boat and watched David fishing, or they sat on empty beaches and looked at the sea, or walked for miles through the heather. They ate in pubs, or Felix fried fish on the Primus or a driftwood fire. And at night they lay together under the green ridge of the tent.

At the end of ten days Felix felt the same calmness and strength that he had experienced outside the barn on the moors. He was grateful to David for having made him a present of it. No more than that. They were separate, after all. David was so sure that he was following the right path; Felix was certain of nothing except, now, himself.

When the end of their holiday came, David went to officer training school and Felix returned to his unit. They didn't see each other again, but Felix thought of him, sometimes, when a movement of someone's head or the way a hand gesture touched the same chord that David had sounded on the bridge over the Yorkshire stream.

Some of this, the bones of it, Felix told Julia while she sat watching the fire and the light faded beyond the window.

"And now?" Julia asked.

"I have to find myself a job, of course. Begin a real life."

Felix was laughing, but Julia stared at him. The idea came to her fully formed, as obvious and immediate as all the best ideas. "You'll have to come and work for George."

One of the young men had left just before Christmas, under a mysterious cloud. Felix had languages, he had his experience from Mr. Mogridge's friend, and he had all the aptitude. In every direction. He would suit George Tressider perfectly. For Julia it was one of those rare flashes of insight in which other people's paths seem clearly set out, smooth and comfortable for them to follow.

If only, she thought forlornly and selfishly, *if only it was as easy for me.*

"We'll see." Felix responded to her suggestion with what seemed to Julia to be infuriating negligence.

In fact, Felix was looking at her, seeing the sharpened angles of her face. Julia had grown up, and she was more beautiful than she had been, but she was unhappy. Yet she had listened to his own confession, accepting it, somehow understanding that she was offering Jessie's acceptance as well as her own. She was sensitive as well as generous.

Felix put his arm around her shoulder, and she rested her face gratefully against his. She felt fragile, and soft. That was all.

"I love you," Felix said.

Julia nodded. She was suddenly afraid that she might cry, and she was trying not to let herself cry these days.

"Is it still Josh?" he asked.

She nodded again.

Felix held on to her, wondering how to make her see differently. "Do you know that I was in love with him too?"

She jerked around to look at him then, full in the eye, and he glimpsed fury and disgust in her face. There was a second's silence, and then she began to laugh. It wasn't comfortable laughter, but it was something.

"I survived it," he told her lightly. "And so can you. Don't carry a candle for him forever. There are all kinds of other people. There's Bliss . . ."

Julia cut him short there. "I don't think so," she said. "No, I don't think so." His hands were still on her shoulders. She looked down at them, frowning a little as if she was wondering how they had come there. Gently, he let go of her. They were friends, but there were still defenses.

"So what will you do?" he persisted.

Julia sighed. "Mattie's doing something, of course. Right at this very minute." She held up her crossed fingers. "And so will I. Soon, I promise you, Felix."

Restlessly, she stood up and switched on the fairy lights on the Christmas tree. The little Woolworth's lanterns shone against the brown needles. Julia put out a finger to the tip of the lowest branch and the dry, falling whisper came again.

TWELVE

The auditorium of the Angel Theatre was small, and it was filled to capacity. Julia glanced up at the ornamental plasterwork garnishing the red velvet boxes. There seemed to be dozens of faces floating over the gilt cherubs, leaning forward, peering down at the curtain. Mattie had been ghostly with fear when she left for the theater, and Julia understood now how she must feel, waiting to come out in front of so many pairs of eyes. She groped to her left for Felix's hand and squeezed it nervously. He nodded at the seats in front of them.

"All the critics are here. That's Hobson, on the end."

Glad to focus on something other than the tension of waiting, Julia wondered how it was that Felix knew so much about everything. She had heard the critics' names only through Mattie, and she would never have recognized any of the impassive profiles dotted along the row of stalls.

On Julia's right-hand side China Bliss sat with her ringless hands folded in her lap. She had arrived at the theater fifteen minutes earlier, escorted by Bliss. Alexander's mother was small, swathed in a thick, dark mink coat, with her graying blond hair drawn up into a neat chignon. She held out a thin, cool hand to Julia and Felix. Her face was smooth, well cared for, and impeccably made up, but when she turned to accept the glass of Tio Pepe that Felix had bought for her in the crowded bar Julia saw that she had the same beaked profile as her son. Her plucked eyebrows made the same sardonic arcs. Her appearance was understated, but Julia understood what Sophia had meant. People automatically turned to look at China Bliss, even though she stood quite still, sipping her sherry, hardly speaking at all.

Julia thought Bliss's mother was unnerving. She found herself overtaken by an unfamiliar desire to be approved of, to do and say the right things in front of this small, straight-backed figure. The result was that she felt awkward and oversized, and suspected that she was talking too much. China's unblinking eyes studied her over the rim of the sherry glass. Julia was relieved when the bell rang and they joined the shuffling crowd making its way into the theater.

There was another thing too.

From the way that Bliss looked at her and listened to the few words that she did utter, Julia recognized what she had already suspected, that he adored his mother. Since she had met him, quite unthinkingly Julia had become used to being the focus of his attention. Now that it was divided, she was faintly but surprisingly resentful.

As she waited for the curtain to go up, Julia sat as still as she could so that her arm wouldn't brush unnecessarily against China's furred one. She didn't try to look at Bliss, seated on the other side of his mother. And then, without warning, the house lights dimmed. An unusual silence fell at once, and Julia didn't think of anything except Mattie. The red velvet folds and gold fringe swept upward, incongruously revealing the set. It was a small, square room, papered with stained wallpaper. There was an old gas oven, a sink with a pail standing in it, an oilcloth-covered table. Mattie was sitting at the table with her back to the audience. Her hair was pinned up so that the white, childish nape of her neck was revealed. In the breathing quiet she began to hum.

The tune was "Greensleeves." Mattie's voice was high and clear, and it was as if it cast a spell. Julia shivered, and the fine hairs stood up all down the length of her back. She slid forward onto the edge of her seat, conscious of Felix, beside her, leaning forward too. After that, Julia didn't move at all. The play, and Mattie's performance, transfixed her.

In the single short interval the four of them sat in their places, not talking but listening to the heightened buzz of talk, feeling the electricity generated in the fusty red and gilt space. Julia couldn't look at the critics. As the houselights went down again, her fingernails clenched into the palms of her hands. *Please, Mattie,* she whispered. *Just go on being as good.* Somehow China Bliss must have heard her.

"She will," she said crisply.

The first act had had its bitter comedy. The second swung into tragedy.

Julia had lost all consciousness that it was Mattie on the stage. Mattie was another person, remote from here, whose laughter and exploits were nothing to do with this Mary or her lover and their fatal disintegration.

At the end, in the last scene, Mary knelt down in front of

the oven's mouth. She showed the same bare, defenseless neck. And then, with shocking distractedness, she began to hum again. It was "Greensleeves" again, but the phrases were broken now and the clear voice was cracked.

The tears ran down Julia's face.

There was a moment of blessed darkness and then there were lights again. And now it was Mattie once more, her hands linked with the other actors', while the applause surged up and broke over them. She was smiling, but she looked dazed. The clapping went on, and on, mixed with shouting and cheering. Half-angrily, Julia rubbed the tears off her cheeks with her wrists and went on clapping until her hands were raw, needing to make some offering to Mattie from herself and all the rest of the people who had seen her. Oddly, she remembered the Showbox. Mattie had been right, she thought. She had uncovered far more tonight than she had ever needed to on Monty's seedy stage.

They were shouting for the author now. Jimmy Proffitt emerged suddenly from the wings, spindly in a black jacket and tight trousers, his neck looking almost too fragile to support his domed head. He nodded, without smiling, with the same dazed look as Mattie. He took Mattie's hand and the actor's who had played her husband and held them up, like a prizefighter's. A moment later, with the applause still thundering, the curtain dropped for the last time. The gold fringe shut out the last glimpse of it, but the sordid room stayed with them all.

The houselights seemed high and hard, and the overblown Victorian decor even more incongruous. Julia blinked, and saw Felix's face. He was still staring at where Mattie had stood.

"She was good, wasn't she?" Julia whispered idiotically. He nodded.

"Oh, yes. She was good. I didn't realize how good."

China stood up, drawing her fur coat neatly around her. She fitted her black suede gloves onto her hands, smoothing each finger in turn before she looked up at Julia. "Thank you," she said calmly. "That was a memorable evening. Your friend, and Mr. Proffitt, have an interesting future ahead of them. I'm sure the critics will agree."

Julia had forgotten them. When she looked, the seats were all empty.

"Gone to do their stuff," Felix said.

Over his mother's head, Bliss was smiling at her. Julia felt a surge of elation, fueled by her relief for Mattie. It swelled into euphoria and she held out her hand to China. "Let's all go backstage," she insisted. "We must go back and see her."

Mattie sat in her dressing room.

The flowers and telegrams that had seemed to fill the space before the performance were obliterated by people. Half of the faces were totally strange, although they swooped down on her and made kissing and congratulating noises. The others were so familiar that they were incongruous in this place; Julia and Felix, looking as happy as if they had just fallen in love, Francis Willoughby grinning like an overfed cat, with his cigar bobbing up and down as he shook hands, Bliss, with an autocratic-looking woman who was unmistakably his mother, John Douglas, Rozzie, with her husband, looking awkward and overawed, Ricky and Sam beaming and nudging each other, Johnny Flowers wearing a clean white vest, seemingly dozens of others. Mattie wanted to hug them all to her, but she couldn't move. She felt as though the viscera had been lifted out of her. She was empty, a shaky bag of skin with a mouth that went on smiling, and murmuring *thank you*.

Someone put a full glass into her hand and she drank gratefully. It was champagne, and the bubbles at the back of her throat made her choke. A hand patted her back, and held her glass while she wiped her eyes. She saw that it was Jimmy Proffitt.

"You did well," he whispered.

"I messed some lines at the beginning."

"Yeah. I wasn't going to mention that until tomorrow." He was smiling. His eyes slanted at the corners and his long top lip lifted from his teeth. Mattie emptied her glass, and it was filled up at once.

Later, there was dinner in an Italian restaurant near the theater. Mattie felt exhausted now, the weight of it all pressing down on her head, but there seemed to be no possibility of escape. She longed to be at home in the square, warming her feet at the gasfire and drinking gin out of a mug, with Julia. But Julia and Felix had gone, presumably to have dinner with Bliss and his mother. Everyone she knew seemed to have gone, all of a sudden, and she had been swept away by the rest of the cast, and the director, and the Angel Company stalwarts, and a lot of strange faces who clamored and squawked around the red table-cloths. Mattie wondered dimly why she didn't share the universal sense of euphoria.

I'm tired, she thought.

"You look knackered," Jimmy Proffitt's flat voice said in her ear. Gratefully, she let her head fall on his shoulder. Here was a friend, at least. His arm came around her as if to prove it.

"I am."

"Well, bear up. We can get away soon."

Mattie drank the glasses of Chianti as they arrived in front of her, and waved the plates of food away. The laughter and voices seemed to reach her down a very long tunnel. But when she turned she could see Jimmy's ear, very close, seemingly larger than life. It had intricate pinky-gray folds, and it lay flat to his head in a way that seemed not quite human. The room was thick with smoke, and the noise seemed unbearable. People were still eating, and she stared at them, wondering how they could force down the mottled red and creamy coils.

Then at last there was a movement. They were standing up and there were bursts of laughter, and she was nodding and smiling and answering. Jimmy's arm was around her waist, half holding her up, half drawing her to him. Outside, on the sidewalk, his face was level with hers. He put his mouth close to her ear.

"Come home with me. I'll take care of you if you want."

Oh, please. Mattie seized at the thought. She knew how exhausted she was, how dazed by the seemingly ecstatic reception of Jimmy's play and her performance, and now, in the cold air, just how drunk. To be taken care of. That was what she needed.

She smiled into Jimmy's slanting eyes. "Yes. I'll come."

He lived in one and a half rooms over a restaurant near Tottenham Court Road. When he clicked on the lights, Mattie saw that the small space was obsessively tidy. There was a bed, a table with a typewriter on it, a few clothes hanging behind a piece of curtain. It reminded her a little of Felix's room, except that there were none of Felix's odd or beautiful objects to decorate it. Jimmy's only ornaments were huge collages made from pictures snipped out of magazines. They were intricate and disturbing, ears pasted to grow out of noses, eyes out of mouths, many heads from a single body. Mattie shivered and looked away.

"Cold?" Jimmy asked. He turned on a one-bar electric fire. His hands were warm when they touched her face, and his mouth was warm when he kissed her. She felt his long, thin lips move against hers. It was very quiet in the room. Mattie wanted to say something, almost anything, to make a bridge of words between them before anything else happened. She lifted her head. "I've never told you before. How brilliant I think it is. *One More Day.* You deserve . . . everything that's coming."

He looked at her, sideways, considering her. "I know. I was never worried about the play after I'd finished it." He took her praise as no more than his due. "I was just afraid of what they'd do to it on the stage. But you did well. I told you." He kissed her neck, pulling the collar of her blouse away from the skin. That was all there was to say, seemingly.

"Thank you," Mattie whispered.

"Are we going to bed?" Jimmy asked.

When she was undressed she tried to wrap the bedcover around herself, but he held it away, looking at her.

"You've got wonderful tits," he said, and buried his face in them.

What Jimmy Proffitt did was not much different from what John Douglas had done, or the one or two men she had experimented with since then, except that it went on for much longer. He came, at last, and rolled away from her, smiling in a way that seemed to Mattie to be inside himself, nothing to do with her at all.

"Did you like that?" he asked.

"Oh. Yes," she said. She was wondering why, on what should have been a triumphant night, when everything was happening to her that she had ever hoped for, why she should feel so lonely and separate, even from Jimmy, who was part of the triumph and whose body had just been part of hers. More than anything else, she wanted to cry, just to lie still and let the tears flood out of her eyes.

"Hey." Jimmy put his arms beneath her shoulder and pulled her closer to him. "Go to sleep now. You're okay. And you can act."

The unexpected tenderness finished Mattie. But Jimmy turned out the light, so her tears were at least invisible. She lay against him, her hand fluttering awkwardly over his flat body and hollow flanks. He caught it and held it between them. Mattie's tears ran into the thin pillow, and then dried.

I can act, she told herself. *I knew I could do it. And I did, didn't I?*

It was her last thought before she fell asleep.

In the morning, when she woke up and blinked in the dirty, early light, Jimmy was already out of bed. He was standing in the middle of the floor pulling a pair of jeans up over his bare thighs.

"Where're you going?" Mattie mumbled.

He stared at her. "The papers. Where d'you think?"

He was gone for only a few moments. He burst back into the room with a thick sheaf of newsprint in his arms. Mattie hauled herself upright, wrapping the bedclothes carefully around her upper half. But Jimmy didn't spare her a glance. He threw himself down on the bed beside her and tore feverishly into the first paper. His lips formed the first words as he read them, and then he shouted in triumph. " 'Mr. Proffitt, the youngest and angriest of the Angry Young Men, has written a remarkable play. His voice is uncompromising, poetic, and as new as tomorrow.' "

Mattie caught the fever. She snatched up another paper and riffled through it. "Here. Listen. 'A tragedy for our times . . . powerful, shocking, mordantly funny . . .' umm, umm, 'Miss Banner is a great discovery.' "

They were like children pulling open Christmas stockings, exclaiming at each new revelation and then throwing it aside in favor of the next. They snatched the reviews from each other, tearing the paper and smudging their hands and faces with newsprint as the pages mounted up in a litter around them.

" 'I am not ashamed to say that I wept, and I don't believe that there were many dry eyes around me.' Jesus, who wrote that?"

" 'A directness that cuts straight to the heart.' "

"Hey, here's one for you. 'I would travel a long way to see Miss Banner in one of our great tragic roles.' "

"How far is a long way? He never came to Sunderland to see me as the debutante in *Welcome Home*."

They were flushed with their success now, shouting and laughing and poring over the best lines again. Mattie was bursting with the elated triumph that had evaded her last night. " 'Miss Banner is a faultless Mary.' "

All the reviewers devoted most of their space to the play itself, and that was how it should be, Mattie thought generously. *One More Day* was a remarkable piece of work, and she was proud that she had recognized it on her first reading, with John Douglas watching her so anxiously. And her own share of the praise and attention was more than she had hoped for, more than she had even dreamed of. She gathered the scattered newspapers voluptuously to her chest and hugged them.

There was only one less than favorable review, in the

Telegraph. The rims of Jimmy's nostrils went white as he read it.

" 'The unpleasantly realistic face of an unpleasant world, and Mr. Proffitt dwells on it with evident relish. The fine acting of the newcomer, Miss Banner, is wasted on the self-seeking melodrama of *One More Day*.' " Jimmy almost spat. "What's he talking about, the ignorant, bloated old bastard?''

Gently, Mattie took the paper from him and dropped it on the floor. "It's only one," she said. "Against all the others."

They went back to the good reviews, rereading them until they knew them by heart. Then Mattie leaned back luxuriously against the pillows while Jimmy went into his kitchen alcove and made bacon sandwiches with thick slabs of white bread smeared with tomato ketchup, and tea in a big brown pot. He brought them back to bed and they feasted together, speculating about what the director would say, and the backers, and on how many weeks the play would run after such reviews, and what Jimmy's share of the take would amount to. Francis's negotiations on Mattie's behalf hadn't secured her any more than a fairly modest weekly wage.

"I'll be rich," Jimmy announced.

At the same moment, Mattie realized with a little jolt that even if she wasn't rich, she was a definite success. There would be other parts now. Lots of them, perhaps even television or films. She had watched it happen to other actresses, and now it was her turn. Just as she had dreamed, ever since Blick Road. A slow, dazzled smile spread over her face.

Jimmy Proffitt saw it and he took her mug of tea out of her hand. "And now, don't you think we should celebrate our mutual triumph?"

He pulled the blankets away and nuzzled his face against the creamy weight of Mattie's breast. Her fists had already begun to tighten when he sat up again and reached for a tin box on the chair beside his bed. Inside the tin was a packet of tobacco and a folded paper of grass. "Shall we have a smoke first?''

Mattie nodded. She watched him while he rolled it and then took the first draw when he offered it to her. There was plenty of marijuana around at the Rocket and elsewhere, but Mattie generally preferred the blues and other uppers taken by the Showbox girls to keep themselves going. The grass made her feel thick-headed now, and her limbs felt heavy and tingly. But it was nice, lying dreamily with her cheek against Jimmy's chest and watching the blue plumes of smoke. She thought that one of the eyes in the collage over the bed winked at her, and she laughed a little.

"That's better," Jimmy said. He put the smoldering butt out in a tin ashtray and pulled Mattie over to lie on top of him.

"Go on," he murmured. "It's not going to bite you, is it?"

After a while, quite a long while, through the usual stabbing and bumping, Mattie began to feel a different sensation. Jimmy had twisted her over onto her back, and her knees were drawn up on either side of his narrow hips. He moved in and out of her with long, slow, rhythmical thrusts. Mattie realized that she was lifting her own hips to meet his. The odd sensation, still dim and unlocalized, was a throb of pleasure. It had nothing to do with what Ted had once done. It belonged to here and now, and Mattie twisted her head on the pillow, trying to reach inside herself for it. It escaped her, tantalizingly, like a point of warmth blown to and fro in a windy space. But it was there, somewhere. It was even intensifying. Mattie was half-afraid to focus on it, in case it vanished.

Jimmy plunged on. His eyes were screwed shut and his face was red. His mouth opened suddenly, a dark, wet square, and he shouted something over her head. Mattie watched him, gripped by an instant of acute anger that the peak of pleasure should be his, and not hers. And then, a moment later, when he flopped down beside her, anger dissolved into tenderness. She was incredulously happy too. This time she hadn't longed for it to end. This time she had begun, a little, to understand what it was all about.

The knot that had tied itself inside her began unsatisfactorily to unravel and the small, local, ordinary sensations of hands and feet, arms and legs, came back to her. It was Jimmy who had shown her the difference. Gratitude washed over her. She leaned over him and brushed the hair back from his forehead. He was panting and he opened his eyes and looked at her, full in the face. He didn't often do that, she realized now. His eyes were an unusual greeny-yellow color.

"Okay," he whispered, and Mattie didn't know whether he meant her or himself.

They lay with their arms around each other for a little while longer. Mattie would have liked a cigarette or perhaps some more grass, but Jimmy jerked himself upright and then swung out of bed, out of her reach. He pulled a shirt over his shoulders and began buttoning it.

"Time to get moving," he said briefly.

"Where . . ."

"People to see. Duties of celebrity to discharge." He grinned at her. "You should have too."

"Yes, of course." She couldn't think of anything she had to do but be at the theater by six P.M., but she slid out of bed, too, keeping the shelter of the covers around her for as long as possible. Jimmy was already dressed. He went into the kitchen alcove and she heard him splashing water and whistling. Mattie looked out of the window into the street. There was a sandwich bar opposite, with office workers taking early lunches already filing into it. She felt supremely privileged. She had no office to go to. She had a part, a wonderful part, and a packed theater. She wanted to put her arms around Jimmy and thank him, but when he came back he was shaved and combed, and he was already shrugging himself into his jacket.

"D'you mind if I push off?"

"No. No, of course not."

"Just pull the door shut. It'll lock itself. See you tonight."

"Yes. Jimmy, thank you . . ." But he was already gone. Mattie stood in the middle of the room, thinking about the way his narrow eyes lifted, the way he had said *I'll take care of you*, the other things he had done. His crumpled jeans were still lying on the floor where he had left them last night, and she picked them up and smoothed them neatly on a chair. Then she made the bed and picked up their breakfast mugs and carried them through into the kitchenette. As she did the dishes she was thinking, is this what it's like? Is this what Julia felt about her aviator? She wondered if her own face glowed in the same way, as if it were illuminated from deep inside. She even tried the words out on her tongue, *I love you, Jimmy*, and didn't stop to laugh at herself.

When the room was restored to its original neatness she dressed herself and pulled the door shut behind her, listening for the click of the lock. Then she walked down to Oxford Street to catch a bus home. She felt different, walking through the crowds, but she didn't know if it was because of her success or because of falling in love.

Julia had been in to work, but George had sent her out to pick up some urgently needed wallpaper samples from the manufacturers' offices in the West End, and she had decided that she would reward herself for the boring chore with a quiet lunch at home in the square. She didn't quite admit to herself that she was worried because Mattie hadn't come home all night, and no one had answered the telephone in the flat this morning. Perhaps she would be in by now, Julia thought as she tramped up the stairs.

The flat was empty when she let herself in, but by the time she had made herself a sandwich in the kitchen Mattie had arrived. Julia glanced quickly at her. She was relieved to see that Mattie looked cheerful, only tired, with dark patches under her eyes.

"And where's the star been all night?" she asked lightly. "Have you seen the papers? George is so impressed, I must be worth at least another thirty bob a week to him just for knowing you."

"Yes, amazing, the reviews . . ."

Mattie looked so uncertain that Julia went and put her arms around her. She had been feeling an uncomfortable sensation that wasn't jealousy, of course it wasn't possible to be jealous of Mattie's success, but still an awkward irritableness every time she thought of the papers, and the three times that the telephone had rung just while she was making her sandwich, each time someone Julia didn't know, urgently wanting to speak to Mattie. She hugged her tightly now.

"Where have you been, Mat? Are you all right?"

"I went home with Jimmy Proffitt."

Julia was startled. "With him?" She hadn't much liked the brief glimpse she had caught of the playwright. "And what was that like?"

"It was nice," Mattie said. "He's really nice. I think. As well as brilliant, of course," she added loyally. "In fact, this could well be *it*."

"Oh, Mattie."

They looked at each other and then they laughed, rubbing their cheeks together. She was still Mattie, after all, Julia thought with relief. Why ever should she have thought otherwise, just because of a few lines in the newspapers? Abruptly, ashamed of her earlier feelings, she said, "I didn't get a chance to tell you properly last night. I was so proud of you, up there. You were better than I'd ever imagined you were going to be. Shows how much I know."

"Thanks," Mattie said, her face glowing.

"C'mon. Have my sandwich. I'll make another. There's coffee in the pot."

"I'd rather have a gin."

Sitting in front of the gasfire in Jessie's room, it was like ordinary life again. Plain and reassuring. Mattie was eager to reconfirm it, convincing herself that the play and the reviews were just delicious icing on top of the solidly familiar cake, and it wouldn't matter if there wasn't to be a second helping of icing.

"Tell me some news of real life. What have you been doing?"

"Since yesterday afternoon? Not much. Being intimidated by Bliss's mother, mostly. Lucky I'm not a hopeful daughter-in-law, isn't it? Oh, yes, one thing. George says he wants Felix to go in and see him. He thinks he just may have an opening."

"No prizes for guessing which one," Mattie said coarsely.

It was so much one of the old jokes that they fell against each other, hooting with laughter. Julia gasped, "Mattie, darling Mattie. You won't get any different, will you, just because you're famous?"

"Nothing's going to get any different," Mattie said firmly. "Just better, that's all."

The telephone began to ring again. Julia sighed.

"Go on, you'd better answer it. It's sure to be for you."

Mattie stood up, brushing the sandwich crumbs away from her mouth as if the caller could see her. She crossed the room to it, in the corner where Jessie's bed had once been, and picked up the receiver.

"Come on, darling. This way. Keeping in step with the poodle, please."

It was the beginning of March, and the few gleams of thin sunshine filtering through the clouds failed to melt the air at all. Julia shivered, stared hard at the rash of yellow crocuses poking out of the grass, and tried to convince herself that she was both warm and perfectly relaxed.

"Ve-ry haughty. Good. Nice. This way, love, can't you?"

She was walking her adorable giant poodle beside the Serpentine in Hyde Park. It was a lovely warm day. She looked marvelous in her new outfit, designed by Yves Saint Laurent for the august house of Dior. She loved the suit in raspberry and black checked tweed, cinched in at the waist with a four-inch-wide patent-leather belt, ballooning out into a skirt that was then pulled into a tight band ending two inches above her knees.

There was a matching tweed hat, divinely shaped like a lampshade. The photographer hopping in front of her was no more important than a fly or a gnat.

If only any of it was true, Julia thought miserably. She thought the clothes made her look grotesque, and the huge earrings they had put on her pinched her earlobes. Her feet were frozen, and the big dog, hideously clipped into balls of black fluff, pulled viciously on its jeweled lead. The photographer was a gray-haired exquisite whose impatience was beginning to wear through his charm, and his assistant and the fashion editor from the magazine looked despairing. Julia had so much makeup on that she didn't know how much of her expression showed through it, but however she looked, it clearly wasn't haughty enough. Not nearly as haughty as the dog.

"Good, keep going, and again, *so* grand," trilled the photographer.

It was Julia's second week as a professional model, and her third assignment. Her photographer friend, surprisingly true to his promise, had shot a portfolio of pictures and they had taken them to a model agency. To Julia's amazement, the agency had agreed to take her onto their books.

"You're a great-looking girl, with a thoroughbred face. You've got the height, and you're slim enough," they had told her. "You're very raw, of course, but time will solve that. Do you want to give it a try?"

It had been a particularly cold and wet February. Mattie was absorbed in *One More Day*, and any free time she had was devoted to Jimmy Proffitt. Suddenly, overnight, they were the golden couple. Every magazine that didn't have Jimmy's face on the cover seemed to have Mattie's.

Felix had joined George Tressider Designs. George had taken him straight behind the door into the design offices, and Julia was left outside in her old place.

"Oh, yes," she told the model agency. "Of course I do."

She handed her notice in to George and waited for her own success to overtake her. It had taken only ten days, ten days divided between sitting in the flat and wishing the agency would phone her, and actual assignments where she spent every second wishing she were back in the flat again, for her to realize that success was elusive.

She had been fine in front of the first photographer. He was a friend, and it was all only a joke. She had strutted and posed with real enjoyment, thinking *as soon as I've done this he'll stop pestering me.* But once it became real work, Julia felt quite different. She was awkward with critical faces peering at her, however much she told herself that she didn't care, and the camera lens seemed to freeze her with its cold fish-eye.

"Good face," she heard one of the photographers say, "but she's as stiff as a board."

Julia seesawed between needing to laugh and wanting to cry. These clothes made her laugh, with their high-flown haute couture absurdity. She supposed that she was lucky even to be allowed to touch them, but the sort of clothes that Julia wanted to wear came from a new little shop called Bazaar in the King's Road. Sadly, Bazaar didn't employ models, nor did its dresses get featured in the glossy magazines. It was failing that made Julia want to cry. She had always hated failure, and she knew that it was facing her now.

"Where are you going?" the photographer shouted in exasperation.

Julia wasn't going anywhere, it was the dog. It had glimpsed an Irish setter in the distance and it shot forward, yanking Julia behind it. And then it stopped dead, unable to contain its malice any longer, with its knotty legs spread wide and its pompom tail quivering. Julia crashed into it, swayed, and lost her footing. She fell heavily, slithered down the wet concrete incline on her bottom, and ended up with her legs in the Serpentine. The dog barked joyously and bounded away, the glittering leash snaking behind it. Murky, freezing wavelets lapped around Julia's calves and soaked the hemline of the hobble skirt. She could imagine the faces behind her, but she sat where she was because she couldn't make herself turn around and see them in reality.

It seemed a very long time before an arm seized her on either side and hoisted her upright. Her sheer nylons were torn to shreds and water ran out of her patent shoes. "Oh, dear," the magazine girl murmured. "Have you got anything there?" she asked her photographer.

"Might have. Just one or two," was the gloomy response. "We'll have to manage somehow with what we've got. That'll be all for today, Julia."

They were all dabbing tenderly at the suit as if it were far more important than she was. *Of course, it is more important,* Julia thought furiously.

When her feet were dry and back in her own shoes the photographer said, "All over now. Cheer up, dear."

"I'm quite cheerful," Julia responded with dignity. "I just hate dogs."

He pursed his lips and raised his eyebrows, reminding her infuriatingly of George.

There was no one at home, of course, when she reached the square. Mattie had already left for the theater, and Felix was absent increasingly often nowadays, about his own mysterious business. Julia made herself a hot drink and sat down beside the fire, snuffling a little and reflecting that no one would care if she caught pneumonia.

When the telephone rang, she almost didn't answer it because she was so sure it would be for Mattie. But she was wrong. It was Bliss. "Would you like to have dinner with me?"

Julia beamed. "Bliss, wonderful Bliss. I'd like to have dinner with you more than anything else in the world."

"Good God. I was going to suggest spaghetti, but I'd better revise my intentions after a response like that."

Julia smiled. She could just see his ironic expression. Bliss was exactly what she needed after a day like today. And the empty flat had begun to feel almost creepily silent.

"I'll pick you up at eight o'clock."

Julia took extra care in getting herself ready. She soaked in a long, hot bath with plenty of L'Air du Temps bath essence. Miraculously, her snuffles dried up. She had recently had her hair cut into a neat, dark cap and she brushed it into gleaming feathers around her face. Finally, she put on her new Bazaar outfit, a short gray flannel tunic with a mustard turtleneck sweater and matching tights.

When Alexander came he looked at her for an extra moment. "You look lovely," he said, and kissed her lightly on the cheek.

He took her to a place she particularly liked, in Kensington. It was small, noisy, and fashionable, full of people who paraded between the tables and stopped to exchange fulsome greetings with one another. Julia knew that it was far from being Bliss's favorite, and she was touched that he had chosen it for her. In return, she tried extra hard to be lively and to make him laugh. He watched her face through the candlelight, seeing the darkness in her eyes. He put his hand over hers and the fingers laced in his, almost greedily.

But they did laugh a good deal over their meal, and later they saw some friends of Sophia's and joined their table for coffee and brandy. Julia thought it had been an excellent evening, and that she had been faultlessly happy and carefree.

But when they were back in the little cocoon of Alexander's red mini, heading home toward the square, he asked her, "What's the matter, Julia?"

They had stopped at some traffic lights and he put out his hand to turn her face to his. There was no question of resisting him. She tried hard to find something light to say, but Bliss's stare was too direct.

"I don't know what I'm doing," Julia whispered.

"Work?"

"Yes, but not just that. I don't have any bearings. Not like Mattie. Or Felix, or you. Everything seems like an empty sea." He was looking at her so closely that she blinked, and bent her head to escape him.

The lights changed and Bliss turned his head too. The car slid forward again.

"Shall I tell you what happened to me today?" she asked.

He nodded gravely. "Yes, please."

She told him the story about the dog, and the Dior suit, and the Serpentine. She made it as amusing as she could, exaggerating the details a little. But at the end he didn't laugh. "Not all that funny," he commented.

Julia was touched. He had seen through her flippant story and understood her humiliation, even though she had imagined it was well hidden. That was perceptive of him, and the power of his perception seemed suddenly at odds with his old vagueness. She looked at him, her eyes wide open, wondering if she had looked before without ever really seeing. "No, I suppose not," she agreed. "Messing things up isn't ever funny, is it?"

Alexander reached out and took her hand again. His felt very large and firm. "I was wondering," he said casually, "if you'd like to come with me to Ladyhill for the weekend. There won't be anyone there. I'd like to show it to you."

"To Ladyhill? All right," Julia said. And then, thinking how lukewarm that sounded, she added hastily, "I'd love to see it, of course. I'll look forward to it."

Alexander drove her down to Ladyhill on a Saturday morning. They set out very early, into a thin mist that masked a featureless world, but as they drove, the sun came out and the countryside emerged in shades of ochre and opal and sharp green. There were new lambs in the fields, and Julia stared blankly at them.

It was a long way, and they stopped for lunch in a country pub that reminded her of the one Josh had taken her to. Those days seemed to belong to another life.

"Are you all right?" Bliss asked her. They were walking down a lane, stretching their legs before driving the last miles of the journey. Julia noticed that Bliss looked right in the countryside. He wore clothes that were the same colors as the fields, and he held his shoulders squarer, as if there were more space available for his height and breadth. Her own thin shoes slid on the hummocks of wet grass, and the pillar-box-red of her coat suddenly seemed too bright. But she didn't want Bliss to have to feel concerned for her.

"Yes, I'm all right." She smiled. "It takes a bit of getting used to, all this . . . space. I can't remember when I was last out of London."

"Dear me," Bliss said mildly.

They reached Ladyhill when the afternoon sun was shining squarely into the windows of the west face. They turned a corner between tall trees, and the house stood in front of them, blazing with reflected light from every tiny pane of the leaded windows. The house seemed to glow with living warmth, and in contrast the clipped yew trees in the paved space enclosed by the wings looked dead black, two-dimensional.

Alexander left his car slewed at an angle in front of the house's magnificence. They crossed the hollowed paving stones in silence. Alexander opened the front door under its stone arch, and they passed through into the dimness. There was a faint scent of lavender and of the soft accretion, in invisible corners, of centuries of dust. Standing in the hallway, where a shaft of light from the high window at the turn of the stairway struck across their heads, Julia looked upward. There was carved oak and the dull gleam of gilt picture frames, a great iron hoop with brackets for dozens of candles suspended by a chain from the dim heights, shadows, and silence. Outside, the birds had been singing and there had been the wind in the elm trees, but there was no sound inside the house.

She couldn't raise her voice above a whisper. "It's beautiful."

To Julia, houses were no more than little boxes like those in Fairmile Road or on the estate, or else they were set out in rows in London terraces, sliced up inside into flats and rooms where the ceiling moldings ended abruptly at arbitrary new walls. Even the flat in the square was home only because Mattie and Felix were there, not because of her own possessions laid out in it.

And Julia, who loved everything new and sharp-edged and iconoclastic, saw how different Ladyhill was. Its beauty was timeless and majestic, dwarfing her and her irrelevant appraisal of it. She followed Alexander obediently through the Long Gallery, looking out at the green view of the gardens beneath the windows, touching the yellow brocade hangings of the great canopied bed in the room beyond it. Alexander called it the Queen's Bed.

There were family rooms as well as formal ones, Alexander's father's bedroom with silver-backed brushes on the tallboy, Sophia's mother's with a lavender silk bedcover, Alexander's and Sophia's rooms still decorated with the clutter of childhood. At the end of the corridor there was a nursery with a dappled rocking horse and shelves of tattered books. They wandered through the rooms together, undisturbed. Julia was glad that he had chosen a time when it was empty of everyone but themselves. The spirit of the house closed intimately around her.

Afterward, she remembered how all her casually acquired impressions of Bliss changed that afternoon. She was impressed by the house—more than impressed, she was awed by it—but she was struck most strongly of all by the difference in Alexander. His sardonic detachment was gone, and his faint, weary vagueness went with it. He was as gentle as he always was to Julia, but he seemed also more forthright, and more able to show her his feelings. As he talked about the house and told her the stories of it, his love for the place showed clearly. She saw it vividly, and her recognition of it provided a missing piece in her understanding of him. Belonging to Ladyhill defined Alexander, and she realized that in London he was different because he was less than himself.

They came back to the ground floor once more by the back stairs, and threaded their way through a seeming warren of stone-flagged kitchens. The house wasn't large, but the succession of rooms was bewildering. Julia had lost her bearings, and she exclaimed with surprise when they reentered the drawing room by a different door. Alexander clicked it shut and the rectangle disappeared into the paneling.

"A secret door," she exclaimed delightedly.

"Only semi-secret. For the servants to make discreet exits. Or perhaps for the hostess to escape her guests for a moment or two?"

With the thought of all the people who must have thronged through this room, all around her like a ghostly pageant in their different clothes, Julia wandered down the length of it. There was a huge open stone hearth, and the scent of woodsmoke lingered pleasantly in the heavy mulberry velvet drapes. There were family photographs clustered in silver frames, but the pictures hanging against the paneling were English landscapes rather than portraits. Books and magazines lay on the tables, and there was a pipe in a rack beside a deep armchair. Julia remembered what Sophia had said about Ladyhill. "It's where we come from, Daddy, Alexander, and me. The most beautiful place in the world."

Julia had thought she was affected, but she understood her words now. For all its size and grandeur, this was a room for living in, redolent of family life. Yet China Bliss had left here, hadn't she? She must ask Alexander about it. Not now, but sometime.

In the tall bay at the end of the room stood a grand piano stacked with sheet music. Alexander went to it and began to look through the piles. He took a sheet seemingly at random, and then he opened the piano and began to play. Julia had heard him play often before, at Markham Square, but never like this. She didn't even know what the piece was, but the notes fell on her as softly as the petals dropping from the scarlet tulips in the vases. As softly as the invisible Ladyhill dust.

Alexander played for a long time, and she watched his head, bent intently over the keys. The light began to fade outside. Julia knew that she liked Alexander very much, and that he was important. It was a rare moment of being quite sure of one truth, its existence untouched and unaffected by the network of other conflicting truths that governed her life.

She envied him too.

She envied his roots here in this place, and the sureness that their secure anchorage gave back to him. It was the sureness that had transformed him for her this afternoon. It made her feel the feebleness of her own grip on the world, the shallowness of the toehold that Betty and Vernon had hollowed for themselves. She understood their fear and their desperation then, with the solidity of Ladyhill's centuries rearing around her.

She looked back at Alexander's bent head and smiled, and the music joined them together as surely as if they were lying down together.

It was almost too dark for him to read the music when he lifted his head again.

"I'll make some tea," he said.

They lit the fire, and then they sat in front of it with the big silver teapot on a tray between them. The logs crackled and shadows thickened in the corners of the room.

Julia said, "It's so quiet. This house needs people. Lots and lots of people. Mad parties."

"Perhaps it does," Alexander said. He came closer to her and they examined each others' faces intently. In London, Julia might have said something flippant to make the moment pass. Here, in the firelight, she put up her fingers to touch his face. The glow from the hearth reddened the blond hair over his ears. Her eyes traveled slowly, seeing each of his features in turn. They had become familiar to her without ever seeming especially interesting, but now it was as if he were a different person, to be rediscovered. Not Bliss, whom she had giggled about with Mattie. Julia wondered a little at her own crassness. This Alexander was a stranger, faintly awe-inspiring. But as she looked into his eyes, Julia saw that he loved her. How could she have been unaware of it before? It seemed very simple, and reassuring, and welcome. He smoothed the hair back from her face, and kissed her. His mouth was more insistent, and her own opened obediently under it. Her head fell back against the cushions and his tongue traced the arch of her throat.

He said, "Julia," and the timbre of his voice reminded her of Josh. She lifted her head again and stared at the log in the hearth. The surface of it was crazed with gray ash, but when the draft fanned it, red veins ran over it like lava. Julia shivered a little and went to close the velvet curtains on the darkness outside. Released from their dull gilt ropes and tassels, they fell in faded but opulent folds. George and Felix would approve, Julia thought. George devoted his life to recreating for his clients just the dim, negligent grandeur that Ladyhill exuded from every corner. George Tressider would die for this place, she realized. And here she was. The irony tickled her, and with her face bright with amusement she went back to Alexander and took hold of both his hands.

"Play some more music. Something silly and loud this time. Let's hear if the house likes the sound of it."

Alexander sat down at the piano and struck up a Scott Joplin rag. Julia beamed her approval, twirled in the middle of the Turkish carpet, and launched herself into a Charleston. Alexander played, faster and faster, until she was panting for breath, and then she collapsed sideways against the piano, gasping and laughing. "Mercy. I can't Charleston like Mattie."

Alexander glanced up at the ceiling. The music seemed to reverberate there still. "I think you're right," he mused. "The old house is too quiet. Lots of people. Lots of parties. Would you like that, Julia?"

Julia didn't know what to say. She didn't look at him, and then when the moment was past she wished that she had.

"I always like parties," she mumbled.

"Hmm." Alexander closed the lid of the piano. "Let's go and forage for some dinner, shall we?"

They found some cold chicken in the refrigerator, and vegetables in a rack in the immense, chilly larder.

"I don't suppose Pa and Faye will mind," Alexander said.

"Where are they?" Julia asked curiously.

"In London. The housekeeper has the weekend off too. Nobody else lives in. There are only a couple of cleaning ladies who come in from the village anyway. Everything has to run on a shoestring nowadays." He nodded cheerfully at the chipped cream paintwork, and then his expression changed. "I like being here alone with you."

"I like it too," Julia said.

"Where shall we eat?"

"In the dining room. Properly."

The room was cold, but Alexander turned on an electric fire and Julia laid the table. There were fourteen high-backed chairs around the length of blackened oak, and she set their two places one at either end. Ransacking the baize-lined drawers of the sideboard, she found the heavy silver cutlery with a worn "B" squirling the handles, and made an elaborate setting with too many knives and forks. Alexander brought up a bottle of hock, and she put out tall glasses with a cloudy spiral trapped in the stems. She enjoyed playing at châtelaine in the somber magnificence of the room.

They sat down, facing each other, so far apart that they almost had to shout. They found it irresistibly funny, and laughed so much that the boiled potatoes went cold in front of them.

Afterward they went back and sat in front of the drawing room fire again, their fingers twined tightly together.

"Will you live here one day?" Julia asked.

"One day," he told her. "After my father dies. That's the understanding."

His London detachment was more comprehensible now. That wasn't his real life. Even his music wasn't quite real, perhaps. His life was here, at Ladyhill. Envy nibbled at Julia again. What was her own freedom, except being adrift?

When they went upstairs, and Alexander showed her into a guest room hung with peacock-patterned fabric, he didn't say good night. Julia undressed, cleaned her teeth and brushed her hair, and took her diaphragm out of its pink box. She put it in place and lay down between the chilly sheets. Alexander knocked at the door and came in, closing the door behind him with a faint click. When he slid into the bed beside her he seemed larger, and strange because of it, but his warmth struck through her and she stopped shivering and turned to him.

Bliss was gentle, more gentle with her than he need have been, and his care heated her response to him. Their lovemaking was good, and she knew that she shouldn't have been so surprised by it.

In the privacy of the dark Julia wondered, *Why did he choose me to love? Why not Mattie, or any of the girls from the Rocket, or Blue Heaven.* . . . She contemplated her own ordinariness, and the narrow confines of her background compared with Alexander's. Then she thought, *You don't choose. I didn't choose Josh. It takes hold, and you can't shake it off.*

Beside her, Alexander breathed deeply, warming her cheek. He tightened his arms around her. "I love you," he said as if he could hear her thoughts.

"I love you too," she answered, offering it hopefully, as if hope could change everything.

Alexander fell asleep. Julia lay very still, her head in the hollow of his shoulder, her physical contentment giving her a sense of stasis, of welcome tranquillity. The wind creaked and groaned in the elm trees beyond the windows, and she tried to imagine the dark gardens, spreading away from the walls of the house. More territory, unexplored. Alexander's territory. She put her hand out to touch him, spreading her fingers over the firm flesh of his thigh.

"I love you," she said again to the safety of his closed ears.

In the morning, with Julia's feet in Lady Bliss's rubber boots, they went out to look at the gardens. There was a high wind, and fretted clouds raced across the cold blue sky. They were both elated and they shouted like children, and ran across the winter-pocked lawns until the blood pounded in Julia's rosy cheeks. She slowed down beside Alexander as they paced along the flower beds, and she listened as he recited plant names like a litany. "Mahonia, magnolia. Anemone, forsythia."

They all looked the same to Julia, and she beamed fondly at him. "Are you a gardener?" Nothing she could have learned about Bliss would have surprised her today.

He laughed. "Pa would be pleased if I was. No, China is the gardener of the family. She restored the old gardens, laid out most of these beds."

Hosta, hellebore. Salix, sambucus.

In a birch thicket at the farthest point from the house lay a sheet of pale gold. The daffodils shivered and swayed, profligate in the sharp chill.

"That is beautiful," Julia murmured, drinking in the sight. Alexander watched her until she turned again, almost high with their color and with the thin, sweet scent. They stood side by side, with the shelter of the birch trees behind them, looking at the house. The shifting sky was reflected in the windows now, so that the house itself seemed to move, sailing before the wind.

Alexander took her hand, weighing it in his own. She had a sense that he had been waiting, waiting for a long time with a kind of calculating patience that had utterly escaped her attention, and that now, at Ladyhill, he judged that the time had come. She felt outguessed and outmaneuvered, and it was an oddly exciting sensation. She looked at him with minute attention, oblivious of the house and the gardens, of everything except Alexander himself.

Even so, she didn't guess what was coming.

"I wanted to ask you if you would like to marry me."

The wind took his words and seemed to spread them over the grounds, seeding them richly, and the house seemed to dip and shimmer in its stately progress. But the ground felt solid under Julia's feet, and the cold still stung her face.

She was thinking, *Not me. You should choose someone better than me. Someone good, like you, not a survivor, which is all I am.*

She was going to say, *I can't marry you,* but she swallowed the hasty words as they took shape in her mouth. With sudden perfect clarity she understood that Bliss did love her, and she began to comprehend the importance of that. To be loved by a man like Alexander made her more than a survivor. It made her full and strong, no more a dirty little baby or even a bad girl, and it made her long to return his love with her own. She did love him now, with an untroubled conviction that was nothing like her grinding passion for Josh. It was simple, and comfortable, and good.

A huge sense of relief washed over her, and happiness swelled up in the wake of it. She was afraid that it would shatter if she moved, but she did move, going to him. The anxiety in his eyes changed to delight. Alexander's arms wrapped around her. The happiness was still there, intact.

"Yes," Julia said. "Yes, if you really want me."

"I want you," Alexander answered her. "I wanted you from the moment I first saw you."

Julia murmured with her face against his, "I'm here. I always want to be here, wherever you are."

THIRTEEN

Julia and Alexander were married in the little church in Ladyhill village. After the ceremony Lady Bliss, or Faye, as she had briskly instructed Julia to call her, gave a small reception for their guests in the Long Gallery at Ladyhill. They were mostly family, villagers, and tenants. Sophia recalled that at her own wedding to Toby there had been five hundred guests and a marquee in the garden.

"At least I'm escaping that," Julia said with relief.

She had wanted to marry in London, in a registry office, and to give her own kind of party afterward in the Rocket Club. Alexander wouldn't hear of it. He wanted them to be married properly, as he put it, at Ladyhill, and for the rest of the fuss to be kept to a minimum. Loving him, and eager to do whatever pleased him, Julia agreed. She was fitted for a ballerina-length dress of cream raw silk, and chose two small Brockway cousins to be her bridesmaids.

"We can have a big celebration for all our friends later, in London, can't we?" she begged Alexander.

"Of course we can," he promised. "Let's just be married first."

The wedding preparations were tedious to both of them, for different reasons, but they were happy and in love, and they cheerfully performed the expected rituals. Once it was over, Julia remembered very little about her wedding day. Betty looked

timid and overawed, swamped by a new two-piece that was too
big and too bright for her. Vernon seemed to be leaning on
Julia's arm rather than the other way around as they made their
way down the aisle. Julia recalled Sir Percy's poker-straight back
in the family pew, and Faye beside him, mistily smiling beneath
the tulle-swathed brim of her hat. China was there, too, sitting
on the bride's, half-empty, side of the church. Her self-possession
was as formidable as a weapon, but Julia warmed to her for her
evident pleasure in Alexander's happiness.

Julia had no doubt that she was far from being the kind of
daughter-in-law that Sir Percy and the second Lady Bliss would
have chosen, had Alexander offered them a choice. Rather sensi-
bly, she thought, they had decided to make the best of her.
Probably they were relieved that Alexander had decided to marry
at all.

As she stood demurely at her new husband's side, listening
to the dull speeches and wishing she could take off the flowered
headdress that was pinching her temples, Julia decided that they
could have been even less lucky. Alexander might have wanted
to marry Mattie, for example. Julia had to bite the inside of her
cheek to stop herself giggling at the idea. Mattie had already
drunk a good deal of champagne, and was creating a disturbance
among the bachelor cousins and uncles at the far end of the
gallery. Julia felt Alexander's arm pressing against hers in sympathy, and she kept her face perfectly straight.

After the wedding, Mr. and Mrs. Bliss flew to Paris for a
week's honeymoon. When it was over they came back to Alexander's flat in Markham Square. Julia unpacked their wedding
presents and tidied up the worst of the bachelor mess. One
morning, when Alexander had gone out to a business meeting,
she sat down and wrote a letter to Josh Flood.

I'm married now, she wrote. *Isn't that strange? I still think
of you, although I love Alexander very much. Is that wrong, do
you think?*

When she had finished the letter she read it through, and
then tore it up. It was all finished, she told herself. It was gone,
like Blick Road and the old square and the frustrating days at
Tressider Designs. The sadness and the sense of loss, of unfin-
ished business, must just be part of being grown-up, Julia thought.
She would learn to live with that, like everything else.

The next thing she did, with her Tressider experience to
back her, was to apply for a job in the homes department of a
glossy magazine. To her surprise, she got the job. Alexander

was pleased and proud, which made her feel proud of herself. She started work, and their life began to settle into a comfortably bohemian routine. Alexander wrote his music and played his trumpet or the piano. In the evenings they gave messy, prolonged dinner parties, mixing new friends with the old ones, or went out to jazz clubs, or sat holding hands in little bistros before hurrying home to bed.

It was a happy, deeply satisfying time.

"I like being married," Julia said to Mattie. "Who'd have guessed it?"

"I would," Mattie said promptly. "I wish I could find someone half as decent as Bliss."

"You will," Julia promised. "Just wait." Neither of them mentioned Jimmy Proffitt.

Then, barely three months after their wedding, Alexander's father had a stroke. It seemed at first that he would survive it, but he died a week later, with Alexander sitting at his bedside.

At first Julia didn't understand what the old man's death meant. It didn't occur to her that after the funeral, after the dismal formalities of wills and settlements had been attended to, they wouldn't be going back to Markham Square to pick up the cheerful threads of their life again.

Alexander was gentle, but he was quite firm.

"We'll have to spend much more of our time down here, now that my father has gone. I have to run the estate, and the farm."

Julia said, "How much more time? Weekends, and so on?"

Alexander put his arm around her. "More than that. Ladyhill is my home." He caught himself, corrected himself almost before the words were out. "Our home. I can't be an absentee landlord, Julia."

She knew, now, what was coming, but she would make him admit it to her. "What does that mean, exactly?"

"I want us to live here."

There was a silence, the particular Ladyhill silence in which there were no sounds of traffic, no voices from a busy street beneath the windows. The quiet was oppressive to Julia, and she broke it by asking, "What about my job, Alexander? I like my job. I thought you liked me to do it?" It struck her now as the only work she had ever shown any talent for, as her great chance, impossible to give up.

Alexander didn't hedge, at least.

"I thought that Ladyhill might be a job too. For both of us, together."

He was looking straight into her eyes, concerned, but with the clear expectation that she would do as he asked. Men like Alexander Bliss—Sir Alexander, she reminded herself, just as she, unthinkably, was now Lady Bliss—were brought up to expect agreement from their wives. Faye would always have agreed. China, presumably, had not. Alexander was clever, and sensitive, and all the other things Julia had learned to love him for, but he had his father in him too. She straightened her back, ready to fight him.

And then she recalled their first visit together to Ladyhill, when she had seen Alexander in the different light of this silent, somber place, and had fallen in love with him. He had told her that he would live here one day. "After my father dies," he had said. "That's the understanding."

She had accepted the provision then. She had known it all along. She had even envied Alexander for his roots, spreading out through the Ladyhill earth. There were, of course, no grounds for dissent now. It was in Julia's nature to understand all that in the few seconds that they stood looking at each other, and to reach her own decision.

"Well," she said lightly, "jobs come and go. If we're going to live here, Alexander, we shall have to liven the place up."

He beamed at her, pleased and happy, and Julia felt satisfaction in her own secret generosity. Alexander wound his arms tighter around her. "Of course we will. You said the house needed lots of people. Everyone will come, you know. We'll make sure of that."

"We owe ourselves a party. A housewarming." Julia slid out of his arms, spinning around the room, suddenly excited. "We'll make it a wonderful housewarming. New Year's Eve. The best party of all time. Shall we?"

Alexander watched her, loving her. "Of course," he answered. "What else?"

So Julia gave up her job, and they closed up the Markham Square flat.

"Don't sell it, or even let it," Julia begged. "There are still weekends, and holidays, aren't there?"

Alexander could afford indulgence. "Of course. We'll keep it for you to use whenever you want."

They moved down to Ladyhill together.

A little to Julia's surprise, Faye quickly moved out to a cottage on the estate.

"Don't want the old folks in the way, do you?" she insisted.

Julia grew to like her, seeing Sophia's innocent good nature in her mother too. She also thought that beneath the perfectly judged display of grief for the loss of her husband, Faye seemed rather relieved to be handing over responsibility for the estate to Alexander and retiring in peace to the chintzy cottage set in its manageable little garden.

Whether or not she had enjoyed it, Faye had filled the public role of Lady Bliss much better than Julia promised to do.

"I'm not Lady Bliss," she wailed to Alexander. "She's someone old. Your mother. Your stepmother."

Alexander was indifferent to his title. "It's only a name," he shrugged. "It doesn't get the roof repaired. I wish it did."

But Julia couldn't get used to hers, nor to the obligations that seemed to go with it.

"It isn't me."

"Yes," Alexander said gently, "it is you, because you are my wife."

At Ladyhill, all the people in the village and on the surrounding farms called her Lady Bliss. "I'm Julia," she insisted over and over again. They stared at her distrustfully.

"Don't you see?" Alexander asked her. "They want you to be who you are. They don't want some way-out London dolly."

After a moment Julia had asked him, "And do you?"

He kissed her then. "I want what I've got, and I don't ever want anything else. I love you."

So it was for the few weeks that they had together before the night of Julia's party. Julia chafed at the conventions of country life and at the matronly role her position required her to play, but in private, within the thick walls of Ladyhill, she was surprised by the depth of her happiness. She loved new challenges, and she was amused and entertained to find herself mistress of a household as grand as Ladyhill. She was full of plans for it, and she rummaged through the silent rooms, moving the furniture and dragging back the curtains. She even went out into the wintry gardens and poked in the flower beds, under the suspicious eye of the old gardener.

"We'll bring the place alive," she promised Alexander.

"You already have," he said softly. He reached out for her and caught her as she pretended to evade him. They clung together, laughing and then breathless and then greedy for each other. Alexander drew her down and they made love on the floor in front of the big stone hearth.

Two weeks before Christmas, Julia's doctor confirmed that she was pregnant.

She kept the secret to herself, without really understanding why. She had planned to tell Alexander on New Year's Eve, at the party.

Then the fire came.

In the aftermath of it, it seemed that the flames had consumed everything. Not just the house, but their hopes, the soft growths of their happiness, and in the end the love itself.

Julia knew that it was all her fault. Everything that happened on New Year's Eve, the terrible things, and everything afterward. Right at the beginning, while the ashes were still smoldering and Alexander and Flowers's girl were lying in the hospital, guilt took root inside her.

The flames were swift and devastating, but the slow spread of guilt was just as deadly, like a malignant tumor, the more frightening for its invisibility. It took a long time for Julia to understand that against the fire and the guilt she and Alexander stood such a small chance together. It took longer still for her to forgive herself for what happened.

And up until the moment when the flames took hold, she might have believed that the two of them were invincible.

Julia enjoyed every moment of the preparations for her party. She invited all the old friends from London, and Alexander's country friends and neighbors. Only Felix couldn't come, because he had gone to New York with George. Julia persuaded a rock 'n' roll band from the Rocket to make the trip to Ladyhill, and she ordered champagne and planned the decoration of the house in minute detail.

The huge Christmas tree was to be the centerpiece. When the men carried it in, Julia clapped with pleasure. The tip touched the ceiling of the paneled drawing room, and the dark, aromatic branches fanned out in perfect proportion. It was Julia's idea to decorate the tree with real candles. She wanted to recreate a Victorian Christmas, like the ones she had dreamed of as a girl at Fairmile Road. Alexander argued in favor of ordinary tree lights, but he gave in to her in the end, as he did in all small things.

The house was decorated and the food was prepared and laid out with the silver and glass in the dining room. The musicians set up their instruments, the candles were lit, and the guests came, flooding into the old house until it shook with music and laughter.

Julia floated among the rooms, watching her party, her creation. If she didn't feel quite a part of it, she believed that was because she had made it, and her sadness was all for the decade that was slipping away.

Then at the best moment of the party when the best guests were drawing closer under the spell of it, and the tree was shining at the height of its beauty, it shivered, and fell in an arc of flame.

The flames burned themselves into Julia's head. Wherever she looked, in the days after the fire, she saw them dancing. They came back most often in her nightmares, bringing convulsions of horror and fear, but even in daylight they leapt in front of her eyes. Over and over again the black outline of Ladyhill reared over her. The windows were obscene red mouths, and their light licked the swelling underside of the smoke pall. The noise was always there too. It was a merry, hungry crackle of flames, and the splinter and roar as old wood and brick succumbed to them.

At first it had seemed that the house was their only victim.

There were the seconds of blind panic as the flames licked up the old velvet curtains and the wood paneling began to crackle, and then the guests choked and stumbled, screaming directions to each other, out into the courtyard. They huddled together, shivering in the cold, seeing the busy flames shoot upward.

It was Julia who remembered Johnny Flowers and his girl. She and Alexander blundered between the huddles of people, searching for them. *The party to end all parties,* Johnny had said. Johnny and the girl were nowhere to be found. Alexander had turned to face the house, and Julia had seen the light of the fire reflected in his eyes. "They must be still inside."

Alexander broke away from her side, unthinkably running toward the house. The heat and the smoke seemed to reach out for him.

Julia screamed, "Stop him. Don't let him go in there."

People ran after him, some trying to pull him back, others beating toward the stone portico behind him.

The others stumbled backward from the fire, defeated by it, but it took Alexander into itself and the noise seemed to grow louder, the red glare intensified.

"He'll die in there," Julia heard herself screaming.

The silence and stillness of the crowd of people seemed the more shocking because of the fire's wild energy.

Mattie was there. The fierce shadows thrown by the blaze made their faces like skulls as she and Julia faced each other. The two of them, as they had always been. They heard the bells of the fire engines.

Julia ran toward the big red engines. The torn tails of her satin dress swished around her calves as she plunged forward.

"My husband's in there. Save him. Oh, save him." Her screams tore her throat. "And Johnny, and his girl. Save them."

The firemen were big, in helmets, and their silver buttons reflected the red light. They put Julia aside and ran past her, their helmets tilted as they looked up at the roof. The black ribs of it showed now as the bright flames broke free. Fire hoses uncoiled like serpents, and a turntable ladder swayed upward. Julia saw the firemen running, as Alexander had, in under the stone arch.

Mattie stood on one side of her, and on the other was the man with the sideburns, Flowers's friend. Julia had danced the conga with him in the candlelight, seemingly an eternity ago. The rest of the guests stood in a silent huddle, frozen with shock. A spout of water arched from the brass mouth of a hosepipe and fell between the black roof beams. The water hissed into steam, seeming no more than a trickle against the fire's triumphant strength. Julia's eyes were fixed on the door arch, and the pulse of its smoky breath. Her mouth and chest burned with the smoke, and tears poured unnoticed down her face.

She didn't know how many minutes they stood there. The hiss and crackle and the fearful red light took control of time and will and left her with nothing but terror. She was still calling out, "Bliss."

She saw a sudden movement in the doorway. There was a beam of healthy light, the yellow glaze of a strong flashlight catching an oilskin shoulder. A fireman ran out of the shroud of smoke, and Julia saw that the bundle slung over his shoulder was the body of a girl. Mattie's hand clutched at Julia's wrist, but she shook it off and ran forward. An ambulance had come, and more dark uniforms dashed past her with a canvas stretcher. They laid it out on the ground in the shelter of one of the clipped yew trees.

The fireman stooped and tenderly laid his burden on it.

What she saw there stayed with Julia for the rest of her life.

The girl was alive, because her head rolled to one side. But the beat of relief in Julia's throat was followed by a spasm of horror. She was looking at her face as it turned, thinking, *Who is she?*

But no one could have recognized Flowers's girlfriend. Her face was nothing like a face. It was a raw slab, like red melted wax, with ragged black holes punched into it.

And then broad backs knelt down in front of it, and hid the burned face from Julia's sight. She put the back of her hand up to her mouth and bit into the knuckles. The pain of it seemed a long way off, belonging to someone else. But it competed with the nausea that rose to choke her, and stifled the moan in her throat. The stretcher was lifted, swaying, and carried away to the ambulance.

Someone was shouting.

Julia turned her head back to the doorway. She saw the gleam of yellow light again, and the firemen with another burden. There were two of them, and they were carrying Bliss between them. His head lolled backward out of her sight. He had lost one of his patent leather shoes, and his foot dangled in its black silk sock. The legs of his trousers were torn, showing smoke-blackened skin.

"Julia . . ."

It was Mattie again, her arm around Julia's waist to support her.

"I want to go to him," Julia said clearly.

She blundered forward and knelt down as they were lowering Bliss onto the second stretcher. Julia ducked her head for an instant, and then looked at his face. It was blackened, and there was blood oozing from a deep graze on the left cheek. The eyes were closed, but it was Bliss's face. His mouth hung open and he took a ragged gasp of air.

He was alive. Julia was shuddering with relief, and they gently put her aside and began to work on him. It was then that she saw his hands. They were drawn up into claws, and they were red and melted like the girl's terrible face. The sleeves of his dinner jacket and the shirt underneath were charred, and the fibers stuck to the burned flesh. Farther up, up to his shoulders, there were little coils of scarlet where the cloth still smoldered. Julia broke free again from the restraining hands just as the rescuers lifted Alexander's stretcher. She reached forward and tried to beat out the burning threads with her own hands.

"Let me go with him," she begged, but they closed the ambulance doors on the two stretchers.

"The police will take you down to the hospital. Let the ambulance get there as quickly as it can." One of the firemen led her away. The blue light on the ambulance roof flashed impartially over the watching faces as it began to revolve. The high white vehicle rolled away and the siren sawed through the darkness. The sound of it was suddenly louder than the fire.

"Flowers," Julia said. Her eyes fixed on the door again, and the firemen. With a sudden surge of hope she saw that the jets of water were stronger than the flames. Wherever new tongues of fire flickered out, water spurted to douse them. The smoke was thicker and blacker, and the crackle of the fire's progress had given way to the hiss of rising steam.

She stared through the rolling smoke at the exposed black ribs of the roof beams. Little blazing fragments fell, and thick, oily smuts drifted in the light wind. The smell of the fire was like a gag thrust into her mouth.

She shouted, "Flowers. Flowers is still in there. Help him."

Mattie and Flowers's friend, and all the other guests stood around her, watching and praying. "They're trying to get him," somebody said.

A fireman loomed in front of Julia, creaking in his protective clothes. "There's a constable here with a car, Lady Bliss. They'll take you to the hospital."

Julia looked wildly around the circle of blackened, shocked faces. The women were shivering in their thin dresses, and it was only then that Julia realized she was trembling uncontrollably herself. She twisted around to face the house. "I can't. I must wait here, for Flowers."

The fireman's face was stiff under his helmet. She understood, *They don't think he'll be alive.* Mattie's hand took hold of Julia's, drawing her away.

"Come on," she murmured. "We'll go to the hospital."

Numbly, Julia let them lead her to the waiting car. She sat in the backseat with Mattie beside her. Someone had brought a red blanket and wrapped it around them, and Julia felt Mattie's bare arm against her own. They looked at each other, and there were tears pouring down Mattie's face.

"He can't be dead," Julia said in a high, sharp voice. "Not Flowers. They'll save him. I know they will."

Her last glimpse of Ladyhill that night stayed with her through the nightmares and the waking horrors. It was a huge, half-extinguished pyre with fear and death trapped within it, and its smoky fingers reached malevolently after the car as it sped away.

Mattie and Julia huddled together as they followed the ambulance through the night. Under the cover of the red blanket Julia's bitten knuckles dug into the pit of her own stomach.

*   *   *

Johnny Flowers died in the fire. The firemen discovered his body, barely identifiable, lying half in and half out of the bedroom door. The post mortem later indicated that he had almost certainly been overcome by fumes before the flames reached him. Alexander's hands and forearms were badly burned. Julia waited in the hospital into the middle of New Year's Day, then went with him in the ambulance when he was transferred to a special burns unit at another hospital thirty miles away. In the ambulance, still dazed with shock and with his face twisted with pain, Alexander whispered, "We'll build Ladyhill again. Every brick and beam. Just a fire can't destroy Ladyhill, you know." He stirred on the narrow shelf bed, as if he wanted to lift his arms from under the protective cages and begin the work at once.

"Of course we'll rebuild," Julia soothed him. Within herself she shuddered. The flames, and Sandy's face, and the last glimpse of the smoky pyre of the house filled her head. Those images would stay with her, she knew that, night and day. And the weight of guilt for what she had caused to happen was already like a stone inside her. She leaned forward to Alexander, letting her mouth brush his forehead. He winced even at the lightest touch, and the nurse who was traveling with them moved her gently aside.

"I'm sorry," Julia said hopelessly. "It was my fault."

Alexander closed his eyes. "No, it wasn't. How could it have been?"

They reached the hospital, and he was wheeled away from her. Later, a specialist came and told Julia that he would need skin grafts, and weeks of special care before they would know if his burned hands could work again.

"He's a musician," Julia said. "He plays the trumpet, and the piano."

"Yes," the doctor said. "It's very early days yet. We can't tell what will happen."

"I see," Julia answered wearily. "Thank you."

Mattie came and took her back to Faye's cottage on the Ladyhill estate. Julia went to bed, but she couldn't sleep because she saw Alexander's hands, and the girl's face, and Johnny Flowers's huddled body whenever she closed her eyes.

Flowers's girl had almost died. For long days after the fire she had been too ill to be moved from the general hospital, but then at last they had been able to bring her to the burns unit.

Julia went to see her where she lay behind white screens. She knew by now, of course, that her name was Sandy. They had met, just once, a long time ago, at the Rocket. Sandy was someone else's wife, and she had slipped away with Johnny Flowers to see the New Year in at Ladyhill. Julia remembered the old conspiratorial brilliance of Flowers's smile when she had seen him at the top of the stairs. The dancers' bright colors blurred like an exotic carpet below them.

Shh. You haven't seen me, Flowers said.

Julia remembered it over and over again, the words and the violent images replaying themselves in her head. Flowers and Sandy had paid everything for their night's truancy.

Julia sat rigidly beside the girl's bed, looking at the burn dressings that masked the destroyed features. Sandy would need months of skin grafts, years of plastic surgery. With an involuntary movement Julia put her fingertips to the smooth skin that stretched over her own cheekbones.

Sandy whispered through the shredded lips, "Tell your husband . . . thank you."

Alexander had saved her life. He had snatched a towel from the kitchen, wrapped it around his head, and then dashed through the smoke and up the burning stairway. He found Sandy lying unconscious, huddled against the wall of the upstairs corridor. The heart of the fire roared behind her. The heat flayed Alexander's skin. Choking and gasping, he had crawled toward her. Sandy's hair and clothes were already on fire. Alexander beat out the flames with his hands and then, somehow, he dragged her to the top of the stairs. The oak treads gaped into red mouths. Alexander pitched himself downward, hauling Sandy with him.

The firemen found them lying at the foot of the great staircase.

Julia pieced the fragments of the story together for herself. Almost nothing beyond the bare details had come from Alexander.

"I couldn't see Johnny Flowers anywhere," he explained. "I just couldn't see him. If only I could have seen him, I could have tried . . ."

"You did everything you could have done," Julia soothed him.

Alexander's bravery silenced her. She loved him for it, but it was awesome and she felt it between them, another distance. Julia knew that she possessed no similar quality.

She leaned closer to Sandy and said in a low voice, "I'll tell him. Of course I'll tell him."

The mask nodded its tiny, painful movement, and Julia's eyes looked through the burn dressings into the red, molten flesh.

In the burns clinic, on the same day as her first visit to Sandy, Julia at last told Alexander that she was pregnant. She could hardly believe that the baby was still inside her, silently growing, oblivious of so much sadness and suffering, but her doctor assured her that it was.

Alexander's delight at the news was almost frighteningly intense. He lifted up his big, bandaged paws in a gesture of impotent celebration. "A baby. Regeneration, you see? Everything will be all right. We'll be a phoenix, the three of us, and Ladyhill."

Julia was ashamed of it, but she had no dreams of regeneration. The fire smoked inside her and guilt stalked her everywhere. She had wanted to fill Ladyhill with people; she had bought the pretty candles for the tree and fixed them to the branches herself. Now Alexander's beloved house was destroyed, and his thin, musician's hands had melted into padded stumps. Flowers was dead, who had been so alive, and Sandy lay along the corridor, unrecognizable. Julia shivered at the thought of Ladyhill and its ghosts. She stayed with Faye in the cottage, going every day to visit Alexander, and never once went back up the driveway between the trees to look at what was left of his house.

Alexander's recovery was so rapid that it amazed his doctors. The grafts on the backs of his hands took, and began to heal, and he grew impatient with the hospital. "I want to go home," he announced. "I've got a wife, and a baby coming. I want to rebuild my house for us all."

Julia was sure that it was his longing to get back to Ladyhill and begin the regeneration that made him recover so quickly.

At last the burns specialist and the plastic surgeon agreed to let him go, weeks earlier than they had first predicted. In time, they said, Alexander would regain almost full use of his hands, even his fingers. But the flexibility would never come back. He could no longer be an instrumental musician.

"I can compose," he told Julia. "I never was much of a trumpeter anyway. Let's go home now."

They left Sandy behind. She was recovering, but she would have to stay in the unit for a long time yet. Her husband had come down to be with her; she had let Julia and Alexander know, without putting it into words, that they would prefer to be left alone together. Julia understood well enough that she wanted no unnecessary reminders of New Year's. She was sure that Sandy had her own inescapable ones, just as she did herself.

Julia and Alexander went home.

They went first to Faye's cottage, but he was hardly into his stepmother's pretty drawing room before Alexander announced that he wanted to walk up to the house. He turned to Julia. "Come with me," he said. Julia knew that it was coming. Their eyes met.

"I . . ."

"Come with me," Alexander repeated.

Julia bent her head. "I'm coming," she whispered. "Faye, will you come too?"

Flustered, Faye mumbled something about getting lunch. Julia and Alexander set out alone together, walking across the park where the crocuses were showing, and cutting into the avenue of trees that curved up to the house. As they came to the corner, Julia glanced at her husband. His expression of fierce concentration seemed to exclude her completely. Then they turned the corner, and the house lay in front of them. Julia saw the gutted wing, the smoke-blackened bricks and stone, and the ruined roof draped in tarpaulin like a shroud. She could smell the smoke again, and see the livid light of the flames. She turned her head, half-listening for the bells of the fire engines.

At her side, Alexander breathed, "It isn't so very bad. I dreamed it would be much worse."

He walked on, quickening his pace, and Julia followed behind him. She clenched her fists in her pockets to stop herself shaking. Closer to the black walls and the blank windows, the fire seemed so real and so near to her that she was afraid her flesh would singe. The reek of smoke made the tears run out of her eyes. The windows in the ruined side seemed to stare down at her, accusing her.

Alexander walked briskly around to the far side of the courtyard. "Are you coming inside with me?" he called.

"I'll . . . I'll wait here," she answered. "I'm afraid to go farther."

Alexander didn't hear her last words. He had already disappeared around the far side of the house, heading for a side door. Julia waited for him for a long time, standing in the courtyard. The rooks that nested in the elms on the other side of the house turned in restless circles over her head, but Julia couldn't see anything but the avid leaping of the flames.

At last Alexander came out again. His mouth was smiling, but there were grim vertical lines at the sides of it. His fierce expression had intensified.

"It's a mess inside, but it can all be put right again. The staircase, the paneling, everything. It's a question of time and money, that's all."

"It would be wonderful if it could be done," Julia offered. She had no conviction that it might.

He rounded on her. "It isn't if. It will be. It must be. Listen, I'll tell you what we can do. The other side of the house, Father's study and the housekeeper's part, all that is almost undamaged. We can move into those rooms, camp there while the restoration goes on. We can watch it every inch of the way."

Julia shrank, but she stopped herself from scuttling backward, away from the threat of it.

"Alexander? Do we have to live in the middle of it? After . . ." Julia's hand moved to the place where the firemen had laid Sandy on the waiting stretcher. They had carried Alexander out between the black stumps of the arch, and sometime on that terrible night what was left of Johnny Flowers too. The images seemed more vivid than the reality of the thin early March sunshine.

"You know we do," Alexander answered. He came to her and she almost flinched, but he put his hand over her stomach. "Not just for us, but for him."

"For him?" Julia echoed.

"There isn't going to be very much money," Alexander added without seeming to hear her. "It seems that the house was underinsured."

"I don't care about the money," Julia said despairingly.

Within days they were installed in the undamaged wing.

Immediately, Alexander flung himself into plans for the rebuilding, and for raising the money to do it. His determination became almost fanatical. He was always busy, and Julia grew lonely, increasingly isolated from him by his preoccupation, her own guilt, and her fears of the house that her husband adored. A distance came between them and widened to the point where Julia could hardly remember or believe in the happiness they had known before the fire. She huddled in their uncomfortable corner of a demolition site, haunted by her bad dreams.

Then, a little while before the baby was due, there was a reprieve. Julia insisted that the baby be delivered at a London maternity clinic, and both Faye and China supported her. Alexander gave way to them, as he was newly prepared to do in anything that concerned the baby. They opened up the Markham Square flat again, and the two of them settled in to wait for the birth.

At once everything seemed almost all right again. Alexander was working on the score for a new film, and Julia enjoyed cooking for him, and pottering in the safe, familiar rooms. Away from Ladyhill, Alexander seemed to look at her with some of the old tenderness.

"I love you," he told her. "I've neglected you because I wanted so much to make the house whole for us all."

"I know," Julie said softly. She felt so heavy and ripe that she could hardly move. It was a huge relief to be in London, to be near to Felix and Mattie and the old places again. She met Sophia, or Mattie, or other friends for lunches, and shopped for the nursery. She wandered through the department stores, picking up toy lambs and fingering the tiny garments, wondering what she was doing there, and if she would really have her own baby soon. At the end, dreamy with late pregnancy, she half-believed that they could go on like this forever.

Early one morning, when they were lying in bed together, the contractions started. "I can feel it," she told Alexander. "The baby's coming."

He knelt over her, then pressed his ear to the bare mound of her stomach as if he were listening for music inside it. "Our baby. A baby for Ladyhill," he said triumphantly.

He helped her to dress, led her downstairs to the red mini, and drove her to the maternity clinic.

* JUNE 1960

FOURTEEN

"Wake up, dear. You've got a lovely baby. A beautiful little girl. Don't you want to see her? Lady Bliss, are you awake?"

That was all right then, Julia thought. They were talking to someone else. Her name was Julia Smith, and it must be someone else's baby. . . .

She didn't want to wake up, because if she did she would start hurting again. She could keep the pain at bay by clinging to sleep. But the voice was insistent. "Wake up, dear."

Through her eyelids she could see the red-gold of threateningly bright light. And across her stomach she could already feel a tight, burning band. She knew that she was awake.

Julia opened her eyes.

There was a nurse in a striped dress and a white butterfly cap, and sunshine stabbing in through the window behind her. The light hurt Julia's eyes, and the rest of her body hurt much more. But the muzzy folds of anesthetic were dropping away, and she remembered why. There had been all the hours of yesterday—was it yesterday?—when the contractions had gone on and on, and the pains had assaulted her until she screamed. The midwives had held her arms and sponged her face, and Alexander had stormed away to find the doctor. They had come then to tell her that after all, her pelvis was too narrow and they would have to deliver the baby by cesarean.

Then even Alexander had been hustled away, and faces in green masks peered down at her through the fog of pain.

After that, she remembered, she had half-woken, sick and exhausted, when they put her into this bed. And now, somehow, it was bright morning and there was a pretty, dark-haired nurse beaming at her.

"Where's my husband?" Julia croaked.

"Oh, he'll be along later. New fathers need their sleep, too, you know." Somehow, the nurse had put her hands under Julia's arms and helped her to sit up. She straightened the pillows behind her head, and Julia found that if she closed her eyes and held her body very still, the pain slackened off a little.

"Feeling some discomfort from the wound, are we?" the nurse asked her.

"I am," Julia said.

"Doctor will probably give you something later. Something mild, for baby's sake. Now, here she is. A real beauty. Are you going to hold her?"

Julia looked to the side of the bed. A white crib had been wheeled there, and the nurse lifted a white bundle out of it. She turned down a corner of blanket and cooed, "There's a girl. Here's your mummy, waiting for you."

Julia's arms felt stiff and heavy, but she lifted them and stretched them out. The bundle was very light, surprisingly warm and soft. She looked down into the baby's face. It was scarlet, and covered with fine, almost invisible down. The eyelashes were minute black spikes, and there was a lot of thick black hair. The tiny chin looked very firm.

So, after everything, there was a baby. It was hard to relate all the pain to this, the wrapped-up product.

"Is it all right?" Julia asked.

"Of course she is. She's perfect."

Julia went on staring at her baby. She was waiting to feel something, wondering what it should be. The little creature was so tiny, but yet such a definite presence.

"Thank you," Julia said politely.

The nurse chuckled. "You two get to know each other. I'll pop back in a little while with a nice cup of tea for you."

Julia felt almost panicky when the door closed behind her, but the baby slept on without stirring. A girl. *My daughter,* Julia thought experimentally. She was certain that Alexander had wanted a boy, although he had never quite said so. She leaned back against the pillows, holding the baby tight, wishing that he would come.

Her first visitor turned out to be Mattie. She erupted into the quiet room, her arms full of flowers and parcels. She dumped them at the end of the bed and wrapped her arms tenderly around Julia and her white bundle. "I came as soon as I'd spoken to Bliss. Let me look at her."

Julia held out the baby.

The little thing fit neatly into Mattie's arms, and she laid a finger against her cheek. She whispered, "Oh, God, she's beautiful. Hello, my lovely." Mattie held the baby as if it belonged where it lay, and there were shiny tears in her eyes. Of course, Julia thought, Mattie understood about babies. She had brought up her own little brothers and sisters. Mattie saw Julia looking at her and sniffed hard, laughing at herself. "Why am I crying over her? Oh, my darling, you're so clever. Was it bad?"

Julia made a face. "But all over now."

"Bliss said that you were shouting for me. And for Jessie."

Julia remembered with shame that she had shouted for everyone, wanting them to come and rescue her from the astonishing grip of pain. "I think I even howled for Betty at one point. I didn't perform very well. It bloody well hurt."

"Bliss says it was their fault. They let you go on and on until he wanted to kill them."

"I knew she was never going to come out. That made it bad."

"But they got her out in the end, and she's wonderful," Mattie comforted her.

Julia rested her head against her shoulder, suddenly feeling that everything was all right. Better than all right; softened and burnished with happiness and relief. "Look, Mattie, her eyes are open."

With their heads close together, they looked down into the baby's black, unfathomable gaze.

After a long silence Mattie repeated, "You're so clever. And lucky." And then, sounding more like herself, she announced, "I've got a bottle of champagne. Let's drink a toast."

She rummaged for glasses, and eased the cork out of the bottle with a resonant plop. She poured the silvery froth and then she looked at Julia and lifted her glass. "To you. Mother and daughter."

Julia thought as she drank, *Is that me?* It seemed a long time, very long, since she had thought of her own real mother, and she wondered what the unknown woman would feel if she knew she had a granddaughter.

The nurse came bustling in with a cup of tea. She clucked at the sight of the champagne and left the cup on the bedside locker. She looked very hard at Mattie before she went away again.

A few moments later Bliss arrived. Julia couldn't see who he was at first, because he was a moving pyramid of flowers. They were all white, white orchids and roses and lilies. They fell around Julia and over the bedcover, and he bent down and kissed her. "Thank you," Alexander whispered, "for my baby."

Julia gathered up some of the flowers and held them to her face. She smelled the spice and honey scents of them. "I thought you wanted a boy."

Alexander said, "I wanted exactly what you've given me." He bent over the crib to look at the baby. Julia had never seen him look so soft, so unmasked, even in the times at night, in bed, their own times at the beginning, before the fire had consumed everything. When Alexander reached to turn back the white covers of the crib, the stretched, glazed pink skin of the burn scars showed on the backs of his hands. Julia breathed harder, watching him, not letting her eyes slide away.

"I sat and held her, you know, in the night," Alexander was saying. "After they had put you to bed. You were safe, and she was alive. Breathing. It was . . . the most precious moment I have ever known."

Mattie stood up abruptly. The legs of her chair squawked on the polished floor. "I must go. Doing a full read-through of the new play this afternoon."

Julia and Alexander nodded, barely hearing; Mattie understood that, she just had to say something to ease her exit. She made herself fix her own attention on the afternoon work as she gathered up her bag. Work was what she had, after all.

Mattie had spent a year in *One More Day,* at the Angel Theatre and then in the West End transfer. She had spent the last three months recreating the role of Mary for the film version. And now she was to read another part in Jimmy's latest work. To directors and producers and backers they were a partnership like bread and butter.

"How's Jimmy?" Alexander asked.

"Oh, he's fine." Only she didn't sleep with Jimmy anymore. He had coolly turned his attention elsewhere, leaving Mattie to feel hurt, and rejected, and then angry. She would have been lonely, now, if she ever had the time to think about it. She bent over and brushed Julia's cheek with her mouth. It was amazing how Julia could still look beautiful even after eighteen hours' labor followed by a cesarean.

And Bliss, looking like a child who had just been given a present that was such an extravagance that he hadn't even dared to wish for it.

They'll be all right together, the two of them, Mattie thought, *in spite of everything.* She found herself praying wordlessly for it. She leaned over the crib once more and breathed in the strange, pungent newborn smell. She remembered it from Rozzie's babies. It tugged in her own stomach and breasts.

Mattie swirled around and drained her glass of champagne. "I really am going now. Bye-bye, my darlings."

But she hadn't reached the door before there was a flutter outside it and Julia's nurse came in, followed by two others. They nudged each other.

"D'you mind us asking? Are you Mattie Banner?"

"Yes." Mattie had a practiced smile for these occasions now.

"Would you . . . could you sign these for us?" They held out bits of paper.

"For my brother, could you? His name's Tony. He thinks you're fabulous."

Mattie scribbled her name, her tongue sticking out between her teeth, just as it used to do when she sat at the desk next to Julia's at Blick Road Girls' Grammar. Julia watched from the sea of her flowers, her hand in Alexander's. The nurses thanked Mattie profusely and rustled away again.

The women's eyes met. They measured each other, for an instant, like strangers.

"I'll come again tomorrow," Mattie said. "If I'm allowed?"

"You'd better," Julia answered.

They blew a kiss to each other. Then the door swung, and closed with a pneumatic hiss. Julia and Alexander were alone together.

"How do you feel?" he asked.

"Sore. It could be worse."

His fingers smoothed the cover over her belly. "You were very brave."

Julia wrinkled her face, and then snorted with laughter. The laugh turned into a wince of pain. "I was awful. I was worse than a baby myself."

Alexander was somber. "I was afraid that you would die."

He had thought of the fire when they wheeled her away, and he could do nothing but sit in a dingy little room and wait. He could hear the fire's roar, and the stench of it filled his nostrils. Death again. He couldn't surrender Julia to it. He would go back himself, into the greedy mouth of it, if it would save her . . .

And then the nurse had come back. "You have a beautiful baby daughter. Your wife is fine."

And now, sitting on his wife's bed in the June sunshine, he tried to slide his hands under the mounds of flowers. Beside them, in her crib, the baby opened her eyes and gave a thin cry.

"She must be hungry."

"What do I do?"

Alexander moved the flowers, heaping them on the chairs and on the floor, and lifted the baby up. With her fingers awkwardly fumbling, Julia opened the front of her nightdress. Alexander held the baby to the breast and she turned her head, nuzzling, but Julia's fingers couldn't connect the tiny mouth to the nipple. She felt huge, and clumsy, as if the weight of her hands alone would crush the fragile skull. The baby's face contorted and her bare gums showed as her lips drew back and she cried louder.

"I don't know what to do," Julia whispered.

The nurse swished back into the room. "Dear, dear. Time to try a little feed, is it? Good girl. Look, it's like this." She grasped Julia's breast and inserted the nipple neatly into the baby's gaping mouth. The gums clamped down at once and the baby began sucking furiously. "'She knows what she wants, all right,'" the nurse said cheerfully.

Julia looked down at the expression that had changed in an

instant from fury to satisfaction. She did know what she wanted, and she was how many hours and minutes old? The bony gums were hard, and the sucking seemed to draw from deep inside Julia. Her innards contracted and she shivered a little.

"That's a picture," said the nurse.

Alexander extricated his camera from among the flowers and asked her, "Will you take it?"

"Smile, then, please."

With Alexander's arm around her and her baby at her breast, Julia looked into the lens and smiled obediently. The shutter clicked.

"The happy family," the nurse said brightly, and left them alone again.

"What shall we call her?" Alexander asked, touching his finger to the back of the dark head. Julia was looking at the flowers. The lilies had curving pure white petals, and golden stamens thickly powdered with pollen. They were cool and sappy, and perfectly beautiful.

"Let's call her Lily," Julia said.

"Lily? I like that. Lily Bliss."

The baby had stopped feeding, and had fallen asleep again with her mouth drooping. Julia and Alexander watched her, and then smiled tentatively at each other.

"I wish I could take you both home now," Alexander said. "I want my family at Ladyhill, where it belongs."

"Ladyhill," Julia repeated.

She turned her face away, not looking at his hands now. She wondered how she could have been so stupid, in the last hazy days of her pregnancy, as to have believed they could go on in the safe suspension of waiting.

"I don't want to go back yet." Her voice sounded shrill and she softened it with an effort. "Can't we stay on at the flat for a while?"

Alexander's hands tightened on hers. "We must go home," he said. "It's where we belong."

Julia looked down again. Their hands were joined, like they were themselves, even more forcibly now by the scrap of life that was half of each of them. But she felt the distance between them all over again, as if they had been sitting on opposite sides of the room.

More softly, Alexander said, "There's work to be done at home. Waiting for us."

Julia nodded, mute. With the unimaginable rite of birth behind her at last, she realized that nothing had changed.

"Are you hurting?" Alexander asked. The corners of his eyes folded into creases of concern.

"A bit."

He put his hand to her cheek, stroking it. Julia wanted to pitch forward into his arms, wanted him to pick her up and hold her, but neither of them moved.

"You should try to go to sleep," he murmured. He did lean forward then, to kiss the corner of her mouth. "I'll come in again this evening. Rest now." He stood looking down into the little crib for a long moment, and then he went away.

After he had gone, Julia lay with her arms resting stiffly over the folded sheet. The room's pale blue walls, hung with innocuous pictures, couldn't contain her imagination, although she longed for its confinement.

The high outline of the house reared over her again. There was a black hole burned through the heart of it, and although there was silence except for the rooks in the elm trees, Julia could always hear the roar of the fire.

She opened her eyes wide, staring at the blue walls and the pictures. She hated herself for her weakness, but the tears came anyway. Alexander wanted to take her and the baby back to Ladyhill, where the nightmares and the guilt followed her like shadows. She shrank under the bedclothes, and she heard Lily snuffle and stir in her crib.

The door clicked open again and the nurse materialized. "Tears? Oh, dear now, there's no need. All new mums feel that they can't cope, you know. And you did have a difficult time, poor love." Her sympathy made Julia feel her inadequacy more sharply, and the tears dripped down her face and ran onto the sheets. The nurse bustled around, finding a handkerchief and pouring a tumbler of water, clearing away the champagne bottle and glasses. Julia sniffed and scoured her face with the handkerchief. "You'll see. You'll be as good as new in a few days, and you'll be able to go home with your husband and the baby. . . ."

Julia looked wildly around. The little blue room was square and safe. "I'm all right here, really," she gabbled. "I don't want to go yet."

The nurse looked at her. "I often think it's better," she mused, "for the mums to be all together, on the ward. They keep each other company and cheer each other up when they get weepy. I suppose you're in here because of who you are. . . ."

Julia stayed in the maternity clinic for almost two weeks. It was longer than was strictly necessary, but she told the doctor that she didn't feel quite strong enough to go home after only ten days.

Streams of visitors came to see her, and to exclaim over Lily, who rapidly lost her redness and became almost as beautiful as everyone declared. Among the visitors was Betty. She brought a pink-ribboned dress for the baby, and a box of chocolates for Julia. Julia put her arm awkwardly around her mother's shoulder and kissed her cheek. "Thank you," Julia said.

"Well, it's not much, I know. But I didn't know what to bring, what with everything. . . ."

Betty gestured nervously at the flower-filled room.

"Thank you for coming."

Betty sat down on the edge of her chair. Since Julia's marriage and the death of Bliss's father, it was as if Betty had become the daughter and Julia the mother. Betty deferred to Julia's opinions, deprecating herself and her circumstances. No one had a better appreciation of social status and its various degrees than Betty, and she made it clear that Julia had moved far beyond her own orbit. It was her evident pride in the fact that disturbed Julia. She had been happier with Betty's approval of her job at Tressider's. That, at least, had been her own doing. Now she was identifiable only as Alexander's wife, and, when she thought about it, she realized that she had come uncomfortably close to being what she herself had despised Betty for.

Julia wondered, a little wearily, how everything had happened so quickly.

She wanted to talk to Betty about it, to ask her if she felt that her sacrifices had been worthwhile, but their relationship was much too remote for that. Betty had turned herself into a distant acquaintance, an acquaintance who wouldn't dream of presuming.

They talked rather stiffly about the baby instead.

"Aren't you proud of her?" Betty asked.

Julia still felt more bewilderment at being asked to accept total responsibility for another human being than pride. But she nodded, and Betty seemed satisfied.

"She looks like you when you were a baby. But you were bigger. We never saw you until six weeks."

It was the first time, since the long-ago day in the square, that either of them had mentioned Julia's adoption.

Carefully, Julia said, "It must have been . . . strange. Like taking delivery of a package."

Suddenly, Betty's face cleared. Her eyes met Julia's, all the stiffness gone.

"It wasn't strange. It was wonderful."

Julia was silenced. She understood that it must have been wonderful, and the sadness that had followed it seemed suddenly almost too much to bear. She looked from Betty's glowing face to the crib beside the bed, and she thought, *Lily*. . . .

She should have left Betty to the comfort of her memories of babyhood, but the moment of intimacy seemed too valuable. She asked, "Do you know anything about my real mother?"

She had thought more about her, since she had been given her own daughter to hold, than she had ever done before. *Does she think of me? On my birthday. At New Year. What would she feel if she knew she had a granddaughter?* She looked at Lily, sleeping. *Are those her features?*

Betty had flinched, and the glow faded from her face.

"No. Nothing at all. The adoption society was very strict. Except that you were . . . you know."

"Illegitimate," Julia supplied for her.

"Yes."

Julia wondered what other words Betty and Vernon would have whispered between themselves. Betty had used some of them that day in the square. *A dirty little baby.*

"Why do you want to know?" Betty asked fiercely. "I'm your mother."

No, you aren't. I'm sorry, but that's the truth. It doesn't matter any longer.

Julia made her voice light. "I just wondered."

They didn't talk about it anymore. After a few minutes Betty gathered up her hat and her gloves and her square handbag and announced that she would have to rush for her train. They brushed their cheeks together, and Julia whispered, "Thank you for coming."

Felix was standing at the window of the Eaton Square apartment, looking out at the afternoon sunshine reflecting off the cars heading westward toward the Kings Road. The view of the trees in the square gardens made him think of the old flat, and he allowed himself a moment's enjoyable nostalgia. Jessie's old room, with its faded photographs and his own precious collection of bric-à-brac.

Felix turned away from the window and walked the length of the drawing room. The triple bay windows were hung with a lily of the valley chintz, one of Tressider Designs' own fabrics, lined with pale gold silk. Gilt-framed French mirrors hung between the windows, and in front of them stood a Regency table with a collection of opalescent Lalique bowls arranged on it. The modern sofas were deep and comfortable, piled up with silk-covered cushions, and in the alcoves on either side of the fireplace stood a magnificent pair of console tables with porphyry tops. With its deft mixing of periods and styles to recreate the haute English country house look in a town apartment, the room was a showpiece for George Tressider's sought-after decorative ability. The only tiny flaw, Felix thought, the single thing that was lacking, was a touch of wit and humor. The perfection was unmarred, and so was faintly sterile. Then he caught sight of his own reflection in one of the gilt mirrors. He was wearing his front-office clothes. The gray suit, tightly waisted, was well cut, and the collar of his white shirt was starched. By contrast with such formality his face looked very dark, and his high cheekbones and full mouth seemed almost wickedly exotic. It occurred to Felix that he provided the requisite touch of eccentricity himself. He smiled, and went on into the bedroom.

George was sitting on the bed, talking on the telephone. "Yes. Yes. Of course the silk must match exactly. If it proves to be necessary, we'll start again and redye a fresh batch for you." He raised his eyebrows at Felix. "Mrs. Lindsay, it will match. You have my assurance. Yes. Yes. As soon as the contractors have finished." Felix could hear the client's high, yipping voice at the other end of the line. He leaned over and massaged the back of George's neck. The telephone conversation took its predictable course, and Mrs. Lindsay hung up at last, mollified.

George looked up, then reached out and caught him by the wrist. "Don't loom over me." Felix sat down beside him, conscious of the inviting expanse of the Chinese red bedcover. He had slept with George for the first time in this bed, one abandoned afternoon after a particularly stiff lunch with a dowager duchess. They had undressed very slowly, and hung up their clothes, like tidy schoolboys, in the walnut armoire. Then they had explored each other with a greedy intensity that Felix hadn't experienced since the twilit barn and David Mander.

And since then, the plain gray walls of the bedroom had witnessed enough exotic interludes. George Tressider had imaginative sexual preferences, and Felix had learned them as quickly as he learned everything else. They had been lovers for more than a year, and they had lived together for the last six months, but there were still frequent occasions when they came together with importunate urgency.

"George?"

"What is it?" The professional George had replaced the private one. He was busy packing design sketches into the little Vuitton bag that he carried instead of an attaché case. "Who wants to look like an invoice clerk?" he had once asked Felix.

"I thought I'd call in to see Julia again for half an hour before I go to the Boltons. Is that all right?"

Even though they slept in the same bed, Felix was careful always to remember that George was his employer.

"Of course. Give her my love, won't you?"

The response was no cooler than he had expected. Felix had stopped hoping that Julia and George would ever love each other.

George went to keep his appointment, and Felix washed and dried the plates and glasses that they had used for their Brie and salad lunch. They didn't often manage to meet at home in the middle of the day, even though they worked in close proximity. When they did, Felix liked to make an occasion of it by setting a pretty table. When the kitchen was tidy he put a bottle of Pouilly Fumé in the fridge for later and then followed George into the sunshine. He was thinking about him as he made his way to Julia's clinic.

He hadn't expected to like George Tressider when Julia had made the first introduction. George had offered him a job and he had accepted it at once, but he had categorized the decorator as a predatory old queen. In the years since his national service, Felix had met enough of those. But in the weeks that followed, Felix discovered that George wasn't predatory at all. He was professionally successful and financially secure, he lived in a whirl of parties and dearest acquaintances, but in private he was surprisingly vulnerable. And he was lonely. George was still fit and slim, and he was good-looking in a silky, feline way, but he was fifty-two years old. Too many of his lovers in the recent past had wanted what George could buy rather than George himself. And he was too clearly aware that nothing was going to get any better for him.

Over and over again, he said to Felix, "With your looks and your talents, you could have anyone you wanted. What are you doing with an old faggot like me?"

"I want you," Felix answered. It was the truth. Everything about George, including their fidelity to each other, suited Felix better than a succession of the doe-eyed boys who hung around the King's Road antiques shops. And then, there was George Tressider Designs. Felix was learning the business from George. He was learning so much, all the time, that he hummed and vibrated with the energy of it. He didn't want anything to change, only to go on getting better. In time he would be able to add the little extra indefinable twists and touches to their work that George was a shade too conventional to introduce. And it would make them the best team there was. Felix was certain of that.

Julia was sitting in the armchair in her room, reading *Vogue*.

"Felix, my love. You look very pleased with yourself."

He kissed her on the forehead. "And you look fully recovered."

"I am. They're sending me home tomorrow."

"To Ladyhill?"

"To Ladyhill."

Felix studied her for a moment, then turned aside. There was a bowl of pink and lavender spikes on the table and he picked out the faded blooms before rearranging the rest.

"I wish we could stay in London," Julia said.

Felix finished the flowers to his satisfaction, and then sat down facing her. "You know I love you, don't you?"

Julia looked startled, but she answered, "Yes, I know you do."

Very softly, Felix said, "Listen to me, then. Go back home, with Alexander and Lily. You can't separate Alexander from Ladyhill, and you shouldn't try to stand in the way of the restoration. . . ."

"You know it was underinsured," Julia broke in. "There isn't the money to restore it the way Bliss wants."

"I think you can assume that if there is a way, he will find it. And that isn't as important as that you should go home with him, take Lily home. Be glad you're all alive, even though poor Flowers is dead. That Sandy survived, at least. Take the happiness you've got. It's enough, Julia, isn't it? Don't destroy anything else."

It was a very long speech, for Felix. Julia shook her head, staring at him. "I . . . I can't forget the fire."

He leaned closer to her. "You can. You must. Do that much, for Alexander."

Her chin jerked up. "You think I'm selfish, don't you?

Well. Perhaps I am. But I look at those black walls, and I hear the roar of the flames. I look up at the sky, and I can't see it for smoke. You weren't there, Felix. You don't know what it was like. And I have to accept, every day, that it was my fault. My fault that Flowers is dead, and Sandy's face is all . . . is all . . . melted. That the house Alexander loves is in ruins, and that his burned fingers are too stiff for him to play the trumpet. That's what I live with, living at Ladyhill. How can I take the happiness, as you call it, being there and knowing all that?''

She pressed her hands over her eyes, but Felix drew them away and held them between his own.

"Is it your fault that Flowers and Sandy were doing what they were doing? That the house was old and dry, and burned like kindling? Or that Alexander was brave enough to do what he did?''

"No," Julia whispered.

"No. But it will be your fault if you don't go back and try to repair what was no one's fault. I don't just mean the bricks and mortar.''

He saw that there were faint vertical lines at the corners of Julia's mouth. He had never seen them before, and they made him feel sad. He remembered the innocent girls he had first seen, trying to be louche at the Rocket.

Suddenly he said, "Were you happy at Ladyhill with Alexander before the fire?''

The glance that Julia darted at him was no more than a flicker of her eyes, but Felix intercepted it. Then her eyelids dropped again, and she studied their linked hands. "Yes, I was.''

He waited, but there was nothing else.

At length, in a different voice, Julia said, "You're right, of course. We'll go back, and I'll try to make it all right. I promise I will.''

"Good," Felix said.

The conversation seemed to be at an end. Julia drew her hands away and stood up. She walked around the room, touching the fading flowers and fingering the books and magazines on the bed table. Then, half-turned away from Felix, she said, "We had this ideal, Mattie and me. When we ran away from home. We were going to be free. We weren't going to let anything tie us down, not us.'' The words spilled out so quickly that they tangled together and she shook her head with impatience. "No conventions, no stereotypes. We were going to make our own rules. The gospel of freedom, according to Mattie Banner and Julia Smith.'' She laughed without a note of amusement. "Well, Mattie's free, isn't she? She's an actress, just like she always wanted. She's famous. Even the nurses in this place come to ask for her autograph. And, you see, I'm Alexander's wife.'' She broke off, and paced across the room. Six steps brought her up against the crib at the side of the bed. Lily was awake; Felix could hear the tiny sounds she made. "And now there's a baby. My baby, Felix. I didn't see her born, but I've got the scar to prove it.'' She laughed again, the same harsh sound. "I'd just like to know how it all happened so quickly. So quickly . . .''

Felix sighed. "Don't you and Mattie talk to each other anymore?''

"What do you mean? Of course we do.''

"I'm not sure that Mattie wouldn't gladly change places with you.''

Julia frowned at him, uncomprehending. "Don't be ridiculous.''

"Well. We're not talking about Mattie now. But you made a choice, Julia. And there are worse losses of freedom than you've suffered. Alexander loves you. Anyone who looks at him can see he loves you.''

She held up the palms of her hands as if to ward something off, but her face crumpled. "I know. That's why I'm going back to Ladyhill. I told you. I love him, and I'm going to be a good mother to Lily, and we'll rebuild the house, and I won't put any more candles on the Christmas tree. Oh, hell. I'm not bloody well going to cry again either.''

Felix stood behind her, folding his arms around her waist and resting his chin on the top of her head. "I'm glad. You're doing the right thing. And the fire will pass, you know. Julia?''

"Yes?''

"If you need me for anything, you know where I am.''

She nodded. Her head was smooth and warm under his chin. "Thank you. I'll remember.''

In her crib, Lily spluttered and began to cry. Julia put her hand to the front of her blouse. "It's time for me to feed her. Not with a bottle, you know. Breasts. Like a real mother. Do you want to stay and watch?''

Felix grinned. "I'd like to draw you, if you'll let me. But not today. I've got to go and measure a house.'' Julia was lifting Lily, cupping the round black head in one hand. "I'll be coming to see you at Ladyhill. You know that Alexander has asked

George and me if we'll help with restoring the interior when the time comes?''

Julia settled herself in her chair again. She undid her bra and Felix saw the faint blue veins on the distended breast, and the enlarged nipple. Lily's cries stopped, and there was a faint grunt of satisfaction. In the quiet Julia lifted her head, and her eyes were clear. "Good. Come as often as you like. It's very quiet down there.''

Felix blew her a kiss, and then she bent her head over the baby again. Outside, the sun was still shining, but Felix didn't notice it. He was preoccupied with the image of Julia feeding her baby. He had a sudden, awed understanding of the change that had overtaken her, the magnitude of it, and the irrevocability. The old Julia, the Julia of Soho and the square, was gone, and she wouldn't come back, however much Julia herself might long for her.

Felix made his way toward the new house in the Boltons, but the cheerfulness of the early afternoon had deserted him.

The red mini swung between the stone gateposts.

Julia blinked once in the dappled shade of the trees, and then again as they came out into the brightness once more. Alexander stopped the car, leaving it at an angle just as he had when he first brought Julia to Ladyhill. As if he couldn't wait to jump out and run into the house.

"Look at the roses,'' Julia said.

The Albertine on the red brick wall that enclosed the garden on two sides was a cascade of coppery pink. Pale gold and gray-green spikes of verbascum reared against the backdrop of roses. It was in her autumn walks around the gardens that Julia had learned it was called verbascum. At the far end of the long border a fine copper beech tree was like a full stop. The leaves had lost the greenish sheen of early summer, and were turning through polished copper to the mahogany-brown of maturity.

"The garden is beautiful,'' Julia whispered.

There was a blackbird singing somewhere close at hand. She turned deliberately and looked at the house.

There was scaffolding enclosing the badly damaged wing now, and masking the whole center front of the house. But it still didn't hide the smoke-blackened brick, and the charred roof beams soared above it. She shook her head imperceptibly, telling herself that she couldn't smell smoke. She mustn't smell it. And there was silence, except for the birdsong.

As Julia watched, a length of new timber was winched upward. A workman at the top of the scaffolding unfastened it and hoisted it away. Now that she looked more closely, she saw that two or three of the huge beams had already been replaced. The raw wood gleamed yellow in contrast with the stark black of the others. Alexander had been staring intently, and now he nodded. "They're making good progress. We must get the roof on before another winter comes."

He bent down and reached into the car. Lily had been asleep in her portable crib on the backseat, but now Alexander lifted her out, swathed in her white shawl. He held her up and her heavy head rolled against his shoulder. "Look," he whispered. "Look, Lily. We're home."

They stood for a moment, the three of them, in front of the stricken house.

Then Alexander took Julia's hand and, still holding the baby, he drew her arm through his. With Alexander setting the pace, they walked briskly toward the gaping mouth of the front door.

There were no flames, of course. No terrible face turning to her. Johnny was gone, but Alexander was fit and well, beside her. Julia made herself breathe evenly, remembering what Felix had said. *The fire will pass.* She looked at Lily in the crook of Alexander's arm. Her eyes were wide open.

The hall was as derelict as when they had left it for Markham Square, seemingly more so since the builders had taken possession of the house. There were tarpaulins spread over the floor, a concrete mixer in the corner, piles of tools. Julia could hear whistling and sawing somewhere overhead. A man in coveralls came through from the back of the house. Alexander shook hands with him, introducing him as the site foreman.

The man said, "Welcome home, sir. Lady Bliss."

"Julia," she responded automatically.

Alexander's expression didn't change. He was quickly absorbed in conversation with the foreman. Julia listened vaguely to the phrases as they drifted around her. Estimates . . . weakened structure . . . new joists. The language was utterly foreign. She took Lily out of Alexander's arms and held her up, like a shield against her own resentment. She rested her cheek against the baby's knitted bonnet and thought, *You're on my side. I know you are. What are floorboards to you? People are what matter, Lily. Remember that.* Julia was surprised by the sudden intensity of her feelings. *This . . . house. This house is a tomb,*

for me and Alexander as well as Johnny. Or just for me now.
She half-turned, shivering, wanting to run.

Alexander saw it, and caught her arm. "I'll come and see
you later, Mr. Minns."

Behind a hanging tarpaulin there was a well-sealed door,
and on the other side was the relatively undamaged wing of the
house where Alexander and Julia had set up home. The little
room on the ground floor had been Sir Percy's den, and now it
had become their sitting room. They had assembled two old
sofas and a pair of armchairs, a bureau and a gate-legged table,
and a Turkish carpet that was much too large and had to be
folded against the walls. Pictures and books and ornaments
salvaged from the farther corners of the house were crammed in
wherever there was space.

Farther along the corridor a kitchen had been created in
what was once the gun room, and above, reached by a back
staircase, there were two bedrooms and a sort of bathroom.

"There isn't much space," Alexander had said when they
returned to the house from his stepmother's cottage.

"More than we had when I lived with Mattie and Felix and
Jessie," Julia had said dully.

Alexander had read it as stoical determination, and he had
kissed her delightedly. "That's my girl. We'll be thoroughly
comfortable here, the two of us. And the baby, when he comes."

Julia hoisted Lily on her shoulder and looked around the
room. It had been repainted in a fresh clear yellow and the
pictures and ornaments had been attractively arranged. There
were flowers in bowls, roses and scabious and stocks from the
garden, in big fragrant bunches. It looked much better than it had
before they left, but Julia regarded it without affection.

"I'm sorry," Alexander said.

She looked at him in surprise and his shoulders lifted awkwardly. He was neither stern nor ironic. The lines in his face had
melted, and he looked like an apologetic boy. "I shouldn't have
kept you standing there while I talked to Minns. I was just
excited to see the work; I wanted to hear what they were doing.
It seems months since we were here." He hesitated, searching
her face, and then his shoulders dropped and he walked away to
the window. He put his hands flat against the glass, staring out
through the small square panes. "I love this house," he said.
His voice was so low that Julia had to strain to catch the words.
"I want to see it, to make it come alive again for the three of
us." He swung around again, coming to her, putting his hands

on her shoulders while Julia wrapped her arms protectively around the baby. "Do you understand?" he asked.

"I will. I'm trying to," she answered him. *No*, her own voice insisted. *How could I?*

Alexander kissed her. "I'll go and make us a cup of tea. Do you like the new paint?"

"Very much. It's bright."

Alexander went away into the kitchen. She could hear water running and the rattle of the kettle under the tap. Julia settled Lily on her spread-out shawl in a corner of the sofa, then wandered across the room. She touched the furled petals of the roses, and looked out of the window as Alexander had. The lawns needed mowing, but the borders were at the peak of their midsummer brilliance. Julia's mouth had lost some of its tautness as she moved on to the walnut bureau. There were neat piles of mail arranged on it, a stack for Alexander, a handful of letters addressed to both of them, perhaps a dozen for herself. She flipped through them. Julia saw the thin blue envelope at once, and the U.S. stamp. She didn't need to look at the handwriting; even though she hadn't seen it for more than two years, it was as recognizable as her own. She held the envelope in dry fingers, hearing the faint, infinitely promising crackle of the paper inside it.

Alexander came back with a teapot and cups on a tray. "Anything interesting in the post?"

"Not really," Julia lied out of a dry throat.

They drank their tea together, and they talked about the house and the progress that Mr. Minns was making with the huge task of rebuilding. Now that Julia was out of the hospital, restored to real life, Alexander was eager to draw her into his great project.

"The assessors have caused very little trouble. Beyond the original facts, and no one can change those. When the insurance company does pay out, the money should cover the structural minimum. The outer fabric, the new roof. I've taken out a short-term mortgage on the land to see us through until it does come. There won't be anything left for the interior, or for replacing the pictures and furniture. The old man's fault, and mine, for not revaluing. But when the time comes, we might think about selling a parcel of land to raise another slice of capital."

With the blue envelope hidden in her lap, Julia nodded her head. She was trying to listen.

"What land?"

"Well. Perhaps the lower four acres. It's convenient for the village. Good building land . . ."

Julia nodded again, dimly imagining bungalows spreading between the house and the village. And the money from that, paying for George Tressider to hang his chintzes and arrange his English oak furniture. Julia laughed, an abrupt bubble of it, then covered her mouth with her hand. "I'm sorry, Bliss. I suddenly thought about George."

He smiled at her. "Go on laughing. I like it. There hasn't been enough for a long time."

"I'm going to feed Lily. If I laugh now, it'll give her hiccups."

Alexander stood up and stretched comfortably. "In that case I'll go and see Minns, and leave you in peace."

When she heard the farther door shut, Julia tore open the blue envelope. She unfolded the thin sheet of airmail paper and began to read.

Dearest Julia, Josh had written.

Harry Gilbert saw the birth announcement in the Times. *I can't imagine you married, and married to a sir, no less. But somehow I can see you with a baby, especially a daughter. Has she got black hair, and eyes like yours? I wish I could see her. And her mother, too, if she would let me. It seems like a long time, doesn't it? And yet no time at all. I think of you often, you know.*

There were more paragraphs, describing Vail and the new ski lodges, skipping on to some flying work that Josh had done in Brazil. Greedily, Julia devoured the words. Josh had no great skill as a letter-writer, but she could hear his voice framing the sentences. He seemed so close that his shape was silhouetted against the light from the window. His vibrancy seemed to spring out at her, a bolt of pure energy. She reached the last paragraph.

I guess Sir Alexander must be Sophia's brother. I told you all that time ago that you should get to like those Wengen girls, didn't I? And now you're one of them. What would you say, that serves me right? I hope you're happy. I'm sure you are. If you will let me, I'd like to come and make certain, and to see your baby and your English manor house in the green country. Do you remember the cottage in the corner of the wood?

Julia, Julia.

I hope you think, once in a while between the garden parties and the summer balls, about your aviator.

Julia looked up, and there was nothing standing between her and the light streaming in through the window. The room was empty, except for Lily on her shawl. She said aloud, "Josh," but nothing answered her except the silence. She began to cry then, desperate and furious tears that didn't assuage the loss or the loneliness.

FIFTEEN

Lily tottered to her feet, took two steps, and flopped down again. She had been installed on a rug in the shade of the copper beech tree, but the moving fringe where shadow met sunlight was irresistibly fascinating. She set off again toward the pattern of leaves, crawling now, rubbing grassy stains into the toes of her new white shoes. The shoes and the pink and white broderie anglaise dress were a present from Faye, and scattered around Lily's rug were the torn wrappings and chewed ribbons from other presents. Lily was more interested in crumpling the bright paper than in playing with the pull-along yellow wooden duck or the woolly elephant, but the circle of adults watched her approvingly. Now she crossed the line between shade and sun and set off toward the blazing colors of the flower beds.

It was Lily's first birthday.

Sophia and Toby and their two boys had come to Ladyhill for the weekend to celebrate it with the rest of the family. The boys were bored with the baby and with baby toys, and had gone to play somewhere in the garden. Occasional whoops and shouts sounded across the grass.

The adults sat around the tea table. Alexander and Toby had drawn their chairs a little way away. They were talking, Julia suspected, about money. The four women faced each other; Julia, Faye, Sophia, and China. China sat still, her small figure upright and her face deeply shadowed by the brim of her straw hat. Faye and Sophia were gossiping, their high voices blotting out the low murmur of the men's. The picture of perfection, Julia thought. Tea on the manor house lawn. White dresses and thin-cut sandwiches. The village church clock was striking five, and she counted the slow strokes and the dragging seconds between them. A stifling sensation clogged her chest and rose into her throat. Her face was suddenly burning and her heart thumped. Julia realized that she was possessed by an ecstasy of boredom. It was distilled by the limpid afternoon to a purity that rushed to her head like a drug. Her hands gripped the wicker arms of her chair and her mouth opened. She had the impression that China was studying her under the brim of her hat.

"The sun's very hot," Faye said.

Julia fixed her attention on containing the boredom. She was becoming expert at it, but this was a powerful onslaught.

"The sun is very hot," Faye repeated more loudly. "I'm worried about it on Lily's head. Don't you think she should have her little sunhat on, Julia dear?"

Julia stood up. The table rocked, and the faces turned up to look at her. Even Alexander and Toby paused momentarily in their low conversation.

"I'll go in and get it, if you're worried," she said clearly. She grabbed the big teapot and held it up. "And I'll make some fresh tea. You would all like some, wouldn't you?" If she stayed in the same position, frozen into her chair and into the contented tableau, she was afraid that she would scream, or swear, or upset the pink and white birthday cake in a shower of breaking china. Bearing the teapot in front of her, she almost ran across the lawn, past Lily, who was happily putting earth into her mouth, over the gravel beneath the yew trees and in through the front door. There was a new door now, in thick, well-seasoned oak. The insurance money had provided that, one of the last items before it ran out. The restoration work had come to a stop, and Mr. Minns and his workmen had departed until Alexander could raise some more funds.

Julia went through into their salvaged wing and put the kettle on in the kitchen. The crusts that she had cut off the teatime sandwiches littered the table. Waiting for the kettle to boil, she folded her arms on the deep windowsill and looked out. This side of the house faced away from the gardens and the village, out over open countryside. The mild, rolling landscape was drowsy under the sun and empty of human life.

Sophia's voice behind her made her start. "You look a bit cheesed off."

Julia turned back into the room. Sophia's choice of words almost made her laugh. But she was fond of her good-natured sister-in-law, and didn't want to hurt her feelings. She said vaguely, "Oh, you know."

"Mmm, only too well. Motherhood's a full-time job, isn't it?"

It was, Julia reflected, not that Sophia knew much about that. Sophia had a Norland nanny, and a girl who came in to help on the nanny's weekends off. "And Faye does fuss a bit. Sunhat in England in June, indeed. When we took Jem and Rupert to Corfu they toddled about all day long in the blazing sun, and it was me and Toby . . ."

In the next room, the telephone began to ring.

"Excuse me," Julia murmured.

"I'll make the tea, shall I?" Sophia asked blithely. Leaving all the doors open between them, Julia went to the telephone and answered it.

"Hello?"

"Julia. It's Josh."

Julia's eyes widened and her breath stuck in her throat. The room went dim, and Sophia's humming faded in the kitchen. His voice was unmistakable, like everything else about him. Julia put her fingers up to shield the mouthpiece, staring imploringly at the open door.

She whispered, "Josh?" and heard him laughing.

"Don't sound so surprised."

"Why not?" Her bearings were coming back. She had answered Josh's letter, sending her reply to the address he gave in Colorado, but there had been no response. She had waited months for another letter, through the frozen Ladyhill winter, and her dreams of the fire, and into the spring. She had stopped hoping, then.

"It's her birthday, isn't it?" he demanded.

"Yes. How did you know?" Julia felt stupid with surprise, and pleasure.

"Harry Gilbert sent me the clipping from the *Times*. I keep it in my wallet. You didn't know I was so sentimental, did you? Tell her happy birthday, from me."

She could see the yellowing fragment of newsprint, tucked

away with the scribbled addresses and business cards and dollar bills.

"Where are you?" Julia breathed. "You sound close."

"I'm in London. I'm going to be here for a while. I want to buy Lily a present. Can I see you, Julia?"

After a year of silence. Years of separation before that. When she had needed him, and he had shaken her off. For her own good, she knew he had believed that. But now she was old enough to know for herself. And she knew that she loved him as much as she had ever.

Without hesitation she said, "Yes."

"When?"

Julia could hear Sophia clanking in the kitchen. She was suddenly terrified that she would appear in the doorway, over-hear everything. *Josh Flood? Golly, how super.*

"It's not a very good time now," she whispered urgently. "Give me a number where I can call you." He recited the digits and Julia gabbled, "Thanks for ringing. I'll talk to you soon. Good-bye."

The receiver clattered into its cradle. She snatched a piece of paper off the desk and wrote down the number. She folded the paper once, then again and again into a tiny square, and pushed it deep into the pocket of her cotton dress.

In the kitchen Sophia was wiping the table top, still hum-ming. She was too well mannered or else too deficient in human curiosity to listen to other people's telephone conversations, Julia thought with relief. But when she saw Julia's face she asked concernedly, "Something up?"

"Um . . ." She knew that she looked blank. "Oh, some-one about the flower rota for the church. I don't know why they come to me. They've always hated my efforts when I've ar-ranged them."

Sophia put her head back and laughed. "Oh, dear me, nothing changes at Ladyhill. After I got back from being fin-ished, with all the weird Constance Spry ideas I'd learned, there were endless feuds about what was suitable for church. They wanted to go on sticking sheaves of purple asters into green enamel buckets, just like always. . . ."

With Sophia still chattering, they went out into the sunlight again. The sun was lower and the walls and lawns and the copper leaves of the big tree were all gilded with the same soft light. A pair of swifts skimmed and looped over the grass, and Julia saw a cloud of midges hovering in the sweet, still air.

It was a beautiful afternoon, she thought. The scented midsummer height of the year. Her boredom had gone, lifting itself like a black depression that had dogged her for months, and leaving her senses cleansed and sharpened. She said to herself, *Josh,* and the tips of her fingers touched the folded square of paper in her pocket.

They reached the group around the table, and she saw Alexander smile. She realized that it was in response to the brightness in her own face. He had taken Lily onto his knee, and her face was smeared with dirt from the flower beds.

"Where is it?" Faye asked.

Julia blinked. "Where's what? There's the tea."

"Her sunhat."

Everyone around the table laughed, and Julia laughed too. She felt light, lightheaded, ready to float.

"I forgot it."

In the midst of the good humor Faye shook her head indulgently. "Well, never mind. It's cooler now."

Composing herself, Julia asked, "Would anyone like some more tea?"

That evening, after the boys and Lily had been put to bed, there was a family dinner. Julia cooked, skimming to and fro in the temporary kitchen and improvising boldly with the ingredients, as Felix would have done. Toby sat with the newspaper and a whiskey and soda, and Sophia set the table and then came to help in the kitchen, devoting herself mostly to peering over Julia's shoulder and exclaiming. "Who taught you to cook so brilliantly?"

"You haven't tasted it yet. It was my friend Felix."

"The black man? The decorator?"

"Yes, that one." Julia's dryness was, as always, lost on Sophia.

"Elizabeth Singer said he did the most lovely room for her. All gray and pink, like being inside a cloud. Clever of you to bring him and George together . . ."

Julia looked out the window. The sky had faded to gray suffused with pink in the west. The trees were lush, heavy masses with impenetrable shadow beneath. Alexander and China were coming slowly across the grass toward the house. They had been out, at Julia's suggestion, to pick herbs from the old bed in a corner of the garden. Julia had taken it over in the spring, looking for something to concentrate on, and to her amazement the chervil and the parsley and all the rest had flourished. China was carrying an armful of green and gray fronds. Her other arm was linked through Alexander's. Their faces were turned to each other and they were talking animatedly. China was hatless now, and Julia could see the line of her throat, and the neat chignon drawn up at the back of her head.

She wondered what they were talking about.

Julia was still jealous of China. Alexander and his mother seemed to share a closeness that excluded her. It might have been easier, Julia reflected, if she had been able to dislike her mother-in-law. As it was, she couldn't even resent Alexander's attachment because she would have liked to possess some of China's cool grace herself. She was calm and at ease even here, at Ladyhill, with Faye and Sophia.

Julia went on chopping vegetables for the salad. Alexander and China passed out of sight again, around the corner of the house.

What chance is there for us? Julia thought. *I'm jealous of Alexander's mother. And of his house. These walls.* The thickness of them, into the window embrasure, confronted her with their solidity. She thought of the other walls, stripped of their scaffolding now, piebald with new and blackened stone. *And the guilt for what has happened to it stalks me around every corner.*

But the buoyancy of Julia's mood didn't change. By admitting them, she felt that for once she had arranged her fear and guilt like hard facts listed on a sheet of paper, and now she was free to turn away to dreams and images. *There is something that's mine*, she thought. *There's Josh. Not just what I remember, but now, today.* She hugged the knowledge to herself as she worked, and the happiness bubbled out of her in little, unconnected snatches of singing.

"You're happy in your work," Sophia said.

Alexander and China came back into the kitchen, and China held out her armful of foliage. "Is this enough? Or far too much? I didn't want to strip your herb garden quite bare, but they look and smell so good."

Julia took them, smiling at her. "Everything grows here. You turn your back, and it's a foot tall. I've never seen anything growing before. It's like magic."

Alexander put his arm around her, proprietorial. "It smells wonderful in here. Thank you for doing everything."

"I'll just put these in," Julia said, "and then it's ready. Are we going to have champagne?"

"Of course we're going to have champagne." Alexander held up two green and gold bottles, and Julia tried not to think of the last time she had seen Johnny Flowers. Going up the stairs, twenty yards from here, with a bottle of champagne in his hand. "To drink a toast to my wife and my daughter. Happiness, and happy birthday."

It was a good evening.

They ate and drank and talked about small things. Faye and Sophia, the daughter looking more and more like her mother, beamed and contradicted each other from either side of Alexander. China and Toby made their different, stately responses, and Julia presided over the table, laughing and encouraging them, and turning her glass in her hand so that the champagne bubbles caught the light.

Alexander watched her, his face softening.

It was late when Faye and Sophia and Toby, carrying their little boys wrapped up in blankets, made their way across the dark grounds and back to Faye's cottage. Alexander went with them, carrying a flashlight, and Julia and China did the dishes together.

"You looked happy tonight," China said.

Julia had to stare down into the greasy water to stop herself jerking around to search China's face. She was afraid of China knowing what was happening. China saw everything, Julia was sure, even though she said little.

"Don't I usually look happy?" Julia answered too lightly.

After a moment China said, "No, not always."

Julia had to say something. She launched into it at random. "Really? I suppose it takes time to adjust to . . . such a different life. To having Lily. I suppose it's lonely here, in a way. Alexander is busy. There's the work on the house, and his music, and he's away a lot."

That was true, at least. While the workmen were at Ladyhill the rebuilding had possessed him. It was not enough for him to watch. He put on overalls and clambered up the scaffolding, lifting bricks or mixing concrete or doing whatever unskilled jobs helped him to assuage his longing for the house to be made whole again. Julia saw his expression, sometimes, as he worked. It was burning with intense eagerness, and she would turn away, facing the familiar circuit of jealousy and guilt.

When the insurance money and the small stock of capital was all gone, Alexander flung himself into earning more money. He took on any work that was offered to him, shutting himself away with his piano and his notebooks for hours on end. He had decided, more recently, that the rewards were much better in America. He had made two long trips, one to New York and one to the West Coast in search of film work. Julia had wanted to take Lily and go with him, but Alexander had refused, saying it would be too uncomfortable for them to travel cheaply. Then Julia had asked him if she could find some work of her own, so that she could contribute, but he had said no to that too. "Lily's your work," he had said, smiling at them both. "More than enough, I should think."

Julia's mouth had set in a thin line and she had changed the subject. She swished the dishmop to and fro in the bowl now, conscious of China waiting for something more. She stayed silent, listening to the silence.

"Is it all as external as that?"

China would express herself succinctly, of course. External. To do with outer things, and not the dangerous ones like Julia's and Alexander's feelings for each other.

"Of course," Julia lied. China's gray-blond head nodded, just once, and she polished a slow circle on a dinner plate that was already dry. Julia was possessed by a longing to tell her the truth. Not just about Josh, but about the long seam that had split open tonight with the telephone's ringing. About how she felt that Alexander and Lily and Ladyhill together had stitched her into a straitjacket, and the prospect of bursting out of it was unbearably enticing. More. About her jealousy—*even of you, China, did you know that?*—and her resentment of her reduction to Alexander's wife and Lily's mother, no more herself, and about her guilt, and her fears of the smoky vault of the house and its terrible ghosts, and how they had come together with all the rest to obliterate the love. She had loved Alexander at the beginning, and now it was gone, leaving her stiff and dry. Nor did she know what Alexander felt, anymore. He was as gentle with her as he had always been, and as stimulating and uncompromising in upholding what he believed in, but it was as if he had simply stepped a little farther away. They went through the motions of being married, that was all.

Julia wanted him back, but tonight had shown her that she wanted other things too. Craved them, with the desperation of an addict.

She lifted her head and looked straight ahead of her. "Were you happy when you lived here?" Julia asked softly.

Perhaps China would give her some clue to help her to interpret her own life.

Alexander's mother put the plate down, very gently, on top of the other five that she had already dried. "My husband was a difficult man to live with," she said. "I don't think yours is."

Julia knew it was a warning.

China had accepted her as Alexander's wife. It surprised her, when she thought about it. There were enough things about her to object to, Julia reflected. But now that she was married, she understood, there was to be no failure. She was Alexander's wife, and that should be enough. Of course China would be Alexander's supporter. She wouldn't want her daughter-in-law to confide her doubts or fears. And to Julia that seemed perfectly natural and predictable.

"Of course not," she murmured. She tipped the water out of the dishpan and wiped it dry. She heard Alexander coming in, bolting the outside door. A moment later he came into the kitchen. Seeing them together, Julia was struck more forcibly than usual by their likeness. It was less in the features themselves than in the lines their features adopted.

"I think I'll go upstairs," China said. Alexander kissed her on the forehead. Julia wanted to shout at him, *But I'm here. Don't you love me as well? More than her?* The pettiness of her jealousy shocked her a little. And then, like an antidote, she thought, *Josh.*

"I hope you'll be comfortable in Lily's room," Julia said politely to China.

"Of course I will. Good night, both of you. It was a lovely day."

China went up to bed, and left Julia and Alexander alone together.

His face was still soft when he looked at her, as it had been across the dinner table. The skin at the corners of his eyes fanned into fine wrinkles. Alexander habitually protected his own tenderness with an ironic shell, but when it showed, as it did now, it touched Julia directly. She reached her hand out to him, but then she remembered all the knot of other things, and turned the gesture into an awkward shrug.

"You were like you used to be, tonight," Alexander said.

"Used to be?"

"Yes. Funny, and alive. Careless, as if it didn't matter what anyone said or thought. I love that in you."

"If you wanted me to go on being those things, you shouldn't have married me. We shouldn't have had Lily." As soon as she had said the sharp words she wished she could take them back again.

Alexander sighed. "Let's sit down and have a nightcap."

They went through into the little sitting room. It smelled of Toby's cigar smoke, and Julia opened the windows wider. She breathed in the earthy chill of the night air, suddenly wishing that she could close her eyes and sleep.

Alexander poured a whiskey for each of them, and they sat down on the sofa.

"Why shouldn't I have married you?" he asked.

Julia lifted her hand, palm upward, and sliced the air with it. The gesture took in the room, the house with its black-shadowed spaces, the gardens and fields beyond it, and the quiet countryside. It took in Alexander, and the baby, and Julia herself. They stared at each other, recognizing what it meant, refusing to acknowledge it. Bitterly, Julia said, "If you hadn't married me, you would still have your house."

Alexander was angry then. His infrequent anger kindled very quickly when it came, burning up his equanimity. He caught her wrist in his hand, jolting her. "If I hadn't married you, I wouldn't have you here with me. I wouldn't have Lily. Houses can be mended. This one will be mended."

Julia looked at him, and saw the familiar expression. Determination that was almost fanatical. She couldn't gauge whether he was determined for themselves, or just for Ladyhill.

"Yes," she said. "I know it will. But at what cost?"

"I thought you didn't care about money," he snapped back at her. "I don't give a damn what it costs."

His misunderstanding was deliberate, Julia thought. There were questions that Alexander didn't want to face.

"Why can't you be happy?" he demanded. "You were happy tonight, weren't you? And your happiness kindled the rest of us. Even Toby, for Christ's sake. Why not other nights? Why not all the time?"

I was happy tonight, because . . .

Julia could have told him the truth, but she knew that she was a coward. Alexander was the brave one, she thought. Deflecting the question, not looking at him, she said, "I asked China if she was happy when she lived here. She said that her husband was a difficult man to live with. Mine isn't." The bitterness had faded, and Julia was smiling faintly. "She was telling me, of course, to rejoice in what I've got."

Alexander rubbed his hand over his face, deepening the lines at the sides of his mouth. "You can hardly compare my father and mother with you and me. There's thirty years, a war, and a social revolution separating us, thank God. I'm sorry, China's very partisan. She shouldn't be."

Julia drank the last mouthful of her whiskey and stood up, looking down at him. "It's all right. Why shouldn't she be on your side? I just wish she were my mother."

That's probably the truth, she thought, surprised by the realization. "I wish I had someone like China to support me. I never have."

Alexander stood up too. He put his arms around her and drew her against him, settling her head against his shoulder. "Julia. I know you haven't had an easy time. Not like I've had, if you want to compare. But you've got me now, and you're a mother yourself. You're twenty-two. You're grown-up. You have to be, for Lily's sake."

No, Julia thought. *I'm not. I don't know how I would be, but not like this. Wouldn't I be happy if I were?*

She turned her face against Alexander, digging her fingers into the roughness of his sweater, hiding herself while Alexander comfortingly stroked her hair. She felt her own selfishness and stupidity, destructiveness like a tumor inside her, but she also knew that she would go to Josh, do whatever he asked, and take what was coming. It was unthinkable to go back to this afternoon, to the suffocation that she had felt under the rustling umbrella of copper leaves.

"Let's go to bed," Alexander said.

They had moved Lily's crib through into their own bedroom, to make room for China. Upstairs they leaned over the bars, looking down at the baby. She was sleeping on her back, her arms and legs spread wide and the satin binding of the blanket clutched against her damp, flushed face. Wet black curls stuck to her forehead. Julia leaned closer and breathed in the scent of her, listening to her faint snores.

Love twisted suddenly and violently inside her, compelling her to reach into the crib and lift up the moist, breathing weight.

"Lily," she whispered, needing to squeeze the baby against her, rubbing her face against the fat creases of the little neck. "Happy birthday. Think of all the years ahead. Just think of them." The smells of baby powder and clean skin and warm flannel mingled with the sharp scent of wet nappy. The baby whimpered and Julia cradled her head, rocking her.

"You'll wake her up," Alexander whispered.

"She needs changing."

Julia laid her on the bed and unbuttoned her nightdress. As she unpinned and pinned on a dry diaper, Lily opened her eyes and stared at her, unblinking, perfectly composed. Mystified, Julia reflected that sometimes her baby was a numbing responsibility, at others no more than a reproach, and yet at other times, like this, Julia knew that she would die or kill for her.

She lifted her up again and kissed the corner of her open mouth, then laid her back in the nest of her crib. Lily's thumb found its way into her mouth, and she sucked noisily at it. Watching her, Julia groped at a silent promise. *I'll try to do what's best. It may not be right, but I will try.*

Alexander came and put his arms on her shoulders.

"It's my turn now," he said.

He took off Julia's cotton dress with the square of paper hidden deep in the pocket and let it fall in a heap on the floor. His hands rested on the points of Julia's hips, then moved slowly to the hollow of her waist, then to cover her breasts. Julia had been proud of her new, voluptuous figure while she was feeding Lily, but now that that was over she had shrunk again, even smaller than before. She put her fingers up to shield the deficit, but Alexander pushed her hand away. He leaned forward to touch his mouth to the nipples, tracing a slow circle around each hard point with his tongue.

"Julia." His mouth moved against her skin. "I love you."

Her body had been stiff, but Alexander's hands warmed it. She had been thinking about the guilt and resentment murkily tangled between them, but a more intense awareness took hold of her now. Her head fell back and she exhaled a long breath. Angrily, she put the other reckonings out of her head. There was this hunger now, sharper than the others, and they shared it. The thread of it was visible through the tangle. This appetite, at least, was simple, and the means of satisfying it was within their reach.

"I want you," Julia whispered.

She stepped out of his grasp and half-turned away, shielding herself, conscious of the lines of her body and Alexander's eyes on them. Then with a quick movement she lay down on the bed, stretching herself out for him. He threw himself down beside her and her body arched against him. Her mouth touched his and then opened, hungry, as his hand parted her legs. His fingers slid over the moist folds and then centered, sending a bolt through her. She gave herself up to the pleasure of it for a moment, and then she whispered, "Wait."

Julia sat up and unbuttoned his shirt, frowning over the cuff links, then unbuckled his belt. Her face was shadowed, intent, as she undressed him. Alexander studied her in the dim light. He had never seen her quite like this before, he thought.

When Alexander was naked she pushed him gently, her hand flat against his chest, so that he lay on his back against the sheet. Then her dark head dipped over him as she took him into her mouth. Her tongue fluttered, drawing itself along the rigid length of him, and Alexander groaned. Perhaps he had caught only brief glimpses of this insistent, imperious Julia in the past. Tonight she had taken control. This was an older, more calculating and more mysterious woman than the girl he had married. Alexander found her almost unbearably erotic. He groaned again, twisting on the sheet, shivering at the point of losing his control. He needed to shudder and burst into her mouth, but he wanted to reassert himself by pushing upward inside her, and feeling her legs twine around his hips. Alexander caught Julia's wrists and rolled sideways, intending to trap her beneath him, but she was too supple and too quick for him.

She twisted with him, pinning him underneath her own body instead. And then when he lay back, giving up to her, she smiled and stretched one long white leg over him. She lifted her body, holding herself poised over him, and then she lowered herself so that they just connected, only just.

Transfixed, Alexander looked up at her. Her dark eyes were as opaque as mirrors, but yet he thought he could see through them, right into her head.

"Wait," she whispered again.

She began to move, very slowly, lifting her hips and then sinking again, dreamily at first, then with sharper thrusts. She sat upright, her back arching and her fingers stretching and curling, and then she crouched over him like a cat, her breath warm on his face and her tongue searching for his. Their eyes locked together, and Julia's imperious expression softened. She was taking him for her own pleasure, dominating him and then withdrawing herself to suit the demands of her own body, but Alexander sensed that she was also giving herself more generously than she had ever done before.

Suddenly, they were equal. There was no domination, and there was no need to yield. They were simply together, and the ease and the intensity of it ignited them. Alexander cried out once, and his body reared upward. Julia's arms spread and her head fell helplessly backward. She forgot Lily in her crib and the image of China lying in the narrow bed in the next room. Her eyes were blind now and she cried out, too, triumphant in the house's silence. The potent waves raced through her and expanded into the soft, remote ripples of satisfaction.

They lay together, tangled in stillness, with Julia's head heavy on Alexander's shoulder.

That was right, she thought.

But already she was losing her sureness of how and why it had been right. If she had imagined equality or made it materialize with their bodies' needs, its absence was reality, and reality always returned. Confusion gathered around her as surely as consciousness itself.

Alexander stirred and settled her head in the crook of his arm. She couldn't see his face, but she thought she could guess what his expression would be. He had a calmness, not quite complacency, but a certainty that she was utterly lacking herself. She didn't want to see that expression. Not now, tonight. They had been right, and the surprising satisfaction of it was still with her.

"Alexander?"

"Ycs."

"What were you talking about? You and China, this evening, when you were walking back from the garden. I saw you, out of the window. You were so busy talking."

She heard the faint murmur of laughter in his chest. "I don't know. I can't remember. Lily, perhaps. Or the house, or the garden. The ordinary things we talk about." His voice was blurring with drowsiness. Julia nodded, her cheek against his skin.

"It must be nice," she murmured.

She watched the white curtains stirring at the dark space of the open window and listened to Lily making her tiny, satisfied noises in her sleep. Alexander's breathing was deep and regular. After a moment or two, Julia fell asleep herself.

"Oh, shit." Mattie had thought that it was the alarm clock, but now she realized it was the telephone.

She couldn't answer it. She couldn't even open her eyes, but it still went on ringing.

"Go away. Leave me alone." Even the silent words stabbed

through her head, and the external noise assaulted her with renewed brutality.

Wincing, Mattie stretched out her hand. There was nothing there, only crumpled sheet. No solid, grunting flesh. She had gone to bed alone, then, somehow or other. That was something.

Fortified by the discovery, she opened one eye. The room was too bright, even though the curtains were lopsidedly drawn. There were clothes all over the floor and the bed; the contents of her handbag were tipped in a heap on the table next to an open half-bottle of whiskey. That was right, she remembered that much. She had wanted to smoke a last cigarette with a last drink, and then hadn't been able to find any matches. At the thought of whiskey Mattie's stomach heaved and her mouth filled with bitter slime. And still the telephone went on ringing.

Mattie took a deep breath and sat up. Trying to move her head as little as possible, she leaned over sideways and groped among the discarded clothes. Her fingers connected with the receiver and she struggled with the weight of it.

"Is that you, Mat?"

"Who else would it bloody well be?"

"I don't know, you sound funny. I thought you must be out."

"I was. Out for the count. I feel much worse now. What time is it?"

"Mattie," Julia said. "It's nearly eleven o'clock."

"So what? You're not exactly an early bird yourself, are you?"

"Lily woke up this morning at half past six. She wakes up every morning at half past six."

"Oh. Yeah. Sorry. How is she? I'm sorry I missed the birthday. Work. You know how it is."

"I know how it is," Julia said crisply. "What is the matter?"

Mattie sighed. With her free hand holding the front of her head in place, she levered herself to sit up against the pillows. The room swung around and then settled again. She wanted tea, two pints of it, but there was no one to make it. "Hangover. A real peach."

"Wish I'd been there. What were you doing?"

"God knows. I wish I could remember. No, I don't. It's probably better forgotten. Not having a show to do in the evenings, that's the trouble. Rehearsing's awful anyway, and there's so much more time left over to fill with drinking."

Julia looked over the side of the desk. Lily was happily playing with her wooden blocks, balancing one on top of another and then pushing them down with a yodel of triumph. Alexander had gone across the garden to the half-overgrown summerhouse. He would spread his notebooks and sheets of music across a white Lloyd Loom table and work in there for hours.

"Go easy, Mat, will you?" Julia's voice sounded concerned.

Mattie shrugged. If only she had a cup of tea. "Julia, what is this? Just a chat? Because if it is . . ."

"No." The sharpness even made Mattie forget her headache for a minute. "I need to talk to you. Josh has come back. He wants to see me again."

Mattie frowned, trying to disentangle what she thought about that. It didn't take long, even in her debilitated condition.

"I hope you told him to fuck off."

There was a brief silence. Then, in a low voice, Julia said, "No. I didn't. I want to see him too."

"What d'you expect me to say? You're married, Bliss is a good guy. You've got Lily, you're lucky."

"Don't say anything." Julia's voice had gone flat. "I'm still me, remember. We're friends. I'm coming up to see you for a couple of days, if anyone asks. That's all."

"Tell a few lies for you, is that it?"

"Will you?"

Mattie closed her eyes. Then she laughed, even though it hurt. "You know I will. It won't be the first time, will it?"

The memories linked them, all the way back to the days of playing truant from Blick Road. The bond seemed indissoluble, even though everything separated them now. They would always have each other, they thought, whatever external circumstances kept them apart.

"Thanks, Mattie."

"I'll just have to hope that you're not really being as bloody stupid as I think you are, won't I? When are you coming?"

"Tomorrow. I'm going to have dinner with him."

Mattie could hear the same old happiness and incredulity and intoxication in her voice. Julia had always been the same about her aviator, from the moment she had set eyes on him in Leoni's. Mattie felt a dull premonition of the hurt that would inevitably come, and also a much keener pang of envy. She wanted to say, *Don't do it*, both to save Julia the pain and to spare herself something too. She could countenance her best friend's marriage, and motherhood, and her possession of Ladyhill, however scarred by the fire, but it was harder to witness passion and ecstasy, even if they were short-lived. *I am a bitch*, Mattie thought wearily. Julia was right. It was better to say nothing at all.

"See you tomorrow, then. You can come here to doll yourself up first, if you want. I'll be back from rehearsal by six. Are you bringing Lily?"

"Don't be daft. Faye's going to help to look after her. She doesn't like doing it because it interferes with her jam making or choir practice or whatever it is that keeps everyone so furiously busy down here. But I told her I had to see my gynecologist and that guaranteed acceptance and silence. Doctors are sacred and we don't talk about down there, do we?"

Mattie grinned. "Heaven forbid. I'll see you tomorrow, you adventuress. Ciao."

After Julia had hung up, Mattie lay still and tried to gather some shreds of strength. Now that she was wide awake there was no point in staying in bed; she knew that from experience. The best thing to do was to get up and pretend that everything was all right, and usually after an hour or two it did turn out to be all right and she could get on with what she was supposed to be doing. There were some days that didn't turn out well, but those were still infrequent enough not to be worth worrying about. Today she was due at rehearsal at two o'clock, so there was plenty of time to discover which sort of day it was going to be.

Very carefully, Mattie sat up and lowered her feet on to the floor. Her head and stomach protested, but not enough to prevent her from standing up. Once upright, she shuffled over to the window and pulled back the curtain. Squinting in the bright light, she rested her face against the cool glass and looked down. There was the usual handful of purposeful-looking people striding past the little row of shops opposite. The second-hand bookseller had lowered his faded blue awning to keep the sunlight off his stock, and the jeweler next to him was standing in his shop doorway watching the passersby. Beneath Mattie's flat there was a dairy, and when she craned her neck forward she could see the empty milk crates stacked up on the black and white tiled frontage, waiting to be returned to the depot. If she looked up again, to the end of the street, she could see a slice of the railings and the pedimented front of the British Museum.

Mattie liked living in Bloomsbury. It was an unfashionable and untheatrical enclave of small booksellers and shabby publishers' offices, conveniently furnished with corner shops and dowdy cafés. She had learned to be at home in the jumbled streets, and felt that they offered a safe retreat. The familiar scene below was pleasing and soothing, and she felt better at once. Mattie hitched her nightdress around her and went across to her kitchen. Her cooking facilities consisted of a hot plate and an electric kettle perched side by side on a narrow shelf beside the sink, but Mattie hardly even used the hot plate. She ate cookies and drank tea, and when she needed to or remembered to she went out to a café and ordered poached eggs or beans on toast. Unlike Julia, she had never acquired Felix's taste for fancy foreign food. After she had eaten her meal she liked to sit in the café, smoking and listening to the conversations around her.

That was in her own, private Bloomsbury existence.

In the other half of her life, she was taken to restaurants before or after parties, usually by someone who wanted to go to bed with her afterward. Usually she prodded at the ornate food, and gave her attention to whatever there was to drink with it. She was as good at resisting the subsequent advances as she always had been, except when she was too weary to bother or too drunk to care. She had certainly been drunk last night, but she had clearly escaped somehow.

Mattie boiled the kettle and made a pot of tea. She sat down at the table with a pint mug, feeling almost healthy again. If she had been lonely and sorry for herself earlier because there was no one to bring her tea and sympathy, she was relieved to be alone now. If there had been a man, she reflected, he would have expected her to bring him the tea. And he would have wanted all the sympathy for himself because he would have felt much worse than she did, of course.

Mattie smiled and gulped her tea. She groped for her cigarettes and then remembered, no matches. She was beginning to remember last night as well. It had started perfectly straightforwardly, in the pub next to the rehearsal room, with two or three of the other actors. It had been a bad day, and they had bought one another rapid rounds of drinks to cheer themselves up. The opening night was still two weeks off, but it seemed impossible that anyone would be able to darn the gaping holes in the production in time.

The play was *Romeo and Juliet,* a dissected version of it to be played in modern dress in a black-painted circular space inside a warehouse near Euston Station. The director described it as Shakespeare for the *West Side Story* generation. Mattie had no particular objection to trying to play Juliet in a black leather jerkin with her hair piled up in an immense beehive on top of her head and finished off with a black ribbon. If that was the director's vision, then she would do her best to interpret it for him. But she was finding it difficult to speak the verse. She had no training, and the rhythms mangled themselves in her mouth, the lines stretching like yawns or telescoping into staccato nonsense. The director was too preoccupied with tinkering with the text and searching for effects to give her the proper pointers, and Mattie was floundering dismally. She knew the director had hated her performance from the beginning, and she suspected that he had cast her in relentless determination only to be avant garde and because he was sourly jealous of Jimmy Proffitt's huge success. Everything was made much worse by the actor taking the part of Romeo, a RADA-trained pansy with all the affectations of Doris and Ada but none of the wit or resilience.

"I'm so bloody awful I could die," Mattie had groaned to Tybalt and Mercutio in the public bar.

"Nah, it's not you," Tybalt had comforted her. "You're not much good, but you're no worse than anyone else. The whole bloody show stinks."

They had made depressed faces at one another, and there had been nothing left to do but to order some more rounds of Guinness.

Later, the gloomy circle had been swelled by the members of a pop group who had turned up to play a booking at a nearby hall and found it canceled. One of the actors knew one of the guitarists, and more drinks had been bought. The conversation had stopped circling around the miseries of the production, and turned to Chubby Checker. Mattie had cheered up immediately. Sixpences were pressed into the jukebox and she and the lead singer obligingly demonstrated the twist to the rest of the pub's customers. After that someone had suggested a Chinese dinner. They had crammed hilariously among the amplifiers in the musicians' van and driven to Gerrard Street. Mattie didn't much like Chinese food, but several bottles of only slightly peculiar-tasting wine had appeared with it, and it was after her share of it that everything went hazy in her recollection. They had left the Chinese restaurant intending to go to a party that someone knew about, but on their way through Soho they had stopped off at the Marquee Club to see another group, and Mattie remembered dancing and then falling sideways to sit on somebody's knee. It was the singer with the group, except she couldn't remember which group, and he had put his hands up under her sweater to knead her breasts. She had dragged his hands away and more or less stood up again, but she was enjoying the noisy company because it saved her having to think about Juliet, or think about anything at all, so she had stayed to have another drink instead of taking herself home to bed.

After that they were outside again and trying to find the van to go on to the party. There were lots of people, although hardly any of them were the ones she had started the evening with, and it was at that moment that Mattie had noticed they were standing right in front of the Showbox. Monty was looming in the doorway, looking for punters. Someone must have paid, or perhaps Monty had let her in with her friends to fill out a thin night, and they had all flocked in to see the show. The rickety chairs and the tatty curtains and the music were all nightmarishly familiar. Mattie had looked around wildly, searching for the way out, but the singer had his arm around her shoulders, dragging her down, and his other hand was crawling up her thigh like a snake. He had muttered something about a cigarette, and she had given him one of hers, and her box of matches, to keep his hands busy for a few seconds.

The girls came on and did their routines, just as they always had. Staring at their creased, unresisting bodies, Mattie felt unbearably sad, for them and for herself. Oily, heavy tears welled up and ran down her face.

Poor women, she thought. *Why should men do this to them? Why should we let them?*

With boozy, sodden ferocity she had lurched to her feet, swiping at the singer and connecting with him so forcibly that he had almost fallen off his chair. Then she stumbled to the front of Monty's dim cavern and shouted something. Something like, "You won't enjoy this as much as girls' tits, but you can bloody well listen."

Sitting at her table with her mug of tea, Mattie put her hands up to hide her face, remembering what she had done.

She had declaimed Juliet's death speech.

. . . I will kiss thy lips.
Haply some poison yet doth hang on them
To make me die with a restorative . . .

"Oh, Jesus," Mattie whispered. "I wish I really was dead."

Monty had rescued her. He had swept her away, bundled

her into a taxi, and she had managed to convey herself from the taxi and into bed.

Mattie lifted her head again, very slowly, and peered around the room. At least there was no one here to witness her shame. Then the corners of her mouth twitched, and she began to laugh. She laughed until she had to gasp for breath, the thought of declaiming Shakespeare in the Showbox was so irresistibly funny. When she had finished laughing she rubbed her eyes and poured herself some more tea.

"I know one thing for sure," she said aloud. "I'm never going to touch another drop. Never. Not ever."

The resolution lasted all the way through what was left of the morning, and until she set off for rehearsal. Then she was just passing the pub opposite the museum, on her way to the bus stop, when it occurred to her that she had had nothing to eat. She went in and bought herself a cheese sandwich, and one drink to go with it. There was no harm in just one, Mattie thought. Afterward, feeling suitably virtuous, she caught the bus to the rehearsal room.

The afternoon was the usual round of bickering and recrimination, and they managed to work their way through barely two scenes.

Mattie had only just reached the sanctuary of her rooms in Bloomsbury when Julia arrived.

Looking at her, it struck Mattie that Julia looked exactly as she had on the day they ran away from home. Hungry and defiant, yet also glowing with anticipation. Ready to be set alight, Mattie thought bleakly. What was that like?

For two or three seconds they confronted each other. Then they swooped together, hugging and exclaiming. "I miss you, Mat." "I miss you too." Then they held each other at arm's length.

Julia shrugged, a little awkwardly. "Thank you," she said. "I know this is different from the old days. I wouldn't have asked you to cover for me if it weren't so important. But it is, you see—" She broke off and turned away. It was unlike Julia not to finish what she wanted to say.

"Is it so important?" Mattie whispered. "Is he?"

Julia turned back then and looked full at her. Mattie saw luminous happiness in her eyes.

Very deliberately, Julia answered. "Oh, yes. I haven't seen him for a long time. But I know exactly what he's like, I know him so well, it's as if he's just gone out of this room. Because he's always been with me, even when I've tried to pretend I've forgotten. I know the shape of his head and the sound of his voice and the smell of his skin, and I love every part of him. It's not an illusion, Mattie. I know what's wrong with him as well as I know everything else.'' Julia lifted her head and spread her hands out. ''The existence of Josh, for me, makes the light seem brighter. It's the difference between being alive, shivering and trembling with it, and being a machine. And I'm going to see him tonight. In an hour.'' As if it explained everything, she finished, in a soft voice, ''You know what being in love is like.''

''No,'' Mattie said flatly. ''I don't.''

Julia glanced curiously at her. ''Not even Jimmy Proffitt?''

''No, I didn't love Jimmy Proffitt. I wanted to, tried to. But he wasn't very lovable. I love you, and Bliss, and Lily, and Felix. Rozzie, and the others. Not men. Men happen to you, that's all.'' Seeing Julia's face, she tried to shrug her confession off with some kind of humor. ''It's all right, darling, I'm not a lezzy. I'd have had a go at you by now, wouldn't I? But you must tell me what it's like, sometime. Being in love.''

''Mattie.''

But Mattie saw her glance flicker to the clock on the mantelpiece. ''Not now, you haven't got time. Do you want a drink before you go?''

Julia had already picked up her little suitcase, was on the way to the bathroom to change. ''No, thanks. Don't think I could force anything down.''

Mattie unscrewed the half-bottle of whiskey that she had firmly put away this morning. Then, half-listening to Julia in the bathroom, she slammed the bottle down again and went to look out of the window. The bookseller's awning had been rolled up again, and the closed sign hung idly inside the glass door. The view of the street was soothing because of its monotony. Mattie watched some pigeons pecking around a trash can that had been put out for the morning's collection.

Julia came out of the bathroom within five minutes. She had changed into a simple polka-dot summer dress. Her face looked clean and malleable, ready to take the fresh impressions. She put her fingers up to her cheeks, explaining, ''I tried some makeup on, but it looked as if I were trying too hard, so I took it off again.''

''You don't need it tonight,'' Mattie said truthfully.

"Well, then." Julia was standing by the door, not wanting to seem to rush away and leave Mattie alone.

"Go on," Mattie said. "Have a good time. Will you be coming back tonight?"

Julia looked almost frightened. "I don't know. I don't know anything, except that I've got to go to him now, and I'll do whatever he asks me."

What must it be like, Mattie wondered again. "If Bliss rings, I'll make up some reason why you're not here."

"Yes. Thank you."

The door was already open when Mattie asked her, "What about Bliss?"

Julia's eyes were wide and blank. For some reason Mattie remembered the fire. "I don't know," Julia murmured. "I told you, didn't I? I just don't know." She turned, the door clicked, and she was gone.

Mattie sat down at the table. *You do know,* she thought. *This will hurt him, you must know that much.* She was afraid, then, that this evening had come between herself and Julia. The suspicion made her feel lonely and cold. Julia was her friend, after all, and Bliss and the aviator and Jimmy Proffitt and the rest were just men who had happened to them. Even Bliss. Abruptly, Mattie reached for the whiskey bottle and poured herself a deep measure.

Josh had been waiting for almost an hour. He had known that he was ridiculously early but he hadn't been able to stop himself from sitting down in the most conspicuous place, watching the big doors every time they revolved. At exactly seven o'clock he saw Julia.

She stepped into the cool, lofty space, glancing quickly upward and then around her, faintly impressed in spite of herself, reminding Josh of years ago when they had arrived in Wengen and Julia had stared upward at the Eiger and the Jungfrau. He didn't know quite why he had chosen the Palm Court at the Ritz for their meeting. Perhaps to acknowledge that they weren't kids, and they didn't need to improvise anymore. Josh had changed from a ski bum into a ski entrepreneur, and Julia, he reminded himself, was Lady Bliss, a wife and a mother, and what else? The idea seemed laughable when he first saw her, all the way across the room. She looked seventeen, exactly the same as when he had first known her. It was impossible to imagine that she had a child of her own.

Then she saw him, and came quickly toward him. There were waiters, and women in cocktail dresses, all obstacles in their way. Josh had stood up when he saw her, and the spindly table rocked in front of him. He held out his hands as she reached him at last.

They didn't speak. They stood looking at each other, their hands clasped. The hum of conversation and the clink of glasses, even the splash of the absurd fountain and the clamor of the rococo gilt decor, faded into silence for Josh and Julia. Josh leaned forward very slowly and kissed the vulnerable point of her jaw. It was at once more intimate than any brash kiss on the lips could have been.

She had changed, Josh saw that now.

It was as if the years had intervened to define her face. The bones had set under the thin skin, to form more noticeable smooth plateaus and shadowed hollows. Josh recognized that the shadows were real, not transitory. She looked older, more grace-ful, self-possessed, and beautiful rather than wilfully pretty.

"I'm glad to see you," Josh said at last.

Julia sat down rather quickly, not letting go of his hands.

"I don't think I really believed, until I saw you at this table, that you were going to be here. I sat in the taxi on the way, looking at the trees in the park, thinking, *If he's not there, I'll order a bottle of champagne. I'll sit and drink it and remember every single day we ever spent together.*"

Reluctantly taking his eyes off her face, Josh realized that someone was standing beside their table. It took him a second to grasp that it was the waiter.

"Sir?"

"A bottle of champagne," Josh said.

When it came, they raised their glasses to each other.

"To you, Julia," Josh said, but she shook her head, smiling.

"I don't deserve a toast. Let's drink to understanding."

He echoed her serious tone, "To understanding," and they drank.

It was hard to know where to begin. Now that they were here, isolated in the sociable splendor, they were almost shy. The champagne helped. It prickled on Julia's tongue, loosening it, and slowly, picking their way around the dangerous corners, they started to talk.

The tables around them emptied as people drifted away to dinner, the ice melted in the champagne bucket, but Julia and

Josh didn't notice. Julia told him about Ladyhill, and the fire, and Johnny Flowers and his girl.

"I'm sorry," Josh said simply. He understood the hollows in her face. He took her hand again and they both looked down at the four diamonds set in a gold band and the thin, plain wedding ring that Alexander had given her. While Julia asked him, he told her about the new trails that were being cleared, and the ski lodges he had borrowed a frightening amount of money to build, that were bringing the skiers into Vail at last.

"Are you happy?" Julia asked him, but she thought the question answered itself. Josh was alive, as vibrant with energy and determination as he had always been. She was almost painfully conscious of his closeness to her, of the way his thumb moved over the thin skin on the back of her hand. Josh generated his own happiness, and she felt the reflected warmth of it within herself, melting her bones.

"I'm happy with what I do," Josh answered. "It's a good life."

But he was thinking, *I'm so careful about keeping it all, just as it is. I have to be most careful of all with you, Julia. Looking at you now . . .*

He didn't ask her about Alexander. Instead, he returned her own question. "Are you happy?"

She tilted her head. Reflections of the shaded lights glinted off the gilt scrollwork and the fountain water splashed softly behind her. Suddenly it seemed that she understood everything with perfect clarity. Infinitesimal structures and complex motivations were laid bare for her inspection, and the simplicity of it all was dazzling. She was here, now, in the midst of her life, with Josh.

She smiled at him. "I'm happy at this minute." That was enough. It had to be enough.

The last of the champagne had gone flat in their glasses.

"Would you like to go somewhere for dinner?" he asked her formally.

Julia looked straight back at him, seeing the color of his eyes, her heart beating high in her throat. "I don't think I could eat anything," she said.

He stood up, holding her chair for her, his hand under her arm.

"Come home with me then," he said.

Out in Piccadilly the sky was royal blue over the streetlamps. Josh whistled for a taxi and they sat with the width of the seat separating them, not touching, not even looking at each other, but the acknowledgment of what they were doing leapt and burned between them. Julia watched the shop mannequins under the display lights, and the tiers of curtained and uncurtained windows in the tall buildings, thinking of the lives behind them, and of her own and Josh's, threads crossing and knotting again. They stopped outside a little mews house in Kensington. Josh unlocked the door and she followed him inside.

The house was almost empty, and in the process of being painted. It smelled of new carpet and wallpaper paste. Everything was white, even the sofa still swathed in its wrappings. Julia walked through the small rooms, touching the new white laminate in the kitchen, raising one eyebrow at Josh. It seemed too permanent to belong to him.

"It's owned by some friends of mine. They're on their honeymoon right now. It's mine until they come back and enter into married bliss." His face changed. "I'm sorry . . ." He was going to say, Of course you're married too.

Julia turned away again, closing her mind, walking back into the living room. She remembered the cottage at the edge of the woods and the way that Josh had touched down in it, hardly disturbing its arrangement and then taken off again. And his friends. So many of them. Everyone loved Josh. Her happiness was less potent for an instant, but she moved quickly, stalking it.

On the low white table there was a large rectangular box wrapped in bright paper. Josh picked it up and presented it to her. "I told you, I had a gift for Lily."

Julia studied the shape of it, weighing it in her hands. Then she looked into Josh's eyes. He was smiling, anticipating the unwrapping.

"Go on. Open it."

"Josh. Were you so sure I'd come back here with you?"

It was important to know. If it was inevitable, or if he had calculated it. But his expression disarmed her at once. He was honest, she knew that.

"I hoped you would. I wouldn't dare to be sure of anything with you." He moved awkwardly, wanting to hold her, but she evaded him.

"Let me open the present first."

It was a doll, almost as big as Lily herself. It opened and closed its eyes and mouth, cried and talked and walked, drank water and the label threatened that it would wet itself too.

"Isn't it great?" Josh beamed. "All the things it can do."

Julia spluttered. "It's wonderfully hideous. Look at its face."

They took one look at each other and started to laugh. The laughter was cleansing and uncomplicated and it reminded them of other times they had shared, blotting out some of the shadows and some of the other memories.

When it was over they faced each other again, aware of the silence, and the anonymity of the white house enclosing them. Josh stepped forward and took her by the elbows. He bent his face to hers and kissed her eyelids and her cheek and the corners of her mouth, and when she turned her head, suddenly demanding, he kissed her throat and her neck under the warm weight of her hair. Julia's fingers tightened on his arms. "I knew I would come back here with you."

He lifted her hand and kissed the knuckles. They went up the stairs, slowly, holding on to each other.

The bedroom was white with a low white bed. The white-painted cupboard doors were closed on the strangers' possessions. Josh's friends. There was one suitcase in the middle of the floor, a pair of jeans over the back of a chair, no other evidence of Josh at all. Stupidly, Julia realized, she had expected skis and ski bindings, books and records and clothes to confirm his solidity. This shadowiness, thrown into even sharper relief by the white rooms, frightened her. She wanted to take hold of him, fix him, as she had wanted in the Pensione Flora with the gold and brown landscape spread under their windows.

Now, in the strange house, her longing translated itself into physical need. A wave of intense desire washed all through her body. She pressed herself against him, her mouth searching for his, and her wide-open eyes saw the pores in his skin, the tiny, sun-bleached hairs, an enlarged freckle at the angle of his jaw.

Love me. She didn't know whether she said the words or not. Josh undid the red and white dress, tearing the buttons. Her fingers felt limp and thick as they fumbled with his. Their clothes dropped, tangled together, and their skin burned as it glued them. She heard Josh gasp, once. He pushed her blindly back on to the bed and dropped on top of her. Their mouths met, ravenous, but they were too desperate for touch or exploration. She lifted herself, aching with need, and Josh was almost brutal as he plunged straight into her. And at once the violent waves rose silently, gathering into a single peak that swept her up and then broke all through her body. Julia screamed, a tearing noise that she had never heard before, and then Josh's cry echoed her own and they twisted together, caught, blinded, and then fell back, their bodies wound together. They were bruised, breathing in shuddering gasps, their faces and their eyelids stuck with sweat and tears.

At last, when the pounding that shook her had become just her heartbeat again, Julia opened her eyes. There were tears on her cheeks, and she saw the darkness of Josh's eyes looking into her head.

"What am I going to do?" she whispered.

To answer her, he rubbed the tears away with the tips of his fingers.

"How much time have we got? Now, here."

"Two days, three days. I've stolen them." And after that, what would there be? Wild, intoxicated hope fluttered. With Josh. She couldn't think of Lily and Alexander now. *Not now.* "Mattie will tell some lies for me."

Josh turned away from her to look up at the blank ceiling. He lay very still.

"Don't lie for me," he said. "Don't lie for anyone but yourself and Lily."

Coldness gathered around Julia's heart.

And if all I want from all my lies is you, Julia thought, *what then?*

SIXTEEN

The white house was a haven, and also a cruel taunt.

They spent four days in it together, going out to eat, or to walk in Holland Park, and coming back again to the silence, and the mocking intimacy. Julia lay beside Josh in the white bed and looked at the blank room, trying to imagine a connubial life lived between these walls, picturing her own clothes, and Josh's, hanging side by side behind the white doors. However sharply she longed for it, the vision stayed dim.

Josh was a perfect companion as well as the breathtaking lover she remembered. His material success seemed to have rounded him. He talked to her about all kinds of things, bridging the spaces of time that had separated them, and he listened intently to her own more halting contributions. He made her laugh, and Julia knew that the fabric of immediate happiness that they wove between them should have furnished the little house for her as comfortably as it did for Josh. But it didn't, and the failure made the happiness seem all the more desirable, and as thin as gossamer. She listened so hard for any mention of their future together that Josh's words began to distort inside her head, changing their significance, becoming almost unintelligible. There never was any mention of it.

She wanted to shout at him, *Yes, this is a magical time. But I want next week with you too. Next year. Ordinary times, Josh, like your friends will share in this house.* She listened to everything he said until her head throbbed, and watched him, but there was nothing beneath the surface except a kind of wariness that frightened her. She said nothing, and she was reminded of the desperation she had felt at Montebellate. It was intensified because there was everything to lose now, and because she didn't understand what she was trying to gain.

On the third day, at the limit of the time she had allotted herself without thinking carefully enough about what would happen when it was over, she telephoned Mattie. "Has Bliss called?"

"Of course," Mattie said evenly. "Twice, yesterday. In the morning I told him you'd gone shopping. And in the evening I told him you'd bumped into an old friend and gone out to dinner. If I'd known where you actually are, I could have rung and passed on your husband's messages. I take it you're still with the aviator?"

"Yes," Julia said. They had eaten dinners in quiet restaurants, holding hands and watching the reflections of the candles. They had filled the white bath with bubbles and soaked in it together. They had slept and woken up again, and reached out for each other. But yet not together. Julia's fingers tightened around the white shell of the receiver. She managed to repeat, "Yes. I'm with the aviator."

"Do you want to give me some instructions about what to say next time Bliss calls? I don't really want to tell him any more lies. He doesn't believe them, in any case."

"I'll call him right now," Julia said. "I'm sorry, Mattie."

"That's all right," Mattie answered before she hung up. "I hope it's worth it."

The happiness hung in shreds now, but the fragments of it were so beautiful.

Julia lifted the telephone again, intending to dial the Ladyhill number. She thought of Lily in her crib, her round face turning up and her fingers stretching out to catch her mother's hands. Julia's shoulders hunched as another kind of longing swept over her. She wanted to lift her baby, cupping her damp, hard head to keep it safe and burying her face in the folds of sweet skin. She knew that Lily would chuckle, and wind her fists in her mother's hair. In that instant Julia missed her so much that it was like an intolerable pain.

For three days, she reflected, she had been using the walls of the little white house like a screen, shutting out reality. Even closing out Lily, who mattered to her more than all the rest of the world.

Mattie had said, I hope it's worth it. And Josh had told her, don't lie for anyone but yourself and Lily.

Julia had to know the truth now. The question must be asked, whatever answer it provoked.

Very carefully, Julia replaced the receiver and walked through into the kitchen. Josh was leaning against the Formica countertop, reading a newspaper.

In a low voice Julia asked him, "What are we going to do?"

He lowered the crackling pages and looked at her. "Shall we go to the Tate and see some pictures?"

There was a summer's day outside. The sun was shining impartially on red London buses and Japanese tourists and George Tressider's shop frontage in the King's Road. It didn't penetrate into the mews house. It was a limbo, without light or shadow, and Julia longed suddenly to burst out of it. She saw Josh very clearly. His eyelids drooped protectively, the wariness much more obvious now.

"I didn't mean now, today. Today we'll do what we did yesterday, and the day before. Hide, and pretend. I want to know about next week, next year."

Adrenaline surged through her. Now that she had asked the question aloud she felt almost elated. She realized how much the waiting and hoping and straining to hear had oppressed her. She wanted to give and take equally, she thought, and not to be meek and submissive. She almost laughed aloud. What hope was there of that, even now? But she could at least ask for what she wanted, and she would do it without pride or pretense. She faced Josh squarely.

"I left Alexander and Lily behind to come to London, to

you. I don't think I should have married Alexander, and I shouldn't have had his baby, but I did do it and I can't change that now. I can change the need to have to lie to them, at least, because of you. I should have told them that I was coming here, you see, but I didn't, because I was too cowardly. I know I'm a coward. I'm trying not to be now. I came here because I love you, and I always have loved you. Right from the beginning, you know that. So I'm asking if I can come with you.'' Julia put her hand up to her face, rubbing it over her eyes as if in disbelief. ''No. I'm asking if we can come with you, Lily and me. I can't leave her behind. I'm not as bad as that, you see. If we can come with you, back to the States. Not to be married, if you don't believe in that. To live with you. To have an ordinary life.'' Julia lifted her hand and pointed at the kitchen shelves, the new white oven. ''Like these people. Because we can be happy. I know that.''

The long speech had left her breathless. The last words came out as a gasp. Josh folded the newspaper, two and then three folds, and laid it beside him. His eyes lingered on it instead of turning to Julia.

''What about Alexander?'' he asked.

''Don't ask me about Alexander.'' Julia's voice sounded harsh in her anxiety. Images jumped up in front of her again. The fire. Their wedding in Ladyhill church. Alexander's bandaged hands, Alexander holding Lily when she was a tiny baby. His work spread out on the table in the summerhouse. Sandy's face.

Julia knew that it was imperative to keep the guilt inside herself for everything that had happened. It was for her to suffer. If she let it leak out, even once, it would taint Josh and herself as surely as it had tainted all the last years. She must not let him even guess at it.

''I'll worry about Alexander,'' she whispered.

Josh began walking around the kitchen. She watched him, noticing the exact gold of his tanned skin, the tiny red tag on the back pocket of his jeans, the way his fingers clenched, the shadow cast by the V of his open-necked shirt. She felt the square, monolithic fact of her love for him, almost angry at its unshakability.

''Do you remember Montebellate?'' Josh asked.

''I've thought about it all the time since we've been here.''

Josh nodded. ''Of course. It's the same, isn't it? You were so hungry then. It was frightening. You wanted everything you hadn't had. Love, experience, the whole lot.''

"I've had experience now," Julia said sadly.

Josh smiled at her, and there was so much warmth in it that she remembered why she liked him as well as loving him. "Nothing finishes," Josh said. "Life is very economical. It recycles the same material over and over again. It's rather comforting. Don't imagine that you've seen everything because you've reached the age of twenty-three."

Julia sighed. She felt prematurely exhausted. "What are you telling me? Plain words, Josh."

"At Montebellate I told you that I can't give you what you want. I couldn't marry you, or promise to love you forever, or give you security and stability then. I still can't. I can't take you back with me because there isn't anything there. It's just a place, work, circumstances, and you expect a home. Don't you? All there is is what we have already shared, in this house." His hands, suddenly unbearably familiar, made a round shape in the air. She could have laughed, again, at the neatly fabricated completion when the truth was so ragged. "I thought you understood that, Julia."

She looked blankly at him, unable to reply.

He went on, floundering a little now. "I thought you came here to enjoy . . . what we have enjoyed. Being friends and lovers. Taking some time together because we matter to each other."

And then moving on, when it was convenient, of course. Josh was right, life did recycle the same material. Only it wasn't comforting. Julia despised the desperation in her own voice when she pleaded, "I can make us a home. It's because your mother left, because you've never had one, you don't know what it's like. We will be happy. I'll make sure we are. Josh, I promise you."

He stepped forward then, taking her by the wrist, folding her against him. His hand stroked her hair, cradling her head to his chest. She heard the vibration of his voice when he spoke again.

"I couldn't promise you, don't you see? I don't want to stay in one place, with one person. It's not my life. I couldn't make you happy. And the last thing I want is to hurt you, or see you hurt. I told you that at Montebellate too."

Julia closed her eyes. Made stupid by disappointment, it took her a moment or two to grasp what he was really telling her. There wasn't any future at all. No wonder she had had to listen until her head hurt. The few hours in the blank house were all there was. Out of her misery, she could only whisper, "Why did you come back then?"

He tilted her chin in his fingers, looking down at her, so close to her that she felt dazed.

"Because I love you, because I wanted to see you." He hesitated for a second, and then he added, "If there was going to be one person, in one place, it would be you."

Anger twisted inside Julia, anesthetizing the hurt for a moment. If. But Josh's consideration of himself came first. For the very first time, it occurred to her to wonder whether Josh was worth loving as much as she did love him.

She didn't ask herself whether she could stop, because she knew that she never had. But the brief flash of anger helped her to lift her head and to produce a smile. "Poor Josh. It must be boring, having women asking you to marry them all the time, when all you want is a few hours of fun."

She had a bitter sense of herself as one of Josh's ports of call, strung out along the line of his travels, and then wondered why the image had never occurred to her before.

"They don't ask, as it happens," Josh said.

"Only the very reckless or the very stupid ones?"

"Don't, Julia. You hurt us both."

But her anger and bitterness had already disappeared. She let her head fall forward against his shoulder again, and he held her tightly, rocking her a little in his arms. She clung to him, thinking that he was still Josh, and nothing had changed from an hour ago except her own expectations, and Josh wasn't to blame for those. He had never been less than honest.

Julia smiled crookedly and, sensing it, Josh kissed the top of her head. "I'm going to telephone Alexander," she told him. He let her go and she went into the other room, closing the door firmly.

Alexander's voice was very cold. He didn't ask her where she was or what she had been doing.

"I'll be home tomorrow afternoon," Julia said. She thought, *I'm going to take one more day, calculatedly, just like Josh would.*

"Which train?"

"There's no need to meet me. I'll get a taxi from the station."

"Lily has missed you," Alexander said abruptly.

Julia hunched her shoulders against the pang that his words gave her. "I've missed her too."

After he had hung up she waited for a moment or two, listening to the empty line. In the kitchen again she said to Josh, "Let's go to the Tate. I'd like to see some pictures today." As if nothing had happened, because nothing was going to happen. And with evident relief, Josh followed her lead.

At the gallery they wandered through the Pre-Raphaelite collection, examining the wide-eyed maidens with their swollen lips and intricate masses of hair. They reminded Julia irresistibly of Mattie trying to look suitably solemn, and she remembered Mattie's wordless disapproval. Julia jerked her head up defiantly and pretended to be studying Ophelia in her bathtub of floating blossoms. Today was today; Josh was still here. There would be more than enough time to reflect on everything else. She put her arm through his and tried to stop her fingers clawing into his arm.

"Let's have lunch in the gallery restaurant," Josh said. They sat facing each other, talking about the pictures and then about other things that they had seen and done, like any couple. Julia felt the minutes like beads on a thread, slipping under her fingers. Josh ordered a special bottle of wine, and when the waitress had poured it he held up his glass to Julia. The silence was awkward because neither of them could think of a toast.

It was only three days since the Ritz, Julia remembered, when they had drunk to understanding. The gulf between their two poles of understanding gaped between them now, and Julia still wanted to launch herself across it and twist her arms around his neck. She lifted her glass and drank half the wine instead, and the skin of her face felt taut and puffy with uncried tears.

Later, in the afternoon heat, they walked along the Embankment in the hope of a river breeze. The slow-running water made Julia think of the night in the Savoy doorway, and of walking with Alexander after their first meeting. The accumulation of memories was like lumber piled around her, too bulky to disperse. I wanted to be free, she thought. And then, *I was deceiving myself.* I wanted to belong to Josh. Am I so conventional, then, after all? The realization of how little she knew herself, coupled with her blindness in running to Josh, oppressed her more than the day's sticky heat. Her feet seemed glued to the melting sidewalk. There wasn't even the faintest breath of air blowing off the river.

"It's too hot," Josh said. "Let's go back home."

Home. For a day, then.

There was a little brick-paved courtyard behind the mews

house, overgrown with dusty ivy and decorated with leggy scarlet geraniums in clay pots. Josh brought out two white chairs, and he made iced tea and carried two glasses outside on a tray. Julia drank hers and then went to sit on the warm bricks beside him. She rested her head exhaustedly against his knee and he lifted the damp strands of her hair from her face. To Julia, the little vista of empty glasses, scattered red petals, Josh's bare feet crossed at the ankles, and the legs of the empty white chair seemed unbearably intimate. His fingers against her face were painfully gentle. We are as tender with each other, Julia thought sadly, as we would be if one of us were going to die.

They sat in silence, listening to the monotonous hum of distant traffic, aware that they were holding on to each other in a kind of desperation.

Julia wanted to plead with him, *Why? When we could make each other happy, just if you changed a word* . . . But she had asked once, and she was too proud to go back to it again.

At last, as the patch of sky overhead lost its brassy light and turned smoky-pale, Josh murmured, "Let's not go out again. Let's stay here together. I'll make us some food."

All right, Julia agreed silently. Let's bury our heads in this playhouse for the last few hours.

Josh went out briefly and came back with a delicatessen bag. He unpacked the contents, displaying steaks and the ingredients of a salad. "You didn't know I could cook, did you?"

She watched him preparing the steaks. "I don't know anything about you, Josh. I just thought I did."

He looked up at her. It was a direct, unveiled gaze that disarmed her all over again and her heart knocked uncomfortably. The impossibility of not loving him was like a vast obstacle, blocking the way to everywhere she turned.

"You know all there is to know," he told her simply. "There isn't anything else. You are the one who wants and imagines more. You are the complicated one."

Julia could find no answer to that.

They ate their meal, and they put the plates and bowls away afterward, cleaning the kitchen carefully to leave no trace of their occupation. As if we'd never existed, Julia thought. In the clean white space that was all that was left, Josh took her hand. He separated the fingers with his own and then kissed the thin skin between them. There was no possibility of resisting him. She knew that she couldn't have done it even if she had intended to. When he drew her closer to him and kissed her, she felt his momentary hesitation. She couldn't have denied her own response, and it was enough of an answer. They went up the stairs to the white bedroom together. Josh could make her forget, as he had always been able to do, even the existence of tomorrow.

A long time afterward, Julia realized that he had fallen asleep. She lay for a while listening to his breathing, and then she slid away from him. Their skin had seemed fused with heat, but it separated with a tiny sound like a faint, final kiss. Julia went and stood at the window, parting the curtains a little so that she could look out into the mews. With a slight shock of surprise she saw that it was pouring with rain. It fell in opaque sheets, and the fat drops bounced up again, silvered by the glow of the streetlamps. The noise of it drummed and gurgled, and the curtains of water closed in, cutting her off behind her pane of glass in total isolation.

Julia shivered, but the day's thundery heat still lay thickly against her bare skin, and she understood that what she felt was loneliness. It intensified as she stood there, until she could have believed that she was the only person in the world left to look at the sudden rivers sluicing over the cobbles of the mews. Josh made a small sound and stirred in his sleep.

Julia let the curtain fall again to close out the rain. She was thinking about the almost deliberate steps she had taken to create such piercing loneliness for herself, even though she had a husband and a baby, a lover, and a friend like Mattie. Her mouth twisted as she crossed the room again to the bed. Josh was deeply asleep, one arm stretched out where she had been lying, his fingers loosely curled. Silently, Julia bent down and picked up his discarded shirt. She put it on, wrapping the folds of it around her. Then she went downstairs to the kitchen and made herself some tea. She sat for a long time, staring at the white countertop and listening to the monotonous pounding of the rain.

In the morning they were still gentle with each other. They even moved too carefully around the little kitchen, as if they were afraid to bump into and bruise each other.

After breakfast Julia went upstairs and folded up the red and white polka-dot dress that she had worn to the Ritz, seemingly years ago. She put it into her suitcase with the few other things on top of it. She was just about to snap the fastenings when she sensed Josh behind her. He was leaning against the door frame and she was struck by his half-penitent, half-wary expression. He looked like a small boy who knew that he was about to get away with misbehavior. He looked sad, truthfully sad, but also relieved. He held out the big doll, her plaits flopping. There was a faint, protesting *Mama*.

"Don't forget this."

Julia put it into her bag with the other things and closed it, definitively.

Josh took her to the station in a taxi. As they walked along the platform to the train, Julia thought that there had already been too many meetings, and far too many pain-racked partings. She knew how they went and what they did to her, and the knowledge made her feel old and tired as well as hurt.

Josh found her a seat and put her suitcase in the rack overhead. They stood facing each other on the platform, watching the other travelers brushing past. Josh moved to intercept the line of her vision and took her face between his hands, forcing her to look at him instead of into the middle distance. She saw that his transitory relief had gone and there was concern, regret, and, she was sure of it, love.

Damn you, Julia thought. *I can't even take refuge in dislike. Will I have to go on loving you forever?*

"I don't want to say good-bye to you," Josh whispered.

Instead of all the things she could have said, Julia answered, "You don't have to."

"We can go on seeing each other, then, sometimes? I don't know how to let you go altogether. You know that already."

His fingers seemed to dig into her face. Julia's eyes flickered. "Josh, you know what I want. If that isn't possible because you say it isn't, I don't know which of the other choices is more painful, having something of you or nothing of you." With a jerk she broke away from him. There were red vertical marks showing on her cheeks. "I can't bear to have nothing of you, that's the answer. You know where I am, or you can find me if you try. When you want to." *When it suits you. To start up and stop again, even if it hurts.* She turned her back on him and mounted the high step into the train. When she looked around again, Josh was still watching her, motionless.

"Go now, this time. Please, Josh."

He turned stiffly and went away down the platform.

There were more long minutes before the train left. Josh stood staring at it from the shelter of the barrier. But even though he was waiting and watching, Julia didn't climb down and come running back toward him. Josh's eyes and mouth burned. He had come closer than he had ever in his life, with Julia's white, tight face in front of him, to saying *Come with me then. I'll try to be what you want.*

He knew that he loved her. But he was afraid that wasn't enough.

Doors were slamming down the length of the train. The guard bustled out and blew a whistle, and the long line of coaches began to slide away. Josh stood in his place, watching unblinkingly, until the swaying tail end of the last car had turned the corner, out of sight. Then he swung around and began to walk, too fast, almost bumping into people. He was going back to the neat white house that he hated, without knowing whether he hated it for what it stood for or because it was empty now. He would pick up his belongings and keep moving, on to somewhere else.

The train seemed to leave London behind very quickly. It gathered lubricious speed and plunged into the countryside. To Julia, staring out of her dirty window, it seemed that the lush meadows and heavy green trees were gorged and somnolent with the previous night's rain. Even the animals in the fields were too drowsy to move.

At last Julia climbed down at the local station, the only passenger to leave the train. With her suitcase in her hand she passed through the dimness of the station, with its posters of Bournemouth and Poole, and found the driver of the single waiting taxi.

She said, "Ladyhill House, please," and he had to ask her to repeat herself because her voice was too low for him to hear.

Under the bright bars of sunlight the countryside seemed to have emptied itself of all relics of life.

Julia made the taxi driver stop just short of the stone gateposts of Ladyhill. She paid him and started to walk up the driveway under the trees. Alternating bands of light and shadow swept over her face, the illusion of rapid change contrasting with the unbroken silence. She stopped again just before the curve in the drive that would reveal the house, conscious of the handle of her suitcase biting into the palm of her hand, and of the pungent rural smells of grass and manure. It was odd, she thought irrelevantly, how she was never aware of the city's smells. They were natural to her, like hard sidewalks under her feet.

Julia took a deep breath and switched off the stream of thoughts. She knew that she was putting off the moment of turning the corner. She was afraid of seeing Alexander. In the past her inborn defiance might have helped her, but it was hard to be defiant at that moment, when she despised herself.

She switched the suitcase to the other hand and trudged on. Around the elbow corner under the last bridge of shade, and there was the house. The new roof glittered rawly, but the empty windows beneath it were blinded eyes that couldn't see her. She glanced to the left, toward the long herbaceous border, at the height of its midsummer magnificence. The blue masses of delphiniums and starry white clouds of campanulas drew her hypnotically, but she made herself walk straight on toward the frowning house.

She went in through the new front door, seeing for the thousandth time the obscene black mouthprints left on the brickwork by the devouring smoke. In their own habitable wing the rooms were tidy, Lily's toys and blocks stacked neatly in their boxes beside her empty playpen. Julia knew where her husband and daughter must be. She went outside again, around to the back of the house, looking across the uncut grass under the apple trees toward the summerhouse. Alexander was there, bending over Lily, who sat on her rug at his feet. Julia went toward them, stupidly still carrying her bag, the reminder of it making her feel like a refugee.

Lily saw her first. She lifted her head and gave a crow of delight. Julia ran forward then. She dropped onto her knees and took hold of one of the fat little fists. She kissed it, and the baby's rosy cheeks, murmuring "Lily. Oh, Lily, I love you." Lily beamed and shouted "Dat!" her single, all-purpose, portmanteau word.

Slowly, stiffly, Julia let go of the baby's soft hand and stood up again. Alexander hadn't moved; their eyes met now. She saw at once how angry he was. She had futilely rehearsed something to say, mollifying and empty words, but they dried up in her mouth.

"Where have you been?" asked Alexander.

There was no point in lying, even deflecting. The truth was the only possibility. "With Joshua Flood," Julia said simply.

Alexander's fists clenched, and for an instant she thought that he was going to hit her. Instead, staring at her, he said, "But you and I are married. You are my wife, Julia."

Her own anger swelled up. Coldly, she said, "I am at least a dozen other things as well as being your wife. But you don't want to take account of those, do you?"

They looked at each other; there was a moment when either of them might have spoken, but neither of them did so.

The silence went solid between them.

It was Lily who broke it, rocking merrily against Julia's legs and shouting, "Dat" all over again. Confused by guilt and anger, Julia bent down once more. She wanted to make a kind of reparation to the baby, but anxiety made her clumsy. She opened her suitcase and took out Josh's enormous doll. Even as she held it out to Lily she recognized the inappropriateness of the gesture.

"Look, Lily. A baby for you to play with."

The doll's flaxen braids flopped forward and her staring blue eyes rolled up into her head. Lily took one horrified glance at it and her bottom lip quivered and dropped. Her face slowly crumpled and she gave a long wail of terror, bumping backward to bury her face against the security of Alexander's legs. He hoisted her against his shoulder and comforted her, and Julia was left with the doll hanging limply in her hand. She dropped it back into her suitcase and it uttered a thin, complaining squeak. "Ma-ma." Lily's face was hidden and two or three of her black curls had caught on the roughness of her father's sweater. Her screams subsided into muffled sobs. Julia wanted to reach out and stroke the curls back into place, and then to hide her own face.

Instead, she stood stock-still for another long moment, and then she turned and walked back toward the house, leaving her husband and daughter under the apple trees. That was the beginning of the end.

It took another year and a half for their marriage to founder completely, but after that day there was never a real chance for its recovery.

In the unhappy months that followed, Alexander seemed to find bottomless reserves of energy within himself. He devoted almost all of it to work and to Ladyhill, the one providing the reason for the other and both of them supplying a kind of comfort. He went everywhere he could possibly go to drum up work, and the commissions began to flow in. A low-budget film he had worked on in the year after the wedding became a sudden, surprising cult success. Alexander's theme music even crept, for one or two weeks, into the bottom of the hit parade. As his name became known and the royalties slowly mounted up, Alexander found that he had more work than he could cope with. He grimly took on more, and he worked even longer hours. The energy he had to spare was devoted to Lily, and the money was plowed into Ladyhill.

Minns and his men came back, and they were followed by

George and Felix. The decorators stalked through the empty, desecrated rooms, frowning and muttering about country house sales where suitable pieces might be picked up, and making cryptic notes for each other.

Julia trailed after them, only half-listening. George and Felix had become a team, she noticed. Their ideas sprang from their mutual enthusiasm and then bounced to and fro between them, gathering impetus like tennis balls in a hard rally. They even finished each other's sentences. They had started to look alike, too, reminding Julia of a pair of sleek pedigree cats in their gray Savile Row suits and silk foulard ties.

"This house is quite, quite beautiful," George said to her. "You know, your fire might turn out to have been a blessing after all."

Julia wanted to protest, *It wasn't my fire*, but she knew that it was, and always would be.

"I'm speaking just in terms of the house. The tragedy, of course . . ." George remembered himself and coughed discreetly. "These old families do neglect their houses," he added in a brighter voice. "Now, with the opportunity to restore this one, and to put just the right pieces into it, we shall be able to see it just as it must once have been. Quite magnificent."

"If my husband can afford Tressider Designs' ideas of magnificence," Julia said stiffly. George glanced sharply at her, raised his eyebrows a millimeter, and wisely said nothing. Out of the corner of her eye she saw Felix moving toward her, protectively. She knew that he was looking at her, but she turned her face away. He had been picking carefully at the charred remnants of some paneling, and the ashy, burned smell that he had released rose in her nostrils. She had to escape from the repellent scent of it, and from the dependent, symbiotic closeness that flaunted itself between George and Felix. She thought, with a bitterness that was no longer new, that they looked almost obscenely happy with each other.

"Excuse me," she muttered, and walked away.

Felix watched her go, his face somber.

George pursed his lips. "Dear me. What can have persuaded a man like Alexander to marry her? Other things, maybe, but marriage?"

"I know why he married her," Felix said softly. "What puzzles me more, now, is why she married him."

He had seen enough, in the course of two or three visits to Ladyhill, to divert almost all his sympathy to Julia. He had seen the way that she lived, in Alexander's frequent absences, alone except for their baby, in the dusty, reproachful shell of his house. She was lonely, and Julia had never been good at being alone. And when Alexander did come home, he was polite but withdrawn. Felix half-guessed that his remoteness was self-protective, and that Julia had hurt him badly in some way, but he also knew Julia's power of contrition and it puzzled him that if there had been a breach, her warmth hadn't succeeded in closing it long ago. Watching the two of them, he began to see another side of Alexander, and he suspected that if he himself had failed to notice it before, then Julia might also have partially over-looked it. Alexander Bliss was an upper-class Englishman.

Felix smiled faintly. In the summer of 1962 the very idea of class seemed quaint, but in Alexander the reality of it suddenly confronted him. Alexander had been reared in the traditions of dignity and conformity. He had made minor deviations, but when the time came he did what was expected of him, and he expected the same of his wife. Only his expectations were marked by a certain hardness and coldness. He had made Julia into Lady Bliss, and now he simply expected her to mother his children and supervise his house, and to help his stepmother to preside over the WI and the WRVS and the Church Wives. He seemed to make no allowances for the fact that Julia had come to him when he was a Chelsea musician, and they shared, however approximately, the common ground of the Markham Arms and the King's Road.

Felix watched Julia's drooping head as she passed outside the windows. He would have done anything possible to comfort her, but he knew that it was beyond him.

"I hope our clients' problems won't affect the restoration," George said briskly. "It's a particularly attractive job." He was looking up at the windows, and Julia had passed out of sight. "I'm sure they had moth-eaten velvet here. We could use the rose chintz, with raspberry swags and tails."

"The enthusiasm for the work is all Alexander's," Felix said, "not Julia's. I don't think anyone would blame her if she hated the sight of the place." He was afraid she did, and afraid that no acreage of chintz could change the fact. "Isn't it rather early to be thinking about curtains? The plasterwork and panel-ing alone will probably take years to restore."

Felix was finding that his interest was increasingly engaged by the architecture and inner structure of their projects, the hard aspects, while George enthused over the richness of soft upholstery and carpets. It was yet another wholly satisfactory aspect of their partnership.

George smiled at him. "You know I like to plan ahead."

They returned to their work.

Julia walked slowly, feeling the sun on her face, frowning a little as if the warmth puzzled her. Lily was having her nap, and for a moment she couldn't remember whether Alexander happened to be away or at home. The recollection came back to her a second later. Of course he was working. In the summerhouse, as he always did in warm weather. Encouraged by the sun, or by stepping outside the dimness of the house, she thought she would walk around and ask him if he would like some coffee.

Alexander was lost in what he was doing. A phrase repeated itself in his head, but the precise cadence that he wanted eluded him, like a fish sliding away under the thick skin of river water. He had had a small upright piano installed in the summerhouse and he sat motionless, hunched over the keyboard, his fingers hanging from the keys.

Then Julia's shadow fell diagonally across his hands and he looked up in surprise, his eyes blank for an instant.

"It's me," she said. He heard the note of bitterness in her voice. It crept into everything with monotonous frequency. As if to remind him, she added, "I live here, remember? I came to ask you if you'd like some coffee. That's all."

Julia might have said something different. It might have been, Can I come and sit with you? It's so light and bright out here after being inside, and Felix and George made me feel miserable.

Alexander might have said, I'd like some coffee. Stay out here and have yours with me.

But with the tone of Julia's voice in his head, and her dark, accusing face looking down at him, he answered curtly. "I'll have some later. I want to finish this piece."

Julia turned on her heel and walked back through the long grass.

They were only tiny incidents, each of them, but they punctuated the days and weeks, and every one drove the wedge deeper between them. As she headed unseeingly for the house, Julia thought that it was already too late. Neither of them knew how to go back and take up the little painstaking stitches that would repair the damage. There had been no big, tempestuous battles. It would have been better if there had, because those would have been easier to reconcile. Rather, there was the slow attrition of coldness and misunderstanding.

Julia reached the wall of shadow cast by the house. It seemed to drop over her face like a veil. Her eyes stung, but she blinked and stared ahead. There wasn't even anything to cry for, after all.

Alexander hadn't bent his head to his work again. Instead, he watched Julia going away, with part of himself still seeing and admiring her lean height and the economy of her movements. The rest of his consciousness went on gnawing at the familiar questions; what had happened to the girl he had married, and why this different Julia, who still looked poignantly the same, couldn't be happy with the here and now. If Julia could be happy, he thought, then he would be happy too. Alexander believed that he understood her horror of the fire, and he was also sure that there was no blame or forgiveness to be bestowed anywhere. What had happened had happened, and all that was needed was work to put the damage right.

What was much less fathomable was the fact that before the fire, long before, at the very beginning, he had brought Julia to Ladyhill. She had surely understood what it meant, and what she would be undertaking, when she had agreed to marry him. Yet now bewilderment, impatience, and boredom seemed to fight for dominance in her, and Alexander felt himself stiffening in defense of the house he loved and the lives that belonged in it.

It would be so easy for them to be happy and comfortable here, the three of them. There should be a son, too, for Ladyhill. Alexander wasn't ashamed of his longing for that. And another girl, exactly like Lily. The shadows of the north wall of the house swallowed Julia up, and Alexander reflected that there wasn't likely to be a son or a daughter because they didn't sleep together anymore, even though they shared the same bed. She had slept with Josh Flood, her comic-book hero, of course. Alexander's anger at that had faded, but a different, colder, less focused resentment had replaced it.

Alexander picked up his pencil and twisted it in his fingers.

He couldn't make Julia want what he wanted, of course. He was becoming increasingly aware that no one could make Julia do anything. In that, she was like China.

And China had left Ladyhill. A weary sense of inevitability settled around Alexander. As if to dispel it, he stared fiercely at the house. The flames had devoured the ancient patch of yellow lichen on the roof. When he was a child, he had thought that the outline of the growth looked like a man's profile. The new roof was bare, the color of it not even softened yet by the weather.

But the existence of it was a minor triumph. It protected the house beneath it. And the walls were intact. As a little boy he used to climb the apple trees and follow with his eyes the patterns made by the old bricks. The same patterns were still there, and the deep crack in one of the stone lintels, and the red rust biting into an iron brace whose bolts had long ago fused to the metal itself. That much of the house had withstood the fire, and he would see that the rest was restored.

There was so much still to do.

The thought was like a goad. Alexander hunched his shoulders over the keyboard again. He brought his forefinger down on middle C, holding the note so that it reverberated in the humming quiet, and then died away.

As soon as she walked into the house Julia heard that Lily was crying. She often woke up irritable after her midday sleep. Julia went upstairs and found her standing up in her crib, gripping the bars with her fists and her face red and wet and accusing. When Lily saw her she stopped crying for a second, then started again, twice as loudly. Julia went to her and picked her up. Lily's legs and arms were stiff, and she wouldn't yield as Julia carried her over to the window and tried to soothe her.

"Shh, see the birds? You've woken them up. Shh, there's my girl. Look, can you see Felix?"

Felix and George were strolling between the wings of the house. George was wearing a panama hat and carrying a silver-knobbed cane. *How bloody affected,* Julia thought. Lily's screams swelled in volume. Suddenly, standing there by the window, Julia felt her like a dead weight in her arms. The paved courtyard below shimmered in the sun, and beyond it the grass rippled. Empty, emptiness everywhere except for Felix and George in the foreground, their arms and legs moving like clockwork figures.

Despair gripped Julia like an iron fist.

Lily's screaming was intolerable.

She dropped the baby awkwardly back into her crib and ran out of the room. Out of the room, down the stairs and outside, without any sense of where she was going except that she must escape.

It only increased her claustrophobia when she stopped running at last, panting for breath, to realize that she had no idea where to escape to.

George and Felix went back to London, to the neat shell of Tressider Designs, taking their notes and their sketches and measurements with them. Alexander went to London and then to the States, and Julia stayed at Ladyhill with Lily. Autumn came, and the borders silted up with the russet and gold patchwork of dead leaves. Julia scraped halfheartedly at them with a wire rake while Lily stumped to and fro in her boots, picking up fistfuls of leaves and letting them fly. They whirled around her head like huge brown moths.

It grew cold, and the first frost came early. At once the landscape took on a dead, closed-up aspect. Looking out at it, Julia said aloud, "I hate this place." She thought of Josh, gleefully waiting for the first fall of snow, like a boy with a new toboggan. He had disappeared just as effectively as he had always been able to, but he was still with her. She had the sense of him wherever she looked, somewhere just beyond the line of her vision.

Alexander came back, but his presence didn't make much difference. They were like strangers now.

In the middle of December, Julia went Christmas shopping. She left Lily with Faye and drove the forty miles to the big town in Alexander's red mini. She made the circuit of the shops, buying toys for Lily and a dashing plum-colored silk dressing gown for Alexander and a Victorian jardiniere for Faye, all the time with a numb sense of isolation from the bustle and glitter of the shops. She felt as if she were standing a little way off, watching her own preparations unbelievingly, like absurd antics. There was a Salvation Army band playing outside one of the stores, but the Christmas music seemed to come from a long way off, filtering through layers of separation that muffled and deadened it. Julia shook her head from side to side, but the misery didn't lift. She went back to the car, tossed the bags of shopping in around the jardiniere, and drove back to Ladyhill. When the bare fingers of the trees along the drive laced over her head, trapping her, Julia found that she was shuddering. When she rounded the corner, the low winter sun behind her was shining into the windows of the house, and it seemed for a fraction of a second that its eyes blazed with flame again. Julia heard the greedy crackle and her throat filled with the acrid taste of smoke. She braked violently and sprang out of the car. Running toward the house, she saw that the windows were reflecting the setting sun, nothing more.

Alexander and Lily were playing together. They looked up as she stumbled into the room. Their faces were alike and their calm expressions mirrored each other.

"Did you get your shopping?" Alexander asked politely.

Julia was breathless from running and her heart was thumping, but she answered with the same politeness. "Yes, thanks. I think I got everything I wanted. It wasn't too crowded."

"Good."

Civility was a weapon, too, the way Alexander used it. They used all the weapons against each other now that they were enemies, Julia thought, except passion. There was too much heat in passion.

She carried her parcels upstairs, but she felt too sad to put them away. She sat down on the wide bed instead, and picked up the telephone from the bedside table. She dialed Mattie's number and listened to the ringing tone, on and on, imagining the small rooms and the view over the Bloomsbury street. Mattie didn't answer. Julia replaced the receiver. Her head was heavy with the weight of tears, but she didn't cry. Instead, she went back downstairs.

She asked Lily, "What shall I make you for tea?"

"Egg," Lily answered stoutly, and Julia smiled at her.

That night Julia had a nightmare of the fire.

She dreamed that the flames had engulfed Lily and Alexander and Flowers and everyone else she cared for, and that as she ran to save herself Sandy pursued her, calling her name out of a mouth that melted and flowed like lava.

Julia didn't scream. Her eyes opened and she stared silently into the darkness. When the trembling had subsided, she sat up. She was wet with sweat, and the cold air struck like ice. Alexander was asleep, turned away from her with his shoulder hunched. His breathing seemed very even. She knew that even if she did disturb him, he would tell her, "The fire's over. You must forget it."

Looking down at him, Julia remembered the night in the white house when she had watched Josh sleeping. She wondered now, as she had often done in the last weeks, if she would feel the loneliness less sharply when she really was alone. As the sweat of terror dried between her shoulder blades, she thought that nothing could hurt more than the parody of closeness that she and Alexander made each other live in at Ladyhill. Carefully, so as not to wake him, she lay down again, but she didn't go to sleep before Lily made her first morning summons from her bed in the next room.

Christmas came closer. On the day before Christmas Eve, Alexander brought home the tree. Julia and Lily met him in the wide hallway among the seemingly permanent detritus left by the builders. Alexander swung the tree off his shoulder and stood it upright for them to admire.

"But isn't it too big?" Julia asked, puzzled. The huge specimen would fill half of their little sitting room.

"I thought," Alexander announced, "that we should put the tree back in the drawing room this year."

Lifting the tree again, and without looking at her, he crossed to the drawing room door and opened it with a flourish. With Lily tugging at her hand and shouting, "Yes, Daddy, yes, Daddy," Julia followed him. The empty room, freshly plastered, seemed a huge, gaunt shell. There was no furniture and on the new, bare floorboards a few wood shavings uncurled. Alexander went across and balanced the tree in its old place, in front of the window, where the ancient velvet curtains had fed the candle flames so generously.

Julia whispered, "No. Not in here. Why not in the little room?"

The fresh, festive scent of the pine needles threatened to choke her, and she could smell melting wax, too, and see the merry points of light twinkling between the thick green branches.

Alexander almost threw the tree aside. He came across the room and Julia shrank a little, drawing Lily's fist, clenched in hers, closer to her side. As if she or Lily could protect each other against him. Her grip must have hurt because Lily whimpered, complaining.

Alexander didn't touch either of them, of course. He came so close that Julia could see a tiny pulse beating at the corner of his eye. She also thought that she could see anger and disappointment half-masked by his anger, but she was angry and very afraid herself, and somehow she found a way to ignore whatever Alexander might feel.

"I think we should have the Christmas tree in this room, where it belongs," Alexander repeated. They were confronting each other now. Julia knew with cold, exhausted certainty that the moment had come. She looked around the room and recognized, with faint surprise, that even though the fire had started here, no visible trace of it remained. The leading in the windows that had melted, and the shattered glass, had been replaced, and the new floorboards of seasoned oak butted together so snugly that there were none of the scything drafts that had characterized the old room. The old oak paneling and the intricate plasterwork of the ceiling had been entirely demolished, and not even George and Felix were proposing to try and copy them afresh. In their place was smooth, as yet unpainted plaster. The smoke-blackened Tudor roses of the carved stone fire surround had been cleaned, and the hearth needed only a new log fire. The room looked just what it was, a big, fresh, airy space, waiting to be lived in again.

But Julia didn't believe that it was waiting for her. It was Alexander's room. She had even seen him run the tips of his fingers over the smooth joints in the floor, as if he were stroking living flesh. It was Alexander's house, and his life enclosed within it, and she was bitterly convinced that she didn't belong in either. She didn't know, after so long, if she hated Ladyhill because she and Alexander had failed in it together, or whether it was because of the destruction and renewal of Ladyhill that they had come to this, their final point, tonight. All she did know was that they had no point of contact left except Lily. Lily, oddly quiet, with her fist still folded in her mother's. And that Christmas here was unthinkable, impossible. She couldn't stay here any longer.

Julia bent her head, looking down at Lily's dark curls and the vulnerable, childish line of her parting drawn through them. She thought what it would mean to Lily and she felt her heart contract.

"I can't," Julia said.

Stubbornly, Alexander took her literally. His voice was brusque. "Julia. The fire was three years ago. We've mourned enough for it, and what happened. It's time for Ladyhill to come alive again."

In this very room, Julia remembered, she had said, *Lots of parties. Crowds of people.* At the beginning, when she had made herself believe that she would love Alexander Bliss.

Numbly, she shook her head. "I said I can't. Don't you understand what I'm saying?"

Even now, she saw, he didn't. All he was thinking about was Ladyhill, and bringing it to life once more.

Julia turned away. Her hand tightened on Lily's and then she stooped down and hoisted the child into her arms. Holding her with her head tucked under her chin, Julia ran out of the room and up the bare wooden skeleton of the stairs.

First, in Lily's room, Julia scooped her clothes out of the white-painted chest of drawers. She flung the little woolen sweaters and kilts into a suitcase. Lily sat on the edge of her bed, watching her mother with wide-open eyes. Pausing and looking desperately around her, Julia saw all the safe, cozy accretions of her daughter's life lining the room. She swept an armful of toys off a shelf and into the suitcase, then lifted Lily's precious toy dog off her pillow.

"Not doggy," Lily said accusingly.

Julia understood that Lily thought her possessions were going somewhere without her. It was as if she already regarded herself as inseparable from Ladyhill. Her father's child.

"It's all right, darling. You're coming with doggy and me. We're going to have a nice time."

Stupid words, an empty promise.

Julia went into the next room and piled haphazard armfuls of her own clothes into another holdall. At the bottom of the wardrobe she saw the presents she had bought for Lily's Christmas stocking. With cold hands she picked them up and put them on top of the clothes. Then she closed the bags and lifted Lily in one arm. As she went down the stairs again, the two heavy cases gripped in one hand, the edges banged against her legs and rattled the banisters.

Alexander must have heard the noise. He came out into the echoing hallway, a screwdriver hanging in his fingers. He had bought fairy lights for the tree, and he had been wiring them up. Julia almost fell down the last few stairs.

"What are you doing?"

Julia thought she had seen Alexander angry before. But now he was incandescent with it. It was impossible to believe that he had ever seemed cold, or had ever been the mild, sardonic Bliss that she had married. His face was burning, twisted with anger. "I can't stay here any longer," Julia managed to say. "We make each other too unhappy."

"Unhappy?" The scorn in his voice bit into her. "What does our relative happiness matter? Have you thought about Lily? Or about everything we're trying to do here?"

The two suitcases slid out of Julia's grasp and banged to the floor, but she managed to hold on to Lily. She tightened her arms protectively around her again.

"Lily will be safe with me. And as for here, I don't care about that. I hate Ladyhill. I hate everything about it. Most of all, I hate it because it doesn't matter, and you make it matter so much. It's only a thing, isn't it? Only a house. Bricks and stones and pieces of wood." The words, at last, came pouring out of her. Her face was wet and her tongue was too big for her mouth. "You love it more than me," she said, almost inaudibly.

"Where are you going?" Alexander demanded.

"I don't know. It doesn't matter. To London, I suppose."

He came closer. One hand gripped her elbow, then wrenched it so that she almost cried out.

"You are a fucking stupid, selfish little bitch."

Of all the things that had happened, all the things that they had said to each other, that was oddly the most shocking and disturbing. Alexander never swore. Suddenly, without warning, Lily gave a long wail of dismay.

"It's all right, darling." Julia tried to reassure her. The same empty words. Trembling, she bent down to retrieve her suitcases, and at the same moment Alexander pulled Lily out of her arms.

"I can't stop you going. But you won't take Lily with you."

Lily's head turned. She looked at Alexander, then back at Julia. What she saw must have terrified her. Her face contorted with fright and she began to scream.

"Mummy. Mummy, here."

She writhed and struggled in Alexander's grasp, stretching her hands out to Julia. Her mother's daughter.

Alexander's face went stiff. He was older in that instant, almost an old man. He held on to Lily for another second while her screams tore into both of them and then, so painfully that it dug deep lines beside his mouth, he handed her back to Julia. Lily buried her face at once against her mother's neck. Even as Julia hugged her, Alexander leaned forward. He rested his cheek against the back of Lily's head, closing his eyes, and then he straightened up again.

"I'll bring her back again, you know," he said dully. "Her home is here, at Ladyhill. But once you go, you don't come back."

It wasn't a threat. It seemed more a statement of the truth that they both recognized. To Alexander, the words rang with a dull familiarity.

"I don't want to come back." Somehow Julia picked up the luggage again, and she struggled to the front door.

It was very cold outside. Over her head the sky was pearl-colored, and in the west the sun floated like an angry red eye in a pink sea.

Alexander's car was parked on the gravel between the dark yew trees. Hastily, afraid that he would follow and stop them, Julia bundled Lily into the backseat. She wedged her in with the suitcases and then clambered into the driver's seat. Alexander always left the keys in the ignition. As the car swung away, Julia realized, with a touch of panic, that she didn't even know the way to get to London. She had been driving for only a few months, no farther than to the nearby towns, for shopping. When they were together, Alexander always drove.

She felt even colder with the recognition of how dependent on him she had become.

I'll have to learn to be independent again, won't I?

"Tell you what, Lily," she said brightly. "We'll drive to the station and catch the London train. That'll be fun, won't it?"

"Ooo, train." Lily beamed.

As they turned the corner in the driveway Julia knew that the windows of the house would be reflecting the blaze of the setting sun again. But she didn't look back to see.

Alexander listened until he couldn't hear the mini any longer. Then, aloud, he said, "I do love you."

It was too late to say it now, of course. Alexander knew that it was his failing, to leave the most important assurances until too late. He threw the screwdriver down, and it rolled away across the floor. As he walked back into the drawing room he remembered why the earlier words had seemed familiar. His father had said exactly the same thing to China, at the end of one of their chilly battles. "Once you go, you don't come back."

He must have been eight or so, he thought, because he had just come home from prep school for the summer holidays. He had listened, frozen, outside the door. The curious thing was that he couldn't remember now whether China ever had come back to Ladyhill. After that, all he could remember was the fun of staying at her flat in town, and how he had imagined that his father's house missed her.

Alexander looked across the drawing room. At the far end, under the propped-up tree in a brilliant, coiled snake, the fairy lights twinkled at him.

Julia parked the car neatly in the station yard. She gave the keys to the station master, telling him that Alexander would collect them, and led Lily across to the ticket window. It was then she realized that in her haste she had come without her checkbook. But she had enough money with her for a ticket to London, and a taxi to Mattie's. Once she had reached Mattie, then she could stop and think.

The train was a slow one, and it was packed with Christmas travelers. Wrapped presents protruded from their bags, and a man in the corner of the compartment brought in a miniature fir tree and stowed in on the luggage rack. Lily sat on Julia's lap. She was cheerful and content at first, but as the train crawled on toward London she became irritable, then hungry. Julia had brought no food with her, and there was no dining car on the train. An old woman sitting opposite offered her an apple, and Lily devoured it. At Reading, Julia jumped off the train and bought some milk from the platform food stand. It was after nine o'clock when they reached Paddington, tired and stiff and hungry. Lily hung in Julia's arms, her arms clasped around her neck. They waited a long time for a taxi.

"We'll soon be at Mattie's now," Julia murmured. "Then you can have a nice hot drink and a big sleep."

They reached the head of the line at last and their taxi threaded through the evening traffic, past the avenues of glittering shops. Julia looked at the people and the lights, and sighed with a sense of homecoming.

When they reached Mattie's street she jumped out of the taxi and stood on the black and white tiles in front of the dairy with her finger on Mattie's doorbell. She stood for a long moment, waiting and then ringing again, and it was only then that she began to be afraid. She stepped back and looked up at the windows.

They were all dark.

Mattie was out. Julia knew that she wasn't in a show, but of course Mattie would be out anyway. It was Christmas. As soon as she had accepted the obvious, Julia wondered at her own stupidity. She had been concentrating so hard on reaching Mattie that she hadn't even taken the time to telephone. Julia felt, suddenly, that her last support had been swept away. She had just about enough money in her purse to meet the figure on the taxi meter, and Lily's round white face was staring at her from the backseat. They were on their own, in London. It was Christmas, and they had no money. Suddenly, it didn't feel like home at all. Unwelcome, unbidden, the memory of the Savoy doorway came back to Julia. The smell, and the shuffling figures passing up and down in the night's anonymity.

"I'm afraid my friend seems to be out," she said.

"Where to then, miss?" the driver asked, not unkindly.

Julia took a deep breath, and then she rattled off the Eaton Square address. She wouldn't telephone there either. If Felix wasn't at home, well, she would worry about it when they arrived.

When they reached the square she counted off the house

numbers, anxiously, as they rattled past them. And then she saw that the tall drawing room windows of the right house were brightly lit behind the elegant first floor balcony.

"Thank God for that," she muttered, and as the cab pulled up again, "Could you just wait?" She hoisted Lily into her arms and ran into the house and up the wide stairs. George Tressider's door was opened by a man who looked like a butler.

Julia blinked. "I'm looking for Felix. Is he at home?"

The man was suitably imperturbable. "Of course, madam. If you would follow me."

Lily began to cry. Along the thickly carpeted corridor, Julia heard music and a babble of voices. They followed the butler toward the noise. He paused, and then flung open the double doors in front of them.

Julia saw a crowd of people. There were cocktail dresses and quite a lot of serious jewels, and men in dark suits or dinner jackets. There were oval silver dishes of complicated canapés, a white and silver Christmas tree, and, right in front of her, George himself in a bottle-green velvet dinner jacket and matching bow tie. George and Felix were giving a Christmas party.

"Julia. This is a nice surprise," George said.

And in the warm, scented room Julia knew that she was grubby and crumpled from the train, that she was white-faced and wild-haired, and that the crying child in her arms was exhausted and bewildered. Everyone in the room seemed to be staring at them, wondering at their bad taste in materializing here and now.

"It's a surprise, anyhow," Julia answered. Her voice was wobbly but bright. And then she saw Felix. He came out of the crowd and kissed her on both cheeks, as if he had been expecting her all evening.

"I expect Lily would like something first, wouldn't she?" he murmured. And he led them away into the kitchen. It was empty except for a maid in a black dress. When she had gone out with another tray of food, Felix asked gently, "What's happened?"

Looking straight at him over Lily's black head, Julia answered, "I've made a mess of everything. I've done everything wrong, and I know what's happened is my fault. I don't want to do any more wrong, that's all. I've left Alexander, because all we can do is hurt each other." It was then that her face crumpled. "I've got a taxi downstairs and I haven't even got enough money to pay it off. And it's your party. I'm sorry, Felix."

To her amazement, and relief, and gratitude, Felix laughed.

"I can, at least, pay the taxi for you." In the doorway, he turned back to her. "Do you remember what I said after Lily was born?"

She nodded slowly.

"I said that if you needed me you would know where to find me."

"Yes."

"Well." He smiled at her. "I'm glad you found me. Party or not."

"Thank you, Felix."

When he had gone, Julia lowered Lily on to a spindly scarlet stool. Then she felt her way around the immaculate kitchen, between the bottles of champagne, finding a saucepan and a pint of milk and a clean teatowel. With the teatowel she wiped the train dirt and the tears off Lily's cheeks and kissed her.

"There," she said. "We'll be all right. Because we've got friends, you see. We're lucky. Very, very lucky."

When Felix and the maid came back, simultaneously, they found Julia sipping at a mug of hot milk and Lily fast asleep with her head against her mother's shoulder.

"She was so tired," Julia said softly, "she couldn't even stay awake long enough to drink her milk."

SEVENTEEN

It was even darker inside the flat than at the bottom of the basement stairwell outside. The three of them bumped against Lily's stroller and peered ahead into the gloom.

"There must be a light switch somewhere," Felix muttered. A second later he found it, and they blinked in the light of the bare overhead bulb.

"Power's still on, that's good," Felix said.

They were in a small, irregularly shaped hallway with four closed doors leading off it. The walls were painted an uncompromising shade of dark, shiny green. Julia marched forward and threw the doors open, one after another. They revealed a medium-sized room and a smaller one, both with grime-coated windows

looking into the well of the building. They were empty except
for some crumpled newspapers on the floor. On the other side
there was a bathroom with an Ascot water heater and a deep,
old-fashioned bath stained blue-green in runnels beneath the
brass taps. And next to the bathroom was a surprisingly large,
almost square room with two windows looking on to the front
basement area. The street railings were visible through the top
half, and the legs and feet of passersby beyond the railings. The
room was as empty as the others, but it was dominated by a
thirties deco fireplace in tile and polished metal.

Through another door at the opposite side of the room Julia
discovered a cupboard of a kitchen.

She turned in the kitchen doorway and smiled at Felix and
Mattie, who were hovering on either side of the monstrous
fireplace. "It's perfect," she said. "We'll take it, of course.
What do you think, Lily?"

Lily scrambled out of her stroller and wiped her hands along
the tiled hearth. She held them up again, the palms black.

"Dirty," she announced superfluously.

"That doesn't matter," Julia told her. "I can soon clean it
up, can't I? I must start doing things for myself now. If Lily and
I are going to survive, I must, mustn't I? This seems a good
place to start. Here and now." Her gesture took in the room, and
the hallway beyond it, and the other rooms under their layers of
dust.

The necessity not only to survive, but to do so alone,
without Alexander, without even Mattie and Felix, had become
Julia's obsession. She had brought Lily here, after the confusion
of the days in Eaton Square and then Mattie's Bloomsbury flat,
and she determined that somehow, whatever it cost, she would
make a proper life for her. She looked down at Lily. She was
rolling her stroller to and fro, crooning to her doll ensconced in
her own place. Within herself, Julia didn't doubt that they could,
and would, survive. But she wanted more than that bare achievement. She wanted success, and part of that was to make Lily as
happy and comfortable as she would have been if she had stayed
at Ladyhill.

It was important that Alexander should recognize that she
could do it.

Julia wanted to make a success of the future for herself and
Lily more fervently than she had ever coveted the old freedom.
She wanted it so much that she shivered, and her teeth chattered.
"That's settled then." Felix was suddenly brisk. "I've got to

go. You can sign the lease on Friday, and take possession as soon as you've signed. Rent six pounds ten a week, unfurnished, as I told you. A bargain at the price, and no key money."

"I know," Julia murmured. "Thanks, Felix."

He kissed them both, and went.

"C'mon, let's go home now. We can come back on the weekend with the floorcloths and Vim."

"Mattie, you don't have to spend your days off doing the scrubbing here. We can move into one room easily enough, and I'll clean up bit by bit."

Mattie turned around, squinting at Julia through the cigarette smoke. "Don't be so bloody stupid," she said. It was an order that didn't allow contradiction.

Outside, in the raw January chill that was being whipped by a wind laden with city grit, Julia buckled Lily back into her stroller and prepared to walk. The new flat, home, she reminded herself, was at the bottom of a gloomy red-brick building to the north of Oxford Street. It lay exactly midway between the old flat in the square and Mattie's Bloomsbury retreat. The geographical symmetry gave Julia a secure sense of place; Bloomsbury was well within walking distance, although a brisk walk. But without hesitation Mattie waved for a cab.

As she unbuckled Lily again and wrestled with the folding stroller, Julia wondered whether Mattie had also noticed the way that their separate decisions marked the difference between them. She supposed that Mattie, who had lately grown used to the studio sending a car and a driver to take her to work, took taxis without thinking about it. Whereas for herself, taxis were just one of the luxuries that were no longer affordable.

Julia climbed in beside Mattie and settled Lily on her lap.

That didn't matter, she told herself. So long as she recognized and avoided what she couldn't afford. Walking never hurt anyone.

Rain spattered against the cab window. Julia leaned back, her arms around Lily, and sighed with relief. They had a home. The second urgent objective had been gained. The first had been to find a job, and George Tressider had provided that, after Felix's coercion.

Julia's solicitors had warned her that unless she had a permanent source of income and somewhere secure for the two of them to live, the chances were that Alexander would be able to win custody of Lily. Equally, Alexander's solicitors had advised him that Julia was Lily's mother, and that the courts preferred children of divorced parents to remain with the mother.

Unless, of course, she should happen to be homeless, feck-less, or otherwise provably unfit.

Julia and Alexander had talked on the telephone. To Julia, perched on Mattie's bed or eyeing her own puffy face in the gilt mirror over George's telephone table, the conversations had been almost unbearably painful.

"I can't come back to Ladyhill," she had said.

"I'm not asking you to," Alexander responded stiffly. "I told you that before you left. It's Lily I want. I'm prepared to take you to court for her custody."

"Alexander, don't do that," Julia had whispered. "It'll cost all the money you can raise, and you won't win. I'll see you don't win. Use the money for your beloved Ladyhill. Don't waste it." She wondered as she spoke, *How can we be saying these terrible things to each other?* She could see Alexander clearly, sitting at the little bureau, the shell of Ladyhill enclosing him. She said, "I don't want to steal Lily from you. We can make an agreement. She can come to you, stay at Ladyhill whenever you want her to. You're her father. But her home must be with me. There must never be any question of that."

I can't give her away, even to you. My mother gave me away. How could I do the same to Lily?

At last, reluctantly, Alexander had agreed.

"Very well. But I want a legal and binding agreement made as to the amount of time she will spend with me at Ladyhill. I expect it to be at least one third of every year, more if Lily herself wishes it. I don't want anything to be subject to your whims. I don't trust you, Julia."

Why should you? Julia thought. *I could have trusted you, but I didn't.*

Alexander was still talking, using his new, lawyerlike expressions. "If you agree to my access requirements, I will pay you for her maintenance during the rest of the year."

"I don't want your money."

"I don't give a fuck what you want. The money is for Lily."

Alexander's voice was cold, but Julia knew how hurt he was.

"All right," she said sadly. "All right. For Lily."

The settlement hadn't been completed yet. Julia knew that even her pride was misplaced. She would need whatever Alexander offered her, to feed and clothe Lily. George was not a generous payer.

As the taxi jolted through the streets and she hung on to Lily's Fruit-Gum-sticky fingers, Julia was thinking about her own mother. In the last months her imaginings of her had changed. She had stopped dreaming of her patrician forebears and of the series of romantic misunderstandings that might have forced her mother to part with her. Now Julia imagined that her mother might have been very young and vulnerable, and alone in the world. Her arms tightened around Lily until the child wriggled and turned around to pat her face. Julia felt the links, stretching backward, drawing her closer to the unknown woman. As she always did, whenever she thought of her, she wondered where she was and if she ever thought of the daughter she had lost.

Mattie looked sideways at her. "Tell you what. Why don't we go out and have a meal tonight? Like old times."

"It can't be like old times. There's Lily."

Julia's retort was sharper than it might have been. But in the week that she had been staying with Mattie, she had felt the difference. Mattie was playing the central role in a film called *Girl at the Window*. It was a big screen part for her, and it promised to bring her some real fame. The theater was what mattered, but it was still a very small world, Mattie reasoned. The film itself was a glossy, contemporary romp, and Mattie affected to disparage it. But in reality she was as committed to her work as she had been since the days with John Douglas, and she was putting real effort into investing the wide-eyed dolly of the director's vision with some genuine emotional force. She worked long hours, and when she did come home she was exhausted but still vibrating with the day's takes. Or else she stayed out, going to the newest clubs and laughing and drinking, and stumbling home when Julia had been asleep for hours.

At night, when Lily had fallen asleep in her makeshift bed, Julia read furiously, history and poetry as well as fiction, relishing the escape and the stimulation that it gave her.

But Mattie's casual mention of old times gave her a sudden, sharp pang of regret.

"I hadn't forgotten Lily," Mattie said. "There's a kid who lives next door, over the baker's. She must be fifteen or so. We could offer her ten bob to come and baby-sit, and you and I could go for a kebab at the Blue Dolphin."

Not the Rocket or even Markham Square, Julia thought. *But tempting enough*.

"Okay." She grinned. "Friday we take possession of the

new flat. Monday I start work full-time again for Tressider Designs. Let's celebrate.''

"That's my girl.''

The teenage neighbor agreed to come and baby-sit. Julia put Lily to bed and Mattie read her a story, with the full range of funny faces and voices that Lily loved. She roared with laughter and clapped her hands, demanding, "More!''

"Tomorrow,'' Mattie said firmly. The small rooms were very crowded with the three of them there. Mattie and Julia squeezed into the bathroom to make up their faces while Lily dropped off to sleep. Mattie stuck on two layers of false eyelashes, applying them in tiny clumps with a practiced hand, then fluttered them at Julia. They made her eyes look enormous under her thick bangs. Suddenly, in the cramped space, Julia realized that Mattie seemed just a little bit larger than life. As if there were really such a commodity as star quality.

"You look fantastic,'' she murmured.

"You don't look too bad yourself.''

"Me? I'm a mother and an ex-wife. I'm twenty-four. I feel as old as Methuselah.''

"Well, I'm twenty-five. For God's sake, let's go and get a few drinks before we're confined to our wheelchairs.''

But although they set out in determinedly high spirits, the evening wasn't a great success.

They went to a pub first. In the beery, agreeably raffish atmosphere Julia tried to work out how long it was since she had last perched on a barstool with Mattie, and was disconcerted that she couldn't even remember.

Mattie was wearing her new boots in shiny, chestnut-brown leather. She crossed her legs, showing her thighs in patterned tights, and lit a French cigarette. She began a story about her co-star in *Girl at the Window*. He was an electrically handsome ex-bricklayer from South London, whose first film, in which he played an electrically handsome maverick photographer from East London, had made him famous.

"There was a poll in one of the film mags. Apparently more people knew Drake's name than Harold Macmillan's.'' Mattie rolled her eyes.

"What's he like?''

"Macmillan? Oh, Drake. As thick as this.'' And she rapped her knuckles on the bar. "Anyway, they'd drawn this chalk line for him to walk along . . .''

Julia had seen the two men, or boys, perhaps. They were

wearing flared jeans and suede jackets, and they had been watching the two of them, or Mattie at least, since she had come in. Men always looked at Mattie. Julia had been aware of that for almost fourteen years. Now, out of the corner of her eye, she saw them shouldering their way across the bar.

"Why don't you two chicks let us buy you a drink?" one of them asked.

Julia saw that they weren't bad-looking. She had an instant of feeling almost flattered, a forgotten sensation, and a brief memory of the days before Alexander, before Ladyhill, when she and Mattie had cut a reckless swathe through the parties and the jazz clubs.

And then, through her rose-pink reverie, she heard Mattie say coldly, "Why don't you two pricks just piss off?" It was so far from repartee that Julia just stared. They recoiled, trying to laugh, one of them mumbling, "Aw, there's no need to be like that . . ."

Mattie drained her glass of gin and stubbed out her cigarette. "Let's go," she said.

Julia had no choice but to follow her.

One of the men called after Mattie, "Here, I know you, don't I? Snooty cow."

Outside, Mattie began walking, too fast, westward, toward Goodge Street and the Greek restaurant. There were bright red spots showing on her cheekbones.

"Why did you do that?" Julia panted, trying to keep up. "You could have said no without being rude."

Mattie stopped and swung around to face her. "I don't like being picked up. I don't like being gaped at, and treated like an object." Julia was going to say, *You're in the wrong business if you mind being looked at,* but she bit her tongue. "Every man, every bloody one of them, wants to pull my tits and get my pants off. I deal with it all day, and some days I deal with it less well than others, that's all. Oh, bloody hell. Half the time I think I get the jobs I do only because of my tits. Just like back at the Showbox." Mattie shrugged. "Men are fuckers. From my dad to Tony Drake, all of them. Or most of them, anyway. With your luck, you managed to marry one of the few who aren't, and for some inexplicable reason you've buggered off and left him. Well. It's none of my business. Come on, let's get to the place. I need another drink."

Mattie was right, it wasn't any of her business, Julia thought.

But the words had struck home. Without proper consideration, she demanded, "Don't you think you drink too much?"

Mattie's mouth opened, showing her teeth and tongue. "And don't you think you spend too much time feeling sorry for yourself?"

They stood on the curb, staring at each other, silenced by shock.

It was Julia, in the end, who spoke first. Slowly, she said, "Perhaps I do. I must try not to."

Mattie rubbed her hands over her eyes, forgetting the false eyelashes. "Oh, shit. Look, I'm sorry. It's just that you've got Lily, and I wish I had a kid. And you had Bliss, and Ladyhill, and seemingly anything anybody could want. But still not enough, because you had to have your aviator as well."

"Don't say anything about him," Julia begged. "Listen, Mattie. You're famous and successful, and you're doing what you've always dreamed of, and everyone wants you."

"Yeah."

"You can't complain either. That's all I'm saying."

"I don't. I just tell men to piss off."

They were still standing face-to-face, measuring up, as if they were going to hit each other. Awkwardly, Julia reached out with one hand, then put her arm around Mattie's shoulder.

"I didn't know you felt like that about men. I thought you treated it all as a joke, like we always used to. Or as something boring but useful to capitalize on, like at the Showbox. And I thought you were still looking for the right person. To love."

Mattie was crying. Her tears ran down her face, carrying her eye liner and the little clumps of eyelash with them.

"I am." Sobs squared her mouth, and she could hardly shape the words. "I don't think I'll ever find anyone."

Julia hugged her and stroked her hair, soothing her as if she were Lily. "Yes you will. Of course you will. There's all the time. Years and years and years." She let Mattie cry for a minute longer, and then ordered her, "We're going to get something to eat now. Lots to eat. And I'll buy you five bottles of wine, if that's what you want."

Mattie lifted her head and sniffed. "Two should be enough."

Slowly, with their arms linked, they made their way to Goodge Street. In the restaurant they sat down facing each other across a blue tablecloth. The shock of Mattie's sudden outburst had shaken them both. Julia saw that Mattie's hands were trembling as she lit a cigarette.

She said, "I haven't seen you cry like that for years." Years. Not since Fairmile Road, when Mattie had turned up with her clothes torn and her mouth bleeding.

"Sorry."

"Don't fend me off, Mat. I didn't know you were unhappy. Talk to me about it."

Mattie looked away, through the net curtains at the window into the street. "I'm sorry," she repeated. "I'm not unhappy. Everything is wonderful. I'm just weary of what happened to-night. And I suppose, therefore, that still hankering after a stale old thing like true love isn't very rational."

"It isn't stale," Julia said. But Mattie's ironic smile didn't reassure her.

"You're a romantic. Your obsession with your aviator is romantic. If you were practical, you'd have stayed with Bliss."

"Thanks."

"Sorry. Again. If that's not what you want to hear." Mattie inhaled deeply, then blue smoke wreathed her head. In a different, lower voice, she added, "Seeing you with Lily this week has made me jealous. Of her dependence on you. You're the center of her world. No one feels that way about me."

They looked at each other then, for a long moment, gauging how much, and how little, they knew.

"Let's not be jealous of each other," Julia said at last.

"Let's try not to be," Mattie amended. Her fingers touched Julia's, briefly, before she picked up the menu with a flourish. "What's that wine that tastes of cleaning fluid?"

"Retsina."

"Let's not have that then." A waiter had materialized beside her. "A large carafe of house red. To begin with." And Mattie smiled at him through the smudges of her makeup.

The man melted, visibly. "At once, madame."

When he had gone, almost running to do Mattie's bidding, Julia laughed. "You're a paradox, Mattie."

"And you've had your nose buried in too many books with long words in them."

They did their best to be lively.

They reminisced about safe subjects, although there didn't seem to be very many of those. They gossiped about friends, especially Felix and George.

"Tell me again about staying at Eaton Square," Mattie begged.

"It was awful. They were trying hard to be kind, and Lily

and I were so wrong. Everything she touched got Marmite on it, or broke. There were different china and napkins and linen cloths for every meal, and I was always trying to help and getting them wrong. Colors clashing, disasters like that. And giving Lily her cereal in George's own special Provençal bowl that he needed for his café au lait. George winced but pretended he didn't mind at all drinking his coffee out of one of the green and gold French bistro ones that they'd brought back from Paris. I was so glad when you got home."

"So was I."

The opportunity for Julia to inquire more closely into Mattie's latest failed affair hadn't presented itself, although she had tried hard enough to find one. Mattie was more secretive than she had once been.

"Not even worth discussing," she had said. All Julia knew was that he was a singer with a group, and that he had been born not far from Blick Road itself. Julia reflected wryly that for all Betty's pride in it, her own marriage had been a move in utterly the wrong direction. Seemingly everyone, nowadays, was a working-class hero. At least everyone who mattered in the restless, kaleidoscopic London world that Mattie was part of, and that Julia thought she had missed so sharply.

Mattie abandoned her pork kebab half-eaten, and leaned back with her glass in her hand. "Are you looking forward to Tressider Designs?"

"Not much, to tell the truth. But it'll do for now."

"And after that?"

"I'll have a brainstorm. Don't ask me what, I haven't had it yet."

"Here's to it, when it does come."

Julia tried to fill and empty her glass to keep pace with Mattie, but she soon fell behind. Mattie drained the first carafe and ordered another, but the wine didn't help them to recapture any of the old conviviality. As the evening went on all Julia felt was a kind of increasing desperation, and she suspected that Mattie felt it too. It wasn't a comfortable feeling, after the first optimism.

Mattie's collapse into drunkenness, when it came, was as sudden as it usually was, but Julia was ready for it. As soon as Mattie's head descended to the blue tablecloth and she gave a comfortable sigh, like a little girl preparing to go to sleep, Julia signaled to the still-admiring waiter.

"My friend is very tired. The bill, and a taxi, please."

Julia paid the bill, but she extracted the money for the taxi from Mattie's purse. Left to herself, she reasoned, she would have been able to walk.

Back at home, Julia hauled the unprotesting Mattie into bed, and the baby-sitter fled. But in the morning Mattie was up, ready for work, even before Lily woke up. Her face was puffy and pale, but she grinned at Julia. "What's the makeup team for, if not to work miracles? 'Bye, my love. On Saturday we'll go and clean up your new home."

But when the weekend came Mattie was called for some extra takes, and in the end Julia took Lily and the buckets and the scrubbing brushes to Gordon Mansions on her own. She installed Lily with her toys and books in what seemed to be the least filthy corner, and set to work.

She had brought Mattie's little red transistor radio with her, and she hummed as she washed the floors, *With love, from me to you.*

Lily was content to play on her own for only five minutes at a time. After exploring the rooms, leaving her possessions scattered behind her, she came back and insisted on helping. Before Julia could stop her she plunged her arms into the bucket of water, and then cried bitterly because it was hot. But she had no sooner stopped crying than she was dipping a cloth into the water and then trailing it over the floor and the walls, soaking herself and the clean dustcloths.

"Lily, you can't help. Stop it," Julia shouted. She grabbed her wet hand and steered her back into her corner. "Now, stay there."

Five minutes later the process started all over again.

Julia was sweaty, and her hair clung in itchy strands to her damp face. The surfaces were all so grimy that the water and the cloths were filthy again almost as soon as she changed them. Lily upset the detergent packet, and trod the spilled powder into blue, gluey trails.

"Stop it!" Julia yelled at her.

She was discovering the impossibility of tackling any major task with a toddler in tow. It wasn't a discovery she had been forced to make at Ladyhill, because no one had expected her to do anything more major than care for Lily.

When Julia dragged her away from the bucket for the tenth time, Lily began to cry. When she had been comforted she asked sweetly, "Go swings now?"

"We can't, not today. We've got to make our new home look nice. Tomorrow we'll go."

When the kitchen and the bathroom were passably clean, Julia unpacked the picnic lunch she had brought with them. They sat on the floor and ate bread and cheese and bananas. "Our first meal in our new house." Julia smiled at Lily. "Is it nice?"

"Nice," Lily repeated obediently.

Julia had resolved to clean all the living room before going back to Bloomsbury. The room didn't look so big, but as soon as she had swept it and they were both coughing and choking in the swirls of dust, she knew that it was too big to finish. But she kept on doggedly, scrubbing and rinsing and wiping dry, straightening up now and then to ease her back and push the hair off her face. The flat seemed empty and isolated, as well as dirty, with only the two of them to occupy it.

Lily was bored and irritable now. She pulled at Julia's hand, shouting, "Lily want swings!"

Julia tried to explain again, as patiently as she could. "Not today. Tomorrow, I promise we'll go tomorrow."

It was late, and getting dark outside, when Lily knocked the bucket of water over. Dirty water flooded over the clean, dry floor. Julia's patience evaporated. Pure, hot, irrational anger flowed through her. With one hand she grabbed Lily's arm, and with the other she delivered a stinging slap across her fat, bare legs. "You're very naughty. Naughty. Look what you've done."

Lily's face showed shock, then disbelief. Her mouth opened and her eyes screwed themselves shut and she began to howl. Shaking, Julia sat her down on the floor with a bump and crossed her arms across her own chest, digging her fingernails into her flesh to stop herself lashing out again. She tried to say, "I'm sorry," but Lily's eyes opened first.

"I want Daddy," she yelled.

Julia dropped to her knees then, so that they were face-to-face. She uncrossed her arms and she took hold of Lily and shook her. The child's head wobbled. There wasn't shock or outrage in her face now. There was fear.

Julia breathed in, gasping for air. "Daddy isn't here. He isn't going to be here. That's why we've done all this. Don't you understand?"

Lily was two and a half years old, Julia told herself through the anger and panic. She didn't understand anything, except that Alexander wasn't there. And that her mother had hurt her.

"Oh, Lily." Julia started to cry with shame and bewilderment. If she was doing all this for Lily's sake, then why must she hurt her at the same time?

Lily put her head on one side, studying her. "Mummy crying." Her face crumpled again, in sympathy, and she held out her arms. "Carry you," she implored.

Julia snatched her up and rocked her, holding her head against her cheek. "Carry me," she whispered. "You mean carry me. I will. Of course I will, if you still want me to."

When they had mopped up the water together, Julia pushed Lily back through the streets to Bloomsbury. When they reached Mattie's, Julia made her her tea and bathed her, and then they sat on the sofa and drank a cup of hot milk each and Julia read the favorite stories. She knew that she was overcompensating with her calmness and motherliness. Lily seemed to have forgotten everything, but Julia was feeling the first stirrings of doubt. Doubt that they would be able to survive, after all.

We will, she vowed. *I'll see that we do.*

Mattie came in later, still high with the day's work, and opened a bottle of wine. Julia shook her head at the offer of a glass. Discarded clothes fell in Mattie's turbulent wake.

"I'm going to meet some people for a drink and a meal. Why don't you come? We can ask the kid to come in again."

Julia thought, half-wanting, and then she remembered and shook her head. "I'm tired. I'm going to bed early."

Mattie looked at them, sitting side by side on her sofa. Lily was in her nightdress, pink and shiny from her bath, and Julia was wrapped in an old bathrobe. Mattie was struck by their likeness. Their faces were the same shape, and their dark hair sprang in the same way. Mother and daughter. "Okay. I'll come with you to the Mansions tomorrow, and we'll blitz the place."

"Thanks, Mattie."

After she had gone Julia put Lily to bed and watched her until she went to sleep. It happened all at once, as it usually did. One minute she was awake, talking and singing, and the next she was asleep with her thumb falling out of her mouth.

Julia sat on the sofa with her knees drawn up to her chin, thinking. It was very quiet, and in the stillness she felt lonely and vulnerable. The responsibilities that she had taken on seemed suddenly daunting. She stood up abruptly. She would go to bed, and sleep, rather than let doubts overcome her.

She bent over Lily once more, drawing the covers unnecessarily tighter, and then she lay down in her own bed. Without knowing it, she adopted the same position as Lily. Julia dreamed that she met her own mother. They were in a vast, cavernous shop, and they were standing side by side piling heaps of groceries into their baskets. At the moment when they turned and recognized each other, Julia realized that the shop was burning. The flames were like a moving curtain behind them. She turned and ran, and she knew that as she ran to save herself she had lost her mother, and that she would never see her again.

On Monday morning Julia started work again for Tressider Designs. She had found a baby-minder for Lily through an advertisement in the local paper. Mrs. Forgan lived in a small terraced house near World's End. She had two children of her own, who were both at school, and she looked after another toddler whose mother was also out at work. Julia noted that her house was clean, and there seemed to be an adequate stock of toys for the children. There was even a little garden at the back of the house for them to play in when the summer came. Julia put Mrs. Forgan's slight lack of warmth down to professional detachment. She seemed naturally fond of children, and Lily went to her quite happily.

To Alexander, Julia exaggerated her qualities a little.

"She's very experienced with small children. She's a mother herself, and she's been looking after children for working mothers for years."

"I don't like the sound of it," Alexander replied.

Julia struggled to sound relaxed. "Everyone does it, Alexander. More and more mothers work nowadays. And I'll be able to tell straight away if she's not happy."

But leaving Lily on that first morning was still one of the hardest things Julia had had to do. "I'll come back and see you at lunchtime," she promised, and then she marched down to the front gate. She tried to close her ears to Lily's howls of protest, but they echoed in her ears all morning.

At Tressider's she found herself occupying her old place at the desk outside the door to the design sanctum. Julia realized that she was probably never going to make it to the other side. The work appeared to be much the same as it had been four years ago, only the clients were either grander or richer—never both at once. The old aristocrats came in droves to George, but they had less money to spend than they once had. And a new elite of fashion designers and pop stars and photographers were beginning to find their way to Felix. They were obsessed with their appearance and their surroundings, and they had more money to spend on creating the right effect than had ever passed through George's coffers in the past. Observing it all, and remembering her own sparse rooms at Gordon Mansions, gave Julia some amusement and, just sometimes, a jolt of pure and passionate envy.

In her first lunch break, Julia dashed back to World's End. Lily was eating baked beans on toast amid a clutter of toys. She clung to Julia on first sight, but then she let her go happily enough when it was time for her to return to work.

It was at the end of the first week that Mrs. Forgan suggested that it wasn't necessary for Julia to come back in the middle of every day. "It's unsettling for her and for the other one, you see, you coming in every day at dinnertime. Best to let her be with me for the whole day."

"All right," Julia said reluctantly. She was thinking about dinnertime, and the irony of returning, full circle, to Betty and Fairmile Road. With its faintly threadbare neatness, Mrs. Forgan's house was beginning to remind her very strongly of Fairmile Road.

Gordon Mansions, Mrs. Forgan's, and Tressider Designs marked the beginning of a long, drab time.

In the mornings Julia and Lily took the tube and bus to World's End, and then Julia rushed back up the King's Road to be in time for work. It was her job to open the shop to the first of the day's avid clients. In the evenings at about six o'clock she collected Lily again, and they made their way back home through the rush hour. Julia realized very early on that she should have found a sitter near the flat rather than near her work. It would have meant longer hours apart, but Lily would have been spared all the traveling. Now that she was settled with Mrs. Forgan, Julia didn't want to uproot her.

As soon as they reached home in the evenings, it was time for Lily's supper and bath. It was a time when they were both always tired and irritable. Julia knew that she saw far, far too little of Lily during the week, but yet by the end of the day even the brief hour that she did have seemed too long. She shouted at Lily when she fumbled and spilled her food or her glass of juice, and she cut down the length of story time because she found herself nodding over the pages as she read.

Lily caught a succession of colds. Mrs. Forgan explained that Warren, the other child, was sickly, and that, in her words, he passed the germs on to everyone else. When Lily had fallen asleep at last, Julia would stand over her bed, listening to her thick breathing and touching the back of her hand to her flushed cheeks. A stab of guilt and love and anxiety would pass through her chest then, so sharp and burning that it would double her up. She would bend over to kiss Lily, almost waking her up again with the oppression of her silent apology.

Without clearly realizing it, Julia was lonely. She had enough friends in London, from the early days of the square and the later times with Alexander, but none of them seemed to be leading a life anything like Julia's own. Most of them weren't married; none of them had children. Julia was well liked and there were plenty of invitations, but baby-sitters were an expense she couldn't always afford, and she refused more offers than she accepted. Soon they began to dwindle, and she spent more and more evenings alone at home, reading, escaping into other worlds.

At weekends Julia tried to assuage her guilt by devoting herself entirely to Lily. They went to play in Coram's Fields, and to the Regent's Park Zoo, which Lily loved. They would spend whole afternoons sitting on a bench in the monkey house, watching the sad gorilla. They went to the local pool, and Julia painstakingly taught Lily to swim. When the weather grew warmer they went to Hampstead Heath for picnics, and they even started visiting Betty and Vernon again.

Lily thought that the short train ride was the best adventure, and that the tidy, draped and ornamented interior of Fairmile Road was wonderfully glamorous and mysterious.

"Like Granny Smith's" was one of her favorite terms of approbation. Betty would let her throw open cupboard doors and prospect through the orderly contents for treasures, as Julia herself had never been allowed to do. Lily could drape the dining table with fringed chenille tablecloths to make a tent, and pile up the interior with cushions and blankets, while Julia watched in disbelief.

"She's only a baby," Betty said fondly. "Poor little thing. Let her play."

Poor little thing, Julia understood, referred to Lily's life without the regular, visible presence of a father who went to an office and came home at exactly half past five, as Vernon did. *Lily's lucky. Luckier than I was,* she might have retorted, but she didn't.

"Whatever's happened?" Betty had whispered, nervous and fascinated and faintly gratified, even in the midst of her disappointment, to be proved right in her belief that the classes didn't mix.

"Alexander and I didn't make each other very happy, in the end," Julia said clearly. "We separated, and I suppose we'll get divorced when the time comes. We'll share the responsibility for Lily, of course."

Vernon, sitting in his armchair with his thin shanks in Sunday slacks and his feet in tartan slippers, said that divorce was a sin. Having delivered his verdict, he folded and refolded the *Sunday People* and went on reading it. Betty nodded, her old, automatic confirmation of *Father's right,* but she also looked at Julia with anxious sympathy.

Julia didn't try to argue or to make them understand. There was no point in making trouble. She was grateful to her parents for the Sunday outing that Fairmile Road provided. The realization depressed her, but she accepted it.

But Lily enjoyed it. She told herself that that was what mattered most.

"Look at her," Betty would say fondly as Lily dragged more cushions across the floor, wrinkling the mats and causing the china spaniels on the coffee table to rock dangerously in her wake. "Bless her lively little heart."

On the train on the way home, Lily said, "I love Granny Smith."

Julia smiled at her. "That's good. Granny Smith loves you too."

It was too late to ask Betty, "What about my lively heart when I was her age?" Nor would asking have provided any answer. Julia reminded herself of Mattie's criticism, and smiled again.

She didn't always succeed, but she was trying.

In the first two or three months Alexander came regularly to see Lily. Before the first visit Julia worked frantically to paint and furnish and turn Gordon Mansions into what would match Alexander's idea of a suitable home.

When he came, she was half-eager for him to approve, half-resentful that she should need his approval. Alexander looked at the serviceable second-hand furniture, and the freshly painted white walls. In Lily's bedroom, where her latest drawings were pinned to the walls, he stood for a long time staring at the colorful blobs and outlines. "She's changed," he said at last. "Just in this short time."

"I know."

They turned away from each other. Lily swung from Alexander's hand. She was shy and excited at the same time, and flirtatious, glancing up at him from under her eyelashes.

"You've made the flat very comfortable," Alexander said. "Is there anything you need?"

"The allowance you make is very useful," Julia answered. "Other than that, there's nothing we need." She was wondering how it was that they had once been close and now were stiff and distant. She knew that it was her own doing, and she felt guilty and helpless.

"Come on then, Lily. Let's go and see Granny." They were going to see China. Alexander was buttoning Lily's coat, his fingers touching each button as if it were precious. Julia waved them off from the doorway. She stood there, rigid, watching them go away together. She wanted to run to Alexander and have him wrap his arms around her too. *Dependent,* she rebuked herself. *Dependent. You have to find a way to stand on your own.* Perhaps, she thought, her need for Josh as well as her need for Alexander were only different facets of her own inadequacy.

I can survive, she repeated.

Julia went back into the silent flat and closed the door firmly behind her. She did some paperwork that she had brought home from Tressider's. Then she listened to a play on the radio because she felt too restless to read, and waited for Lily to come home again.

After the first one, Alexander's visits were fairly frequent, but they were always to collect or deliver Lily. He took her on outings, or to China's flat in a grand block overlooking Albert Bridge, because Markham Square was let. Sometimes he took her home to Ladyhill for a whole weekend. Julia watched her carefully when she came back, as if she were expecting Ladyhill itself to have seduced her daughter's loyalty. But Lily seemed exactly as she always was—lively and inquisitive and impartially lavish with her love.

Spring came at last, and the time that Julia had agreed with Alexander, right at the beginning, for Lily to go to Ladyhill for a whole month. She notified Mrs. Forgan, who pursed her lips, and she washed and ironed Lily's clothes and packed them with her favorite toys and books in a big suitcase. The night before Alexander was to come to collect her, Julia sat by Lily's bed for a long time, watching her sleep. She reached out and twisted one of her black curls around her finger, trying to unravel the knots of love and possessiveness, jealousy and responsibility and resentment, that tangled inside her.

Alexander came to take her away, and Lily threw her arms around him. "See the cows?" she asked, and Julia realized with a pang that she remembered Ladyhill, and already understood that the pleasures of it were to be shared with Alexander, not with her mother.

"Yes, we'll see the cows. And there are baby lambs as well. Granny Faye's feeding one with a bottle because it's lost its mother. Are you all ready?"

"Ready now." Lily beamed. "See Granny Faye." Lily accepted it as part of life's natural generosity that she had three grandmothers.

Julia hugged her, then let her go.

When she had gone, the empty rooms seemed full of imprints of her. Julia had told herself that she was looking forward to a month of freedom. She had made plans, and promises. Now she sat on Lily's bed, holding one inside-out white ankle sock, and cried out of loneliness and despondency.

When she had finished crying, Julia found that it took an effort to relearn the ground rules of a life of freedom.

"Relax," Mattie told her. "You can't pack everything into one evening. Leave something for tomorrow."

Julia wanted to go to a restaurant, and then to go to a party to dance, then as soon as she had arrived and restlessly scanned the room, to move on somewhere else, another party, another place. She seemed fueled by a kind of wild energy that was close to desperation. Privately, Mattie thought she looked gaunt and feverish.

"I can't keep up with you," she complained.

Julia stared at her. "But you're used to it. This is what you do, isn't it?"

"Not really."

Men gathered around Julia, drawn like moths to the bright light of her new energy. She hadn't slept with anyone for months and months. She thought that motherhood had obliterated sex. Now, in quick succession, she had several lovers. It was exciting to discover that she could have whomever she wanted, choosing with deliberate care or with reckless rapidity from the King's Road parade. Suddenly, it seemed, that springtime, everyone was doing the same thing. Julia was shaken by the depths of erotic intensity that the rediscovery stirred in her. She woke up in the mornings and reached out for whoever was lying beside her, greedy for a feast of lips and fingers and warm, unfamiliar flesh. All day long, at Tressider's, she hummed and crackled with the electric charge of sex. She looked out of the tall plate-glass windows of the shop front at the men going by, noticing the length of their legs and the bunch of muscles under tight jeans. George Tressider arched a disapproving eyebrow. But Felix remembered the time that he had spent in Florence and what had happened to him there and was briefly piercingly jealous. And then when the evening came and Julia left work, going to a bar with Felix or meeting Mattie somewhere, it was time to choose again. She chose a cleft chin or an outré pigtail or a glimpse of a suntan under an open-necked shirt, and she spread herself out like a feast for the favored one.

Her appetite lasted for almost the whole of the time Lily was away.

Then she woke up one morning and after they had made love she discovered that she couldn't think of anything to say to the blond boy in bed beside her. She hadn't cared to talk before, but this morning she wanted to share confidences, and lovers' laughter. The blank-faced boy confronted her instead.

"Wasn't it any good?" he asked her.

"Oh yes, it was fine," Julia lied. She got rid of him as soon as she could. *You're still dependent,* she told herself. *A mass of men, that's no different from one, is it?*

She went to Soho, to a shop displaying surgical corsets and bottles of patent medicine with faded labels in its dusty window. A sign in the corner of the window announced MARITAL AIDS. The irony of that didn't seem particularly amusing. She bought a vibrator and used it, grimly conjuring up faceless fantasies. The charge running through her rapidly lost its electricity, then disappeared altogether.

"Come with me to rehearsal tomorrow," Mattie said.

"They won't want spectators hanging around at rehearsal, will they?"

"This is different," Mattie told her.

She had finished work on *Girl at the Window.* It had been a relief to kiss good-bye her own vapid role, even more of a relief not to have to simulate passion for Tony Drake every day. Mattie had been out of work for weeks afterward. Deliberately, she had turned down the parts her agent had tried to persuade her to audition for. There had been a supporting role in a silly West End musical being staged only as a vehicle for a much older, bigger star, and the chance of playing a student nurse in *Emergency, Ward 10.*

"Bread and butter," Francis Willoughby's successor had said, shaking his head. "You can't afford to turn down bread and butter."

"I'd rather have gin and eclairs," Mattie had told him.

She had stayed at home in Bloomsbury, reading magazines and watching her new television, and going out to eat in her favorite cafés at erratic hours. As an economy measure, because she was out of work, she drank Spanish burgundy instead of gin or whiskey. The wine made her sleepy, and she often woke up stiff in her armchair with the blue eye in the center of the television screen staring balefully at her.

Then, without any warning or preliminaries, a woman called her.

"Mattie Banner?"

"Speaking."

"My name is Chris Fredericks, of the Women's Stage Group. We've seen your work. Are you interested in coming to read for us? It's a new play, by a new woman playwright. It's an all-female production." Her low, slightly hoarse voice was attractive.

Mattie thought for a moment. She had never heard of the Women's Stage Group. She looked across the room and saw the pile of magazines on top of the television set, and three empty bottles of wine beside it.

"Yes," she said. "I think I would be interested."

Chris Fredericks gave her an address, a place that sounded like a warehouse, south of the river, a date, and a time. Then she hung up.

Mattie raised her eyebrows in mock surprise. "I'm supposed to be the famous actress," she told the dead line. "What happened to *please, please come and read for us*?"

She found herself looking forward to the reading more keenly than its relative importance might have warranted.

When the day came she found her way to the address in Lambeth. It was, as she had imagined, a warehouse. After hammering at the big metal doors and shouting for several minutes without making herself heard, Mattie was beginning to assume that she had come on the wrong day. Then she heard a rattle on the other side of the doors and one of them slid open to leave a narrow slit. A head popped out of it. It was a girl's with a bush of curly dark hair.

"Oh, hi," the girl said, smiling at her. "Sorry. We were talking. Didn't hear you. Come on in."

Mattie followed her. They passed through the shadowy warehouse space, which as far as she could see was still filled with bits of machinery, and through a door in a partition at the far end. The partition closed off a small high room furnished with a table and a few packing cases. There was a layer of dust over everything, including a kettle on a tray. Coffee mugs, playscripts, a relatively undusty bottle of milk, and an open packet of chocolate crackers were scattered over the table. There were perhaps a dozen women perched on the packing cases, all talking. Two or three of them glanced up at Mattie and grinned; one of them stood up and held out her hand. She had a young face, but her black hair was thickly streaked with gray. She was wearing jeans and a man's shirt.

"You must be Mattie Banner. I'm Chris Fredericks."

Mattie was used to recognition and acknowledgment, in professional encounters at least, just as she was used to the studio car and driver. But the members of the Women's Stage Group hadn't offered her any acknowledgment beyond ordinary, casual friendliness. Mattie dismissed the twinge of pride and decided that she liked them for it. She shook Chris Fredericks's hand warmly.

"We're a women's group, as I told you. We're also a democratic group. All decisions, artistic or administrative, are taken collectively. I have been nominated director because only one person can make a telephone call, for instance. But I have no more authority within the group than anyone else." Chris pushed a copy of the script across the table to Mattie. "Here you are. *Everywoman's Odyssey*. Shall we start reading? Is everyone ready?"

Mattie interrupted. "One question before we start. Why have you invited me?"

"Alison read an interview with you. You said in it that you think women are more interesting than men. Also, having you in the cast will make sure that we get proper attention."

It was the oddest read-through that Mattie had ever attended.

There was no directorial suggestion or control. As a result everyone chipped in with what they felt and how they thought a line should be spoken. If there was a serious disagreement, it was put to a vote. It took five and a half hours to complete a read-through of the piece.

Mattie thought the play was pungent and funny in parts. She also thought it was too long and much too wordy, and she said so. By linking a series of short scenes from myth and history, it aimed to illustrate the difference between men and women.

At last, at long last, they came to the final line.

There was a small silence while the words echoed in the dusty space.

Then, "What do you think?" The question was timid. It took Mattie a moment to realize that after all the democracy, they were asking for her opinion.

"I think it needs a lot of work. It's rough, and it needs to be sharpened. Democratically, of course."

There was another small silence.

"So? Are you in?"

"Yes, I'm in," Mattie said.

They stood up and crowded around to shake her hand.

"Welcome to the group," Chris Fredericks said. "What d'you think? Shall we all go to the pub to celebrate?"

In the pub they spread around two tables and talked and joked and wisecracked. In the center of the big, easy group of women Mattie felt warm and invulnerable. Looking beyond Jocelyn and Chris, at the couples sitting at other tables, at the knots of men lounging at the bar, Mattie experienced a new sensation. It was the feeling of being on the inside, looking out.

On the day before Alexander brought a taller, rosier Lily back to Gordon Mansions, a young man with a big suitcase walked into George Tressider's shop. He had a lively face, long hair, and a denim jacket over a stripy T-shirt. He was so much not a Tressider-looking customer that Julia frowned discouragingly. But he stood squarely in front of her desk and announced, "I've got a new product here. I want an exclusive outlet to sell it through."

"You're in the right place if it's exclusivity you want." He was gleaming with enthusiasm, and it was infectious. "You'd better let me see this wonderful product."

Out of the suitcase, with a flourish like a magician's, he produced fold upon fold of bright pink plastic. While Julia stared, he attached a foot pump to a nozzle and began to inflate the plastic. In front of her eyes the shapeless plastic took on a shape. It grew, and became an armchair, with arms and a back and even a neat plastic antimacassar.

Julia applauded, and sat down on it. It was squeaky, but perfectly comfortable.

"Blow-up furniture," he said. "It's cheap, and it's fun."

"Do you know, I think you're right. It is fun."

It was as bright as a child's balloon, and as rude as a raspberry blown in the faces of all the serious gilt and old oak and mahogany pieces that lined the walls of George Tressider's shop.

The door to the inner sanctum opened and George himself came out. His gaze flicked over the salesman and his T-shirt, the suitcase and the shiny pink chair underneath Julia.

"Look, George," she exclaimed too enthusiastically. "Blow-up furniture."

Silently, George surveyed the three of them.

"What do you think of it?" the blow-up man asked.

"I think it's the tackiest thing I've ever seen," George answered. He walked past them, past the glowering gilt and mahogany, and out into the street, as though out in the King's Road he could breathe in air that was at least uncontaminated by inflatable pink armchairs.

Inside the shop Julia and the salesman looked ruefully at each other, and then they started to laugh.

"Well, it was a bit of a long shot," Julia snorted, "coming in here with it."

"I thought you were supposed to be decorators to the new rich. Pop stars and photographers and hairdressers. I read about you in *Queen*."

"That's Felix," Julia said. She held out her hand and the salesman shook it. "I'm Julia Smith."

"Thomas Tree. Do you really like the armchair?"

"Yes, I do." Julia didn't stop to think. "If you can produce them, I'll find a sales outlet for you."

And that, although she didn't recognize it, was the start of her brainstorm.

It was also the tiny, chance-sown seed from which Garlic & Sapphires grew.

EIGHTEEN

It started in a small way. Through her contacts, Julia found one or two retail outlets who were willing to take a chance with Thomas Tree's blow-up chairs. Thomas was surprised, although Julia insisted she wasn't in the least surprised herself, when the first few samples sold at once. The shops clamored for more, and Thomas went back to his workshop to produce them.

"Quickly," Julia ordered him. "It's no use turning up with

them in six months' time when everyone's forgotten.'' She looked speculatively at Thomas and at the patches on the knees of his jeans. "Do you mind me telling you what to do? There's no reason why you should take any notice, of course.''

"I'm grateful,'' Thomas said. "Looks like we make quite a good team.''

"Have you got the money for materials?''

"I'll find it.''

Julia had none to offer him. At his insistence, she had taken a tiny commission on the sales. The shops had sold the chairs at a huge markup; she knew that Thomas must have made hardly anything out of them.

He came back three weeks later with three dozen chairs in pink, green, orange, and scarlet. The colors glowed when he unpacked them in Julia's living room and Lily bounced gleefully on the orange chair that he blew up for her. Thomas had big dark rings under his eyes, and he looked even thinner than he had when he first turned up in George's shop.

"I've been working all hours. It's glueing the seams that's the problem,'' he said. "The cutting, all the rest, that's easy. But heat-sealing the seams by hand takes forever. I need machinery if I'm going to produce in quantities.''

"See how these sell first,'' Julia advised him.

"And I've got this,'' Thomas announced. From the big suitcase he produced a multicolored coil of plastic. Attached to the foot pump, it blossomed into a nine-foot plastic palm tree, complete with coconuts and a parrot. Lily's face turned into three O's of astonishment. "Only a prototype,'' he said proudly. "But with half a dozen of these you could transform your living room into a desert island.''

Julia stared at it, for one second feeling like George Tressider as she imagined a roomful of waving plastic fronds. Then she started laughing again. "Why not? Have you got any more ideas?''

"Hundreds. Just no money to put them into practice.''

"Sell these chairs, then get a bank loan. I'll see if I can persuade Felix to guarantee it.''

"I hope it'll be worthwhile for both of you,'' Thomas said.

Julia went out with him to the foot of the basement stairs. "I'll try to get you a better deal from the retailers,'' she promised. "But you mustn't pay me any more commission. The chairs sell themselves.''

Thomas held out his hand, and after a moment she shook it.

She noticed that he was looking at her, and that the look was admiring. She stepped backward, away from it, with the memory of her month of freedom still sharp.

" 'Bye," Thomas said. "I'll be back soon."

The chairs sold. Julia made the retailers pay more for them than for the first batch, and passed the difference straight to Thomas Tree. That made the final price higher, but they still sold almost as soon as they reached the shops.

There's a market, Julia thought. The hairs prickled down the nape of her neck as she contemplated the potential size of it, and the corresponding size of her idea. The young people who swarmed down the King's Road every Saturday had money to spend. Julia reckoned if they had so much to spend on their clothes, they might spare some for their rooms. If, that is, they were offered merchandise that was cheap, fun, and new. It was the newness that was the most important.

Through that spring and summer she looked carefully for goods that fulfilled her criteria as brilliantly as Thomas's did. And as soon as she began to look, she saw possibilities everywhere. In Peter Jones she almost fell over a range of self-assembly tables and tub chairs. They were shoved away behind the garden furniture, and the cardboard was too thin and the colors were nasty, but the idea was good. A design magazine that she picked up from Felix's desk featured a space-age chair, the square white plastic shape upholstered in scarlet vinyl, and Julia thought, *That's it too. Only it costs too much. Could it be done more cheaply?* In a lighting shop she saw Japanese paper lanterns to use as lampshades, big white globes that gave a soft, simple light. On a handicraft stall at a market she saw hand-colored candles in the shape of apples and ice cream cones and Coca-Cola bottles, and at the same market a month later she met a girl selling lurid satin cushions in the shape of lips and ears and fists.

She liked whatever made her stop short to look harder. And she particularly liked the witty, irreverent or punchy things that would make George raise his eyebrows and shudder delicately.

Julia knew that anything she had already seen somewhere else wasn't nearly new enough. It was no good copying: originality was the key. She would have to sniff out her merchandise at its source, but she was sure that if she had the time to devote to it, and the backing, she could do it. And the trick would be to display it all, a stun-the-eye collection, under one roof. A shop. A shop that would be a meeting place and a talking point, and that would do for rooms just what *Bazaar* had done for clothes. *Blow-up*, she dreamed. Or *Bang*. Or just *Designs*.

Thomas Tree insisted on taking her out to dinner to celebrate an order. The bank had agreed to a substantial line of credit, a guarantee had proved unnecessary.

"If I opened a shop," Julia said, "how many things could I find to sell that are as mad as your chairs?"

Thomas glanced at her. She was stirring her coffee one way, then the other. Her eyes seemed very bright. "Dozens," he answered. "People I was at college with are inventing things, making all kinds of weird stuff. It's finding the right outlet that's difficult. People are conservative. Like my mum. She likes shiny brown wood and flowered covers."

Julia grinned. "So does George Tressider, except his are glazed chintz and inlaid walnut." She looked steadily at him and then said, "Thomas, if I open a shop, can I have the exclusive right to sell your furniture?"

"Yes. All of it."

"Will you be my partner, then?"

"Yes."

They shook hands again. This time Julia didn't draw away.

Her first plan was to persuade George and Felix, somehow, to set her up under the Tressider umbrella. If they would help her to find and stock her shop, just by lending her the money, then they could share the profits with herself and Thomas. From the very beginning Julia had no doubts that the profits would roll in. And she knew perfectly well that Tressider Designs could afford the investment. They had just enjoyed the most successful year in the company's history.

Wisely, Julia decided to put the idea to Felix first. "Come and have lunch with me," she asked him. "I want to talk."

They strolled away from the offices together, with the sun warming their faces. Julia looked around her, at the crowds and the shop windows. When she breathed in she thought that she could taste and smell newness and excitement and energy. It was the first summer of the Beatles; girls were flooding out of shops and offices to buy records and posters and clothes. Everyone they passed seemed to be swinging a shopping bag with their latest purchase.

"You look happy," Felix said.

"I'm excited," Julia answered. "I've got an idea."

She hardly touched her food and wine. She talked and talked, drawing shapes in the air with her hands, trying to ignite

Felix's enthusiasm with the heat of her own. As he sat and watched her, Felix thought what a pleasure it was to see the old, vivid Julia again. He remembered how the same Julia had affected him in the confusing days when she had first come to the square with Mattie, and with the taste of wine on his tongue and his own food going cold in front of him, he remembered the night of Jessie's funeral. He remembered it with surprising clarity, the lightness and fragility of Julia in his arms. He had thought that sadness and responsibility had aged her, but now the years seemed to have dropped away and she might have been fifteen again.

She leaned forward, touching his hands. Without thinking, he took hold of hers and held them tight. Love was a difficult commodity, but he knew that he loved Julia.

"Don't you think it's a good idea?"

Her vehemence startled him. "What?"

"What I've been telling you about for the last hour, that's all."

Felix thought carefully. He would have to disappoint her, but he would do it as gently as he could.

"It's a brilliant idea."

He was sure that it was. There was no shop like the one Julia described, and he knew from his own clients that anything irreverent and original would sell. Julia had style herself—he had admired it from the moment he first glimpsed her in the Rocket— and if she could recognize it, she could almost certainly sell it. Her shop would probably work.

"But I don't think George is the right person to back you." The truth was that George didn't trust Julia. Felix knew that his dislike was rooted in jealousy. George was sensitive enough and clever enough to suspect the closeness of the bond between his lover and his shopgirl. Julia was tolerated at Tressider Designs only because Felix wanted her to have a job that would support her and Lily, and because George couldn't refuse anything that Felix wanted. Within reason, Felix mentally corrected himself. Setting Julia up with Tressider money in a shop selling pop furniture and plastic artifacts wouldn't count as within reason.

He did his best to explain to Julia without any suggestion of disloyalty to George. Felix loved George too, and would have defended him against anyone, but he was beginning to feel the weight of George's fierce possessiveness. As he talked, his eyes wandered beyond Julia to the restaurant windows. Outside, he could see people passing by. The way a head turned or a hand lifted seemed charged with eroticism. Like Julia, he felt the season's vibration of energy carried on the dusty city air.

"It would make good commercial sense for George," Julia pleaded. "His name needn't be associated with it, for God's sake."

"George doesn't need any more money," Felix said gently. "Put your efforts into getting backing from somewhere else. If it's any help," he added, "I've got two or three thousand of my own that you can use."

Her intense expression fractured into a brilliant smile of gratitude. She leaned across the table and kissed him. "You angel."

"It won't be enough," he warned her. "Find some premises that would be suitable, work out the rent and taxes, do your figures on the basis of those costs. You could try to raise a corresponding amount from your bank."

"Just what I advised Thomas." She beamed at him. "And Thomas did it."

"Mmm. Is there anyone else you could try? Mattie?"

"I think Mattie should hang on to her money. Rainy day, all that. I don't think she's going to make much from the Women's Stage Group. Financially, that is."

Felix and Julia looked at each other, then mutually avoided the subject.

"What about Alexander?"

The light faded from Julia's face. "Of course not Alexander."

She had seen Alexander only the day before. He had come to take Lily away to stay at Ladyhill.

Julia had recited all the truths to herself. It was good for Lily to be in the country in the middle of the summer. The Gordon Mansions flat was dark, and the streets outside were heavy with dirt. At Ladyhill she could play under the trees in the orchard, and pedal her tricycle in the sheltered courtyard. Julia could see so clearly exactly how she would be, making darting rushes on the red trike, her dark head bent low over the handlebars. It was good for her to be with her father. Alexander would give his time to her more generously than Julia ever did. And the freedom would give Julia time to work. To look for premises and stock, once she had raised the problematic money. When the necessity of taking care of Lily stopped Julia from rushing to see a new designer, or from going with Thomas to look at some exciting work, she longed for the same freedom with desperate impatience.

Yet when the time came for her to hand Lily over to Alexander, she could hardly make herself do it. But she had promised. That was the deal, and she couldn't go back on it now.

Lily went happily. She looked from one of them to the other, somehow aware, with all her three-year-old perception, of the power she possessed. Then she put her hand in Alexander's. "Let's go in the car." She loved cars, and because Julia didn't own one a ride was a treat.

"Be good for Daddy and Granny Faye. Have a nice time." *I won't cry. They mustn't see me cry.*

Julia and Alexander didn't look at each other. They said polite things in neutral voices. Alexander admired the orange plastic chair that Thomas had left behind for Lily. "It's made by a friend of mine. I've been helping him to sell them."

"Good."

Even after they had gone, Julia could hear other words in her head. But they couldn't have been uttered, not between the two stiff, colorless people that she and Alexander had become. She was left with the physical ache of longing for the sound and the touch of Lily. Work, Julia thought. Work would anesthetize it. Turning a slippery idea into solid reality.

"I couldn't ask Alexander," she repeated.

"Well then, someone else. I don't think it'll be too difficult."

Julia smiled at Felix. She could smell his expensive, lemony cologne mingled with the scents of coffee and garlic and French cigarettes. The existence of such things that could be measured and bought and consumed was comforting compared with the frightening equations of love and need.

"You're a good friend. I hope your faith in my commercial sense is justified."

"I think it will be."

They finished their glasses of wine, sketching a toast, and went out again into the August sun.

The bank manager peered at her across the expanse of his big, shiny desk. There was nothing on it but her own neatly typed proposals and figures. His frown seemed to melt into his horn-rimmed glasses.

Julia had done exactly as Felix had advised. After a week of intensive searching, she had found a little shop to let just off the King's Road itself. If she missed that one, she thought, she could find another similar one without too much trouble. She had figured out the rent and taxes over a year, and added those figures to some minimal shop equipment and the major capital outlay on stock. Staff would be herself. She would have to pay herself something in order to live, but that would be as little as possible. She calculated that if she opened in time for Christmas, she could hope to break even in a few months. And she had come to lay her figures in front of the bank manager.

To Julia the careful calculations suddenly felt like little more than wishful guesses. But Felix and Thomas had assured her that they seemed businesslike enough.

The bank manager turned his Parker pen over and over in his fingers. "What will you call your—ah—shop, Lady Bliss? Your proposed business doesn't seem to have a name."

Julia almost smiled. The importance of a name. Lady Bliss might, after all, impress a bank manager more than Julia Smith. "I'm going to call it Garlic & Sapphires."

The man blinked. "But, as I understand it, you are not intending to sell either continental foodstuffs or precious stones?"

Julia knew then that she wouldn't get the loan.

"It's from a poem. Quite a famous poem, actually." She had brought the volume home from Holborn Library and read it in Mattie's Bloomsbury flat. "For the shop, it's just supposed to sound different and intriguing."

"I see."

It was very clear that he didn't see anything at all. Julia guessed that the last poem he had read was "Daffodils," in the fourth grade. And that different and intriguing were not business-like adjectives. He drew her papers together in front of him and tapped them to align the edges. Then he told her why he wasn't prepared to give her a loan. Not even to match her own capital of two and a half thousand pounds. She had decided that it wasn't necessary to mention that the money was really Felix's.

"It is my sad experience," he concluded, pompous to the last, "that women do not make successful business people. Particularly in ephemeral enterprises of this kind. Perhaps if your husband . . ."

"My husband is not connected with this proposal," Julia said coldly. She found herself standing up, holding out her hand for her papers.

"If I happened to be a man, would you think differently?" she asked.

The man didn't even hear the significance of the question.

"It's possible," he answered. He made a note for himself and screwed the cap back on his pen. The interview was over.

Julia strode past his minions at their desks outside his door. They reminded her of herself outside George Tressider's door, and she promised herself that she wouldn't stay in that subordinate position for a day longer than she had to. She walked out of the bank and straight down to the river. The muddy breeze blowing off it cooled her hot face. When her rage had subsided, she leaned over the parapet and looked down at the water.

The color of green olives, as it had been the day she met Alexander . . .

Julia jerked her head up. She was renewing her promises to herself, and this time not just to survive, but to be a huge, blazing incandescent success.

She had a moment of understanding of Mattie, and of Mattie's early craving to be an actress, a Name, a Somebody. Mattie had done it, and on her own. The recognition was like a bond, tightening, making her long for her friend's company. And if Mattie could do it, Julia could do it too. Not even though she was a woman, but because of it. She would find the sinew to do it without a husband or a lover, a prop or a screen. And it would be something that she could pass on to Lily, even though she couldn't give her grass or space or the protection of ancestral walls.

Not yet.

The determination to raise enough money to match Felix's became an obsession. Julia went to see everyone she could think of and begged and flattered and cajoled. And when Sophia's husband, Toby, couldn't stand it any longer, he introduced her to a banker friend of his who had some private funds to invest. He read her proposal carefully, asked her some searching questions, and then, to Julia's triumphant joy, agreed to the loan.

She took a deep breath, gave George notice, and went out and signed the lease on the shop premises.

"I've done it," she told Thomas Tree. "We're in business."

"I've done it," she told Mattie. "You are talking to the proprietor of Garlic & Sapphires."

Mattie shouted with delight. "Now we're doing it. Now we're going places."

She came to see the shop, with Chris and Freda. Mattie looked happier than she had for months. Her face looked rounder, and her hair waved wildly. She had discarded her tight skirts and boots in favor of jeans and shirts, like the others wore. But most noticeably of all, the old aggression had softened. In the past Mattie had wisecracked and attacked to defend herself. She was still funny and witty now, but she laughed more at herself because she was relaxed enough to see the joke.

Seeing her with her new friends, Julia kept her jealousy rigidly contained. She thought, *Mattie's happy at last. That's what counts*.

After the shop had been admired, the three of them took Julia to the pub. They made mild fun of her gin and tonic beside their beers, and Julia smiled to hear Mattie, who she couldn't remember ever opening a newspaper except to read her horoscope, discussing women's freedom and workers' freedom and Karl Marx.

Felix asked Julia, "Are you going to let me help you design your shop even though you turned me down for your flat?"

She hugged him. "I hardly dared to ask."

They had a wonderful time doing it.

"I want white and silver," Julia said. "Space-age silver. The color of the sixties."

They painted the inside shell of the shop white, and from an Italian lighting designer Felix bought a dozen silvery anodized spotlights. Julia eyed them skeptically when they were delivered, but when the electrician had wired them in and Felix switched them on, she gasped in amazement. Bright, pure pools of white light shone on the floors and walls.

"Your merchandise will look as good as sapphires," Felix said. Within a year the newest shops and rooms and restaurants were all spotlit.

Felix made low wooden plinths and pyramids and sprayed them silver, and Thomas bought aluminum sheeting and smoothed it and polished it to make the shelves for the walls.

"It's going to look wonderful," Julia breathed. "I hope I can find goods to do it justice."

In the busiest, shortest days of her life she borrowed a beat-up car and set off on a circuit of art colleges, workshops, import companies, and wholesalers. She rejected most things, but when she saw something she wanted she bargained, chiseled, and begged for delivery dates. She discovered that she had undreamed-of talents. She could beat a glass importer's price down without agreeing to take any more of his greenish glass wine goblets on firm order. She could make a reluctant designer promise to deliver another half-dozen of his shiny PVC licorice allsort cube seats by guaranteeing that they would just walk out of her wonderful new shop.

For most of the goods she had to pay in advance because she was new and unknown, and she was frightened all the time as she wrote out the checks in the brand-new company checkbook. But she was also exhilarated. The excitement of finding something she loved and longed to sell was unlike anything she had ever known.

Then, in a slow stream just as the furnishing was completed, the merchandise began to arrive. Felix and Thomas and Julia were like children at Christmas. They stayed in the shop until late at night, unpacking the boxes and carrying the newest treasures around in their arms, from silver plinth to silver shelf, to find where they looked their very best.

Very late one night, after even Felix and Thomas had gone home to bed, Julia stood looking at her white and silver creation, the bright colors of her stock shining like jewels. Thomas's palm tree stood in the window, its plastic fronds dipping against the blackness outside. For once she wasn't thinking about the money it had all cost and counting up in her head the sales that must be made before she could begin to recoup any of it.

Instead, she told herself with elation, *This is right*. For a moment she was clearly aware of the frustration and boredom that had muted and stretched the last years. They were tangible, like a thick, wrinkled skin. She was frightened and exhausted now, but she was awake. She was lonely, but the loneliness fueled her.

With the awareness she thought of Alexander, and of how little happiness she had succeeded in bringing him. Coldly, she thought of Josh too. I'm learning to be tough, she realized. She didn't know whether that was what she wanted, but she was sure that it was happening.

She made a last circuit of the shop, touching a gleam of silver, moving a glass so that it caught the light. Then she went to the bank of switches. She extinguished the white circles of light one by one, and the shop crowded with shadows. Julia locked the doors on them and drove home in her borrowed car.

At the height of Julia's rush to make the shop ready, Alexander had brought Lily back. He was going abroad to do some lucrative work, he explained regretfully.

Lily ran down the steps to the basement front door at Gordon Mansions and launched herself into her mother's arms. She was bigger and heavier, and she was wearing an unfamiliar pink dress with a Peter Pan collar that must have been bought by Faye. Julia held her and pretended to stagger under her weight.

She rubbed the curly hair and kissed her while Lily pinched her cheeks and nose and shouted her news. Julia had hardly had time to miss her, and she knew that she was too busy to spend enough time with her now. The familiarity of guilt and anxiety knotted with her love and pleasure.

"There's a pony, and I rided it!"

"Did you really? I can't ride a pony."

"Why didn't you come and see me?"

Over Lily's head their eyes met. "I have to stay in London, Lily. I'm busy making our new shop. Wait till you see it, it's so beautiful."

Alexander followed them into the flat. Lily ran to and fro, finding half-forgotten possessions and bouncing on the beds and chairs. Watching Julia pour him a drink, Alexander told her the truth without thinking about it first.

"You look happy, Julia."

She handed him his glass before answering, carefully, "I'm very busy. I don't know about happy." She was afraid of his probing, and she added, as if to deflect him, "How's Ladyhill?"

He accepted the deflection, changing the subject to an important sale of English furniture to be held the next month. "There's some linenfold paneling, and some fine chairs. I want them quite badly. Felix is going to the sale for me. Didn't he tell you?"

"No, he didn't."

Felix was tactful. He never mentioned the work at Ladyhill unless Julia asked directly, and she rarely did that.

"Well. I hope you get the pieces you want." *Obsessions*, she thought. *Alexander's with Ladyhill, now mine with Garlic & Sapphires. Both of us, putting our love and energy into inanimate safekeeping.* It was the first time that the similarity had struck her. Lily ran back into the room, dragging an armful of toys with her.

Except for Lily; we both love Lily. What would happen when she was older? Anxiety flicked her again, like a cold finger. There was no safekeeping between parents and children, any more than between men and women. Julia was rawly certain of that. She shivered, and tightened her fingers on her glass so that a drop of wine spilled over the rim. She licked it away, hoping that Alexander wouldn't see. "Lily seems to have enjoyed herself."

Alexander smiled. "I think she did."

The summer at Ladyhill had drawn them close. Lily had

seemed much older when she arrived, suddenly an individual instead of the unpredictable baby he had taken on weekend outings and for the first long visit to Ladyhill. Then, she had been a mystery to cajole and placate. China and Faye, with their female expertise, had been essential assistants. But this time, the two of them had made friends.

Alexander had put off all his own work until the evenings, when Lily was in bed. Through a succession of long, hot days they had explored the grounds and the fields around the house. They had picnicked, and waded in the river, and Lily had demonstrated her swimming in the deep pool under a line of alders where Alexander had learned to swim as a little boy. He had watched her rounded arms and legs moving strongly under the water with a mixture of pride and amazement.

He built her a house in the low branches of an oak tree, and taught her to climb the ladder to the little door. Lily helped herself to plates and cups from the kitchen, and gravely invited him into her house for banquets of shredded leaves and rose-petal tea. He found that he enjoyed the games of pretend almost as much as Lily did herself, and wondered why he couldn't remember playing in his own childhood.

"I've been grown up for much too long," he told her, and she nodded sympathetically.

"Never mind. Have a nice cup of tea."

Lily loved Ladyhill, Alexander could see that. It was one of the surprising, potent pleasures that her company gave him. She followed him through the house, unafraid of the black, remote corners that were still waiting to be restored, unawed by the echoing spaces of the rooms and the shadowy passages. Her own voice echoed through it as she shouted after him. The house and the gardens were her playground, and she took possession of them without hesitation. Alexander was delighted.

"She did enjoy herself," he told Julia.

Julia looked from one to the other of them, but she saw the house with its blackened walls and the exposed rafters like bony fingers. The walls were clean now, of course, and the roof was whole again. It was fanciful and morbid to think of the fingers reaching out for Lily. It was jealousy again, no more than that. The wine slopped once more in Julia's glass.

"Good for her to be in the fresh air," she said with a show of briskness.

Alexander prepared to leave.

"I'm opening the shop in two weeks' time," Julia told him. "There's a party to celebrate it."

He nodded politely. "Good luck. I'm sorry I won't be here. But this job will pay for the paneling."

"Of course." She would have liked him to be there to see it, but she wouldn't let him know as much. Even then the pettiness of her motives dismayed her.

After Alexander had gone, Lily said, "Let's play now."

Julia peered around the flat and saw the limitations of the walls and windows looking out on the murky streets. For the last weeks it had been no more than a place to sleep. Now it would have to be home to both of them again. She tried to smile reassuringly. She had a pile of paperwork to do and half a dozen telephone calls to make. "Tell you what. Why don't you do a painting?"

And with Lily installed at the other end of the table with her paintbox and a glass of water, Julia did her best to work. Irritation at the constant interruptions gave way to a mild panic. She could do her accounts at night, all night if necessary, but suppliers wouldn't welcome midnight telephone calls.

"Lily, I'm busy."

"Daddy doesn't be busy."

Julia's head jerked up. Staring across the table into the child's clear eyes, Julia read the signs of a new, strong will, and the beginnings of defiance. She looked like her father. "Daddy isn't here, is he?" Dismay made her voice sharp. In her own ears she sounded as childish as Lily herself.

Lily's stare didn't waver. "I want to play. Not paint."

Julia's patience deserted her. She snapped, "We can't always do what we want to do. Whatever you and Daddy think." *There. Now I've put them both on one side and ranged myself against them. All in the space of an hour.*

She dropped her pen with a clatter and went around the table. She lifted Lily from her chair and held her. "I love you," she whispered. The violence of it made Lily stare harder, and Julia knew that she was only confusing her.

Out of nowhere the thought came to her. *If I had a real mother, would I be a better mother myself?*

The riddle seemed unanswerable. Wearily, Julia focused on the present battle. "Tomorrow you can go to Forgum's." Forgum was Lily's name for the baby-sitter. "And play with Warren and all the toys."

"Don't want to," Lily wailed. "She's horrid." She knew

that she had the advantage, and she was pressing it home. Like a full-grown adversary. If she hadn't been caught so badly off balance, Julia might have laughed.

"No, she isn't. She's your friend, and Warren is too. Come on, let's go to the park now if you want to play."

And Lily, all smiles again, beamed up at her through her wet black eyelashes.

In the morning, at Mrs. Forgan's, she cried and hid behind Julia's skirt. The woman pursed her lips. "It's disruptive, Mrs. Bliss. Taking her away for weeks. No wonder."

Cowardly, Julia said, "I'm sorry. It's the only way." She disentangled her hand from Lily's and ran away, trying not to hear the screams from the other side of the door. She raced to the shop and worked with all the concentration she could muster until it was time to go back to Mrs. Forgan's again.

The last two weeks of preparation before the opening of Garlic & Sapphires were a whirlwind. Lily quickly realized that the shop was her rival for her mother's attention, and she marshaled all her resources to divert Julia from it. She tried everything, from saccharine charm to temper tantrums, and then alarming, convincing illness. She's only three years old, Julia told herself. She needs me, and she needs to be shown that she can't win.

She dismissed the images of Betty that came back to her, and did her best to be consistent and gentle. She gave Lily medicine for her complaints, waited patiently until the tantrums burned themselves out in gales of sobbing, and lived every day with the guilt that Lily's sweetness brewed in her.

But the effort cost her, and she knew that sometimes she hated her own child, and felt the weight of her like a stone around her neck. Love and guilt seemed ugly, inseparable partners.

Then, one afternoon, Julia came home with the worries of the business aching in her head and the prospect of an evening poring over some figures ahead of her. Lily, dragging her sandaled feet beside her, suddenly wound her arm through the iron railings of the basement steps and refused to let go.

"Come on, Lily, I'm tired," Julia begged her.

"I'm stuck," Lily announced with pleasure.

The anger that suddenly flashed through Julia's body was as powerful as lightning. In that instant she had enough wild strength to tear the railings out of the stone steps. But what she did was grasp Lily's hand and pull her. The small arm twisted through the rails and then came free. Julia dragged Lily down the last steps behind her. Violent. She wanted to hurt her.

Julia felt her own strength, boiling and bursting inside the package of her flesh, overwhelming Lily's irritant frailty. She felt mad, and wicked, and triumphant. Then Julia's heel caught on the bottom step, and she tripped. They fell together in a heap on their own doorstep. Julia lay, panting like an animal, the power drained out of her limbs. She opened her eyes to look at Lily, beginning to struggle upright, and she saw the child flinch. Her face was stiff. She was too shocked and frightened even to cry.

Julia looked down at her arm. The skin was crimson, except for the long white rake of a fresh graze. Three tiny red beads of blood stood out of it. "Oh, God, Lily. Look what I've done. I'm sorry. Mummy's sorry."

She began to tremble violently. Her teeth chattered and her hand shook as she fumbled in her handbag for the door key. Somehow she wrenched the door open and scooped Lily up. She glanced up the steps like a criminal. Nobody there. Nobody had seen the terrible thing. Julia kicked their scattered possessions through the open door and tottered into the hallway with Lily in her arms. With the familiarity of home around her, Lily found her voice. She opened her mouth, took one breath, and began to scream. Julia sank down to the floor and rocked her, trying to soothe her and to control her own scalding tears.

As soon as she could think again, and Lily had quieted a little, Julia carried her to the telephone. With their wet faces still pressed together, she dialed Mattie's number. Miraculously, Mattie was at home.

"Please come," Julia said. "Please. I need some help."

Mattie sat with Lily on her lap. Nowadays Mattie wore her spectacular hair bundled up and tied with a brown bootlace, but Lily had managed to undo the knot and she was playing with the shiny gold coils. Mattie examined the bare arm, and the graze that had turned angry red.

"Nothing broken," she said cheerfully.

She hadn't suggested a drink, the usual remedy for all ills. Instead, she had made Julia a cup of tea, ladling sugar into it. Julia drank it without tasting it.

"I wanted her to be hurt," she whispered, driven by the need to confess. Disgust filled her mouth, hotter and stronger than the tea.

Mattie eyed her. "The thing you mustn't do," she told her, "is make a great fuss about it. Everyone does it, or nearly does it. You're not a monster, or unique. I've seen Rozzie with hers, my ma with us, when we were little, before she gave up on us. Myself with Phil or Marilyn or one of the others. Just sometimes everything drives you too far.''

"I might have hurt her badly. Even worse . . .''

"Doubt it,'' Mattie interrupted. "Drink your bloody tea. But that doesn't say you don't need some help.''

"Oh, Mattie.''

"What about an au pair girl, or whatever they're called?''

Julia waved at the three rooms. "Here? And I can only just afford the Forgum.''

Mattie reached out and patted her shoulder.

"Don't worry,'' she said. "We'll think of something.''

Soon, much too quickly, the day of the opening came. Julia felt like a walking assembly of lists. She had lists of stock, a list of people who had promised to come to the opening, lists of vital tasks, probably, somewhere, a list of the lists. She was high with anticipation, and as keyed up as if she were opening a department store instead of a little shop off the King's Road.

With Lily she had established an uneasy truce. Lily allowed herself to be taken to Mrs. Forgan's, but she misbehaved there and the baby-sitter's limited supply of patience was clearly wearing out. Her lips pursed tighter every day and Warren, clinging to her skirts, looked more deflated.

"It's a bit hard at the moment,'' Julia conciliated. "After the shop's open, we'll both be better.''

"I hope so,'' Mrs. Forgan said thinly.

The party was to be in the evening. More people would come then, of course, Felix had said. Julia spent the day tidying the immaculate shop and looking nervously at the rows of polished glasses waiting for her guests. She took Lily home early and gave her her tea, and she was just zipping up her own red silk tunic ready to dash away as soon as the baby-sitter arrived, when the girl telephoned. She said that she was ill and couldn't come. Julia knew the truth was more probably that she had a date, but there was nothing to be done about it.

Lily blinked angelically over a well-sucked banana.

"Lily, you're going to come to Mummy's party. Will you be good?''

"Can I wear my party dress?''

Julia found it and buttoned her into it and they raced to the shop together.

Thomas Tree was already there, humming and uncorking bottles of wine. Julia was so glad to see him, she put her arms around him and hugged him. She had almost forgotten that she had a partner, even a nonactive one. The jokes about sleeping partners had already been made, not quite as easily and naturally as Julia might have hoped.

"I had to bring Lily. The bloody baby-sitter let me down."

Thomas grinned down at Lily in her frilly dress. "The more the merrier. You're only small, so you need a special seat, where you can see everyone. What about this one?"

He hoisted her into a transparent inflatable chair. One of Julia's kaleidoscope of memories of the evening was of Lily seemingly floating in the white and silver cavern, her feet sticking straight out in front of her, watching wide-eyed with her thumb in her mouth.

Felix arrived with George. George announced that it all looked very amusing.

Mattie came, with Chris Fredericks, but she also brought Tony Drake and the luminous fashion model who was his latest girl.

Mattie winked. "Bumped into each other, just like that. Didn't we, Tone?" And in a sibilant whisper, "I thought he'd add a bit of color. Don't ask him to say anything."

The film star and the model lounged decoratively among Thomas's palm trees, and within seconds, it seemed, the shop was full of people. There were photographers with flashbulbs, and gossip columnists as well as the trade writers and fashion commentators that Julia and Felix had invited.

The news of something new and exciting going on traveled faster than a forest fire. Chelsea was still a village, and for an evening the party at Garlic & Sapphires was the hub of it.

"Everyone is here, darling," Felix said.

In the melée, Julia shook hands, kissed cheeks, and took orders.

"I love it. We'll feature it."

"Can we bring some girls, do some fashion shots?"

"Has Tony seen it?"

"I want a dozen chairs."

Suddenly, people were buying. Julia retreated behind her cash register and took money, real money. Her hands were shaking. Tony Drake loomed over her with a portfolio of glossy photographs. The furniture illustrated was much too expensive for Julia to stock—the portfolio and a promise were all she could manage. But Tony Drake's beefy, tanned fingers prodded the page. "I want this table."

It was an octagonal dining table carved out of Perspex and mounted on a Perspex column.

"It's three hundred pounds."

"Yeah."

"Up to ten weeks to deliver."

"Yeah. You in the selling line, or not?"

Julia laughed. Tony Drake was right. If she was going to sell, she would have to sell hard. "Yes sir. And as it's for you, I'll see if I can make them produce it in ten days." Everything was selling. Best of all were the little things, the witty candles and cushions and china . . . not a big margin, but with a big enough volume turnover . . . here I am, *I'm in business*. Joyfully, in the midst of the hubbub, Julia looked up and saw another familiar face. It was Ricky Banner, Mattie's little brother. Except that he wasn't little anymore, he was six foot two and wore his hair brushed forward in bangs just like the Beatles. Ricky was the bass guitarist in a group called The Dandelions who were playing the pub and club circuit. Mattie had bought him his first guitar with money earned from *One More Day*. Like all the Banners, Ricky attracted children as infallibly as a jar of sweets. Lily was perched on his shoulders, her head brushing the ceiling.

"Long time, Julia," Ricky said.

"A very long time." She remembered Mattie's kitchen on the estate, the first time, with Rozzie frying onions and children tumbling everywhere.

"Mat said you wouldn't mind."

"Of course I don't. And if you're looking after Lily, you're more welcome than Drake and the editor of the *Sunday Times* mag put together."

Mattie materialized beside her brother. She put her arm around his waist, proud and pleased. "We've got an idea, me and Rick. It came to us, just like that. It's called Marilyn."

"What?" Noise was pounding off the white walls, and another popping flash intensified the white and silver light. The party was in full swing.

"Our little sister. She's seventeen now. She wants a job in London, she loves kids, and she doesn't expect gracious living. What d'you think?"

How long ago, when Mattie and Julia had huddled together in the Savoy doorway? To comfort Mattie in her anxiety for

Marilyn and the rest, Julia had promised her, *They can all come and live with us. When we've made it.* Now, with Garlic & Sapphires reverberating around her, she thought that she hadn't made it yet, but there was a chance. And there wasn't room at Gordon Mansions for all the Banners, but somehow, by squeezing herself, she knew she should make room for Marilyn. A slow, delighted smile spread over Julia's face.

"What do I think? I think you might have saved our lives." And she looked up at Lily. Her face was flushed with overexcitement, and there were dark rings around her eyes, but her expression was unreadable. She gazed unblinkingly back at her mother. The graze on her arm had disappeared long ago; there were no other marks to see. None to see, but Julia knew how badly she still needed help. She reached up to stroke Lily's bare knee.

"It's all right," she said inaudibly. "I may not be very good, but I'm doing my best. I think we'll be all right, the two of us."

Someone twitched at her sleeve. "Julia, Julia. There's someone here you must meet."

She gave Mattie and Ricky a quick hug. "Tell Marilyn to come and see us as soon as she wants."

At last the crowd began to thin out. The celebrities and the hangers-on and the paparazzi filtered out into the street, most of them carrying their purchases in Julia's special sapphire-blue wrapping paper. George had gone much earlier; eventually Felix followed him. Ricky had left with another boy from his group, Mattie and Chris had disappeared, perhaps with Tony Drake. In the end, Julia and Thomas were left alone. Lily had fallen asleep, and had been put to bed on two chairs in the back of the shop. Julia let out a long breath and stared around at the debris. The girls who had prepared the food and poured the wine had gone too. She was almost surprised to see that the stock was still there. She had been afraid, halfway through the evening, that there would be none left. But there was enough, still on the silver shelves and plinths, for tomorrow. The first real day, opening to real customers at ten o'clock.

"Was it worth it?" Thomas asked. "Is it worth it?"

She bent down to pick up a glass lying at her feet and straightened up again. "Yes." She smiled at him. "It was worth it. It is worth it."

Her eyes went to Lily, asleep under their two coats.

"Come on," Thomas said. "We'll clear half of this lot now

and come in early in the morning to do the rest before opening-up time.''

"Thank you,'' Julia said gratefully

They did as much as they could find the energy for and then, without warning, Julia found herself in one corner of the shop with Thomas in front of her. She tried to slip around him, but he moved to block her way. She noticed, seemingly for the first time, how tall he was. He put his hand out and touched her fingers. "May I come home with you tonight?''

Oh, no, Thomas.

The words sprang up automatically, but she didn't say them. Thomas's old car must be parked outside; without him Julia would have to carry Lily off in search of a taxi. Suddenly, desperately, Julia longed for some help. Just ordinary, simple help and support. The efforts of the last weeks felt too much, an unscalable height rising in retrospect. If she went home with Thomas, he would put his arms around her, after Lily had been put safely in her own bed. Thomas had shared tonight with her. She didn't want to go home from this party alone.

Julia knew that it was shameful to say yes to him for comfort's sake, but she was lonely and tired, and she knew that Thomas was kind. She saw his wrists, protruding from the cuffs of his best shirt, and she also saw the hungry way that he looked at her.

She bent her head. "Yes,'' she whispered, not quite willingly, thinking, *Sleeping partner.* "But Lily mustn't know anything. She must think you stayed in the living room.''

With one finger Thomas touched the angle of her jaw. "You mustn't let Lily be the law you govern yourself by. You have a life of your own to lead.''

"I'll work it out with Lily without your help.'' Julia's voice was very sharp. And then, "I'm sorry. I didn't mean to sound like that.''

He kissed her, awkwardly, like a boy. Julia stood still. Something had made her think of Alexander. Loneliness swooped around her again. Thomas let her go, and went to pick Lily up out of her nest of coats.

"Let's go home,'' he said gently.

NINETEEN

On Sunday mornings the house filled with the sound of church bells, as if it stood on some village green instead of in a London terrace. In fine weather the sun reflected off the canal and cast ripples of light on the tall ceilings, heightening the rural atmosphere.

Julia stood at the long window on the half-landing, looking down into the little yard. The daffodils in the tubs had faded, but the muscari still lay in sheets of Oxford blue. In the shade beneath the fences were the plum-dark clumps of hellebores, to Julia the most beautiful of all flowers. Around them, overnight competition for the unemphatic hellebores were the new spikes of brash green growth. At the end of the garden was the Regent's Park Canal, and the willows along the towpath showed the first pale fronds of green.

The house was quiet, except for the bells. Julia stood watching the water and the movement of the leaves, and when the bells had wound after each other through the last peal and into humming silence, she turned away from the window and went slowly downstairs. As it always did, the scented, insistent stirring of English springtime made her feel restless.

The ground floor had been opened out, at Felix's suggestion, into one big, L shaped space, kitchen and living room and dining room all together. There was a chesterfield under the tall windows that looked out over the garden, and an old pine table with a wicker-shaded lamp hanging above it. The sun shone in through the windows that faced on to the quiet street, making yellow squares on the floor, and the stripped and polished boards felt warm under Julia's bare feet.

Lily was sitting at the table, in the T-shirt she slept in instead of pajamas, reading. She looked up when Julia came in. Her hair was cut short now, emphasizing the shape of her face. Lily was almost nine, and the adult lines were beginning to emerge from the babyish roundness. Her coloring was her mother's but her features, even to the high bridge of her nose, were Alexander's. She resembled him in other ways too. She could be reserved to the point of detachment, and then blaze into sudden anger. Alexander and his daughter were very close. Julia and Alexander had been divorced for four years, but with Lily she lived, schizophrenically, with his constant presence.

"I've had my breakfast," Lily said.

"That's good," Julia answered, refusing to interpret her daughter's words as a complaint or as a criticism of her own late appearance. Some days, they could make the simplest remark into material for a battle. Not today, Julia thought, not with the spring sun shining. On good days Lily's company was more enjoyable than anyone else's. Julia went to the hob to heat herself up some leftover coffee. Lily had brought in the Sunday newspapers and they were lying in a neat pile on the table. With her mug of coffee in one hand, Julia flipped through them. Then she stopped short. Mattie's face stared up at her from the cover of the *Sunday Times* magazine. The picture must have been taken the year before, in Mattie's high hippie phase. Her hair was knotted with flowers and colorful scarves, and she was wearing some sort of flowing ethnic robe. Julia looked at it carefully, and then held it up for Lily to see. "Look at this."

Lily's face broke into smiles. She loved Mattie. "Hey, that's great. D'you think Marilyn's seen it? Shall I take it down?"

The basement of the house was Marilyn's separate domain. Hastily, Julia said, "Wait until I've read the article. Anyway, it's a bit early for Marilyn on a Sunday."

She wasn't quite sure who Marilyn might have down there with her, and she preferred Lily not to know either. Or, at least, to appear not to know. There was very little going on around her that Lily missed.

"What's it say?" Lily asked now. They sat down side by side on the chesterfield and read the piece together. It was a standard show biz interview, pegged to the release of Mattie's latest film. It touched only lightly on Mattie's reputation as a feminist and political activist, and made no mention of her private life at all. Julia guessed that her PR agent had seen to that. The interviewer did retell the story of her Oscar nomination for her last role as the heroine of a lush Thomas Hardy adaptation. Mattie had made no secret of her intention to refuse the reward as a protest against American involvement in Vietnam, but anyway, the Oscar had been shared by Hepburn and Streisand, and Mattie had been deprived of the chance to make her defiant gesture.

"Not very interesting," Lily pronounced. "It doesn't make her sound like Mattie."

"These things never do," Julia answered. "Not to those of us who know her."

She closed the magazine again and studied Mattie's face. Seeing it there reminded her of Mattie's first spurt of fame, with *One More Day*. Kitchen sink dramas, and Jimmy Proffitt. How long ago, and how quaintly archaic, viewed through the distorting glass of the sixties. Julia remembered how equivocal she had felt about Mattie's success, and how guilty for not being able to rejoice completely. She was just married to Alexander then, just pregnant with Lily. Before the fire. When Ladyhill was seemingly invulnerable, and Flowers was still alive.

Julia tried to remember why her memories were of unhappiness. *I could have been happy. There was no reason not to be, except for Josh.*

When she thought of him now, still too often, it was with a mixture of impatience and skepticism, but added to those were more powerful elements of sadness and loss. There was a kind of reverence, too, for something that had once been valuable and was still too precious to bundle up and throw away like an outmoded dress.

She hadn't seen Josh since the days in the little white house that had marked the effective end of her marriage to Bliss. Julia frowned at the rawness of the memory. They had written to each other once in a while, but they had never met. Strangely, Julia had once been invited to a party in the little mews house. She had recognized it with a painful shock. Josh's friends, whoever they were, must have sold it and moved on long before. The white walls had been painted over with psychedelic designs and the white furniture had been replaced with Afghan rugs and beaded cushions. The cushions had come from Julia's shop. The new owners were customers of hers. The odd cycles that life moved in. Julia felt old as she leaned forward and laid the magazine on the floor. Mattie still stared at her sideways through the tangled hair and scarves.

At least, she reflected, she felt only pride and pleasure in Mattie's success nowadays. Perhaps greater equanimity was one of the few compensations for getting older. At the height of a generation's youth-worship, to turn thirty had seemed almost a criminal offense. And Julia had her own success too. If she was neither as rich nor as famous as Mattie, she was at least established and comfortably off. She had opened a second Garlic &

Sapphires in Kensington High Street, then others in Brighton and Oxford. Astute Julia had recognized the appeal of Eastern mysticism almost as soon as the Maharishi did. She traveled to India and on to Afghanistan, buying up the necessary beads and fringes, mirrorwork fabrics and tinkling bells. The prevailing scent in Garlic & Sapphires now was slow-burning joss sticks. Even the shop name, so ridiculous to her first bank manager, had the right hippie-mystical overtones.

Julia traveled widely, searching out stock, leaving the shops in the care of capable managers, and Lily in the care of Marilyn or Alexander, depending on whether it was school time or holidays. Marilyn had come to Gordon Mansions and she had stayed. She was neither a nanny nor a companion nor a housekeeper, but she was good for Lily and, in her own way, she managed to organize the house in NW1 that Julia had bought with her business profits.

Usually, Julia and Marilyn worked together amicably. Julia could make up the domestic shortcomings herself, shopping when Marilyn had forgotten to do it, scrubbing the bathroom floor when she could no longer stand the grime.

"I'm glad you're not my real wife, Marilyn," she would joke, still able to acknowledge that the younger sister's presence, a pale imitation of Mattie even down to the domestic slovenliness, was welcome for the sake of the reminder. Especially when Mattie was away, which she often was. It was only over Lily that they disagreed. Once, at the beginning, Julia had had to work late even though Lily had been ill with a feverish cold. She had come home to find the Gordon Mansions flat empty. She had leapt to the conclusion that Lily must be worse, and that Marilyn must have rushed to the doctor's with her. She was dialing the office number when the two of them came in. They had been out to a boxing match. Marilyn's current love was an amateur boxer, and they had been to see him fight at a hall in Finsbury. Lily had sat on Marilyn's knee in the front row and had been petted and fussed over by all the managers and their female hangers-on. Her eyes were wide open with excitement and the reflected drama.

"She enjoyed it," Marilyn said. "Made her forget her cold. Dave won his bout."

Julia was furiously angry, and she had vented it on Marilyn. "You're not fit to look after a child," she had stormed. "You're thoughtless and selfish and careless."

But Marilyn had retaliated. She had drawn herself up,

looking more like Mattie, and shouted back. "I'm fitter than you are. And you're supposed to be her mother. Never here, are you? You put your shop first, and your own life, don't you? Don't think you can tell me off just for taking her to see a fight. You could take her a few more places yourself, only you're afraid she'll be a nuisance."

They had stared at each other, shocked into mutual silence. *She's right,* Julia had thought. *Half right.*

The overfamiliar chains of guilt, self-justification, and fierce love had clanked morbidly around her. Only it wasn't that she didn't want Lily with her. The truth was that she wanted to keep her apart from Thomas Tree. Thomas was her mother's lover, but Julia believed that the empty space of father, for Lily, could only properly be occupied by Alexander. She didn't want Thomas even to begin to usurp that place, even if Lily might have let him. She kept her loyalties to Lily and to Thomas separate, doubling her obligations and the necessary efforts to fulfill them. Even when Thomas had lived with them in the house overlooking the canal, she had tried, deviously, to keep a space between them. Julia knew that was one of the reasons why Thomas had moved out, almost two years ago.

"We just split," she told her friends, anyone who asked, even Mattie. "One of those things. Time to move on, you know?"

Back at the beginning, Julia had accepted Marilyn's criticism. It had never been mentioned again, but she never forgot it. On her part, Marilyn tried harder to fulfill Julia's conventional ideas of how Lily should be looked after.

All through that one argument that they had had in front of her, Lily had watched them in silence. Even then, she seemed to have the mature ability to watch, and assimilate, and judge for herself. Lily's ideas and opinions were always all her own. Julia was sometimes frightened by the vehemence of them, more often made angry by her calm stubbornness. She was like Alexander in that too.

"What are you thinking about, Mum?"

Lily stretched her legs, hitching the T-shirt around her. She was already tall for her age; she would have long legs and a slim figure. Teazle, the fat little pony kept at Ladyhill for her to ride, had long ago been replaced by a neat cob that Lily adored. There was a photograph of Lily cantering, in a hard hat and a hacking jacket, in a silver frame on the mantelpiece. Julia joked about it and called it the National Velvet, but she was proud of the picture.

"What am I thinking about? Nothing. Time. Getting old. Boring things like that."

Lily looked critically at her. "You aren't old. Not compared with some people's mothers. You're still quite with it."

"Thank you, darling."

Lily was fidgeting, pirouetting around the room, picking things up and putting them down again.

"What can we do today?"

Julia sighed. Sundays like this one should be peaceful, empty of obligations. But Lily needed to be busy. Julia knew where her daughter's restlessness came from.

"We could call someone up, ask some people to come to lunch. Would you like that?" There were plenty of friends. She had made sure that the house was always welcoming, that it was often filled with people who came to eat and to talk. Nor, after the years that had just gone by, did many of them belong to tidy, static families. Even Sophia and Toby had separated. Almost as soon as Sophia's boys had gone off to boarding school, Sophia had met a painter and moved in with him. Lily had never felt odd because her father and mother happened to lead separate lives. Nor had she ever felt trapped with Julia in an empty house. Julia remembered too vividly how no one had ever come to Fairmile Road, and how Betty had kept the little rooms stiffly arranged for a celebration that never happened.

"Can I cook something?" Lily asked.

"You'd better. I'm not doing everything. Well, who shall we ask?"

But before they had decided, the telephone rang.

"Julia? It's Mat." There was a busy silence before the words, static crackling over them.

"Mattie? How fabulous, where are you?"

"New York, of course."

"Must be telepathy. We were talking about you. Also your face is all over the color mag."

"Is it this week? Is it that picture that makes me look like a freaked-out gippo?"

" 'Fraid so."

"Bloody hell. Just when I'm trying to look straight so someone'll offer me some Shakespeare or something decent." Mattie was talking too quickly, and laughing a lot. She sounded slightly drunk, or high. Julia peered at the kitchen clock. A bar of yellow sunlight lay across the face of it.

"Mattie, what's the time there?"

"Um. Ten past six. In the morning, dear."

"Up early, aren't you?"

Mattie laughed louder. "How many dollars a minute is this chat about my bedtimes costing? I haven't been to bed, actually. Came back from a party, and knew I wouldn't be able to sleep in this hotel room. So I've watched an old movie on the TV—they have old movies all night, isn't it clever of them?—and then I thought I'd telephone my old friend." Mattie's real voice suddenly broke through. "I just wanted a talk. Felt a bit lonely, to tell the truth. It was a straight choice between ringing you and having another scotch. What's it like in London this morning?"

Smiling, Julia told her. She told her the news of mutual friends, and the snippets of gossip that Mattie loved. She told her about Lily's part in the school play.

"That's my girl. She'll knock their socks off," Mattie crowed. She was never afraid to let her pride or partiality show, as Julia was. Mattie thought Lily could do no wrong, and regularly said so.

"Go on," Mattie prompted. "What else is new?"

And so Julia told her about the latest buying she had done for the shop, about the house Felix was decorating for Bill Wyman, anything else she could think of that would make Mattie feel closer to home. They had always been able to do it. All through their successful years that had kept them apart more than they had been together, they had kept the links by telephoning each other. Even when Mattie had been inseparable from Chris Fredericks, and Julia had been wary and awkward with the two of them, they had been able to talk on the telephone when they couldn't do it face-to-face.

At last Mattie sighed. "That's better. I feel a bit less mad now. Hey, there's something I haven't told you. I'm coming home, to dear old Bloomsbury. I can't bear this town any longer."

And into the hum of the transatlantic connection, as if the idea was fully formed instead of just having stirred in her head with the restless reminders of spring and the enticing sunshine, Julia said, "Well, that's a pity. Because I'm coming to the States." Across the room, blurred by the bright light that showed the winter's accumulation of dust, Julia saw Lily's head jerk up. Just for an instant, her small face seemed set in an alarming mask of anger and anxiety.

"I haven't been before, that's why," she answered into the receiver. "I want to look for some new ideas, make a few contacts. Look ahead to the next decade, like a shopkeeper should.''

''And see the aviator.''

Lily had bent her head again, seemingly to her book. Julia was relieved, because she could feel the foolish flush of color rising in her own cheeks. Like a teenager, she thought angrily. Watching Lily's dark, smooth head, she thought that the strange expression must have been a trick of the light.

''I honestly hadn't thought of that. It's very old history, Mat.''

Far away, Mattie chuckled. ''D'you know how often you still talk about him? And you've sat there all these years, just like Patience on her bloody monument, waiting for him to come back for you. Not very liberated of you, is it?''

''That's your department, not mine,'' Julia said tartly, but Mattie only laughed again.

''Think about it. D'you know, I think I could go to sleep now. Thank God for that. Can I have a talk to Lily first?''

''Sleep well, my love. I will think about it, although I wish you'd never mentioned it.'' She held the receiver out to Lily. ''Here. Talk to the wild woman.''

Julia went out of the room, and when she came back Lily had already finished the conversation. She was sitting calmly on the sofa, cross-legged, waiting. Julia opened the address book she had been upstairs to fetch.

''Who would it be nice to see today?''

''I don't care,'' Lily said politely. ''You can choose if you like.''

The friends came to lunch, two women and a man, and three children of various ages. Julia made lasagna and they sat around the pine table talking, the adults drinking wine after the children had disappeared upstairs to Lily's room. At the end of the afternoon they went to Regent's Park and walked in the sunshine. It was a cheerful, convivial day, like dozens of others Julia and Lily had spent. Julia liked inviting people, and feeding them, and making them feel comfortable in her house. The parties were different now, she reflected, but there still were parties.

Lily was quieter than usual, but if anyone except Julia noticed it, no one mentioned it.

The light was fading when Julia went out to see the last pair of guests into their car. After they had driven off she stood for a moment under the plane tree outside the house, watching the lit-up windows of the houses opposite, and her neighbors passing to and fro behind the uncurtained glass. The little tableau made the street seem cozy. She breathed in a satisfying lungful of damp, leafy air and then went back up the five steps to their front door.

It was dim in the big living room after the brighter light outside. Julia blinked and hesitated, and then saw Lily sitting on the rug in front of the chesterfield. Her knees were drawn up to her chin and one cheek rested on one knee. Her shoulders were hunched forward as if to hide something, or protect something. A corner of the rug was pulled up underneath her. Julia was particularly fond of the rug, an old Anatolian kelim in soft, faded garnet reds and cobalt blues. It had long, hand-knotted, bobbled fringes, and an expert had told her that the design represented the tree of life. She was proud of the rug too. She had bought it on one of her first trips, when she was still nervous traveling alone, from a market in a little hill town. She had haggled and bargained with the old man who was selling it, and then had walked away because his price was too high. Then she had turned back because she knew she wanted it, and he had disarmed her by accepting her offer and rolling the rug up to press it into her arms, as if he knew it was going to a good home. There had been no question, after that, of it going into the shop. It exactly fit the space on the sanded floor.

Julia went across and put her hand on Lily's shoulder, intending to say something about supper and there being school tomorrow. Then she saw that Lily was methodically snipping off the knotted fringes, one by one, with the big pair of kitchen scissors. A pathetic pile of fraying ends lay on the floor beside her.

Julia snatched the scissors. They fell, and slithered out of sight under the chesterfield. Julia gave Lily's hand a stinging slap. She didn't flinch, but stared up at her mother, her face a set, triangular mask of defiant unhappiness. Julia saw the unhappiness, but her own possessive anger was much stronger. After the instant she was ashamed of it, but then it was too late.

She held on to Lily's hand, and shook her. "You stupid girl. Why have you done it? It's a beautiful rug, and you've wrecked it. You're a thoughtless, stupid vandal. Just to sit there and cut it up. Don't you care about people's things? It's not your rug to ruin. It's mine, I . . ."

Coldly, Lily cut her short. "Everything's yours. Your house, and your shops, and your friends. Well, I'm not yours, so there. I'm Alexander's. I wish he was here. I hate you."

Lily broke free and scrambled to her feet. She bent down and scooped up the severed fringes, then flung them across the room.

"It's only a mat," she shouted. "It's not a person." The coldness had gone. She was crying now, and the puckering of her face made her look as she had when she was a baby. Helplessly, Julia held her hand out to her, but Lily pushed it away from her and ran out of the room.

I'm Alexander's, Julia thought heavily. There had been other times, many other rows, of course, when Julia had forbidden something or enforced some discipline, and Lily had wished for her father. The bond between them had always been strong, and it was strengthening all the time as Lily grew up in her devotion to Ladyhill, and the green, folded countryside around it. Lily's pride in the rebirth of Ladyhill's splendor, artfully aged and faded by George and Felix, was no less fierce than Alexander's. After each visit she came back full of the details of the latest room that had been cleaned and reopened or of some nineteenth-century oil of the house that had passed out of the family and Alexander had managed to buy back again. Julia had accepted it all, as she had made herself promise she would at the beginning, and she had encouraged Lily to talk about her father as well as to think of Ladyhill as home, her other home.

But this was the first time that Lily had said, *I'm Alexander's.*

I hate you, Julia comforted herself, that was ordinary enough, wasn't it? All daughters told their mothers that sometime. But not, *I'm his, not yours.*

It had begun, then, as Julia had been afraid that it would. The measuring of one of them against the other, and as soon as measuring had started there would be judging, and then choosing. She didn't want to think of what that would mean. To push the thought away, she moved, stiffly, to pick up the scattered ends of fringes from where Lily had thrown them.

She is mine, she thought. *I was there when she was born, out of me, even though I don't remember it. Even though I'm a bad one, I am her mother.*

She looked down at the shreds of wool and silk in her hands. They smelled of dust, and there were pieces of fluff trapped with the fibers. *It is only a mat. Lily's right.*

She went quickly and threw them into the trash. Then she

retrieved the kitchen scissors and put them away in their proper place.

Suddenly a memory stirred and revived. A wonderful fire-work display of colored stars, spreading across some flowered wallpaper. The gummed stars that she had brought home, as a little girl, from somebody's birthday party. And then had stuck all over the bedroom wall. Julia remembered Betty's boiling anger, and her accusations, and the way that she had shouted, "It's our house, not yours." Julia realized that always, up to this moment, she had believed that she just thought the stars were pretty, that the bright colors improved the insipid wallpaper.

But now, as if she had become someone else altogether, she realized that she had wanted to deface the order of Betty's house. She could see herself, licking and sticking the stars, knowing that they would make a mess, knowing what Betty would do. She had wanted to assert herself, and distance herself, testing Betty and rebelling against her at the same time.

Poor Betty, Julia thought. All along I made her the villain of that story. I told it to Jessie, once, and I made myself out to be the innocent little thing who saw no farther than the bright, beautiful stars. How much did Lily understand of what she had done, how much did she mean? The same? The same test, and rebellion?

Julia frowned, trying to tease out the threads of signifi-cance. Lily had no need to rebel against petty domestic tyranny. Julia wasn't house-proud. She had been, briefly, very angry about her kelim, as surely anyone would have been. She liked and valued pretty things, and clearly remembered the days when she hadn't been able to afford them. But the moment was past now. It wasn't the mat that was important.

She could talk to Lily, at least. Betty had never talked to her.

Julia went slowly upstairs. Lily was lying on her bed, stiff, looking very small. She had been crying, but her eyes were dry now. Julia sat down at the edge of the bed, looking down at her. "What's the matter?" she asked gently. "Can you tell me why?"

Lily turned her head away to stare at the wall.

Julia waited, but the silence began to solidify between them. She knew from experience how stubbornly silent Lily could be when she was angry or sulking about something. It was quite possible that she wouldn't speak until tomorrow morning, and Julia didn't want to let that silence happen, not this time. To break it, she began talking herself. "Do you know something that happened when I was a bit younger than you? Something I did to Granny Smith? I went to a birthday party, and I was given a packet of colored sticky stars. The kind that teachers stick in exercise books, for good work . . ." She knew that Lily was listening, although she kept her face turned away. "Until tonight, you know, I always thought Granny Smith was wrong. But I've just understood that I knew what I was doing. I wanted to serve her right for something, although I didn't know what it was. Not properly."

Julia stopped again, and waited. Lily was quick enough and perceptive enough to draw her own conclusions.

Without warning, in a little, toneless voice, she said, "You didn't tell me you were going to America."

It was so unexpected that it left Julia breathless. "I . . ."

"You didn't tell me. You just said it on the phone, to Mattie. Like it didn't matter whether you were here or not."

Julia peered into the windy expanse of misunderstanding that seemed suddenly to have opened between them. Lily was still frowning at the wall; her hand lay loosely, palm up, on the bedcover. Julia took hold of it and squeezed it between her own hands. "I've been away before," she said. "To Turkey, and India, and Thailand, and all the other places. I didn't think you didn't want me to go." Julia tried to recall. Lily had always let her go quite cheerfully. Seemingly cheerfully. Sometimes she had said, "Wish you weren't going, Mum," but that was all. She had seemed happy with Marilyn and Alexander, relaxed and welcoming when she came home again. Julia had even congratulated herself on that. "I didn't know," she said sadly. "I'm sorry." She was thinking of the cut-up rug, the vehemence of the silent protest.

"I hate it when you're not here," Lily burst out. "You shouldn't have to go away."

"Lily, I've had to earn a living, to support us both." That was the truth, she reflected, but only the partial truth. Lily ignored it.

"You're my mother. You should be here."

The selfishness made Julia ache for both of them. Lily's need and her own, Betty's and her own colliding head-on. Poor mothers, she thought. Can't ever get it right. And poor daughters too. We want things from each other, and we want to give them, but the gestures are so clumsy that they knock themselves awry. Gently, she let go of Lily's hand and stroked her hair. As she seemed to do more and more often, she wondered about her own natural mother. Where was she, and what would she say? "I won't go to America," she promised.

She felt the stiffness of Lily's neck and shoulders, knew that she was trying not to jerk her head out of reach of her mother's hand.

"Oh, go," Lily said, dismissing her. "Just tell me properly. I don't like hearing about it when you're having a chat with Mattie."

"I'm sorry," Julia said again, humbly. "The idea just came to me there and then, and it seemed a good one, so I said it."

My own selfishness, equal and opposite.

Lily had picked up a book and was staring at the jacket picture. Julia knew that she wouldn't say any more. She stood up, saying something about supper, and went to the door. As she reached it, Lily mumbled, "I'm sorry about your rug."

Julia was surprised, and grateful.

"You were right, it's only a thing, not a person. Anyway, it's our rug."

"Not mine. I don't care about stuff like that."

Julia half-smiled. "You do if it belongs to Ladyhill."

The answer came back without a second's hesitation. "Ladyhill's different."

Julia nodded. She waited for a second or two, but neither of them said any more. She closed Lily's door and went downstairs, moving as if her limbs hurt. The light had faded, and the big room seemed gloomy and cold. Julia wrapped her arms around herself and walked to the window, staring out without seeing anything. She wanted to talk to Alexander. She wanted to pick up the telephone and say, "This is happening. What can we do?"

She wasn't surprised, anymore, to recognize the importance that Alexander still held for her. She had told herself that he was still her friend, even after all that had happened, and much more than that, he was Lily's father. But it was only recently that Julia had understood that she needed the reassurance, however remote, of his influence on her own life, as well as on Lily's. Alexander had become a kind of measuring scale, a mark of permanence and stability. She would judge, Alexander would like this, or believe in that, or enjoy the other. The link with him was comforting, and strengthening for Lily's sake. She thought it was harmless, after so long. They saw each other rarely in London. Julia had never been back to Ladyhill. She avoided it out of a kind of superstition, although there had been times when she might have gone, to see Lily compete in a gymkhana, or to Faye's sixtieth birthday party. But she had never gone, and they met when Lily was on her way to Ladyhill or coming back again, or when Alexander happened to be working in town.

Julia valued the loose unspoken but continuing ties. She wondered if perhaps Alexander did too. He had met Thomas Tree but he had never spoken of him and he must have noticed his disappearance, but he had never commented on that either.

It never could have worked, with Thomas, Julia thought wearily. There were too many ghosts.

And now, when she wanted to share tonight's particular fears with Alexander, it was impossible. Because Julia was certain that the truth of this evening was nothing to do with the Anatolian kelim, nothing, even, to do with America or her own absences from home. The truth was, *I'm not yours, so there. I'm Alexander's.*

Everything else, whatever Lily might protest, because she didn't yet understand it herself, was just a symptom of that.

Lily had begun to compare, and to judge, just because she was old enough. Her parents were separate, unconnected, and so represented different choices. And if a choice offered itself, wasn't the childish instinct to make it? Children didn't equivocate, or conciliate, Julia remembered, thinking of herself and what she had done to Betty. The thought of Lily with her fierce, childish allegiances, choosing between herself and Alexander, was unbearably painful. But it seemed, equally unbearably, quite inevitable. Julia felt cold, swung away from the window, and walked the length of the chilly room.

She was thinking that everything, this pretty house and its careful contents, Garlic & Sapphires, four shops with their window displays and managers and staff, the warehouse full of stock and the office and filing cabinets, even the Triumph Vitesse parked in the street outside, had been assembled for Lily's sake. She had been a bad mother, she thought, in her efforts to be a good mother. Without Lily, nothing mattered, and yet everything else had been made to matter.

And none of it made any difference. She couldn't tie Lily to her, or insist on her love and loyalty, or stop them flowing away elsewhere. Nor could she confide any of these terrors to Alexander because, in this, he was her enemy.

Julia was lonely, and loneliness made her helpless.

Then her arms dropped to her sides. If the room was cold,

then she should turn the heat on. Lily would need supper, and to be reminded to find the contents of her gym bag, get it ready for school in the morning. Julia turned the lights on and drew the curtains to close out the street, then deliberately fixed her attention on the little domestic jobs that would fill the spaces for this evening, for a while longer. She made boiled eggs and toast, and called Lily down from her room. She came jumping down the stairs and then sat in her place at the table, her feet folded under her, munching toast and watching the television.

Looking at her, Julia thought that she was as oblivious as she had been herself, blithely sticking the stars on Betty's wallpaper. Nor had she recognized the little truth under the layers until the great age of thirty-one. Why should Lily be any different?

Julia reached across the table to clear the plates.

It took a long time to grow up, she told herself. *A bloody long, painful time.*

"I'll send you a postcard of the Empire State Building."

"And the Statue of Liberty. And I want some proper American T-shirts, that everyone will know you can't buy here."

"Status snob," Julia teased.

"Why not? What's wrong with wanting groovy gear no one else has?"

Lily faced her, wide-eyed, perfectly serious. Remembering the expeditions to Brick Lane market, the rummaging in Jessie's old finery and the inexpert dressmaking of years ago, Julia had to smile. "Nothing at all. I used to be just like you."

"Really, Mum? Even in your day?"

Alexander was sitting on the chesterfield, with his long, thin legs stretched out in front of him. Alexander's wardrobe seemed to have changed very little since 1959. He still wore corduroys, sweaters, and Tattersall check shirts, and in winter a tweed coat that had belonged to his father. "I'm so out I'm in," he used to proclaim with clear satisfaction.

Julia appealed to him. "That's true, isn't it, Alexander? Even in my day. Distant though that is."

He lifted his head, looking at her. "Quite true. When I first saw your mother, Lily, she was like some exotic butterfly. She always had extraordinary clothes. Either very complicated or perfectly simple, but always completely different from what the other girls were wearing, and about fifty times more glamorous. And she had wonderful legs, which she still has."

"This is Mummy?"

"Of course."

Julia had already turned away, hiding her face from Alexander's scrutiny. The floor was heaped with Lily's bags and possessions, ready for the trip to Ladyhill, and she rummaged gratefully among them, wondering what she was pretending to look for. "Yes, well. Thank you. A hundred years ago now, Lily darling."

She knew that Alexander was still looking at her. She felt awkward, disconcerted, and separated by much more than a hundred years from the exotic butterfly that Alexander remembered. She glossed the moment over with unnecessary fuss over Lily's belongings as they were stowed into Alexander's car.

But then, when that was done and Lily's bicycle was safely roped to the roof rack, they had to go back into the house to fill the empty moments before saying good-bye. Lily ran down the basement steps to look for Marilyn, and Julia and Alexander stood by the window looking into the yard. It was full of roses, and lavender, and honeysuckle, and the wash from pleasure boats on the canal slapped and rippled against the towpath.

"Your garden looks pretty," Alexander said.

"Thank you. It's funny, I enjoy it now. Who'd have thought I'd turn into a gardener?" She laughed. "It must be old age."

"You talk too much about getting old. You're still young, Julia. Everything could happen."

With sharpened hearing she listened to the words, thinking, *what could?* She was very aware of him standing beside her, his arm almost touching hers. *Don't be a fool*, she warned herself. *You're getting weak and sentimental as well as middle-aged.*

Alexander sighed. "The long border at Ladyhill looks a mess."

"Does it?" Julia said neutrally. "You should get a proper gardener again." *That was better*, she thought. *Safe ground.*

"Yes. Perhaps I should." He put his hand on her shoulder. She had to turn to him, smiling, or seem unnaturally stiff. "Don't work too hard in the States." He was looking at her far too closely.

"No, I won't work too hard."

"Do you have friends there? People to see, who can look after you if you need it?"

"Oh, friends of friends. Contacts. I'll meet people, I always do."

It was impossible to say, "I thought I'd look up Josh Flood." How could she be honest with Alexander when she

BAD GIRLS, GOOD WOMEN / 419

wasn't truly honest with herself? Julia moved away, distancing herself, seemingly fixing her attention on securing the open window.

"That's good," Alexander murmured ambiguously.

Lily raced into the room, followed by Marilyn. Marilyn was wearing jeans and a Marvin Gaye T-shirt with her hair pulled back in a knot behind her head. She looked like a younger, simpler Mattie, and Julia saw Alexander glance at her.

"Come on, Daddy," Lily was shouting. "It's time to go."

"Can't wait to get away from us, can you?" Marilyn joked. "Here, give us a proper hug. How'm I going to bear eight weeks without you?"

Marilyn would take care of the house while Julia and Lily were away. For the tenth time, Lily embarked on the complicated instructions for managing the hamsters that lived in a cage in her room.

"Have you seen Mattie?" Alexander asked over their heads.

"We had a boozy lunch last week," Julia said. "She's been offered a play that she's excited about. A tryout at Chichester in September, then perhaps a West End transfer."

"Give her my love," Alexander said.

"You're more likely to see her than I am. I'm just off to the States for six weeks, remember?"

"So you are."

They all went out into the sunny street. Lily hopped from one leg to the other, and Julia bent down to her level and put her arms around her shoulders.

"Have a lovely summer holiday. Be good for Daddy."

Lily hugged her back. However hard she searched, Julia could see nothing in the child's face but happy anticipation. As it always did, the moment of parting seemed much harder for Julia.

"You know you could have come to New York with me?" There was no need to say it, but she couldn't stop herself. She had planned the trip. They could have traveled together. Lily was old enough now. They would have enjoyed sharing the adventure, and Julia would have fit in the business when and where she could. But Lily had refused even to be tempted. "I couldn't miss Ladyhill," she had said. "Not in the summer."

Slowly, Julia straightened up and opened the car door for her. Lily scrambled inside. A shadow fell, and Julia gave a nervous start. But it was Alexander, moving between her face and the sun. She couldn't see his expression against the brightness. He kissed her on each cheek. He never usually kissed her when they met or parted. She smiled, confused, shading her eyes against the sun. Then Alexander was in the car beside Lily, and Julia and Marilyn were left side by side on the sidewalk. The car slid forward, and they waved, calling good-bye, until it had turned the corner of the street.

"She's lucky," Marilyn said. "Having Alexander for her dad."

Julia remembered Ted Banner. Ted had died of drink, at last, four years before. Mattie and Marilyn had gone to the bleak cremation and came back white-faced to Julia's house. And Vernon. Vernon Smith, folding his newspaper into neat creases, with the clock ticking behind him. Vernon had just retired from his accounts office, and Julia wondered how he and Betty were stepping around each other in the house in Fairmile Road.

"Yes, Lily's lucky," Julia answered. Marilyn glanced at her, and her broad smile faded away into puzzlement. Julia took her hand and squeezed it. "I suppose I'd better go and finish my own packing."

"Do you need any ironing done?"

They went back into the house together. It felt empty and silent, as it always did when Lily had gone away.

Lily watched the road intently as it unwound in front of the car. There were familiar, important landmarks to be greeted, secretly and superstitiously, as they flashed past. The journey was an essential part of each holiday, the time when she transformed herself from London Lily into Ladyhill Lily. It always seemed a very long way from London to Dorset, but even though she was hopelessly impatient on other trips, Lily always sat quietly through this one. She turned her head to look at Alexander. His face was red with the sun, which meant that he must have been doing his work outside. Perhaps by the summerhouse in the orchard. Lily liked it when he did that, because she could see him while she played. He was wearing one of his ordinary shirts with frayed bits around the sleeves and no tie, and his thin, fair hair was brushed smooth. Her father had never grown his hair long, like some of the other girls' fathers. Even Felix had let his grow into a round ball called an afro, at the time when he wore colored caftans like women's dresses, but he had cut it short again now and wore gray suits like Alexander's.

Alexander always looked the same. That was one of the safest things about him, and he always behaved the same too. He could be very strict, and fierce if people didn't do what he told them to do, but the things that made him strict or fierce were always quite reasonable and obvious. And it was easy to guess what would make him laugh, and what he would enjoy. Usually they were the things that she enjoyed herself, like Ladyhill.

All that was what made him different from Julia.

Lily drew a strand of hair across her mouth and sucked it, thinking about her mother. She loved her, of course. Everyone loved their mothers. And Julia was much prettier and more interesting than most people's. It was being different, even looking different when she came to school, Lily supposed, that made her dangerous. It was only lately, perhaps since she had turned nine, that she had described it to herself as dangerous. But the knowledge had always been there, ever since she could remember. Julia could change so quickly. One moment she might be laughing and playing, and the next she could be blazing with anger. Lily was afraid of the changes. Julia could be gentle, and cuddly, but she could also whip around with a slap that stung and made her cry, or—worse—with words that made her feel small and wicked. And after that, almost always, she would look sad. Even cry sometimes. It was confusing, and it made Lily wish for the ordinariness of a mother that people didn't stare at, however admiringly.

Alexander was never like that. He didn't cuddle, but he didn't boil up and overflow with hot temper either. He was always just the same. Like Ladyhill itself. Love for her father and the house knotted pleasurably, inseparably, together. Lily sighed with anticipation and settled deeper in her seat.

It was early evening when they reached Ladyhill. Long shadows lay behind the stone gateposts and the avenue of trees, and midges hung in clouds in the patches of buttery sunlight. In the paddock beyond the trees Lily's pony stood in the deep grass, idly swishing his tail.

"I'm home," Lily shouted.

Alexander carried in her belongings while she made the circuit of the quiet house. He could hear her feet scrambling on the floorboards over his head, and the doors along the gallery banging in her wake. It was like having a crowd of people surging through the rooms instead of one child.

Crowds of people. Mad parties.

Abruptly, Alexander put down the armful of luggage. There was another housekeeper to take care of the house now, living in the rooms where Alexander and Julia had camped in the years just after the fire. She came through the inner door, looking for

Lily, and Alexander shook off the memory of the crowds and the party. He told Mrs. Tovey that Lily would have supper in an hour or so, when the excitement had worn off a little, and went into the drawing room to pour himself a drink.

The carved paneling, bought at a sale of the contents of a much grander house, had been ingeniously adapted by Felix. It looked as though it had never belonged anywhere but here, in this room, and the ceiling plaster had been replaced, remolded to echo the motifs in the paneling. It had cost thousands of pounds. Alexander had met the bills, somehow, most recently by selling land. With the tumbler of whiskey and soda in his hand he studied the room instead of opening the newspaper.

Bits and pieces, he was thinking. Carefully put together to make the house look the same as it always had. He had given it all his attention, and there had been satisfaction in seeing the room finished, and the pieces of furniture being brought in, one by one, from the sales and auction rooms. There had been satisfaction, but it was a dry, finite sort of pleasure.

Drinking his evening whiskey, alone in here, over the last few months Alexander had wondered whether the recreation of his childhood's shell was a worthwhile achievement or merely a refuge.

Lily's reappearance broke the somber chain of thought. She stood in the doorway, panting, her flushed face split by a huge smile. She ran across the room and rubbed her cheek against his, bumping and spilling some of his whiskey.

"I do love you."

She ran out, and when she had gone he wondered why he hadn't hugged her and told her that he loved her in return. Julia would have. His own reluctance was his father's legacy, his father's and China's.

Julia was never afraid to let her love show. The expression of it came naturally to her—the obviousness of her love for Josh Flood was what had hurt him so deeply long ago. He had seen another manifestation of it today as they stood on the sidewalk outside her house. Love radiated out of her, all directed at Lily. Julia had lost none of her directness over the years, nor any of the intensity of her reactions to the people she cared for. Her loves and fears and needs were as unconfined as they had always been, in contrast to his own, ever more carefully preserved invulnerability.

It was Julia's clarity that made her lovable; he had loved it from the day Sophia brought her to meet him. The fresh recognition of it had made him want to kiss her today. He had wanted to do more than that, but her startled expression had convinced him that he should step back, return his hands to his pockets, and concentrate on Lily and the drive to Ladyhill.

And now he was home again, in his impeccable re-creation of what had been before. Alexander stood up and walked to the window. The paving of the courtyard still shimmered with warmth. Beyond lay the yew trees and a sweep of gravel, then mown grass dipping in the shade of trees. Ladyhill was beautiful, but he knew that it needed Lily, other people, too, to bring it alive. As Julia had said, long ago. Without them it was empty, dry of juice, like a museum. Like himself, Alexander reflected. He had turned forty. It seemed that the chances were all Lily's now, not his own. He felt stiff, and awkward from having been absorbed in the house for too long, and dull from having worked too hard without diversion.

There had been other women, of course, since Julia had left. Two or three of them had been connected with the music business, but they had been based in London, and one of them in New York, and in the end the distances to be traveled and arrangements to be made had outweighed the satisfactions, and the affairs had petered out. After that there had been a local girl, the schoolteacher daughter of a doctor, and their discreet relationship had lasted more than a year. But in the end, with her charity projects and her community work and her noticeably proprietorial enthusiasm for Ladyhill, Jenny had reminded him much too strongly of his stepmother. Alexander had disentangled himself as gently as he could, and since then, for the last seven months, there had been no one at all.

He was lonely, but he reminded himself with irritation that he had no one to blame for that but himself. If he really wanted company, it wasn't too difficult to find. Abruptly, he turned away from the window. Contemplation of Ladyhill's summer-evening tranquillity was giving him no satisfaction at all. Alexander went back to his chair with its cushions covered in a needlepoint fragment rescued by Felix from a junkshop in Salisbury, and very deliberately picked up the newspaper.

Lily was here, at least, for the two months of the summer. Her warmth would animate the dry bones of the house.

He heard her coming back long before the hour was up. He put his paper down again, smiling, but when she burst into the room he saw that her face was red with anger, and smudged with the grubby marks of tears. "Those bungalows," Lily wailed.

Eighteen months ago Alexander had sold six acres of land on the border of the estate with Ladyhill Village. The land had been bought by a developer who had, in record time, sought planning permission for a small estate of eighteen bungalows. The local Council had granted the permission, and the excavators and site levelers had moved in just after the end of Lily's last stay at Ladyhill. The bungalows were almost complete now. They had steep pitched roofs and picture windows, and neat little plots of garden around the neat little boxy buildings. Two or three of them had been bought by young couples or pensioners from the village, but most of them would be occupied by incomers.

If he had had a choice, Alexander would have preferred the land be left unbuilt. He had put off the sale for as long as possible, but the point had come when he knew he couldn't undertake more work, and a further injection of cash into the house had been essential. The developer had paid very good money. The village had accepted the development as a symptom of modern times, and Alexander had got used to seeing it as it rose on what had once been open ground.

Lily's outrage surprised him for a moment.

"There are houses on our fields. And fences all around them."

"I know, I'm sorry, I should have told you about it."

She stared at him, uncomprehending. "But why? What are they doing there?"

Alexander drew up a stool and made her sit on it, next to him. She perched on the edge of it, still watching him intently, as if her concentration could make the houses disappear.

"You remember that there was a fire at Ladyhill, long ago, before you were born?" Lily nodded impatiently. The fire was rarely mentioned. Almost all the talk she had half-listened to as a child had been of mending and restoring. She had one fragment of a memory, of wandering in dark, crumbling places in the house that had smelled frightening, making her choke in the back of her throat. Then Julia had come from somewhere and lifted her up and then taken her away.

"The fire damaged the house very badly. It burned the beams that hold up the roof, and melted the lead of the windows and gutters. The smoke blackened everything, and the water the firemen used to put out the flames soaked the furniture and the pictures and the covers. Those that hadn't already been burned."

Lily watched her father, forgetting the bungalows for a moment. His voice was quite calm and level, describing the terrible things. He didn't sound angry, or sad. Yet, for the first time, Lily imagined what it must have been like. A fire, with all the heat and greedy speed of logs blazing in the hearth, only a thousand times bigger. Running away, and devouring their house. She looked up, involuntarily, as if she expected to see the orange tongues of it licking over her head.

"The fire was put out, of course," Alexander comforted her.

Lily looked down again, and saw the mysterious puckers of shiny pink and grayish skin on the backs of her father's hands.

The truth suddenly fit together, like an adult eye opening. "Your hands were burned."

"Yes. But I was lucky. They healed."

"Then what happened?" Under the adult eye everything seemed clearer, but with cold, sharp edges.

"Then the house needed to be healed. I wanted to make it the same as it was before. It's taken a very long time, and a lot of money. The last money, because I couldn't get it from anywhere else, came from selling the village fields. And the man who bought those fields has put up the houses for people to buy and live in. People need houses, Lily." But she wouldn't accept the sugaring of the pill. Her face turned red again and she was almost crying.

"But they're horrible. They're like . . . like chicken pox. And you can see them from everywhere, once you get past the garden. That means they can see us. And I used to ride Marco Polo in those fields. I don't want the houses there."

"Lily," Alexander said firmly. "Those houses are needed, and we needed the money that comes from having them there. I understand that you're angry, and I'm sorry, because I should have warned you that they were being built. But you are also being selfish. You have plenty of room to play, and to ride your pony. We're very lucky. Don't forget that, will you?"

Lily raised her miserable face. "I didn't mean that," she whispered. "They make everything different. You can't stop looking at them, wherever you turn, because they're so new. And . . . bare. I want everything to be the same forever. And now it isn't." Tears ran down her cheeks. She wasn't nine anymore, but a thwarted, uncomprehending baby.

"Oh, Lily." Alexander put his arms around her. They felt as stiff as the rest of him. "Listen. I've spent years, almost all the time since you were born, think how long that is, trying to make Ladyhill the same as it was. So that it will go on forever like it was when I was your age, for you, and your children. I've only just begun to realize that you shouldn't try to make everything the same. It's a . . . it's a kind of weakness, wanting them to be. If you're brave, braver than I am, you can let things change and make the best of them. Felix made the Long Gallery look beautiful with some of the land money, and I did all kinds of valuable things with the rest of it. Can you be glad about that, and try to accept the bungalows? I promise you, in a month or two you won't even remember that they weren't always there.''

"I will," Lily said stubbornly, but she was scrubbing the tears away. "Yes, I will." She didn't protest anymore. Perhaps, Alexander thought without Julia's softness, that was a valuable lesson learned.

Lily had one more question. "Felix helped to mend Ladyhill, didn't he? Why didn't Julia?"

He paused for a moment, considering. Then he said, "Julia believed that I cared too much about it. In the end, because I didn't make her happy, and neither did Ladyhill, she chose to go and live somewhere else. That was her right, you know. And we agreed to share you between us."

Lily nodded, digesting the information. And then, surprising him, she asked, "You said that you weren't brave. What would you have done if you were?"

"I suppose I would have gone with Julia."

Alexander wondered why it was easier to admit it to Lily than to himself.

Immediately, she said, "I'm glad you didn't."

"Why?"

"Well, then we wouldn't live here, would we?"

He smiled at her. "Is it so important?"

"Of course it is. There's nowhere in the whole world like Ladyhill."

He looked at her eager, tear-grimy face. That was what he had wanted her to feel, wasn't it? The satisfaction seemed less rounded than it might have.

"Go on," Alexander said gently. "Go up and wash your face. Then I think you should call in on Mrs. Tovey. Your supper is probably ready."

He telephoned Julia, to tell her that Lily was safely at Ladyhill. The conversation was brief. "Bon voyage," he said at the end of it.

"Thank you." There was a pause. "Alexander?"

"Yes?"

Another pause. Then, "Nothing. I'm sorry, it doesn't matter. Have a nice summer, both of you."

The days of Lily's vacation rapidly fell into their usual pattern. Alexander worked in the mornings while Lily went to see her friend Elizabeth, or Faye, or helped Mrs. Tovey. In the afternoons the two of them picnicked, or walked, or swam in the river pool. Lily didn't mention the bungalows again, but she refused to ride Marco Polo near them.

At the end of the first week Felix arrived.

His visits were rare now that the house was almost fully restored, but he still came for a few days in the spring, and again in the summer. He would bring pictures or rugs or pieces of porcelain, collected over the intervening months, for Alexander's approval. Usually they were much too expensive, but they were always chosen with an exact niche in mind, and often looked so exactly right that Alexander ended up paying for them, protesting mournfully throughout. It was Felix's achievement that Ladyhill glowed with more subtle splendor than it ever had in Sir Percy Bliss's dingy day.

And if the visits to Ladyhill weren't strictly necessary any longer, Alexander understood that they gave Felix a proper pretext for leaving Eaton Square for a few days. George Tressider had developed a muscular disease that gave him considerable pain and limited his mobility. He suffered it tetchily. Felix ran the business and took care of George with perfect good humor, but they weren't lovers any longer. Felix pursued his affairs discreetly but intently. Legality and opportunity were on his side, and the generous choice reminded him of Florence, all those years ago. He didn't come to Ladyhill in search of boys, however. There were enough of those in London. He came because he enjoyed the rosy English beauty of the place, and because he and Alexander, for all their dissimilarity, had become friends.

Alexander was expecting him, and when he heard Felix's white Alfa accelerating under the avenue of trees, he strolled out into the courtyard to welcome him. To his surprise, he saw that the car, instead of being loaded down with precious pieces nested in wood shavings, contained a passenger. He was even more surprised when she stepped out, and he saw that it was Mattie.

Simultaneously, Lily appeared. "Mattie, Mattie, Mattie!" she yelled, and launched herself at her. Felix looked at Alexander over their heads, smiling and shrugging.

When she had disentangled herself, Mattie took Alexander's hands and kissed both his cheeks. After Chris Fredericks, Mattie had discarded her jeans and working shirts and reverted to Mattie-esque dresses. Today she was wearing a very short, shocking pink shift and pink leather gladiator's sandals. She had heavy Indian silver bracelets and a matching necklace, and outsized round sunglasses pushed up over her head.

"Bliss. Are you horrified? I had dinner with Felix, and he said he was driving down, so I came for the ride. There must be a pub in the village I can stay at for a night or two?"

Her face was turned up to him and so he kissed it. Her mouth was slightly open, and the soft brush of it sent a jolt all through him.

"There are at least a dozen bedrooms in this house, all crying out for occupation. Stay for as long as you like. We're very pleased to see you, aren't we, Lily?" Somehow, that seemed an understatement. Looking at Mattie, he saw that her milky skin, too pale to tan, was powdered with faint freckles. The down of fine hair was pale gold. He made himself look away again, shake hands with Felix.

"What's the time? Past twelve. Pimms on the grass, don't you think? You must have left very early." Inane remarks, Alexander thought. More like a boy of fourteen than a man of forty.

"Before dawn, darling." Mattie's throaty giggle was exactly the same as it had always been. "I'm ready for a Pimms."

They sat on the lawn, facing the house. Mattie tilted her head to look up at it, and Alexander watched the line of her throat.

"It's so long since I've been here," Mattie murmured. "Do you know, this house is too beautiful to be real. You expect to step through the door and find it's a Pinewood mockup."

"It's real." Felix laughed. "Every bloody brick and beam. It's taken almost ten years of our lives, hasn't it, Alexander?"

Ten years, at the end of this year. Since the fire destroyed . . .

The shadow lay across the grass, as though a cloud had passed over the sun.

It was Alexander who swept it away again. He lifted his glass, sprouting the blue borage that Lily had run to pick from the garden. "Here's to the completion of a magnificent undertaking."

He leaned over to clink his glass against Felix's, but Felix amended hastily, "Of course, these things are never really completed . . ."

Mattie and Alexander snorted with laughter, and after a moment Felix joined in. Mattie was thinking, There are only about three men in the entire world who are truly worth loving. And two of them are sitting here, under a blue sky.

Mattie and Felix stayed for five days. The sun shone, and in the sleepy heat they explored the countryside, walking and driving, played games with Lily, dozed on the lawns, and swam in the river. They drove to Chesil Beach and collected a perfectly graded set of pebbles for Lily, and they wandered through the little towns, where Felix rummaged in the antique shops and complained, as he always did, that the prices were higher than in London. In the evenings, after Lily was in bed, they ate and drank and talked, and Mattie sang while Alexander played the piano.

"If only Julia were here," Mattie sighed, "it would be just like old times."

On the fifth evening Alexander asked, "Can't you stay a day or two longer?"

"I must go back to George," Felix told him.

That evening Alexander opened two bottles of champagne and they drank them outside, with the scent of nicotiana drifting across the grass and bats dipping under the veil of the copper beech tree. Looking at their two faces, Felix felt for the first time that he made a crowd.

After dinner Alexander played Chopin. Mattie, half-drunk, swayed dreamily to the music.

"Do you have to go?" Alexander asked in a low voice.

Mattie stood still. The fanciful chiffon points of her skirt floated around her. "No, I don't have to go. I'll stay if you would like me to."

Sitting a little apart, as dark and immobile as if he were carved from polished wood, Felix wanted to whisper, *Be careful*. But he didn't deliver his warning because he guessed that it was already too late for that.

In the morning Lily and Alexander and Mattie stood waving until the white Alfa had disappeared under the tunnel of trees.

And that evening, when Alexander went to lift the lid of the piano, Mattie put her hands over his, closing it again. "Don't play tonight."

"What then?"

But Alexander answered his own question. He put his hands on her shoulders, let his palms slide down over her bare arms. Her skin seemed soft enough to melt as he touched it. He kissed

her, probing insistently with his tongue until her head fell back
and her mouth opened to him. And then, as he had longed to do
all week, he undid the front of her dress and let her breasts fall
loose. They rested in his hands, ripe and heavy, moon-pale in
the dim room. He put his mouth to them, tasting her rich, musky
sweetness. He wondered why, in all the years, he had never
noticed how sexy Mattie was, until now. He wanted her so badly
that he could have pushed her to the floor and torn her clothes,
stabbing himself into her and crying out, *Mattie.*

"Come to bed, Mattie," he implored her.

She smiled at him, a surprising, crooked and sad smile.
"Bliss. I'm not very good at sex, Bliss. Lots of other things, but
not sex."

With an effort Alexander controlled himself. "You are, my
darling. Look." He gestured at the pale, satiny smoothness of
her. "You are so beautiful."

"I don't want anything to be spoiled," Mattie whispered.
"I've enjoyed these days with you so much."

"Nothing will be spoiled," he murmured. "Nothing. I
promise." He kissed her neck and her throat, thinking that if he
could take bites out of her flesh it would taste of ripe golden
melons.

"Bliss . . ."

He took her face between his hands. "Just answer one
question. Is it the truth that you prefer girls?"

Her eyes were very soft now. "The truth is that I don't
know what I prefer."

He smiled at her. "I'm not arrogant enough to say *I'll show
you.* Come to bed, Mattie."

Almost inaudibly, she answered, "Yes. If you want me
to."

To Alexander, the naked abundance of Mattie in his bed
seemed miraculous. Mattie had never been slim, and now the
melting folds of her seemed to turn inward and inward, enclosing
him and drawing him closer, submerging him in mounting sensu-
ous waves of pleasure. She filled his hands, and his mouth, and
he wanted to feast on her, blind and greedy, until he couldn't
devour anymore.

But Alexander clung to the last remnants of control. He bit
his teeth together, and counting grimly from one to a thousand,
as he taught himself to do with the first girl he had ever made
love to, he focused his attention on Mattie's pleasure. He stroked
her and cajoled her, and put his lips to the soft button of flesh,

drawing it into the heat of his mouth. Mattie sighed, and smiled faintly behind the mask of her closed eyelids, but he couldn't drive her any further.

Alexander reached one thousand. He knew that he couldn't count much longer. He put his lips to her ear.

"Mattie, I want you to come."

Just perceptibly, she shook her head. "I can't. But you can."

Her smooth hand grasped him, and he groaned aloud. Then she guided him into her, lifting her hips to give him more of herself. It took just six long thrusts before Alexander came, his back arching and his breath shuddering out of him.

He was still for a long time afterward, his eyes closed and his arms wrapped tightly around her, as if he were afraid that she would try to escape. Mattie lay still, thinking, *Alexander. You're as loving and generous as I knew you would be. I'm glad I found that out. I'm glad this happened, after all this time. I like you very much. Why didn't I tell you?*

"Mattie," he whispered. "Why can't you come? You gave me more pleasure then than I think I've ever had before."

"Hmm. That's a paradox, isn't it?"

He shifted his weight so that he could look into her eyes. "A paradox? How many film stars talk about paradoxes in bed?"

Brightly, Mattie said, "None of the ones I've had."

They laughed, softly at first and then louder, gasping with it, lying in the darkness with their arms wrapped around each other.

TWENTY

Julia looked around the SoHo studio. Stacked all around the walls were originals and prints by the three young artists who shared the loft, but there was none of the other familiar painters' clutter. Instead, there were drawing boards and airbrushes, plan chests and a boy in very clean OshKosh dungarees frowning at a computer terminal. The neat beige space looked more like the art department of a glossy magazine than anything else, Julia thought.

"I like this stuff," Julia said. "I'm tired of flowers and beads."

The boy looked up. "Yeah. All that faded shit."

She prowled back along the line of pictures. The ones that interested her particularly were gleaming airbrush paintings of jukeboxes, cars with grilles like sharks' teeth, girls with overpointed breasts and tight dresses that emphasized the V between their thighs. They were all realer than the real thing, sharp and shiny and cynical. There was nothing gentle or optimistic or pretty about them, and they made psychedelia seem as dated as the pennyfarthing. Julia smiled with satisfaction. She liked the prickle down her spine when she recognized a seller.

And interleaved with the super-realist paintings of space-age artifacts, there were computer graphics in which a circle composed of circles and dots transformed itself by stages into a leaping panther, and then back to a circle again. By the same progression, a Coca-Cola bottle became the Apollo 11 space rocket that had, in that week, deposited Armstrong and Aldrin on the moon.

It was a wonderful week to be in America.

"And these," Julia said. "These are brilliant. Is there anything you can't do with that computer?"

"Nope." The boy leaned back in his chair. "Or, at least, not much."

Julia took out her notebook and unscrewed her fountain pen. It was gold-nibbed, and filled with sepia ink. Mattie had given it to her for Christmas. "Biros don't go with silk suits and leather briefcases," she had pronounced. Julia smiled at the memory, and held the pen poised.

"I'd love to buy some of your work, of course," she said. "But I can only think of unlimited editions for my market. I've got a chain of shops in England, not a gallery."

"Posters?"

"That's right."

The boy yawned. "Well, I guess it's not out of the question if the price is right. You'd have to hack all that out with my agent."

Cheerfully, Julia clipped the cap back on to her pen. She liked dealing with agents, and enjoyed the almost formal gavotte of agreeing terms. There was always a deal to be made, and she was good at getting what she wanted. She knew that the fifties Pontiacs and Coke bottle Apollo 11 would hang well on the walls of Garlic & Sapphires, and would sell as fast as she could see them produced.

"Thank you for showing me your work. I'll call your agent this afternoon. Can I take you somewhere for lunch now?"

The artist looked under his long eyelashes at Julia in her buttercup-yellow tussore silk safari suit. "Sure you can," he murmured. "Let's go right away."

They went out into the street, and Julia felt the sun striking hot on her head. She had been almost cold in the air-conditioned studio, and the noise of traffic seemed doubly loud after its humming quiet. The constant contrasts of the city stirred her blood. She had to make conscious efforts not to dash to and fro, admiring and exclaiming, as if she were Lily's age.

"Where shall we go?" she asked. The heat of the sidewalk struck up insistently through the soles of her buttercup-yellow pumps.

"I know a place."

They went uptown, to a bar restaurant called Al's. It was cool and dim inside, and Julia blinked at the further contrast. She blinked again, when her eyes readjusted themselves to the light. The interior was a cavern of thirties Deco, and it was impossible to tell at a glance whether it was original or a clever recreation. There were peachy-pink walls lit by fan-shaped lights, cream leather and chrome sofas and barstools, and a white piano complete with a black pianist playing Cole Porter.

It was muted, and opulent, and so modish that Julia laughed out loud. "Oh, joss sticks and beanbags and temple bells, where are you now? I should be wearing a cream crepe-de-chine teagown with a river of pleats, and marcel waves in my hair. I feel out of place in this." She held out her arms in the yellow suit. Her companion laughed with her, and stuck his thumbs in the straps of his overalls.

"And a white tux for me. But who gives a shit? Let's get ourselves a drink."

He greeted ten people on the way to the bar, and they settled themselves at last on the tall chrome stools. There was a cocktail menu, with Deco lettering and a silhouette of a sinuous dancing couple. Julia sighed over the White Ladies and Manhattans and Deep Seas. "It's got to be a Manhattan, hasn't it?"

The bartender mixed their cocktails in a silver shaker, and poured them into black-stemmed cocktail glasses with frosted rims.

Julia said, "I want everything. I want the shaker, and the glasses, and the lights and the ashtrays and the barstools, all shipped back to Garlic & Sapphires, right now. Off with the old, and on with the new. Or the retro-new."

The painter lifted his glass in an admiring toast. "You Brits. You're supposed to be cool. But when you like something, you get out and get it. Here's to your enthusiasm."

"I like your graphics." Julia lifted her glass in return. The frosted rims touched with a faint *ping*. The painter's long eyelashes lifted again.

"And I like you."

Oh, New York, Julia thought. *You're very good for me.*

It made her feel young, and hungry again, as she hadn't done for a very long time. They had another cocktail apiece, and Julia ate a BLT and her new friend had a hamburger and they talked about Warhol and the men on the moon.

When they had eaten, two or three of the painter's friends came to join them, and one of them said that there was a party that night, and why didn't they both come along? The painter raised one of his thick black eyebrows at Julia, and she said yes, that sounded like fun. In the evening she put on her Ossie Clark dress of flowered crepe with ribbons and panels of silk, and wide trumpet sleeves and took a cab to another loft. Moving between huge polished-metal sculptures, she met and talked to more painters, and potters, and poets, and their friends who were television directors and copywriters and script editors. They were friendly and interesting, and she told them about her shops, and in her handbag she collected a little sheaf of cards and addresses. They were new designers, and artists, and people who other people insisted she must meet, and talk with, because their stuff was just so great, she'd be crazy not to go and see it for herself.

Julia drank her white wine, ate dolmades, and shared a joint or two, and at the end of the evening her painter friend didn't seem too perturbed when she told him that, on the whole, she thought it would probably be better if she just went quietly back to her own hotel bedroom.

"Another time, baby," he said.

In the peace of her room in the Algonquin, Julia took off her dress and hung it up in the closet. She felt tired, and drunk, and thoroughly satisfied. That was how her trip had been. The few names she had armed herself with via friends in London had been the pebble dropping into the pond. The ripples had spread outward, carrying her with them. She had seen more things that she wanted to buy than she could ever hope to ship home, and she had seen the direction she wanted Garlic & Sapphires to follow into the seventies. It had been a thoroughly satisfactory expedition.

Julia had flown to Toronto, and out to the Coast. But in comparison with New York, Canada had seemed provincial, and San Francisco was still tangled in hippiedom. She had come back to the East Coast with a sense of relief and renewed energy to fix up a last two or three deals before going home. She was beginning to look forward to seeing Lily, and seeing Lily would also mean meeting Alexander. But she knew that she needn't go yet, not quite yet. She had a little time, and enough money, and at last she was in the same country.

Lying back on her bed, with her eyes fixed unseeingly on the Celia Birtwell print of her dress inside the open closet, Julia picked up the telephone beside her. She spoke to long distance information, and a minute later wrote down the number on the headed pad next to the telephone. She didn't dial the number at once. Instead, she stood up and walked to the window. She stood for a moment, looking down into West Forty-fourth Street. The city's electricity seemed to crackle up to her. She breathed in sharply, and stretched upward, as though a line through her body drew tauter.

Then she went back to the bedside telephone and picked out the digits. She listened to the ringing tone. She was already thinking, *He's not there,* when he answered.

"Josh Flood."

"Josh, it's Julia."

A pause, and then laughter. The same lazy, warm laughter that she remembered. "Well, what d'you know? When can we see each other?"

That was like Josh too. No *How are you?* or *Where are you?* No mention, either, of how long it had been, or how much had been missed. Just *Hey, here you are.* Now was what mattered to Josh, now, this minute.

And, charged with the potency of success and freedom, Julia felt, at last, that she could match him. She smiled at the empty hotel bedroom.

"Tomorrow, if I can get a flight."

"From London?"

"New York."

"Here I am, waiting for you. Hearing your voice is the best thing that's happened to me for months."

"Oh, Josh."

"Julia Bliss."

"Julia Smith. Alexander and I are divorced."

He cut her short. "Don't tell me any more now. Save it for tomorrow when I can see your face."

"I'll look forward to it."

"Me too. Julia? I'm glad you called."

The next day Julia flew to Denver.

Josh met her at the airport. He stood at the gate, waiting for her to come through, and although he saw her at once, walking briskly in the midst of a mixed convoy of nuns and businessmen, he had to look again to assure himself that she really was Julia.

And then she was standing in front of him, smiling, her head on one side. Josh held out his arms and she stepped into them. He held her tightly for a long moment, before moving back to look at her again.

Julia had discarded her miniskirts, although only a year ago she had sworn she never would. Now she was wearing a sand-colored Saint Laurent suit with a slim knee-length skirt. She had on a plain white shirt, and pearl studs in her ears. Her five-point Vidal Sassoon bob had grown out long ago, and her hair waved thickly around her face, as it had when Josh first saw her in Leoni's. Her face was thinner, but there seemed to be a new luminosity beneath the surface of her skin. She looked older, but she also looked as if she had grown into herself. She was no less beautiful than she had ever been, but she was different, and that was why he had had to look again as she came toward him, to make sure. If he had to choose a single word for this Julia, Josh thought, it would be *formidable*.

They stood there, holding hands, while the departing passengers ebbed away from them.

Julia was thinking, So I did it. I turned up in Josh's life instead of he in mine. I'm the traveler, the initiator. And Josh is the same as he always was. He looked exactly the same. The bright fairness of his hair might have faded a little, and there might be an almost invisible net of fine lines in the tanned skin at the corners of his eyes, but he was as lean and muscled and quick-moving as he had always been. Even the clothes were the same, jeans and a thick leather belt, and a denim workshirt. He looked tough, and handsome, with a streak of warm good humor, as he always had.

Deliberately, she put her hand behind his head, and drew his face down to kiss the corner of his mouth. His eyes half-closed, and she saw the sun-bleached tips of his eyelashes. The current hadn't flickered either. It ran between them as powerfully as it ever had.

"Come on," Josh said. "The car's outside. Give me those bags."

He hoisted her neat executive luggage and Julia followed him.

The car, negligently parked at the doors, was a white Mercedes 220SL convertible. Julia whistled at the sight of it, and Josh grinned.

"Neat, hey?"

She settled into her red leather seat, sighing. "How senior we all are. Cars, and houses, and businesses."

Josh looked sideways at her, amused. "Don't class my car with all that other shit. This is a pair of racing skis, or a jet plane. Watch."

They had left the tangle of airport traffic behind them. The car's long white nose pointed on to a freeway, and Josh accelerated. They whirled past a truck, and another, and howled past a line of family sedans. Julia felt herself pressed backward into the seat's leathery grip. The wind sliced over the windshield and pinned her skin to her face, peeling a smile out of it as tears smarted in her eyes. Her hair whipped around her cheeks, and she lifted one hand to draw it back into a knot. Josh was smiling too. The wind blew his hair off his forehead, and his eyes narrowed with concentration as they sped faster. Julia remembered that that was how he had looked when he was skiing. Absorbed, and exultant.

They went faster. The roar of the engine drowned out the rest of the world, and speed enveloped the sight of it in a featureless blur. Suddenly Julia thought, *He's like a boy showing off his car to impress his girl. If we were in a plane, he'd be looping the loop. He did that once, didn't he?* The realization touched her, and made her want to laugh, but it was also oddly startling. She filed it away in the back of her mind, to reexamine later. Then she reached out and put her hand on Josh's arm.

"Josh! I'm sorry!" she yelled. "Forgive my classing your car with the other trappings of middle age. It's faster than a jet, more frightening than skis. Now, will you bloody well slow down?"

She had been watching the speedometer. The needle had held steady, somewhere way past the one hundred mark. Now Josh lifted his foot and the red finger obligingly fell back again.

"Are you a trapping of middle age, my Julia?"

"It looks like it," Julia said dryly.

"In that case, I forgive you everything."

At a sedate sixty miles per hour, Julia could look around her. They were outside the city now and the clear air shimmered.

Ahead of them, between the billboards that lined the freeway, she saw mountains. Even in midsummer, the peaks were seamed with white.

"The Rockies?" she asked Josh.

He nodded, whistling, his forearms lazily crossed over the wheel.

"Where are we going? To Vail?"

Through all the years, summer and winter, she had somehow imagined him out on the ski trails, or in the glittering powder snow of some huge mountain bowl.

"No. I try to keep out of it for some part of the summer. I've got a place up here, although I don't use it much. How did you know to call me there?"

"I didn't. That was the number information gave me, that's all."

He looked at her again, an open, reflective glance this time, undisguised by laughter. "Then it must be fate," he said softly.

And Julia felt her tender, innermost muscles secretly contract and loosen again. Her response to the aviator was just the same as it had always been. He disarmed her effortlessly, and left her helpless. *But I didn't come here to defend myself,* Julia thought. *I came because I wanted to, and because I wanted Josh. Because I'm old enough to understand that if you want something you have to gauge how badly you want it, and then you have to reach out and take it.*

Surely we both know why I'm here. We don't need to dissemble after so long.

She knew that her face had reddened, and she stared ahead at the green and blue and gray rockfolds of the mountains.

They left the freeway and followed a smaller road past scattered motels and diners, linked by the taut black lines of telegraph wires like apron strings. They were climbing steadily. They passed through a small town and Julia glimpsed the storefronts and two trucks pulled up on the forecourt of a filling station. Beyond the town, higher up, there were fewer buildings along the roadway. They passed farm wagons and timber trucks, and the driver of one of them raised his arm and waved to Josh.

"Almost there," Josh said.

They turned off again, along a road that was hardly more than a rutted track. They were in trees now, a heavy green canopy that knitted over their heads. Josh slowed the car to walking speed, and they bumped slowly over the grassy ridges.

The engine's echo thrummed back at them. Through the beat of it Julia could hear birdsong, and the splash of water.

Josh swung the wheel again, and the car nosed past a rough timber gate. He drove up a track for a little way, and then they stopped. When he reached and turned off the ignition, the silence suddenly yawned, seemingly immense.

Ahead of her, Julia could see the wall of a timber shack.

Josh came around and opened her door for her, helping her out. She stood up in the green stillness, stretching, her legs stiff after the long flight and the drive.

Josh folded her arm through his. "It's up here," he said gently.

They walked on up the steep track, leaning against each other. The low, dark wall of the shack looked like a frown among the greenery. Julia caught her foot in a hollow and stumbled.

"City shoes," she said.

"City girl," Josh teased her.

They reached the shack wall and skirted around it, Josh leading the way. Julia was breathing heavily after the uphill scramble. He pushed the branches aside as they walked so that the fingers of them didn't catch at Julia's clothes. Then they turned the corner. Julia looked up and gasped. Josh's summer house was built on a little plateau in the side of the mountain. The trees grew up to each side of it, and reared above and behind. But in front of the cabin a space had been cleared, and the magnificence of the view dropped away, unobstructed, beneath their feet.

Julia stood at the edge of the clearing and looked down over the variegated canopy of trees, over the silver thread of a waterfall that broke between them, and on down to the yellow-green expanse of open grassland, rolling away farther to the bluish hump of a little town in the distance and, beyond that, a blue haze that melted into the indistinguishable skyline. The colors were different, and the air had a sharper bite to it, but the memories stirred just the same. It was like Montebellate, and she had half-turned to Josh to say it when she felt the warmth of his breath on her neck.

"I know," he said, reading her thoughts. "It reminds me of it too."

"Only there's no old woman in a black dress, and no tethered goat up here," Julia said softly. "No cracked bell ringing the hours."

Josh touched her arm. "Come inside," he said.

Julia followed him. Under the shallow pitch of the shingled roof there was a porch, open on three sides. There was one wicker chair, facing outward. Josh had to stoop to pass under the lintel of the door. The inner part of the cabin was divided into two rooms. The larger was furnished with a table and a couple of upright chairs, two armchairs, and some shelves and a wood-burning stove. Through an open door beside her Julia could see a bed with a turned-back blanket, and some of Josh's clothes laid neatly on a chair. In a corner, propped against the wall, were two fishing rods and a shotgun. On the shelves were a handful of paperback thrillers, a radio, and a telephone incongruous even though it was a heavy, old-fashioned black one. There was almost nothing else. No patina of accumulated possessions, no pictures or photographs or mementoes, nothing to decorate the bare walls.

Julia thought of her little house by the canal. It was full of things, reminders and pleasurable acquisitions, arranged and laid out as if to reassure her of some necessary permanence.

Josh had none of that. This cabin on the side of the mountain was the same as the cottage in the angle of the Kentish woods, uninhabited by memories, a place to sleep in and then leave behind.

"Is this all there is?" she asked, and then blushed. "I didn't mean that, exactly . . ."

He smiled at her, undeterred. "There's a kitchen out back, and a perfectly good bathroom, if you aren't too particular. There's water from the well, and that runs dry only if there's a drought. I've got electricity, canister gas for cooking, and the telephone. As you know. What more could anyone want?"

"What do you do here, Josh?"

"I fish, do a little shooting and stalking, drink a few beers. That's all."

Julia tried, and failed, to imagine herself in such self-contained isolation. "Don't you feel lonely?"

He laughed. "You always like to be with people."

To reflect myself back at me? Julia wondered.

"No, I'm not lonely. My nearest neighbor is only a quarter of a mile on up the track. These woods are full of people vacationing, trying to get away from one another. If I need company, I can drive down into Honey Creek and sit in a bar, talking about baseball."

Honey Creek must be the little town with the trucks and the

shuttered storefronts. Thinking about it, and about Josh sitting in a bar with the farmers and loggers, Julia had wandered across the room. She put the toe of her city shoe in the powdering of wood ash around the legs of the stove.

"What's your proper home like?" she asked. "In Vail?"

"Oh, it's a modern apartment. If you're asking me whether it's got pictures on the walls and ornaments on the mantel, then, no, it hasn't."

She went back across the room to him, put her fingers on the rolled-back cuff of his shirt. "Don't you ever want to put down roots?"

Josh looked down at her. She thought that she was seeing his face, clearly, without the camouflage of good humor or detachment or charm, for the very first time. She wondered if she had ever really known Josh at all.

He said, "I have spent so long evading it, I don't think I know how to begin now."

She asked him again, "Are you lonely?"

And this time he thought about it, and then he answered, very quietly, "Not all the time. Not even most of the time." After a moment he added, "I'm glad you called when you did." Then he touched his forefinger to the tip of her nose, the old, teasing Josh again. "I'm not looking after you very well. My cabin isn't as primitive as you think it is. There's no English tea or anchovy toast, I'm afraid . . ."

"Do you imagine I spend my life sitting on rolling lawns sipping lapsang souchong and nibbling toast?"

". . . But there's cold beer, or coffee. Which would you like?"

Julia accepted the deflection. For Josh, even so much openness was startling.

"I would like a beer, please."

"Let's sit on the porch."

He brought two cans of beer from the kitchen refrigerator, and settled Julia in the wicker chair. For himself he dragged out one of the upright chairs and sat with his feet hooked over the porch rail.

The light was fading from blue to dove-gray, and the splash of the waterfall below them sounded louder in the stillness.

Julia was watching the dusk thickening under the trees, and she sighed with satisfaction. "It seems a long way from New York."

Josh's eyes had been on her face. "Tell me about it. Tell

me everything you've been doing. And about lovely Lily. And Mattie. I saw one of her movies. The girl I was with wouldn't believe me when I said I knew her."

Julia took a long gulp of her beer. "All kinds of things have happened," she said. "And yet, in another way, hardly anything has happened at all."

While the darkness crept out from under the branches of the trees, she told him about Lily and Alexander and Ladyhill, about Mattie and Chris, and about Garlic & Sapphires and Thomas Tree and the house by the Regent's Park Canal.

Josh listened, and nodded, and when their beers were finished he went in and brought two more.

The sky over their heads lost the last pinky-gray glimmer, and he lit the lamp in the window of the cabin. The glow of it lay thickly on the old boards under their feet, and big, pale moths came drifting out of the darkness to bat their wings against the glass.

"A long time," Julia said at the end.

Josh stood up. He came to perch on the rail beside her, and the old wood creaked in protest. He leaned over and kissed the top of her head.

"What now?" he asked.

"I don't know," Julia said softly.

But she was thinking, *I do know*. She wanted to go home, to Lily and Alexander. The thought of them, together at Ladyhill, pulled sharply at her. And the thought of Alexander himself was more important still. It seemed to have grown in her consciousness, always demanding more of her attention, although, superstitiously, she had refused to give it. He had been in her head in New York and he was present even more strongly now, while Josh sat beside her on the porch rail. She had dreamed of coming here, of seeing Josh again, but with sharpened perception she wondered if she had come out of a need to knit up loose ends. To draw a neat line, freeing herself. So that she could see Alexander again? She didn't expect him to say anything, or to do anything, any more than he ever did. She knew his mild, dry, English demeanor well enough by now. But she suddenly understood that she was ready, at last, to go to Ladyhill again, without fear of the black fingers of the old terrors snatching at them again.

She would like to visit them, to see Lily and Alexander happy together in the old house. That was all, wasn't it?

But she could no more confess to Josh what she felt now

than, in London, she could have told Alexander that she was going to look for her comic book hero.

Subterfuges, Julia thought suddenly. *I'm tired of them. I want everything to be simple.* She turned her face up to look at Josh in the yellow light of the lamp.

It was Josh who was here with her. He was still her aviator, and she felt the force of the old attraction. It had followed her like a shadow for so long, but now she felt that she had the power to reach down and roll up the shadow, to put it away in a drawer with the other, musty keepsakes from long ago, or to take it out, and examine it at her own pleasure.

The recognition of that power released an erotic charge inside her.

Deliberately, she reached up and put her mouth to his. She held herself still for an instant and then she leaned back again, breaking the connection.

It was an added satisfaction for both of them, she understood, to play with the moment before it overtook them. They were old enough now to postpone it, and so to heighten the eventual satisfaction. Once, they would have fallen on each other, incapable of any delay.

"Do you remember the Swann Hotel?" Julia asked, her voice ripe with amusement.

"And the Pensione Flora. And the signora in the next room, who must have heard everything."

His fingers touched her cheek. "Shall I cook you some dinner?"

Postponement, imagination, recollection; the delicate refinements of adulthood.

"Yes, please," Julia said.

Josh made a simple meal in the bare kitchen, and Julia watched him, leaning against the door frame and sipping the glass of red wine that he gave her. He moved economically in the cramped space, and she knew that she liked watching the turn of his wrists, and the set of his head on his tanned neck.

They sat facing each other across the small table, talking, leaning back in their creaking chairs to look at each other. From the darkness outside the moths went on batting against the windowpanes. When they had eaten they carried the dishes out into the little kitchen. Julia washed them and Josh took them from her and dried them and put them neatly away. She remembered how the parody of domesticity had been so painful in the empty white house in London, and she wondered how the pain could have evaporated. She understood that the net of longing and wishing that she had tangled around herself had simply dropped away, and set her free.

She was glad to be with Josh. She felt a girl's excitement, and an adult's satisfaction in their closeness, but she didn't want, or expect, any more. Not any longer. She felt just as Josh must have, she thought, in Wengen and in Montebellate and in the times afterward. And all through those times she had been beating herself against his indifference to the future as hopelessly as the big pale moths beat themselves against the glass.

Well now, Julia thought, she wasn't indifferent to the future herself, but simply understood that her hopes for it lay elsewhere.

The recognition of her own blindness, and the simplicity of the vision that replaced it, dazzled her for a moment. And the happiness that came after it added to her pleasure in her freedom and her power.

Josh was looking at her. He took her hands, twisting his fingers in hers, and kissed the skin inside her wrists.

"I love you," he said.

"I love you too," she answered, and for the first time she thought that she was recognizing the different kinds of love, subtle and infinite and changeable gradations, instead of dreaming of one shining version that would transcend everything else if only she could catch it, and make it.

They went out on to the porch, and in the doorway the moths swooped around their heads and plunged toward the yellow lights. The blackness was thick enough to make Julia feel that she could reach out and touch it, pressing the cool, earthy folds of it against her skin, disturbing the unimaginable creatures that rustled and stalked under the invisible trees. Listening to the sound of them, she shivered in her thin shirt.

Josh turned abruptly and put his arms around her.

They felt each other's heat through the thickness of their clothes.

The bedroom of the cabin was so small that there was room for only the bed, the chair with Josh's folded clothes, and a rickety chest of drawers. In the eagerness that they had kindled between them, Josh bumped against the chest and knocked over the lamp that stood on it. The light went out, leaving them in the dense dark. Josh swore, but Julia put her hand to his mouth.

"Leave it. I like the dark."

He felt for her instead. His fingers moved over her neck to her throat, and to the V of bare skin below it. He unbuttoned her shirt and discarded it. The white linen glimmered as it fell at their feet. Impatience made him clumsy. He whispered, *Julia,* and she helped him, stepping out of her city clothes and letting the wisps of silk and lace underclothes drop after them.

They lay down together, matching their bodies, touch intensified by the absence of sight.

Julia remembered the weight, and the taste, and the texture of him, as vividly as if they had been lying together like this last night, instead of years ago, in the sad little white house. But the old Josh had been imperious, taking the lead and letting her follow, because there had been no question that she wouldn't follow, giving whatever she could offer, because she wanted him to have everything. That had been part of their contract in bed, and it had fueled their physical pleasure. This different Josh was more tentative. With unusual gentleness his hands touched the points of her hips, and the tips of his fingers smoothed the white skin inside her thighs. It was as if he were afraid that she might not respond.

There had never, before, been any element of doubt.

With her mouth against his she whispered, "Josh, I'm here."

His arms tightened around her. The word he whispered back might have been *stay.* Julia smiled. She lifted herself and lay down on top of him, taking his wrists and pinioning them above their heads. With small, precise movements she kissed his cheeks and the corners of his mouth, his eyelids and his throat and the curling mat of hair on his chest. She stretched and their toes touched, their faces and their mouths, blind, rediscovering hunger. Julia sat up, and with one movement she fit herself around him. The pleasure was as intense as it had ever been. For an instant she crouched over him, motionless, possessing him. She remembered other times, the Swann Hotel with the shouts and laughter in the snow under their windows, the Pensione Flora when she had longed to possess him without understanding that she already did, and London, and the sadness there, and all the years since.

Josh's hands gripped her waist and lifted her, triumphantly, holding her poised before he drove upward into her again.

The tentativeness, if it had been there, was gone.

Julia gave herself up to him, as she always had, and if there was a part of her that she held back, then that little separateness only heightened her pleasure in what they could and did give to each other.

And at the end, when the fierce waves possessed her and her eyes opened without seeing the dark, there was only Josh. She called his name and heard him answer, whispering and shouting, the intimate voice that she had forgotten. It was over so quickly.

There's no reason to be sad, she told herself.

Afterward they lay companionably with their heads together, watching the darker square of the window at the end of the tiny room. The unknown animals in the trees sounded louder, and closer. There was the call of a bird, perhaps an owl, and then a high, eerie sound that was neither a bark nor a yelp.

"What are they?" Julia asked.

She felt Josh's smile against her cheek. "Deer. Perhaps coyote."

"Not wolves?"

"No, darling. Not wolves."

"Aren't you ever afraid?"

"Of wild animals?"

"Just afraid, I meant."

He was silent, thinking.

"Sometimes. More than I used to be. What are you afraid of, Julia?"

"I think I'm afraid of making mistakes." Looking back, there seemed to have been so many. Made almost willfully. She wondered if recognizing the ones that had gone made any difference to the ones that would come. If there were enough chances left, now, to put any of it right.

Alexander, she thought. *Lily. If I can come home. Just to see you there, at Ladyhill.*

Josh settled her head more comfortably against him, drawing the covers around their shoulders. "You're safe in my cabin in the woods," he said. "Safer than you would be in London, or in New York."

"I know," Julia said, turning her face to him and closing her eyes. "I'm not afraid of the wolves."

Waiting to go to sleep, she listened to the noises of the trees beyond the wooden walls. There was no resemblance, and there were thousands of miles separating them, but the eddies of wind and the scraping branches and the sudden, mystifying animal cries reminded her of Ladyhill. She had been afraid of Ladyhill, of course. Even before the flames and smoke came. She had imagined that she was mistress of it, playing with the furniture and curtains and dressing it up for her fantasy Christmas, but in reality it had mastered her. She had been too young, and too silly, and too impatient for it.

"I'm not afraid now," she repeated.

Julia stayed with Josh in his forest cabin for three days.

In the Honey Creek store Julia bought Levis and a pair of boots, and they went walking. "Scrambling," Julia gasped, following Josh up the steep wooded slopes. "I'm getting old."

Josh held out his hand to help her. "I don't think so."

For all her mild, citified protesting, Julia enjoyed the blue, empty days. It occurred to her that she had never spent so many hours at a time out of the shelter of roofs and rooms. Her cheeks and arms flushed in the sunshine, then turned pale gold. She tied her hair back with a piece of string, and wore Josh's frayed shirts with her Levis.

"You look about seventeen," he told her.

"I'm glad I'm not," Julia said soberly.

In the pale evenings, when the sun's glare had faded, Josh went fishing. The streams and waterfalls that netted the mountainside ran down into a wide, mirror-faced lake. Julia sat on the bank beside Josh, watching the ripples that spread lazily from his casts. She was surprised by his absorption, and by his ability to sit still for so long.

Her images of him, well-defined by reexamination over the years, were all active. She remembered Josh racing in the Inferno, his face briefly turned toward the spectators as he skimmed past, and Josh at the controls of the Auster Autocrat over the green and brown patchwork of English fields. She had no recollections of times like this. Josh had always been a coiled spring; it was his energy that she had fallen in love with. She loved it still, but it was as if the clarity of the mountain air was allowing her to see more clearly what was missing.

Sitting beside the reflecting water, with her chin resting on her knees, Julia tried to unravel the threads. They had been knotted together for so long that they were difficult to unpick, but she made herself do it, dispassionately following the strands.

Of course she loved Josh. She always had. From the beginning, from the first night. She had fallen in love with the dash and sparkle, but she had wanted to do it. Had almost determined to do it.

It was the day that Betty had come to the flat in the square. Julia could see her hands nervously folded over the clasp of her old handbag, the brown felt hat pulled tightly down over her colorless hair.

A dirty little baby, those were the words.

Julia had lifted her chin and pretended not to care. Pretended relief, even. And that night she had gone out, with Jessie's five pounds, to dinner with her best friends. Hungry, and defiant, she thought now.

And there Josh had been.

She had transferred all the weight of her love and need to a bright-haired American pilot. He had bought her a bottle of pink champagne, and taken her to a nightclub, and he had been kind to her. He had always been kind to her, Julia reflected, within his own definition of kindness.

She turned her head on her knees so that she could look at him.

Josh was watching the motionless tip of his rod, then glancing away to the black arc of line. His face was half-hidden by the peak of his cap, but she knew every line of it.

Fifteen years had blurred the sharp angles a little, that was all.

Julia sighed, thinking of her own sixteen-year-old naïveté. She had fallen in love in an hour, and she had made Josh carry the weight of it for all the years because the love had seemed too big and deep-rooted to dislodge.

She turned her head sharply again, and stared out over the water. It made her feel guilty to think of the responsibility she had thrust on him. Josh wasn't made for responsibility.

He had told her that over and over, but she had been deaf.

She thought of the little shock of recognition that she had experienced in his Mercedes, racing up toward Honey Creek. Josh was a boy, showing off his car to impress his girl. He had always been the same, with his airplanes and his skis. Not quite grown-up. *Your comic-book hero.* Alexander's words.

Josh was the perfect hero for a girl of sixteen. No wonder she had loved him then; the sadness was that she had made the love into a totem.

And now she was almost thirty-one, too old for heroes.

Julia contemplated the threads that she had untangled, without pleasure and without liking for the images of herself that were revealed.

She had clung to the romantic ideal of loving Josh, with a schoolgirl's fervor. She had been sure that it would last forever, at whatever cost. She had allowed herself to feel tragic, luxuriating in her own passion.

What it had cost her, she understood, was her marriage.

And because of that, what had Lily lost?

Julia wrapped her arms more tightly around her knees, containing herself. She couldn't jump up and run to Ladyhill, not yet. The threads must be set straight, finally, so that they could never tangle again.

Alexander had always been too grown-up, that was the difference. He was simply himself, not a hero, except when heroism was necessary. Alexander had run back under the stone arch at Ladyhill, into the smoke and heat. She closed her eyes on the image of that. When she opened them again she saw that the last light had gone. The lake had turned from a mirror into a sheet of cold, black glass.

Has it taken until now, she wondered, all this time, for me to grow up enough myself? The thought shamed her, but it was also an encouragement.

She had needed the struggle, for her own independence and for the success of Garlic & Sapphires. The old restlessness had gone, at least. Only it was Lily who had suffered. Thinking of her, Julia smiled a little. Lily was resilient, almost in the same way as Josh himself.

Perhaps even the flare of sexual energy that had overtaken her in New York had been necessary. It had meant that she had stopped dreaming of Josh, and waiting for him like Patience on her monument—clever, sharp Mattie—and had come to find him instead. And it was coming here, to the cabin under the trees, that had made her see the way that she should go.

If she could follow it, all the way back to Ladyhill, and find Alexander and Lily there, then that would be enough. She didn't know how much she could hope for beyond that. Slowly, Julia uncoiled her arms. She stood up, stiff with sitting still for so long, and touched her hand to Josh's shoulder.

"It's gone dark," she said.

Josh must have been as absorbed in his own thoughts. He started, and then squeezed her cold fingers.

"Time to pack up." He began reeling in his line, the rapid *ticktick* of the mechanism very loud in the stillness. He seemed more like a boy than ever, frowning intently over his task. Watching him, Julia felt the draft of guilt again.

Don't be guilty, she warned herself. Josh's self-protective mechanisms must be well enough developed by now.

She bent to help him to pack the scatter of equipment into the fishing basket. Josh lifted it, and held out his hand. She took it and they turned to walk together, along the rutted track to where the white nose of the Mercedes glimmered in the dimness.

Even in the late evenings they sat outside on the porch. Josh put away the fishing tackle and came out with two glasses of Jack Daniel's. Julia took hers and wrapped her fingers around it, looking away into the infinity under the trees. The noises that had seemed threatening on the first night were familiar now. She felt that she had been here a long time, and had reached a crossroads. The way that she had glimpsed beside the lake seemed clearer still, beckoning her.

"Josh, I've got to go home soon."

He didn't answer for a moment. He stood up and went to lean on the porch rail, staring intently out, as if he could see something that Julia couldn't. When he turned back again, she could see his face lit by the glow from inside the cabin.

"Won't you stay a while longer?" he asked softly.

Was that what he had asked her, when they were lying with their arms around each other on the first night? *Stay?*

"I don't mean here," Josh said, the movement of his hand taking in the cabin and the height rising behind it. "Come to Vail with me, perhaps. You've got managers for your shops, haven't you? Lily could come out. We could teach her to ski before she gets too old to be a champ—"

"Josh," she interrupted him. "What are you asking me?"

"Well." Another movement of his hand. This time it was just for the cabin, the bare shell of it enclosing bareness. Julia knew that the same gesture was for his apartment, where he had told her that there were no pictures on the walls and no ornaments on the mantel.

Josh said, "I always told you. If there was ever going to be anyone, it would be you."

Julia might almost have laughed. The irony was so complete, and so unexpected. But sadness touched her too quickly, and the tiny splutter died in her throat.

She didn't want to contemplate Josh's solitude, not now, because she knew that she couldn't dispel it. Whatever he was hoping for, asking for. The quiet, reflective Josh that she had glimpsed here in the mountains wasn't hers, not her aviator.

Hastily, she pushed the net of questions aside. Selfish. Her mouth tasted bitter.

"Josh," she repeated, "I've got to go home."

She stood up, facing him, and put her hands on his arms.

"To London?"

She lifted her head, looking at him through the dim yellow light.

"To Ladyhill."

At last he nodded. Julia's eyes were stinging and she blinked, angry with herself.

"Lily will like that," he said. "Did you . . . did you know what you were going to do when you came here?"

"No. I didn't know anything. I know a little bit more now."

He put his hands up, cupping her cheeks. "Thank you for coming."

"Thank you for asking me. I'm glad I came."

He kissed the corners of her mouth, very gently, and she let her head fall forward to rest against his shoulder. She felt the stolid reality of affection, and the impotence of love.

All the infinite gradations of it, she thought. *How long it takes to recognize them.* Then Josh kissed her again. She knew, as she had always known, how sharply she wanted him too.

"Come to bed," Josh ordered her. "I'll drive you to Denver tomorrow." The old Josh.

"I'm coming," Julia answered him.

In the morning Julia lifted the few clothes she had worn off the hooks behind the door of the cabin's bedroom and folded them into her suitcase. Their removal emphasized the bareness of the small rooms as she looked around them for the last time. Josh stood watching her, his hands seeming empty and awkward by his sides. She knelt down to snap the locks, then stood up again. Now that the time had come, she felt herself pulled two ways, the clarity that she thought she had achieved deserting her again.

I don't know, she thought angrily. *Why don't I know, after so long?*

She wondered if Josh had felt like this, at their separations in the past, while she had clung to him.

No, she decided. Not like this. Josh's instincts for self-preservation had been too well-developed then. She was less sure about now, and the irony of the reversal touched her again. She might have held out her hand, taking his awkward one, but she didn't. Instead, she gripped the handle of her suitcase, testing its weight.

The means of hurting each other are within such easy reach, she thought. Not just for Josh and me, but for all of us. For a moment, sadness seemed heavier than the real weight in her arms.

Josh looked at his watch. Uncharacteristically, he said, "We should go now, if we're going to make your plane." In the past, Josh had never worried about times or days. When he was ready to do what he wanted to do, he did it. Julia knew that he was filling the silence with conventional words, but she still noticed the change, disliking it.

"I'm ready," she said quietly.

He took her suitcase from her and carried it out to the Mercedes. The car rolled smoothly down the track, and the cabin was swallowed up by its curtain of trees. Julia didn't look back at it. She didn't want to think of its emptiness. Instead, she fixed her attention on the road as it unfolded, in reverse, through the new familiarity of Honey Creek, down again, and at last out on to the freeway. She thought of the distance ahead of her, beyond Denver, and New York, to the village in the hollow of green English countryside.

It was only when they had reached the airport, and found the New York flight already boarding, that Josh said, "I'm glad you came. I told you that already." And then, abruptly, "I shouldn't have asked you to stay on. Or hoped that you could have. That wasn't part of the contract, was it?"

"No, I suppose it wasn't," Julia said.

"And I think I set the terms of the contract." Josh was smiling, making her want to reach out and hold on to him.

"Yes," she agreed. "We kept to it, more or less, didn't we?"

And the other contracts? she wondered. *With Alexander, and Lily. Betty and Vernon, even. Those were harder to keep. Because they were real. What I imagined with Josh never was real. Gilt, instead of guilt. That was what I was chasing.* The recognition made her smile, a small, thin smile.

"It's time to go." Josh took her hands and kissed the suntanned knuckles, then turned her toward the departure gate.

"Come and see me in London," Julia said. *Me, not us,* although the plural could have included Lily, or Mattie, or the whole wide spread of the city rather than herself and Alexander.

"Of course I will."

They kissed, touching cheeks, like friends. *The contract of friendship,* Julia thought. *Mattie and I kept ours. That's one truth. Perhaps Josh and I will achieve that now. But only perhaps.*

She was walking away from him now, patting the pocket of her Rive Gauche suit to check her boarding card, hearing the busy click of her high heels on the wide shiny floor, carried along, a traveler. When she looked around, before turning the corner, she saw Josh's bright head over the other heads moving past him. He looked exactly as he had across the room at Leoni's. When she was sixteen, half-drunk, a dirty little baby.

Josh lifted his arm and waved.

Julia turned the corner, her own *click click* accompanying her.

She flew back to New York, and transferred to the first available London flight. As soon as she was airborne, she felt the threads of eagerness pulling at her. She leaned forward in her seat, as if that would make the jet fly faster through the curve of blue sky. She reached London in the gray-white light of early morning, but by the time she was climbing the five steps to her own front door the sun was streaming down the length of the street. London was welcoming, a city of top-heavy trees and homely corners, but Julia hardly registered it. The rooms of her house looked pretty and unusually clean and tidy, but she didn't stop to admire them. She tipped the contents of her suitcases on to her bedroom floor, intending to sort through them, but impatience took hold of her before she had begun and she pushed the heaps into a corner. She went downstairs and flipped through the piles of mail that Marilyn had stacked on the pine table, but there was nothing to catch her attention. She went back up the stairs and ran a bath, scenting it with Floris oil.

Lying in the water, looking through the steam at the coral branches and conch shells ranged on the shelves above her, Julia thought, *I couldn't sleep now even if I wanted to. I've come this far. I'll go straight on to Ladyhill.*

She sat up abruptly, sending a little wave of scented water splashing over the floor. An hour later, with the damp ends of her hair still curling around her neck, Julia turned her scarlet Vitesse into the traffic at the end of the street. She hadn't telephoned. *I'll surprise them,* she thought. *Lily will like that.*

She hadn't driven to Dorset for so long, but she remembered the way without effort. She knew that she was very tired, but the road seemed to unroll in front of her, hypnotic in its steady familiarity. When she left London behind, the fields opened on either side of her, yellow and gold, patched with knobs of trees and little clusters of houses, doll-like after the scale of Josh's America. Julia laughed, tightening her grip on the steering wheel. She sang to keep herself alert, snatches of songs

that she had hummed to Lily on similar journeys, "One Man
Went to Mow" and "Buttercup Joe."

Her mind wandered. How did she know songs like that
herself? Had Betty or Vernon ever sung to her?

*I'm as fresh as a daisy, that grows in the fields, and they
calls I Buttercup Joe.*

Did Lily still remember the words? They could sing it for
Alexander. It would make him laugh.

Basingstoke, Andover, Salisbury. After Blandford, over the
Stour, almost there.

"Nearly home," Alexander used to say, almost always at
exactly the same point in the road. Julia remembered that his
pleasure had irritated her. *Why was I so jealous?* she wondered.
She rubbed her eyes with the knuckles of one hand, yawning.
Blinking, looking around, she thought she understood Alexander's satisfaction perfectly. It was very beautiful, this corner of
England. Little hills, and open fields, and wooded hollows, each
little valley with its own stream. The villages with their low-
browed cottages were sunny and sleepy. How had the vertiginous spaces of Josh's mountainsides reminded her of this?

Julia knew that she was only two miles from Ladyhill. She
had just passed the fingerpost that announced *Ladyhill, 3*, and
that was on down to the village itself. A tractor materialized
ahead of her and she slowed to a crawl in its wake. Her memory
served up a picture of straight, open road ahead of it, dipping
down to the stone gateposts of Ladyhill House.

Julia pressed her foot down and the car surged forward,
swinging out parallel with the tractor. The road was clear, as she
remembered, of course. The roar of the Vitesse's engine swirled
in through the open window and she caught the scent of hay
from the tractor's load. In the same instant, the threat of it
frighteningly at odds with the reassuring country smell, a car
shimmered up in her path. It was big and gray, and it swept up
out of a dip in the road that her memory had obliterated. It was
traveling fast, coming at her like a silvery bullet. She knew that
she couldn't brake hard enough to get back behind the tractor. Its
huge wheels turned beside her head.

Julia stamped her foot hard. The car howled in protest, but
it leapt forward. The tractor seemed dragged back behind her.
She wrenched the wheel and the car rocked under her, slewing
across to her own side of the road. The gray car whirled past her
in a dazzle of headlights and a deafening blast of the horn. She
caught a glimpse of the driver's angry, red, frightened face, and

then he was gone. They had missed each other, she guessed, by less than a yard.

Julia drove on, her hands damp and shaking, and sweat sticky in a patch at the small of her back. Relief made her legs feel weak and her head too heavy for her neck. She was tired, and she had been driving recklessly, but she had been lucky. Lucky this time. Ahead of her were the stone gateposts of Ladyhill.

With an extraordinary, grateful surge, her spirits lifted. She knew that life was precious; she felt it like a smooth stone, miraculously veined, warm in the palm of her hand. She would hold it, keep it safe, value it. From now, this moment.

The shadow of the trees lining the driveway dappled her face. She slowed the car, lifting her head to the coolness. She turned the corner and saw the house in front of her. Her head held a hundred different images of Ladyhill, but none of them matched this afternoon's. It was as if she had known but never before acknowledged that it was beautiful.

She let the car drift to a standstill and climbed out. She walked on, up to the house, her eyes fixed on it. The gray stone was gold-tinged in the sunlight, the brick was warm coral-pink. Beside her now was the wing where the fire had started. The black stains of it had been cleaned away. The windows had been releaded, and the small panes of glass shone. There was no sign, anymore, of the devastation.

The blanket of smoke and fear had drifted away.

Julia's footsteps scrunched on the gravel. She walked on, to the paved court enclosed by the two projecting wings. Lavender and nepeta had been planted in blue-gray drifts in the beds against the gray walls. The front door under its portico in the short central arm of the house's E-shape stood invitingly open.

Julia wondered where Lily and Alexander could be.

On the threshold, as the shadow of the house fell over her face, she hesitated. She hadn't been here since she had run away, with Lily in her arms.

Did she have the right now to walk past the bees humming in the lavender and into the dim silence of the house?

Julia looked up. Above her head, over the door, was a stone tablet with the family motto carved in it. It was the single word, *Aeternitas*.

She put out her hand, tentative, as if she were feeling her way in darkness. The heavy door, warmed by the sun, swung open. Julia walked into the stone-flagged hallway. She looked up, surprised. The walls were washed pale ivory, bringing light into the heart of the house. Sunlight streamed through the restored glass of the high stairway window, lying in patterns over the clean stone flags and the new oak boards of the stairs. The intricately turned banisters looked just as they always had, instead of the bitten-off black stumps of her nightmares. There were new pictures on the walls, landscapes and a tiny, glowing still life, and a pair of fine Gothic hall chairs faced each other from opposite sides of the front door.

So Alexander had done it, she thought.

He had remade Ladyhill. It was as lovely, more perfect in itself, than it had been before.

Julia stepped forward, the patterns of light breaking over her feet. There was one wrong detail, just one tiny flaw in the picture of perfection. At the foot of the stairs she bent down and picked it up.

It was a high-heeled gold sandal. Not gold, rather. Gilt. Rather a tarty piece of work, Julia thought.

What was it doing here?

Then the answer, satisfyingly obvious, came to her. It must be Lily's, one of Lily's dressing-up shoes. At school rummage sales Lily always bought the cast-off evening slippers, and stumbled around in them at home, dragging a wake of chiffon scarves and floppy hats and beads behind her.

Swinging the shoe by its strap, Julia went on through the house. Of course, Lily and Alexander would be outside, in the sun. They would be sitting in the orchard, by the white-painted summerhouse.

The back door had been replaced. There were six glass panels in it now, letting new light into the once-dingy flower room with its big stone sink and hanging row of gardening jackets and fraying straw hats.

Julia saw them through the glass panels.

Alexander was sitting in a Lloyd Loom chair, reading, and Lily was lying on her stomach, a little way away from him, drawing on a sketchpad. The tip of her tongue stuck out between her teeth. It was then that Julia remembered that Lily had stopped dressing up years ago.

Mattie was sitting on the grass beside Alexander's chair. The other gold sandal, discarded like its partner, lay next to her. And as Julia watched, Alexander looked up from his book and let his hand fall on to Mattie's shoulder. His fingers touched the nape of her neck, where she had bundled up the heavy mass of her hair.

At once, immediately, Julia understood everything.

She stood frozen into stillness, her hand on the latch of the door. A second later, their attention drawn by her guilty, horrified stare, the comfortable trio on the grass looked up and saw her.

Julia turned away and ran.

Without knowing where she was going, she ran up the stairs, her feet thudding painfully on the oak boards. She ran down the gallery to the big bedroom that she had shared with Alexander. At the beginning, when they were first married. When Alexander was a boy, he had told her, the room had been his parents'.

The room looked different now. The first thing she saw was a new dressing table, oval, with a looped skirt of unusually pretty chintz. Felix's touch, she thought dully, automatically. The top of the table was protected by an oval of thick glass, and on the glass there was a dusting of spilled powder. Julia swept her hand over it and stared down at the pinky-white crust edging her palm.

The powder told her everything she already knew, hammering it brutally home. There were other things too: another pair of high-heeled sandals, a lace-edged slip turned inside out, flung over a chair with one of Alexander's familiar Tattersall check shirts. But the powder on its own was enough.

Julia turned, and saw that Mattie had followed her. Her cheeks were too pink, and her hair was escaping from its combs.

Standing in the doorway, seeing Julia's gray face and burning eyes, Mattie said, "Why didn't you tell us you were coming?"

Julia was shaking. She felt cold and stiff and sick with anger and shame. She found the words, any words, out of the torrent that boiled up in her. "And why didn't you tell me? I thought you were my friend, Mattie. I thought you were."

"I am your friend."

Julia's hand flew up, and then she found herself looking at it, wondering why, as if it didn't belong to her. She was still holding the silly gilt sandal. She let her arm drop again, stiff, to her side and the sandal fell at her feet. "No. No, you aren't. How could you be?"

And then they heard Lily and Alexander, coming after them.

Mattie began, "Julia, I want to . . ." but Julia turned on her, cutting her short.

"I don't care what you want. How could you do it, Mat? Here. With Alexander. After . . . after everything."

"It's nothing," Mattie said helplessly. "It's just friends."
The blaze of anger in Julia's face frightened her.

"Don't ever say it's nothing," Julia warned.

Lily was shouting. "Mummy, Mummy, where are you?
Where have you gone?"

"I'm here," Julia managed to say, her eyes fixed on Mattie
in disbelief. "I'm here, Lily."

A moment later Lily appeared at Mattie's side. She had
grown. Her brown legs, netted with bramble scratches, looked
longer and thinner than ever. Julia felt a treacherous space of
jealousy and secrecy yawning between them. She wanted to rush
into it, headlong.

"Mummy, why are you here? Is everything okay?" Lily
was surprised, not alarmed.

Julia said, "I thought I'd surprise you all. I did, didn't I?"

She was tired now. Exhaustion and misery pulled at her,
dragging at her limbs. Lily came and hugged her, the perfunctory, dismissive greeting of security.

"It's a fab surprise. Isn't it, Mattie?"

"Yes, love," Mattie said. Julia wouldn't meet her eyes.
They could hear Alexander coming along the gallery toward
them.

TWENTY-ONE

For Lily's sake, they made the necessary pretenses.

Alexander held out his hands to Julia, large warm hands
that enveloped her own cold ones and she saw the concern in his
face. She also saw that he was awkward, and unhappy at the
position that she had put him in. She had never seen Alexander
awkward before, and she knew that when her anger and shock
had subsided, she would be sorry for having made him so. She
withdrew her hands and pushed them, defensively, into her
pockets.

"Did you have a successful trip?"

The question was so strangely formal that she stared,
uncomprehending, for a moment. "Oh. Yes, very successful. I

met all sorts of people, saw all kinds of interesting things for the shops.''

They were like polite strangers, Julia thought bitterly, newly introduced at some less than successful cocktail party. This reality, compared with the rosy, romantic dreams that she had permitted herself as she drove through the summer country, made her want to duck her head to hide her shame and embarrassment. She held it up defiantly, and saw Mattie gathering up her rolls of hair that had escaped from their combs. She was straightening herself, putting on a public face after the intimate scene that Julia had glimpsed in the orchard.

A public face, for me. The sense of exclusion cut through her, sharp as a knifeblade.

"Shall I go and make us all some tea?" Mattie asked.

Mattie as châtelaine, graciously dispensing the hospitality of Ladyhill. Furiously, childishly, Julia hated her, knowing that there were no grounds for hating Mattie except for puncturing an illusion. She turned away from the sight of her, to Lily, who was hopping with impatience by her side.

"Mummy, come to the paddock and see Marco Polo. You've never even seen him." She took her mother's hand, swinging it. "Alexander put up some jumps. I'm so pleased you're here."

Julia looked down at her oval face, noticeably printed with Alexander's features as well as her own. Lily was pleased. She made herself smile, feeling it as a grimace. "Of course I'll come. I'd love to see Marco Polo."

It would help to leave this bedroom, with its little bits of sordid evidence. Had Lily seen them, she wondered. What had Lily guessed? Perhaps she would be able to breathe more easily outside these walls. Perhaps she would be able to straighten the tangle of jealous questions without Mattie confronting her, without the gold sandal lying on the floor between them.

She held out her hand to Lily. "Come on then. Show me the famous Marco Polo."

They went down the stairs together, out into the sunshine. Lily led the way, skipping, talking, full of news of the summer.

We went to Weymouth . . . we had a picnic . . . Julia half-listened, not daring to ask the questions that throbbed in her head.

When they reached the paddock, Lily climbed the gate and ran to put her arms around her pony's neck. He nuzzled at her hand, looking for sugar. Julia heard Lily telling him, "Mummy's here."

She watched her scramble on to the pony's back and then urge him to a trot. There was a circuit of little jumps made of brushwood and fencing poles, and Lily and Marco Polo hopped neatly over them. Julia stretched her arms along the top of the gate, feeling the splintery wood against the palms of her hands. Lily looked so happy. Her face, and the pink shirt she was wearing, made her a bright, moving spot of light in the soft green landscape.

I was a fool to come here, Julia thought.

She had been right not to come before, through all the years. Even to see Lily's happiness. Because that brought her face-to-face with her own jealousy. She could feel it, shifting and rolling its weight inside her, ignited by what she had glimpsed this afternoon. The only possibility is to get away again, she told herself, as quickly as possible. And to take Lily with her.

She wanted Lily. She wanted to see her happy at home, in the house by the canal, as well as trotting in the Ladyhill paddock. And she didn't want Mattie and Alexander to have her.

She's mine, Julia reassured herself fiercely. *My daughter.*

Lily and the pony wheeled in a tight circle and trotted back to the gate. Lily was pink with pride and pleasure. The pony snorted and tossed its head and she bent over its neck, patting it and praising it. "What d'you think, Mum?"

"I think you're very clever. I didn't know you could jump half as well as that."

"I've been practicing. Elizabeth and I have jump-offs. We do three circuits each and Alexander times us . . ." She swung down off the pony's back, vaulted the gate again, put her arm through her mother's, still breathlessly chattering.

She's only a child, even now, Julia realized. How much longer have I got her for, like this? A sense of the preciousness of time gnawed at her. She drew Lily's hand through her arm more tightly, turning her away from the house. "Let's have a walk. Tell me everything."

They swished through the grass. Julia listened carefully now. There was no hint, in any of Lily's outpourings, that Mattie had become anything different from what Mattie always had been. A friend, part of the family.

My friend. Julia remembered how, with Josh, she had reflected on the durability of that. Well then. That had been wrong.

At least they had concealed their love affair from Lily. Even though Mattie had carelessly left her underclothes and her face powder strewn in Alexander's bedroom.

"What's the matter?" Lily asked. Julia saw her clear eyes.

"Nothing's the matter. I sat on an airplane all night, and so I'm tired."

Such necessary lies.

They had reached the point beyond the walls of the garden where the land sloped gently down to the village. Julia stopped short, staring ahead of her. "What's that?"

She could see what it was. There was a rash of tiled roofs and rendered walls. It was a cluster of bungalows, their picture windows looking out onto neat plots of backyard, a child's swing in the nearest fenced square. Once there had been only a field. Dimly, Julia remembered that Alexander had called it the lower Four Acres.

Lily scowled. "Horrible houses, on our fields. I don't look at them. Daddy just said that people need somewhere to live, and he and Felix needed the money for Ladyhill. Since the fire, you know."

"I know."

Julia turned away. So Alexander had sold land to pay for the restoration work. Of course, he would have had to.

The lurid images swirled up, unwanted, inescapable. Flowers, and Sandy. Alexander running away from her, into the smoke.

"They make everything look different," Lily complained. "I wanted Ladyhill to be the same always."

We all want things to be the same, Julia thought sadly. *It takes a long time to understand that they can't be. Alexander, I've done everything wrong. I'm so sorry.*

"They're perfectly nice houses," Julia said automatically. "And people do need somewhere to live. If Daddy needed the money for Ladyhill, he was lucky to have something that he could sell, wasn't he?"

"You sound just like him," Lily sniffed.

They began to walk back toward the house. They could just see the tops of the high chimneys, over the sheltering screen of trees.

"Why did you come?" Lily asked abruptly. "You never have, before, have you?"

"I wanted to see you and Daddy. Here, together, at Ladyhill. And now I have done that." A measure of adult truth, Julia decided. Just a measure, to be added. "Perhaps it would have been better not to come, not even this time. I don't seem to belong at Ladyhill like you do. It makes me feel . . . left out."

There was a small silence. "Mattie doesn't feel like that," Lily said after a moment.

Julia answered, "Mattie's only a guest. She isn't part of the family." How much too much sharpness in her voice?

Lily nodded. "Like Felix, when he comes?"

"I suppose so." Julia took a deep breath. "Lily, I'm going back to London in the morning. I want you to come with me."

There was a long, protesting wail. "But there's another whole week. I can't go yet. I want to take Marco to the Middleham show. . . ."

Julia listened in grim silence, all the way back to the house, to the remonstrances that Lily flung at her. As they passed through the garden, Julia saw Mattie in the distance, apparently engrossed in studying the flower border. She wondered what hasty colloquy she and Alexander had had.

When they reached the front door Julia said, "Just the same, Lily, I want you to be ready to come back with me in the morning."

To get away from here, that was the important thing.

Alexander was sitting in the drawing room. His arms hung loosely on either side of the chair's arms. He looked baffled, and exhausted. Julia wanted to walk across and touch his shoulder, but she stood stiffly in the doorway. Lily pushed past her.

"Mum says I've got to go with her in the morning. I haven't, have I? Tell her I haven't."

"If your mother says you must go, then you must," Alexander told her.

Lily never argued with him. She whirled around and ran out of the room. They listened to her feet thudding up the stairs, and their eyes met. When a door had slammed, somewhere a long way off, Alexander stood up. He crossed the room to the drinks tray and held up a bottle of whiskey, inquiringly.

Julia nodded wearily. "Thanks."

They sat down with their drinks, facing each other, unthinkingly taking up the places that had always been theirs. Julia drank half of her whiskey, and then let her head fall back against the cushions, closing her eyes.

"I shouldn't have arrived without telling you. I'm sorry, Alexander."

"There's no reason why you shouldn't have come if you wanted to. It would just have been easier if we could all have pretended that nothing was happening. Nothing has happened, by the way, as far as Lily is concerned."

"I gathered that. Thank you."

"Julia? None of this was planned, you know. Mattie came to stay, with Felix—"

Julia cut him short. "I don't want to hear about it. I don't want to be told."

She sensed rather than heard a movement, knew that he was leaning forward, looking at her. It was comforting to keep her eyes closed, like being under a warm red veil.

"Mattie would tell you the same."

"I particularly don't want to hear about Mattie."

She heard him sigh. "You hurt yourself, you know. Couldn't you learn to be kinder to yourself?"

"I don't see how," Julia said coldly. And then, after a second, "Do you love her?"

It seemed to take him a long time to consider. "Not in the way that you mean."

"And does she love you?"

Much quicker, this time. "No. I'm sure she doesn't."

Julia opened her eyes. The room looked golden, the late sun pouring through it like syrup. It was different now, Felixified, but it was still the room where they had sat on her very first visit to Ladyhill, still the room where her Christmas tree had shone in its nimbus of candlelight.

"So it was just a casual fuck?"

Alexander was cold now. "You know it wasn't that."

She did, and she was ashamed, but she wouldn't let him see the shame. It seemed, suddenly, imperative to hide the fact of being hurt. If she could only be dignified, she thought, just until she could extricate herself from here. After that, where they couldn't see her, it wouldn't matter. She drank the rest of her whiskey.

"I don't know anything," she said, and it struck her that it was the truth. "May I stay the night, Alexander? I got in from New York only this morning. I don't think I could drive back now. Lily and I will go first thing in the morning."

"Of course. Whatever you like. Does Lily have to leave before the end of her holiday?"

"Yes," Julia said very softly. She put her glass down, carefully, stood up, noticing with detachment the ache of tiredness in her arms and legs. "I think I'll go and"—what to do, to fill in the painful time?—"have a bath, tidy myself up. It's been, it's been a long day."

"There are three bathrooms now," Alexander said. "All of them bearing Felix's signature."

They smiled at each other, briefly forgetting.

"The whole house does. It looks very beautiful," Julia told him. "You must be proud of it."

"Less proud than I thought I would be." He said it so quietly that she wondered, afterward, if she had heard correctly.

Julia reached the door, and then turned back again. She was driven by some impulse to tell Alexander the truth so that out of all this unhappiness she would have at least that small satisfaction.

"I saw Josh Flood when I was in America."

He nodded. "I thought you would."

Alexander wouldn't make a gibe. He would never say *Just a casual fuck.* But he knew her far better than she ever allowed for.

"We usually have dinner at about half past eight," Alexander said. That was all.

"I'll be down in time."

We, and *usually,* Julia thought as she trailed up the stairs. Did that mean *Mattie and I?* Even if it did, she reminded herself, she had no claim on Alexander. But Mattie should have known what she had stupidly allowed herself to hope for. Mattie should have known, with the osmotic understanding of long-standing friendship. Yet Mattie had either not seen it, or she hadn't cared.

It felt like a betrayal of all the years.

Julia ran a bath that she didn't want, in a bathroom tiled with blue-patterned Portuguese tiles. She lay in the water, staring at the blue painted fish.

Afterward, at half past eight, when Lily had gone upstairs to her bedroom in a ferocious sulk, the three of them had dinner together. They sat, formally, at one end of the long polished table in the dining room. It was a stiff reflection of other, happier meals that they had shared.

Mattie did most of the talking. She had bolstered herself with a hefty gin before they sat down, and while they ate she emptied her wineglass as quickly as Alexander refilled it for her. She talked, apparently at random, about the Ladyhill Village fête and the new play she was learning for Chichester and a moth-eaten second-hand shop in Weymouth where she had found an almost perfect 1930s Persian lamb coat for ten pounds. Julia listened, and to Alexander's brief responses, but she said little herself because she couldn't think of anything. She watched Mattie's face, seeing that she was miserable, too, and half-admired her ability to keep on filling the silence through the wretched meal.

But at the end, when she had drunk too much to hold on to the pretense of civility any longer, Mattie dropped her dessert spoon with a clatter. "Oh, Christ, can't we have a proper bloody row and get it over?"

"Mattie . . ." Alexander warned her, but she ignored him.

"So, Julia? You don't like to come down here and find me and Alexander together. Well, no one likes that sort of thing, do they? It's like not being picked for rounders at Blick Road, is it? But there it is, it happened. I came with Felix, for the ride, and I stayed. We've had a happy few weeks here, as a matter of fact. We've seen the green fields, sat in the sun, all that." She drank some more wine, spilling a little that collected in a shiny globule on the mahogany tabletop. "Alexander and I also went to bed together. It was very nice, thank you, if you were thinking of asking. I like Alexander very much. He's one of the minute number of decent men there are in the world."

"I know that," Julia said almost inaudibly.

"But you didn't bloody want him, did you?"

"Be quiet, Mattie," Alexander said.

Mattie turned to him. She swept her arm out in a big, loose gesture. Her wrist was loaded with gilt bracelets, and they glittered dangerously. "I'm sorry, darling, if you're embarrassed to have all this said in front of you. Not very restrained or middle-class, is it? But then, Julia and I aren't. *Arrivistes,* that's what we are. Scratch us, and it shows."

Alexander leaned across the table to take Mattie's hand, but she shook him off.

"So, Julia. Here you find us. Not particularly nice for you, I agree, but then, not so very terrible either. How long have you and Alexander been divorced exactly? How much longer have you and I supposedly been friends?"

She stared at Julia, as if she were waiting for the pedantic answers to her questions. Julia shook her head, frozen, and Mattie shrugged. She picked up her glass and emptied it again, but her mouth twisted, as if the taste disgusted her. Then she laughed. "Funny, this love and friendship business, isn't it? It doesn't seem to mean much. I was lonely when I came down here. I expect Alexander was lonely, too, although he's never quite said so."

We're all lonely, Julia thought, remembering Josh. The recognition and the fear of solitude crept around her, chilling her. It made her think of Betty and Vernon, in their separate solitudes inside the tiny rooms of Fairmile Road. The unwelcome insight of the moment convinced her that what lay ahead of all of them, Mattie and Alexander as well as herself, was no more than middle age. The passion of friendship, as well as love, would cool, and go on cooling until it froze altogether. They would move on, all of them, in increasing isolation. Then, finally, they would be old.

The prospect seemed unbearably sad and perfectly irrevocable.

It made her long for Alexander, and for what she had once possessed and stupidly rejected. The reality of what was happening now, by contrast, bit savagely back at her.

She turned her head to look at Mattie again, and saw that she had dipped over the edge into being definitely drunk. Her extravagant earrings, matching the gilt bracelets, swung lopsidedly.

"Meanwhile," Mattie went on, clearly unstoppable, "you were in America. With Josh Flood, no less. Patience hopping off her dreary monument at last. God, that little item has run on and on, hasn't it? Are you going to tell us the latest? No? Well, never mind. Plenty of time. I'm sure it was all very exciting. But the point is, isn't it, that you can't afterward turn up here and act all grieved and injured because your best friend and your ex-husband have warmed their creaking bones a little. Or on the other hand you can, but you should know that it makes you seem a selfish bitch. Darling." Mattie listened to her own words echoing, and then she laughed, without conviction. "Oh, Julia. Aren't you going to say anything?"

The fact that what Mattie had said was true, Julia reflected, didn't make her like her any more for having said it. But it was important not to let them see that she was hurt, to keep what was left of her dignity until she had escaped from Ladyhill.

"What do you want to hear, Mattie? Haven't you said it all already?"

Julia stood up. Her hands rested on the carved back of her chair. "You're quite right, of course, about everything. And selfishness is worse than disloyalty, I agree." She turned, abruptly, away from Mattie, to Alexander. "I'm sorry, Alexander. Lily and I will be going first thing in the morning."

He nodded stiffly. Clearly, he had hated the scene, hated having to witness it in impotent silence. Mattie had been right about that too. Alexander was middle-class. China would never have initiated a row like this one.

Carefully, tidily, Julia pushed her chair into the table, aligning the back of it with its unoccupied fellows. "I'm going to bed now. Good night, Mattie. Thank you for the room, Alexander."

As she reached the door, Mattie put her hand out to her glass once more. Alexander hadn't refilled it, and so she had taken the bottle and done it herself. But now she misjudged the distance, clumsily swept the glass over. Wine flooded over the table, and dripped between the leaves and on to the floor.

Alexander sat motionless, watching it.

"Shit," Mattie said. "Oh, shit. Why am I so stupid?"

Julia went up to her bedroom, along the gallery at the far end, and left them there. She undressed and lay for a long time, looking up into the darkness. Later she heard Alexander and Mattie, separately, coming upstairs. Her room was too far away for her to hear, even if she had remotely wanted to, whether Mattie went to Alexander's or to her own separate bedroom.

In the morning, unemotionally, she gathered up Lily's clothes and belongings and packed them into the car. Lily tramped down to the paddock to say a tearful good-bye to her pony, and by nine o'clock they were ready to leave.

Alexander came out to say good-bye. Lily pillowed her puffy face against his shirt and he hugged her, assuring her that there would be other holidays, and that Ladyhill would remain exactly where it stood.

"No holidays as good as these," she wailed.

"Exactly as good," he told her robustly.

In silence, Julia admired the way that Alexander dealt with Lily. As Marilyn had perceptively—if unflatteringly—pointed out, Lily was lucky in her father, at least.

With Lily at last in her seat in the car, Julia said for the last time, "I'm sorry."

"Don't keep apologizing," Alexander told her. "I haven't said that I'm sorry, and neither has Mattie. Why should you?"

They didn't touch each other. Julia wanted to ask, *What will happen now?* but she was too proud. Instead, she got into the car. Alexander stood back to let her drive away.

Mattie hadn't appeared at all.

They drove in silence for two or three miles, with Lily huddled in her place, before she asked suddenly, "Did you and Mattie have a quarrel or something?"

"No," Julia lied faintheartedly, "of course we didn't."

Drearily, they reversed the journey of the day before. Over the Stour to Blandford. Salisbury, Andover, Basingstoke, and back to London.

* * *

Mattie stayed at Ladyhill for only one more day. As if to emphasize that the precarious holiday had come to an inauspicious end, the weather changed suddenly and conclusively. Huge, solid slabs of cloud mounted up and slid across the sky. A cold wind flattened the grass and then the rain came, driving from the east. Mattie took her thin dresses from the hangers, one by one, and folded them into her suitcase.

She had returned to the single bed, with its Provençal cotton cover, in the spare room she had used in the first five days. It seemed a long time ago.

"Don't," Alexander had said gently. "Unless you want to."

Mattie had thought carefully. "We can't always have what we want," she had told him. She had gone back to the spare room anyway.

Alone, doing her packing, Mattie sighed and looked out of the window at the rain. She pressed the flat of her hand to each eye socket in turn, and then swept a jingling heap of bangles and earrings off the dressing table and into the suitcase.

Alexander drove her to the station. She wouldn't let him come out on to the platform with her to wait for the train. They said good-bye in the windy parking lot.

"I'm sorry if I fucked things up for you with Julia," she said.

Alexander looked down at her and touched the metallic-bright strands of hair where she had scraped it forbiddingly back behind her ears. There was no frivolity in Mattie today.

"You didn't fuck anything up. That happened long ago."

"Did it?" And then, "What a mess we all make."

"What are you going to do now?"

"Get to work," Mattie answered crisply. The prospect wasn't enticing, but she didn't want Alexander to guess that. He put his arms around her, in the car, and held her against him.

"I loved these weeks," he said. Mattie thought how much she liked him for the simplicity of the acknowledgment. She liked him, too, for not holding out any false hopes. No *if it had only happened differently*, or *next time we see each other* . . .

There are only two or three men in the world worth loving, she remembered.

"I've got to go. The train will come before I've bought my ticket."

He held on to her for a second longer. They kissed, soft-mouthed, full of regret. Then Mattie picked up her suitcase and walked away into the ticket office.

On the train, wedged on her own among the returning vacationers, Mattie stared out of the rain-washed window.

She was telling herself, *I didn't know Julia wanted to go back to him. Why didn't I ever realize it?*

Julia has been a fool, Mattie thought. And then, wearily, *Why did she choose the most important thing to be stupid about?*

There were three small children crammed with their parents into the compartment. Mattie looked at them, the smallest perched on its father's knee, wondering whether to smile at them and make friends for the journey. She decided at once that she felt much too gloomy. Her thoughts turned to whether there was a bar on the train, and if there was, at what time it was likely to open.

Julia went back to work.

There was plenty of it waiting for her in the Garlic & Sapphires office. She plowed through the paperwork that followed her American buying trip, unpacked and inspected samples as they arrived, and drove around to the three other shops to inspire the managers and staff with enthusiasm for the new goods. Everything was the same as it always was, only duller. Business was slack, as it always was over the weeks of the summer holidays, and the autumnal surge of shoppers looking for something amusing to enliven their bedrooms or living rooms hadn't begun yet.

Julia telephoned Felix at Tressider Designs.

"Come to lunch."

"George is in hospital."

"I didn't know. Is it bad?"

"Not yet. But it isn't getting any better. I don't think it will either."

"Felix, I'm sorry. Is there anything I can do?"

"Buy me some lunch. Cheer me up."

"I'll do my best," Julia promised, not very hopefully.

George Tressider wasn't a good patient. He was being treated privately, in a private room, but he complained that it was the ugliest he had ever been in. The walls were painted a pale shade of shiny turquoise, and there were blue and magenta contemporary print curtains and screens.

"Shall I bring in some Tressider chintz and rehang?" Felix asked him, only half-joking.

"Perhaps just a blindfold would do," George responded with a pale echo of his old wit.

Felix smiled at him. George was brave, for all his ill temper.

The muscular disease had progressed to the stage when George could no longer walk without assistance. When he was out of bed he sat in a wheelchair, with a blanket folded over his knees. He looked like an old man. Aware of it, he lifted his hands and held them out to Felix. Felix came, stooping down to his level, and held the knotted fingers. The rich color of his own skin made George's look even grayer.

"I don't like this," George said.

"I know."

Felix held his head, cradling it against his shoulder. He looked down at George's gray hair, and saw the scalp showing beneath the thin strands.

It was after this visit that Felix and Julia met for lunch.

"How is he?" Julia asked.

"They say they can let him come home soon."

"Does that mean he's better?"

Felix couldn't answer the question. "I'd rather look after him at home. He hates the hospital so much."

Julia looked at him gravely. She understood what was happening. She had never been fond of George Tressider, but the prospect of his death seemed monstrous, a terrible injustice. She tried to imagine what it would mean to Felix. Across the table, staring blankly at his menu, he was as handsome as he had ever been, but there were lines of anxiety at the corners of his mouth, and the first signs of gray were showing in his black, springy hair.

"May I go and visit him?" Julia asked.

"Of course." He gave her the details, and Julia wrote them down and put the piece of folded paper into her handbag. "It's aged him," Felix said abruptly. He was warning her what to expect. "He's only sixty-two. He looks ten years older than that."

"Poor George," Julia said, ashamed of the inadequacy of her sympathy.

"We've been married for eleven years. That's a long time."

"Has it been a happy marriage?" Julia asked softly.

"I haven't been a faithful wife." He smiled at her, an

acknowledgment that they understood each other. "But yes, we have been very happy. We are a good partnership."

A partnership, Julia thought. Of course, that's what pairing was. After so long, after the passion. She knew what it was to be without it, and sadness for Felix washed through her.

"Hey." Felix touched the back of her hand. "This is a cheerful lunch, remember?" He discarded the menu in favor of the wine list. "Let's order some wine," he said. "A lot of wine."

"You sound like Mattie."

He looked sharply at her. "Are we going to talk about Mattie?"

"You know about it?"

Felix remembered Alexander playing the piano, and Mattie dancing with her dress swirling around her. "I guessed."

He would have warned, *Be careful*, but he knew that it was too late for that.

"No," Julia said briskly. "We aren't going to talk about Mattie or Alexander. Not today." It seemed too small, for all the hurt of it, compared with what was happening to Felix and George.

So they talked about Tressider Designs instead, and about Garlic & Sapphires and the American art market and the latest decorators' gossip. They drank two bottles of wine and turned giggly, then serious again, when it was time to leave. Julia insisted on paying the bill.

"I'm an independent woman," she said, presenting her credit card with a flourish. "I've fought hard enough to be. Too hard, do you think, Felix?"

"Only if you feel that it has cost you too much."

She didn't look at him now. She bent her head, folding her purse away. "Perhaps it has," she whispered. "Perhaps after all I should have stayed at home and had babies and made jam for the WI."

"I don't think it would have worked," Felix said truthfully. "But you look tired, Julia. Why don't you take a holiday?"

"I've just had one. New York, San Francisco, Toronto, Colorado."

"I thought that was work."

And so it mostly had been, except for seeing Josh. And if she did go on vacation, where should she go, and with whom? "It's an idea," she said, dismissing it.

They parted on the sidewalk outside the restaurant. Felix kissed her, and she held on to him for a moment.

"You're a good friend, Felix."

"As good as you are."

She watched him as he walked away. But I'm not good, or much of a friend, she was thinking. She looked at her watch. Half past three. She should have been back at work long ago. Over the next weeks, she thought two or three times about Felix's suggestion.

Julia's eye for a witty or original piece of merchandise had never deserted her, and over the years of running her shops she had developed into an efficient administrator as well. The Garlic & Sapphires operation ran smoothly, but for Julia most of the uncertainty and so most of the excitement had gone. She knew what pieces would sell, and she knew how to price them and how to display them. Sitting at her desk, she remembered the anxiety, and the thrills, of the very early days, when she had done everything herself, and had snatched bites of sandwich for her lunch in the little cubicle behind the first shop.

She didn't often, nowadays, experience the charge of excitement that she had felt in New York. It occurred to her that perhaps Felix was right, in a sense. Perhaps she needed not so much a holiday as a change of scene, and the different perspectives that a change would bring.

It was a long time, too, since she had been away for any reason not connected directly with the shops. Lily never wanted to go anywhere on holiday except to Ladyhill, and Julia had taken the opportunity provided by her absences to work harder, for longer hours.

For what? she thought now with sudden bitterness.

She would go away, she decided. For a proper holiday, sometime soon.

In the end, it was George Tressider who provided the final impetus.

Julia had been to see him in the hospital. She had taken him a huge bunch of extravagant, creamy lilies, and a big, plain white cylindrical vase from the shop to display them in. George was touchingly grateful for the offering. It was the vase, even more than the flowers, that pleased him. Julia arranged the lilies in it and set it on his bed table.

He lay back, gazing at them. "You've no idea," he said. Even his voice sounded thinner, drained of all the fluting emphases. "People bring exquisite flowers, and the nurses take them and dump them in Woolworth's green cut glass, or bulbous purple pot. I would rather not have flowers at all than see them made hideous. You have given me such pleasure by bringing the right container. It is all a question of balance, and proportion, isn't it? In the big things as well as the small ones. It's the search for the right balance and the correct proportion that has made my work so pleasurable.''

The next time she saw him, he was much happier. Felix had taken him home to the old flat in Eaton Square. It was a relief to see him once more ensconced among the Lalique bowls and the Regency furniture, the French marble mantels and the billowing Tressider chintzes. There were flowers everywhere, perfectly arranged, and bowls of potpourri on the tables contributing to the scented atmosphere. George was sitting in an armchair. He was wearing one of his immaculate, waisted, lavender-gray suits, and a high-collared pale pink shirt. His hair had been cut and brushed back, and he looked almost himself again. Almost well, Julia thought, until his hand held hers. His flesh felt dry and papery, as if it would flake off the bones.

"My dear. Here we are again," George said. "Restored to grace."

They had tea together, the three of them. Felix brought in a tray, laid with the full works. Georgian silver teapot, sugar bowl and cream jug, although they all took their tea with lemon. Silver tongs, and a little spirit lamp to keep the water hot. Meissen china, white and gold, practically transparent in its thinness, and lawn and lace fragments too delicate to be called napkins.

"Pretty," Julia murmured, accepting a tiny triangle of cucumber sandwich.

George and Felix treated each other with a kind of watchful tenderness. Julia was moved, but she felt like an intruder. She stared at the tiny plate on her lap while her eyes burned.

George drank his tea, but he ate nothing.

Afterward Julia helped Felix to carry the precious paraphernalia back into the kitchen. "He likes beautiful things," Felix said. "He has collected all these, over the years. It would be a pity not to use them, now, wouldn't it?"

"Of course," Julia reassured him.

George wanted to talk. She listened while he described the early days of Tressider Designs, after the war, when there had been no money and even fewer materials. "Make do and mend. The best training of all, having to make something from nothing.'' He looked around his glowing room with clear satisfaction. "That, and never missing an opportunity. The only trouble with getting old, you know, is that you regret the opportunities that you did miss.''

He didn't talk about being ill, only about getting old. Julia didn't know if he understood that he wouldn't live very much longer. His eyes settled on Felix. "I didn't miss all that many," he said. Felix smiled at him. Julia saw that they were happy, and understood that it wasn't the amount of time left that was important, only the quality of it. And she saw clearly that the quality of her own time, however much of it remained, was about as precious as the green glass hospital vases. At the same time the opportunities, unrecognized and unreached for, were slipping past her.

"I thought I'd take the chance to go away," she said suddenly. "Now that the business is ticking over. For a long, open-ended holiday."

"You lucky girl," George said immediately. "You must go to Rome, of course. The most fascinating, the most erotic city in the world."

And so Julia made her plans.

She consulted Lily first. "I think you should go, why not?" Lily said, surprising her. "You never have a holiday. Marilyn and I will be okay."

She told the shop managers, and her assistant. They echoed Lily's words. Julia's conviction of her own indispensability began to weaken. It was unnerving, but she also felt her spirits lifting. It was an opportunity, and she would take it. She took a precise, grown-up pleasure in planning the holiday to suit herself alone. She booked a flight, and a room in an elegant, expensive hotel recommended by George. She spent half an afternoon in a bookshop choosing maps and guides, and another day buying clothes that she didn't need. She enjoyed the tidy, finicky preparations without, she realized afterward, ever quite believing that she was really going.

Then, one afternoon in the middle of October, she found herself airborne in an Alitalia jet. London and England dropped away behind her. Lily and Marilyn had waved her off; she had told her staff that she wasn't sure when she would be back, only that it would be well before the Christmas rush started.

Julia unfastened her seat belt and looked down at the indeterminate meal placed in front of her. Staring at the individual plastic portions, she felt an upsurge of loneliness so powerful that she was afraid that it would choke her.

She had no idea where she was going, and no idea what she

would do when she reached her destination. She didn't even have any fixed return date to look forward to. It was one of the bleakest, most bewildering moments she had ever known.

In the Rome airport she took control of herself. She told herself that she was a traveler, after all. She was independent and potent and free, just as Josh had seemed to be. She summoned a taxi and rode to her luxurious hotel, unpacked her new clothes and hung them carefully in the empty closets. She took a bath in her big marble-lined bathroom and ate a deliberate dinner in the hotel dining room. The food was good, and the maître d'hôtel and the waiters were attentive. Afterward she went back up to her room and looked at the guidebooks. Tomorrow she would see the miraculous sights. She undressed calmly and lay down in the big, wide bed.

She slept badly, in fitful snatches shot through with vivid, uncomfortable dreams.

Julia did her best to be a conscientious tourist.

She visited the monuments, the Forum, and the Palatine Hill. She toured the Colosseum and St. Peter's and the Vatican museums. In between she ate meals and drank cups of cappuccino that she didn't want. She could see that Rome was fascinating, but she didn't feel herself drawn into it. It was a duty that she fulfilled mechanically, ticking off the objectives in her books. She recognized that it was erotic too. Men looked at her, in the streets and restaurants, but she brushed off the glances and the lingering stares like darts that threatened to pierce the slow, thick cloak of her isolation.

After four days, she realized that she couldn't bear it any longer.

In the street one morning she saw a long distance bus crowded with Italian families. The destination board at the front announced NAPOLI. At once she thought of the days she had spent there with Josh. The teeming, pungent streets had fascinated her. The memory of them now offered a welcome contrast with the cosmopolitan elegance of Rome.

I'll go to Naples, Julia thought. *Why not?*

She went back to her hotel, packed her belongings, and checked out.

In Naples the summer's heat still hung in the air and radiated from the crumbling walls, but the sky was veiled with a thin layer of cloud. From her visit with Josh, Julia remembered the watery brilliance of spring sunshine, and this humid grayness depressed her spirits that had risen as she left Rome.

She chose a hotel near the Piazza dei Martiri, as different as it was possible to be from the doss house she had stayed in with Josh. In spite of herself, she smiled at the memory of how Josh had hated the Neapolitan dirt and the inhabitants' eagerness for tourists' money.

In her new room, not much different from the one in Rome, Julia half-unpacked and then, after considerable difficulty, put a telephone call through to Lily in London. Lily was full of news of school, and of her best friend's latest exploits. Julia listened, smiling. The small details were comforting, the sound of Lily's voice even more so. "Are you missing me?" she asked, half-hopefully.

"A bit. But I'm okay. Alexander's in London. He took me to *Swan Lake*, it was fab."

"And is Mattie there?"

"Mattie? No. She's working somewhere, isn't she? Why?"

"I just wondered." Hastily, Julia said, "Just think, I'm in Naples."

"Are you having a nice time?"

"Yes, very nice. Quite nice. Thinking of you, and our house, and London."

"Do you know what? Katie's mum has bought her a new stereo. It's so fantastic. Can I have one for my birthday? My record player's so ancient."

Julia laughed. Lily was all right. She was almost certain that Lily always would be all right. "We'll talk about it when I get home. It's a long time until your birthday."

After talking to Lily, Julia went out and equipped herself with another set of maps and guides. She sat down at a café table in the center of a square to study them. The tables were like an island, cut off by a high tide of bellowing traffic. All around her there was the noise of it, and the talk of the drinkers at the surrounding tables rose and fell with the waves, singsong Italian and the confusing dialect of Naples. Julia drank her coffee and read her guidebook. She was relieved to find that she felt more comfortable here, amid the cheerful confusion.

In the next days she ignored the recommendations of the green Michelin. The one excursion she did make was to Pompeii. She quartered the ruins, looking up at the broken pillars and cracked lintels, stopping to gaze at the huddled shapes that had once been people, overtaken by the flow of lava. Skeletal dogs, themselves barely alive, wandered between the lava shapes of their ancestors that had been trapped in the same way as the people. Julia looked at the messages and graffiti carved in the excavated stone, frowning in her efforts to unravel the Latin. The suddenness of these deaths under Vesuvius seemed no less moving, no less immediate than those of her own times. Her perception of time and humanity became momentarily elastic, embracing these anonymous remains together with Flowers, and Jessie, and George. The recognition of individual insignificance, certainly her own, was oddly soothing. She walked among the lava shapes as if they were friends, and then made her way calmly back into the din of Naples.

The inhibiting pressure of loneliness eased after that. She found that she could exchange small talk with the other guests in the hotel lobby, even join a pleasant trio of Americans for lunch in the dining room. She met a languages student at a café table, a dark-faced boy with a faint look of Felix, and the excellence of his English made it a pleasure for her to sit and talk to him in the warm twilight. When at last she stood up to leave he took her hand and kissed it.

The rest of her time she spent in wandering at random, deeper into streets that narrowed in turn until they seemed impassable. She walked slowly, with lines of wash flapping over her head and ancient, black-dressed grandmothers peering suspiciously at her from their stools set in the shelter of doorways. Julia breathed in the smells, and watched the endlessly changing tableaus of street life. She felt invulnerable, but alive, as if all her senses had been sharpened.

Slowly, as she walked, she became aware that she wasn't aimlessly drifting at all. She was filling in decent intervals, playing a waiting game with herself, but all the time she was being drawn onward.

She never finished her unpacking in the hotel near the Piazza dei Martiri. She replaced the top layer in her suitcase and obeyed the compulsion to move.

She traveled south, by train, to Salerno and then to Agropoli. The view from the windows of the train was familiar. From Agropoli, admitting the truth of her destination at last, she took a taxi to Montebellate.

Looking behind her, as the Fiat wound its way upward toward the crown of houses on top of the conical hill, she saw that the view was unchanged. Away from Naples the sky had turned blue again, and the sea mirrored it. She followed with her eyes the thread of gold that fringed the sea, the ribbon of white houses along the beach that had thickened only a little, and the spread of the land, lemon-yellow, silver-gray, sage-green, and umber.

With difficulty, shouting above the engine's protesting whine, Julia directed her driver through the angles of the narrow streets. At the end of each street the sky opened and the view spread itself.

She thought she might have forgotten, but she had not. They reached the Pensione Flora without a single wrong turn. Julia paid for her taxi and watched the driver reverse away, irritable with the awkward corner she had led him into. When he had gone, she turned to the door again. It was still discernibly harebell-blue. But when she tilted her head she saw that the hand-painted sign that announced it as the Pensione Flora had gone. Julia hesitated, and then knocked at the blue door. The woman who opened it was certainly the signora. She had brought Julia and Josh their breakfasts, warm bread and honey and wonderful coffee, nearly fifteen years ago. She looked blankly at Julia now. *"Si?"*

The signora had barely changed, but Julia knew that she had. And how could she expect to be remembered, one couple who had spent a few days, out of so many summers? The effort of trying to explain, to stir up a recollection, was unthinkable. Awkwardly, Julia asked "Pensione Flora?" She explained that she was looking for a room, just for a few nights. The woman shook her head, pursing her lips. Out of the rapid flow of Italian Julia caught the word *finito*. The signora was no longer operating Flora's hotel. Perhaps times had got harder, or easier.

Julia was momentarily disconcerted. The possibility that she might not be able to stay in the room with the two iron bedsteads and the marble-topped washstand had, absurdly, never occurred to her.

Haltingly, she asked where else she could stay. Was there a hotel in Montebellate? The signora nodded, and then shook her head more vigorously. There was another flood of words, and Julia distinguished *chiuso,* and *stagione.* There was a hotel, but it had closed with the end of the season. For all the warmth of the sun and the air's softness, it was almost the end of October.

"Is there really nowhere?" Julia asked without much hope.

The woman thought for a moment. She looked up, peering at Julia as if she might, almost, recognize her, then she pointed up the street. Julia turned, but she could see nothing but the steep rise of cobbles and the angles of whitewashed walls. She struggled to understand the signora's instructions, and failed. They faced each other, helpless.

"Again. Slowly," Julia begged. The words were repeated, but they were no more intelligible. The signora shrugged, ready to abandon the struggle, but then she saw a man turn the corner, on the shady side of the street, and walk toward them. She called out, "Signor Galli?"

Julia watched him as he crossed over. He was tall, dressed in a white shirt and khaki trousers, and his face was hidden by the wide brim of a straw hat. He moved easily, loosely, like a young man. But when he took his hat off, with a sweeping gesture, Julia saw with a little shock of surprise that he was old. His hair was completely white, and the dark irises of his eyes were circled with a milky rim. He must be in his mid-seventies, she thought, although he moved like a man of forty.

Signor Galli and the woman conferred. Then he turned to Julia, holding his hat by the brim. "I speak a very little English."

She smiled at him. "You are very helpful."

"The signora here is suggesting that you might ask the sisters for a bed for the night."

"The sisters?"

Signor Galli pointed to the top of the hill.

Julia remembered the high stone wall enclosing the neglected grounds of the palazzo, and the cracked bell tolling.

"I remember that there are nuns, up at the palazzo."

"You have been here before?"

"A long time ago."

He nodded, looking properly at Julia and her luggage. "Our sisters of Montebellate belong to an open order. Many good works. They have now an *ospedale*."

"A hospital?"

"More, perhaps, an infirmary. For the old, the sick, all ages, children, who do not get better. In Italy, you understand, we have the family. We care for our old and ill people, and there is no need for them to be sent away. But here the sisters make a service. They take for some days, perhaps for a week or two weeks, the very sick ones. And so a mother may rest, a daughter may be free for her own children."

"I understand," Julia said. "But I'm not old, or ill."

The man laughed. Julia felt his warmth. The signora beamed proudly at him.

"I can see that for myself. We have many tourists, now, at Montebellate. They come in their cars and buses to the sea, and

they make the excursion up here. At the end of the day, they go
away again, to their hotels. We have very few travelers, but I
think you are a traveler.''

Julia stood up a little straighter, swelling with an unjustifi-
able pride.

"For travelers, the sisters keep one or two beds. It is a
tradition, I think. There is a small charge of money, perhaps they
ask for some simple work to be done. There is no luxury. If you
want that, perhaps you go down to the sea, or back to Agropoli.''

Julia shook her head.

"Then I will walk with you to see the sisters. They are
good friends of mine.''

They left Julia's luggage with the signora. She followed
him up the street between the white walls, her steps feeling stiff
beside his looseness. He had put his hat on again, and the brim
shadowed his face.

"Have you lived here for a long time?'' she asked, unimag-
inative, but wanting to know.

"I was born here. I have gone and come back and gone
again. But now I think I will stay. And you?''

"I am just traveling.''

"And that is either an escape or a discovery.''

Which? Julia thought.

They had climbed the last of the way beside the high wall
that enclosed the palazzo grounds. Now they came out into the
square at the hill's summit. The plane trees were there, their
leaves dulled with dust, and the seat built around the trunk of
one of them. There was the tiny patch of grass, but the old
woman and her tethered goat had gone. They crossed to the tall
gates. Julia's guide gripped one of the rusty iron curlicues and
pushed. The gate swung open, and they passed through.

The box hedges that lined the path were ragged and shapeless. Weeds grew underfoot in tufts and plumes. Julia didn't see
the neglect, then. She was looking ahead, at the solid, square
walls. In places the pinky-brown plaster seemed to have melted
away, exposing the huge blocks of stone from which the palazzo
had been built. The walls were pierced at intervals by small
windows, and at the nearest corner there was a high, arched
entrance flanked by round turrets. Lank and unpruned bougain-
villea and plumbago scrambled up the turret walls and the sky-
blue and purple flowers twined and nodded from the keystone of
the arch.

"It was built by the Bellate family as a fortress palace in the sixteenth century," Julia's companion told her. "The history of it has not always been happy. There are many legends. Many quarrels. In the last war, even, it was occupied by both sides." He shrugged eloquently, distancing himself from either. "I think now it is well."

They passed under the arch, into a square lodge with a domed roof and a hollowed stone floor. The shadow cooled Julia's face, and the dazzle of light beyond the corresponding arch seemed blindingly bright. She blinked, squinting into it, and saw that the palazzo's square enclosed a courtyard. A nun in a gray and white habit was pushing a wheelchair across it. In the wheelchair was a girl of perhaps Lily's age. Her feet twisted and her head lolled to one side. Her hands pulled compulsively at the folds of her dress. Beyond the girl and the nun, as her eyes accommodated themselves, Julia saw another chair placed in the shade of the high walls. There was a tiny, shriveled bundle propped up in it. It was impossible to distinguish, under the layers of wrappings, whether it was a man or a woman.

Julia had never encountered severe handicap, or illness except for George's, or even extreme old age, at close quarters. Her first, shaming impulse now was to turn and run. The chairs and their occupants seemed out of place under the bright sun.

"An infirmary," Signor Galli murmured beside her.

They heard brisk footsteps descending stone stairs. From a low doorway in one of the turrets another nun appeared. She wore the same gray and white habit, with the addition of a starched and folded white coif. A plain wooden crucifix lay on her breast. Signor Galli and the nun were already greeting each other. It was too late for Julia to run away.

A moment later she was drawn in. The nun held out her hand and Julia took it. "La Suora Maria degli Angeli," Signor Galli said.

Sister Mary of the Angels had a pale, smooth face and dark eyes. The stiff folds of the coif suited her, Madonna-like. Julia guessed that she was not many years older than herself.

"I am Julia Smith."

The nun made a small, courteous bow. "We have a room. Not much comfort, I am sorry."

"I am very grateful," Julia said gravely.

Signor Galli left her, promising that he would send boys with her suitcases. Julia followed her new guide up the turret stairs and along a lofty corridor. The flaking whitewashed walls were sparsely hung with holy pictures, and in a niche at the far end a red light glowed in front of a plaster Holy Family.

They turned the corner into the southern side of the square and came to a door. Sister Maria opened it, and signaled Julia inside. The room was high and square. There was an iron bedstead, like one of the pair in the Pensione Flora, with a crucifix on the wall above it. The bedcover was plain white, and well darned. The only other furniture was a chair, and a washstand with a tin jug and basin. There was a row of hooks behind the door.

It was the window that drew Julia. She rested her hand on the wooden shutter and looked out. Beneath her she could see the blue sea with its fringe of white and gold, and all the shades and undulations of the land to the remote gray-blue horizon.

She turned back to Sister Maria. "Thank you," she said.

"You are welcome here." At first Julia couldn't understand the rest of the nun's response. Finally, from their combined efforts in English and Italian, she gathered that the community and their guests, those that were well enough to come or to be brought to the table, ate all together at six o'clock in the refectory. They would be happy if their visitor would join them.

"Thank you," Julia said again.

Sister Maria went briskly away.

Julia crossed back to the door. Opposite it, in the corridor wall, there was another window. It looked down into the courtyard. She saw that there was a greenish metal basin in the center, ornamented with dolphins' heads. It must have been a fountain, once. The basin was surrounded with terra-cotta pots in which straggling geraniums grew. A man loped in a diagonal through the sun. His body shook and his head twitched, and he was shouting and laughing. Julia couldn't decipher any words. Against the courtyard wall opposite her there were more chairs. The occupants were of all ages, some seemingly alert, others motionless bundles. On the east and west sides there were arches instead of walls, making open loggias. There were white beds drawn up in the deeper shade. Nuns were moving to and fro, or sitting beside the chairs. Two of them had their heads bent over a white cloth spread across their knees. They were mending, or embroidering. Watching from her window, Julia wondered why she had wanted to run away from her first glimpse of the palazzo's inhabitants. Now that she saw them again, she recognized that they belonged in the sun's warmth as much as she did herself. Their faces, sighted or blind, turned up to drink it in.

When she listened, she heard a comfortable buzz of sound. There were voices, overlaying each other, some talking and some singing, uncoordinated but happy. From somewhere else came a high, braying laugh. And looking straight beneath her, Julia saw the girl of Lily's age, in her wheelchair. She was banging a child's drum with a stick, a rhythmic tattoo, her head nodding with the beat of it.

Julia watched for a long time before going back into her white room. The rhythm never flagged or varied itself.

She sat down on the bed with her hands loose in her lap. It was odd that it should be here in this place, that the self-pitying loneliness should release her. But it did. She felt the weight of it, lifting, letting her see clearly again. She saw herself, thrown into sharp focus against the people in the courtyard. The picture was unappealing, but she studied it carefully.

And then she realized that the restlessness had gone too. She had come to Montebellate, and she knew that she could stay here. If they would let her stay.

Close at hand, so close that it seemed directly above her head, the palazzo bell began to toll. Listening to it, counting the long, slow strokes, Julia realized that it wasn't cracked at all. It was the warmth-thickened air that took up the notes, muffling them and stretching them and delivering them up, distorted, over the tiled roofs. It was a pleasing discovery. It made her feel that, after all, after her mistakes, all would still be well.

She sat on her bed and the bell echoes faded over her head.

Just before six o'clock, two young boys appeared with her suitcases. They seemed to know and feel comfortable in the palazzo, although they shuffled and giggled with embarrassment outside her door. Julia thanked them, and gave them small-denomination lira notes, at which they looked amazed.

Julia changed her dress and laid out her toilet things on the washstand. Then she went down to dinner.

The refectory was bare, arched, and wooden-beamed. The community sat at long tables, on benches at one side, in their wheelchairs on the other. Sister Maria led Julia to an empty place. She was greeted with smiles, or welcoming glances devoid of curiosity. A handbell rang, and those who could stand stood up for a Latin grace, simply delivered by a young nun. The nuns took their places among their charges, and the food was served. It was coarse but good. There was a soup of vegetables, tasting strongly of olive oil, *penne* and tomato sauce, then figs and rosy grapes and lumps of pecorino.

Julia never forgot her first meal at the palazzo.

She had been placed between a tiny old woman with fingers like a bird's claws and a young man who mumbled incessantly and made fishlike movements with his knobby red hands. Covertly, Julia peered at the nuns. They spooned up their charges' food for them, held their jerking limbs steady while they ate, talked and listened and smiled.

Julia's old lady seemed too frail to lift her spoon. Julia crumbled her bread for her and was rewarded with a darting glance from bright eyes in a pucker of seamed brown skin. The spoon was not, after all, too heavy. The bread was soaked in soup, to soften it. The boy on her left was harder to help. His arms began to shoot out in uncontrollable lunges. At last, before all her own food had descended into her lap, Julia discovered how to keep them pinioned between them with one hand while she fed him with the other. She didn't know whether his mumblings were for her or not. She talked back to him, in English, about her journey from Rome to Naples to Montebellate. Her lack of Italian was, at last, no handicap. Looking around her, she reflected that each one of them at these long tables, except for the calm-faced nuns, was inarticulate in their own particular way.

And yet the hum of their talk rose from the tables and companionably filled the space under the rough beams.

Julia discovered that she was very hungry. She ate everything rapidly, in the intervals that were left between helping her neighbors. She noticed that by the end of the meal Sister Maria had stopped watching out for her from her place at the other end of the table.

That pleased her too.

Julia stayed for a month with the Sisters of the Blessed Family at Montebellate. Over the days and weeks she came to know and admire them all, the different Marias and Martas and Teresas of the Innocents and the Martyrs and the Holy Blood. Few of them spoke more than a word or two of English; Sister Maria of the Angels and the Mother Superior herself were the rare exceptions. But they were all used to obstacles in the path of communication and to circumventing them. Their friendliness and interest and warmth did not, in any case, need words in order to express itself. Julia felt it surrounding her, as well as the more deserving guests who were brought up to the palazzo in ambulances and buses and dusty Fiats. Sometimes they stayed for only a few days, sometimes for much longer. They came, mostly, from the poor villages that spread down from Naples into Calabria, from families that had no other resources to turn to for help. For all their suffering, Julia saw clearly how much the visitors benefited from their stay. The palazzo community was a deeply happy one. The recognition of the nuns' goodness was chastening for Julia, but it was also profoundly soothing.

She did what she could to help them in their work, frustrated at first by how little it was. She had no nursing skills, and not many more domestic ones.

At last she found her niche with the small group of little children who occupied the upper floor of one of the wings. Most of them were incurably handicapped; more happily, there were two or three who were convalescing, and one boisterous little boy who was well, but whose parents were unable to care for him. Julia discovered that her emergent, infantile Italian was just right for the children. They could understand one another perfectly. She knelt on the linoleum floors of the ward or on the stone flags of the courtyard and drew pictures, or helped with jigsaw puzzles, or sang songs with them. More patiently, more willingly, than she had ever done with Lily.

They grew fond of her, even the ones who could barely recognize anything. The stronger ones hung on her hands, shouting, and put their arms around her neck. The healthy Raimundo became her lieutenant in their games.

When she was not with the children, Julia was too tired to do much else. She walked in the palazzo's ruined gardens, down the steep terraces that fell away beneath her window to the south side of Montebellate's hill. She tried to make sense of the once formal grandeur, and wondered about the unfamiliar plants that sprang and straggled along the overgrown walks. One of the nuns knew a little about the garden's history. She told her that at the beginning of the century, the palace and its land had been bought by a wealthy family, a manufacturing family from the north. The lady had had the gardens laid out in the grand Italian manner. But, Sister Agnes had shrugged, the times had changed. Perhaps the family had lost their money. In any case they had gone away, and the palace had lain empty for years. Then, in the war, it had been a garrison for the military. Sister Agnes crossed herself. Since the war, another absentee owner, and then the convent had taken possession of it.

"Better," Julia said, nodding and smiling.

But the sight of the neglected gardens disturbed her.

Sometimes, in the evenings after the early meal in the refectory, she walked out through the iron gates and into the darkness gathering in the steep streets. On one of the first of these walks a voice called to her from a balcony over her head. She looked up, and saw Signor Galli. He invited her up to his rooms, and she sat down between high shelves of books and drank strong coffee out of a blue and gold cup. Her new friend, she discovered, was an architect who had worked in Paris and London as well as in Rome and Milan. He was a widower, with grown-up children now scattered across Italy.

It was comfortable to sit and talk in the warm light of red-shaded lamps. After that first visit, Julia found her way back on other evenings. Nicolo Galli was an easy and stimulating conversationalist.

"Ah, Montebellate. I came back to my birthplace to die," he said cheerfully on one occasion.

"You don't look on the point of death."

"No, indeed. But here I shall stay until the day comes. How pleasant it is not to have to think of traveling farther."

"Yes," Julia said softly. She felt a little of his stability herself. She had been happy here, this time. And if she had not come to Montebellate, she would have spent the weeks wandering through Europe, waiting for enough time to elapse before she could decently allow herself to head for home again. "I wish I could stay here. But I must go home soon."

She had been thinking of Mattie. Here, in the quiet village on its hilltop, the memory of Mattie and Alexander at Ladyhill was losing its sharpness. Julia wished that she could show the palazzo and the gardens to Mattie. One morning she had bought a postcard at the little tobacconist's shop, scrawled a few neutral words, and signed it, *Your old friend*. When she had posted it, she'd felt the links tighten again.

Nicolo looked at her. "Who do you go home to?"

"My daughter. And my business."

"Oh, yes. Of course."

Rain came, whipping down from the north and then drifting inexorably in from the sea. Julia knew that it was time to go. In London, the shop windows would already be piled up with tinsel and parcels and fake snow. She told Sister Maria and the other nuns that she was leaving. They would be sorry to lose her, they said, but Julia knew that they wouldn't really miss her. They were too closely bound by the needs and neces. ies of the community, too secure in their faith, to miss an outsider. It was she who would miss them.

Julia went to see the Mother Superior, to thank her for the convent's hospitality. She gave her, as tactfully as she could, as much money as she could afford. The nun accepted it gracefully. Julia knew that the state provided only a small amount of money for the work done at the palazzo. The Infirmary of the Sisters of the Blessed Family depended on the church, and charity.

The hardest part was saying good-bye to the children. Raimundo wrapped his arms around her waist and sobbed. The others flocked behind him. Julia disentangled herself, gently, too close to tears herself.

"I'll come back," she promised. "I'll come back one day, and see you all. You will be a big boy, Raimundo. You won't cry then."

She left them, blindly running down the stone steps. Her suitcases, full of the now unsuitably light clothes, were packed and waiting in the lodge between the two turrets. A taxi had come to take her back to Agropoli.

The sisters crowded around her. They kissed her, and commended her to God's keeping. Nicolo Galli had come, too, to say a last good-bye. He took Julia's hands and kissed both of her cheeks. She turned and climbed into the battered Fiat.

When she looked back, as the car drove away, her last sight was of Nicolo. With the arrival of winter, he had exchanged his straw hat for a black fedora. He took it off, and waved it over his head, saluting her.

TWENTY-TWO

Mattie walked down to the harbor. It was cold, and the wind stung her face. The sea was gray, greasily flecked with white, and she could taste salt spray on her tongue. She walked slowly with her hands in her pockets, trying not to think of the play, of her opening lines, trying not to think of anything. The cold was distracting: that helped.

Most of the sailing dinghies that flecked the summer harbor had been lifted for the winter, but a few still rode at their moorings. She watched them dipping and rearing with the small, vicious waves, then looked away again because even contemplating the motion made her feel sicker than she did already.

Mattie walked on a little farther, then perched on a bollard to watch the gulls. She liked the deserted feel of out-of-season English towns. The shuttered kiosks and wet-slicked quaysides reminded her of her days on tour with Francis Willoughby's repertory company. She flapped her arms against her sides to keep warm, remembering Great Yarmouth and John Douglas, who had taken her to bed in a salesmen's hotel. John Douglas had eventually retired, taking his bitterness with the theater back to his wife in Burford, and for all Mattie knew he was there still. She thought of him with distant, incurious affection. All of it seemed a very long time ago.

It was too cold to sit down. She stood up and moved on, to the edge of the quay. The tide was out, and she liked the look of the shiny mud netted with salt channels, and the stiff tufts of marsh grass. It was better to be outside, anyway, than in her hotel or waiting in her dressing room at the theater. Mattie shivered.

She was still afflicted with nerves. Every time, before every performance, fear gripped her stomach and her blood froze. She was certain that she would remember nothing, be unable to utter a syllable. It was worse, if anything, this time. It was more than two years since Mattie had appeared before a theater audience. Film work was different. It still induced fear, but it was a diffuse, more controllable variety.

Mattie concentrated on her well-practiced routine for containing the fright. She breathed deeply, in and out, feeling the rise and fall of her diaphragm. She told herself that the play was good, and that she could do only what she had been doing in rehearsal, with all her heart. Then she made herself dismiss all thoughts of the performance. She emptied her mind, letting her face muscles slacken, the corners of her mouth drooping.

She saw that a man was watching her, from a few yards away, along the quay. She looked away quickly, and noticed the first few spots of rain pocking the stones.

"Got the place all to ourselves," the man said.

Mattie noted, automatically, that his north-country vowels were overlaid with a faint mid-Atlantic drawl. It was a pleasant, friendly voice.

"The summer sailors have all gone home," she responded, moving past him. That was enough. They had acknowledged each other's existence in the empty landscape; now they could walk on.

To her irritation, he turned in the same direction and began to walk with her. *Dammit,* she thought, *he must have recognized me.* In a moment there would be a request for an autograph, for his wife, or daughter, of course, never for himself; a handshake; questions. She didn't want that, intruding into her isolation out here on the harbor wall.

"I don't mind the place being empty," the man said happily. "I like looking at the birds and the mud. See the patterns they make, walking in it? Like little stars."

Mattie looked. The birds' prints were like a child's drawing of stars, scribbled over each other on the gray-brown mudbank. "I've never noticed that," she said.

"I saw it when I was a boy. I didn't have much else to look at." He laughed, pleased with the memory. "I grew up in Whitby. North Yorkshire. Do you know it?"

Mattie had played there, with John Douglas and Sheila Firth and the others. It had been another town, smelling of fish and chips and bottled Guinness. "I've been there."

"It's a grand place."

She looked sideways at him. He was squarely built, not very tall, zipped up in an anonymous greenish jacket. With the addition of a map and rucksack he might have been a hiker, with binoculars perhaps a birdwatcher. Except that a birdwatcher would have talked about gulls, not birds in the mud. The man was balding, probably in his late fifties. He wore glasses, and the lenses were spotted with raindrops. He took them off and wiped them with a clean white handkerchief.

"What are you doing here?" Mattie asked rather reluctantly.

"Vacationing." The transatlantic word sounded odd.

It was raining harder. The wind batted it into their faces.

"Getting ugly," the man announced. "Shall we go and have some tea? I saw a teashop a little way back. It might even be open."

Mattie looked at her watch, preparing to decline the invitation. It was four o'clock. Three and a half hours to curtain time. Too late to go back to her hotel, too early to go to the theater.

"Thank you," she said. "Tea's a good idea."

The man held out his hand. "Mitchell Howorth. Mitch." They shook. His grip was firm, unlingering.

"That sounds American. Are you from the States?"

"Nope. Lived there for a long time. But my mother was a Mitchell, my father was a Howorth. Both from Whitby."

Well, here goes, Mattie thought. "I'm Mattie Banner."

Mitch's face didn't flicker. "Hello, Mattie."

He doesn't know, she thought. She was just a woman caught in the rain. The notion delighted her.

They reached the teashop after a stiff walk. It was just like the ones Mattie used to sit in with Lenny and Vera, on rainy afternoons identical to this one. There was a plastic open sign hanging on a chain between the glass door and a frilled nylon curtain caught in a double V-shape. Inside there were red gingham tablecloths and plastic cruets, and a bored waitress in a sauce-spotted apron. It smelled, rather too strongly for Mattie, of lunchtime fried egg.

Mattie undid the headscarf that she had knotted under her chin. Mitch looked at her hair, and at her face. The frankness of his sudden admiration was endearing. For the first time, Mattie smiled at him. They were standing too close together in the narrow entrance, they realized. Mitch stepped backward to help her off with her coat.

They sat at a table in the window, cut off from the rainy street by more net curtaining. They were the only customers.

Briskly summoning the waitress, Mitch ordered tea for two and toasted teacakes. Evidently, he had clear ideas about what tea constituted.

The teacakes came very quickly. They were thickly spread with butter, yellow clots of it swimming in its own melted halo. The smell of fried egg seemed to thicken around Mattie, and her stomach heaved. She stood up at once.

"Excuse me," she muttered.

She made for the door at the back of the tearoom. In the pink-distempered cubicle of the Ladies she was very neatly sick. Afterward she washed her face and combed her damp hair, staring briefly at herself in the mirror. Then she made her way back to Mitch. He stood up at once. To her relief, she saw that the teacakes had been removed. He held out her chair for her, settled her into it, touched her shoulder briefly.

"Have some tea," he ordered her. "Weak, no milk."

"Thank you." Mattie took it, thinking that what she really needed was whiskey, strong, no water. But she sipped the tea anyway, and it warmed her.

"Are you ill?" Mitch asked. She liked him for not fussing her.

"No. Just frightened. But I'll be all right now."

He looked at her, over the top of his glasses, a mock-quizzical expression that made her want to laugh. "What can someone like you possibly be frightened of?"

To her surprise, Mattie told him.

She told him about the well-made tragedy of manners that was trying out for the West End. She told him about her own starring role in it, and her agent and her publicist and the director and the theater management, about the critics who would at this moment be irritably *en route* for Chichester, and the writer who thought she was too tainted with Hollywood for his precious play. She told him about the telegrams and the flowers and the witty little presents that would be waiting for her in the star's dressing room, and about the painful clutches of her stage fright.

At the end of the recital she sighed. "Now you'll think I'm a self-obsessed hysterical actress."

Mitch Howorth poured her another cup of tea. "Does it matter what I think?"

Mattie blushed like a schoolgirl, all the way up into her scalp. "Not a bit," she answered.

"I'll tell you anyway. I don't know anything about plays, or about movies. But I don't believe, from looking and listening to you, that you would be capable of doing anything badly. That's what I think. You're frightened for nothing, Mattie."

It isn't nothing, she was going to snap back at him. *Do you think it's nothing, going out in front of all those people?*

Then their eyes met.

His mild, level gaze disarmed her. It wasn't nothing, she knew that, but it wasn't everything either.

Mattie laughed. "If you say so." She noticed that behind Mitch Howorth's glasses, and the neutrality of his rounded, unremarkable face, there was sympathy and intelligence. She leaned back in her chair and lit a cigarette. "That's enough about that. Now you tell me who you are," she ordered flatly.

"Nothing remotely as impressive."

Mitch told her that he had left Whitby after his discharge from the Royal Navy. He had spent time as an engineer in the merchant marine, working routes to the Far East, and to Central and North America. "A drifter, not a mover," he said. But then, in Baltimore, he had met and struck up a friendship with a young American, another engineer.

"We liked each other. And I liked the States a whole lot

better than Britain in 1950. We went into partnership together, in Baltimore.''

Mattie blinked at him. "Doing what?"

"Manufacturing metal casings.''

"Oh." Mattie knew that she wasn't equipped to pursue a conversation about metal casings.

"I stayed put,'' Mitch continued. "Applied for citizenship. I've been a Yankee for seventeen years.''

"Was your manufacturing successful?'' she asked, mostly because she couldn't think of anything else to ask about it. Mitch grinned at her. He shrugged his shoulders, and the corners of his eyes and mouth turned up. From a solid middle-aged man he was suddenly transformed into an impish schoolboy. It was very attractive.

"You could say that.''

And that was it, Mattie thought. There had been something about him that she had been unable quite to define, and now she had it. Mr. Howorth from Whitby via Baltimore was a successful man. She glanced at his watch. It was a Rolex, a not-too-ostentatiously gold one. He was wealthy, and he was used to people doing what he told them to. Not just tearoom waitresses. He probably had a chain of metal casings plants or factories or units, or whatever they were, stretching halfway across North America. Mattie decided that she had the complete picture now.

Her new friend was over here on his vacation, touring around little England, chuckling and reminiscing, and looking up fading Mitchells and Howorths in their retirement flats and council semis. His wife, bored to tears, was at this minute back at the Holiday Inn having her hair seen to. Where, Mattie wondered, was the nearest Holiday Inn to Chichester? But Mitch surprised her.

"I'd had enough. I retired early and handed over to a bunch of kids with letters after their names. I've no management control, although I'm still a stockholder. My partner died a couple of years back." He tapped his green jacket, superstitiously, over his own heart. "And now I'm free. I came home. I started at Whitby, and I've traveled right around the coast to here. I like seaside towns.''

"So do I,'' Mattie said. She turned her head away and stared through the drooping swathes of net curtain. "What about your wife? Does she like them too?''

There was the briefest of pauses. Mattie watched the rain.

"I'm divorced. Evie was a mover, and she moved on.''

"Children?"

"No. Never happened. How about you?"

"Neither. I've already told you all there is to know about me. I'm an actress."

Why have I, Mattie wondered. To a manufacturer of metal casings, in a teashop? Belatedly, her defenses rose again. She became aware of the waitress ostentatiously rattling and locking up in the background. The bill on its saucer had been slapped down in front of Mitch ages ago.

They had been sitting in the teashop window for a long time.

"I've got to go," Mattie said. "They'll be wondering where I've run off to."

Mitch stood up, held her chair again. "May I come and see the performance?" His faintly formal manners reminded her of Alexander.

Mattie headed off the thought. "Oh, no, for God's sake."

They laughed, and the waitress scowled at them.

Outside, to forestall any further approaches, Mattie held out her hand. She shook Mitch's like a fellow metal casings trader.

"Thank you for tea. You stopped me thinking about tonight, and I'm very grateful. Enjoy the rest of your holiday."

In his mild way Mitch studied her. "It's raining very hard. Wouldn't you like . . ."

"Oh, no thanks. It's no distance. Good-bye, and thank you."

Mattie turned and almost ran. Cold water oozed into her shoes and splashed up the backs of her legs. She was glad to reach the theater, even with what it held in store for her.

Her dresser was waiting for her with more tea when what she really wanted was whiskey. Mattie tried, not always successfully, never to drink before a performance. The flowers and messages were there, too, and she tried to concentrate on the good wishes. Julia's first night greetings were usually the best, but this time there were none; Julia was abroad, of course.

There was a knock at the door and the director stuck his head around it. He was followed a few minutes later by the orotund Shakespearean actor who was playing opposite Mattie. She went through the rituals, obligingly, because she was so used to them. Fear churned inside her and she thought of Mitch, probably driving his rented Ford back to wherever he had sprung from.

Mattie sat down at the mirror and made up her face. Her

dresser brought her costume, and then she spent the last minutes sitting in silence, letting the scenes of the play flick through her head.

Then it was time. "Miss Banner? Five minutes, please." She was being called, just as she herself had called Sheila Firth and the others, years ago. Mattie went down to the wings and waited, the murmur from the audience beyond the curtain like thunder in her ears.

The first-night performance was no worse than any of the week's previews, perhaps even a little better. Everyone claimed to be thrilled with its reception. There were kisses and congratulations afterward, the formalities no less familiar although she had been away from them for two years. Mattie didn't go to the party that followed. She excused herself, saying that she was getting a migraine. She took a sleeping pill and went to bed.

The reviews were good enough.

One critic implied that Mattie's performance was muted, another wrote snippily that overexposure to the camera lens and the dictates of commercialism had coarsened her technique.

"Bollocks," Mattie said to that one, and tore the review in half.

"That's right, dear," her dresser agreed.

The company settled down into the run, and as it did so Mattie's fear evaporated. She was working, burrowing inside the part, and the process engaged her, as it always had. The houses were good, and there began to be optimistic talk about the West End transfer.

A week passed. Mattie wondered what had become of Mitch Howorth. After all, he might have come to see the show regardless of the fact that she had begged him not to. She was admitting to herself now that she would have liked to see him again and had to accept, with exasperation, that it was her own fault she wasn't going to. By this time he must have moved on to Gosport, or Lymington, or to Weymouth, where she had picnicked on the beach with Lily and Alexander. He would have forgotten the bilious actress and her first-night nerves.

Two weeks after the opening night, a bunch of roses was delivered to her dressing room. They were shaggy, golden yellow, and richly scented, like the ones Julia grew in her garden overlooking the canal. Where could he have found such flowers in October? The card attached read simply, With best wishes, Mitchell Howorth.

Mattie spun around, holding the card aloft. Then she tore down the telegrams and tucked it into the mirror frame in their place. Before she left the room to go onstage, she buried her face in the depths of the golden petals.

When she came back, after her curtain call, the dressing room was full of the heady scent. She knew that he would come even before she heard the knock.

He came in, bulky and solid in the small space. Even so, she wanted to touch his arm, to make sure that he was real.

"I told you you weren't capable of doing anything badly," he said.

"Mitch, where did you get roses like these?" she asked him.

He had been staring at her, trying to marry the image of this Mattie, wrapped in a Japanese kimono with her hair loose over her shoulders with the stage image that still filled his head.

"By magic," he said.

In that minute, looking back at him and seeing a square-set man in a raincoat, and seeing much more because her skin burned under the Japanese silk, Mattie believed in magic.

"May I take you out for dinner?" Mitch asked.

Mattie's smile was luminous. "I'll be hurt if you don't."

He looked surprised, and pleased, as if he had prepared himself for her refusal and hadn't dared to hope for the opposite.

When she had changed and pinned up her hair and gazed in mystification at her reflection in the mirror before turning her back on it, Mattie followed him.

His car, parked at the theater doors, was not the rented Ford she had pictured. It was a pale gray Bentley, with aristocratic lines and creased leather seats. Mattie supposed, without reluctance, that she had better stop imagining him at the Holiday Inn. Mitch Howorth was not predictable at all. Or perhaps, more seriously, it was her own reaction to him that was unpredictable.

He drove her, without consultation, to a country restaurant. Mattie liked the way he took it for granted that he would deal with the arrangements for their evening. After her years with Chris, when the motivation behind every choice was minutely examined, choosing anything at all bored Mattie. And she had been alone for long enough to make pleasing herself seem less than a luxury.

The restaurant was not unlike the one John Douglas had taken her to long ago. The waiters were French with equal ostentation, and as many flambé pans flared and sizzled beside the diners. Mattie remembered how hungry she had been, and how impressed by the grandeur. Now her eyes met Mitch's, and they smiled at each other.

"The teashop is closed at this time of night," he said.

Before their food came Mattie curled her fingers around the drink he had ordered for her, but she didn't lift it. It was odd to realize that she wanted to talk to Mitch more than she wanted to reassure herself with the woolly detachment that whiskey brought.

Watch it, she warned herself. Mattie was wary now. Since Alexander, warier still. But she asked, just the same, "It's two weeks since we had tea together. Why didn't you come to see me before this? I thought you'd gone. To Swanage, or Weymouth, or somewhere."

Mitch shook his head. "No. I passed the theater every day. Looked at your pictures outside. I found out how famous you are. I felt like a fool for not knowing you in the first place, I guess. And I supposed you'd be busy. Why should you have the time to see some middle-aged retired manufacturer of metal casings? Even though you'd let him accost you on the harbor."

"Mitch," Mattie said softly, "don't talk like an idiot. I know you're not one. I hoped you'd come. If I'd known where to begin looking for you, I'd have been out searching. I can't bear to think of you being outside the theater every day, and me not knowing." *I've been lonely,* she thought, *without needing to be.* It was extraordinary how unlonely she felt now.

He took her hand then. They both knew that they were missing out the proper stages, galloping past the milestones, and neither of them cared. He took her untouched glass away and folded her hand between both of his own.

"I've been to see your play three times," he said. Mattie stared at him. "Tonight was the third. I couldn't stop looking at you. What you did made me cry. You were that man's wife, and I believed everything you said and did. And yet you were you too. The girl in the teashop. I thought you were magnificent."

"It's my job," Mattie said lamely, touched and shaken by the sincerity of his praise. "Being another person. Pretending. Not pretending, that's not true. Creating. All falsehoods, I suppose, but as true as I can make them."

"Are you pretending now? Creating?"

There were no straight lines in Mitch's face, Mattie saw. His mouth curled, bracketed by lines, and his eyes were softened by folds of skin that drew them down at the corners. She wanted to reach out and follow the curves with her fingertips. Mattie shook her head. "No. What you see is what I am."

His hands tightened on hers. "Talk to me," he ordered.

There seemed, suddenly, so much to tell.

Their food and wine came and they ate and drank, not noticing it. The room glowed around them, and then emptied slowly and became quiet. They were the last diners, and the waiters yawned and muttered in the corners. Mattie and Mitch blinked and looked around. They had focused on nothing but each other's faces, the tiny movements of muscles and the flickers of feeling, and it was disconcerting to remember that they were part of a bigger world.

Mitch laughed. "We've overstayed our welcome again." He paid the bill, and they went out together into the night. It smelled of the sea meeting the land, of salt and rain together.

They leaned back in the Bentley's leather arms, not looking at each other. Mitch's finger rested on the ignition keys. "Shall I take you home?" he asked. "You'll have to direct me to your hotel."

Mattie was thinking about pretending and creating again, and about falsehoods. *Don't pretend now,* she warned herself. She wanted Mitch to decide this too; but she also wanted to go half of the way to meet him.

"I don't want to go home," she said. "It isn't home. It's a hotel room. It's square and empty and there's a gray television eye in the corner."

"Then come with me," Mitch Howorth said.

The Bentley slid forward. Mattie let her head fall back against the leather cushion. They drove for a little way, Mattie didn't try to distinguish where. She watched the steady glow of the lights on the walnut fascia, and the shadows making hollows in Mitch's face. She felt happy and dreamy in the car's opulent cocoon. She could have driven on, all night, anywhere he chose to take her. But they turned and drove up a steep hill, swung around, and came to a standstill. As she stepped out of the car, Mattie had a brief impression of gardens on a slope, and a tall house with a lighted porch. Mitch took her hand and led her.

Inside the house she peered around, her eyes slowly acclimating themselves to the light. She saw polished floors and Persian rugs, portraits and serious furniture and porcelain. Mattie laughed delightedly.

"What's funny?" Mitch asked, half-offended.

"I imagined a Holiday Inn."

"What? This is an English country house. Like I read about when I was a kid. Okay, it's only a small one. But the real thing."

That was it, Mattie thought. *It was like Ladyhill.* She felt happy and secure enough in Mitch Howorth's company for the irony only to add to her amusement.

"Is it yours?"

He was too good-natured to take further offense at her incredulity. "No. Of course not. I rented it a few days ago. I was staying in digs before, not very gracious ones. Fine for me, but I couldn't have taken someone like you back there."

"Wait a minute . . ." Mattie countered. "You said . . . you said that you were afraid I'd be too busy and glamorous to have time to see you again. How come you felt confident enough of me to rent a whole manor house?"

Mitch crossed the little space of polished floor that had opened between them. He put his hands on either side of her face, turning it to his. Mattie looked steadily back at him. His eyes were surprisingly clear, close up, the eyes of a much younger man. Quietly, Mitch said, "Everything that can be arranged should be. I never leave manageable details to chance. But I never confuse what I can make happen with what I can only hope for. It's an important distinction in business as well as in affairs of the heart." *He rented a whole manor house,* Mattie thought, *on the chance that he would need somewhere to bring me. If he was going to bring me anywhere, he wanted it to be the place he dreamed of when he was small. His own Ladyhill, his fantasy possession, to which to bring an illusionist.* The aptness as well as the grandeur of the gesture touched a deep chord inside her. It made tears prickle behind her eyes.

She knew that she shouldn't ask, but the words came out just the same. "Am I an affair of the heart?"

"Oh, yes, Mattie. Body and soul as well, if you want. Only if you want."

"I do want."

He kissed her then, a very gentle kiss. She put her arms around him awkwardly. When he lifted his head to look at her again, Mitch said, "The owners have gone away to the South of France. For the whole winter. Isn't that thoughtful of them?"

"Supremely thoughtful."

He kissed her again, but then pulled back once more.

"The car is mine. I don't want to confuse you." He was laughing at her.

Mattie groaned. "I don't give a damn about houses or cars. I don't care if you went to a gents' outfitters and hired your suit and your sober tie and your clean white shirt. I don't even care if your glasses belong to the theater props department. Just so long as it's you inside them. You are real, Mitch, aren't you? You won't vanish in a puff of smoke?"

He didn't laugh anymore. He took hold of her, almost roughly now, and bent her back against him. "Come to bed," he ordered her.

After that, Mattie didn't see the paneled walls or the reproving portraits. They stumbled up the stairs together, and in a dim room with a four-poster hung with dark red curtains Mitch undressed her and then took off his own clothes. He was unabashed, gentle, and inquisitive and unhurried. When he held her against him she felt that his solidity was hard muscle, not fat. She ran her hands over his shoulders and his hips, and put her mouth against the thick, curling gray hair that covered his chest. Mitch's naturalness made her natural too. He didn't appear to feel that it was necessary to be overcome with passion, or to hurry her on before she was ready. Mattie didn't wish that she was thinner, or had a suntan, or try to pull in the rounded swell of her stomach. Mitch knelt down and kissed it, and then gently parted her thighs with his hands. He seemed to expect that she would explore him in the same way. Mattie had never, ever since the times with Ted Banner that she had hidden away inside herself and forgotten, felt that it was comfortable to look at a man who was aroused by her.

Even with Alexander she had closed her eyes or looked away.

With Mitch, inexplicably but clearly, it was different. She knelt down in her turn and took hold of him. She drew back the skin and touched the rosy head that was revealed, lifting itself toward her.

It seemed quite simple, as natural as it was for her to feel his arms around her, his mouth against hers.

Mitch lifted her up and laid her on the bed. Very slowly, but allowing no interruption, he began to work on her toes. He kissed them, and flexed the joints, and then traced the arch of each foot with his tongue. His lips closed over her ankle bones, gently sucking, and then his fingers locked around each ankle, measuring it, pinioning it. He moved to her shins and her calves, meticulously exploring the white skin, and then buried his face in the warmth of the hollows behind her knees.

"Mitch," she begged him, "stop. I can't bear it." She felt awkward that he should be so patient, convinced that no part of her was worth such undivided attention.

"Don't interrupt," he reproved her.

She lay back and followed the loops and folds of the bed curtains with her eyes. Mitch's fingers, surprisingly light, made feathery strokes over her thighs and her hips. He knelt over her and kissed her belly again, and then spanned her waist with his hands.

"You have beautiful skin," he told her. "It feels soft enough to melt away altogether."

"I'm perfectly solid." She smiled at him. She locked her arms around his neck and drew him closer so that she could reach his mouth. Mitch had taken his glasses off, and folded them tidily on the carved chest beside the bed. Without them his eyes had the vulnerable, faintly puzzled softness of short sight.

"Wait," he ordered. "I'm not ready yet."

Mattie lay back again. Mitch wasn't vulnerable, not in that way at least. He was too sure of what he wanted.

He turned his attention to her breasts. He weighted his hands with them, then brushed the nipples with his fingers, watching them harden. He put his mouth to them and gently sucked, then turned his face against the white, abundant flesh.

"They're too big," Mattie whispered, putting her forearm across them.

"No," Mitch gravely contradicted her. "If there is the slightest flaw, it's that they are not quite big enough." He removed her arm and went to work with his mouth again.

Mattie closed her eyes. She sighed, faintly, with pleasure and she felt his mouth curve in a smile of satisfaction.

He lifted her hands and kissed each of her fingers, circled his tongue in the crook of her arm and buried his face in her armpits. He stroked her shoulders and her throat, and kissed the thin skin under the angle of her jaw. And then he turned her over to continue his painstaking journey from the nape of her neck and down the length of her spine.

Mattie felt warm, and dreamy, but at the same time every inch of her skin tingled, and burned, and she felt the tiny pull of the muscles and the rush of blood in her feet, and the tips of her fingers, as well as in the aching center of herself.

When he reached the small of her back, Mattie moaned.

Unhurriedly, Mitch turned her over again. He parted her

legs and knelt between them, looking down at her. Their eyes traveled over the other's face.

And then, of her own accord because she wanted him, Mattie reached up for him. She lifted her hips to meet him, guiding him into her.

For the first time in her life she wasn't afraid of the size of a man. For the first time in her life she didn't close her eyes, hoping out of fear, or affection, or boredom, that it would be all right, and quickly over. Her eyes stayed open, fastened on Mitch's. Her mouth searched for his, and found it.

As soon as he came inside her, Mattie knew that she would come. And as soon as she knew it, it began. It was nothing like the hasty, bruising, brief burst of externally centered pleasure that was all she had ever known. This was inexorable, spreading from a fierce bud that swelled inside her, but very slowly, exquisitely slowly, as they moved together. She whispered his name, then called it aloud. Her fingers clutched at him, then loosened and fell open. Mattie was lost, and it was a joy to be lost, within herself, apart even from Mitch. The bud grew, and became a dark red flower, full-blown, and the petals fell back. The wonderful shock waves that it released raced all through Mattie, to the tips of the fingers and toes that Mitch had caressed, in a hundred thousand shimmering and refracting ripples. She cried out, a sound she didn't recognize that came from deep in her throat, and the cry died away into a long, shuddering sob.

It was only then that Mitch let himself respond. Mattie held on to him, rocking him in her arms and rejoicing in his pleasure, because it was part of her triumph in her own. To be absolved from the necessity to pretend, or to joke, or to cajole, was a revelation of lightness.

They lay still, half-enclosed by the red curtain, holding on to each other. Mattie felt so happy that tears swam into her eyes and she let them roll down her cheeks. "I hardly ever come," she whispered. "And never like that."

Lazily, watching her with satisfaction, Mitch propped himself on one elbow. He rubbed the tears away with his thumb and then tasted the salt of them.

"Why not?" he asked softly.

Mattie sighed and settled her head against his shoulder. The hair on his chest tickled her cheek. The rest of the world seemed comfortably remote, suitably irrelevant to their curtained enclave. She felt blissfully safe, and secure, and pleased with the two of them. "I'd better tell you," she said reluctantly, "in case you don't want to go any further."

"Don't be ridiculous. But you'd better tell me anyway."

She began at the beginning. She told him what she had never told anyone else, except for Julia, about Ted Banner and his sad, shameful advances, and her own guilt, and the way she had locked all that away.

Mitch's face went dark. "Jesus Christ. My poor love."

"It's all right," she told him. "I was a tough kid." It was easy to see it like that, with the luxury of Mitch's sympathy on her side. More confidently, she told him about John Douglas, and Jimmy Proffitt, and the men who had come after that. Mitch listened without interrupting her.

"I never liked it," Mattie whispered. "Perhaps I didn't want to let myself like it."

"I'm no psychologist," Mitch answered, "but it's possible."

Mattie told him about her long affair with Chris Fredericks. He nodded patiently. Last of all, she came to Alexander. It was only then, when she talked about Alexander, and Ladyhill and Lily and Julia, that Mitch showed any flicker of jealousy.

"Where is Alexander now?"

"At Ladyhill, I think."

"Will you see him again?"

Mattie studied his face, then she shook her head. "No. Not like that. How could I? Alexander is a friend. I should have had the sense, for both of us, to keep it that way."

Mitch nodded, satisfied. Then he put his arms around her, holding her against him. "Is that all?"

Suddenly Mattie laughed. "Yes. Not very much, is it?" The sense of lightness came back to her. She could have floated up off the big bed, except for Mitch's arms holding her down. She felt his mouth against her ear. "Enough to be going on with." He was laughing too; she heard it in his voice.

Mitch reached out and turned off the lights. He folded himself against her back, tucking his knees into the crook of hers. "It's all right," he told her. "Everything's going to be all right. You're safe now. Go to sleep, my love."

For so long, Mattie thought, she had been waiting for someone to say that to her. It seemed so simple, and so obvious, now that Mitch Howorth had finally done it. Obediently, Mattie closed her eyes and went to sleep.

In the morning, with thin autumn sunlight flooding the room, she turned to him again. She had woken up with the old, disbelieving cynicism dulling her happiness, but she reached out to Mitch with it. She touched him, smoothing her hands over his belly and the rounded muscles of his chest and arms, with the beginnings of familiarity. He blinked at her sleepily, and then lifted her on top of him. Mattie crouched over him, like a frog, and her hair fell around them, a more intimate curtain.

He made her come again. The easiness of it, the reverberating depths of the pleasure it gave her, startled Mattie into silence. Afterward she lay curled up in the warmth under the covers, incubating her happiness.

Mitch touched her cheek, then climbed out of bed and put on his dressing gown. He walked over to the window and stood with his back to her, his hands in his pockets, looking down into the garden. He stood without moving for such a long time that Mattie began to be afraid. She imagined that he was going to turn around and tell her something terrible, that he had to go away, that after all it wasn't any good, that she wasn't safe after all. She scrambled out of bed and went to him, greedily putting her arms around him, knowing that if he said it she wouldn't be able to bear it.

In the garden beneath she saw yellow leaves, and russet ones, shining with the night's rain and bare branches poking up between them.

Mitch said, "Mattie, will you marry me?"

She listened to the words, inside her head, before she understood them. And then she felt a shock of relief and joy and certainty that was far stronger even than the physical pleasure that he had given her.

"Yes," Mattie answered.

Mitch lifted her up and carried her back to the shelter of the absurd four-poster.

Mattie and Mitch were married at the beginning of December, a little over a month after they had first met. They were married at the St. Pancras registry office, just around the corner from Mattie's Bloomsbury flat, on a Monday, the only day on which Mattie didn't have to be back at the theater the same evening.

"We want to do it very quietly," Mattie said firmly. But she relented in the face of Lily's disappointment and made her the bridesmaid. Lily wore an ankle-length pink Empire-line dress with puffed sleeves, and sheltered under a white fur shoulder cape, which she was delighted with. The bride wore a black maxi-coat with puffs of black fur at the collar and cuffs. It was not unlike the one that John Douglas had paid for to keep her warm through her first winter on tour. Mattie's amazing hair rippled out from under a gold crochet pudding-basin hat. She looked like Ophelia, but she carried no flowers. Only Lily had a bouquet, of daisies and carnations in a pink frill to match her dress.

Mitch Howorth, blinking with pride behind his glasses, wore a double-breasted dark blue suit with a rose in the button-hole. Julia had had to work hard to contain her astonishment when Mattie introduced him. He seemed so unremarkable, a small, balding man with a slight paunch and an amiable smile. But there was no question that Mattie was in love with him, and he with her. On their wedding day they seemed to see no one else. Their eyes were fixed on each other, greedily, as if they couldn't wait to be alone again. To Julia the obvious intensity of their passion seemed too naked, almost indecent. She shivered a little, beyond the impervious circle of their intimacy.

There was only a handful of other guests at the brief cere-mony. Mattie's brothers and sisters came, and Felix, looking very dark and spare in morning dress. Mitch's only supporter was his younger brother, a fisherman from Whitby, who was his best man. But afterward, when they all shuffled outside again led by Mattie and Mitch with their hands glued together, they were confronted by a knot of press photographers waiting on the sidewalk. The news had leaked out despite Mattie's insistence on secrecy. Flashbulbs went off, their incandescence making the December light seem even grayer when it descended again.

Mattie half-hid behind Mitch. She was thoroughly relieved to discover that the photographers were there as much for Ricky as for herself. In the last years, Ricky had achieved some fame as the lead guitarist of the Dandelions. He had appeared at Mattie's wedding in trumpet-legged white trousers and a ruffle-fronted overshirt, his forehead and cheekbones painted with flowers. He waved the photographers away and cheerfully fended off the reporters' questions.

"Nah, I'm just giving my sister away, aren't I? It's her day. You've got your pics, haven't you? Now, off you go."

Mitch and a giggling Mattie were bundled into Mitch's surprisingly elegant car, and the rest of the wedding party into the lineup behind it. They drove away to lunch in a nearby Italian restaurant, a favorite of Mattie's.

Julia had wanted to give the party at her house.

"Please let me," she begged Mattie. "I'd love to do it."

"It'll be too much work for you," Mattie said.

Julia stared at her. "How could it be too much trouble? It's your wedding."

The two of them had come together again, almost as friends. With an effort Julia had made herself happy for Mattie's happiness, and put the memories behind her.

Gently, but allowing no possibility of contradiction, Mattie said, "I'd rather just go to the restaurant, without any fuss. You see, it's being married to Mitch that's important, not all the ballyhoo of a wedding."

Julia was hurt, and her sense of exclusion deepened, but she knew there was no point in renewing her offer.

A few more people had been invited to the lunch party. They were mostly theatrical friends of Mattie's, but Julia was relieved to see one or two familiar faces from the world that she and Mattie had once inhabited together.

Alexander had been asked, but he had telephoned to say that he was sorry, he had to be in New York. Julia thought that it was cowardly of him, but she could hardly talk to Mattie about his failure to appear. Neither of them mentioned Alexander, or Ladyhill, in the brief conversations that Mattie had time for before her wedding.

The wedding lunch, in the restaurant's upstairs room, was satisfactorily convivial. Julia sat near the end of the long table, with Felix, and Rozzie, and the familiar faces. There was plenty of gossip and champagne. Lily drank two glasses, becoming endearingly giggly, and then sleepy. Mitch's brother made an excellent droll speech, and presented a yawning Lily with a gold locket on a chain, on behalf of the bridegroom. Mitch's response to the toast was brief.

"I never expected to find happiness like this. I know I haven't deserved it. I want to thank Mattie for giving it to me, and all of you for coming to celebrate it with us."

Julia gulped her champagne, blinking back her tears and smiling through them at Mattie, who saw no one but Mitch.

The party ended, amid laughing and clapping. Julia went down the stairs with everyone else, following the bride and groom. The newlyweds looked dazed, and relieved to be escaping back into their own company.

Mitch's car was waiting at the curb. Ricky had tied white ribbons and tin cans to the bumper. Mattie and Mitch were going to spend one night at the Savoy, and the next day they were returning to Chichester.

"We'll go abroad for Christmas, when the show closes for

the pantomime season," Mattie explained. On the sidewalk, in the little crowd, Mattie and Julia kissed each other, brushing cheeks. Julia was sure that Mattie didn't distinguish her from any of the other guests. "Good luck," she whispered. "Be very happy, both of you."

Mattie's face was radiant with it. "I'll be happy so long as I've got Mitch."

Julia hugged her. Mattie smelled just the same. Although her scent was more expensive than the old Coty, it was still emphatic, a little too sweet, faintly overlaid with cigarette smoke. Julia felt bereft at the prospect of losing her.

"Good-bye." They held each other at arm's length, for a last look. Mattie winked, and for an instant she was her old self. Then she was inside the car, beside Mitch, waving at all of them left behind outside the restaurant. Julia waved back until the car was out of sight, trailing the ribbons and cans behind it.

"I've had enough," Marilyn murmured beside her. "I'll take Lily back if you want to go somewhere with all these."

"Thank you," Julia said, not wanting in the least to go back to the quiet house. Felix went home to George. Julia fell in with Ricky and the actors and the familiar faces.

She didn't remember much about the rest of the day. It ended in a club, somewhere, where she danced with an actor and took his hands out of the front of her dress. Alone in a taxi, going home at last, she sobbed stupidly, her sadness unblunted by all the drinking she had done to celebrate Mattie's wedding.

Christmas came, after the annual tornado had torn through Garlic & Sapphires. The shops took a record amount of money and were almost cleared of stock.

"Thank God that's over for another year," Julia exulted on Christmas Eve, as she always did. But in her heart she didn't care much about the takings, or the stock.

Julia and Lily spent Christmas in the house by the canal. In the morning they opened their presents together in Lily's bed, and at ten o'clock Alexander called to wish them a Merry Christmas. Julia knew that at ten-thirty, following the stately parish rituals, he would go down to Ladyhill church to read one of the lessons at morning service. She could see the little stone church, packed with people and scented with pine branches and mothballs, and hear the choruses of "Hark the Herald Angels."

Ten years ago, she thought.

Lily grabbed the receiver almost before Julia had returned

Alexander's brief good wishes and bombarded her father with talk. After she had finished she hung up, without asking Julia if she wanted to say any more.

Later Julia cooked a traditional dinner and friends came to eat and drink with them, Felix and George among them. George sat by the log fire with a blanket over his knees, and folds of it draped so that they partly hid the wheelchair. He sipped at a glass of Vouvray and ate a small piece of turkey breast. His present to Julia was an exquisite marquetry box. She had admired it many times, on his desk and in the inner sanctum of Tressider Designs.

"George, you can't mean to give me this," Julia protested, but he put his hand over hers.

"It's to keep your precious things in."

They were sitting a little apart from the others, where it was quieter for George. Julia looked sideways at him. "The trouble is that you can't put the really precious things in boxes."

George's gaze moved to settle on Felix. "That's true. Luckily we both recognize that, don't we? And we can also innocently enjoy the bibelots that do fit in boxes. Aren't we fortunate?"

Yes, Julia thought, looking at her pretty room warmed by the company of friends and the spirit of Christmas. Fortunate, after all. She squeezed George's hand, wondering that she had ever dismissed him as a waspish old queen, wondering at all her other mistakes. After dinner they played charades. After everything Julia still clung to her notions of what a proper Christmas should be. Felix and Lily were demons at the game. It was after midnight when the last guests left. Julia went upstairs to see Lily into bed. She lay under the covers and held up her arms.

"Thank you for my presents. It's been a lovely day. I love you, Mummy."

You can't put the really precious things in boxes. Lily was the most precious.

"I love you too."

Lily was to go to Ladyhill for the New Year. She didn't usually go during the Christmas holiday but she had asked if she might this time because her summer visit had been cut short, and Julia saw no reason to refuse her. Alexander had accepted the suggestion eagerly, and it occurred to Julia that he might not want to see in 1970 alone in the house. She wondered how often he thought of the New Year ten years ago, and how vivid the memories of it still were for him, even though Felix and his minions had removed all the black traces from the fabric of Ladyhill.

When he arrived to take Lily back with him, two days before the end of the year, Alexander and Julia greeted each other stiffly. It was their first meeting since she had driven away with Lily and left him. They didn't know how to confront each other, and they took refuge in chill politeness.

"Do you mind parting with her for a few days?"

"Yes," Julia answered, "but she wants to come, and I've never stopped her, have I?"

"No. Thank you. What will you do for New Year yourself?"

For Julia, it was a night to be survived rather than celebrated. If she guessed at Alexander's concern for her, she didn't grasp at it, in case it was an illusion. She shrugged. "There are two or three possibilities. One of those, or none of them. It isn't important."

"You could always come with us to Ladyhill," Alexander said.

For an instant Julia thought of it almost longingly. But then the pall of smoke rose up around her. It burned in her throat and blinded her eyes, but still through the folds of it she saw the old, horrifying images, all of them still weighted with her guilt.

"I couldn't do that," she said quickly. "Not this time."

Alexander nodded, masking his disappointment. "If Lily's ready, I think we'll go."

Julia went out into the street to wave them off. Then she climbed into her red Vitesse and drove away to work, where she spent the day interrupting the post-Christmas torpor of some of her suppliers with unnecessarily brisk telephone calls.

In the end, improbably, Julia saw the New Year in with Betty and Vernon. Betty had telephoned to suggest it, so tentatively that it was hardly a suggestion at all, and Julia had accepted the invitation. She knew exactly how the evening would be, and the certainty of dullness was more reassuring than the parties or the solitude that were her alternatives.

There was no one else at Fairmile Road, of course. Betty and Vernon didn't entertain. Julia wasn't sure what they did in Vernon's retirement. When she arrived she saw that the newspaper on the coffee table was folded open at the television pages, and Vernon had already marked his choices of prepacked heatherflavored celebration for the evening. He had been a late convert to television from the Third Programme, but Julia guessed he had become an enthusiast. Probably he sat in his chair watching it while Betty looked after the house, as she always had.

The old people seemed glad to see her. They settled her in the best chair, placed squarely in front of the set, and Betty brought her the first in a series of cups of tea. Julia noticed, as she had on other visits over the last months, that Betty had become the power now. It was Betty who decided when the kettle was to be put on, and when the room was warm enough for one of the bars of the fire to be switched off. Vernon had control of the knobs of the television, but in everything else he deferred to Betty. He called her Mum, and she fussed over him mildly. Julia was reminded of the way that Betty had mothered her, as a very little and obedient girl, before she had turned rebellious. She saw that Betty was at her best in looking after a not very demanding dependent. She seemed happier than she had once been, and no longer even remotely afraid of Vernon.

At a quarter to midnight Betty asked, "Would you like a glass of wine, Julia? To toast the new decade?"

Julia blinked. She couldn't remember there ever being any alcohol in the house. "Yes, please. That would be . . . nice."

She picked up the teacups and put them on the flowered tray, followed her mother into the kitchen with it. Betty held out a clear bottle of yellowish liquid and Julia read the handwritten label. It was homemade elderflower wine, the bottle bought or more probably won at a church bring-and-buy, and saved. Betty was making a tribute, bringing it out for her.

"Thank you for coming," Betty said. "It means a lot to your dad, you know."

"Does it?" Julia wished that Betty could say it meant a lot to her, but to be open or demonstrative wasn't Betty's way. It wouldn't change now.

"How's Lily?"

"She's very well. She has written to thank you and Dad for the sweater . . ."

"That's all right. Gone to Ladyhill, has she?"

Betty knew that already, of course. "Yes."

"She's a lovely girl."

"I know."

After a little pause Betty said something that astonished Julia. She asked, "Do you ever think of her? Your real mother? At Christmas and New Year, times like this?"

"Always," Julia said softly. "Betty, do you know anything about her? Who she was, or where she came from?"

She had asked the question only once before, just after Lily's birth, although it had often been in her head. Betty had answered, *I'm your mother. Why do you want to know?* And then, *I don't know anything about her anyway.*

Now, after a small silence, Betty said, "I told you. You came to us from the adoption society. They were very careful, those people. They wouldn't want trouble, would they?" Julia shook her head. She reached out and covered her mother's thin hand with her own. From the next room Vernon called impatiently, "Come on, you'll miss Big Ben."

Betty drew her hand away, picked up the tray with the glasses, and bustled out with it.

When the twelfth stroke of Big Ben had died away and the studio erupted into "Auld Lang Syne," probably prerecorded months ago, Julia and her parents kissed one another and lifted their glasses of elderflower wine.

"Happy New Year," Betty said.

"Happy New Year," Vernon and Julia agreed with her.

It was 1970.

Outside, Fairmile Road was dark and silent. There were no visible signs of celebration. The utter predictability of her surroundings blanketed Julia's terrors. There was no log fire here, no pretty candles, no music or dancing or sudden cannibalistic crackle of flame. She thought of Ladyhill, quiet in its gardens, and she knew that Lily would be fast asleep in her bed, because Alexander was far too strict to let her stay up. Happy New Year, she wished them, and Mattie and Mitch, and Felix and George and Marilyn and Nicolo Galli, and all the others. Happy New Year.

Twenty minutes later Vernon fell asleep in his chair. Julia sat on for a little while with Betty, and then said she would drive home. She didn't feel afraid of the prospect of home any longer. Betty came to the door and stood in the rectangle of light until Julia had driven away.

The roads on the way back were almost empty, slick with rain. Julia drove steadily and carefully, relieved that the night was almost over. She saw only a few other cars, and occasional knots of directionless revelers on the street corners, until she reached London.

Alexander looked down the length of the table. He had been invited to a neighbor's house for dinner, and he had left Lily and Mrs. Tovey and come to the party because he didn't want to be alone at Ladyhill.

He had hoped that Julia would be there with him, but it seemed clear now that he would have to stop hoping for the ghosts finally to be laid to rest. Another, newer ghost had glided between them. It was an added, bitter twist that the ghost should be Mattie. And now Mattie was married, and he had no idea where Julia was tonight, or what she was doing.

Alexander was too much of a realist to wish that what had happened had not, and he valued the memory of the happiness that he had shared with Mattie. He missed her, when she had gone. He still missed her, even now. But he did wish that that timing might have been different: that they could have been luckier, all three of them.

Julia had looked away when he had asked her to come home for the end of this ten years.

I couldn't do that, she had said.

It struck Alexander with cold force that all their years, together and apart, were finally over.

And now he found himself part of a merry party, as if to celebrate his acceptance of the truth at last.

Alexander knew that he had had enough of being alone. He felt tired, with another ten years ahead of him, and on the brink of getting old.

The girl opposite him leaned across the table. She was in her thirties, he guessed, and she had fair hair and big gray eyes. She had been introduced to him as Clare something.

"Penny for your thoughts," she invited him unstartlingly.

Alexander smiled. "They're not worth half that."

The girl laughed as if he had delivered an epigram of Wildean polish. Her top lip lifted attractively when she laughed, showing her gums. "They're worth twice as much as mine then," she told him.

"It sounds to me," Alexander said, "as if the two of us should give up thinking."

At midnight, when they all joined hands, he noticed that Clare made her way around the circle so that she could be next to him.

TWENTY-THREE

The office was a welter of boxes, spilling wood shavings, and crumpled tissue, with the enthusiastic girl burrowing among them. After a moment she found what she was looking for. She unwrapped the object from its tissue layers and held it up.

"Look at this."

Julia studied it. It was a teapot, made in the shape of a black kitten with a tartan bow around its neck. One upraised paw formed the spout, and its curled tail made the handle. The creature's expression was sickeningly winsome. The girl rubbed it with her sleeve, beaming at it.

"It's wonderfully kitsch," she assured Julia.

"I can see that it's kitsch."

Julia transferred her attention to the girl. She was wearing very short pink velvet shorts with a bib front, and a pale T-shirt with the message, Kiss me Quick. She had very long, tanned legs, ending in polka-dot ankle socks and a pair of platform-soled clogs. She was in her early twenties, almost straight out of college. She was Julia's newest and brightest buyer.

"It's funny," she insisted. "People want things that will make them laugh."

Julia sighed. "I'm not sure that I want pussycat teapots or ashtrays shaped like lavatories, or plaster ducks to hang on the walls of my house, even though they make my family and friends *choke* with laughter."

"Well . . ." The girl hesitated. She was much too bright actually to suggest that her employer was too close to senility to hope to understand what the young wanted nowadays. But it was clearly what she was thinking.

Julia laughed in spite of herself.

"Oh, all right. Two dozen. You can try them in Oxford. Are they funny enough there? We'll see how they go before putting them in the other shops."

"What about the ashtrays?"

"No."

"The ducks?"

"Two dozen of those as well. On your own head." Suki had been right before, Julia had to acknowledge that.

"Great. Fantastic. Now, wait till you see this . . ."

Julia looked at her watch. "It'll have to wait until tomorrow, whatever it is." A leopard-skin umbrella stand? A poker-work poem addressed 'To Mother'? "I haven't got time for any more now."

"Okay, whenever you say." Suki hesitated, then she added, "I think people are getting tired of wholesome good taste. Pine cupboards and glass and steel tables and that sort of stuff. They want something a bit tacky and decadent." Suki loved her job, there was no doubt about that. Her pretty face was radiant, and she couldn't have looked less like the decadence she was advocating.

"Maybe you're right," Julia said. She watched Suki bounding away on her towering platform soles and was reminded of Lily. Lily would certainly love the pussycat teapot. Only Lily didn't have any spending power. Not yet. But Lily had just turned eleven. It wouldn't be long before she did.

Julia turned in her swivel chair to stare out the window behind her desk. It made her anxious to think of Lily. Julia had hoped, without thinking particularly hard about it, that as Lily grew older their defined mother-daughter relationship would soften into a more sisterly friendship. She imagined that they would develop the kind of closeness that she had never achieved with Betty. Julia was ready to accept confidences, holding herself open for them in the way that she believed she had wanted Betty to before it was too late. But they never came. If Lily had confidences to bestow, she saved them for Alexander.

Or perhaps for Clare.

Julia stared out into the street. The windows opposite were so thick with summer dirt that she could hardly see into the depressing offices. She peered downward, into the traffic. The busy street was baldly ugly.

She didn't want to think about Clare, even now. The view offered no distraction. But Lily. Lily was growing up, and away from her. Julia was afraid that, to Lily, she was *only* her mother. She was the one who enforced the rules about bedtimes, and made unwelcome strictures about clothes, and homework, and friends. Just as Betty had done. Julia's mouth twisted. She could appreciate the irony, at least. But it didn't make her anxiety any less sharp. *If I had stayed at home*, she thought. *Like Betty did. Would that have made the difference for us, for Lily and me? Would she be mine, then, instead of her father's?*

But Julia had asked the same questions too many times lately. They were hypothetical, unanswerable.

The only fact was that Lily was increasingly rebellious as Julia's anxiety for her increased. Alexander's was the only voice she listened to. And Clare's, sometimes, because Lily liked Clare.

Julia turned abruptly back to her desk. Her in tray was piled high, and her secretary was waiting in the outer office to take dictation. Julia pressed the intercom button and asked her to come in.

After they had done the letters, Julia pulled the stack of papers toward her and worked at full stretch for an hour. Then she realized that the offices had become quiet around her. She looked at her watch. Six-thirty, and everyone had gone home. She would have to go herself, because she was meeting Felix at seven. They were going to have dinner together, and Julia was looking forward to it.

Julia went through into the bathroom that was part of her office suite, smiling briefly, as she often did at the memory of the dingy, all-purpose cubicle behind the first shop. Julia stood in the shower for five minutes, letting the hot needles of water ping against her skin, then rubbed herself briskly down. She noted with an automatic sidelong glance into the mirror that her stomach was still flat, there was no loosening of the skin under her arms or over her thighs. The she redid her face and her hair, and stepped into her dress. It was a Thea Porter, with a tight bodice and a skirt made of panels of Oriental silk. Julia wore it with a wide, beaded choker, but even as she did up the ribbons that fastened the choker and turned her head from side to side, she felt dissatisfied. The dress had been expensive, and looked it, but she was afraid that it lacked the certainty of style that Suki had managed in her velvet shorts.

Perhaps I am losing my touch, Julia thought. *Like with the bloody teapots. What do I know anymore?*

Or care, she retorted to herself. She marched back into her office, picked up one of the teapots, and stuffed it into her bag. She would ask Felix what he thought of it. As always, the sight of him cheered her up.

He was waiting for her at a corner table in the mirrored bar and he stood up at once and kissed her on both cheeks. Then he held her at arm's length to look at her.

"That dress is wonderful."

If Felix said it was, then it was. He could still criticize, while managing to remain beyond criticism himself. Tonight he was wearing a cream raw silk Nehru jacket. The pale color made his skin look darker, the bones of his face more prominent.

George Tressider had died twelve months before. He had survived longer than the doctors had predicted, but even so the loss of his partner had shocked Felix deeply. For a time he found it too painful even to go into work at Tressider Designs. He grew alarmingly thin, and saw almost no one except Julia. Then he disappeared. Julia didn't know where he had gone, but she guessed, approximately. When he resurfaced he was dead-eyed with exhaustion, but he went back to work. He reorganized some of the systems at Tressider's, and he began to gain weight again. Felix had dealt with his grief in his own way. Julia loved and admired him for his strength.

Now that Mattie was away working so much of the time, and so occupied with Mitch even when she was in London, Felix had become Julia's closest friend. They saw each other often, and she still glanced half-anxiously at him when they met. But she knew that Felix was all right.

Tonight they sat at their corner table exchanging their small snippets of news. *As if we were married,* Julia sometimes thought.

Felix asked her about Garlic & Sapphires. She reached into her bag and brought out the bundle of tissue paper. She unwrapped it and put the teapot on the table in front of Felix.

"There now. What do you think of that?"

He stared at it expressionlessly. Then he raised one eyebrow. "Do I have to think anything?"

"You certainly do. It's funny, it's wonderfully kitsch, it's what people want."

"Then God help them. Another drink?"

While she drank hers, Julia told him about Suki, and the new stock. "You remember what the first shop was like. Remember Thomas's armchairs? I promised myself that I'd never sell anything I wouldn't have in my own house. It was all supposed to be so clever and original and daring. It was supposed to be"— she broke off and eyed him—"the opposite of everything you and George were doing, but just as good. Yet now I find myself selling stuff I hate, on my buyer's excellent advice. I'm running a chain of gift shops, aren't I? It isn't what I planned."

The black cat sat on the table in front of them, its heart-shaped sugar-pink nose gleaming with apparent satisfaction. Julia made a face at it.

"You've expanded," Felix said dryly. "Once you employ other people, you accept their contributions. As for the teapot itself, I'm sure it will sell. This, and the ducks and all the other bits you dislike, are briefly fashionable. The fashion will pass."

"There will be others," Julia replied. "Felix, am I too old?"

"Do you feel too old?"

Too something, Julia realized. *What was it?*

"You've got three choices." Felix held up his fingers. "You can let Garlic & Sapphires go on the way it is. Getting bigger and more successful. It'll make you rich, probably. Or you can cut it back to being what it once was. So you don't have to sell anything you don't personally admire. Or you can sell up and come back into Tressider's with me."

Julia was amazed. At first she was sure he was joking. And then she was afraid that he was serious. She was warmed, and flattered, but she knew she couldn't do it. It would be going back. Stepping around George, and all kinds of other memories, and going in the wrong direction.

"Tressider, Lemoine, & Smith," Felix mused. "What do you think?"

Julia put her hands over his. "It sounds like an ad agency."

"You can choose the name."

"Thank you for asking me, Felix. But no. I don't know what I should do next, but I don't belong in Tressider's. George knew that."

Felix's face changed, saddened, before he looked directly at her again. "Are you sure?"

"I'm quite sure." Of that, at least.

Felix nodded. "Okay. Let's just go and have dinner then, shall we?"

They enjoyed the meal, and each other's company, as they always did. At the end, Julia asked him, "Would Jessie be proud of us, do you think?"

Felix thought for a moment. "Jessie admired material success. But it was contentment that she valued."

Julia smiled. "Still a little way to go then."

"A little way."

Felix kissed her good night and put her into a taxi. His

touch was light and his skin, brushing hers, was cool. Brother
and sister. It was a long time since Julia had looked for anything
different from anyone.

Sitting in her corner on the way home, looking out at the
lights, Julia thought about Jessie and Felix, and about Mattie.
Not about Lily at all. But when the cab drew up outside her
house, Julia frowned. The downstairs lights were still on. It was
eleven o'clock, and a schoolday tomorrow. Lily should be in
bed. Unless it was Marilyn sitting there, although Marilyn always watched the television in her own rooms.

Julia paid off the taxi and ran up the steps.

Lily was sitting curled up in an armchair facing the television, but the screen was blank.

"Lily, what are you doing? Do you know what the time
is?"

Slowly, Lily uncurled herself and stood up, facing her
mother.

"Hello, Mum. How's Felix?"

"Fine. He sends his love. Did you hear me, Lily? Where's
Marilyn?"

"Downstairs. She saw me into bed, then I got up again."

"Why?"

Lily squared her shoulders. Her T-shirt was an old one and
there was a three-cornered tear in it. Her skin, brown from the
summer, showed through. Her small, suntanned feet emerged
from the flares of her jeans. She had painted her toenails with
silvery polish, from one of Julia's bottles.

"I wanted to talk to you."

Julia hesitated. "Well, good. But it's late now, Lily, and
you shouldn't have waited up all this time."

"I want to talk to you now," Lily repeated.

Julia looked at her again. Lily thrust her hands into her
pockets, her shoulders hunching to make deep shadows at the
base of her throat. But the protective stance didn't quite hide the
beginnings of her breasts. The new roundness contradicted her
bony shoulders and skinny legs. Not a child anymore, Julia
thought sadly. Not a woman either.

"What is it?" she asked. Perhaps trouble at school, with
one of her friends. Nothing else, yet, surely?

Lily looked straight into her eyes. "I want to go and live at
Ladyhill."

Shock made Julia stupid. "What?"

"It's a good time," Lily said clearly. "I needn't start the

new school here. I can go to the one down there instead. Elizabeth is starting too.''

Julia sat down, hard, against the corner of the scrubbed pine table. The edge of it dug savagely into her thigh with the impact. Lily had thought it out. It wasn't an impulsive idea, blurted out to test her. "You live here, Lily."

Lily put her head on one side, studying her. Julia saw determination, something else too. Pity? Sympathy? Had she looked at Betty, once, like that? It was Lily's awareness of her strength that made Julia feel cold, and helpless, and terrified now. She remembered feeling her own strength in just the same way. She had defeated Betty with it, of course.

"You can't go to Ladyhill. You live here, with me."

"I want to. I know I couldn't before, when Alexander was just on his own with Mrs. Tovey. But Clare lives there now. She was there all last summer. She . . ."

Julia held up her hands, fending it off. "They aren't married, Lily."

"They could get married."

Julia stood up again. There would be a bruise on her thigh where it had hit the table. Her chest, and her throat, and her eyes all hurt her.

She saw Jessie's old room. A paisley cloth over the back of a sofa, and oranges in a blue bowl. Betty, standing up to her, but already beaten.

"Have you talked to Alexander about this idea?"

"He said that I would have to talk to you. Daddy is fair."

Anger swirled up inside Julia, all of it directed against Alexander. Fair, in his house with all the acres, that Lily had loved since babyhood. Fair, with his new girlfriend comfortably installed in it, who would be glad to look after Lily and go to her sports days and applaud her in her school play, because it would cement her more firmly to Alexander himself.

Fair, to take my daughter away from me.

Julia heard and hated the childishness and the jealousy of her own response, but the recognition of her weakness only fueled her determination to fight.

"I won't let you go," she whispered.

Lily held out her hand. Not to Julia, but to take in the room with a single gesture. They both looked at the blank television and the empty chair, the chesterfield with its plumped cushions, the day's newspapers, delivered but not unfolded.

"You aren't here. You've never been here, really. It'll be easier for you."

Julia stumbled to her, wrapping her arms around the knobby shoulders. They stayed stiff, resisting her. "I will be here from now on. Lily, if that's what you want, I'll sell the shops . . ." The words ran on. She was begging now, but she knew that it was too late.

Lily stepped backward, looking at her with Alexander's level gaze. "I want to go. I want to go with Daddy and Clare."

The clear, high voice slashed into Julia, sharper than knife blades, colder than steel.

"You have to live with me."

"What kind of life will it be if you make me?"

The terrible, inexorable clarity of youth and strength. That strength, that she had once possessed herself. Experience took it away, and gave back only endurance. Lily was too old, and yet she knew nothing, and she had everything ahead of her to endure. Pity for her, and for herself, and Betty made Julia catch her breath. The tears started, and ran down her face.

"Lily . . . I'm sorry. For all the things I've done to you, and the rest I've failed to do. I didn't mean any of it, because I meant it to be different. I should have known how to make it different."

"I'm sorry, Julia. It'll be better, I know it will." And Lily turned away from her. She was part acting, Julia knew that. She was making moves that she had rehearsed. She even had that advantage, while Julia still gasped with the shock of it.

Julia wanted to run after her, to pick her up and smother her with hugs, now that she was too big to be lifted. She wanted to love her differently now that it was too late to change anything.

The door closed. Julia was left, staring unseeingly at the familiar room, seeing the other room overlooking the square, helpless in the face of the inevitable. She poured herself a whiskey that she didn't want, drank it looking down into the darkness of the garden, then went upstairs. Lily's light was off and her door was closed, and although she waited outside it, Julia could hear nothing.

She went to bed but not to sleep. The mistakes that she knew she had made with Lily came back to her, magnified by the darkness and the silence. Her impatience stalked her as cruelty, her preoccupation as neglect. In the wash of guilt Julia clung to the single comforting truth—the evidence that Lily herself was all right. She was strong and determined, and she knew what she wanted. She would get it, just as Julia had herself.

It was only much later, Julia told herself, when the truths became blurred and the hard-edged certainties melted, that life became difficult, and painful, and seemingly unchangeable.

In the morning Lily's resilience showed clearly. It was like any other day. Lily gulped her breakfast, gathered up her belongings, and kissed Julia as she rushed past, then departed for school. After she had gone the house seemed dry and stale. Julia flung open the windows, but the weight in the rooms seemed immobile. She went to telephone Alexander. Her anger and bitterness focused itself on him. Alexander must have encouraged Lily with her idea.

"I did nothing of the kind," Alexander said. "It was Lily's own suggestion."

"You must have worked on her. You and Clare."

"Clare wouldn't presume to do anything of the kind either."

No, of course not. She's too good, too nice. But I know what she wants. She wants you, and Lily's a part of you. She's not as stupid as she seems, Clare isn't.

"I won't let her go, Alexander."

There was a pause. Then Alexander said, "It was always part of our agreement, wasn't it, that Lily should choose for herself when she was old enough?"

Oh, yes. But I never thought she wouldn't choose me. Even I, knowing what I know, took my own daughter so much for granted.

Julia's anger crumbled away, and her defenses with it.

"I love her."

"We both love her."

They listened to each other's anxiety and to the distances between them, and then Alexander said, "I'll come up and talk to you. Expect me by lunchtime."

Clare was in the kitchen. He went back to the smell of coffee and toast.

"That was Julia."

Clare's head jerked up. She was wearing a yellow shirt, the brightness of it making her eyes and hair look pale by comparison. She looked at Alexander, saying nothing.

"She's upset. Lily has told her that she wants to come and live here."

"Poor Julia."

Alexander went to her and held her against him. He was

used to Clare; they had been together for a year and a half. She didn't goad him, or reward him. She was good-humored, and her predictability made their life tranquil. He smoothed her hair with one hand and looked over her head, out of the window. He could see a long vista of the garden, and a corner of Marco Polo's paddock.

"I'm going up this morning to see her. It's important to work it all out properly. For Lily, for all of us." He looked away from the garden and down into Clare's face. "Do you mind Lily coming here, if it's what she really wants?"

"Of course not. You know I don't. I'm not her mother, but I can take care of her."

Alexander bent his head and kissed her. Clare smiled and went to the percolator to pour him another cup of coffee.

When he was ready to leave, she went out and walked with him to the car. He kissed her again and then drove away, waving out of the window without looking back. Clare stood still, watching him go with the sun in her eyes. The brightness made them water.

Clare wanted to marry Alexander, but he hadn't asked her. She would like to think that he might, but she didn't believe that accepting the responsibility for his daughter would make any difference to whether he would or not. Nor would she suggest it to him. That wasn't Clare's way.

As he drove, Alexander wondered irritably why he was driving two hundred miles to see Julia when he could have stayed at Ladyhill and tried to unravel the problem by telephone.

Julia was waiting for him. When she opened the door he saw that she was white-faced, with gray patches under her eyes. Sympathy dispelled his irritation. Julia could be a harsh judge, but she judged herself most harshly of all. He thought, with a touch of sadness, how well they knew each other and to what little effect.

It was an uncomfortable meeting. In her hurt Julia was convinced that Lily and Alexander had conspired against her. Alexander accepted her hurt, knowing that he couldn't salve it, and was gentle with her. But he couldn't make her see the truth, which was that Lily had made her decision without reference to any of them. Soon enough, Lily wouldn't need them at all.

"Listen," he tried to persuade Julia. "Let's say that she can come, just for a few months. Then if it doesn't work, she can come back again. The school's a good one. And perhaps it will be safer for her to do her growing up at Ladyhill than in London."

Julia lifted her swollen eyes to meet his. "We've already chosen a good school for her here, remember? And I think I could have kept her safe while she was growing up. I wanted to. I was looking forward to seeing it happen."

She wouldn't cry, not in front of him. But Julia knew that she was defeated. They faced each other across the pine table, with the greatest distance between them that there had ever been.

By the time that Lily came home again from school, Julia had accepted that she would go to Ladyhill for the summer holidays, as she always had done, and that this time she would stay there. Lily stood at the end of the table in her striped uniform dress, meek and conciliatory now that she had achieved what she wanted. It seemed to Julia that Lily and Alexander could both afford to be gentle and gracious now that they had beaten her. It deepened her sense of exclusion and she turned away, to the kitchen, saying that she would make supper before Alexander drove back to the country. Lily perched on the arm of the chesterfield, swinging her legs in her hated white ankle socks, talking about her part in the school play. Julia couldn't believe that everything was so ordinary, when she had just lost it all. She clattered blindly with the knives and pans.

She cooked the food almost without knowing what it was, and put it on the table. They sat down to eat, the three of them, as if they were any ordinary family at the end of the day. To Julia, it seemed the bitterest moment of all.

Afterward, Lily let Alexander go without any of the fuss she habitually made. She came back from seeing him off and sat beside Julia on the chesterfield. Julia sat with her hands lying heavily in her lap and her head bent. Seeing her, Lily realized that she had never known her mother at a loss before. That had always been part of her otherness, what set her apart from other people's mothers. Julia had so much power. It was startling to realize that her power could desert her. Lily leaned forward and put her cheek against her mother's, trying for the right words.

"It won't be any different, will it? Not really? Just the other way around. I'll be coming to you for the holidays. If I can. If you want me to."

Julia looked at her. "I want to see you as often as we can arrange it, whenever you want to. I also want you to know, Lily, that I love you very much. Granny Smith never told me that she loved me, and I never realized she did until I was grown-up. It was too late then."

Lily understood that her mother was talking to her like a

person, not like a little girl or a daughter. The change seemed to mark an important stage in her life. She nodded, her face solemn.

"I understand. I love you, too, only in a complicated way. At Ladyhill nothing's complicated, and I like that."

"I think I understand," Julia said slowly, in her turn. She stood up and walked to and fro, while Lily watched her. At last she sighed, a big gusty sigh that seemed hopeless. "Lily, will you mind very much if I sell this house? I don't think I can bear to live here without you."

Lily did mind, because the house by the canal meant home as much as Ladyhill did. But she shook her head, understanding that it was important for the altered dealings between them. "You ought to do what makes you happy. It's only a house, isn't it?"

Julia wanted to turn and seize Lily, fasten on to her, but she made herself go on walking, slowly up and down the Turkish kelim that Lily had once hacked the fringes off.

After that the days went quickly. Julia went to the school play and watched Lily's bloodcurdling Captain Hook through a glaze of tears.

"You must be proud of her, Lady Bliss," the headmistress said at the noisy party afterward. "I know we all are."

"I am," Julia answered.

At home she helped Lily to clear her room. They took down the pop posters, and they opened the closets and ordered the fate of picture books and woolly lambs and dolls. Among the dolls was the flaxen-haired monster that Josh had bought for Lily so long ago. Lily had never liked it, and its simpering face was hardly marked. Julia bundled it into the rummage sale bag, not wanting to meet its empty blue eyes.

Lily dealt solemnly with the accretions of her childhood, but Julia found the rite almost unbearably painful. She found herself stealing things away, taking "The Tale of Tom Kitten" and a rag doll and a china pig from the discarded piles and hiding them among her own things. At night, with her knees drawn up and the pillow pressed into her face, she cried as if she were a child herself.

Alexander came to drive Lily away. Julia had dreaded the moment, but when it came, almost the worst thing to bear was his gentleness. She felt his sympathy and understanding of her loss as sharply as she felt her own pain: her anger with him evaporated immediately.

When Lily was out of the room he came to her, taking hold

of her wrists and looking down into her eyes. "It was Lily's choice," he whispered. "I can't deny her what she wants. But I'd do anything if it meant not hurting you like this."

Julia wanted to cry, to throw herself against him and let her tears wash away the barriers between them. She felt how close he was; she didn't feel any longer that he could afford to be generous because he had won Lily. Lily wasn't a trophy, after all. Alexander was generous, just as he was honorable and loyal and kind. She saw him objectively now, after so many years of confusion.

Julia didn't cry.

Instead, she looked straight back at him, finding a smile within herself. It occurred to her that if she managed to be unselfish now, she would truly have achieved something.

"I know," she said. "It's all right. Just look after her, will you?"

"You know I'll do that. I wish I could do the same for you."

Julia laughed then. "I'm much too old to be looked after. Too old and too selfish."

Alexander touched her cheek. "You think you're selfish, but you aren't. Don't be so harsh to yourself."

Lily came back then, and almost at once it was time for them to leave. After they had gone, Julia felt that a piece had been cut away from her. She remembered waking up, in the clinic, after Lily's birth. She went slowly up the stairs to Lily's bedroom. It had always seemed empty when she went away; now it was dead. The posters and the photographs had left rectangles like mocking shadows on the faded walls. She stood on a chair and unhooked the blue and yellow curtains from the rods. At once the room was unfurnished. Standing back, she saw that there were cobweb filaments blowing from the window frame, and a layer of fine dust on the sill. She folded the curtains carefully, into exactly symmetrical squares and then into smaller squares, and left them lying in the middle of the bare mattress. The real estate agent's valuer had already been to look at the house. He had surprised her with his estimate of how much it was worth.

Mattie searched for the key, then unlocked the front door with its diamond-shaped leaded lights. The hall smelled musty. Mitch followed her with the first of the suitcases, and she heard the mini-cab driver bringing the rest.

"Welcome home," she said to Mitch.

"Does it feel like home?"

"Immediately." Mattie had been in Nice for a month. The filming had lasted for only four weeks, and Mitch had been with her, but even so it had seemed too long to be away. The house was waiting, and she wanted to be in it.

Mitch had bought it. Mattie had claimed to be uninterested in houses. At the beginning of their married life Mattie had been reluctant to relinquish her Bloomsbury eyrie, but then she had been forced to admit that it was too small for both of them. For the first year they had made their base in London in a characterless flat, and when the West End run of the Chichester play had finally come to an end there had been several months in Hollywood, and then the film in France.

It was Mitch who had insisted that they needed a proper house, near enough to London for easy commuting, far enough away to have a real garden and countryside within reach. After a proper search he had found the house in Surrey. It was a solid example of thirties stockbroker Tudorbethan, with black and white timbering and tall chimneys and an extensive garden that came complete with a gardener who had tended it two days a week for seventeen years. It had wood paneling and inglenook fireplaces and luxurious bathrooms installed by the last owners. It was called Coppins.

Mitch was delighted with it. "I'd buy you a manor house, Mattie, but you need to devote your life to that kind of a house."

Mattie thought of Alexander and Julia, and the imposing bulk of Ladyhill. "I don't want that," she said quickly. "I don't want anything to be more important to you than me."

"We need a good, solid house that's convenient, comfortable, and undemanding. Coppins is all those things. And not a bad price either."

Mitch was always businesslike.

"Take me to see it, at once."

At first glance, Mattie laughed. Coppins sat in its gardens like a picture in an old-fashioned children's book. *William*, perhaps, or *Greyfriars*. It needed a parlormaid in a lace cap to open the front door. It seemed so improbable that she should own anything of the kind. But as they explored it, calling out to each other up and down the stairs, she recognized its character. Coppins was enormous, but it had a doll's-house quality. It made her want to settle down and play house, with a china tea set and miniature sets of reproduction furniture.

From the kitchen, which had a stone-shelved larder as well as a pantry, she called out to Mitch again. "Let's buy it!"

Mitch was also an excellent negotiator. Within three weeks Coppins was theirs, at a slightly reduced price. While they were in Nice the painters had been at work, and the minimum of furniture had been delivered. Now they had come home.

Mitch stepped around the heap of luggage and held out his arms. Mattie walked into them. They went upstairs to the big bedroom overlooking the garden.

Later, Mattie said, "It will be a good house for children to grow up in."

Mattie was trying to have a baby. Mitch raised himself on one elbow to look down at her. "Lots of children. Running up and down the stairs, round and round the garden. We'd better have a couple of sets of twins."

She grinned at him, winding one arm around his neck. "How shall we do that?"

It was easy to play house in Coppins, as Mattie had guessed it would be. She was no better at the domestic details than she had ever been, but Mitch quickly found a local woman who came in every day to cook and clean. Mattie discovered that what she enjoyed was shopping, and then arranging and rearranging her purchases. She made expeditions up to town, and came home with curtain fabric and kitchen utensils and china. Department stores' vans began to arrive with armchairs and coffee tables. Mattie combed the local antique shops and brought her finds triumphantly back home with her.

"I've never had a real house," she said. "Doesn't it make you feel safe, owning electric blankets and pictures of water meadows?"

"You are safe," Mitch answered. "I told you."

"I love you. I don't want anything except you, but I quite love my house as well. Look, Mitch, do you think this little chair looks nice here?"

Mitch would put his head on one side, seeming to look at the chair but really looking at Mattie's glowing face. Then he would nod.

"I think it does. Yep, it's good there." He put his arms around her waist, and she let her head fall back against him.

They were happy. At first Mattie had almost been afraid to move in case the happiness broke, or disappeared as quickly as it had come. The very ordinariness, that other people took for granted, seemed a miracle. Then, with Mitch's certainty to reassure her, she began to accept it. Mattie found that she loved routine, and at Coppins they slipped comfortably into patterns that even half a year ago she would have dismissed as impossible.

In the mornings Mitch worked. He liked to have time to attend to his investments, to make telephone calls, and to read the financial press. While he was busy Mattie shopped or read scripts. She turned them all down, but she did have lunch with her agent, although she had to rush away afterward to a sale at Phillips. In the afternoons sometimes Mitch played golf, or they went for mild walks, or else pottered companionably in the big garden. It made Mattie laugh to find herself wondering which were weeds and which were plants growing in the cracks of the crazy-paved terrace. In the evenings they ate quietly at home together. Occasionally, they went to the local cinema; even less frequently, they went to the theater in the West End. They saw almost no one, because they didn't need any company beyond their own. The peace and contentment, to Mattie, seemed almost magical.

One of the few people they did see was Felix. He came down at Mattie's invitation to give some advice about the house. She showed him around it from top to bottom, and Felix listened politely to her plans. But when they came back to their armchairs in the drawing room she saw his face, and started to laugh.

"Poor Felix. You hate it, don't you?"

"Of course I don't hate it. It's a fine house."

"But not your kind of house."

"You've . . . made it all very much of a piece. The style suits the house. You don't need me to help."

Mattie was still laughing. "I suppose not. I've found out that I like big, fat armchairs and lampshades with fringes and pictures that you can look at and see straightaway what they're supposed to be pictures of. I suppose I've had a kind of image of what a proper house should be ever since I was a little girl. The opposite of my mum and dad's house. I shouldn't need your approval of that, should I? Felix, I must need it because I like you so much."

Felix crossed to Mattie's chair, then knelt down in front of her so that their faces were level. "I do approve. Of the house, and everything. I've never seen you look so pretty. Being happy suits you."

She smiled at him. "Doesn't it? Come on, put your notebook away. Let's go and find Mitch and have a drink."

Felix had noticed that when they had been apart for more

than a few minutes, Mattie began to look anxiously around for Mitch. He also noticed that she poured herself a drink, and then forgot about it. It was good, he thought. All of it, even Coppins itself.

Almost the only other visitor was Julia. She came to lunch, one Sunday in early September, driving up to the house in her red car. Mattie was in the garden. There was a half-moon-shaped rose bed beyond the terrace, and Mattie was snipping the dead heads off the Blue Moon and the Wendy Cussons with a pair of shears. Her face and arms were faintly freckled with the sun and her hair was tied up in a damp, heavy knot at the nape of her neck. She saw that the car was Julia's, and came running to meet her. They hugged each other, and over Mattie's shoulder Julia saw Mitch come out of the house. He was wearing a golf pullover and checked trousers, and he lifted his arm to wave to her.

Mattie and Julia had met, when they could, after Mattie's marriage. But there was a constraint between them. They had never talked about Alexander, and it seemed unlikely now that they ever would. The omission left treacherous openings at the end of every avenue of talk.

Today Julia knew that it was Mattie who seized her hand and led her in a tour of the house, and then presided proudly over drinks and lunch, but it was a different Mattie, almost a stranger. They talked, and Mitch joined in, but the old understanding between the two of them that had never needed any words seemed to have gone for good. It was as if Mattie had grown slightly deaf, and Julia wondered if she had lost her own hearing too. It was hard not to feel that her oldest friend had gone away somewhere, and that Mitch Howorth had taken her.

There was just one flash of the old Mattie. The meal was very good, a chicken dish with lemon followed by apple charlotte.

"Did you make this, Mat?" Julia asked.

Mattie shrugged airily. "It's very simple." Her face stayed perfectly straight for a second, then melted. "Nah, of course not. Mrs. Hopper does it. I knew you wouldn't believe me even if I tried to pretend."

"I might well have," Julia said faintly. "Thank God you didn't."

After they had eaten, Mitch announced that he was going upstairs to read the papers for an hour.

"Go on then, my love." Mattie reached up to touch his hand as he passed. She winked at Julia. "Have a sleep, he means." Julia had the impression she was longing to go with him. They went outside and lay in the sun on canvas loungers. There was a sheen on Mattie's skin, and her figure looked full and ripe. She sighed and let her head fall back, giving herself up to the sun. Julia knew the resonance and sweetness of physical satisfaction. She was glad for Mattie, but her contentment made Julia sharply aware of her own loneliness.

Mattie opened her eyes again. "Talk to me. Tell me the news. Is Lily at Ladyhill?"

Carefully, Julia said, "Yes. She's not coming back. She's chosen to go and live with Alexander and Clare."

Mattie's eyes opened wide now, and she sat up. "Bloody hell, Julia. I'm sorry."

It was hard to talk about it without talking about Alexander. Mattie knew about Clare, of course, but only in the most general way. Now she asked directly, "What's she like?" Julia could have opened up then. She might have told Mattie that she felt alone, with no sense of direction or purpose. But Mattie looked so radiant that she couldn't expose her own desolation. Afterward she regretted the weakness.

"She's my age, or a bit younger. Quite pretty in an insipid way. A good committee woman. Sensible and responsible, not very clever."

"Gawd," Mattie said.

"She'll be good at looking after Lily's school uniform, I suppose. And Alexander says that it will be safer for Lily to do her growing up at Ladyhill anyway. No dope or acid in Ladyhill Village, is there?"

"More's the pity," Mattie drawled. "Shh. Don't let Mitch hear that. So what will you do, Julia?"

"I thought I might sell the house. It's too big for me, and it's worth a shocking amount of money. Oh, don't worry about Marilyn. I'll fix her up with another flat, and she's such a good nanny, she could get a job anywhere."

"I wasn't worrying about Marilyn. I don't worry about Ricky, or Sam and Phil either. Do you remember that night in the doorway, and the two of us huddled there in the dark worrying about what would happen to them? We should have been saving all our worrying for ourselves. And so should you, Julia."

Julia smiled, but somehow in the Coppins garden even the memory of the Savoy doorway didn't draw them close together again.

"What about your business?"

Julia told her about Suki. Mattie put her head back and laughed. "I love the sound of the teapot, and the toilet ashtrays as well. I'll take six of each."

"I think I'm going to take a break from it," Julia said abruptly.

Mattie stared. "And do what?"

"I don't know. Felix asked me not long ago if I felt too old for Garlic & Sapphires. What I do feel is tired. I'm tired of myself, most of all."

"That doesn't sound like you."

They looked at each other, separated by sun-warmed stones.

"No," Julia said quietly. "I think it's time I wasn't like myself anymore."

Mattie sat up, wrapping her arms around her knees. "Are we still friends?" she asked.

With the big house looming above her, and the suburban scents of mown grass and roses thickening the air, Julia said, "Of course we are," and the reassurance denied itself. Mitch came out again, and drew up his deck chair to make a circle. They wouldn't talk now, Julia knew that. A sense of her own smallness oppressed her.

Mattie and Mitch pressed her to stay to dinner, or at least to have some tea before driving back, but Julia said she must get home. Before she climbed into the car they both kissed her, and then they waved, standing shoulder to shoulder in their graveled driveway, until she had gone.

Julia had no reason to hurry back to the house by the canal, but it was a relief to be alone again.

Perhaps I'm learning, she thought. *Not to depend, after all. Bloody freedom takes a lot of earning. Or does it come only when you know that you don't want it?*

The exhausted irony seemed too stale to bear thinking about.

The first thing that Julia did the next morning was to put the house by the canal on the market. Within four days she had a buyer who offered a higher price than the agent's recommendation. The speed disconcerted her briefly, but the momentum pushed her on. Very quickly, hardly even bothering to view it properly, Julia made an offer for a flat in Camden Town. It had two bedrooms; she would need somewhere for Lily's visits. Julia described it to her on the telephone.

"It sounds fine," Lily said.

"Are you all right?"

"Yes, Mum. I'm fine. Are you?"

"Oh, yes. Busy, that's all."

Arranging to have her business taken care of proved to be no more difficult. Julia took the most senior of her shop managers out to lunch and suggested to her that she might like to try her hand at managing the entire business for an unspecified period of time.

"I'd like it very much," the woman said promptly. "I know I can do it."

Julia nodded. She had deputized for her successfully in the past.

The manageress was looking curiously at her. "But why do you want me to do it?"

"I'm just tired," Julia told her, unable to find a better answer.

After that there was a transition period during which she worked side by side with her deputy, handing Garlic & Sapphires over to her. Julia went through the motions of ordinary life, but she felt as if she were watching herself from some way off. She looked like a stiff little marionette.

Some things pierced her detachment. There was the day when Lily should have come back from Ladyhill. There was another day, too, when she happened to pass the school that should have been Lily's new one. The street outside it was flooded with girls in bottle-green uniforms. Julia sat in her car, watching them as they passed. Twice, she thought she saw Lily among them. She had to rub her eyes savagely so that she could see to drive on.

Compared with that, leaving the house by the canal seemed easy. She kept just enough of her furniture to furnish the new flat sparsely, and sold everything else. She almost sold the mutilated kelim, but in the end she rolled it up and took it with her. When she closed the door on the empty house for the last time, she walked away without looking back. She felt lighter as she did it.

She kept the white walls of her new home completely bare. It was easier to look at clean, empty spaces.

By the middle of December, at the height of the Christmas rush, Julia knew that the shops no longer needed her, and that she was only getting in the way of her replacement. At the end of one afternoon she cleared her desk and said the briefest good-byes. She walked out of her offices into the icy wind. A Salvation Army silver band was playing carols at the end of the street. Julia stopped to listen, and then emptied her purse into the collecting bag. She walked home to Camden Town, and the feeling of lightness grew stronger. Watching herself, Julia thought how small she looked as she threaded her way through the jostling shoppers.

Julia spent Christmas Day with Felix, at Eaton Square.

He had decorated the high drawing room with dark ivy and branches of blue spruce, frosted with silver, as George had always done. The tree was the same, too, hung with silver and sparkling with white light. It made her see again how much Felix missed him.

They were deliberately lighthearted. They exchanged their small, well-chosen presents and drank champagne. They ate Felix's wonderful Christmas dinner off the gold-rimmed Meissen china, and filled George's crystal glasses with Château Latour. It was a long time since Julia had had so much to drink. She kicked off her shoes and sank back into the sofa cushions, holding out her brandy glass for a refill.

"Perhaps we should get married, Felix. D'you think we'd make each other happy?" Julia laughed, but she meant it.

He came to sit beside her, lacing his fingers through hers. Julia rested her head against his shoulder, but the movement made her spill her brandy.

"Whoops."

"Would we make each other happy?" he repeated. "I don't think so. Not in the way that counts."

She laughed at that, but then he put his hand up to stroke her hair, and the unexpected tenderness made the laughter dissolve into tears.

"Oh, dear. I'm sorry, Felix. I'm not crying because you don't want to marry me."

"I know that."

He gave her a silk handkerchief, too beautiful for Julia even to contemplate blowing her nose on it. She sniffed firmly instead. "I'm going back to Italy," she said. "For good, I think. I don't really want to live here anymore. And there doesn't seem to be any point in it without Lily."

"I'll miss you very much," Felix told her.

They held on to each other tightly. After a few minutes Julia fell asleep. Much later, when she woke up again, she found that Felix had covered her with a blanket. He used to look after her in just the same way, years ago, when she and Mattie collapsed after their sorties into Soho.

"I can't drink like I used to," she moaned, putting her hand to her head.

Felix was prim. "I'm relieved to hear it."

Lily came for two weeks of the Christmas holidays.

She seemed to be delighted with the spare, compact Camden Town flat. "It's like a ship," she announced. "Sailing over the street. My room's like a cabin on a liner."

Before she came, Julia was nervous. She didn't have work to go to anymore, and she wondered how they would fill in their time together. She worried that they might not have enough to say to each other, that Lily might have edged even further away from her, even become like Clare.

But Lily was just the same. She unpacked, and scattered her own room and the living room with clothes and records, and seized the telephone to call her friends. Julia loved her for her ability to make easy what she herself had looked forward to with apprehension.

"Still my daughter," Julia said.

Lily grinned up at her. "What did you expect, Mum?"

They enjoyed their time together. Looking back on it, Julia thought it was the happiest they had ever known. She took Lily shopping, and to the ballet, and to see Felix. They visited Marilyn in her new flat, and admired the newborn baby she was looking after. "You were exactly like that," Julia told Lily. "You're much nicer now."

Lily looked amazed, and pleased. "Am I really?"

Julia invited friends to the flat, and cooked meals for them. She thought she had forgotten how to cook. If Lily was surprised that none of them seemed to have visited Camden Town before, she kept her surprise to herself.

The times when they were alone together, with no particular distractions, were the best of all. It was as if, without responsibilities, they were able to see each other more clearly. They talked to each other, and listened. Julia's detachment left her.

She was Lily's mother, after all. There was simplicity in the bare fact. Perhaps she could use it as a foundation block.

Lily was good at listening. Julia explained why she had extricated herself from Garlic & Sapphires as well as selling the old house.

"I didn't care enough about the business just now." Lily nodded wisely. "It was a good thing to realize. I've cared about it too much. You told me that."

"Only because I was angry. I was always really proud about it when I was little. You had all those people working for you, and fabulous things in the shops. All the other mothers just made cakes."

Julia thought, *Our perspectives all change, all the time. Where's the truth? Where should I stow my guilt, now, and you your resentment?* But she only said, "I never was any good at baking. And I'm glad the shops are off my hands for a while." She took a breath. "Lily? I want to ask you something. Are you happy at Ladyhill with Daddy and Clare?"

Lily stared levelly back at her. Julia remembered the old, wary look. "Yes, I am."

"Will you mind, then, if I go to live in Italy?"

"To where you were before?"

"Yes. To Montebellate."

"It's a long way. I'll miss you."

Julia took her hand. It was small and warm, with dirty fingernails. She wanted to crush it against herself, but she made herself let go of it again.

"You can come out there to me whenever you want. Or I'll come home, anytime you need me. I can be home in a day. But I do want to go."

"Were you happy there?"

"Yes."

"Then you should go," Lily said. "I'll be all right."

"I know you will."

And so they arranged it between them. Julia let herself think of the palazzo with its iron-framed beds in the shade of the loggia, and the neglected gardens stepping down the side of the hill toward the sea.

At the end of Lily's visit, gathering her courage, Julia took her back to Ladyhill. The house looked stark in its winter-bare setting as they approached it. Julia felt Lily's warm breath on her face as she leaned forward, smiling at the sight of it.

Alexander and Clare were waiting for them.

They were very polite to one another, all of them. They drank sherry, then sat down to lunch like remote relatives gathered for some uncomfortable family ritual. Julia felt suddenly impatient with it all. She was anxious, now, to get on her way. Clare was wearing riding clothes, with her hair pulled back in a ponytail. Julia thought it made her look like a hamster. She longed for Mattie, and then remembered that Mattie was at Coppins with Mitch. After lunch Clare announced that she would have to go. Julia imagined her pulling on her hard hat and trotting away. Clare shook her hand without looking at her.

Women as rivals, Julia thought with a flicker of amusement. Even Mattie and me. Except I'm no one's rival any longer. I'm noncombatant. The feeling of lightness came back to her, pleasurable now. She was cut loose, ready to float away. She caught sight of Alexander, watching her.

When Clare and Lily had gone, they went into the drawing room with their coffee. There was a pewter jug filled with wands of winter jasmine on the table in the window. Julia imagined Clare going out into the garden to cut them.

She told Alexander, "I'm going back to Italy."

Alexander didn't say anything. He put his cup down and stood looking out into the garden over the golden spikes of the jasmine. Then he turned around and came to Julia. He stood close to her, and she saw the indentations of fine wrinkles at the corners of his eyes, and the minute fading of fair hair into silver stubble at his cheekbones and over his ears. The collar points of his open-necked shirt were frayed.

Julia nodded almost imperceptibly. The animosity had faded. Alexander put his hands on her shoulders, looking into her face. She met his eyes, and she felt the lightness that lifted her up also sharpening her sight. She knew that she was seeing Alexander clearly. And she knew that she still loved him. Anger and bitterness had been her own smoke screens. She hoped that she had learned enough, at last, not to let them obscure her sight any longer. There was that self-awareness, at least; an achievement of a kind. She had lost Alexander first to Ladyhill and then to Clare—not to Mattie, because of course Mattie had never really betrayed her, even though her own anger and jealousy had convinced her of it—but it occurred to Julia that she could finally accept her loss so long as Alexander himself was happy.

"Are we still friends?" he asked her. The question was half-ironic, because Alexander had always deflected the truth with irony. The echo of Mattie, unconscious, twisted the knot of it tighter in Julia.

Not less than friends, she thought. *Not more than that, not now.*

"Of course."

His arms came around her. His hand stroked her hair, holding her head against his shoulder, and she let it rest there. He held her differently from Felix.

With her eyes closed, without moving, she recited the

instructions about how to reach her in Montebellate if Lily should need her. And then, when there was no reason to stay there any longer, she stepped back again.

"Lily's all right, you know," Alexander said.

"Yes. Thank you. It will be good for her to come to Italy to see me," she added. "She'll be able to learn the language." They smiled at each other, acknowledging their mutual pride in her.

I am her mother, and Alexander is her father. Simplicity in the bare fact.

Then, all over again, it was time for her to go. Alexander stood with his arm around Lily's shoulders, then Lily ran forward to Julia. Julia held her, then let her go. The wrench was like a pain in her chest. She thought of her own mother, and the vaguest intention crystallized, in that moment, into determination.

"When do you leave?" Alexander asked.

"Almost straightaway. I just have to go and see Betty about something."

She was on her way again, turning away from the square face of Ladyhill. "Be happy, all of you," she ordered them.

"See you soon," Lily called after her. "Bon voyage."

Julia smiled as she turned the corner under the bare trees. *Bon voyage.* She must have read that in a book.

Alexander and Lily stood watching until the car was out of sight, then went back into the house under the stone arch.

"Do you miss her?" Lily asked abruptly.

"I always miss her," Alexander answered. "I expect I always shall. There's no one like your mother, Lily. No one at all."

Vernon was in his usual chair, drawn up in front of the television. He smiled vaguely at Julia, then returned his attention to *Top of the Pops.* She wondered if he remembered who she was.

The only place for Betty and Julia to talk was in the kitchen. Julia sat at the blue Formica-topped table with the cup of tea that Betty had handed to her. Betty was wiping the drain board. Every worn surface gleamed.

"Won't you mind living with all those foreigners?" Betty asked her.

"I'll be the foreigner," Julia said.

"I'll miss seeing our Lily."

Julia felt guilty. They had managed only a brief visit to Fairmile Road during Lily's holiday. But there was no resentment in Betty's voice. She went on rhythmically wiping, looking out over the net half-curtain at the backs of the houses in the next road.

"I'll tell Alexander to bring her to see you as often as he can."

"It's funny, for a man to be bringing up a young girl."

"He has Clare there with him."

But Betty shook her head, as if she couldn't be expected even to try to understand such oddity.

"There's something I want to ask you," Julia began. "I've wanted to for a long time. I want to try to find my mother."

Betty didn't turn around. Julia wasn't even sure that she had heard, except that the wiping stopped. "Every time I part with Lily, I think about her," Julia went on, knowing what she must do, now that she had begun. "I wonder what she felt when she gave me up. I try to imagine what she feels now. I told you that, didn't I? I just want to know. I've felt the need of it ever since . . . ever since Lily went to live with her father. It isn't that I don't think of you as my proper mother. I do. I always will."

She didn't mention the adolescent dreams she had had, of tragedy and aristocracy, and Victorian family Christmases with one empty place kept in memory of a lost baby girl. Those were over, but the intense visceral pull that she felt toward an unknown woman was not. It grew stronger every day.

Betty hadn't moved. Julia got up and went to her, put her hand on her wrist. "Please," she said softly. "You must know something."

Betty turned sharply and left the room. Julia waited, wondering what to do. From the next room Vernon's program blared out cacophonous music. Then she heard Betty coming back.

"It's too loud, Dad," she said. The din softened a little. Betty came back into the kitchen with a tin box like an old-fashioned deed box. Julia had never seen it before. It must have lived for years in the recesses of Betty's cupboard, between the folded woolens or under the underwear and old-fashioned brassieres. Betty unlocked it and handed her a piece of paper, neatly folded.

"This is all there is. You came to us from the adoption agency when you were six weeks old. I told you that. We never knew your real mother. We didn't want to either. You were ours from the day you were handed to us."

Julia unfolded the thin sheet. It was a birth certificate. She had seen her own birth certificate, of course. It gave her date of birth and her name as Julia Smith, adopted daughter of Elizabeth and Vernon Smith. This certificate was for a child born on the same day as herself. Her name was Valerie Hall, and her mother's name was given as Margaret Ann Hall. The space for the father's details was left blank, and the registrar's office was in Colchester, Essex.

"We called you Julia," Betty said. "We thought Valerie was a bit . . . well, you know."

Julia's hands were shaking. The yellowed paper crinkled faintly as she held it. Valerie Hall was no one, but she had her mother's name in front of her. Margaret Ann Hall, of Colchester, Essex. Or of Colchester thirty-three years ago.

Betty intercepted her thoughts. "It's not very likely that she'll still be there. She might not even have come from there in the first place. Girls who got themselves into trouble in those days went to homes to have their babies. Quite often somewhere away from where they lived. Because of what people said."

A dirty little baby. Had Margaret thought that?

"It's a common name," Julia said. How many Halls in the country? How many Margaret Anns who had given birth to an illegitimate daughter in a home in Colchester?

Very carefully, she folded up the certificate again. "May I keep it?" she asked.

Betty nodded and picked up her cloth once more.

Julia recognized that the chances of her ever finding Margaret Ann Hall were impossibly slim. But she had her name, at least. It was a link, and the pull inside her seemed to slacken a little.

She put the slip of paper into the innermost recess of her handbag. She went to Betty at the sink and kissed her. "Thank you," she said. "It makes it more imaginable, just knowing this much."

Her mother felt very thin and small. Julia was aware of the contrast of her own height, and the size and shape of her bones. They were so different. Was Margaret Hall tall and dark-haired too?

Julia stayed for sandwiches and tea in front of the television. Before she left, she tried to persuade Betty, "When I've found a proper house out there, will you and Vernon come for a holiday?"

"I don't think so," Betty said, without considering it. "I don't think your dad would like it."

*   *   *

A week later Julia came back to the Palazzo Montebellate.

Another ramshackle Fiat taxi deposited her at the gates, and she walked through into the courtyard. It was cold, and there were no chairs or beds in the shelter of the arches, but it was still just the same.

Julia had written to the Madre Superiore, and Sister Mary of the Angels and all the others greeted her warmly, but without surprise. Julia thought that they would have been equally unsurprised if she had arrived unannounced. The sisters were too tranquil for surprise, and too busy for speculation.

She had told the Mother Superior that she would find her own house, if she could, in Montebellate. But they assured her gracefully that she was welcome to the old white room for as long as she needed it. Julia went up the hollowed stone steps and down the long corridor past the Holy Family in its lighted niche. Different children, but with the same wide eyes, sidled past her and then ran away.

In the little room there was the same darned cover on the bed; the view beyond the shuttered windows was only winter browned.

Julia unpacked the first of her belongings and hung them on the hooks. In London, getting ready to travel, she had disposed of almost all her clothes. She had given away the necklaces and bracelets and all the clutter of ornaments that had littered her dressing tables and overflowed from her jewelry boxes for the years of her adult life.

The only thing she had kept was George Tressider's marquetry box, with her wedding and engagement rings folded inside Valerie Hall's birth certificate. Being free of possessions made Julia laugh. It was more intoxicating than champagne, the lightness lighter than the bubbles.

After the first refectory dinner, where she sat again among the wheelchairs, Julia went out into the garden. It was dark, and she felt her way until her eyes accustomed themselves to the blackness. The air had an unfamiliar rawness. But it was still enough for her to hear the sea, far below, patiently chafing at its invisible yellow and silver fringe.

Stripped of their summer leaves, the bones of the neglected shrubs seemed more intricately tangled and knotted at her ankles and over her head. Julia walked slowly down a wide flight of shallow stone steps. Hedges of clipped box had once descended here, but now they had swelled to undulating humps through which the weeds climbed and sprawled. Julia reached up to push a sinewy branch out of her path, and then pulled back with a cry of pain. Thorns had gouged into her arm. She nursed it in front of her, watching the blood well up into black droplets, and then run in glistening trails over the white skin.

She pushed the pain down within herself, and felt it spring up as silent, swelling elation.

All her detachment had gone, in that instant. She wasn't standing apart any longer, condemned to watch her own stiff, puppetlike movements. She was inside herself once more, and she felt the warm, intricate fit of moving parts. She put her arm to her mouth and licked off the salty blood.

"I am alive," she told herself. "I'm here."

Happiness buoyed her up, swelling and spreading to take in the rampant gardens and the thick-walled palazzo on the crest of the hill above her. She turned her head and the claw of a twig scraped her cheek. She reached out to grasp at it, pulling down against her lips and tasting clean raindrops on the cold bark.

TWENTY-FOUR

It was the palazzo gardens that took possession of Julia.

At the beginning she walked only along the terraces when she had finished her day's work with the children, or sat on a step or balustrade to look down at the point where the sea met the land. Then slowly she explored the four corners, and traced the grand design under the dereliction.

Her favorite place became a little space enclosed against the west wall of the palazzo. It was walled but roofless, and the walls were pierced with arched windows to frame the view. There were stone seats against the walls, set in twisted arbors of leafless roses and wisteria. Even on a cold day it was safely sheltered, and when the thin wintry sun shone into it, it caught the warmth and generously amplified it.

Sister Agnes told Julia that it was the palazzo's *giardino segreto*, the secret garden. It was very old, the nun thought. Much older than the rest of the gardens, and perhaps constructed at the same time as the palazzo itself. It would have been an outdoor room, where the ladies sat with their work or took their exercise by walking between the intricate beds. Julia used to sit on the mossed stone of one of the benches and imagine them, until she could almost hear their murmuring voices and the rustle of their silk skirts over the raked gravel.

When the spring came, Julia watched the green fronds of the wisteria unfurl like feathers, and the bronze leaves of the roses unwrapping themselves in the sunlight. She began to pull up the weeds that sprouted through the gravel paths. At the four corners of the garden there were big stone pots, heavy with stone garlands of flowers and fruit. Julia had never looked closely at the gnarled and shapeless trees that grew in the pots, but now they budded and the buds swelled and burst into white flowers flushed with red. The strengthening sunshine distilled their fragrant scent, and Julia realized that they were lemon trees.

She saw that the secret garden was beginning to divulge its secrets, and she let herself be drawn into it, forgetting her imaginings of the *settecento* ladies.

She turned her attention to the beds that formed the heart of the garden. They had been laid out in the intricate, geometric shapes of diamonds, circles, and lozenges, the lines marked by low box hedges and narrow intersecting paths. Julia remembered, although she had no idea how she had first come by the information, that the formal arrangement of beds was called a parterre. But the once-crisp outlines were sadly blurred. The lines that should have been dark and straight had become hummocks that grew together into ungainly mounds, and the plants in the bed sprang out of their circles and squares to choke the paths.

Julia remembered from her first visit that the sad gardens had disturbed her. But then she had only been a visitor, and she had only seen October fade into November. Now she saw the sharp spears of narcissi trying to break through the sheaves of smothering ivy, and a single scarlet tulip standing in a nettle patch, where there must once have been a blazing crescent filled with them.

One evening she went to Sister Maria and asked if any of the palazzo's shadowy storerooms might yield some gardening tools.

"The garden has always taken care of itself," Sister Maria said. "The children like to look after the plants in the courtyard, but there is no time to do any more."

"I have time," Julia said.

The nun looked at her steadily. "Even after what you already do?"

Julia smiled at her. "Even after that. It isn't very much. I wish it could be more. If I was a nurse, or a teacher . . ."

She felt her inadequacy sharply, but Sister Maria cut her short. "All hands are valuable. Come with me, and I will see what I can find for you."

In a windowless room filled with the lumber of decades, they uncovered some ancient implements. There was a hoe and a rake, and a huge, heavy spade. Julia struggled out to her garden with them.

She spent a few moments raking the gravel of one of the paths. The detritus of broken twigs and clods of earth grew into a mound, and the weeds came away with it. The raked lines swirled behind her, and Julia's blood sang with the pleasure of it.

But there were dozens of tiny paths, and after a few minutes she picked up the spade instead. She thrust at it with all her strength, but the edge wouldn't even bite into the baked earth under the matted vegetation. She let it fall with a clatter, and dropped to her knees beside one of the box mounds. She grasped a handful of the coarse grass that smothered the bed, and pulled it up by the roots. At once she smelled a hot, pungent, and familiar scent. She leaned forward, groping among the grass, and found the source of it. It was a clump of thyme. The hoary green leaves gave up their scent as soon as her fingers brushed them.

Of course some of the beds would have been planted with herbs, Julia remembered. There would have been medicinal and pot herbs here, interplanted with other varieties grown simply for their scent or for their beauty. She explored a little further, frowning with concentration, but she could recognize only fever-few, and the gray branches of lavender. The scent of it brought back the memory of Betty's tidy cupboards, the shelves lined with folded paper and perfumed with lavender sachets from the old-fashioned chemist's in the High Street.

Julia sat back on her heels, twisting a lavender sprig in her fingers. The tiny, unlooked-for link between the secret garden and Fairmile Road was oddly pleasing. And the scent of the thyme made her think of Felix's cooking, long ago, when she had watched him, overawed, in the kitchen over the square.

The forgotten herbs were suddenly important, uniting her with home as well as belonging here, in the walled garden. She bent down again, and worked busily at the weeds.

The thought came to her that she could cultivate the plants

once more. If they had been useful once, they could be so again. She went on, digging bare-handed, until her back ached and her fingernails were clogged with the reddish earth. The task reminded her of the herbs that she had grown in the corner of the Ladyhill garden.

The strands of recollection spread outward and then returned again, anchoring her in her place. It was a comforting sensation, to be pinned to the fertile soil. When she straightened up again, pressing her hands into the small of her back to ease the ache, Julia frowned critically at the little patch she had cleared. It was one corner of one of the geometric beds, and even so she wasn't sure that she had uprooted weeds rather than precious plants.

She would have to get Nicolo's help.

Julia and Nicolo Galli had resumed their friendship as if there had been no two-year interruption. When she first met him, after her return, she was relieved to see that he was exactly the same. He held himself just as straight, and moved with the same looseness. He had taken her hand, holding it in his own lean, brown one and smiling at her.

"So, you are back again?"

"I am. I'm going to stay and work at the palazzo, if the sisters will have me."

"I'm happy to see you, Julia."

He had asked her about Lily, and she had told him the story. Nicolo nodded. "You are wise to let her do as she wishes. It will be better for you both, at last."

"I hope you're right."

Julia resumed her evening visits to Nicolo's house. As the weather grew warmer they took to sitting in the courtyard behind it. Nicolo grew a few kitchen herbs in pots, and a vine scrambled up a trellis and hung its serrated leaves over their heads.

On the next visit after her efforts in the secret garden, Julia asked him if he would teach her to cultivate a plot at the palazzo.

"It's different from gardening in England," she said. The fierce heat and the summer's drought contradicted the little she had learned in the lush greenery of Ladyhill.

Nicolo laughed at her. "I make buildings, not gardens. I know nothing."

"At least come up to the palazzo and look at the garden with me," she begged him. Nicolo took his straw hat off its peg and strolled up the hill with her.

The nuns stopped to greet him as they crossed the courtyard, and the visitors in the wheelchairs followed him with their eyes. Nicolo was well-loved in the community. In the secret garden he walked for a long time between the ruined beds, and then sat on one of the seats under the hanging purple banners of the wisteria.

"It is a long time since I came out here," he said at last. "I had forgotten it is so beautiful."

Eagerly, Julia told him, "I could clear the parterres, couldn't I? If I could learn what to plant, I could grow vegetables for the kitchen. That would bring the garden alive again, and it would be useful too."

"If you are interested in the history, it would not be quite accurate to grow vegetables here. There would have been some herbs, yes, but mostly flowers for the ladies to enjoy."

"I don't think the families who once owned the palazzo would mind the nuns being here now. I'm sure they approve of the work they do. Perhaps they won't mind if I adapt their garden, too, just a little?"

"Perhaps you are right."

They left the secret garden and walked around the walls to the main part of the gardens. They caught the spicy scent of the cedars that spread on the lowest terrace, and Julia sighed. "I wish I could have seen it all. Before the last owners went away and left it."

"This part is not so very old," Nicolo said. "Perhaps only the same age as me, although I do not remember how it was then. But it was made as a copy of the great gardens of our Renaissance. If you are interested in those, I have a book. But it is in Italian."

"I can puzzle it out," Julia said.

"Perhaps this garden is lucky to have been left just as it is," Nicolo went on. "At just the time that it was made, many of the old gardens were being destroyed. To make way for a new fashion. The English style."

Julia thought of the sweet, damp profusion of an English border wilting under the eye of the Italian sun, and shook her head.

"And, Julia, if you wish to learn how to grow for food, I will take you to meet Vito."

"Vito?"

"Vito is a gardener, but he will not thank you for pretty flowers."

Nicolo took her down to the lowest point on the skirt of

Montebellate, where the last houses of the hill village clung above sheer rocks. Vito was a very old man with a wrinkled nut for a face. The last few teeth left in his gums were as brown as his skin, and his hand as Julia shook it felt like a paw. He looked as if he had sprung from his own earth. When he led them out to the back of his house, muttering in Italian of which Julia could decipher one word in ten, she gasped in astonishment. Vito's garden seemed no more than a series of tiny lips chiseled out of the hillside. But above and below the house, in their precarious lines, fat, bursting vegetables sprang and sprouted. There were early tomatoes ripening below the scarlet flowers of bean rows, tiny crisp lettuces, and swelling marrows nested in straw, little knobby cucumbers and strawberry plants and other glossy leaves and urgent shoots that Julia didn't even recognize. There were espaliered peach trees against a wall of rock, and on a tiny plateau a fig tree and a walnut tree reached upward, with dusty brown hens scratching at their feet. There were tangles of canes, shelters constructed of flapping polythene, and snaking coils of hosepipe underfoot. It was makeshift, without a single ornamental concession, but it was one of the best gardens Julia had ever seen.

She put her hand out to the earth in one of the beds. It crumbled in her fingers. It was dark, and rich, and seamed with straw. It couldn't have been less like the unyielding crust of her parterres.

Her nursery Italian was hopelessly inadequate, but she tried to explain what she wanted. Vito listened, and then said something to Nicolo. It sounded to Julia like a series of snorts and whistles.

"What does he say?"

Nicolo was trying not to laugh. "He says, approximately, that he can't teach you. The only way you'll learn is by watching. And if you must watch him, you'd better not get in the way."

Julia beamed at them both. *"Molto grazie,"* she said, and meant it.

From then on, Julia divided her spare time between the secret garden and Vito's vertical wonderland. She sat on an upturned bucket beneath the fig tree and watched as he dug and pruned and irrigated. Occasionally, and then more often, he would grunt over his shoulder in her direction. She learned the Italian words for all the vegetables, and began to understand what he was telling her. She sampled the first tomatoes, and tiny sweet strawberries hot with the sun.

One day she went with Nicolo to the market in Agropoli. From a stall clanking with agricultural tools she bought two shiny spades and a pair of shears, and some trowels and hand forks and a big coil of hosepipe. They hurried home again, armed with her trophies.

In the evenings, when it was cool, she clipped the box edgings of one section of the parterre. It was hypnotically fascinating to see the crisp shapes emerge. Julia felt as close to the intricate pattern as if she had drawn it and planted it herself. She worked on and on, promising herself that she would just get to the next corner, but then the curve beyond that enticed her, and the satisfaction of the complete shape that the next angle led to. It was pitch dark when she finally gave in, but the new black lines were sharply etched against the colorless gravel. In the morning she could hardly straighten her back, and there were oozing blisters in the palms of her hands. She was impatient to continue the work, but it would have to wait a little. She opened the history of the gardens that Nicolo had lent her.

She gazed in fascination at the illustrations of the Villa Lente and Isola Bella. The formal magnificence of stone and statuary and massed plants clipped and trained into architectural discipline was unlike anything she had ever seen, only guessed at under the wilderness that had engulfed Montebellate. She turned to the descriptions, but with constant references to her dictionary it took her half an hour to read a single paragraph of the scholarly text.

Sadly, she realized that she needed an English book if she was to make any headway. She wondered how far she would have to go to find one—to Naples, or all the way to Rome? It would probably be easier to order one from England.

It was then that Julia thought of China.

China had sold her flat in Cheyne Walk, claiming that she was too old for London, and bought a cottage in Wiltshire. Julia had seen little of her in the last years. It was Alexander who took Lily to visit Granny Bliss now. He had told Julia once that China spent her time in her flower garden, and Julia had pictured her small, straight-backed figure moving between the blue delphinium spires. But it was also China who had revived the Ladyhill gardens years ago, and during Julia's brief regime the old man who came in to work on the grounds used to talk with uncharacteristic enthusiasm of China's knowledge and expertise.

Julia sat down in her little room one evening and wrote a long letter to China describing the secret garden and the rest of the wilderness. To her surprise, almost by round trip, a letter came back. It was followed by a package of books that seemed to offer Julia more information than she could ever hope to absorb. She read everything eagerly, and wrote back to China with a dozen questions that she had been unable to ask Vito. China replied, and they began a correspondence.

They wrote only about gardening, and the problems that Julia faced at Montebellate in undoing the neglect. There were just two lines in one letter, when China asked if Julia remembered a particular corner of the Ladyhill garden, that were painful to read. They touched a memory, as clear as a photograph. Julia remembered Alexander, with Lily as a baby in his arms, sitting in the same corner. He had settled the brim of the baby's sunhat to keep the sun off her face. There was an expression of mystified pride in his face that made Julia jealous. I was always jealous then, she thought. I'm not anymore. I wish I could show them that. She felt her isolation at Montebellate, thinking of them.

She folded the letter over so that she couldn't see the particular words, and focused her attention on China's instructions for preparing a bed for planting.

The work began very slowly.

Julia enlisted the help of two of the palazzo's longer-term residents. One of them was mentally handicapped, but he was a big man with brawny arms and shoulders. Julia showed him how to dig, and he seized her spade and began to work. He tossed the clods of earth, matted with weeds, into a big heap behind him. His big, loose smile showed that he was enjoying himself.

Her other helper took longer to interest himself in the project, but once he did he became more enthusiastic than Julia herself. Tomaso was fourteen, the oldest of the children. He wasn't ill or handicapped, but like her original lieutenant Raimundo, he had nowhere else to go. Sister Maria told Julia that he had come from Naples, where he had lived with an ailing grandmother. Tomaso had got into trouble with the police, and his grandmother had been unable to control him. He had been removed by the authorities and at last he had ended up at Montebellate, under the care of the nuns.

He was a difficult resident. At the palazzo he was bored and unruly, and he was disruptive at school. But he attached himself to Julia as Raimundo had, and through Julia he had found his way out into the gardens. At first he was dismissive of her efforts, but before long he was unable to conceal his fascination. He had a natural feel for plants that surprised Julia. He seemed to know more by instinct than she did after all her poring over China's books.

She told him that he had green fingers, translating the expression literally, and he stared at his fingers and then back at her with an expression of bafflement that made Julia laugh. Tomaso looked angry for a moment, then began to laugh too.

Tomaso would have worked in the garden all night if she had let him. He was particularly good with the willing, clumsy Guido, directing his onslaughts to the right place, and away from the beds that had already been cleared and planted.

Julia gratefully took whatever plants and seeds and cuttings Vito was prepared to offer her, and tomatoes began to ripen against the wall of the palazzo. It was a proud moment for her and Tomaso when they took the first small crop of tomatoes with some strawberries and fresh basil leaves to the kitchens. The nuns and the women who worked there accepted the tiny offering with grave congratulations.

Julia had pruned the roses, following the instructions in her books, and now the pink and white damasks and albas and fragrant centifolias bloomed in great drifts against the old walls. By contrast the earth in the parterres, although it had been cleared and then manured and lightened with straw just like Vito's, looked barren and reproachful. Julia had managed to save very little of the original growth from Guido's enthusiasm, and her precious vegetables filled only a fraction of the geometric pattern. The freshly clipped box edgings and smooth paths seemed only to emphasize the emptiness.

She began to dream of the flowers of the original design. Her books showed her geraniums and marigolds and petunias in carpets of color. Nicolo gave her geraniums from his own plot, but the space of the secret garden swallowed them up.

Next year, she told herself, I will have planted my own seeds. I'll take cuttings and propagate them, somehow, and I'll have enough of everything to fill the beds. But what can I do now?

China had warned her that every novice gardener made the mistake of wanting rewards at once, and she smiled to recognize the failing in herself. But the recognition didn't stop her from pursuing what she wanted.

She overcame her diffidence, and her mistrust of her Italian, and began to ask around the village. "Can you spare some plants, signora, for the nuns' garden?"

The wheedling and persuading reminded her of the beginnings of Garlic & Sapphires. She found that the small victories in Montebellate gave her even more satisfaction. At first she was greeted with shrugs, or blank stares, but Julia was careful always to call it the nuns' garden, and the sisters were deeply respected in Montebellate. And the villagers were interested in what the peculiar Englishwoman was doing behind the palazzo walls. Slowly, bearing straggling greenery and lumps of earth, they began to wander up to the palazzo. They peered into the secret garden, warily at first and then more confidently. They met one another, and gestured with admiring surprise at the roses and the parterres. The residents followed them, and the walled garden suddenly became a social focus. The nuns nodded and smiled, and Julia and Tomaso and Guido found themselves welcoming visitors with gifts of plants at all hours.

Julia accepted everything that was offered, and put it in the beds. The empty circles and diamonds filled up under her care and Tomaso's watering, sprouting a blanket of random colors and scents that should have been hideous but was unexpectedly vivid and satisfying.

Next year, the year after, there would be time to make a white bed, another of misty blue, and the circle that formed the eye of the design would be a great splash of solid scarlet.

Julia realized that her plans would take a long time to bring to reality. She looked forward to it calmly. If her life in Montebellate lacked the intimacy of real happiness, it had its own different satisfactions, and a kind of richness that she had never known before.

By the time the summer came, she felt that she was woven into the life of the palazzo. If the garden occupied her thoughts, most of her time was still spent with the children. The fitter ones followed her as if she were the Pied Piper. They sat in the secret garden while the shade of the morning still lay on it, and Julia taught them songs and clapping games. Another parcel came from China. It contained dominoes and checkers and snakes and ladders, *For your Italian children,* China said. The thoughtfulness of the gesture touched Julia, and made her wonder why she had never made friends with China before. At the palazzo, the acts of friendship seemed simple. She wrote back at once, a warm letter that described her days in the children's wing, and enclosed some of their drawings done as thanks. The games became a craze, and Tomaso proved to be so good at checkers that not even Nicolo could beat him. Nicolo taught him to play chess, and in the evenings they solemnly faced each other in one of the rose arbors while Julia weeded and watered her flower beds.

The children who could walk and play games were the lucky ones. There were others who had to be pushed in their cumbersome chairs, and whose lolling heads didn't lift to look at the bright splash of the flowers. Julia took them close to the beds, hoping that the rich scents, at least, would find their way to them.

There were other children too. Julia saw less of these, because the nuns nursed the chronically sick ones. But sometimes she went into the two small wards to read stories, or to help with bathing or changing beds, or to walk a few shuffling steps, taking the weight of a seemingly weightless little body. Julia had learned to accept the suffering that she saw in the adult wings. When an old woman died, sitting in her chair under the arches of the courtyard, she watched the nuns' faces as they lifted her up. There was no pain in them. Julia couldn't share their faith, but she tried to find some of their serenity. But the sight of the children filled her with pity and anger.

When she bathed a little girl whose ribs were like sharp fingers and whose head barely turned as warm water dripped from Julia's sponge on to her skin, there was no calm in her. She thought of Lily, and her round, firm arms and legs, with a mixture of terror and need and love.

Pia was seven or eight years old. Her body was covered with the oozing scabs and patches of eczema, and her fingers raked constantly at the inflamed skin. Julia used to cut and clean her fingernails, and bathe the red flesh with cool water to soothe it. Pia always wanted to hear the same story. Julia read a version of "Rapunzel" to her over and over again. The little girl was fascinated by the idea of Rapunzel's long ropes of golden hair. She would pull at her own, the stiff dark spikes parting to show the blotched scalp, as if tugging at it and wishing hard enough would make it change color and grow.

Julia tried to interest her in "Cinderella," but she only ever wanted "Rapunzel." Pia suffered from asthma too. One evening, when Julia went into the ward to say good night, the curtain was drawn at the side of her bed. Pia was having an attack. Julia stood for a moment, listening to the pitiful struggle for each breath, her fists clenched at her sides. She turned away again and walked slowly out of the ward. Sister Maria was with Pia; Julia had heard her voice.

Julia was carrying the Rapunzel book. She looked at the faded cover, then slipped it into her pocket.

She had reached the foot of the stone stairs and walked out into the evening light when she heard running footsteps behind her. It was Sister Maria, with the white folds of her headdress billowing. It was the only time Julia ever saw one of the sisters run. Sister Maria reached the door of the rooms where the palazzo's doctor lived. A moment later the two women were running back again.

Julia sat down heavily on a bench under one of the arches. She watched the shadows lengthen on the stone flags, listened to the sounds from the open windows overhead. When she looked up again, she saw the priest crossing the courtyard with his bag. He was a young man with spectacles and a pale, serious face. He was a friend of Nicolo Galli's. Julia waited without moving. It seemed a long time before Sister Maria reappeared in the doorway that led up to the children's wards. She didn't see Julia. She stood with her head bowed, then lifted her face to the light. The sky overhead had faded from blue to pearl.

Julia felt like an intruder, but she couldn't sit motionless any longer. She walked across the courtyard and touched the sister's arm.

"Pia is dead," was the answer.

Pia's mother lived in an inland village a dozen kilometers away. Her daughter had died before she could reach her.

Julia shook her head. She could hardly take in the words, even though she had known what must be happening. "Why?" she asked stupidly. "She was well yesterday. I read 'Rapunzel' to her."

Sister Maria looked at her. The nun's oval face was smooth and her eyes were clear. "It is God's will," she said.

Seeing nothing, her eyes hot, Julia went out into the secret garden. Guido was brushing petals from the paving. He saw her, and his face split into his empty, happy smile. There was no sign of Tomaso. He must be playing chess at Nicolo's house, Julia thought mechanically. She would have welcomed his company. She went back through the stone doorway and out into the main part of the garden. She walked faster, then began to run. She ran down the steps of the terraces, her feet catching in the brambles. The prickles tore at her bare ankles. She was thinking of Pia, the beads of blood that her scratching brought welling out of her

552 / ROSIE THOMAS

skin, and the rending gasps for breath that were now silenced. The pity for her short life brought grief and anger welling up in Julia, bringing with them all the other angers and grief that she had known.

The world turned black, and hostile.

She was sobbing when she reached the last terrace that hung out over the smooth sea. She wanted to lash out against the amorphous weight of injustice. As if her efforts could affect the disposition of justice in Pia's favor, in favor of any of the others, she began to pull at a mass of bindweed and thistle that grew at her shoulder. Something was hidden beneath it. With her bare hands she went on tearing at the weeds until she caught a glimpse of greenish marble. The tears dried on her face as she worked.

At last, the forgotten statue was revealed again. It was a boy, with plump limbs and a sly, secretive face. Julia smoothed her hands over the cold marble, wondering if he was Mercury, or Pan, or Cupid. He stood like a wicked sentinel, guarding the terraces from the sea. She looked upward, over the cracked stones and the laced fingers of green, invading shoots.

It is God's will.

She had none of Sister Maria's faith. She would have to search for her own answers to the enormity of a child's gasping death.

And as she stood there, a kind of calm possessed her. She listened to the sea, and spread her fingers out over the stone wall. The earth under her feet was warm, and she could hear the faint rustle of the spreading leaves. She could almost have believed that if she listened hard enough, she would hear the blind roots burrowing beneath her feet, and the music of the earth turning.

There was a solace in that. The turn of the seasons was lovely, and immutable. The cycle renewed itself beyond human reach. Beyond Pia. Beyond herself.

Julia stood up straight. She was convinced, as she went on looking upward, that it was not enough to play in her walled garden with a boy and simple Guido to help her. Nothing less than a complete restoration of the whole garden would be enough. She would make it live again. That would be her challenge, and her offering.

Julia stayed out in the garden until it was completely dark. Then she went back up the ruined terraces to the black bulk of the palazzo against the midnight sky. She let herself silently into the chapel. There was a nimbus of candlelight glowing around the Blessed Family. She knelt down in front of it and said her own kind of prayer for Pia.

Before she went to bed in her bare room, she put the Rapunzel book away in George Tressider's marquetry box. She didn't want to read the story to anyone else.

Julia went to see the Mother Superior, and they talked about the ruined gardens.

"It will be a very great job," the Mother observed. "It will need men, experts as well as workers. And money."

"I'm not an expert," Julia said slowly. An idea was beginning to take shape. "But experts can always be found, and workers too. It takes only money." She went on quickly, the idea already more than an idea. She was convinced of what she must do. "If I could find enough to pay for everything, all the work, should it be spent on the garden? Or would it be better given to the *ospedale*, to assist the work that you do here?"

The nun considered, then she smiled, a surprisingly worldly smile. "I think that our *ospedale* will continue in any case. And perhaps if some generous person were to give us money for it, we would lose our little assistance from the authorities. But a benefactor for the gardens, that could affect nothing, could it?"

"No, of course not," Julia said gravely.

"Do you have all this money, Julia? You do not have the look of a rich woman." There was no surprise, or curiosity even. Only the calmness that Julia loved.

"I have a business, in England. Some shops. I gave many years to them, perhaps too many. I think that now the time has come to sell. If I did sell, Mother, I would like to use my money to pay for the gardens."

More than like, Julia thought. It would give me more happiness than almost anything else I could imagine.

She said, "The work would take a year, perhaps. We could employ local men, and Signor Galli might advise us where to turn for expert assistance. And once the restoration is complete, I think that the gardens could be maintained by two, perhaps three workers. Maybe one man with help from some of the residents here, like Guido and Tomaso. And myself, of course."

The plans came to her mind ready-formed, as if her subconscious had established every detail.

The Mother Superior looked at Julia. "Do you intend to make our gardens your life's work?"

Julia thought of the simplicity of life in the palazzo, the friends that she was beginning to make inside its walls and in the houses that clung around them, and then of the sweep of the terraces overlooking the sea. She remembered her empty flat in Camden Town, and the dull, busy streets. There was nowhere she wanted to be except Montebellate.

Only Ladyhill, and that was impossible.

"If you will let me," she answered.

The nun smiled again. It was agreed that Julia and Nicolo could begin to plan the restoration of the entire garden.

The sale of Garlic & Sapphires was less easy. The business was doing better than it had ever done, since the very beginning. For Julia, in her isolation at Montebellate, it had been both reassuring and saddening to read the reports and balance sheets that were forwarded to her, and to realize that she was no longer needed. It would be a relief, in a way, to cut herself off altogether. But Julia still cared enough about her business to want to find the right buyer. It had taken enough years of her own life, and too much of Lily's childhood, to be worth less than that.

The sale took weeks of long distance calls, while independent valuations took place, then more talks, and finally haggling between solicitors. Julia made two brief trips to London, seeing no one while she was there and feeling each time as though she were visiting a foreign city. At last, at the beginning of the summer, a deal was struck. Julia's shops would be owned by an astute, cold-eyed young businessman and his warmer, vaguer, artist wife. Julia thought that they would do well together. At least her creation would not be swallowed up and obliterated by a bigger chain.

The contract was signed, and a very large sum of money was credited to Julia's Italian bank account. It arrived none too soon. The money left over from the sale of the house by the canal had already been poured into the gardens. Julia flew back to Italy with the sense that she was going home for good.

Then it was July, and Lily's summer holiday. To Julia, it seemed a painfully long time since she had seen her, and yet the months had gone so quickly that she had had no time to look for the village house that she had intended to make into a home for herself and Lily. Julia went to see the Mother Superior again.

"I could ask Signor Galli if Lily might stay in his house . . ."

"But you would like to have your daughter with you here,

of course. There are other guest rooms. We have no shortage of space for our friends, Julia.''

"Thank you," Julia said.

She borrowed Nicolo's car, and drove to Naples to meet Lily's plane.

Lily came out in a press of other travelers, but Julia saw her immediately. They ran to each other, and as she hugged her, Julia felt Lily's new height, and her adult shape emerging from the childish roundness.

"You've grown," she said.

"And you're thin, Mum. And you're so brown."

"I've been working very hard. Look at my hands." Julia held them up. The fingers were stained with earth and the nails were cracked and split. Lily looked at them, amazed.

At the parking lot, beside Nicolo's rusty Fiat, Lily asked, "Is this your car?"

Julia laughed. "It's a special occasion; I borrowed it. I haven't got a car. I haven't got a house either. You're coming to stay at the palazzo."

In her letters Julia had described everything. She had telephoned Lily, too, and told her about the sale of Garlic & Sapphires. To her surprise, Lily had received the news as if she had been expecting it.

"You didn't care so much about the shops anymore, did you?" she said. "Not like the way you used to when I was little. I thought you loved them more than me."

"I didn't. I was doing it for you."

"I know that now." Lily had laughed, the laughter sounding close at hand, for all the miles that separated Ladyhill from Montebellate.

Now Lily was in the car beside her, peering between the hurtling airport buses at the press of Neapolitan traffic. At Julia's words she turned around in dismay. "We're staying in the palazzo? With the funny people?"

"They're not funny, Lily. They're ill, or damaged, or old. Otherwise just the same as you."

Julia had spoken sharply. It was an inauspicious beginning. "Never mind," she said quickly. "You haven't said anything about you. Tell me everything you've been doing."

Lily's letters had already told most of it. With amusement, Julia noticed fewer references to Marco Polo, many more to Lily's friend Elizabeth and their doings together. It made her think of Mattie and herself, at Blick Road Grammar School.

"Have you seen Mattie?"

"Yes, she came with Mitch. He's nice. Mattie's got a Jaguar, a white one."

"Mattie has? Can she drive it?"

Lily laughed a lot. "Not very well."

Julia had written to Mattie, but Mattie had never been a great correspondent. Her notes in return were superficial, sometimes illegible. The veil that had descended between them showed no signs of lifting.

Lily chattered on as they drove. When they came to the coast she leaned forward in her seat. "Look at the sea. Isn't it blue?"

Julia pointed at the conical hill rearing ahead, with Montebellate crowning it. As they began to wind up the hairpin bends, with the scents of wild thyme and curryplant drifting through the open windows of the car, Lily's talk died away. She looked nervous, peering upward. She asked abruptly, "Mummy? Are you all right?"

Julia touched her hand. "Everything is all right."

But the first days of the visit were not a success.

Lily stood in the doorway of Julia's room. She looked at the narrow bed and the single chair drawn up to a table spread with gardening books and plans.

"Is this all there is?"

"Yes, because it's all I need. Not everyone lives in nice houses in London, or in manor houses in Dorset."

"I know that," Lily said mulishly.

"Do you?"

At the refectory supper she sat in silence, hardly touching her food.

Julia had her work to do, and she went calmly on with it. During the day Lily shadowed her, or else she sat apart in the secret garden. Julia knew that she was sulking, felt angry with her, and then relented. It was Lily's holiday, after all.

"I'll take you down to the beach this afternoon," she offered. "We can take some of the little ones too."

"I don't want to go anywhere with all those kids. People will stare at us. You're *my* mother."

"And you're my daughter. But we don't own each other, do we? You have proved that for us both."

Lily tried to outstare her. "I don't like it here. All these old people, and sick kids, and nuns. It's creepy. I can't eat my food with them slobbering and grunting all around me. I thought I'd be coming to your house. Like it used to be."

Julia's expression didn't change. "I'm sorry, Lily. I can't remove the people. They belong here, and we don't. And you are twelve years old. You can face a little uncomfortable reality, can't you?"

"Not if it's drool and prayers and snotty kids," Lily muttered darkly.

It was Tomaso who saved the day.

Julia had noticed him watching Lily. He eyed her pale skin and her pretty clothes, and then turned away scowling when anyone caught him at it. Lily pretended not to notice him at all.

Lily had been at the palazzo for ten days when Julia, driven to the breaking point by her sulks, sent her out into the secret garden to do some work. She gave her the shears, and told her to clip some of the hedges. It was an easy if laborious job. It should keep Lily usefully occupied for an hour or so. It was much later when Julia finally finished what she was doing and went in search of her. She wasn't in the walled garden, although the shears were lying in the middle of the parterre. Some of the box had been clipped, surprisingly well. Julia went out on to the highest terrace and looked down. The sea was the pale opal of early evening, and the sky above an infinitesimal shade paler. Lily and Tomaso were leaning against the wall at the bottom, looking out over it.

Julia turned aside and went back up the steps to the palazzo.

Later she said, "I'm glad you've made friends with Tomaso."

"He clipped the hedges for me, that's all." Lily tried to be dismissive, but her need to talk overcame her. If Elizabeth were here, Julia thought, hiding her smile, I'd never hear about anything. Casually, Lily added, "He's okay-looking, don't you think? For an Italian?"

Tomaso had black curly hair, and limpid brown eyes. He had a broken tooth that made his smile rakishly appealing.

"Oh, for an Italian," Julia agreed.

After that Lily's mood changed dramatically. She devised an ingenious hiding and chasing game for the stronger children that led them up and down the garden terraces. And at one refectory supper she took a place beside Guido and talked to him while he crumbled his food into his awkward mouth. And she and Tomaso pretended to bump into each other everywhere, and then glanced quickly away, blushing.

"How do you talk?" Julia asked. Lily knew no Italian, and Tomaso didn't know a word of English.

Lily looked surprised. "We manage fine."

After some thought Julia agreed to let Tomaso take Lily down to the sea on the old blue bus that left the Montebellate square twice daily. And after the first time, the expedition was regularly repeated.

"Does Alexander let you go out with boys?" Julia asked. "Be sensible, won't you?"

Lily looked levelly back at her. "I know what you mean. And I'm not silly."

Not half as silly as I was, Julia thought.

She wrote a letter to Josh. She didn't have to describe Montebellate to him, or the view that spread beneath her open shutters. Josh did reply to the letter, many months later. He told her that he had been working in Argentina, and then had traveled back very slowly, through Peru and Colombia. Josh had no more ties than he had ever had.

There was the inevitable evening when Lily came home with her red mouth swollen and her eyes starry.

Julia sat with Nicolo with the planting plans and designs from the experts in Rome spread out in front of them. She told him about Lily and Tomaso.

"What do you feel about it?" he asked.

Julia put her hands over her face, rubbing under her eyes. "Old," she answered. "I'm thirty-three."

Nicolo put his hand on her bare shoulder. His touch was dry and light, like a falling leaf. "How old do you think it makes me feel, to hear you say that?"

Julia took his hand between her own. "You'll never be old."

"I am quite ancient," Nicolo said cheerfully. "Too old, sadly, for anything except friendship."

"Friendship is enough."

Nicolo sighed. "Try to tell that to Lily and her Tomaso."

Lily spent six weeks at the palazzo. By the end of the time she was as brown as Julia, and she seemed to have grown up again. To Julia, she seemed to be on the very heartbreaking edge of the divide between girl and woman.

On the morning of her departure, everyone who could came out into the courtyard to say good-bye to her. Tomaso waited at the edge of the crowd, hanging back to the very last moment. Then, when Lily looked around for him, he edged forward. He kissed her, very formally, on both cheeks and then stepped back again. Lily hesitated, and then nodded. Her smile had turned shy again. She held her head up and walked quickly after Julia. In the car, on the way down the hill, she cried a little, very quietly. Then she dried her eyes and watched the sea receding.

"I can't wait to see Elizabeth," she announced at last.

At the airport, on the point of saying good-bye, Lily asked suddenly, "Can I come back another time?"

"Of course you can. Whenever you want. Next time I'll have a house for us. Perhaps I shouldn't have expected you to spend your holidays in the hospital."

Lily beamed at her. "I'm glad you did."

After she had gone it occurred to Julia that they had, all unexpectedly, come close to friendship.

All through the summer and on into the autumn the consultations with experts and the garden planning went on. Nicolo had found a garden historian in Rome, and he came and spent a week among the palazzo papers researching the original plantings. Through his discoveries the Montebellate gardens were linked back to the classic gardens of Northern Italy on which they had been modeled.

Designers and horticulturists came, bringing with them stone-masons and marble masons who examined the cracked pillars and urns, and began the exhumation of the classical statues from their crypts of weeds.

When the summer season was over, the workmen moved in to begin the job of clearing the ground. Fredo, Vito's nephew, who closed down his beach pizza bar in mid-October every year, came to lead the gang of laborers. Rotavators were towed in, and trucks loaded with topsoil and fertilizer and fresh gravel ground their slow way up the hill to the village.

Julia and Nicolo and the nuns watched with childlike excitement as the magnificent bones of the garden were raked bare. And as the work of clearing went on, plans for the restored planting arrived. In the late evenings, under Nicolo's red-shaded lamps, they pored over the lists of santolinas and lavenders and helichrysums, cistuses and helianthemums and hundreds of bulbs.

Julia paid the huge bills, signing the checks with a flourish of satisfaction.

At the end of the autumn the first batches of plants arrived from the nurseries. These, and the spring bulbs, would be planted out while there was still some warmth in the ground. The rest would wait until the end of the short winter. She walked out in the sharp early mornings, with the thin mist wrapping around her ankles and the white sea like flat metal under the colorless sky. Fredo and his uncle Vito knelt to unwrap the earthy balls of plant roots, and pressed them gently into the planting holes. Julia worked beside them, firming the moist earth around the neck of each plant, touching the crowns of cropped shoots as if to bless them. Fredo smiled at her as she sat back on her heels and rubbed her forehead with earth-blackened hands.

In the first summer after the planting the garden lay fresh and raw, with the statues standing blindly in the haze of new green. Julia watched with fierce pleasure as each new shoot uncurled. She walked the terraces, up and down, seeing the hard lines of the long walls and wide steps soften with foliage, and the gray and white of stone and marble fade by contrast with the brilliance of blossom.

Under the hot sun she felt the garden's vitality inside herself as well as all around her. She felt an erotic charge that made her lift her head and straighten her back, aware of the pressures and recesses of her body under her faded cotton dress.

Fredo came up from his beach bar in the evenings to help with carrying the tubs of dirty water from the palazzo for siphoning on to the beds. He watched her all the time, smiled at her more often.

One evening, when the late darkness was falling, he caught her alone on the lowest terrace just within the sound of the sea. She was working not far from the point where she had first seen Lily and Tomaso together. She stood up as soon as she heard him approach, but he was already close and they almost bumped together.

"*Sera*," Fredo murmured. She twisted her head away, then looked back at him, feeling the heat in her cheeks. Fredo had muscular, thick shoulders and damp black hair showed at the neck of his shirt. The hair tangled with a gold chain on which hung a crucifix. She had often seen it dangle while he worked, before he tucked it away again in his shirtfront. There was a white, crescent-shaped scar in the brown skin at his jawline. She had never noticed that before. He was so close that she thought she could see the blood pulsing beneath it. She could smell his clean sweat, and see the sheen of it in the hollow of his throat.

Dizzily, she thought, *I could put my mouth there. Taste the salt.* And she thought of the other things too.

Her heart thumped in her chest, and her head swam. It would have been easy to let her head fall forward, by slow, slow degrees, and let it rest against him. The heat of their skins would flash and burn.

Fredo moved the one half-step that brought their bodies into contact. He put his hand at the small of her back, heavy and hot, moving her hips against his. He put the fingers of his other hand on her breast. Julia almost screamed. Fredo's white teeth showed as his mouth opened.

Fredo had a wife and several children down on the coast. Julia put her hand up, closed her fingers around his wrist, and lifted his hand away. She stepped back, into coolness, into safety. She nodded at Fredo. Not angrily, not dismissively. A neutral, concluding gesture. Then she turned away and managed to walk up a flight of stone steps. Another and another, and up to the palazzo. She reached her room and closed the door. There was no lock, so she leaned against it, the palms of her hands pressed to the panels. She realized that she was panting like a dog. After a long time she crept across to her bed and lay down. She lay on her back, stretched out, staring up at the white roof. She ran her fingers over the taut skin inside her thighs, touched herself.

Julia was grateful to Fredo.

It was a long time, longer than she could remember, since she had felt the imperative, unspecific ache of physical need. It made her feel young, after she had decided that she was old. She was regenerated, like her Italian garden. Julia thought, with amusement, of the sap flowing again.

After that she was careful not to be alone near Fredo. Not because she was afraid of him, but because she didn't trust herself.

Before Lily's summer holiday that year, Nicolo found Julia a house. It was a little way down the cobbled street from his own, a small white building full of awkward angles sheltering in the corner between two higher walls. It belonged to an old woman who was moving inland to live with her daughter. Nicolo helped Julia with the legal formalities involved in the purchase, and Julia sold her Camden Town flat to pay for it. When the house became hers she repainted it with fresh white paint, and put small iron bedsteads in the two bedrooms. She left the primitive kitchen just as it was, and left the walls bare because she had forgotten how to make magpie collections of things to adorn them. But she did paint the front door the harebell-blue that she remembered from the Pensione Flora.

She wrote another letter to Josh, and after a long time he wrote back.

Julia never wrote to Alexander. Sometimes he sent her short, formal notes, enclosing Lily's school reports or other evidence of her progress. She always read his letters very carefully over and over, but they never yielded more than the bare words.

Julia thought that it was as if they had both retired behind their own ramparts, herself to the remoteness of Montebellate, and Alexander deeper into the old stronghold of Ladyhill. He never mentioned Clare, but Julia imagined her as a newer fortification.

Clare wrote, too, sometimes. Clare evidently thought that it was her duty to keep Julia informed about Lily's elocution lessons, the date of her first period, her first dance dress. Clare's handwriting was as unformed as Lily's own, her spelling even more erratic.

Lily herself came out for her second summer, and her friendship with Tomaso renewed itself. He used to come down from the palazzo to visit them in the little house. By the next year in the gardens the thin shoots had swelled into branches, and the flowers lay along the terraces in hot, shimmering sheets of color. Marigold, peony, pinks. Julia moved among them, sometimes half-dazed by the abundance.

Against one wall of the palazzo a functional greenhouse was built. Julia and Tomaso learned to strike cuttings, to propagate seeds. Tomaso was much better at it, but Julia loved the fecundity of the seed trays and earthenware pots.

She was happy; a passive, unfocused happiness.

Another year. Julia sometimes lost track of days, even of weeks. Her calendar became the seasons, measured out by the demands of the gardens. They were reaching their full, forgotten glory now. They began to attract visitors, and an entrance fee was charged for the benefit of the *ospedale*. Julia and Tomaso worked full-time on the terraces and parterres. Tomaso was paid a wage, by Julia. For herself, she lived very frugally. She ate in the convent refectory, burned wood in winter in the stove in her little house. Tomaso moved out of the palazzo into a room across the square. He acquired a moped. That was the summer that Lily was fifteen.

At first Julia forbade her to ride with Tomaso on the moped. Then she saw that the other girls rode behind the boys, and she relented. The boys and girls used to gather in the evenings, in the square beyond the palazzo gates. They stood in the shade of the plane tree, where Julia had first seen the old woman and her tethered goat, laughing and talking and listening to pop on tinny transistor radios. The mopeds coughed and whined around and around the square. Julia saw Lily absorbed into the crowd. She was proud of Lily; of her ease among the Italian girls and boys, of her natural good spirits, of her beauty. She liked to see her with Tomaso and the others, enjoying the evening and the summer's richness.

Julia would wave, and walk on down to her little house. Sometimes Nicolo would come to have dinner with her. He looked older now, and his joints had lost some of their elasticity, but he was as acute as he had ever been. Julia loved his company. Without him, for all her friendships with the nuns and the patients and the villagers, she would have felt her isolation.

It was during the moped summer that a letter came for Julia. The stamp was Italian and the print on the back flap read Hotel Garibaldi, Rome, so at first she didn't register the handwriting on the envelope front. Then she looked more closely and saw that it was indeed from China.

China announced that since she was, as she put it, getting so horribly old, she had decided to take one last continental holiday. Traveling alone, she had been to Paris and Florence and Siena. She had visited old friends, and been to the Louvre and the Uffizi, had looked for the last time at Brunelleschi's dome. She was now in Rome, and would Julia be willing to show her the famous gardens if she came to Montebellate for a night or two? She would put up in a hotel, of course. And at the same time she could see Lily, and Julia herself if that would not be an inconvenience.

From Nicolo's house, because she still didn't have a telephone of her own, Julia called the hotel at once. She told China that she must come to stay in her house, and that it would give her more pleasure to show the gardens to her than to anyone else in the world.

Two days later Julia and Lily drove to Naples to meet her.

China was in her seventies, but she still held herself erect, with her head up. She commanded the same speculative glances too. She was immaculate after the short journey. Her gray-blond hair had turned silver, but she kept it in the neat chignon. She was wearing an uncreased cream suit, with crocodile shoes. Her ankles were still trim, in fine, pale stockings. She made Julia feel, acutely, her own complete lack of grooming. But China kissed her cheek and murmured, "You look well, Julia."

Lily's bedroom in the village house was little more than a cupboard, so Julia gave up her bedroom to China and slept downstairs. China demurred, but she was clearly touched by Julia's hospitality.

Julia smiled at her. "There are no proper hotels in Montebellate."

"Thank heaven," Lily said. "Otherwise the place would be full of tourists, wouldn't it?"

The three of them laughed, and sat down to eat the meal that Julia had prepared.

Afterward, when Lily had gone off with Tomaso and the others, China and Julia walked slowly up the hill to the palazzo. They made a slow, complete circuit of the gardens. Julia was proud to show them off, and China was a knowledgeable observer. She knew the plants, and their histories, and the formal disciplines of the Italian gardens. The bridge that their letters had established between them held firm, strengthened by Julia's pleasure in her achievement, and China's admiration of it.

At the end of their exploration they stood on the top terrace again, looking at the symmetry spreading below them. China said, "And this was really a wilderness before you came?"

"The skeleton was here, covered in decay. I only put the flesh back. With much help from everyone. From you, China."

China inclined her head in acknowledgment. *I like her stateliness,* Julia thought. *I assumed it was coldness before, but it isn't. She is uncompromising, that's all. When I first knew her I couldn't even see clearly that people exist as themselves, and not just in relation to myself. That's why I never understood her.*

"How long have you been here?" China asked.

"Four and a half years."

China thought for a moment, then inclined her head again. "I congratulate you on your achievement. It is magnificent. And unusually generous."

Julia knew that she meant what she said. She felt a fierce flush of pride. "Thank you."

They passed the arches that looked inward into the secret garden, and the concentrated scents drifted out to them. They went on, back to the courtyard, and Julia took China to meet the different children who still played with her presents of checkers and snakes and ladders.

Nicolo Galli entertained them at dinner with great success. They dined in the refectory, the next night, with China sitting straight-backed next to the Mother Superior. But Julia and Lily were unable to persuade China to stay in Montebellate for longer than three nights.

"I'm keeping you from your bed," China said firmly. "And it is time I went back to my own garden."

Julia understood that.

On the third evening, after their refectory supper, Julia and China sat on one of the stone seats in the secret garden. The last of the summer's great flush of roses hung raggedly over their heads. Behind them, the chapel bell tolled. As always, the warm air muffled the peals. Lily had gone with Tomaso, down to the coast to see a film at the open-air cinema.

"Are you happy here?" China asked.

"As happy as I need to be."

Julia had the sense, as she had done all through the three days, that China was observing her.

"Is that a riddle?"

Julia laughed briefly. "I didn't intend it to be. It's just that the necessity for happiness—my own happiness, I suppose—seems diminished here. Through seeing the nuns and what they do, and the lives of the people who come to the *ospedale*. And in watching the gardens. Perhaps I've learned to be a little bit, a very little bit unselfish." She laughed again, trying to dispel the seriousness. "Not before time, you might say."

"When will you come home?"

"Home? There's nothing to come home for."

"And if there were?"

Julia was silent for a moment. Then she said, "I can't imagine what it would be."

"Alexander, perhaps."

The words were spoken lightly, but Julia had the sudden, vertiginous conviction that all China's visit had been leading up to them. Had she come from Rome to suggest as much? From Paris? All the way from her green Wiltshire garden? Julia's heart lurched, and the blood buzzed in her ears.

She managed to say, "Alexander and I have been divorced for a long time."

"Yes. Do you know, Julia, that one of the realities of old age is that one's perspectives change? The problems of other people begin to look very simple, because one's own are over. One begins to imagine that one can solve them. The arrogance of that.''

Listening to her, Julia was trying to remember. What was it that China had said, long ago, at Ladyhill? On Lily's first birthday. *My husband is a difficult man. Yours is not.* Alexander was not simple. None of the knots that he and I have created, Julia thought sadly, can be easily unraveled.

She waited for China to go on, but there was nothing. China was not arrogant, of course. Nor would she interfere.

Julia began to wonder if she made more of the few words than China had intended her to. There was no message from Alexander in them. Alexander would send his own message if he wanted to.

They began to talk about other things, and then they stood up and made a last slow circuit of the secret garden. In the arched doorway, looking back, China said musingly, ''I think you used to be jealous of me, all that time ago. Perhaps we can be friends now? I have enjoyed being here with you and Lily.''

Julia took her hand and held it. ''I'd like that. I was jealous of you and Alexander. I was jealous of everything, once. But I'm not anymore. I don't think I'm even jealous of Clare.''

China's profile was immobile. But she said, ''I don't think you need to be jealous of Clare.''

They walked back through the dusk to the little house. When they reached it, China said she was very tired, and went straight up to bed. Julia sat up, pretending to read, waiting for Lily to come home. The significance of China's words flickered and faded.

There was nothing to go home for. This was home.

When it had been dark for a long time, and she was just beginning to worry, Julia heard Tomaso's moped bumping over the cobbles at the corner.

Lily had followed Tomaso, walking in his footsteps over the sand although she knew the way as well as he did. The sea lay directly behind them, and the moon made a silver streak over it that pointed at their backs.

They were heading for their special place. The sand was soft underfoot now, and they scrambled up the lip of a sand dune with coarse grass brushing their bare ankles. The canopy of pine trees closed over their heads, and Lily breathed in the resinous scent. A few yards ahead there was a hollow, enclosed by the pines. Tomaso jumped lightly down, and held up his arms to Lily. He took her hands and swung her down beside him. They looked around, into the dim emptiness, and then laughed, a little shakily.

Then, very slowly, they knelt down facing each other.

"I love you," Tomaso said in English.

Lily answered him in Italian.

Tomaso took off his jacket and spread it out for her. Lily lay down. Her fingers brushed the sand. The evening air had cooled the surface, but as she burrowed downward she found the stored warmth of the sun. Farther down it was cool again, and damp. She turned her head a little.

They had come here, to the hollow in the pines, often before. They had kissed each other in the sand, licking the salt of the day's swimming off each other's cheeks like warm animals.

Tonight was different. They had decided it. Tomaso had brought a packet of things in the pocket of his jeans. Lily didn't ask where he had got them from.

"Are you sure you want to?" he had asked. "With me?" But his face had split into the disbelieving, delighted smile that Lily loved.

"I do," Lily had said seriously.

It was the truth. Lily loved Tomaso, but even though she would have denied it fiercely, she knew that she wouldn't go on coming back here to him, every summer forever. It was partly because of her sense of the fragility, the impermanence, that she wanted to seal something between them. The first time would always be there.

They had come to the sand hollow by mutual silent agreement. Romantic Lily wanted the place to be right, and there was no righter place than here, with the black pines meeting over their heads and the sound of the sea cutting them off from the cinema, from Montebellate on its hill, from the world.

Seeing her mother and her father's mother together had given Lily a sharp sense of time, of years beginning to click past all of them like the beads on the nuns' rosaries. There was no *always*, Lily realized. Not even at Ladyhill. Especially at Ladyhill. In the last few months there had been another change. Clare had gone, stayed away, then come back again. Lily had begun to see that Clare and her father didn't make each other happy. The recognition had come with a chilly, adult awareness. She had folded it away, never mentioning it to anyone. Here in Montebellate, sharing the little house with her closest female relatives, Lily had understood what shaped her and linked her to the two older women, and because of it she had felt the imperative need to separate herself, and make her own individual claims to experiences and memories. She felt hungry, and jubilant, and melancholy, all at the same time. Granny Bliss looked frail and Julia herself had acquired a sort of unexpectant patience that made Lily unaccountably sad. Simultaneously, she felt inside herself the bursting knot of her own strength and eagerness. Fiercely she whispered, "Tomaso, I love you."

It lasted barely a minute. Tomaso was helpless, and when he came his head reared up and he shouted her name. Lily held him, his weight on top of her, feeling the pressure seeping away inside her. She had felt almost nothing after the first urgency, and then the brief shock of pain, but she didn't care about that. Her fingers fluttered over Tomaso's back. Sweat had gathered in the indentation of his spine, trapped by the developed muscles. She had a sudden memory of Tomaso working, shirtless, in the palazzo gardens. The muscles contracted as he bent and straightened. Julia was there, too, her sunhat shading her face. They both stopped what they had been doing and turned to look at her as she came down the steps. The vision seemed very precious, clear-edged, and significant. Lily screwed her eyes more tightly shut, to store the memory, guessing presciently that it was the one that would come back to her, not this sandy clearing, when she thought of Tomaso.

When she was Julia's age. When she was China's age.

Lily found that she could easily imagine it, now, the way in which the years would click past. She had lost the careless, childish expectation of eternity. I have grown up, Lily thought portentously, and half-smiled at the obviousness of the occasion.

She opened her eyes. The stars were faint points of light between the lacings of the pine branches. She realized that she felt happy, lying there, with Tomaso still inside her. She was glad it was Tomaso. She was glad it had been as she had imagined it. Lily was romantic, but she was also a child of her generation. She had never expected pulsing tides and soaring violins. She and Tomaso had done it together, sealed it between themselves, forever. That was what mattered. There would be other times, other sensations. Other men, Lily was sure of that. But only this first time.

Tomaso stirred, lifted his weight. They separated, very carefully, looking down at themselves. Tomaso tied a knot in the rubber and buried it in the sand.

"We should make a stone, to mark the spot."

"We'll remember anyway," Lily said.

Tomaso took her hand, as if they had only just met, as if she were a princess released from a tower. He thought she looked like the signora. Tomaso always thought of her as the signora, never as Julia.

"Thank you, Lily," he said.

"Thank you, Tomaso," she repeated.

The seriousness burst like a bubble. They laughed, a little wildly, looking at each other's nakedness in the sand. Tomaso brushed the crusting of it from Lily's cheek and stomach.

"Hey. Ouch," she shouted at him. When they had stopped laughing Tomaso seized her by the wrist, hauled her to her feet.

"Swim?" he asked her.

"Race," Lily answered.

They scrambled over the lip of the hollow and ran, over the soft sand, down the beach. The black water was laced with silver foam. They plunged into it, whooping, and the coldness took Lily's breath away. She swam, fierce strokes, then rolled over onto her back and felt the salt wash scouring her. She dived, slick as an eel, and touched the rippled sand. When she burst to the surface again, with Tomaso splashing beside her, she trod water with the cold drift of the sea between her legs. She felt sharp, and clean, and exultant.

After their swim they dried each other with Tomaso's T-shirt. Then, with Tomaso bare-chested, they straddled the moped. Sheltered by Tomaso's warm back, Lily breathed in the hot, vegetable scents of the south as they rode up to Montebellate, where she knew that Julia would be waiting for her.

"Good film?" Julia asked, putting aside her book and smothering a yawn.

"Yes, really good," Lily answered composedly.

"Where's Tomaso?"

"He's gone straight home." Lily went to her, put her arms around her mother's neck. "I love you, you know."

Julia smiled, to Lily's opened eyes suddenly seeming almost shy. "That's good. That's very important. I love you too. You're a good girl, Lily."

Lily looked over her head, out at the darkness pressing against the uncurtained window. "I hope so," Lily said, wondering.

TWENTY-FIVE

The two women had been sitting at the corner table for a long time.

The waiters glanced speculatively at them. When the blond came in, one of them had sketched a suggestive little gesture to his colleagues, but she didn't see it. She had gone straight to the dark one, who was sitting in the corner waiting for her. They had put their arms around each other, holding themselves apart still so that they could look at each other. Then they had started laughing and crying at the same time. When the blond took off her dark glasses and nested them in her mass of hair, one of the waiters insisted that she was a film star, although he couldn't remember her name. The others shrugged. This was Naples's best restaurant. Film stars were not exactly thick on the ground, but they were not unknown either.

The two women made an odd couple. When the blond came in she was swathed in a long, furred jacket against the January cold. Then she took the jacket off, to reveal a tight, dark dress that bared the tops of her breasts. They were full and white, with a blue shadow between them, and when the waiters brought up the silver dishes they leaned forward to peer into the inviting cleft. The dark one was quite different. She was tall, and thin to the point of gauntness. Her clothes were tidy, but slightly faded, as if she required nothing from them but decency. Her hair was cut short, not very expertly, but the ragged points of it framed her dark, arresting face. She had high cheekbones and a long, mobile mouth bare of lipstick. She ordered their food in idiomatic, locally accented Italian, gesturing with her brown hands. The fingers were ingrained with dirt like a laborer's, in bewildering contrast to her friend's shiny crimson talons. But together the two of them spoke English, torrents of it. And they drank too. The blond tipped it back, although the dark one only sipped warily, at the beginning. But then the first glass warmed her, and she began to keep pace with her friend. The wine waiter brought a second bottle, then a third.

They laughed, too, the two of them. Their laughter grew

louder, attracting covert glances from the other tables, but by
then the long Neapolitan lunchtime was almost over, and the
restaurant was beginning to empty.

"Oh, Mat," Julia sighed, leaning back in her padded chair
with a full glass. "Why has it been so long?"

Seeing Mattie across the table, with her same hazy, sexy,
reckless and shortsighted smile, and the light behind her turning
her hair into a fuzzy halo, Julia thought she looked no different
from when they had first known each other. At the very beginning of their real lives. And their real lives had twisted together,
still knotted and curled together. The breach was forgotten. It
seemed long-ago and trivial, now that they were here together.

"Five years," Mattie answered. "A bloody long time. But
we wrote, didn't we?"

"I wrote."

"But if you insist on interring yourself out here, and never
come home . . ."

"Home is where you are, Mat," Julia said sentimentally.

Mattie raised her glass. "Here's to home sweet home."

They drank gleefully. Five years seemed no longer than an
afternoon.

The elegant room was deserted when their waiter brought
the elaborate bill at last, and laid it between them.

"Mine," Mattie said firmly. She unfolded it, then shrugged
and dropped a credit card on top of it. "I'm not much good at
bills and all the rest of it. Mitch does them, or the studio, or
somebody."

"I'm glad you're happy," Julia said, meaning it. They
squeezed hands, rough against smooth, on the white tablecloth.

"Let's go home," Julia begged.

"I thought you were home."

Outside, walking into the fresh bite of the brief southern
winter, Julia lurched against Mattie.

"Oh, dear. I'm not used to drinking." Mattie was none too
steady herself. "Good thing I didn't drive up here."

"Didn't you?" Mattie asked, surprised.

"I haven't got a car. I used to use Nicolo's, sometimes. But
it's broken, and we can't seem to get it mended. And the two of
us have stopped being able to think of reasons for ever leaving
Montebellate."

They steered each other to a taxi, asked for the station, and
sank back into the smoky interior.

"Julia, what do you do for money?"

Julia blinked. "I haven't got any. I did have, you know that, from the house and the business. But most of that went on the gardens. Do you have any idea what good topsoil costs down here?"

"Not at all," Mattie said dryly.

"Well. Lots of money. And marble masons, and contractors, and hundreds of dozens of beautiful bulbs. And now the gardens are all lovely. People come to see them, you know? They pay money, and that keeps one gardener. Then there's me, and some of the men from the *ospedale* are able to do some of the work. That's all all right. The gardens will be kept up, whatever happens."

Julia had evidently worked it all out. She had worried about it, and then rationalized it for herself. Mattie looked at her again. Her thinness and her odd clothes seemed suddenly to do with need rather than deliberate eccentricity.

"Jesus, Julia. How much do you want?"

Julia laughed, bewildering Mattie with her obvious, genuine amusement. "I don't need anything," she said. "Nothing at all. It makes everything very simple. I have reeducated myself." She was as triumphant, in her own way, as Mattie had been. They linked hands once again, and looked at each other.

At the station they found the train, and seats side by side. They had barely left behind the heaped-up, teeming Naples tenements before they fell asleep, their heads resting together. At Agropoli Julia jolted awake again, and shook Mattie. They yawned and rubbed their eyes, dazed and somnolent.

"Just like old ladies," Julia protested.

"Well, I'm staring forty in the face," Mattie said gloomily. "Do you feel it?"

They were standing on the platform, surrounded by Mattie's expensive luggage.

"Do I?" Mattie's face split into her smile again. "Most of the time I feel just the same as I did at the Blick Road first years' party." And then, with the blue-overalled workmen and black-shrouded old ladies trudging past them to the exit, they faced each other, struck a pose, and sang *Ma, He's Making Eyes at Me.*

In the second taxi, grinding up the hairpin bends to Montebellate, Mattie peered upward and then down at the gulf behind them. The sea was shrouded in its white winter mist, and the land lay indistinct under a fine veil of it.

"It's like a fortress in a fairy tale," she said.

"My fortress," Julia answered. She didn't know herself, now that Mattie was here, whether it was a strength or a weakness.

In the little house Mattie looked disbelievingly at the bare walls pressing in on them, the two chairs on either side of the cold stove. She shivered a little, even in her furred jacket, because some of the plains' mist seemed to have followed them and seeped between the blue-painted shutters.

"You're right. You have reeducated yourself."

"I'm sorry," Julia said simply. "You're not seeing it at its best, that's all. It's a summer house. But I don't think much about comfort anymore. Look, I'll light the stove. It takes only a minute to get hot. Are you hungry? Do you want a glass of wine? There's some local stuff. It's not bad."

They sat down, facing each other in the two chairs. The stove's belly glowed a dull red, and the room grew comfortably warm. Mattie took off her jacket and propped her feet on a wooden stool. They drank the bottle of wine and they talked.

They talked, seemingly, without stopping.

The avenues had opened up again, and they wandered down them.

"When I was at Ladyhill, with Alexander," Mattie said, "I wasn't trying to make him mine, or exclude you, or help myself to anything that I knew was yours."

"I know that, Mattie."

Mattie stared at the stove's red center. "We always liked each other, Alexander and me. And we were just there together, in that beautiful place. It was a happy time, that's all." She looked up suddenly. "We were both lonely, I told you that. It wasn't meant to last, although it was sad when it didn't. Most of all, it wasn't meant to hurt anyone."

"I understand," Julia said.

Mattie went on, determined to say now what they had never touched on before. "I didn't know, you see. I'd never thought, until the moment I saw you watching us through that glass door. That you still loved Alexander. Even though I knew you so well. Thought I knew you so well."

Julia cut her short. "It's long ago, Mattie."

But Mattie persisted. "Do you still?"

Julia gestured at the room, the bare essentials that furnished it, illustrating from it the bare essentials by which she had learned to exist. "I'm here now."

"You don't have to be."

Julia smiled. "I don't think I know how to do anything

else, after five years." She stood up, leaving her creaking chair and crossing to Mattie's side of the stove. She put her arm across Mattie's shoulders and rested her cheek against the familiarly scented, intemperate hair. "I'm so glad you're here. I've missed you so much. We're still friends."

It was a statement at last, not a question.

"Yes." That was all Mattie said. They wouldn't need to talk anymore to fill the breach.

Julia said later, as lightly as if it were any piece of gossip, "Lily told me that Clare isn't at Ladyhill anymore. She told me, in fact, that Clare is on the point of marrying someone else."

Mattie raised her eyebrows. She peered at Julia, focusing as sharply as she could through the haze of local wine. "And so?" she demanded. But Julia's face looked smooth, and perfectly tranquil.

"And so here we are in our separate strongholds. Me in Montebellate, and Alexander, I imagine, at Ladyhill. It's safe, Mattie." She brandished her glass at the thick walls, to the wintry silence beyond them. "It's perfectly safe, living like this."

"Oh, well," Mattie answered, despairing of her. "If it's safety you want. I'm going to go upstairs to bed."

Julia led the way up the narrow stairs, into her own bedroom. She had moved out into Lily's space, in Mattie's honor. She showed her the rudimentary bathroom, and Mattie eyed it without enthusiasm. Julia remembered the flush of dolphin-headed taps and tinted double handbasins at Coppins.

"Hmm. Does Felix approve of this?" Mattie frowned.

"He does rather, as a matter of fact."

Felix had visited Montebellate when he could, although not very recently. Apart from Lily, Felix was still Julia's most reliable link with the world that had once been hers.

"He would. He's gotten very minimalist lately."

"You wouldn't go for that. No one could accuse you of minimalism, Mat."

That seemed uproariously funny to both of them. They laughed so much, standing in the cramped angle of the stairs, that they had to hold on to each other for support. Julia was still smiling when she fell asleep, with the curling photograph of Tomaso pinned to Lily's wall staring down at her.

In her short stay at Montebellate, Mattie seemed to re-create the old days so vividly for Julia that they became almost more real than the palazzo and the terraces and parterres. Julia took her out into the gardens. They leaned over the top terrace, looking down at the bare earth and the pruned branches, the startling green of the first spring shoots showing between the cold statues. Mattie shook her head in amazement.

"I can't connect all this with you."

"You're not seeing it at its best, exactly," Julia defended it.

"I can imagine how beautiful it must be. But it's a life's work, Julia."

"Tell me about your work," Julia asked. There were fewer questions for Mattie to ask. Julia's life lay around them, clear to see.

"I haven't done much stage work lately," Mattie sighed. "Mitch doesn't like it when I'm out every evening for weeks. I don't like being away from him either. A month or two of concentrated film work is better, because then he can come with me. But I get sent a lot of shit to read. I did a James Bond a couple of years ago; that was the biggest thing. Did it show out here?"

Mattie mentioned the film's title and Julia frowned. "I'm sure Lily and Tomaso saw that one. They never mentioned seeing you in it."

"Probably didn't recognize me. You should have seen the clothes they made me wear. You think these are tarty." Laughing, they stood up and took a last turn between the parterres, then walked through the silent courtyard and down the cobbled street to Julia's house.

It wasn't until almost the end of Mattie's visit, lubricated with wine again, that Julia said, "Mitch. Tell me about Mitch now."

She had seen it as the last taboo between them, the fact that they hadn't talked about Mitch. She knew that it was in order to get back to Mitch that Mattie was leaving Montebellate the next morning, and she had an uneasy sense of the shadow of him still between them. Julia didn't want anything separating herself and Mattie. Not now, not anymore. And in her turn, Mattie had been sensitive to Julia's isolation. She hadn't wanted to talk too much of her own happiness.

Now she said, "He's a good man. There isn't anything about him I don't love. Nothing I can't admire. There aren't many people to say that about, are there?"

"Almost none," Julia said softly.

"He makes me happy. He's always there, like a rock, whatever happens." She laughed, half to herself. "It's not like at the beginning, when we could hardly get out of bed."

"I remember."

Mattie blushed a little. "That changes. But it's better, even. Coppins is a place for us. We go out if we have to, then we come back, to be together. Mitch does little things in the house, mends things, you know. It's very comfortable. It's very simple, when everything used to be so complicated. You always seemed to know what you wanted, Julia. Even when I was working, I was bouncing from one thing to the next. Men. Sisterhood. Political platforms. Booze."

"I remember," Julia said again.

"With Mitch, I'm solid. He makes it possible for me to do everything else. That's all there is."

Looking at Mattie, at the smooth swell of her calves, and the rings on her fingers that Mitch had given her, and the way her hair coiled and sprang behind her ears, and most of all at the light in her eyes, Julia saw the proofs of happiness and love. And she had come herself to the point of equilibrium, at last, when she felt neither envy nor bitterness. The shadow lifted.

"I'm so glad, Mat," Julia said.

They held on to each other again, wordlessly, as they had done under the waiters' eyes in the Naples restaurant.

"I wish you didn't have to go," Julia whispered.

"Come with me." Mattie gripped her arms. "Why don't you come home?"

There was a silence, and then Julia shook her head. "No, Mattie. I'm going to stay here."

I know where I am, here. I know that because there's no further to go.

They had drunk a lot of wine on that last evening, and before they went to bed they went out into the little street to breathe in the cold air. There were lights in Nicolo's windows, and the voices and music of a television program were audible through another window beyond it.

"The joint is really humming tonight," Mattie murmured. "Hoo. Wow."

They were giggling, leaning against the wall with their hands pressed to their mouths, like schoolgirls. Then they heard someone coming toward them. Julia recognized the faint click of beads before she saw the nun's gray and white habit. It was Sister Maria degli Angeli.

"I've been trying to take Julia away from you, Sister," Mattie called boldly. "Telling her to come home."

Julia's voice was much lower. "I've told her I won't go. I'm going to stay here forever." She knew that the nun must have heard their laughter, and that she saw their unsteadiness as they held on to each other. Sister Maria's face was a calm oval in the darkness. Nothing would surprise or shock the Sisters of the Blessed Family, Julia thought. Nothing that she or Mattie could do.

"Forever? There is only one certainty about forever," Sister Maria said tranquilly.

In the morning Julia went back to Naples with Mattie. She stood watching the Alitalia jet as it tipped its nose upward, kept her eyes on it until it slid into the clouds. Mattie was gone, and Julia was left standing on her small patch of ground. She tried to fix her thoughts on it; on the gardens, waiting for her, and the safe horizons of Montebellate.

Mattie opened her eyes and saw Mitch. He was standing beside the bed, holding a cup of tea. "Hello, my love," he smiled at her. "Tea."

Mattie sat up and took the cup. Mitch often brought her tea in the mornings. They would sit together, drinking it and talking about the day. Mitch sat down on the edge of the bed. He was still in his pajamas and his tartan robe, and his thin hair stood up in feathers at the back of his head, where he had slept on it. Mattie stroked it flat for him.

"It was a stormy old night," Mitch told her. "The wind's blown some tiles off the roof."

"What a nuisance," Mattie said comfortably. They looked after Coppins with as much care as if the house were alive. It was part of their coziness together.

"I might go up and have a look at the damage later on."

"Be careful," Mattie warned him, and he leaned across to kiss her.

She drank her tea, and watched Mitch go across to the bathroom for his shower. When the tea was finished she lay back against the pillows and drifted into sleep again.

She didn't know how much later it was when she woke up again. She lay on her side, with her arm crooked under her head, looking at the room. The blue silk peignoir that Mitch had given her was folded over the dressing table stool, where she had left it last night when she undressed for bed. His plaid robe now hung behind the door that led into the bathroom. While she was asleep, Mitch must have put his clothes on and gone outside.

The room was full of thin bright light. It gleamed on the row of gold-topped bottles ranged on her dressing table, then faded, then strengthened again. It was windy outside; she could hear the wind, and there must be March clouds raggedly crossing the pale sun. Mattie didn't like windy weather. It made her feel cross-grained and restless.

She pushed back the covers and swung her legs out of bed. She went across and picked up her peignoir, wrapping it around herself and tying the belt, luxuriating in the folds of the silk as they fell against her skin. She turned to the window.

The bare branches of the trees lashed and writhed in the wind. The capricious gusts flattened the grass beyond the bare rose beds, and drove dead brown leaves out of their winter drifts under the laurel bushes. Mattie saw that the clumps of daffodils would be beaten flat too. She frowned, with her fingers at her throat, then looked back into the room.

Afterward she remembered its stillness after the tossing branches outside. Its stillness, and the order of everything, her bottles and brushes mirrored in the shiny glass tabletop, the line of Mitch's jackets on their hangers, just visible past the open door of the dressing room.

She was walking toward the bathroom, thinking of hot water and the way that a trickle of bath essence would puff up into fragrant bubbles, when she heard a noise.

She knew at once that it was a terrible noise.

It was a sliding clatter and then a thump. The sound of something heavy, rolling and thumping. There was a silence and a cry bursting through it, then another thump. The silence that followed it splintered in her head. It had been Mitch's cry.

Mattie screamed, just once. "Mitch!"

She ran to the window. Her hands were like melted wax. The catch was stiff, and she couldn't open it. She pressed her face to the glass. All she could see below was a strip of graveled path and the crescent of the rose bed. The roses had been pruned and the stumpy twigs stuck up like bony fingers.

Mitch. Oh, God, Mitch.

She looked wildly around her. The room was silent. Mitch wasn't in the tumbled bed, or in the bath, or standing in front of the empty clothes in the dressing room.

Mattie began to run. Barefoot, she ran down the wide

staircase and across the hall where he had picked up the newspapers from the mat and laid them on the side table. The heavy front door with its diamond-shaped light banged open when she fell against it. Outside, the wind whipped into her face, and a spiral of brown leaves blew past her into the hall. She ran over the gravel, unaware of the chippings digging into her feet. Ahead of her, projecting beyond the angle of the house, she could see the end of a ladder lying on the ground.

Mattie's hand came up over her mouth. As she ran the last few yards she was moaning, "Oh, please, oh, please, God."

She turned the corner.

Mitch was lying with his legs still tangled in the metal rungs of the ladder. She half-fell beside him. She put her hands to her cheeks and turned his head so that he looked up at her. His glasses were broken, and they hung at a comical angle. There was blood on his face. Lumps of gravel were embedded in raw flesh.

Oh, Mitch.

Mattie put her arms under his shoulders, trying to lift him. He was a big, warm, familiar weight and she couldn't move him. Her struggle only shifted the lightweight ladder, and it clanked tinnily against the stones. Mitch's head fell back.

She was sobbing and gasping, but she scrambled to her feet again.

Mitch. Don't worry. I'll get help.

Where? No Mrs. Hopper today. Neighbors. The road, that was it.

Mattie stumbled as she fled, the blue folds of her robe tangling between her legs. She dragged open the ornate gate that had Coppins on it in wrought-iron lettering, and ran into the road.

Help me, somebody.

It was the milkman who found her. He drove around the corner and saw a woman standing in the middle of the road. All the front of her dressing gown was darkened with a big wet stain.

Mattie ran to the truck. The milkman was very young, pale and freckled, with ginger hair sticking out under his peaked cap. She looked at him, then put out her hands. Mattie could only think that she must clean the gravel off Mitch's face. She must clean it off and bathe the broken skin.

"Please come," she said clearly. "My husband is hurt."

They went back together. The milkman was wearing a

leather bag on a strap across his chest and the pouch banged and jingled against his hip as he ran. They knelt down again beside Mitch. When the milkman looked up again his face was whiter still.

"Where's the telephone?"

"Inside, on the hall table." Mattie spoke in the same clear voice.

"Get a neighbor," the milkman begged her. "The nearest." He was running toward the front door, hitching his bag over his shoulder.

Mattie hesitated, wondering which way to go. The big houses were widely spaced behind their high hedges. She couldn't think of anything except Mitch's face, and the need to sponge the dirt off it. Then she saw a man in coveralls come around the corner from the gate, and a woman following him. She recognized the woman. She lived in the big half-timbered house across the way. Sometimes Mattie and Mitch met her in the supermarket. Mattie's neighbor and the workman both had the same shocked but inquisitive expressions of lookers-on at an accident. They were staring down at Mitch. *He'll be all right*, Mattie wanted to say. *He'll be all right*. She was shaking now, and her teeth chattered. The sensible words didn't come out of her throat.

The man knelt down beside Mitch. The woman came and put her arm around Mattie. "Come on, dear," she said meaninglessly. "Come on, now."

The milkman ran out of the house again. "They're on their way," he said. He had taken off his leather bag and his white coat, and he stood holding the coat out as if he wanted to wrap Mitch in it.

Mattie saw the workman shake his head. She noticed his big hands, grimy with oil. It seemed a very long time since she had heard the noise. She could hear it still in her head, clatter and rolling thump. But she realized that it wasn't very long at all. A minute or two, just a minute or two ago she had been standing at the bedroom window, watching the wind.

Mattie looked down. Mitch hadn't moved; he was lying looking up at her with blood on his face.

It came to her with a rush of terrible fear that he wasn't all right at all.

She dropped to her knees, bending over him, but he still didn't move. She tried to lie down with her head against his chest, to cradle him and comfort him, but the hands of the people she didn't know took hold of her and held her back.

Blindly, Mattie lifted her head. The March wind blew her hair into her face.

"I can hear it," the milkman said. "I'll go to the gate."

She wondered what he was talking about, and then she heard the ambulance siren. Of course, it was a part of this tableau, as much as the faces of the people waiting for it. It was Mitch and herself who didn't belong here. It shouldn't have anything to do with them, or with the security of Coppins. She looked around for Mitch to confirm it for her, and then she remembered that he was lying at her feet.

The ambulance swung toward them. It rolled over the gravel, curiously stately except for the urgency of its blue flashing lights. It stopped and two men jumped out. The milkman and the housewife and the man in coveralls stepped back to make room for them. Mattie was left, standing with her hands loose and helpless at her sides.

The ambulance men crouched down beside Mitch. Mattie watched what they did to him, their busy hands and their intent faces. She felt childishly relieved, as confident as a child that these officials would take care of Mitch for her.

But a moment later one of them looked up, then straightened so that he stood close to her. He put his hand on her arm.

"I'm afraid he's dead. Death was almost instantaneous."

Mattie stepped backward, shaking his hand off her arm. In her clear, strange voice she said, "Oh, no, that can't be right. Mitch isn't dead."

And then the housewife came to her again, putting her arm around her shoulders and trying to turn her away. "Come on, my love," she said. "Come in the house with me."

Mattie stared at her without comprehension. Then she looked around again, searching the circle of faces for Mitch's, so that he could explain to her how this blank horror had descended on the ordinary day.

Mitch had gone. One of the faces had pronounced the words, *I'm afraid he's dead*. The first brutal blow of understanding struck her.

"Oh, no. Please."

It wasn't a contradiction now. She was begging them.

The faces closed around her, and another sound came out of Mattie's mouth. It was an involuntary noise, neither a cry nor a moan. The people took hold of her, one on either side, and they led her away. She looked back, over her shoulder, to where Mitch lay still on the ground. The pain of understanding twisted tighter. He wouldn't move anymore because he was dead.

The big house with the high roof was empty. Why were they leading her back to it? It was so quiet inside after the bluster of the wind. They walked over the dead leaves that had blown into the hall, past the folded newspapers waiting on the side table. The mail was there too. Mitch would pick the letters up again, after they had had breakfast together, and open them in his study. Only not today. He wouldn't, today, because he was dead.

The hands, unwelcome hands, led her into her own bright kitchen. There were copper saucepans, a neatly diminishing set, hanging on the wall, and flowered window shades with scalloped edges. Mitch should be here, humming to himself as he moved to and fro.

They made Mattie sit down at the breakfast table.

She looked down at her own hands and saw that they were shaking. She wanted Mitch to take hold of them. Everything she thought of, everywhere she looked, had Mitch in it. He couldn't die, he couldn't simply stop being while the copper pans stayed in their places on the wall, while all the evidence of their life stayed solidly around her.

She turned her head to look out the window at the patchy blue sky. There were the same shredded clouds that she had watched from their bedroom window. Mattie frowned, hunching her shoulders against the spreading pain. Just this little loop of time had elapsed. It was still only minutes, surely, since she had heard Mitch fall. That's what it was, he had fallen. If she could only stop her hands from trembling, she could catch the time between her fingers and wind it back again. She would walk on into the bathroom, and she would hear Mitch pass under the window, whistling, on his way back into the house. Mattie closed her eyes. Inside her head she took the few steps to the bathroom door and heard the reassuring scrunch of Mitch crossing the gravel below. But then she opened her eyes again and she was sitting in the cold bright kitchen, the woman from the house across the way was there, and Mitch was dead.

She knew now that he was dead. He wouldn't be lying there with blood and grit on his cheeks and his head twisted if he weren't dead. She wished that she had taken off his glasses instead of leaving them crooked, as if he were making a joke about dying.

The neighbor and the man in coveralls were both moving about in her kitchen. The man filled the kettle at the sink, and the woman opened and closed the cupboard doors. They were trying to make tea. That's what they gave people at times like this, Mattie remembered. She felt a wave of anger at their intrusion, and a fierce determination to hold herself together in front of them. They had seen Mitch, beyond their inquisitive help, with his glasses broken. They shouldn't see anything else. That was for Mitch, and herself. "The tea is in the blue caddy on the left," Mattie said. "And you will find the cups in the end cupboard."

They gave her a cup of tea, too strong and much too sweet, but she drank it, not noticing that it scalded her tongue.

"Shouldn't we call the doctor? And the police?" Mattie made her voice steady, wondering in a remote corner of herself that she could sit here, holding a teacup, when Mitch was dead. "I know it was an accident, but the police will have to see, won't they?"

"The police are coming," the woman soothed her. "Tim Wright's your doctor, isn't he?"

Mattie nodded. Mitch played golf with him sometimes. The workman had finished his tea. He put his cup down on the drainboard, and Mattie noticed the marks that his oily fingers had made on the china. She seemed to see them, and everything else, with lurid and painful clarity.

A car was coming. She heard the crunch of gravel again, and her neighbor bobbed up to look out of the window.

"The police," she murmured. She sounded relieved, glad to be handing over some responsibility.

After a few minutes they came in, putting their caps down on the breakfast table. Mattie looked up into their faces, but their eyes didn't meet hers. They were calm, doing a job, and the tragedy was her own. Mattie kept it to herself, wrapping her arms around her chest and compressing the pain. There were only a very few questions. Mattie told them that Mitch must have gone up on the roof to fix tiles that had blown off in the night's wind. He had slipped, or the ladder had slipped, and he had fallen from the high roof. The fall had killed him. Death was almost instantaneous, the ambulance man had told her that.

The absurdity, the pointlessness of Mitch's death rose up in front of her. The sickening pressure of a sob swelled in Mattie's throat, but she lifted her head, denying it. The senior policeman closed his notebook.

"Dr. Wright is here," somebody said. Mattie looked over the shoulders of the policemen and saw Tim Wright's round, reddish face. It belonged in the clubhouse, not here in the Coppins kitchen. Mattie wrapped her arms tighter, holding in her secrets. The doctor drew her to her feet, led her away into the drawing room. As he closed the door she glanced around. There were plumped cushions and photographs in frames, a ticking clock. Just the same, but dead. The room felt dead, and time seemed to be stretching and compressing itself. None of this is real, Mattie tried to convince herself. But she knew that it was real, and her whole body was shaking with the shock of it. She didn't know whether it was hours or minutes since Mitch had died, only that he was gone. She felt her sob rising again, like vomit, and she swallowed it down once more.

"Can I have a drink?" she asked.

"Of course."

Tim Wright went to the silver tray that Mitch's brother had given them as a wedding present. He poured whiskey into a glass, and splashed soda into it from the siphon. To Mattie the familiar, sociable little process seemed obscenely out of place, but she took the glass when he held it out to her, and drained it. The doctor was talking about shock, she realized, and about arrangements. She interrupted him without apology.

"What have they done with Mitch? I want to stay with him."

"They have taken him in the ambulance. There will have to be a coroner's inquest. Only a formality." He was apologizing, and trying to avoid the word mortuary. Mattie watched him, thinking that no one wanted to contaminate themselves with tragedy.

"Did you take his glasses off?"

"I'm sorry?"

"It doesn't matter." Mattie went to the drinks tray herself, this time, and poured a much bigger measure. The whiskey didn't warm her, but she drank it just the same.

"You mustn't be on your own, you know. Just say who you'd like me to telephone, and I'll do it for you now." The doctor waited, kindly. "A friend? A relative?"

Mattie sat down, knitting her fingers around the empty glass. She tried to think of someone and then, without warning, like a dam cracking open to let out the floodwater, the full truth and its significance washed through her. Mitch was dead. He had gone, and she was alone. There was no one else she wanted to call on. No one she wanted here, at Coppins, where Mitch had been. Not for a week, not even for a day.

Mattie bowed her head. She felt that all the painful, swelling need for Mitch, and anger at his futile death, and fear of loneliness was only just contained in the leaky, fragile shell of her body. If she moved, it would burst out of her. And that mustn't happen in front of Tim Wright, with his concerned, professional manner. Not even in front of Julia, even if she were to come from Italy. It was private, private. Her own, and Mitch's.

"There's our housekeeper," she said at last. "Mrs. Hopper. It's her day off. I think she goes to her sister in Crawley. The number is in the book on the table."

That was all.

"Are you sure?" the doctor asked her.

Mattie gritted her teeth. "Certain."

He did what she asked, and then came back. He gave her a sedative and she took it, carelessly. The doctor glanced at his watch, then snapped his bag shut. They agreed that Mattie's neighbor should stay in the house until Mrs. Hopper came back.

Mattie wanted them all to go, to leave her.

After the doctor had driven away she went upstairs, away from her neighbor's sympathy. She went into the dressing room, and with a little noise like an animal's whimper she hid her face against Mitch's clothes, hanging empty on the rail. After a long time, with her body aching from the awkward position, she crept back and stretched out across her bed. A little while later she fell asleep.

When she woke up, she had forgotten. She lay blinking at the room from the unfamiliar angle, dazed by the sedative and wondering at the dark weight that seemed suspended above her. The oblivion lasted for only a second. When she remembered what had happened, reality fell around her in poisonous folds. It lay against her face, suffocating her. Blindly, Mattie drew her legs up to her chest and rocked herself. The silence around her was complete, and terrifying.

Mitch was dead. Mitch had gone, and he would never come back.

Panic rose in her chest. It made her gasp, and lash out. She heaved herself upright, kneeling on the creased satin bedcover.

"Mitch," she called out to the empty, heavy air. "Mitch, I don't know what to do."

* * *

In the end, it was Alexander she turned to.

Every hour of that day reared up in front of her, a pointless obstacle to be pointlessly surmounted, only to dwindle and turn into another, and then to stretch away into the night. When it grew dark, Mattie wouldn't have Mrs. Hopper with her. She sent the housekeeper away to her own rooms, and then she walked through the silent house, turning on every light so the big house blazed. But the darkness still pressed in on her. She was visited by images of Mitch lying in a cold steel drawer, with his poor face still unwashed and his glasses hanging crooked.

Mattie went into the brilliantly lit drawing room and drank the rest of the bottle of whiskey. It made her feel sick, and she shook so much that her teeth rattled. And at midnight, out of fear that the night would never end, she telephoned Alexander.

"Mitch is dead. He died this morning." She wondered that she could say the words.

Alexander came at once, driving through the night.

Mattie sat waiting for him, with a new bottle on the table in front of her and her fingers clenched tight around her glass. She imagined that when he came she would be able to run to him, and that he would give her some comfort. When she heard his car rolling up in the lowest, deadest hour of the night, she jumped up and whiskey flooded over the white rug at her feet. She ran to open the front door.

Alexander had pulled a sweater and corduroys on over his pajamas. His fair hair stood up in unbrushed wings and his beaky, ironic face was gray with concern. As soon as she saw him, Mattie knew that she had made a mistake. He was warm, and solid, and he was her friend, but there was no comfort here. He was only Alexander, and Mitch had gone away.

Alexander held her. She felt the rough wool of his sweater against her face, and after a second she moved carefully away. The shock of grief separated her from Alexander as surely as it cut her off from everything else. It began to dawn on her that it was ineradicable.

"Come in, Alexander," Mattie said. "I'm having a drink in the drawing room."

Alexander followed her. All the way from Ladyhill he had been preparing himself, but even so the sight of Mattie shocked him. In their puffy sockets her eyes were flat, and she looked at him as if she didn't recognize him. The bright drawing room stank of whiskey. He put his arm around her shoulders and made her sit down. He realized that Mattie was half-drunk, and insensible with shock and exhaustion.

He looked angrily around the room, as if the silk-covered walls might explain to him how Mattie could be so alone, now of all times.

The toe of Mattie's shoe poked at the sodden rug.

"Give me another drink," she begged him. And then added, in bewilderment, "I don't know what to do."

Alexander filled her glass, watched as she emptied it, then took her hands.

"You need to go to sleep now."

"I can't."

He saw fear in her face. "I'll stay with you. I'll be here."

He led her upstairs. In the pink marble bathroom he sponged her face, and undressed her as if she were a child. He was ashamed of seeing that her body seemed as richly perfect as it had six years before, at Ladyhill. He found a nightdress, and covered it up. He straightened the creased bed, and drew the covers back for her. Like an obedient robot, Mattie lay down. Alexander closed the dressing room door, so that she couldn't see Mitch's empty clothes. Then he sat down in a velvet chair and watched until her face sagged, the lines in it softening, and she fell asleep.

In the morning, it was Alexander who made the necessary, painful telephone calls. He spoke to Mitch's brother in Whitby, and to Mattie's family and her agent. He fended off the reporters and photographers who had heard the news and gathered in the Coppins driveway, and he dealt with police and solicitors. He broke the news to Felix in his office at Tressider & Lemoine, and he answered the telephone's increasingly insistent ringing.

"Thank you," Mattie said to him. "I couldn't do any of this myself, you know. I never could do anything like this. That was why Mitch was so good for me." She shook her head, turning her flat eyes away from Alexander's sympathy. She seemed to watch the sad arrangements being made as if they concerned someone else, he thought, and half-wished that she would cry so that he could make some attempt to comfort her. The bluff, golfing GP came back and confided to Alexander, "Grief manifests itself in a dozen different ways. We can only let it run its course."

He left a prescription for tranquilizers and sleeping tablets and Alexander, irritated, watched him drive away again.

In the evening Alexander sat beside Mattie on the slippery

sofa in her drawing room. Every lamp was lit, and the house-keeper had taken away the whiskey-stained rug.

"Let me call Julia," he pleaded. "She'll want to come and be with you. You should have her here, Mattie."

Mattie didn't even look at him now. She turned her wedding ring to and fro on her finger. "What can Julia do?" She added, almost conversationally, "Better to leave her in peace. Her garden is beautiful, you know."

But when Mattie had taken her sleeping pills and gone to lie in her wide bed, Alexander picked up the telephone on Mitch's desk. The news would be in the papers the next day, and he didn't want Julia to have to learn it from them. As he waited through the complications of reaching Montebellate, his eyes wandered over the neatly arranged documents in front of him. Copies of Mitch's will, insurance policies, and everything else that was necessary had been immediately at hand. Mattie was right, he thought. Mitch had been very good for her. Grief, and anger at the pointlessness of his death, struck him simulta-neously. Alexander had to rub his face as the call went through at last. He found himself trying to explain to an elderly-sounding Italian man that he must speak to Julia Bliss at once.

"Julia Smith?" Nicolo Galli asked. "There is no trouble, I hope?"

"Tell her it's Alexander here. It's not Lily, tell her."

"Thank God," Nicolo replied. "I will fetch Julia for you."

Alexander waited for a long time. He tried to imagine the little hill town and Julia's house, but he could see only Mitch's tidy desk, and the photograph of Mitch and Mattie on their wedding day that stood at one side. Julia was in the picture, too, but a shadow partly hid her face. Alexander found that he couldn't even remember exactly how long it was since he had spoken to her. He rubbed his knuckles wearily into the sockets of his eyes.

"Alexander?"

Julia's voice came from a long way away, but he could hear the sharpness of anxiety in it. Quickly and quietly he told her what had happened.

There was a moment's silence.

"Poor Mattie. Oh, God, Alexander. Poor Mattie."

They talked for a moment longer. It struck Alexander that Julia spoke English too carefully, as if her command of it were slipping away. But yet there was no hesitation between the two of them. They were drawn together by their love for Mattie, and the common bond of the years.

"I'll come as soon as I can," Julia promised. "Tomorrow sometime."

"She's very shocked," Alexander warned her as they hung up.

Julia's face had gone white. She looked across his piles of books to meet Nicolo's concerned gaze. "I've got to go home. I've got to go home right away. Mattie's husband is dead."

Outside, Montebellate was silent. Julia remembered how she and Mattie had huddled against one of these walls and laughed together. Tonight's darkness had extinguished the first warmth of the southern spring day, but it would be warm again tomorrow, and then warmer. But Julia felt England pulling at her. The urgency of her need to be there tightened and twisted inside her so sharply that she could smell the green March winds and feel the sting of driven rain in her face. She ran down the steep hill to her own house, as if by running she could reach Mattie more quickly.

Alexander walked slowly through the glossy, ornamented rooms of Coppins. He was thinking of the time that Mattie and Mitch must have taken to accumulate all these things, and of his own pursuit of the pieces for Ladyhill. The futility that he had grown to recognize at Ladyhill confronted him again, sharpened by the arbitrariness of tragedy. And he thought of Julia again, and the estranged, Latinate cadences of her voice. Yet still, for all the distance and the time, he knew her better than he knew anyone else. He reached under the silk shades of the lamps and turned them off, one by one. The darkness seemed to move faster than he did. Alexander was used to empty houses, but he had never learned to be happy with the emptiness. His own vacancy seemed to stretch ahead of him.

In Coppins, now, Alexander shivered and turned off the last lamp.

Mitch was buried in the graveyard of the church where he had been christened. It stood on a headland overlooking the sea, and as the group of mourners watched the coffin being lowered, the salty wind blew inland and wrapped the loose strands of Mattie's hair against her cheeks. It made her think of Chichester harbor and the soaking rain in her face, and then the teashop where she had taken shelter with Mitch. Her face and her eyes were dry now.

She watched the ropes being removed and the bearers, Mitch's brother and the other Whitby fishermen, stood back with their heads bowed. The vicar's surplice billowed as he motioned Mattie forward. Mattie dropped her wreath of roses into the hole and stepped back again. Julia put a hand to her arm, but she didn't need steadying. Felix and Alexander stood at her other side, but she felt separated from them by thick, invisible walls. She wasn't thinking about them, or even about Mitch. The smell of the sea reminded her of fish and chip suppers in northern towns, and the zigzagging, cross-country progress of Francis Willoughby's touring company. But that was all finished, long ago. Mattie had a sense of many things being finished.

The funeral tea was held in her brother-in-law's terraced house in one of the little streets not far from where Mitch had grown up. Ruddy-faced Mitchells and Howorths crowded into the living room, holding teacups and staring covertly at Mattie. She was pale but perfectly in control of herself. She nodded gravely in acknowledgment of their condolences, and made sure that she spoke to everyone who had come to remember Mitch. Once or twice she glanced at Felix and Alexander, who sat on upright chairs by the window, talking in low voices. Julia was in the kitchen, fiercely buttering sliced bread and helping Mitch's brother's wife to refill the emptying teapots.

Mattie felt that she was delivering a finely judged performance as the young widow. Each moment she wished that the performance would end. If only it would end, Mitch would come into her dressing room and wait while she removed her makeup, tell her that the show had been wonderful, and then take her back home again.

Mattie's performance concealed all the rage and terror and grief that wound up inside her, and the invisible walls that separate the victims of tragedy cut her off even from Julia.

Another hour, Mattie was thinking, *then this tea will be over. What shall I do then?*

Mitch was in his coffin, under the wreath of roses and the salty earth. They had cleaned his face and taken off his broken glasses.

"Thank you," Mattie murmured to a Howorth cousin. "Thank you for coming." At last the proper ritual of the funeral tea was over. When the people had all gone, Mattie said suddenly that she wanted to go back to Coppins. Julia and Alexander tried to persuade her to stay another night with Mitch's family, but she was adamant.

"I'll drive you," Felix offered. In the Howorths' living room Felix looked alarmingly exotic. "I must get home too."

Felix was in love. He had only met William Paget a few days before Mitch's death. William was Felix's own age, the younger son of a grand family for whom Felix had done some work at their country house. William had never been there when Felix had visited it. Then by coincidence, they had met at a private showing in London. William was a painter, although the exhibition was of someone else's work. He had turned his back on the packed gallery and stretched his hand out to the wall, as if to exclude everyone else and to stop Felix from escaping.

"I wondered what you were like," William said. "Now I see."

Felix was slightly drunk. "And what am I like?" he inquired.

William put his head on one side, considering. And then he answered, "Extremely exciting."

They left the gallery and went back to Eaton Square.

William laughed at the serious paintings, and then he closed the door of Felix's bedroom behind them. For more than a week they had hardly been apart.

Felix had stood on the windy North Yorkshire headland thinking of William, and then of Mitch, who wouldn't have the chance of any more beginnings. He wondered how Mattie, standing so stiffly beside him, would find her way on her own again, and he was conscious of Julia and Alexander and the inexplicable distances between them. Tasting the salty air, stirred by the freshness of it, Felix was possessed by a furious longing to get back to London and to William, and to seize his own chances while they still lay within his reach.

"I must get home," he repeated in the street outside the Howorths' house.

Mattie went with him. "I'll be all right," she said in her composed way. "I'm going to get back to work in a day or two. Everyone says it will be for the best. I'm sure that's what Mitch would think."

They let her go. Julia and Alexander stood watching as Felix's latest Alfa growled out of sight.

"Will she be all right?" Julia asked, not expecting an answer. Alexander didn't give one. They felt Mattie's removal from them, and their inability to help her. The street's windows, overlooking them, suddenly seemed like prying eyes.

"Let's go for a walk," Alexander said.

He drove them southward, along the coast, to a wide, flat

cxpanse of glittering sands. They walked parallel to the low
waves as they tipped over and slid back again under the netted
foam. It was the first time that they had been alone together
since Julia's return to England, but they talked very little because
there seemed to be no need. *The common bond of the years,*
Alexander thought again. *That's what Julia and I have. Time is
rubbing us smooth, like stones in the sea.*

A seventh wave ran up and engulfed Julia's feet. She
laughed briefly and took off her shoes, emptying the water out of
them. She unrolled her black stockings and walked barefoot in
the sand, and Alexander put her shoes in his pockets. He watched
her as she walked, a little ahead of him, her head turned to look
out to sea.

Alexander had looked at her often since she had come
home, but he seemed to see her with perfect clarity in this
strong, coastal light. Julia was older, and there was a look to her
as if she were too used to the hard sun and the slow demands of
her Italian garden. But if the work had worn her, it had also
softened her. The lines of bitterness that had begun to set in her
face had all been rubbed out. Her tranquility, and the efforts by
which he guessed it had been gained, gave the old Julia an added
dimension of sweetness. As they walked, Alexander thought
how much he liked her.

He knew her, and he liked her better than he ever had. If, at
the beginning, he had ever truly liked her, beyond loving her too
insistently. Alexander understood that he had tried to replace
her, with Clare and the others before her, and he had failed.
Now, with Julia beside him at the edge of the gray sea, Alexander felt the soft, dead weight of regret. He might have tried to
push it away, taking her hand in his or even trying, with awkward inappositeness, to kiss her. But as soon as he thought of it,
Julia turned around to him, walking backward and leaving deep,
dissolving footprints in the wet sand.

She said, "I should get back to London too."

Her glance held his for only a second, and then her eyes slid
away again, back to the sea.

Alexander drove them the distance back to London.

They talked about Lily, and about the gardens at Montebellate,
and about Alexander's late success in his work.

In the long intervals of silence, Julia looked out at the
length of England. She was sharply conscious of every green and
dun contour, of the little gray huddles of villages and the sudden,
stridently ugly outcrops of the towns. And she believed that she

could feel, under the road, the firm flint and chalk backbone of it. It was hard and inhospitable, in its coldness quite unlike Italy, but she felt herself luxuriously drawn against it, like a baby to its mother.

Alexander was part of this landscape. She peered at him, almost furtively, as he drove. There was an English hardness in Alexander, an uncompromising strength beneath the undramatic surface. She had seen enough now to recognize its worth at last. Julia suspected that she had fought against that strength, in their early days, as she had fought with herself. If she had won the battle with herself, she thought sadly, she had lost Alexander's. She loved him, but she was almost as deeply afraid of what loving him might mean. She had no idea what Alexander felt, and it occurred to her that she never had. The retrospective vision of her own selfishness made her feel cold, and she drew her coat around her in the farthest corner of the car.

She closed her eyes, and made the journey inside her head from the harebell-blue door of her house, up the cobbled street under Nicolo's balcony, across the square and through the gates of the palazzo. She knew the steps across the courtyard, and the scents trapped in the warmth of the secret garden. She knew the view from the stone-framed window, down over the terraces to the sea. But in her head there was no sun shining. The sunlight all seemed to be here, invisibly brightening the unspectacular outlines of England.

But Italy is safe, Julia whispered to herself. Italy is safe.

Alexander glanced sideways at her, and thought she had gone to sleep.

Felix had lent Julia a Kensington flat that Tressider & Lemoine was renovating for resale. He hadn't wanted Julia at Eaton Square, witnessing his incredulous happiness with William, and he felt ashamed that his roundabout lack of generosity drew gratitude from Julia. She took the keys from him with cheerful relief.

"I don't know where else in London I could have stayed. I've neglected my friends, haven't I? Mattie doesn't seem to want me at her house, although I wish she'd let me look after her. And I haven't really got the money, anymore, for hotels."

"It's yours for as long as you want it," Felix said quickly.

It was midnight when Alexander stopped his car outside the door. Julia reached into her bag for the keys with their Tressider & Lemoine label. They both found themselves looking at them, under the car's dim courtesy light, as if they had some signifi-

cance. Alexander thought of Mattie's set, pale face, and in
another, deeper recess of his mind he thought again about kissing
Julia. She opened the door of the car, letting in the cold air, and
slid out. She had to lean down to see his face as she spoke.

"Good night. Thank you." The rusty, Italian sound had
come back into her voice.

"There's no need to thank me," Alexander said. Julia
ducked her head, a quick, acquiescent nod, and then ran up the
steps to the door.

She closed it behind her, letting out a large breath of relief
and regret. Then she picked her way past the ladders and paint
pots that filled the hallway. She heard Alexander driving away,
remembering that she didn't even know where he was going.

TWENTY-SIX

"The law changed," Lily said. "Didn't you know?"

"What law? I've been away a long time. There must be all
kinds of things I don't know about."

Julia and Lily were perched at opposite ends of the make-
shift dining table in the Tressider & Lemoine Kensington flat.
They had been drinking instant coffee and talking. George
Tressider's marquetry box was open on the table between them.
Lily looked up from Valerie Hall's birth certificate.

"The adoption law. If you're adopted, you're allowed to try
to find your real mother. They give you all the papers and files,
and help you."

Julia shook her head. "I didn't know that," she said softly.
"I've wanted to find her, you know, with part of myself, ever
since you were born."

Lily stood up, came around the table to Julia, and gave her
the birth certificate. Julia folded it up and put it back in the box,
on top of the envelope that held her two rings and Pia's Rapunzel
book. In all the haste of packing to get back to Mattie as quickly
as possible, Julia had still remembered to put the marquetry box
in her suitcase. The box and its contents had become a kind of
talisman.

"I'll come with you, to start looking for her, if you want me to," Lily offered.

Julia looked up at her in gratitude. Since she had been back in London, since Lily had come up from Ladyhill to stay with her for a few days, Julia had noticed yet another change in their relationship. Julia had found that London was different, and that it seemed more than ever like a foreign city. It seemed bigger, dirtier, and vaguely threatening. Lily noticed her uncertainty and she had become oddly protective, almost maternal to her own mother. The gap in years between them seemed to have diminished. They were more nearly equals now. And in their most recent hours together, Julia had observed her daughter with a mixture of incredulity, amusement and pride. At almost seventeen, Lily seemed to have made the transition into adulthood with admirable panache. She had her own life, her own well-considered opinions, and a startling sense of style. To make the trip to London to stay with her mother, she had chosen her haute-punk mode. She was wearing tight black plastic trousers, a torn black vest, and a festoon of chains and pins. Her dark hair was teased into sticky points, each one tipped with what looked like an arrowhead of red ink.

Julia had eyed the ensemble, knowing that she should probably disapprove of it. But the effect was much too reminiscent of her own and Mattie's early Juliette Greco phase. In fact, Julia reflected, with her pale face and black eye make-up Lily probably didn't look much more outlandish than she had herself twenty years ago.

She felt a moment of sharp, sweet nostalgia for the Rocket, and her own girlhood. "What does Alexander say about your clothes?" she asked.

Wordlessly, Lily had rolled her eyes and bared her teeth. They had both laughed.

"You're okay, Mum," Lily had added. "Lots of people's mums would go crazy."

"I remember," Julia murmured.

Julia put her hand up to touch Lily's now. The chains round Lily's wrist rattled merrily. "I'd like it if you would help me. We're looking for your grandmother too."

Lily stood with her head on one side, twisting one of the red-tipped points of hair. "Don't do it for me, Julia. Do it for yourself." She smiled, a sudden pretty smile that was entirely at odds with her fierce maquillage. "Besides, I've got three grandmothers already."

Julia put her hands on the warm, satiny wood of George's box and sighed. "Where do we start? 'Colchester, Essex,' isn't very much to go on."

"Granny Smith will know the name of the adoption agency. If the agency still exists, they should have kept your file."

Julia was impressed. "How do you know all this?"

But Lily only shrugged. "I know all kinds of things."

I'm sure you do, Julia thought. *Only don't tell me all of them. I don't think I'm ready for that. I trust you, Lily. Is that enough?*

So it was, with Lily's encouragement, that Julia embarked on the search for Margaret Ann Hall. The provisions of the 1975 Children's Act were in her favor.

They began by visiting Betty at Fairmile Road, and sat drinking tea at the blue Formica table while the television boomed from the living room. Julia tried to assure her that even if the search was successful, finding her real mother would make no difference to her feelings for Betty.

Betty pursed her lips and glanced at Lily. And Lily, who had toned down her appearance for Granny Smith's sake, nodded slightly. At once, the lines of anxiety in Betty's face eased a little, and her eyes stopped darting nervously around the room. Watching, Julia remembered that she had always been surprised by Betty's and Lily's fondness for each other. Surprised, and faintly resentful, in her heart. But now it seemed both natural and thoroughly pleasing. Getting older, she reflected, was like seeing baffling and frustrating pieces of some vast puzzle beginning to fit smoothly together to make a recognizable picture.

Betty found a sheet of paper and wrote something down for them. It was the address of a private adoption agency in Southwark. Julia noticed that she remembered the address perfectly. Over the years it must often have been in her head.

The adoption agency had vanished without trace from the Southwark address. The site had been redeveloped, and was occupied by a new supermarket. They were deeply disheartened, until Julia hit on the idea of contacting the borough social services. She clung to the telephone, being transferred from department to department, until at last she was put through to the right social worker. Betty's agency had been amalgamated with another, larger concern. The business had been transferred, along with all its records, to Guildford. Julia wrote down another address.

She made a second, lengthy telephone call, and this time she was successful. She had found the right place, and the records of her adoption were indeed available.

She was advised that she would have to attend counseling before any further details could be released to her.

When she replaced the receiver her hands were shaking. She seemed close enough to her mother to be able to reach out and touch her.

"Yippee," shouted Lily, her eyes sparkling with the excitement of the hunt. "I know we can do it."

The hunt took a little time, but it was a short and unmysterious trail.

Julia went to see a social worker for the obligatory counseling session. The woman faced her across a desk, on which lay a file with a faded blue cover. Julia could hardly take her eyes off it. Inside it, written on those slips of yellow-edged paper, was her mother's story. The old, romantic dreams and fantasies seemed a long way off. All she could think of now was how she would find her, an ordinary woman and a stranger, yet as close to her as she was to Lily. She had to force herself to listen to and answer the counselor's questions.

At last the woman nodded. She told Julia that she seemed to have thought out her reasons for searching for her mother very clearly. Julia felt dimly surprised. She wasn't aware of anything as cogent as reasons, only of a pull that grew more intense the closer she came, and which she knew must be satisfied.

Her counselor put her hand on the blue file, opened it, and sighed. "I'm afraid we can't give you very much to go on."

Julia looked down at the fragments of her history.

The first document was a fuller version of the birth certificate that Betty had kept hidden among her underwear. Julia saw that Valerie Hall had been born at St. Benet's Home for Unmarried Mothers in Goodmayes Road, Colchester. She had been Valerie, there was no mistake. The date of birth was her own. Her mother was Margaret Ann Hall, of 11 Partington Street, Ilford, Essex.

Julia stared in amazement. Her real mother had lived only a few miles from Fairmile Road and her date of birth was given as January 17, 1923. She had been sixteen when she had given birth to her daughter in St. Benet's Home. She would now be only fifty-four. Almost twenty years younger than Betty Smith.

Julia lifted her eyes from the certificate. The counselor was watching her with sympathy, but the sympathy seemed almost an intrusion in this moment of revelation. "She was very young," Julia said softly.

In the space for the father's details the words *father not known* had been written. Whoever he had been, he had left Margaret Ann Hall to go through her ordeal alone. Julia put the certificate aside. Underneath it was the letter that Betty had written to the agency, asking for herself and Vernon to be considered as prospective adoptive parents. A note clipped to it stated, *Accepted*.

Next was a copy of the certificate of adoption, on which the baby girl's name was given as *Julia Smith*. And from the last document in the little pile, Julia learned that she had been fostered for the first six weeks of her life by a couple in Colchester. She had been collected from their house by an employee of the adoption agency, and taken to Fairmile Road.

There were tears in Julia's eyes. She felt no pity for the six-week-old baby who had been handed over to Betty and Vernon and a safe life of dull security. Her sadness was all for sixteen-year-old Margaret, in the bleak-sounding church home, who had been forced to give up her child. *She must have wanted to keep me,* Julia thought. *But how could she?* Sixteen was the age she herself had been when she found her way with Mattie to Jessie and Felix. They had been barely able to take care of themselves, let alone a baby. How could Margaret Ann Hall have done anything different?

Julia sniffed hard and rubbed her face with the palm of her hand. There was one item left in her file. It was a folded sheet of writing paper, the cheap gray kind with ruled lines. She picked it up, feeling a tightness in her chest.

The counselor said, "It's not much, but I think it gives you your best chance of finding her. St. Benet's closed down years ago."

Julia read the letter.

It was written from another address in Ilford, and dated August 1942. Margaret Ann Hall had become Margaret Rennyshaw, and she was writing to the adoption agency to ask for some news of Valerie. The short sentences were hastily scrawled, with words misspelled or left out altogether, but the urgency of the plea was clear and painful to read.

> *Me and Derek have got our own little lad now, but I still think all the time about what happened to my Valerie.*

On my birthday, Julia thought. At Christmas, and New Year, and all the other times.

I no that I did wrong, but I just want to no that she is alright now. Derek is in the Navy. He doesn't no nothing about Valerie. If I could just see her the once, Id be happy.

There was no copy of any answer to Margaret's letter in the file. Julia looked up again. Her mother had wanted to see her. She had a mother, and a half brother, and while she had been growing up in Fairmile Road they had been so close to her.

"What would have happened?" she asked the counselor.

The woman pursed her lips. "Nothing very enlightened, I'm afraid, in those days. I've seen similar cases. I imagine the copy of the reply to your mother isn't in the file because it wasn't something to be proud of. She would have been reminded, rather brusquely, exactly what adoption meant. She would have been told that she could not hope to see or hear from you ever again."

There was a brief silence in the bare cubicle of a room.

"But now she will," Julia murmured.

"If you are certain that it's best for you, and for her." The counselor was kindly, but only doing her job.

Julia was reminded suddenly of Montebellatc, and Sister Maria's calm face. She smiled. "Only one thing in life is certain. But I must find her. I know that."

The counselor held out her hand. "Good luck, then. I'm here if you need me." The interview was over. Julia pointed to the letter.

"May I keep this?"

"Of course. It's yours."

Lily was waiting in a café across the street. To pass the time she had been shopping. Another ripped and zipped black garment protruded from the shopping bag at her feet.

"Well?" she demanded cheerfully. Julia sank down on a mushroom stool. She took out the sheet of grayish paper and handed it to Lily. When they looked at each other again their faces were somber.

"She's real," Lily breathed. "Until right now I'd thought of her only as the prize in a treasure hunt. Granny Smith was your mother. But this Mrs. Rennyshaw is a person. You were her Valerie."

"She was sixteen years old. A few months younger than you are now."

"It's sad." Lily reached across the table to Julia. She seized her hand in both of hers. Underneath the black warpaint her face had crumpled like an anxious child's. "Julia, you won't go and leave me, will you? Will you always be here?"

Julia smiled again. Not everything had changed. She was still mother as well as daughter. Lily was still her child as well as her friend. "I'm thirty-eight, and you're nearly seventeen. We've done our leaving and our coming back to each other. We're here now because we like each other, not because we owe each other things. I'll always be here."

Lily nodded. "I'm glad. I'm glad for everything."

They were still holding on to each other across the greasy table.

"So am I," Julia said.

"What are we waiting for then?" Lily demanded. "Let's go"—she glanced down at the letter—"to Seventy-six Forrester Terrace, Ilford, Essex."

It was Julia who wanted to hold back now that they had come closer still. She wanted to give herself some time, but she was afraid that she didn't have very much to spare. She thought guiltily that she ought to be back in her gardens, working with Tomaso to make them ready for the summer. She was in London, where she could no longer really afford to live, and she was holding up the work on Felix's flat. It was almost the end of the Easter holidays, and Lily would have to go back to Ladyhill, and to school.

It was years since Julia had felt herself to be making a crossing, observing the distances between one life and another. Anxiety, and a timid desire for the certainty of Montebellate, gripped her again.

But in the face of everything else, Julia knew that she was in London for Mattie's sake, and that she would do her best to stay until she was sure that Mattie didn't need her any longer.

It wasn't easy to know what Mattie did need. She had retreated to Coppins, and had politely refused to let anyone come to stay with her. She insisted that Mrs. Hopper would look after her, and that she would soon, in any case, be going back to work. Two weeks after Mitch's funeral she had agreed to do a television commercial.

"It's for underwear, or deodorant, or something," she told Julia on the telephone.

"Don't you know which?"

"Does it matter which?" Mattie's voice sounded blurred. She had admitted that she was sleeping badly.

"Are you all right?" Julia asked impotently. "Can't I come down and keep you company?"

After a little pause Mattie said, "I'm not all right. But I'm trying hard, you know. I'm better on my own just now. Mitch loved this house."

Julia pressed her. "Have you got this number written down? Will you promise to call if you want anything? Even if it's in the middle of the night?"

"What? Oh, yes." Mattie was vague, as if in her mind she had already hung up and immersed herself again in Coppins and its memories.

"Please, Mattie."

"Oh, Julia," Mattie whispered. "If only he wasn't dead. If only he was still here. But there's nothing you can do. Even you. You can't bring him back, can you?"

So Julia stayed on in the half-grandeur and half-desolation of Felix's flat, and Lily kept her company. And one afternoon they went out to Ilford together.

They quickly discovered what they could equally well have found out without leaving the Kensington flat. The even-numbered side of Forrester Terrace had suffered a direct hit from a wartime bomb, and what was left of it had been cleared in the postwar years. A line of early fifties council houses stood in its place, facing the odd-numbered houses that had survived. The terrace showed signs of gentrification, with brightly painted front doors and plants in tubs beside the doorsteps. The houses would be mostly owned by young couples, who would spend their weekends cleaning the layers of distemper out of the cornices in the cramped Victorian living rooms. Julia had no hope that anyone now living in them would remember Margaret and Derek Rennyshaw and their baby son.

"What if she was bombed?" Lily asked.

"If she was, she didn't die," Julia answered. "I'm sure of that."

They walked the mile and a half to Partington Street, to what must have been Margaret's family home. *My grandparents,* Julia thought without much conviction. Her apprehensive eagerness was almost entirely fixed on Margaret herself.

Partington Street was intact, but it was less prosperous-looking than the good half of Forrester Terrace. There was a run-down stationer's at one end, and a bare pub with empty potato chip packets blowing about on the sidewalk at the other. Number eleven was four houses down from the pub.

Julia and Lily glanced at each other, took a breath, and marched up the cracked path. There was no bell. Julia's knock was answered, after a very long time, by an Asian woman in a sari. She held a baby with shiny brown eyes against her chest. She spoke almost no English, but it took very few words to convince Julia and Lily that the present occupants of Number Eleven had never heard of Mr. and Mrs. Hall from 1939, or of Margaret and Derek Rennyshaw. "Let's try next door," Lily insisted.

There was no one at home at Number Nine. The door of Number Thirteen was opened by a glowering skinhead. He had swastikas tattooed on his pallid forearms, and a studded dog-collar around his neck. He ignored Julia, but eyed Lily with a degree of approval.

"Ain't no one livin' in this street now but fuckin' Pakis," he told her. "You from the social, or what?"

"Just looking for some friends," Lily said hastily as they retreated.

"'Ere," he yelled after them. "You can come back any time you fancy. Don't bother bringing yer friend, though."

Julia and Lily were too disappointed even to catch each other's eye. They turned the corner by the pub and gazed down another identical, littered street. Julia wondered if it had always been so ugly here, and if so, why she had never noticed it before. But she was sure that violence like the boy's was new, and it chilled her. "What now?" Lily asked.

"I don't know," she said sadly. "I don't know where to go from here. There must be millions of Halls. But Rennyshaw isn't a common name, is it?"

"Isn't there some sort of list of all the people living in a place? Or if they still live in the area?"

Julia's head jerked up. "Of course. The electoral roll. I should have thought of that." They went to the town hall and asked to see a copy of the roll. And they found her at once.

There were three Rennyshaws listed, and the third was Mrs. Margaret A. Rennyshaw, of Sixty Denebank.

Margaret Ann was alive, still living in Ilford. Now that the search was over, Julia realized how slim their chances had been, and their great luck that the trail had been such a short one. She felt a retrospective despondency that had never touched her while they were still searching. It made her legs weak and heavy and she sat down suddenly on a bench in the busy hallway. One or two of the passersby eyed her curiously.

Lily was dancing with delight and triumph. "We could go and see her now, right away."

"We can't, Lily. We can't possibly. Think of the shock it would give her."

"Well then, we could look up her number in the directory, and telephone her."

Lily saw a row of telephone booths in the town hall foyer and ran across to them. A moment later she was back, holding out an envelope with the number printed on it in big red numerals. Julia looked at it, thinking, *In one minute from now, I could be speaking to her.* Then she took it, folded the envelope in half, and put it away with Margaret's letter and her present address. Lily's face fell.

"Lily, I need to prepare myself. And I should try to prepare her . . ." Julia couldn't call her *Margaret,* or *my mother.* She realized that, in truth, she hadn't thought much beyond just finding her. Different, newer fears began to assert themselves.

Lily nodded, mastering her disappointment. "It's okay, Mum. I understand."

"I'll take you to see . . . her, as soon as I can," Julia promised, aware of her own evasion. She felt guilty because of Lily's generosity, but she wanted to make this very last step on her own. She wanted to see Margaret alone, for the first time. And Julia was impatient. She had meant to wait and think a little longer, perhaps to write a careful letter. But just two days later she was on her way back to Ilford. She borrowed Felix's car, thinking that she could hide herself in a car rather than standing exposed in the open street. It wasn't until she turned into Denebank itself that it occurred to her that a brand-new white Alfa Romeo might provide more advertisement than camouflage.

Denebank was a long, straight cul-de-sac. The double row of council houses looked flat and tired. Some of the windows were dressed with bunched frills of nylon curtain, grayish-white or bright pink, but just as many were bare and dusty. There were cars parked with their wheels half on the sidewalks, but none of them was anything like Felix's. The front yards of the houses sloped into the street, separated from the neighbors' by low wire fences. Some of the fences had sagged, in other places they had rusted away altogether, giving all the yards a dispirited air. Some of them were planted with rosebushes and tiny circles of grass, but the rest sprouted weeds and drifts of litter.

Julia let the Alfa slide slowly forward, conscious of its gleaming white shell around her. The children stared at her as she passed them. She counted the house numbers. Forty, forty-two. She stopped the car well short of Number Sixty, but as she shrank back against Felix's black leather upholstery, feeling like a dirty voyeur, she could see it clearly.

It was one of the bare-windowed, littered-yard houses.

A dull, stale feeling of perfect familiarity possessed Julia as she gazed at it. This house was just like the one that Mattie had run away from, back on the old estate. This estate was much newer, and stained high-rise blocks poked up beyond it instead of hundreds of identical streets spreading in unrelieved flatness. But exactly the same air of exhausted inertia stalked between the houses. None of the people who lived here were going anywhere else.

Julia closed her eyes, then opened them again. Nothing had changed. The children had edged closer, but they ran off when they saw her watching them.

Oh, Mattie, Julia thought. *Full circle. If you were here.* She wanted Mattie badly then, and knew a moment's selfish resentment of the grief that had taken Mattie into itself. *It shouldn't,* she resolved. *I won't let it, however much you try to fend me off. You need me, and I need you.* Love and sympathy for her friend spilled over inside her, gratefully warm in the chilly street.

She sat in the car for a long time, wanting to move but rooted by fascination. At about half past five a man walked past. He was wearing a worn jacket, carrying a bag over his shoulder that might have held an empty lunchbox. He was graying, bulky, with a wide, pale face. He went up the sloping path to Number Sixty and let himself in.

Julia shifted in her seat, afraid that he might be staring out at her through the dirty windows. She started the car's engine, swung the wheel, and turned away down Denebank. She was stiff and cramped from sitting too long in the same position.

She saw a woman walking along the sidewalk toward her. She was black, very fat, with a headscarf, and a coat gaping across her front. She had a cheerful face, the only one that Julia had seen in Denebank. Julia stopped the car again and wound down the window, confident that she wasn't unknowingly approaching Margaret Rennyshaw.

"Excuse me. Number Sixty." She nodded covertly back at the house. "Is that where Mrs. Rennyshaw lives?"

The woman shifted her heavy basket to her other hand and peered along the road. "Let's see now. Sixty? No, my love, that's the Davises' house."

"Oh." Julia gripped the steering wheel. "Has Mrs. Rennyshaw moved then? I'm sure that was her house."

The woman shook her head. "Don't know no Rennyshaws. Them's the Davises living there. Been there since the estate was built, same as me. Thirteen years next month. Gawd help us."

Julia was stunned. She couldn't even make herself return the woman's smile. "Thank you," she whispered. "I must have made a mistake."

She drove slowly on, turning into clogged high streets, past garish shopfronts, not knowing where she was going. A wild, silly hope fluttered inside her, that she would find her mother living somewhere else altogether, in a pretty cottage in the country with lavender and hollyhocks in the garden. The old romantic dream twisted with the fear that she had lost her again and that there were no more clues to follow up. And lying over it all she felt a heavy certainty that Margaret Rennyshaw *did* live at Number Sixty Denebank, and that for some reason she couldn't explain, the cheerful neighbor was wrong and she had been right all along.

At last she reached home, and told Lily the story.

"It must be a mistake," Lily said sadly. "The list thing must be wrong, mustn't it?"

"I don't think so. There's just something we don't understand."

"What was the place like?"

Julia hesitated. "It reminded me of Mattie's old house. Where she lived with her father, and Marilyn and Ricky and the others, right at the very beginning." Julia could see the two houses, one superimposed on the other. The similarity was eerie. "Lily. Will you be all right here on your own if I go to Coppins tomorrow to see Mattie? I must go and see her. Whatever she says." As she spoke she felt sharp, irrational anxiety. "Ma." Lily exhaled patiently. "You know I'll be all right."

Julia begged Felix's car again and drove to Coppins.

She didn't know, or wouldn't admit to herself, what she was afraid of. But she craned her neck forward to see the house as she swung through the gates. It looked much the same as it had always, except that the curtains were drawn at some of the windows. The grass had started to grow in the April sun, and the lawns needed mowing.

Mattie answered the doorbell. She was dressed, but she didn't look as if she had given much regard to her choice of clothes.

Julia said, "Hello, Mat."

"Julia? We didn't fix anything, did we?" Mattie looked around in bewilderment. She had been in the empty kitchen, telling herself that she should eat some of the food that Mrs. Hopper had made for her. And now Julia was here, standing bright and urgent and out of place in the listening garden.

"I just came. I wanted to see you."

Julia took her arm, and Mattie let her guide her back inside and across the hallway. Mattie didn't like crossing the hall. She always thought that she could feel the crackle of dead leaves underfoot, and see the mail lying neatly where Mitch had left it on the hall table.

In the kitchen she made a vague gesture intended to be hospitable. "I was just going to have something to eat. Do you want it? It smells quite good," she added in encouragement. She decided that she would get a drink for herself. It was only the second, or perhaps the third of the morning. The bottle was standing handily on the countertop. Mrs. Hopper tended to put it away, but Mattie always got it out again. She poured herself a full glass, and another for Julia. She held Julia's out to her, carefully not spilling a drop.

"Here you are. Helps the lunch go down."

Julia took the glass but set it aside without tasting it. She came across the kitchen and wrapped her arms around Mattie. Mattie held herself stiff for a second, then let her head fall forward to rest against Julia's shoulder. Julia stroked her hair. When she spoke again, her voice was muffled for Mattie by the stroking.

"Oh, Mat. Are you drinking very much?"

"No. Yes, I suppose I am. It helps." And then, after a moment, "Actually, it doesn't even bloody help, but I don't know what else to do. I miss him so much that I hate him."

Julia went on rhythmically stroking her hair. "Poor Mat. Poor Mattie, poor love." After a little while Mattie sniffed. At once the mucus in the back of her throat tasted of stale whiskey. "Give me my drink," she begged. "There's a dear."

She drank, and straightened up. Julia led her to the kitchen table and made her sit down. She poured two bowls of soup out of the pan on the stove and set them on the table. "Go on. Eat some," she ordered. She began spooning up her own, setting an example, but Mattie left hers untouched. She lit a cigarette instead and let the smoke curl up through her thick hair. Julia watched her.

"I don't want you to go on living here on your own, Mattie, when you're like this."

"I'm better on my own." There was a sharp edge in her voice. Mattie knew it was the truth, and she was defending it.

"Mitch wouldn't want you to."

"You don't damn well know what Mitch would have wanted."

Julia reddened slightly, but she didn't look away. Mattie leaned awkwardly across to her. "I'm sorry, I didn't mean that. Take no notice, I don't mean anything. You see? I am better on my own."

She could see Julia mustering her arguments, ready to try again.

"It doesn't matter what you say, Mattie. Say anything. Just listen to what I'm saying too. Won't you sell this house? Buy yourself one somewhere else, on your own if you must, but in town. I'd rather you came with me though. Come back to Montebellate. Just for a little while, won't you?"

As if she hadn't heard, Mattie repeated, "Mitch loved this house."

She didn't love it herself anymore. There was nothing in it that she could look at without seeing him, nowhere in it to hide from his absence. But she couldn't sell it, or even leave it. To sell it would be to sell Mitch himself. She felt the house sucking her into itself.

Julia did bend her head now, to hide her face. She finished her soup, not even noticing what it was. Mattie ate nothing, but she drank her whiskey.

Afterward Julia made some coffee. She carried the tray through into the drawing room and Mattie brought the whiskey bottle. The thick velvet curtains were closed, but otherwise the room was formally neat. The cushions were all smooth and the silver-framed photographs were set squarely on their tables. Julia felt the atmosphere and shivered a little. She went to the windows and pulled back the curtains. Mattie squinted in the shafts of sunshine but said nothing. When she sat down Julia pulled up another chair so that she could be close to her.

She asked gently, "What are you doing here, all by yourself? You've got friends who love you. We want to look after you."

Mattie frowned down at her hands. "What do I do? Try to go to sleep. Wake up again. I watch television quite a lot."

Deliberately, willfully, she took the question at its literal value. She knew that Julia was asking *Why? Why not come and grieve with us?* but Mattie didn't want to give her that answer. The truth was that the performance of friendship called for more than she could give. Mattie felt that the loss of Mitch had left her with no assets, no store of emotions, even selfish ones, that she could offer as currency in return. And worse. With the sharp perceptions of grief—perceptions that stayed painfully sharp however much she tried to blunt them with whiskey—she could hear the silent demands under Julia's kindness. *Look, see here, I'm your friend. Don't pull away, because I need to help you. I'll make you feel better, and that will make me feel better. That's how it works, isn't it?*

In her desolation Mattie couldn't hand over anything, but she didn't want Julia to know what she was thinking. Because that might hurt her, mightn't it?

Mattie tried to marshal her thoughts, momentarily regretting the whiskey.

Then she attempted a laugh. "I can't give you anything, Julia."

"What?" Julia looked stunned.

"What did I say?" The laugh wasn't a good idea. But perhaps Julia would just think it was the drink. *I'm better on my own. I knew I was.* "Sorry. I'm not thinking very straight."

Julia left her chair and knelt down in front of Mattie. She was too close, looking at her too hard.

"It's going to take a long time, I know that, Mattie. Try to be gentle with yourself." For her own part, Julia felt the clumsiness of her attempts at condolence. In frustration, she felt that the right words, the key to the help that Mattie needed, lay close at hand, somewhere just out of her reach. But every word that did come into her mouth shouted its inadequacy at her.

"It will get better," she whispered. "I know it will."

Mattie stared miserably over her head. This distance from her oldest friend made the hurt worse, if that was possible. Only it couldn't be possible, because it was already the most terrible thing in the world.

Mattie longed to be alone again.

But to be alone, she must convince Julia that she was all

right. That was the token that she must hand over, wasn't it? "I have been doing things other than drinking and watching the telly. I went to do the commercial, for a start."

Julia looked pleased. Her pleasure touched Mattie. "How did it go?"

Mattie couldn't help the laugh this time. "Not all that brilliantly. I was rather pissed, actually. They were quite nice about it."

Julia didn't laugh with her. "You don't have to work, do you?"

"I'm reading a script just now. It's quite good." *And if I don't work, what else is there? Has it come to this?* Mattie thought. *Has everything, all of it, finally come to this?* She stood up abruptly.

"This room's getting on my nerves a bit. Whenever I try to mess it up, Mrs. Hopper comes in and tidies. Let's go and walk around the garden."

They went outside. The April sun was thin but bright. They walked slowly over the uncut grass, passing between the rosebushes with their swelling red knobs. Mattie kept her face turned away from the corner of the house, from the patch of colorless gravel. "Talk to me about something else," she ordered without much hope.

Julia began to tell her about Margaret Rennyshaw.

She described the adoption agency, and the first two Ilford streets. Mattie walked beside her, her head down and her hands pushed deep into the pockets of her woolen jacket. Julia came to the point, only the day before, when she had sat in Felix's car in Denebank. Mattie listened, trying to imagine it. She couldn't think what it must have been like for Julia to sit outside a stranger's house, a stranger who was also her mother. It occurred to her that her perceptions of herself were hideously clear, those concerning other people blurred, or nonexistent. She tried to care about that, and couldn't. Her sense of isolation deepened.

Mitch. Why did you have to die? So stupid. So cruel.

Julia was talking about the street her real mother lived in. She said it had reminded her of Mattie's old home. Mattie tried to grasp why it seemed so significant.

"Full circle," Julia said in wonderment. "It was as if we tried so hard to get away from it, the estate and Fairmile Road, and all the time it was lying in wait for us. You can't run away. Perhaps that's what we're supposed to learn. Perhaps you haven't ever really gotten away, until you know it. And afterward you're free."

"Free," Mattie echoed. She had no sense of circularity. She imagined that it would be comforting to recognize such a definite pattern. For herself, the estate, and Ted Banner, and everything else lay dimly, a long way off, reduced to irrelevance. Life seemed like a long, dull thread, perilously thin, easily severed.

She couldn't see that it would make much difference now whether Betty Smith or Mrs. Rennyshaw was Julia's real mother. Not after almost forty years. And it mattered even less than that that a street on a council estate in Ilford looked like another street, on another estate, from almost as long ago. After all, everything, all of it, came to this. And this was what? As little as nothing?

"So will you go and see this Mrs. Rennyshaw?"

"Oh, yes. I'm afraid of doing it, but I must."

Mattie nodded. "Of course. Yes, of course." They made another circuit of the lawns before Mattie shivered. "It's cold out here. Let's go inside again."

In the dusted and polished drawing room she made straight for the whiskey bottle. "Don't frown, Julia. It keeps out the cold. Cheers."

Mattie didn't remember much about the rest of the day. She dimly recalled Julia and Mrs. Hopper fussing in the kitchen, and then sitting down at the kitchen table with Julia for more food. She might even have eaten some of it, because she wanted Julia to know that she was all right.

And then it must have been the end of the day, at last, because Julia had helped her upstairs. She found herself lying on the bed, but she sat up at once. Her head had cleared for a moment. Treacherous. She didn't like these clear intervals, and she didn't like waking up after being asleep. The hurt swung in harder then.

"I don't need to be put to bed like Lily, you know."

"Lily doesn't need to be put to bed nowadays either."

"God. Isn't it weird?"

Julia came and sat down on the bed beside her. "Will you go to sleep now?"

"Sure."

She looked skeptical. "Do you have anything to help you sleep?"

"Brown bottle in the bathroom. Half a tablet only."

Julia went, and came back with a halved tablet and a glass of water. "Here. Mattie," she begged, "Won't you let me stay?" Lily needed her less, she was sure of that.

Mattie gulped, swallowed the pill. Her eyes met Julia's and Julia was relieved to see her smile, the old Mattie.

"I'm all right, I promise. I just need to work through it in my own way."

Julia hesitated. "All right, Mat. If that's what you want."

She picked up the pad from the bedside table, wrote her number, left it beside the cream telephone. "I'm going to call in the mornings and in the evenings. And any other time, you're to call me."

"I will," Mattie murmured.

"Mrs. Hopper knows where I am. I've talked to her."

"Good."

Their hands met, Julia's squeezed. "Go to sleep then."

Mattie lay down. They smiled at each other, then Mattie obediently closed her eyes. Julia crept out of the room, closed the door behind her.

As soon as she had gone, Mattie's eyes snapped open again. Sleep didn't come as easily as that. No matter how she stalked it and tempted it. And when she did fall asleep there were the dreams, and after that there was the waking up again.

Julia made her morning call to Mattie. Mattie told her that she was still in bed, reading the newspapers.

"Fine. I'll talk to you tonight."

Julia put the receiver down, picked it up again at once. She dialed Directory Assistance. The number they gave her was the same as the one Lily had written down in the town hall. Margaret Rennyshaw did live at Sixty Denebank. There was no question about that.

Julia dialed the number. She didn't wait, or think about it again, in case her courage deserted her.

"Hello?"

It was her, she knew it was. It was a thick, rather husky voice.

"May I speak to Mrs. Rennyshaw, please?"

"This is Mrs. Rennyshaw." She had a strong London accent. She sounded suspicious, and defensive.

"Mrs. Rennyshaw, I'd like to talk to you about a personal matter. A very private, personal matter."

There was a long silence. Julia wondered if she had even heard her, or if she had heard her and gone away.

Then she said, "You're Valerie, aren't you?"

"Yes," Julia whispered. "Yes, I'm Valerie." To her dismay, tears began to roll out of her eyes. They ran down her cheeks and she scrubbed them away with her wrist.

"I knew it was you. I knew, as soon as my neighbor told me you were asking. A woman in a posh white car, talking about a Mrs. Rennyshaw. They call me Mrs. Davis 'round here."

"I know. Do you mind? Do you mind me finding you?"

There was another pause, a shorter one. "No, my love. I don't mind, if you don't." Julia thought she wasn't going to say anything else. She was about to start talking, wildly, to fill the silence, when Margaret added slowly, "I thought you'd come someday. After they changed that law. I didn't give you up, you know. Not in my head. I thought about you. Wondering what you were like and what you were doing, all that."

"I know. I know you did. I was thinking about you too. More and more as the time went. I needed to find you so badly. I can't believe it, now that I have. Now that we're talking." It was so strange, Julia thought. To talk like this, and to cry, with a woman she had never known. Never even seen.

"How have you been?" Margaret asked. She sounded awkward now, embarrassed by Julia's tears. Just as suddenly, Julia wanted to laugh. *What has your life been like for almost forty years?*

"Fine. Lucky, I think." Too late, Julia caught herself. "I didn't mean lucky that you had to give me up. Lucky in what came after. Only I didn't realize it at the time." That was her acknowledgment to Betty. She owed her that.

"I know what you meant." The husky voice had gone flat. Julia thought her mother sounded as resigned as the rest of Denebank.

"Can I come to see you?" she asked. "It's hard to talk on the telephone."

"You know where I am," Margaret answered, neither encouraging nor forbidding her.

"Would you like me to come?" Julia persisted.

There was another of Margaret's silences, then she said brusquely, "Yes, I would. Don't come this week. Eddie's on evenings and he's in the house all day. Eddie's the man I live with. He's on the buses."

"I think I saw him."

"Yes. Well, come next week. Monday if you like. Twelve o'clock, he'll be out by then. He . . . doesn't know about you, Valerie."

"I'll be there," Julia said. "My name's Julia now." She hadn't yet called her mother anything.

Margaret tried it out. "Julia?" Then she gave a wheezy laugh. "Better class of name than Valerie, isn't it? Well then, Julia, I'll see you on Monday."

After she had talked to her mother, Julia sat for a long time in the window of the flat. Looking out, she could see the ordinary comings and goings of the quiet street. A woman went by pushing a pram, and a builder's van stopped to unload bags of plaster. Two girls of Lily's age passed, arm in arm, and the builders whistled at them. Julia liked the ordinariness. Life was ordinary, after all. The discovery of Margaret confirmed that. Julia was still watching the street when Alexander's car drew up, and Lily and Alexander got out. She knew that he had been working in London, but she hadn't seen him since the day of Mitch's funeral. He was going to drive Lily back to Ladyhill, and the new school term.

It was almost May. Soon it would be summer. Julia thought of Montebellate, telling herself that she should go back. It drew her, but less strongly than before.

"I talked to her. I just dialed her number and spoke to her," Julia said when they came in. Lily had told Alexander about the hunt, she knew that. They looked at her, expectant. Lily gave a little snort of excitement. "What did she say? Was she amazed?"

"Not exactly. She sounded . . . resigned, I suppose. Curious about what I might be like."

Lily ran across the room to her. Over her shoulder Julia looked at Alexander. She saw that they were concerned for her, and the concern made her feel warm, and strong. Life was ordinary like the street outside, but it was precious too.

"It's all right. I wanted to find her, and now I have. I'm going to see her on Monday. I'm glad I've done it," Julia reassured them.

"I think we should go out to lunch," Alexander said. There was to be a celebration, but nobody tried to explain what they were celebrating.

They went to an Italian restaurant, because Lily loved Italian food.

"It's not as good as real Italian food," Julia insisted, and Lily groaned.

"Mum, you always say that."

Around the table, Julia thought, they were a family. Enough of a family for anyone. *More than she deserved*, she told herself. Whatever she discovered at Denebank, and whatever came after that. Her eyes met Alexander's and she felt her luck, the luck that she had clumsily tried to explain to Margaret, and a strengthening pulse of happiness.

Alexander lifted his glass to her and they drank without pledging anything.

"I wish Mattie was here with us," Julia said. It was hard to think of being happy without Mattie's happiness.

"Is she all right?"

She shook her head. "She did her best to convince me that she is. All she did make me believe is that she wants to be left alone. I ring her in the morning, and at night. I don't know what else to do, except to let her know that we're here for her."

When she looked up she saw that Alexander was still watching her. There was the softness of affection around his mouth and eyes.

Julia understood that Alexander was there for her.

The revelation changed the colors and the contours of everything. It filled the bustling, crowded restaurant with light and gilded the heads of the Kensington shoppers, and it made Lily and Alexander look as beautiful and serene as Olympians.

Julia blushed. She looked away again, suddenly as shy as a girl.

"Ahem," Lily said, out of mischief, seeing everything. "Can I have zabaglione for dessert? Does anyone care?"

"Not a jot," Alexander answered. "Today you may have twenty zabagliones."

Afterward, when Lily was already sitting in the car ready for the drive back to Ladyhill, Alexander and Julia turned to face each other. It was almost the end of the afternoon and office workers were beginning to stream past them toward the tube station.

"There have been so many times like this," Julia offered him. "Too many to count. They always did make me sad."

"There needn't be any more. Don't be sad."

She looked straight at him, smiling. "I know. I won't be."

Alexander leaned forward and touched the corner of her mouth with his own. Then he got into the car and drove away with Lily. This time Julia knew where he was going, and she knew that he would come back. They had grown up, and they knew each other, and there was no need to hurry or to be afraid.

Julia stayed on in Felix's flat.

She wrote to the Mother Superior and explained that she would stay in England for a little longer; she didn't know yet how long exactly. With the letter she enclosed a lengthy list of instructions and advice for Tomaso. But she finished up by writing, "You don't really need me to tell you any of this, do you? We learned it together, and you're ready to do it yourself. Good luck, Tomaso."

She also telephoned Nicolo Galli. His voice sounded thin and brittle, but she heard him chuckle. "I'll miss you, Julia. But you are doing what is right. I am glad of it."

"I think I am right. I'm happy to be here. Nicolo?"

"What is it?"

"I miss you too."

Three or four more times Julia went down to Coppins. Each time Mattie tried to fend her off, greeting her with blank silences or with angry outbursts, and then retreating into incoherence as that day's whiskey took hold.

Julia could do little more than sit with her, or try to persuade her to eat, and Mattie objected even to that. She insisted that Julia didn't really want to be there, that she was doing it only out of a sense of duty, and that she herself didn't need her.

"I'm all right on my own. I need to be by myself, don't you understand? I'm no good for anyone," Mattie cried. Her face was blotched and swollen.

"You don't need to be anything for me," Julia told her. "You don't believe it will get better, Mattie, but I know it will. I'll stay with you until it does. Won't you let me come and live here so that I can look after you?"

"No," Mattie whispered. "No, Julia, please."

Julia ached for her, wishing that she could take on some of her suffering. She tried to see beyond the vehemence of Mattie's rejections, accepting the rebuffs with what she hoped was some of the Sisters' calm.

On one of the days, Mattie wouldn't even open the door to her. Either the housekeeper was out, or Mattie had persuaded her that she didn't want to see Julia. Julia waited on the gravel path for a long time, imagining Mattie inside the dark house, pierced with pain for what she was enduring. At last she stepped back and called up to the dead windows, "Mat, I'm here if you want me. It doesn't matter if you don't, I just want you to know that I am. I'll be back tomorrow. And if you won't let me in then, I'll keep on coming back until you do."

The next day Mattie opened the door at once. Julia could only guess at how much she had already had to drink.

"I'm sorry," Mattie whispered. "I'm hurting so much I don't know what I'm doing."

Julia put her arms around her. "I know. Let me help, Mattie."

Mattie shook her head wearily. "You can't." But that day she let Julia make them some food, and sat down with her in the kitchen to eat it. They talked about Felix and William, and Julia saw a ghost of the old Mattie. She left her that evening with a lighter heart.

To fill in the time when she couldn't be with Mattie, Julia went shopping. She had forgotten how to buy things, even if she had had the money, but she enjoyed looking in the shop windows. Everything seemed very new, and bright and shiny. She also had dinner at Eaton Square with Felix and William, and she admired William's paintings that hung on the freshly painted walls in place of the old, important landscapes and somber portraits. She liked William, and guessed that he was very good for Felix. She saw other old friends, too, and remembered some of the London she had loved in the old days. Her fear of it receded, and she began to feel at home again.

She telephoned Mattie every morning, and every evening, whether they had seen each other that day or not.

"I'm all right," Mattie would lie. "I have to work my own way through it."

"Call me if you need me," Julia said on the Monday morning. She didn't say that she was going to meet Margaret Rennyshaw, nor did she mention Alexander. There were things she felt she couldn't say to Mattie. Not now, not yet, until she was better.

Julia was getting ready to leave for the station. This time she would go to Ilford by train. She didn't want to take Felix's car down to Denebank again. But even before she saw his shadow blurred by the rippled glass in the door, even before the bell rang, Julia had half-guessed that Alexander would come.

She opened the door to him. He was wearing corduroys and a sweater that was unraveling at the shoulder seam, as if he had just walked in from the garden at Ladyhill. He was completely familiar, and welcome to her, and she could only stand and smile at him.

"I thought that if you were going to meet your mother, you might like me to come with you."

"I would like it," Julia said. "I'd like it very much."

On the way she told him about the short, unromantic search for Margaret Ann Hall that Lily had called their treasure hunt. She described Denebank to him, so that he wouldn't be shocked when they reached it.

"Do you mind?" Alexander asked, looking ahead at the traffic and the unlovely shopfronts of the outer urban high streets.

Julia thought. "I mind for her if I find that she isn't happy. How can I mind for myself?"

He put his hand over hers, covering it where it lay in her lap, without looking at her. Julia glanced down and saw the glazed, discolored skin of the old scars. She was overtaken by a sudden longing to make him happy, in compensation, and to wipe out all the sadness of the years.

They passed the end of Denebank and Alexander stopped the car farther away, in another street. Alexander drove an unremarkable, mud-splashed station wagon, but Julia felt his tact.

"I'll wait for you," he promised.

Julia got out and slowly retraced the way to Denebank. She felt conspicuous as she turned into her mother's street, as conspicuous as she had in Felix's car and without the polished shelter of it. The two or three people that she passed looked blankly at her. It seemed a long way to Number Sixty. When she reached it she went up the path, past the broken-down metal fence, and knocked on the door. She had only a moment to stare at the splitting wood under the flakes of old paint before it opened. Margaret Rennyshaw must have been waiting in the hallway.

They looked at each other, greedy, defensive, eager, and appraising all at once. No one seeing them together would have guessed at their relationship, but Julia and Margaret knew immediately that there was no mistake. Julia was Margaret's daughter, as incontrovertibly as Lily was her own.

"You'd best come in," Margaret said in her husky voice. "We don't want the whole street knowing our business, do we?"

Julia followed her in and the door closed behind her.

Beyond the hallway was a living room, filled up with a

three-piece suite in black leatherette with red piping and a big television set. On a low coffee table with upcurved ends two cups were laid out with chocolate cookies arranged in a fan shape on a chrome dish.

In this enclosed space they could look at each other. Julia saw dark hair like her own, only seamed with gray. She saw a strong face with deep lines running from nose to mouth, dark eyes that had begun to fade with age, a body that was indeterminately shaped under a colorless sweater and skirt. She had imagined herself comparing their features, cataloguing the precious similarities that would prove their relationship, finding triumphantly that their hands or their mouths were the exact same shape. She was dismayed, now, to find that there was no need to do so. Their features were different, but the underlying physical resemblance was clear. Her mother looked like an older, wearier version of herself, or as she might have become already if she had been different, less lucky.

Until the last moment, Julia thought with a wry sadness, she had clung to the romantic dreams. It was only now that the rosy clouds finally drifted away.

"Let's get a look at you," Margaret said. And after a moment, "You look fine."

"And you too," Julia answered. "So do you."

"Sit down then," Margaret ordered. "I'll make a cup of coffee." She was formal, as if Julia had come from some authority to inspect the life that she shared with Mr. Davis. She went out into the kitchen, leaving Julia to look around her, and came back very quickly. Julia sat with her cup and saucer balanced on her lap. A chocolate cookie that she didn't want was thick and sticky in her mouth.

"I'm sorry about the state of the place," Margaret began. Julia glanced around her, noticing for the first time that the embossed wallpaper was stained and ripped away in places. The orange and brown patterned carpet was threadbare, and from the worn patches in it, it appeared that it had come from another, bigger room. "Only Eddie's had some money problems over the years. We haven't got ourselves straight, yet."

Julia felt the exhaustion and the hopelessness of the street outside creeping in, and lying heavy in her mother's house.

"It's a nice room," she lied. Margaret didn't waste her energy in contradiction. She lit a cigarette, inhaled, then tapped the nonexistent ash in her saucer. She looked at Julia under lowered eyelids through the smoke. Then she smiled. The smile made her seem warmer and suddenly familiar, then Julia realized that it was because it was like her own. There would be other similarities that would catch at her too. This was what it meant. This was what she had come looking for. A confirmation of where and what she had sprung from.

The sense of circularity came back to her.

"Funny, isn't it?" Margaret said slowly. "We don't know each other. Don't know anything. Where do you start, after you've said you're sorry?"

Julia moved closer to her. The damp palms of her hands stuck to the black sofa.

"Don't be sorry. Don't let either of us be sorry, right from now."

Margaret nodded. "But I was sorry then. Didn't you think I was? I didn't want to let you go. I cried, more than I've ever cried for anything since. They left you with me for a day after you were born. I held you, and looked at you. Then they came and took you away. I could have stopped them, couldn't I? I often thought, after, that I could have."

"No," Julia said firmly. "You were too young."

Margaret looked older than her real age now. Julia felt sad that she had never known her when she was still young, still hopeful. There was a small, lonely silence.

"Tell me about yourself," Margaret said. "Go on. Everything, all about it."

Julia did her best. But as she talked, she knew that she wasn't doing it right. A divorcee, with one daughter who lived in the country with her father, wasn't what Margaret wanted. Nor did she much want to hear about a remote job in Italy, with sick people and nuns and an unimaginable garden. Margaret sat listening, and smoking, without comment. Julia saw her glance at her earth-ingrained fingers, and her plain, faintly dated clothes. She seemed not very interested in Lily, or in Julia's present life. If she had still owned Garlic & Sapphires, Julia thought, it would have been quite different.

"I used to have a business, a chain of shops. But I sold them. I've been much happier since then."

"Hmm. I suppose that's the main thing. What about your nice car?"

"I haven't got a car. I borrowed that one, from a friend." If she had still had the scarlet Vitesse, even, it would have helped. She tried to tell her some more about Montebellate, and the triumph of her gardens.

"Well," Margaret said at last. "You've had the advantages, haven't you?"

Have I? Julia thought. *And wasted them?* Her mother looked baffled, and disappointed. Julia almost told her that she had once been Lady Bliss, mistress of Ladyhill. Margaret would have been proud of that, as Betty had briefly been. She might be impressed, too, if she talked about Mattie. But Julia didn't want to bring Mattie back here, to the estate with her, even in words.

"It's your turn," she said at last. "Tell me about you now."

Margaret turned down the corners of her mouth, gestured around the room. "You can see for yourself. Haven't had much luck, have I?"

Julia felt suddenly, hotly impatient with her. "Why not? Tell me what got you here. Tell me about my father. Your other children."

Her flash of irritation seemed, oddly, to enliven Margaret. She tossed her head with a touch of coquetry and lit another cigarette. "Your father, now. He was clever. Been to college. He was a teacher. Keen on me, he was." She chuckled with pleasure at the memory. "Dirty devil."

Margaret must have been attractive once, Julia saw. Not pretty, any more than she was herself. But magnetic. Perhaps even beautiful. Margaret wouldn't ever have been short of a man to keep her company, Julia guessed.

"Why didn't he help you?"

Margaret glanced at her. "Why do you think? He was married, wasn't he?"

She told the story willingly, even with some relief. He was a teacher at the secondary modern that had been Margaret's school until she left at fifteen. And he had lived at the other end of the same street, with his wife.

Partington Street, Julia thought. She remembered the Asian woman, and the skinhead who had shouted after Lily. The street would have been different then, in the last year before the war. It would have been a tight-knit, homogeneous community. One day, Margaret told her, on her way home from her job in a shop, she had met the teacher. They knew each other, and they were going the same way. They met again the next day, by accident, and then by arrangement. Soon they were meeting at times and in places that were nothing to do with the walk home from work.

Margaret was looking out of the window, beyond the dismal road. "There was an empty house, on the way back to our street.

And it was getting on for winter then. Dark by teatime. We used to slip into the old house together. No one ever knew. He used to call me his wicked little Meg. If I was wicked, it was him who taught me to be." Margaret laughed, a throaty, reminiscent, knowing laugh.

A not-very-bad girl, Julia thought. *Half-knowing, risking it. Like Mattie and me.* Circles again.

"What happened?"

Margaret shrugged. "What I should have known would happen, if I'd had any sense. He got another job. Moved away before I even knew I'd fallen pregnant. He said he'd write, send for me when he'd told his wife that we loved each other. Never did, of course. And I never gave him away. My dad went mad, but I never told a soul."

Margaret was proud of her loyalty. She had gone through what needed to be done all alone.

Julia felt no stirring of longing to know the handsome, deceiving teacher who had been her father. She felt that she knew him already, and disliked his weakness.

"Never told a soul," Margaret repeated, "until you."

Their eyes met. There was the first faint stirring of a real bond between them.

"Go on," Julia said softly.

As she talked, her mother seemed to soften. She told her story without the self-pity that Julia had detected at the beginning.

Within three years of the birth of her illegitimate daughter, Margaret had been married to Derek Rennyshaw, with a baby son of their own. They had had a rented house in Forrester Terrace, and Derek's navy pay. At home without her husband, Margaret had written her pleading letter to the adoption agency.

"They wouldn't tell me anything," she said.

"I know."

Julia took the folded letter out of her bag, handed it over the low table to her mother. Margaret read it, her face expressionless, and then passed it back again.

"You see? I did try. I didn't just let you go."

"I know you didn't."

The slack bond stirred again, like an anchor chain pulled by the tide.

After Derek's discharge at the end of the war there had been two more children, both girls. Derek had had a good job as a long distance truck driver. And then he had been killed in a head-on collision with a bus.

Margaret had gone out to work as a barmaid. The work suited her, but the family had hardly made their way. Much later, after uncomfortable years, she had met Eddie Davis. He was a builder, with a small company of his own. He was married, too, and his wife had never divorced him. Undeterred, Margaret had moved on as Mrs. Davis. There had been a brief, prosperous interval. Then Eddie's business had collapsed.

"He went bust. In a big way," Margaret said flatly. "That was it then."

Julia learned that Mr. Davis was still an undischarged bankrupt. The council house, the telephone, and the rented television and the hire purchase agreement on the black suite were all in Margaret's name, as Mrs. Rennyshaw.

Julia saw, and understood.

Margaret's mouth went tight again. "Easy to end up with nothing, isn't it? But Eddie's all right. We've been together a long time."

"You didn't have any more children?" Julia asked, needing the history to be complete.

Margaret shook her head. "Four is enough for any woman."

Julia accepted her own inclusion in the total, and accepted the weariness of the admissions. She asked about her half brother and sisters. The two girls were married. They had moved away with their husbands, one to the north and one to Plymouth. Mark was married, too, but he still lived in Ilford.

The other Rennyshaws on the electoral roll, Julia remembered.

"Mark's a good boy," Margaret said. "He's a gas fitter now."

Mark was clearly the favorite child. Julia accepted that, too, as she knew she must and could accept everything else about this family that was hers and not hers at all. There were seven grandchildren. She accepted that Margaret had only a little interest to spare for the unknown eighth, for Lily.

Anyway, I've got three grandmothers already, Julia heard Lily say. She felt an unsteadying rush of love and gratitude for her own daughter.

"So there you are," Margaret finished. The softness had gone again. "I'm sorry I can't give you much to be proud of. You were expecting something better."

Once again she made Julia feel like an inspector from an unwelcome authority.

"I wasn't expecting anything. I'm not what you were looking for either, am I?"

Once more her directness seemed to please Margaret.

"I've no right to look for anything." She looked down. Their cups of coffee had become cold on the table between them. They had been talking for nearly two hours. Almost in a whisper Margaret added, "I'm glad you came. I'm grateful. It can't have been easy for you."

Julia glanced around the bare, chilly room. It was a room that had been given up on. As its centerpiece the chocolate cookies arranged fanwise on a chrome dish seemed almost unbearably sad. Julia stood up abruptly and went to her mother. She put her hand on her shoulder and Margaret looked up into her face. Then Julia bent down, awkwardly half-knelt, and put her arms around her. Their cheeks touched.

"I'm glad I found you," she whispered. "We needn't lose each other again."

In that moment Julia knew that the bond between them would never grow taut. It would never be a lifeline, like hers to Lily, but it would still join them. Their acknowledgment of it over the cookies and cold coffee, this awkward embrace, was the coda to her years of dreams. There would be no more dreams, and none of the luxury and pain of speculation, because the truth was here.

In time, Julia guessed, she would meet Eddie Davis, and be introduced to Mark and his sisters. The announcement of her existence would be a shock, but the shock would be quickly forgotten. There would be visits to Denebank, as there were to Fairmile Road, perhaps with Lily. There would be exchanges of presents at Christmas and birthdays, telephone calls at the festivals that called for family unity. The times of the year when she had dreamed of her real mother, when she had convinced herself that she was longed for in her turn.

She would be assimilated, as all truths came in the end to be assimilated. Her recognition of that, Julia thought, showed her that she wasn't young anymore. She didn't feel much regret for youth as she knelt beside her mother's black leatherette chair.

Margaret patted her shoulder. It was a tentative caress, as if the display of affection didn't come easily to her. Julia nodded her head. The brief embrace was over. She stood up, went back to her own chair, but didn't sit down.

"I think I should go now," Julia said quietly. Margaret looked up, but she made no move. "Thank you for coming." She seemed exhausted. Julia was suddenly tired too. Her bones ached.

"May I come again?"

"Of course you can, my love."

She had called her *my love* on the telephone as well, Julia remembered. It was the barmaid's casual phrase, nothing special for herself, of course. Jessie had used the same endearment but differently. *If Jessie had been my mother,* Julia thought with a moment of intense longing that she quelled immediately. She told Margaret that she mustn't get up, turned at the door to smile at her, and let herself quietly out of the house.

She went back along Denebank, walking quickly, aware of Margaret's stricture that the neighbors shouldn't know all her business. As she walked, Julia's tiredness left her. Her head came up, and she straightened her shoulders. She felt loose, and light. The few people who passed stared at her, and she realized that it wasn't because she was conspicuous, but because she was smiling.

It was relief that buoyed her up. She had the truth, and her possession of it added another dimension to her freedom. The truth was neither tragedy nor miracle, but as ordinary as life. As precious as life.

Julia turned at the corner to look back at the street and at her mother's house. She saw it clearly, stripped clear of the fascination and fear that had shrouded it. The outlines were all sharp, as if a summer thunderstorm had washed the dirt from the city air.

She turned again and almost ran to where Alexander was waiting for her.

He was sitting in his car reading, but he closed his book as soon as he saw her. Julia slid into the seat beside him. When she looked into his face she felt another surge of love. It consumed her, and it burned up her fears. She felt brave, and sure, and grateful. Her face was as bare as the truth, and she offered it humbly to him. She knew, too, that if he refused her now, she was finished.

Alexander leaned closer, then touched his mouth to hers.

That was all.

A moment later the traffic flowed past them, they fumbled with the mechanism of seat belts, Alexander started the car and swung the wheel. They were both smiling, dazed with their good fortune. Light danced on chrome trims and reflected into their eyes from the windows of buses. And when they looked again, they saw each other as clearly as Julia had seen Denebank, without the veils of romance but with all the dust of bitterness and jealousy washed away. They had the chance to be new again, and they had learned enough to know that they must take it.

"Tell me what happened," Alexander asked her.

As they drove, without much idea where they were going, Julia described her mother and the house in Denebank, and told the story that had deposited her there.

"What do you feel?" Alexander asked. Julia loved him again for his unobtrusive sympathy.

"I feel relieved," she answered. She told him about the circularity that seemed to have brought her back where she had begun, with Mattie, and her acceptance of those patterns of truth, at last, because she knew that she couldn't change them.

"I'm free," Julia said. "It's taken a long time, hasn't it?"

Alexander stopped the car. He pulled in very carefully to the side of the road, each movement meticulously completed. Julia waited, and then he turned to face her.

"I want you to come back to me," Alexander said.

Julia didn't hesitate. Her face dissolved into a smile that Alexander couldn't remember ever having seen before.

"I can come back, if you will have me," she told him. "I can, can't I, because I'm free?"

He took hold of her and kissed her then, and a little knot of passing schoolgirls looked into the car and giggled among themselves at the glimpse of such old-age, incongruous passion.

Through the haze of oblivious happiness, Julia saw that they had parked beside the tentative spring green of a big public park.

"Let's go and walk in there, under the trees."

They left the car, and walked through high wrought-iron gates. They followed bare earth paths between the plane trees, and they crossed the wide grass spaces to a lake fringed with weeping willows. Alexander took her hand and held it in his own, protected in the pocket of his coat. They sat on a bench, talking in low voices and watching the silent anglers and the ducks trailing V's of ripples behind them. They knew that the passage of years had left them with yawning spaces to fill, but they talked only about small things, leaving the rest to find their own time.

When the cold wind drove them on, Alexander put his arm around Julia and they walked in step, their hips touching. They passed beds full of scarlet municipal tulips, and Julia thought of the seductive warmth of Montebellate. She loved it still, but she wouldn't have exchanged the most beautiful place in the world, and all her achievement in it, for the windswept regimentation of the London park, with Alexander. She smiled, and gazed at the tulips. Their brightness seemed to bleed into the air. The color was as hot and sharp as her own blood. Physical longing took hold of Julia, a sudden need that was fiercer because she had half-forgotten it. Alexander saw it, and felt it with her.

They left the park and drove on.

The flat in Kensington greeted them like a refuge. Julia and Alexander locked its front door behind them, half-laughing and half-awed by what was happening. The flat was exciting in its empty anonymity. Here, for now, there were no memories and no reproaches. They felt that they had made an assignation, and had come creeping here to steal their time together. Alexander saw the flush under Julia's brown skin, and the light in her slanting eyes, turned up to his. The laughter faded, replaced by hunger, and he drew her against him. She was as pliant as a reed, thinner and lighter than he remembered. She was hot, and the taste of her made him want to push himself deeper into her, staking a final, irrefutable claim.

Only Julia drew back, holding him away with her hands. Alexander was briefly certain that, after all, there was another obstacle.

"No," he said. "Not now."

"Listen. I wanted to tell you that I was always wrong. I was selfish, and I put myself first instead of you and Lily. I never did anything for you, did I? Not one thing. I'm ashamed of that, Alexander. I'm sorry for the fire, and for what I did with Josh Flood, and for trying to take Lily away from Ladyhill. If I could undo any of it, I would."

Alexander said, "I wanted you to love my house as much as me. I know you did love me, Julia."

"I love you still."

She seemed very sweet then. He loved the sweetness because it must have been there all along, while he had been too certain of his own rightness to see it.

"I was wrong too."

Julia moved her hands. "No," she echoed. "Not now."

They went into the bedroom and lay down together.

Julia had been afraid that her body had forgotten its rhythms. She had used it for so long as an instrument of work instead of pleasure. But the rhythms came back to her, clearer and more intense than they had ever been. There was an added resonance, too, because they were also Alexander's, and they found that the music of familiarity was better than any novelty.

Afterward they lay in the still room together. They studied each other's faces, seeing the marks that the years had made and triumphantly discounting them. There was no need, yet, to talk very much.

It began to get dark outside, the quick and mysterious spring dusk overtaken by the orange glow of the city night. Julia looked at her discarded watch. It was almost nine o'clock.

"I must ring Mattie," she said.

Alexander yawned luxuriously. "I'll get us a drink," he offered. He padded away to the kitchen, and Julia dialed the Coppins number.

Mattie was sitting on her bed. She didn't know quite how long she had been there, but her limbs were stiff and heavy. It must be a long time. She looked down, frowning, and saw an empty bottle nestled in the bedcover's satin folds. As the telephone began to ring she remembered that earlier she had stood by the window, watching the wind tossing the trees. She hated the wind. She had drawn the curtains to shut it out, but she had still heard it clawing at the roof.

"Mattie?"

"Yes."

"Mattie?"

"What is it?" Her voice came out thickly. Even in her own ears it sounded rusty, as if she hadn't used it for a long time.

"Are you all right?"

The howling of the wind was so loud, she could hardly hear what Julia was saying. How long was it since her last call? It was impossible that it had been only this morning. A very long time seemed to have gone by since then, only she had no idea what she had done with it. "What's the time?"

"Nine o'clock," Julia answered in her enviable, clear voice. "Mattie, are you a bit pissed? You don't sound very well. Have you had anything to eat?"

"Nine o'clock at night?"

"Of course. Listen, is Mrs. Hopper there? Can I talk to her?"

"I can't hear you very well. Is it windy there?"

"Yes, it is." The wind had pulled at the willow branches and shaken the red tulips in the park.

"It's very windy here," Mattie said slowly. She was glad that it was real, at least. She had begun to be afraid that it was only in her head. But now it seemed to threaten its way into the bedroom with her. It stirred the heavy curtains at the windows. Mattie turned away from it, hunching her shoulders. "Mrs. Hopper's gone down to the village to a whist drive. I'm okay. I'm going to have dinner now. On a tray in front of the TV. There's a play I want to see." She had used to do that with Mitch. Mattie built up the little details for Julia, as if with her loving accuracy she could make them come true.

"That sounds nice. What time's the play? Shall I drive down and watch it with you?"

Mattie stared around her. She didn't know what was on television. She hadn't watched anything for days. She looked down again, and saw that there were stains of spilled whiskey on her clothes. She felt afraid of Julia's intrusion. Even Julia was an intruder here, behind the curtains that couldn't close out the wind. Julia would see the whiskey stains. It was difficult enough to allay Mrs. Hopper's suspicions.

Mattie smiled, with a kind of new cunning. "No, don't bother with that. It'll be over before you get here."

As they talked, she could hear Julia's anxiety begin to fade. Regret swam like a quick fish in Mattie's head, as if she had missed a vital chance. But she didn't want Julia down here, did she? She was trying to keep them all away, because then it hurt less, didn't it?

Sitting up in her own bed, listening to Alexander hunting for glasses, Julia made a last try.

"Mat, Alexander's here. Shall I put him on?"

"What? Oh, don't worry, I'll miss the beginning of the play. Give him my love, will you?"

"Yes. Yes, of course I will. He sends his too."

Mattie stared unseeingly at the crumpled satin and the Johnny Walker label. Then a thick wet mist of tears rose up and washed everything out of sight.

"Good night, then, Mat. I'll call in the morning."

"Good night. Thanks for ringing."

"Sleep well."

Mattie uncurled her stiff fingers. She put the receiver down, knocking it sideways. She pushed the telephone off the bed and on to the carpet. The thick pile muffled the purr of the dial tone, and the blast of the wind seemed to engulf everything else. The tears ran down Mattie's face. She shook her head from side to side, too weary even to stop them dripping from her jaw. The wind mocked her with its noise, and she wanted nothing more than to go to sleep. She had hardly slept last night, whenever that had been, and in the intervals of it when sleep did come she had dreamed of Mitch, lying in his cold steel drawer and then under the earth in the windy churchyard.

Mattie stumbled to her feet. She needed another drink. In her luxurious bathroom she took another full bottle out from under the towels in the linen chest and unscrewed the cap. Then she took the brown bottle of sleeping pills down from its place on the shelf and ate one with a swig of whiskey, and then another.

If she could only sleep, Mattie thought. *If she could only sleep, and not have to dream anymore.*

A little while later Mattie went downstairs. She knew that she should eat something now. She moved clumsily in the kitchen, knocking a dish off the worktop and sending a knife skidding across the polished floor. She found a loaf of bread, and tore some ragged chunks off it. She put a plateful of it on a tray, and carried it through into the television room. Then she sat down in front of the dead screen and ate the dry hunks, chewing them slowly until they slipped heavily down her throat. She didn't think of the other suppers that she had eaten here with Mitch, their trays balanced companionably on their laps. She concentrated on swallowing the bread, lump by lump.

When it was all gone she stood up. The tray and the plate crashed to the floor. Her legs had begun to fold beneath her, but she made her slow, painstaking way up the stairs to her bedroom. Then she lay down across her bed and closed her eyes. The wind had stopped blowing at last.

TWENTY-SEVEN

It was the beginning of September. It was as hot as midsummer; hotter, even, with the reverberating heat stored in the earth and stone, but the light was already changing. The shadows, infinitesimally lengthened, made Julia think of autumn, and the Italian winter following it.

She was standing on the lowest terrace of the garden, her back against the stone balustrade that protected the paved walk from the sheer drop down to the sea. Far below her was the restless water with its white and gold fringe, and in front of her the serene terraces rising up to the palazzo walls.

Mechanically, Julia's eyes followed the lines of them. She knew each lemon tree in its terra-cotta pot, the face of each statue and the contours of each step. She knew the welcoming shade of the vine and jasmine pergolas, and the exact music of the fountains. She knew them and she loved them with fierce pride, but she was going to leave them for the last time.

Yesterday, Nicolo Galli had told her that she must go home before it was too late. She had come out into the gardens at last to breathe in their sweetness, and to think, but she had found that there was no need even for that. Julia knew already what she must do. She felt that she could see clearly again, after the months of grief, all the way to the horizon.

Mattie was dead.

She had died alone, on the same night that Alexander and Julia had slept together in the Kensington flat. Her housekeeper had found her, and it was the housekeeper's telephone call that woke Julia as she slept in Alexander's arms. They had gone at once to Coppins, but there was nothing they could do for Mattie. They could only arrange to bury her in the Whitby churchyard, with the wind blowing across it off the North Sea.

They reopened Mitch's grave to put Mattie in beside him. Their friends stood in a little huddle around its open mouth, Julia and Alexander and Lily and Felix, and Mattie's brothers and sisters. Lily had cried, big choking sobs like a child's. Julia had stared straight ahead of her, her eyes wide and dark with grief.

Afterward they had stumbled blindly away, unable to believe that they were leaving Mattie's brightness behind forever on the windy headland.

Julia left the Kensington flat. She gave the keys back to Tressider & Lemoine, and went to Coppins. She stayed in the big, desolate house, living like a wraith herself in the sad rooms, until all Mattie's accumulation of belongings had been sorted and removed. The furniture and the prints of popular works of art and the fringed lampshades were all sold or given away, and then the house itself was put on the market. There had seemed to be no place for Alexander there, nor even for the faint expectation of their own happiness, while those painful rites were being completed. When it was over, exhausted and torn too many ways by guilt and grief, Julia fled back to the bare simplicity of Montebellate.

The nuns had received her kindly, but Tomaso was surprised and Nicolo was shocked. For the first time, Montebellate failed to provide the expected balm. Julia walked through the perfection of her gardens, and up and down the steep cobbled streets, and thought of Mattie. She dreamed of her, talked to her, and cried because there was never the whisper of an answer. She was never able to unravel the secret that Mattie had taken with her. None of them ever knew whether Mattie had wanted to die, or simply to sleep.

All through that Montebellate summer, Julia lived with the memories of their friendship. The act of remembering made a tribute to Mattie.

She went back over the years, picking out the threads that linked the two of them and that stretched all the way back to hated Blick Road. She tried to recall each moment with perfect honesty, because she wouldn't have the shadows of guilt any longer. There were times when they had neglected each other, and times when they had been less than generous. Julia counted them over with clear sight, and set them on one side. Even at the end, Julia knew, she hadn't failed Mattie. She had given all that she could, and Mattie had not found it enough. She had gone her own way, and not even Julia could see that way clearly.

On the opposite side of the reckoning, after all they had lived through, there was the friendship that had endured. The friendship had been strong, and they had drawn their own strengths from it. They had been mother and sister to each other as well as friend, and Julia was orphaned by her loss more truly than she had ever been by Betty or by Margaret Hall.

It took all the early summer months, when the garden walks and the palazzo shadows seemed full of Mattie, for Julia to realize that the fact of their friendship hadn't disappeared. It was still with her, and it would always remain with her, even though Mattie herself had withdrawn.

Julia's strength returned, and she was surprised by the measure of it. Even before Nicolo warned her, she knew it was time to leave her refuge and go back to her own world.

Nicolo had a chest infection that would not respond to treatment. The nuns had done their best to nurse him, but at last he had been taken to the big hospital in Salerno. Only a few months before, he would have resisted the move with every ounce of himself, but he was an old man and he was beginning to fail.

"Don't bury yourself here any longer," he urged her. "Go

home now, to Alexander and Lily, or it will be too late for you."

Julia sat by his bed. "I know," she said. "I'm going, my old friend."

She would go back home for Mattie's memorial service. It was important to do that.

Now, in her garden with the sun hot on her head, Julia knew that she didn't need to think anymore. She had done enough of that, in her solitude.

She didn't owe any debt to Mattie. Mattie and Mitch were dead, but her own choices and discoveries lay ahead of her. Her debts were only to the living, to Alexander most of all.

If she had never before done anything just for him, Julia resolved, she would do it now. She would leave her gardens behind, for the nuns and their patients and Tomaso, their real owners. She would leave the safety and the simple, limited satisfactions, because she was strong enough, and go back to Alexander and Ladyhill. If he wanted her, still and after so much, she would be there for him.

Julia said her good-byes. It took only a very little time. Nicolo held her hand in his thin, dry one. "You are doing right," he told her.

"At last." Julia smiled at him. She kissed him on the forehead and walked away down the ward without looking back.

On her last evening she walked with Tomaso through the secret garden, and out onto the highest terrace. The air was so still that they could hear the whisper of the sea, and the stillness distilled and intensified the flower scents. Julia felt the full beauty and magnificence of what she was leaving behind.

"You will miss your gardens, I think," Tomaso observed.

"They aren't mine," Julia answered. "And you are here to look after them. I will always know that they are here."

Like the memory of Mattie. Like our friendship itself. They had not ceased to exist anymore than the gardens would just because Julia was no longer there.

Julia and Tomaso went down the flights of steps and leaned over the warm stone coping to look down at the sea, and then they walked back up to the palazzo together. The nuns came to the palazzo gates to see Julia off. The children ran with them, and a handful of residents. The Mother Superior kissed Julia on each cheek.

"May God be with you."

"Thank you, Mother."

Looking back, as the taxi took her down the hill, Julia saw the nuns' white coifs moving like butterflies in the garden.

Alexander and Lily were at the airport to meet her. Julia saw them at once, as if they were the only people in the arrivals hall. Lily was shouting.

"Mummy! Oh, Mummy, welcome home. We thought you'd never come."

Alexander was standing behind her. Alexander was no chameleon. Julia thought he looked just as he had when they first knew each other. Even the checked shirt and old jacket might have been the ones he had always worn.

He stepped forward and put his hand to lift her chin so that he could see into her face. She met his eyes, and they smiled at each other.

In Alexander's car, the same dirty station wagon, Julia asked, "Where are we going?"

"Lily and I have rented a flat in Fulham," Alexander answered. "It's rather suitable. We use it whenever either of us needs to be in London."

"Neutral territory," Julia murmured.

"Exactly," he agreed. They were both thinking that Ladyhill wasn't neutral, not yet.

They reached the Chiswick flyover. Julia looked at the tangled buildings and the streaming cars, all bathed in pale, murky sunlight. Montebellate already seemed far behind her, but she felt no regret. She turned to look at Alexander's profile, filled with affection for its familiarity.

"Do you know what I was thinking on the plane?"

"Tell me."

"I was thinking that we should have a party, for Mattie. Not a solemn business like her memorial service will be. But a real old noisy party, like there used to be."

To her delight, Alexander caught the shimmer of the idea and tossed it back to her. "Yes. And I know where we should have it too. The only possible place. The Rocket. It's been turned into a bar now, rather a louche one, and there's a little dance floor downstairs."

Lily leaned forward between them, her arms spread along the backs of their seats. "A party," she chanted. "a wonderful, wicked party."

Later, when they were alone together, Julia sat with Alexander's arms around her and her head resting against his shoulder.

"I couldn't come back any sooner," Julia said. "Not straight after Mattie died. I didn't see how we could start again with shadows still between us."

"I know," Alexander answered. "I understand why you went away. It's part of your strictness. We didn't deserve our happiness then, when Mattie was dead. That was what you thought, wasn't it?"

He understood more, at last. He understood Julia herself. "You lost her too."

"Yes, I lost her. I loved her as well."

To her infinite relief, Julia realized that there was no bitterness left between them.

"Julia, are you here to stay?"

"If you will have me."

He held her tighter, answering her.

Felix was standing in his dressing gown at one of the tall windows that overlooked Eaton Square. There had been weeks of rain, but now there was the promise of an Indian summer. The angle of the sun had already declined, and it filtered through the tired trees to cast long, autumnal shadows.

Felix was thinking of the old days, with Julia and Mattie, and the other flat with a view of London plane trees. He remembered how their female mystery had seemed to exclude him, but how the three of them had still drawn closer together, until he loved them both.

He had kept the drawings that he had done of them, all that time ago.

And this April, after Julia had telephoned to tell him the unthinkable news, he had gone to the dusty folder and taken them out.

The first drawing showed the two of them sprawled on Mattie's bed. Mattie was reading a magazine, Julia a fat novel. Mattie was all loose curves, and her bare thigh showed where her robe had fallen open. Beside her, Julia was dark and angry-looking, with sharp bones showing under her thin skin. Looking afresh at his work, Felix realized that he had unknowingly drawn her as a boy. And he also saw that they were only children, trying hard to look like bad girls.

It was twenty-two years since he had done the drawing, but he had found that he could still remember their reaction when he showed it to them. "You haven't made us very pretty," Julia complained.

And he had told them that they were more than prettiness, they had style. They had kept their style, the two of them, individually and in the convolutions of their friendship. He had taken out the second drawing and studied that. It showed the three of them, Mattie and Julia and Josh. They were listening to "Rock Around the Clock." Such a long time ago, even the music seemed innocent.

Felix had liked the second drawing. He had kept it pinned to his wall over the mantelpiece. He found, oddly, that he couldn't remember exactly when he had realized that it was there because he liked to look at Josh.

Since the dark day at the end of April, he had often gone back to the folder and taken out the two drawings. But on this morning, in the oblique yellow light of the beginning of autumn, he went only as far as his desk between two of the high windows. He touched the folder with the tips of his fingers, then walked on through the quiet flat. He didn't turn his head to look at George's Lalique glass, or at the modern pictures, or any of the juxtaposition of old and new things. But he was still conscious of the continuity, and the changes.

After William had come, the faintly old-maidish order of the place had disappeared. William made lively, healthy disarray. He left open books and magazines on the marble consoles, and he lay with his feet up on the pale silk sofas. He emptied the loose change out of his pockets and dumped it in the Lalique bowls, and left a trail of coffee cups and sketches and thrown-off shoes wherever he went.

Felix went into the kitchen and made tea. Then he carried the tray through into the bedroom.

William blinked at him and yawned. Felix put the tray down beside the bed and opened the curtains to the slanting sunshine. William hauled himself upright and leaned back against the bedhead. He was always a heavy sleeper, and it took him a long time to wake up in the mornings. Felix took him tea, and William was always grateful. It was one of William's most likable traits that he demonstrated his gratitude for even the smallest things that were done for him. It made him an attractive companion. They had lived together for almost six months, and Felix was still discovering the extent of their pleasure in it.

Felix poured the tea and gave William his cup. He drank it quickly, with the open appetite that he brought to everything. Then he folded his hands behind his head. Thick, dark hair

curled in his armpits and across his chest. Felix put his hand over
William's breastbone. He was very warm, and the sheets of
muscle pulled smoothly under Felix's fingers. They smiled candidly at each other.

"What time do we have to be there?" William asked.

Felix's face changed, turning somber. "Eleven o'clock. I'd
better go and have my shower."

When he came back, he was carrying one of his dark gray
suits on its padded hanger.

"It's a celebration," William reminded him gently, "not a
funeral."

"I know it's not a funeral," Felix answered.

Today was the day of Mattie's memorial service. And
tonight, at the Rocket Club, there would be the party that she
would have wanted. The shock and despair that they had felt at
her funeral had faded enough to let them celebrate her.

He hung the dark suit up again and took out a cream one.
He tucked a blue silk handkerchief into the breast pocket and put
on a shirt in the same shade of blue. Beside him, William
shrugged himself into his blue and white seersucker summer
jacket.

When they were ready, they went out across the square in
their light, bright clothes. Felix's white car was parked under the
trees. They got into it together and drove across London.

The Actors' Church in Covent Garden was already almost
full.

Felix and William hesitated for a moment when they came
inside it, letting their eyes grow accustomed to the dimness after
the sunlight, breathing in the churchy air. Then they walked
down the nave to their places near the front.

A moment later Julia slipped into the seat next to Felix. She
was wearing a little hat with a veil that reminded him, for some
reason that he couldn't quite place, of Jessie. They kissed each
other, then Julia stretched her hand across to touch William's in
greeting. Her fingers and thin wrist were tanned from the Italian
sun. Beyond Julia was Lily. Alexander followed her, smiling
over their two heads at Felix.

Felix was glad to see that Alexander was there.

They bowed their heads, shuffled in their decorous line, and
folded their hands, inexperienced churchgoers except for Alexander, who was used to the rituals of Ladyhill parish. Julia was
thinking that Mattie would have giggled and whispered behind

her service sheet, and that when she bent her head to bring it closer there would be the old scent of Coty and cigarettes. She closed her eyes, folding the memory of her within herself. The service took the form of readings from what were supposed to be some of Mattie's favorite books. Ricky Banner, Chris Fredericks, and Tony Drake read in turn, and a film producer who had been a frustrated long-term admirer of Mattie's gave a short address.

They sang the Twenty-Third Psalm, and finally the hymn "He Who Would Valiant Be." The hymn had been Julia's choice. She and Mattie had sung it at Blick Road together, two little girls nudging each other behind their hymn books.

To be a pilgrim. As they sang, Julia was aware of the people all around her. She had seen John Douglas, and villainous old Francis Willoughby, Jimmy Proffitt, and other faces that were familiar from films and the theater. She remembered some of the women from Mattie's feminist theater group, and among the others she didn't know were Lenny, and Doris and Ada, and one or two unplaceable middle-aged women who had once worked Monty's strip-club circuit alongside Mattie.

They had all come here to remember Mattie. Except that there was no real memory of her here, in these tasteful, sanitized proceedings. Julia couldn't remember Mattie ever having expressed admiration for the Shakespeare sonnet that Chris Fredericks read so movingly. All of this was to make this gathering of Mattie's friends feel that they had done the right thing for her, only none of them had been able to do it at the right time. They had all loved Mattie. It was one of her special talents to command love, and yet in the end none of it had been enough for her.

Painfully, Julia turned her head, trying to shift the weight of her guilt. Guilt was futile and destructive; Julia knew that after the summer that had just passed. But still she couldn't escape the knowledge that of all these people Mattie had loved her best, and yet she hadn't been there when she was needed.

If she had gone to Coppins that night, instead of sleeping in Alexander's arms.

If. There was no comfort or validity in *if*.

Standing in the crowded church, with their schoolgirls' hymn rolling around her, Julia suffered her loss once more. Mattie was gone, and no amount of respectful celebration could bring even an echo of her back.

They started on the last verse. People were thinking of cups of coffee, early drinks and lunch, and the promise of the living day outside the church. Their voices rose cheerfully. Julia could hear Alexander's firm musician's tenor and Lily's soprano. On her other side Felix's head was bent but William was singing with his chin well up, showing a well-bred public schoolboy's familiarity with the words.

And then, looking away in the opposite direction across the nave, to where a shaft of light struck through one of the windows, she saw Josh's blond head.

He was singing, isolated in the midst of a contingent from the agency that had used Mattie in its deodorant ads.

Julia shook her head slightly, turned her eyes down to her service sheet, then lifted them to where she had last seen Josh. He was still there.

After the first shock of surprise, Julia recognized the inevitability of it. It had always been Josh's ability to appear and disappear with theatrical suddenness. It had hurt her, long ago.

Josh had loved Mattie, too, in his way. He had materialized here to celebrate what passed for her memory, along with everyone else. There was nothing particularly startling in that. But Julia felt her heart thumping unpleasantly.

Lily glanced at her mother. Then she followed the direction of her gaze across the nave.

The memorial service was over. They knelt, with a rustling of paper and skirts, for the priest's final blessing. Then, with the triumphal burst of an organ fugue dismissing them, they stood up and began to crowd into the aisle. There were greetings, and handshakes, and as they streamed out into the sunlight of the piazza there were kisses and discreet ripples of laughter. They were like the congregation at a rather somber wedding suddenly released to the prospect of champagne and gossip. They felt alive, each one of them, straightening their shoulders and peering ahead into the brightness.

Julia's mourning for Mattie wasn't complete, even after the summer she had spent alone at Montebellate with her memories of her. She guessed that the sense of loss would always stay with her. But now, coming out of the Actors' Church in the press of Mattie's friends and colleagues, Julia knew that she was alive too. Mattie and Mitch were dead, but her own choices and discoveries lay ahead of her.

Julia smiled, uncertainly, her eyes stinging behind her veil.

Someone stepped in front of her, isolating her from the crowd. She looked up at Josh. Julia lifted the wisp of net away from her face and he kissed her, small, light kisses on either side of her mouth.

"What are you doing here, Josh?"

His face was still the same, only there was more silver than gold about Josh now. She remembered just what it was about him that she had loved, and why it had been so helplessly.

"I was in England. I knew that Mattie was dead, of course. I'm sorry." Formally, he offered his condolences to her, and Julia nodded. "I saw the notice of the memorial in the paper. I wanted to be here. Harry Gilbert wanted to come, too, you know. But he's in the hospital. He's not very well. He saw all Mattie's films, although I don't think he ever told Joyce why. He even came to see her in the West End, once or twice."

Julia nodded again, absorbing the idea of Harry Gilbert's making an icon out of Mattie. Nothing could seem odd or incongruous today.

Josh said, "I didn't know where to find you. I knew you would be here this morning." She lifted her eyes to Josh's. "Did you still want to find me, after everything?"

"I did."

She remembered the loneliness that she had seen in the mountain cabin, the threads she had glimpsed of a life that hadn't changed in twenty years. Josh didn't change, or grow. But he had the same, compelling effect. Lightly, Julia rested her hand on his arm. "Look," she said, "Here's Lily. Would you have guessed?"

Lily delighted in her chameleon changes. Today her hair was a black, glossy cap. The hem of her raspberry-pink linen dress fell below her knees, and she was wearing a pair of her mother's pearl studs in her ears, like any debutante.

"I wouldn't have guessed," Josh answered. "But now I see." He studied her candidly. He held out his hand, and Lily shook it. "You're the aviator," she breathed, her eyes widening.

"Your mother and Mattie called me that, long ago."

Your comic-book hero. Those were Alexander's words.

"Josh, here's Felix. And this is Felix's friend, William Paget."

There was more handshaking, followed by the good-humored greetings of friends who were silently conscious of their fortune in being here, and of the absences.

Julia shielded her eyes with her hand. The day's beaten brilliance seemed suddenly too bright for her.

"And this is Alexander Bliss. Alexander, this is Josh Flood."

Alexander saw a lean, suntanned man with an open, good-humored expression. He looked pleasant, but Alexander would never have picked him out of a crowd as a comic-book hero. *How odd it is,* he thought, *when legends finally take shape.* Yet Julia had left him for this man, the willful tenacity of her love for him had been hurtful and baffling. Once, Alexander might have wanted to hit him. Now he felt nothing but curiosity.

Julia was watching them. He sensed her anxiety and it touched him. He loved her now, and he was almost sure of her. The appearance of Josh did no more than convince him that he must make certain of her, at once.

He held out his hand. "Hullo, Josh."

Josh took it in both of his, shook it warmly. "Alexander. Good to see you."

They stood, the six of them, in the wide space outside the church while the pigeons hopped and pecked between their feet. They talked lightly about the ceremony, but not about Mattie's absence from it. And then the conversation faltered. They began to glance around them, wondering what it was proper to do next.

Felix said, "Would it be a good idea if we all went back to have lunch at Eaton Square? It would be our own private party before this evening."

Julia smiled at him. "Mattie would have liked to be with us."

"I know she would," Felix said softly. Julia knew that they were both remembering how Mattie had loved smoky rooms, refilled glasses, and the laughter and conspiracies of friendship.

Alexander's fingers touched Julia's wrist.

They drove back across London in their cars, and sat down among the pale cushions in Felix's drawing room. William poured glasses of wine, and Julia lifted hers.

"To Mattie," she said proudly.

"To Mattie," they echoed her.

They drank their wine, and they talked, like any group of old friends. Josh and Alexander talked about skiing and the Concorde. Julia and William talked about painting, and Felix described Paris to Lily. Lily was going to Paris in the autumn, to live for a year, to work and to learn French. At her insistence, Alexander had allowed her to leave school.

Lily's brightness shone and crackled in the muted elegance of the room. She laughed, and she made the rest of them laugh with her. Julia saw the flicker of Josh's admiration from the moment that it kindled, and she also saw Alexander's frank pride in his daughter.

The angle of the sun declined further still. It struck through the windows in long, gilded bars and then the bars narrowed and disappeared altogether as the sun slid behind the roofs across the square. Soon it would be time for their little group to move on to the big party at the Rocket.

Felix stood up and went over to his desk between the windows. He undid the ribbon that tied it, and opened the blue folder. He lifted a drawing in each hand and held them out, the one of Julia and Mattie to Julia, the other one to Josh.

They took them. Felix said, "I've held on to these for a long time. I think I'd like you to take them now. As a different memorial."

Josh took his, then held it out for Lily to see. Her glance went from the face in the picture to the one in front of her.

"A long time ago," Josh murmured. He smiled at Felix. "I'd like it, very much. I remember we were listening to Bill Haley."

Julia imagined the picture tacked up on the bare walls of the cabin in the mountains, or in the impersonal Aspen apartment. She looked down at her own drawing. A few months ago she might have folded it and put it lovingly in her marquetry box. But she was trying to live without her talisman now. Life was to be lived, its chances seized, and not to be propitiated as she had tried to do. She had thrown away Valerie Hall's birth certificate because she had no need of it, and she had replaced the Rapunzel book in the palazzo library. Her engagement and wedding rings were still in the box. If she was right, if she was lucky, they could be taken out again.

And then, because she had started to buy them once more, she could keep her strings of pearls and pairs of garish earrings in George's marquetry box.

She held the picture out to Lily. "You take it, Lily," she said. "When Felix made that drawing, Mattie and I were the age that you are now. We knew that we had everything to happen to us, but we still thought that we were such clever, bad girls."

"You became good women," Alexander said. "Both of you did."

They came together, all the old friends, in the white-painted cellar for Mattie's party. Julia had searched them out, and tracing the networks of marriages and moving and remarriages made her feel at home again in London.

Ricky brought a reformed version of the Dandelions, and a little crowd of fans followed them. They were closer to Lily's age than to Mattie and Julia's. Rozzie's children were among them, and the Banner party was completed by Rozzie herself with Marilyn and Sam. Phil had gotten married and gone to live in Canada. Mattie hadn't left a will, but most of Mitch's money and her own considerable estate had been divided among the five brothers and sisters. Marilyn put her arms around Julia. The waves of blond hair were just like Mattie's.

"I'd give anything in the world to have her back again," Marilyn sobbed.

"I know," Julia soothed her. "All of us would."

She looked around the crowded cellar. The noise of talk and laughter swelled as the drink began to flow. It was comforting, and an affirmation, to be here with Mattie's friends, enjoying themselves as Mattie once would have done. *My friends too,* Julia thought, feeling the invisible threads of familiarity, common experience, draw her close to them all. She could see Ricky talking to a group of men who had once played trad jazz in this same cellar. With Mattie, she had tried to dance to it all night. She could see Thomas Tree with his wife, in a corner with Marilyn and her husband, and she could see the two boys, husbands and fathers now, who had driven Johnny Flowers to Ladyhill for a party to celebrate a new decade. One of them had long sideburns, Julia remembered, and she had danced the conga with him. She could see Jimmy Proffitt lounging against a wall, arguing with Chris Fredericks. Jimmy had just published his autobiography, with the story of *One More Day* and Mattie's great success in it. Julia had picked the book up in a bookshop, and turned the pages, looking at the photographs. There was one of Mattie, in the last scene of the play. Her face stared up from the page, peering across a great distance. Julia had put the book back on the glossy pile and turned slowly away.

Julia saw Felix, sinuously moving through the crowded space. In the dim light, in his sweater, he looked hardly any older than when she had first seen 'him. He caught her hand in his.

"A good party," Felix said. "Do you think Mattie would be happy?"

"I know she would. Felix, do you remember the party we gave after Jessie's funeral?"

A sad day. Somehow, miraculously, this day wasn't sad.

"I remember," he answered.

She saw the tilt of his head, his white teeth, and the flicker of candlelight emphasize the high planes and deep hollows of his face. Julia and Felix remembered what had happened afterward. He lifted her hand and kissed it, then went on into the clamor of the party, looking for William.

It was Felix who had decorated the restaurant for the party. There were candles in Chianti bottles, and travel posters set at angles on the walls. With just a few touches, he had brought the Rocket back for them. Everyone was finding their places now, sitting down at tables with checked cloths to eat chili and French bread, a meal like the ones that Felix used to cook in the flat overlooking the square.

In the crush Julia saw Lily sit down firmly next to Josh and, at the farthest point, where she stood herself, she saw Alexander.

She had brought Alexander to the Rocket as a test. He had passed it as he had passed every other test, except for one, and that had required him to be Josh Flood. Julia flushed at the thought of it, and felt a great rush of love for Alexander.

Feeling her eyes on him, he looked across at her. His mouth twisted, briefly and humorously, an acknowledgment and the most private greeting to her. The old, ironic Alexander, irony masking his tenderness.

Yes, Julia thought. *Yes, now, at last.*

All the way away from her he sat down, and she saw him incline his head to listen courteously to something that Rozzie Banner was telling him.

Julia sat down, too, very suddenly, at a table with the Dandelions and some of Lily's friends and a jazz trumpeter. Or perhaps he was a saxophonist. The memory of Jessie's stories made her smile, and suddenly Julia felt a warm bubble of happiness swelling up inside her. It pressed against her rib cage, making her breathless and causing her heart to knock in her throat. Julia swept up her glass and drank, toasting the Dandelions and Lily's friends and the trumpeter-saxophonist. The cheap red wine curled her tongue, and the taste of it launched its own flotilla of memories.

She wanted to drink, to laugh and to dance and to celebrate the years that had brought them all here, back to the Rocket again. To celebrate, because tonight was not a night to mourn.

After they had finished eating, the tables were pushed back against the walls to make room for the dancing. Julia drank the wine, and danced, and as the wine and the heat and the candlelight worked on her she felt dreamy and yet abundantly alive. The dancers' shadows flickered on the white walls. Watching them as she danced, seeing only the bold puppet shapes blacker than the cruel faint shadows of reality, Julia could have believed that they were all young again, that she was seventeen once more, that she was Lily's age, after all.

Julia was jiving with the trumpeter-saxophonist. It was a long time since she had danced at all, and much longer since she had tried to recall the intricate rhythms of twenty years ago. But the jazz player was a good dancer, although not as good as Alexander, and dreamily she matched her steps to his. He swung her out in a flamboyant twirl, and as she whirled, past the dancers, beside the kinder shadows on the white wall, Julia saw Lily. Tonight Lily was a punk princess again, but even the willfulness of her self-presentation failed to disguise her beauty.

She was standing right against the opposite wall, turned away from the dancers, so that Julia saw only her profile. She was looking up at Josh, and Josh was listening to her, smiling. Easy, fatal Josh, Julia remembered.

The movements and the music slowed around Julia. The moment seemed to freeze, and stretch itself, as time lost its familiar dimensions. Lily and Josh were captured in Julia's eyes under a white light, held in a black frame that shut out everyone else.

Lily reached up and put one hand at the back of Josh's neck. Julia saw him hesitate, neither drawing back nor reaching forward. Then Lily laughed. She tilted her face up and drew his down so that their mouths met.

Then her bare arm uncoiled and she stepped back again.

It was the briefest of kisses, but there was no mistaking it. It told Julia how much Lily knew, and the mocking, confident ease of the kiss stirred a contraction of protective jealousy in Julia that was as fierce as a birth pang. She dropped the musician's hand and stood still, staring at them. Josh put his hand to

Lily's cheek, turning her head to look into her eyes. Lily laughed again, teasing, mistress of herself. In that instant Julia was sure that it was Lily who led and Josh who stumbled, hopeful and bewildered.

Then the picture shuddered in its frame and began to move again, faster, catching up with reality. The frame itself dissolved and the party recomposed itself, flowing around Lily and Josh and hiding them from Julia's gaze.

Someone's arm came around her shoulders, half-supporting her. She thought it was the jazz player and turned, startled. It was Alexander.

"My dance, next, I think?" It was the first time he had spoken to her since the beginning of the party. Helplessly, Julia looked back, to the place where the shadows leapt against the wall. Lily and Josh had gone, swallowed up into the party's heart. Alexander drew her closer, making her turn to him again. He looked into her face and she felt his scrutiny penetrate her, keen enough to peel the flesh from her bones. The trumpeter slid past them, leaving them to each other.

"I don't think we need to dance, do we?" Alexander murmured. "We don't need to make any beginnings, you and I. Let's go now. Come on, come with me."

Julia turned her head one more time. "Lily," she whispered. "I saw Lily . . ."

"Forget about Lily now," Alexander ordered her. "She is her own self."

His grip on her wasn't gentle any longer. It hurt, and she almost broke away from him. She was going to say, *I can't let Lily* . . . but the words stopped in her mouth, and Alexander saw that they did.

"Yes, you can," he told her. "You must."

Julia stared at him, amazed, and he laughed at her.

"Julia. How many years, and you haven't learned?"

She thought of Betty and Vernon, and Margaret Hall and China and Jessie. Parents and children.

"Not with Josh," she begged.

Alexander wouldn't let her turn away, not even look away from him. "Are you afraid?" he asked. "Or are you jealous?"

The noise of the party seemed a long way off, even though it was all around them. Julia felt the importance of this one moment, as if all the years were being called to account. It frightened her, but it also made her brave.

"I'm not jealous. I've known for a long time that I don't want anyone but you."

"Then are you afraid?"

For Lily? But Lily wouldn't make her mother's mistakes. Recognizing that, admiring it, Julia knew that she, in her turn, must not fail her daughter as Betty had. She took a breath, tasting the forgotten, familiar smoke of crowded rooms.

"No, I'm not afraid either."

Not for Lily. Not even, she realized in wonderment, for Lily with Josh. It was Lily who had the strength, after all. She must use it for herself.

"Then let her be."

Julia looked around once more. There were dancers, shadows flickering on the white walls, no sign of her daughter, or of Josh. It was a party, the kind of party that Mattie would have loved, and Lily was somewhere in the thick of it. Suddenly, Julia smiled.

"Come with me," Alexander repeated.

Without turning back again Julia followed him up the narrow basement stairs.

Outside, in the street, the air was cold. Julia stumbled and Alexander held on to her. The passing traffic dipped and hummed, at a distance.

"I think I must be a bit drunk." *Oh, Mattie.*

"Let's walk a little way."

Arm in arm, leaning inward as if there were a much stronger wind blowing, Julia and Alexander made their way through Soho. Over twenty years the continental grocers frequented by Felix, and the glovemakers and musical instrument shops had mostly disappeared, replaced by brasher establishments, but to Julia it seemed just the same place. The Showbox was still open, offering Girls, Girls, Girls. It was hard to believe that if they went inside they wouldn't find Miss Matilda snapping her cane.

They held tighter to each other and walked on, leaving Soho behind them. With no thought of where they were going, they came at last to the Strand. The north entrance of the Savoy filled its cul-de-sac, glittering with revolving lights and polished metal. Julia and Alexander turned aside and plunged into the dark, steep alleyway that led down to the river.

The light from the single old-fashioned streetlamp was dimmed by the mist off the river, and their footsteps were loud in the close quietness.

Opposite the doorway Julia stopped. The floor of the recess was lined with flattened cardboard, and a bundle wrapped in a sack was pushed into one corner. The space was unoccupied but it was claimed, and before long one of the old men who crouched under the bridges along the Embankment would shuffle back to his refuge for the night. Overhead, the grille in the wall puffed out the smell of stale food. Julia closed her eyes, trying to see herself and Mattie curled up together in the dingy space. Lying there, she had glimpsed Betty's fear of the disorderly unknown, and made her own naïve promises to herself. With a beat inside her that seemed almost indecently triumphant, Julia realized that, more or less, she had kept those promises. What had Mattie's promises been? Already with sad finality, Mattie seemed to have melted away. There would be no answer now.

"We were so desperate to be free," Julia said. "And so dismayed to find that it could mean sleeping in a doorway."

"You told me about it," Alexander answered. "The first time we met. Do you remember?"

"I exaggerated everything."

They had walked down to the river then, too, and looked over the Embankment wall into the olive-green water.

Julia glanced again at the doorway, at the shreds of a nest that announced someone's claim on it. Her own claims on a wider world seemed as ephemeral, as easily swept away, and of equal importance. No more, no less. The chances of happiness remained with her, intact as they had been on the night when she and Mattie had sheltered here. That was her good fortune. Mattie's was gone.

"I miss her so much. I wish she would come back," Julia said.

"Mattie's dead. She won't come back. Do you think I don't miss her too?"

Abruptly, Julia turned to face Alexander. "I know you do. I'm sorry, I was selfish. It was selfish to shut myself in at Coppins after she died, and then to run off back to Italy. I'm here now, if it isn't too late. If you want me. I'm afraid to ask, Alexander, but I must, mustn't I?"

In the dim light Julia tried to read his face. But he took her arm, leading her away. "I don't want to talk here."

They walked on, out of the alleyway and up some stone steps, to a point overlooking the river. It smelled, as always at low tide, of alluvial mud thatched with decaying weed. Side by side they leaned on the cold, smooth stone wall and looked over into the Thames. The depths beneath them seemed very black, but in midstream and on the opposite side the surface was braceleted with chains of reflected light, like a silent fairground. And then a riverboat, itself a layer cake of lights, plowed through and scattered the reflections as it carried a noisy party on up the river toward Kew.

Alexander said, "I was wrong, too, years ago." It was time to make certain of her now. Josh Flood had made him aware of that. "I tried to tell you before, do you remember? The night we were together, the night Mattie died."

"There was no need," Julia murmured. "It was enough to find each other, after all."

"I was wrong at Ladyhill, before the fire, as well as afterward. I shouldn't have expected you to adopt my life in place of your own."

Julia listened intently to the calling to account. If their debts couldn't be settled now, beside the dark river, then truly she and Alexander had nowhere to go on to together.

"I shouldn't have been disappointed in you because you didn't want to. And I might justifiably have been angry, but I shouldn't have been so amazed when you left me for Joshua Flood. Felix understood you better than I did."

Julia nodded, surprised. "Felix did, and Mattie didn't. Not then."

"Mattie wanted what you rejected. I don't mean me, although Mattie and I loved each other in a way. She wanted a house, and a family. A place to belong."

Alexander and Mattie, sitting with Lily under the apple trees in the Ladyhill orchard. Mattie's gold sandal, discarded, and her underclothes dropped on the bedroom chair. Mattie had found what she wanted, with Mitch at Coppins, and then she had lost it all. It was cruel, but there was no place for guilt among those who were left. Julia lifted her head. "Wait," Alexander said. "Something else. I shouldn't have expected you to marry a house. Or to live with my passion for rebuilding it. I spent years, after you'd gone, trying to make love to roof beams and oak boards and plaster moldings. Then I tried to find a substitute for you. I worked quite hard at it, Lily knows that. But I couldn't replace you. Least of all with Ladyhill."

Alexander took Julia in his arms. He looked at each of her features in turn, as if he wanted to relearn them. The generosity of his admission, and the importance of it, caught Julia's breath in her throat. She held out her own painful contribution, her breathlessness chopping the words.

"I was helpless as far as Josh was concerned. I needn't have been, but I half-wanted it I convinced myself that I would follow him anywhere, if he would only let me. I was in love with the very idea of my infatuation. It was only quite lately that I found I could see Josh clearly enough. I saw, and I came running back to Ladyhill. That's when I found Mattie there with you."

"Yes. And now it's Lily's turn to see, do you think?" The old, ironic twist when Alexander smiled. He had seen that kiss in the Rocket, too, of course.

"If I'm afraid for anyone, it's Josh. I don't think Lily's heart will break."

"Neither do I."

They laughed, and just as quickly as it had come, the laughter died away. Alexander's mouth was close to hers, but she held him away as long as she could.

"Listen. I did everything wrong. I know I did. To you, and to Lily. I was jealous of Ladyhill and Lily, even of China. And then after the fire, when I'd ruined it all and run away, I had a feast of guilt." She tried again to read his expression, but his face was too close to hers. She found herself laughing again. She didn't know how appropriate her happiness was, but she couldn't suppress it. "Guilt and jealousy," she managed to murmur. "Two essentials I'm trying to live without."

"That's good." Their mouths did find each other then, and another riverboat carried its noisy cargo past them unnoticed.

Julia and Alexander knew that they had simplified their confessions, that the years couldn't be scraped away so easily and that there were layers, accretions of misunderstanding and failure and obstinacy, that they would have to penetrate. But they knew also that there was still time. Miraculously, there was still time left to them.

Alexander put his hands up to her face, holding her so that he could fix his eyes on hers. "Will you come back to Ladyhill?"

He remembered Josh outside the Actors' Church. It seemed much longer ago than only this morning. He had known then that he must make certain of her.

Urgently, he said, "Come with me now. We can drive down, and be there when the sun comes up."

Julia was going to say again, "But Lily . . ." Lily was still at the Rocket, with Josh. Alexander had said, *She's her own self.* Instead of the protest she said simply, "Yes, I'll come with you. I'd like to see Ladyhill in the dawn."

A river patrol boat swept past, the beam from its searchlight slicing a path ahead of it over the black ripples. On either side of them the traffic rolled over the bridges, the bright red of the buses and the orange of the streetlights incongruous over the water's impenetrable depths. Julia and Alexander didn't look back. They walked quickly, retracing their steps, back to where Alexander's dusty car was waiting.

Light came before the sun. Julia watched the sky as Alexander drove, and she saw the dark turning to washy gray in the east. The shadows rolled away behind them as they drove westward. The light strengthened, and color crept back into the fields. The trees were raggedly yellow and brown, spiky branches showing, and there were drifts of russet leaves over the grass verges. Beyond the hedges the bare fields were winter-furrowed. Julia wound down her window. There was a frosty savor in the air that she had never encountered in Italy. She watched the countryside, thinking that it was more beautiful now with the bones showing than it ever was in its summer opulence.

They reached the old signpost. *Ladyhill, 3.* The sun was up behind them, and the tops of the hedges were spangled with sudden brightness. Alexander put his hand over Julia's. They drove between the Ladyhill stone gateposts and along the curve of the drive. The trees laced overhead were losing their leaves, and the tunnel they formed seemed no longer threatening. When they turned the corner Julia faced the house. It looked mild and unemphatic in its fold of land, soft pink and gray against gray-green.

She kept her eyes fixed watchfully on it as they came closer, but she could see nothing more. It was a manor house of English brick and stone, unpretentious but beautifully proportioned, carefully preserved and comfortable in its wide gardens, neither threatening nor demanding anything more than a due acknowledgment of its history.

There was no flicker of flames behind the windows, no taint of smoke.

The fire had been put out and Julia knew that the guilt and fear that had blazed as damagingly for much longer had also been extinguished. Johnny Flowers was dead, but Sandy had divorced and remarried and her children were growing up. Mattie and Mitch were dead, but Julia was alive, and Alexander and Felix and Josh, and Lily was growing up. Ladyhill was just a house, a particularly beautiful house, and it was a home only if they could make it one.

Alexander stopped the car. They climbed out, stiff with the long drive and blinking in the strengthening light. Julia looked at the yew trees enclosed in the courtyard, and at the stone portico with its carved motto, *Aeternitas*. They made no move to go inside. Instead, they walked away, across the wet grass and into the garden. In the sunken center they came to the sundial, and they stood looking down at the long shadow cast by the uplifted metal finger.

Julia lifted her head. "I'm glad we came today," she whispered. "I'm glad to be here. It looks more beautiful than it ever did."

"Julia," he said abruptly, "we don't have to stay here. If you don't want to live at Ladyhill, I'll sell it and we can find somewhere else. Wherever you would like."

She took that, that went beyond generosity, to hoard for the future as if it were solid gold. "I want to stay at Ladyhill. If you will have me."

Alexander drew her closer, his hand at the hollow of her back, holding her against him. "I'm getting to be an old man. I'm nearly fifty . . ." Julia put her hand over his mouth, an impulsive gesture that made her seem almost a girl again. He took her wrist and drew it away. "And if you don't stay with me now, I don't know what I can do."

Very slowly, Julia let her head fall against his shoulder.

"Are you afraid?" he asked her again. She had been afraid of Ladyhill, even before the fire had devoured it and their love together. She wasn't afraid anymore, but she knew that he was asking her something else, too, much more important now. He was asking her if she was afraid to try again, after all they had done to each other.

"No," Julia told him. She felt the last cold touch of fear, and the need to dispel it.

"Are you afraid, Alexander?"

He smiled. "I love you," he told her.

"I love you too."

Her head was still against his shoulder. It was the greatest luxury she had ever known to let it rest there. Now that it was lifted, the weight of hoping seemed too heavy to bear. Looking back, the threads between them looked much too fragile to hold, too thin to draw them back together again. But they had held, and the drawing was done. Alexander lifted his hand and smoothed her hair.

The sundial shadow seemed to point away to the long border. The dead arms of the summer plants were tangled with bindweed, and spiders' webs stretched between dry brown spikes that had once been flowers. Julia saw that there was work to be done, and the simplicity and satisfaction of it, turning with the seasons, filled her with pleasure. The earth was rich, and she enjoyed the fruits of it.

Alexander's arms were still around her. "I never saw your Italian garden," he said.

"It's very different from this one. And it's Tomaso's garden now." Julia spoke of it fondly, without regret. "We could go to see it one day."

"One day," Alexander agreed. "Do you know what I would like now?"

Thinking that he was going to say some breakfast or a cup of hot coffee, she smiled at him and asked, "What would you like?"

"I'd like a son. For Ladyhill."

Julia stood very still. Alexander's hand moved to rest over her stomach, as gently as if there was already a son inside it. She thought, I'm not forty yet. It's possible. She had believed that she was empty and dry, like the old leaves, but suddenly she understood that if she wanted it, she could be as rich as the earth itself.

"A baby. Is that what you really want?"

"I do."

Julia laughed, amazed and delighted. She let the idea carry her. "Sir Felix Bliss," she murmured, joking.

Alexander went one better. "Sir Joshua Bliss. No, perhaps not. And I'm afraid that at least one of his names must be Percy."

"Sir Percy Alexander Bliss," Julia echoed. "And what if it's a girl?"

"You know that Lily has given me more happiness than almost anything else in my life. I can't imagine loving any other child as much as I love Lily, but I know that other fathers succeed."

Julia looked into his face. There were lines, and the corners of his eyelids had begun to droop, intensifying his sardonic air. His hair was gray at the temples, and thinning, but Alexander wasn't an old man. She felt that he was still young, that they both were, and that she loved him unreservedly. She wanted to give him happiness, and to set the sadness of the years behind them. That was in her power. It had always been in her power, if only she had known it. The muted English gardens would grow green again, and they would make the lovely, silent house alive once more.

If Alexander wanted a son to run through the rooms, and out under the trees, then she wanted the same with all her heart.

She looked beyond him, at the sweep of the garden and at the tall chimneys and pointed eaves of the house.

Ladyhill. Home.

"Well," Julia said, composed in her delight. "Well. We'll have to see what we can do, won't we?"

Now, beginning on the next page,
you can read a special preview
of ROSIE THOMAS' new hardcover novel,
A WOMAN OF OUR TIMES,
WHICH BANTAM BOOKS
WILL PUBLISH
IN FALL 1990.

It's the unforgettable story of a remarkable woman of substance, whose passion is building an empire from the ground up—and making it her own. Independent, creative, and above all daring, Harriet Peacock is very much a woman of her time—determined to play a more exciting role in the world than her mother did . . . and to choose the destiny that is uniquely hers.

A WOMAN OF OUR TIMES is a story of mothers and daughters, passion and purpose, friendship and betrayal, jealousy, revenge, and redemption. Rosie Thomas has once again written a novel of intricate and complex relationships, and filled its pages with characters of astonishing depth. No one who reads this richly satisfying tale will soon forget it.

And now—*A WOMAN OF OUR TIMES*. . . .

* * *

Landwith Associates occupied a stucco-fronted house in a quiet side-street. There was no marble entrance hall, and no opulent fountain. A discreet brass plate gave the company's name, and an equally discreet bell placed beside it brought an immaculate girl to open the door.

"Harriet Peacock," Harriet announced herself.

She had christened her embryo company Peacocks, and since the meeting at Morton's she had resolved that there would be no more Mrs. Gold. Nor would she go back to calling herself Harriet Trott. The direct identification of herself with her company gave her logical pleasure. "Mr. Landwith is expecting me."

Armed with an introduction from Henry Orde, and once past the barrier of an ingeniously defensive secretary, Harriet had found it quite easy to achieve an appointment with Martin Landwith. It had been harder to find the time in her own schedule. The Toy Fair opened the next day. Harriet knew that she should have been on her stand, organizing the pinning and draping and positioning.

"This way, please, Miss Peacock."

The hall was panelled, and empty except for a Persian rug on the floor and an oval table with a big bowl of fresh flowers. Harriet followed the girl up the shallow curve of the stairs, passing three serious, gloomy still lifes in weighty frames. Harriet suspected that they were worth, individually, about as much as the total amount she was trying to borrow.

The girl opened the double doors facing the top of the stairs. Harriet saw Martin Landwith stand up at once, and come round his desk to greet her. He was a stocky man, not very tall, but dressed in a dark blue suit of such magical cut that he seemed perfectly proportioned. He was wearing a pale blue shirt and a sober tie. Narrow, shiny hand-made shoes emphasized the smallness of his feet. His dark hair was graying at the temples; it seemed sculpted rather than mundanely cut. The silver threads glittered as he turned his head. He had dark eyes, and his naturally dark skin had the healthy polish of a real suntan. Harriet judged that he was in his early- or mid-fifties. The fingernails of the hand he held out to her were professionally manicured.

"Please sit down, won't you?"

His voice was friendly, his smile followed the invitation only a second or two later. Martin Landwith made no attempt to disguise his scrutiny of her. Harriet accepted it, looking coolly back at him, and then sat down in the chair opposite his desk. She glanced around the room. To her right there were tall windows overlooking the street. They were framed in curtains of some honey-colored material, with deep, soft scallops above and long rippling tails that were fringed in dull gold. Opposite the windows stood a Chinese Chippendale cabinet, the glass front reflecting the light in lozenges over the plain walls. Over the mantelpiece was a Victorian portrait. The whiskered subject might have been Mr. Landwith's grandfather. His grandson, if he was his grandson, sat beneath the picture at a partners desk probably inherited from the old man. Only the telephones, dictating machine, computer terminal had been added at some later date. On the floor there was a rug whose subtly glowing colors and intricate pattern spoke to Harriet of tiny silk threads, and thousands upon thousands of hand-knots. There wasn't much else in the room. It was a masterpiece of understatement that still shouted *money* as clearly as if the walls had been pasted with layers of notes. It made the glass and steel temple of Morton's seem by comparison like a hamburger bar in a new shopping district.

Harriet's mouth curved. She sucked the corners of it inwards to contain her smile. But she saw at the same time that Martin Landwith had noted her inventory, and her amusement, and seemed to approve of it.

"This is my son, and partner, Robin Landwith."

Harriet turned. He must have come silently in behind her.

He was taller, and thinner, than his father. He had the same dark colouring, but there was no grey in his hair and it was thicker and more casually cut than the father's. Clearly they shared the same tailor, but Robin's lapels were two hairsbreadths wider, and there were discreet pleats at the front of the trousers. His hand, when Harriet shook it, was larger and warmer.

He looked her over, just as Landwith senior had done. There was more open appreciation in his smile, but afterwards his glance flickered back to his father, as if for approval. Only that made Harriet notice how young he was. He was younger than herself. Perhaps only twenty-five, twenty-six at the most. Not quite ready, yet, to be given free rein. It struck Harriet, seeing him take his place beside his father, that Robin looked like a particularly fine thorough-bred colt. He had been sired for this particular course, for races in which the stakes were pure risk and the prizes were all the multiplication of money. Clearly the bloodlines were faultless, whatever the running he would finally make.

For now, father and son together made a formidable combination. Martin Landwith was sitting with his chin resting on one hand. With the other hand he made a small, polite gesture of invitation.

"Won't you tell us how we can help you?"

Harriet told.

She left nothing out, nor did she add anything, but she avoided the operatic performance that had failed her at Morton's. If the proposal was good enough, she reasoned, these two would spot it even if she made her pitch in Swahili. She spoke quietly, without emphasis, letting the information do its own selling. When she took out the game and set it up on the broad desk, they examined it carefully and asked half a dozen questions about the manufacture, but they didn't try to play it. Instead, when they had finished with the board itself, they scrutinized the box and the point-of-sale roughs and all the leaflets and promotional material that the design studio had expensively prepared for the Toy Fair. But the time expended even on all of that was brief.

"The package is probably good enough," Martin Land-with judged. Then he moved on with practiced speed to her business plan.

They went through the figures line by line, and they accepted none of her forecasts without query. Harriet was glad of the thoroughness of her preparation, and relieved that they couldn't fault her calculations. She wouldn't care to have stumbled in front of the two Landwiths. But she had to admit, under their questioning, that she had only investigated the performance of roughly similar products.

"There's nothing on the market quite like this," she told them. "A direct parallel between potential performance and real sales is impossible for that reason. But that is the game's strength, too, isn't it?"

She saw that they didn't glance away, but kept their attention fixed on her. She felt a small beat of triumph. She was right, it was herself and her own capabilities that she was trying to sell. If the Landwiths would buy her, she would show them that she could make the world buy her game.

"I think we should discuss your marketing strategy now," Martin Landwith said. That was more difficult. Without having tested the water at the Fair, Harriet wasn't quite sure what direction her marketing thrust would follow. But she brought out the research notes that showed the performance of the most nearly similar products out of the big chains, and talked about targeting W. H. Smith, Menzies, Toys 'R' Us, and the rest.

Father and son listened attentively, but without any encouraging sign.

When she finished, she saw Martin glance at his watch. Then he put his fingertips together, looking at her over the crest of them.

Harriet's heart began to thump unpleasantly.

"I like your game," Martin said. "It may well be a seller. But I wouldn't want to try to predict how strong a seller, or how durable. I don't see any convincing way of doing so and—I'm sorry—I don't see that your due diligence succeeds either. The FMCG world is unpredictable . . ."

Fast moving consumer goods. Harriet translated silently. *Oh, please.* ". . . . and we prefer our risks to be calculated. Can you demonstrate the value of your game other than theoretically?"

Harriet wondered if she should tell him about her Sundays on the top deck of the 73 bus, and the enthusiasm and friendliness she had met there. But she doubted that Martin Landwith would know where to go to catch a bus, and doubted even more strongly that he would accept the vote of its passengers. And Robin Landwith, with his long legs stretched out to one side of the desk, didn't look as though he had ever ridden a bus in his life.

"Only by having the opportunity to sell it. I shall be doing that for the next four days, at the trade fair. Why don't you come and take a look?"

Martin was consulting his watch again. The meeting had reached an inconclusive finish. Harriet stood up briskly, so that she could appear to control the endgame.

"Thank you for your time. I hope you'll decide in my favor, Mr. Landwith. Peacocks could work well for us both."

He looked up at her; it was an odd, sidelong glance. The atmosphere in the room changed with it. It had been cool and crystalline, now it became warmer, as if thick velvet curtains had been drawn somewhere. Harriet understood that Martin Landwith had finished his appraisal of her investment potential. Now he was examining her as a woman. His eyes traveled from her mouth to her breasts. Such practiced attention might have angered her, but she was interested to discover that it did not. She let him look, even squaring her shoulders and holding her head higher.

If he wants to play the game this way, she thought, *I can do it too. I can play any way he likes, for the right stakes.* The realization of how much she would do for the sake of the game didn't shock her. She felt charged by it, rather, as if Martin Landwith's deft, over-dainty fingers had already worked on her. But it was the recognition of her own freedom, to do what she wanted with herself, that had excited her, not anything Martin Landwith would or could do.

Robin had seen the shade of Harriet too, through the opaque business dress. They had stepped, an awkward three-some, on to different ground. Harriet looked from the father to the son, meeting their eyes squarely. *Funny,* she thought. *Do they compete, or run together?*

"Thank you for coming, Miss Peacock," Martin said quietly. "We'll consider your proposal."

It was Robin who touched her elbow, guided her back through the double doors and down the staircase to the paneled hall. There was a scent of clove carnations from the flower display that Harriet hadn't detected on the way up. She breathed it in luxuriously. She felt light-hearted, now that she was released from the strain of the meeting, and Robin became a part of the lightness. When he smiled at her they were almost co-conspirators, released from the oppressive company of the grown-ups. They shook hands, still smiling.

"Try to come to the Fair," Harriet repeated.

"I'll do my best for you," he said. Harriet wasn't sure

whether he meant the Toy Fair, or persuading his father to back the game. She went down the steps into the street, knowing that he was watching her go.

"Harriet? Where have you *been*? They wouldn't let me in without an exhibitor's pass."

Harriet was hot and flustered and guilty. Jane, loyal Jane, had freed herself from school for an afternoon in order to help her and she had kept her waiting for three-quarters of an hour. She gasped her apologies, waved her pass at the security man, and they were inside. She took Jane's arm and steered her forward.

"I'm sorry, I'm so sorry. Landwith Associates took longer than I thought, then there were no cabs. I thought I'd never get here."

They were half-running, half-stumbling down a long aisle. On either side there were stands where giant teddy-bears reared up, where ranks of dolls smiled sweet persuasive smiles, and the rattle and whirr of mechanical toys mingled and multiplied. The dim roofspace overhead was noisy with the drilling and hammering and sawing of last preparations.

"Slow down. Calm down," Jane ordered her, but Harriet rushed them faster. At last they reached a bare rectangle of space with packing cases tipped haphazardly in the center. Harriet consulted a docket, looked at the number fixed to the stand frame, and back at the docket again.

"This is it," she said. "This is ours." She couldn't keep the flatness out of her voice.

The space was so bare, and dusty, and uninviting.

"Not even a giant teddy to lend a hand," Jane said. Two young women in red and white Queen of Hearts costumes were eyeing them curiously from an apparently complete display across the aisle. "Come on, we'd better get started."

It seemed impossible that they could ever make the stand look like anything. When she unwrapped the parachute silk and draped the creased swathes over the chipboard walls, Harriet thought she saw the Queens of Hearts covertly smiling. If it had not been for Jane, she would have turned tail, even at that last moment, and run away from the exhibition hall, right away from the game itself.

But Jane raised her eyebrows by a fraction and twitched

the corners of her mouth, conveying her opinion of the Queens with such perfect economy that Harriet laughed, and instead of running she climbed a stepladder with a staple gun ready in her hand.

"How'd it go this morning?" Jane called, over a mouthful of pins. Harriet perched on her ladder, dipping her splayed hand from side to side.

"The smoothest pair of operators you ever saw. They're thinking about it."

Jane returned to her pinning. It seemed the wildest optimism to have come this far, with prototypes and printed glossy leaflets and swathes of bloody parachute silk, on the strength of two smooth operators consenting to think about further funding. Harriet had cheerfully spent all of her own capital, Jane was sure of that. If she had been in the same position she would have been too frightened to become absorbed in getting white folds of fabric to hang just so. But then, Jane reflected, she was no entrepreneur. If she were it might have been Harriet patiently waiting on the steps and herself arriving, with blazing eyes and cheeks, in a crackle of energy that made everyone turn round to look. The image didn't attract Jane in the least. Even trying to teach *The Catcher in the Rye* to recalcitrant juniors was more appealing.

By the end of the afternoon, working without stopping, they had mocked-up black shiny pillars and puffy white clouds. The air in the hall stirred just enough to make the clouds drift. It was also warm enough to have caused the creases to drop out. The Queens of Hearts had stopped smirking and yawning. Before they left they had begun to stare quite openly.

Harriet and Jane only ran into trouble when they unpacked the painted styrofoam blocks from which to construct the ambitious sunburst. There had been a measuring or a making error, and they didn't fit together. The structure lurched at a drunken angle, offering slopes instead of smooth display shelves.

Harriet pushed her knuckles against her teeth. She closed her eyes and opened them again but instead of disappearing the list only seemed more pronounced.

"I can't believe it," she whispered. "We'll have to get a saw and cut the blocks at one corner to even the thing up."

Jane understood that Harriet contained her own kind of fright, and that she was close to letting it spill out. She left her and went to the exhibitors bar, full now of exhibitors who had finished putting up their stands and were greeting each other with annual boisterousness. She pushed her way through them and bought two plastic tumblers of gin, carried them back to Harriet and put one into her hand.

"Drink first, problem-solving afterwards," she commanded.

"I don't know how to solve it," Harriet moaned.

Before they had finished the gin, Jenny arrived on her way home from her publishing house. She took one look at the mismatched heaps of painted styrofoam.

"Oh dear," she said.

"We're going to try to cut the blocks to make them even," Harriet told her.

Jenny had a strong practical streak. "Don't *cut*, whatever you do. You'll never get them even, and you'll end up cutting off more and more until you've got blocks the size of matchboxes. You'll have to shore up with something." She glanced around, and then cocked her head to the sound of sawing, "Hang on here."

Five minutes later, she was back with a handful of rough wooden wedges. It was fiddly work, but an hour later the sunburst stood level. Game sets and the sunburst-bright boxes had to be balanced on it with infinite care, but they stood level too.

"Finishing touches now," Harriet commanded.

She had rented black folding tables and chairs for each side of the stand. When they were put in place there were boxes of leaflets and information folders and printed order books to be unpacked.

They worked silently, because it was ten o'clock at night and they were tired and hungry. But they were not too tired to notice that the other exhibitors, the last ones who were straggling out towards the exits and their hotel beds, all stopped to look at the stand.

At last, the job was done.

They stood back, shoulder to shoulder, to admire it. Their backs and arms ached, and their faces were smeared with dust. Harriet completed her scrutiny.

"It's all right," she said slowly. "In fact, it's more than all right."

"It's bloody brilliant," Jenny corrected her. "So long as no-one breathes on the sun thing."

Jane stuck her hands into the pockets of her overalls. "I'll get us another drink. We've earned it." She went to the bar, but came back with the news that it was closed.

"This is all I could get from a machine." She held up three tins of fizzy orange and three vending-machine packs of sandwiches.

They sat down on the stand, very carefully in case they upset any of their handiwork.

"Thank you," Harriet said. She was dirty and exhausted, but she felt full of hope. Tomorrow she would be able to show off her game. Tomorrow would tell.

"Harriet Peacock. Mr. Landwith, I hoped you might be able to come to the Toy Fair to see the game on display. The Fair closes this evening, so this is your last chance." She tried to sound warm and humorous, feeling neither of those things.

"One of our companies has gone public this week. It's been a busy few days for us."

"I'm sure," Harriet said, then reminded herself that she would gain nothing by sounding scratchy. "Look, the exhibition is hardly any way from you by cab." *If you can get one. People like you invariably can.* "The fair's open until six. Come on your way home." She heard him laughing, a rather suprisingly nice laugh. "On my way home, at five-thirty? What kind of hours do you think venture capitalists work? Don't expect me, but I'll try to get there. How has the game been selling to the trade?"

"Very well indeed. There'll be more orders later, of course."

"Hm. Harriet, we haven't made a decision either way, yet, you know."

Harriet? Had he called her Harriet? "That's all right. I can wait, for the right answer." After she hung up, leaning against the wall of the booth, Harriet was overtaken by a cold wash of terror. She couldn't afford to wait at all, not even a day. She was taking orders for thousands of games that she didn't have the funding to manufacture; and if she managed to get the money she didn't have enough orders to push herself into profit.

It took Harriet two minutes to stop herself shaking. In the end she drew a deep breath of the overused air. *Sell,* she told herself. *That's what you're here for. You're not far short of break-even, not disastrously far short.*

Back on the stand, the salesgirl greeted her with a triumphant smile. "He took two hundred and fifty. I put the order in the book."

Harriet nodded wearily. She knew that the order should have been for five hundred, the buyer was responsible for a group of shops. The game was selling, but it wasn't selling enough. The game was good. It deserved a better response, so what was she doing wrong? She stood back now, and looked at the stand she had been so proud of. Perhaps, a suspicion gnawed at her, perhaps it was *too* wholesome and bright? What the buyers saw was all there was. There was no story here, there was nothing to beckon or intrigue. The challenge rekindled a little fire in her. *What can I do?* Harriet wondered. *What's the extra little thing that will make them all take notice?*

"How much longer?" she was asking the photographer, when she saw Robin Landwith. He was picking his way through the debris, his expression of interest tinged with mild surprise at finding himself in an unlikely place. Amongst the salesmen in chainstore suits his handmade gloss seemed doubly exotic.

"I'll finish the roll," Leo said, his head bent over his lens.

Harriet was pinned against her sunburst, in her buttoned outfit with the two identically-dressed girls posing on either side, while the lights clicked and flared. Robin stopped to watch, off to the side in the welcome shadow. Harriet endured the humiliation for a minute longer, then said brusquely, "That should be enough, shouldn't it?"

She stepped off the stand. Leo straightened up with a shrug of irritation, but his eyes followed her. Harriet held out her hand and Robin Landwith shook it.

"Thank you for coming."

He looked at the stand. "It's impressive." His tone

seemed to indicate to Harriet that it was anything but. Seeing it through his eyes she noticed that the silk was grubby and marked with hand- and footprints, and even torn in places so that it hung down in little sulky mouths.

"It's seen a lot of hard wear, the last few days," she defended it. "Crowds of buyers and sightseers. When we first put it up it stopped everyone dead." She was conscious of the girls in their dresses the same as her own, and Leo with his paraphernalia of lights and tripods. She could hardly avoid introducing them.

"This is Natalie, and Caroline, who have been helping with selling and PR on the stand. And Leo Gold, the photographer."

Harriet didn't know who stepped awkwardly sideways in the narrow confines of the stand. It might even have been Robin Landwith. All she did know was that someone trod on the corner of the precarious sunburst. It had survived for four days but now there was a small crunching sound, and then a much louder rattle and bump as the colored platforms tilted and fell forward, domino-like, and unstoppably. The boards and boxes that had been arranged on the ledges slid and bounced to fall over the four people beneath. For a few seconds it felt as if they might all be buried beneath an avalanche of shiny black frames and rainbow-colored boxes and counters.

And then there was a moment of appalled silence as they stood in the wreckage. It was funny, but it was too catastrophic for any of them to laugh. Natalie and Caroline caught each other's eyes, and looked quickly away again. Harriet moved stiffly, over to the collapsed sunburst, and pushed it roughly upright again. Styrofoam and plastic crunched under her feet. A small crowd of people was gathering in front of the stand. "Grand finale, eh?" one of them called. She bent down and began to collect spilled counters in the cup of her hand, her eyes and her face red.

"That's right," she answered. "Big finish."

Afterwards, when it was all done and the stand had been stripped to an empty slot once more, Robin took Harriet out to dinner. They were dusty beyond repair in the exhibition center cloakrooms, but the restaurant was small and satisfyingly dim.

"Thank you for helping with that," Harriet said.

"Why didn't you want me to?"

"I didn't want to see someone I'm trying to borrow money from picking up embarrassing wreckage. Of course."

"If you're embarrassed by wreckage, perhaps you shouldn't be trying to borrow money in the first place? Disaster's always a possibility."

"I should. I want everything to fit, not to fail. Failure should be private, success is for celebration. I'd prefer to be successful."

Robin looked at her through the meretricious candlelight. He saw a face that was too angular for beauty, but which seemed to offer other interesting possibilities. Robin liked woman as well as enjoying them, which marked a difference from his father, and he liked what he had seen of Harriet. Her declaration of preference impressed him less, because he had heard the same from every would-be entrepreneur he had ever encountered.

"I think you'll be successful," Robin said. If he could influence Martin, he added silently, and he was almost sure that he could.

They didn't talk any more about money, or about Peacocks and its prospects.

Robin ordered champagne, a marque that Harriet had never seen before in a bottle that appeared to have been hand-painted with scattered flowers. She was susceptible to champagne. The bubbles always went to her head, and tonight was no exception. She had thought, when she chose her food from the rather startlingly expensive menu, that it would be impossible to forget the anxiety of the Fair and the final catastrophe. But after two glasses of champagne, and with the arrival of Salade d'artichauts et cailles aux noix, pretty as a picture on a plain white plate, the obcessions of the day drifted away. They were replaced by an unlocalized sense of well-being, and a sharp appetite.

What the hell, Harriet thought.

Robin watched her with approval as she attacked her food.

After the quail and artichoke came Faisan de mer au basilic, and more champagne. Harriet sighed and leaned back in her chair, releasing her heels from her shoes. Her feet seemed to have grown after four days spent standing on them. Her shoulders and back ached too, but champagne bubbles prickling at the back of her throat dispelled the pain.

"You were hungry," Robin commented.

"I haven't had time to eat. Sandwiches and filthy coffee, that's all."

Robin gave an automatic, gourmet's shudder. He was interested in food and wine in almost the same knowledge-able, academic way that he was interested in the movements of the money market. Both were there to be studied and their benefits, in different ways, to be enjoyed. Tonight, however, he had barely noticed his food as he concentrated on Harriet. He had seen her soften, as they talked and drank, by slow degrees. So far, but no further. He wondered what it was that she kept so tightly contained, and the speculation excited him.

"You must have some pudding," he told her, "They're very good here."

Because he was so young his assumption of authority over what she ate amused Harriet, but she submitted grace-fully.

"What shall I have?"

He chose for her, and ordered wine for them both. When the wine came it was dark gold and viscous-looking, but on her tongue Harriet tasted honey and flowers.

"It's good," she said.

Robin smiled. "It is, isn't it?"

Her pudding was five different tiny puddings, with petals of marbled raspberry sauce fanning between them. Food that looked as beautiful as it tasted was new to Harriet. She closed her eyes as she sampled each separate taste, and broke the pink and cream ribs of the petals with the edge of her spoon. As she ate, it struck her that her pleasure in it was sensual, as in making out-of-the-ordinary love.

She looked up, and met Robin's eyes. She held out her spoon for him to taste. He acknowledged both the food, and her enjoyment of it.

"That was all wonderful," she said.

Robin inclined his head. "And now?"

"Now I have to go home. Work tomorrow." Back to her neglected store, and to a dismal re-examination of order books. Back to the necessity to decide, and plan, and to find a way of selling more games. The cold touch of anxiety was the more unwelcome in the glow of the restaurant. Harriet pushed the thoughts back, examining the faces at the other tables instead, deciding that she would allow herself to escape just for tonight.

"What is this place called?"

Robin told her, and she guessed that she should have heard of it.

"I don't know it."

"You do now. I'm glad it was me who brought you."

"Thank you," Harriet said, meaning it. She had enjoyed his company. He had let her talk, without cross-examining her, and he had told her a little about himself. Not very much, his style was hardly confessional. He had steered the evening, for all its unpromising beginning, with rather likeable adroitness. "I think we probably live in quite different worlds," Harriet said, half to herself. She was still looking at the sleek customers at the other tables. *Money* was written as clearly here, in its penetrable code, as it had been in Martin Landwith's office. With Leo, she had eaten for years in noisy Italian restaurants, along the Greek strip of Charlotte Street and in garlicky little French places. Too late, she realized that Robin might imagine she was offering him an opening to invite her a few paces further into his enviable existence. But if he did think anything of the kind, he was too subtle to show it, let alone to respond. He only said, "I wouldn't care to try to define *worlds* in terms of restaurants. It's a tempting idea, but much too superficial. I go to all kinds of places. I'm sure you do too."

"All kinds," she agreed, liking him even better. "Robin, I must go now."

He paid the bill, which Harriet estimated must be huge, after checking the addition. Then he drew back his chair, and guided her towards the door, hand under her elbow, as he had done from his father's office. He had perfect, faintly old-fashioned manners. It was raining outside, and it felt very exposed after the restaurant's intimacy to be standing on a wet pavement in the cold wind. Robin unfurled a big black umbrella and held it over their heads.

As Harriet might have predicted, a yellow-lit taxi rounded the corner a second later. When it stopped Robin opened the door for her, asked for her address, and relayed it to the driver.

"Will you be all right?"

"Of course. I enjoyed this evening."

What happened next she also might have predicted, but it still surprised her when it came. Robin bent his head and kissed her on the mouth, very lightly, and then he placed two more kisses, one to each side of her mouth. The whole exchange took no more than three seconds. Harriet scrambled into the taxi and he closed the door, and the cab carried her away. She sat back in her seat, catching her breath, trying to work out what had happened to her.

"I was stuck all of a heap," she told skeptical Jane the next time they met. "Like a teenager, with the class heart-throb."

The right word came to her as the taxi wandered in the approximate direction of Belsize Park. It was *tender*.

Robin Landwith had treated her with tenderness, and she had responded to it. But by the time she reached the basement flat, with its unwashed dishes waiting in the sink and hungry, complaining cats, she had control of herself again.

Don't be a fool, she had told herself. *He's years younger than you are. He's not much more than a boy. And he's a venture capitalist, from whom you want to borrow a hundred thousand pounds. Don't let three kisses blur your sight of that, will you?*

DON'T MISS
THESE CURRENT
Bantam Bestsellers

☐ 28390	**THE AMATEUR** Robert Littell	$4.95
☐ 28525	**THE DEBRIEFING** Robert Littell	$4.95
☐ 28362	**COREY LANE** Norman Zollinger	$4.50
☐ 27636	**PASSAGE TO QUIVIRA** Norman Zollinger	$4.50
☐ 27759	**RIDER TO CIBOLA** Norman Zollinger	$3.95
☐ 27814	**THIS FAR FROM PARADISE** Philip Shelby	$4.95
☐ 27811	**DOCTORS** Erich Segal	$5.95
☐ 28179	**TREVAYNE** Robert Ludlum	$5.95
☐ 27807	**PARTNERS** John Martel	$4.95
☐ 28058	**EVA LUNA** Isabel Allende	$4.95
☐ 27597	**THE BONFIRE OF THE VANITIES** Tom Wolfe	$5.95
☐ 27510	**THE BUTCHER'S THEATER** Jonathan Kellerman	$4.95
☐ 27800	**THE ICARUS AGENDA** Robert Ludlum	$5.95
☐ 27891	**PEOPLE LIKE US** Dominick Dunne	$4.95
☐ 27953	**TO BE THE BEST** Barbara Taylor Bradford	$5.95
☐ 26892	**THE GREAT SANTINI** Pat Conroy	$4.95
☐ 26574	**SACRED SINS** Nora Roberts	$3.95

Buy them at your local bookstore or use this page to order.

Bantam Books, Dept. FB, 414 East Golf Road, Des Plaines, IL 60016

Please send me the items I have checked above. I am enclosing $_____
(please add $2.00 to cover postage and handling). Send check or money
order, no cash or C.O.D.s please.

Mr/Ms _____

Address _____

City/State _____ Zip _____

FB–4/90

Please allow four to six weeks for delivery.
Prices and availability subject to change without notice.

60 Minutes to a Better, More Beautiful You!

N ow it's easier than ever to awaken your sensuality, stay slim forever—even make yourself irresistible. With Bantam's bestselling subliminal audio tapes, you're only 60 minutes away from a better, more beautiful you!

__ 45004-2	**Slim Forever**	$8.95
__ 45112-X	**Awaken Your Sensuality**	$7.95
__ 45081-6	**You're Irresistible**	$7.95
__ 45035-2	**Stop Smoking Forever**	$8.95
__ 45130-8	**Develop Your Intuition**	$7.95
__ 45022-0	**Positively Change Your Life**	$8.95
__ 45154-5	**Get What You Want**	$7.95
__ 45041-7	**Stress Free Forever**	$7.95
__ 45106-5	**Get a Good Night's Sleep**	$7.95
__ 45094-8	**Improve Your Concentration**	$7.95
__ 45172-3	**Develop A Perfect Memory**	$8.95

Bantam Books, Dept. LT, 414 East Golf Road, Des Plaines, IL 60016

Please send me the items I have checked above. I am enclosing $_____ (please add $2.00 to cover postage and handling). Send check or money order, no cash or C.O.D.s please. (Tape offer good in USA only.)

Mr/Ms _____

Address _____

City/State _____ Zip _____

LT-12/89

Please allow four to six weeks for delivery.
Prices and availability subject to change without notice.